"Dominance and submission is complex Kara. It's different for every couple that does it. I cannot explain what it will become for us, partly because it will depend some on what you want it to be too. It's the kind of thing you'll have to experience to really understand."

"Yes, but I'm afraid I'm going to mess everything up before I get there," she sighed.

Her voice was so solemn that it cut at him. He stroked her cheek. "There is nothing to mess up Kara. I know I dumped a lot in your lap the day I asked you to marry me but really all I want from you right now is to earn your trust and get to know you better. The rest of it will fall into place over time. Okay?"

She didn't know how it happened or when she had stopped fearing him and had started trusting him, at least a little but his reassurance soothed her.

He stroked her cheek and she nodded her understanding. Then his mouth pressed against hers. She tensed, anticipating the breathlessness and the terror as the memory of being held down, her breath cut off by someone larger and stronger teased the edges of her consciousness.

Alyssa Aaron has created two wonderful characters that will involve you in their story of tenderness, fear, dominance, submission and what happens when all of the emotions involved come to a head. Slade and Kara are believable and the depth of emotions shared and hidden will strike at the heart of any who have considered the BDSM lifestyle, or even thought about it. To be truly mastered… to truly submit… gifts or horrors you can find on the internet? Which is right? Who will be proved correct? *His Perfect Submissive* will show you the way this particular dominant teaches his chosen sub, but will she be able to learn? Can she set aside a history of pain and anguish and follow his path?

Lee Rush – Author — *Bound by Fate* and
Love of a Pendant Heart from *The Crimson Z*

His Perfect Submissive was a delight to read. The depth of some relationships is tricky to portray, but this is debut book, from this stunning author, captures it beautifully. Once I picked up the book, I did not want to put it down. The characterization was sensitive and I found myself empathising with both hero and heroine. The plot is a triumph of subtle twists and turns, showing the trust that goes into a domination and submission relationship. I can't wait to read Alyssa's next book.

Richard Savage – Author – *Temporally Yours & The Key*
and *The Anniversary* from *The Crimson Z*

www.blackvelvetseductions.com

Alyssa Aaron

His Perfect Submissive

ISBN 0-9774682-0-8

Published 2008
Printed by Black Velvet Seductions Publishing
Company in the United States of America

Visit us at:
www.blackvelvetseductions.com

Dedication

This book is dedicated to my husband Orville without whose unwavering support and acceptance of frequent take-out it never would have come to fruition.

Acknowledgments

I would like to thank several people without whose impact this book would never have been written. First of all, I would like to thank Mr. Burdick who was a student teacher in my 9th grade business class. It was his praise of the my rather lengthy responses to essay questions that gave me the confidence to believe that I could write in the first place.

I would like to thank Mr. Sudol, my 10th grade English teacher, who read my earlier (much tamer) works and critiqued them.

I would also like to thank Members of the Heart of Iowa Fiction Authors and the members of the critique group I belonged to in Cedar Rapids. Without their constructive criticism I would never have understood point of view, dialogue, or any of the other hundred and one things that go into writing a book.

Last but not least I would like to thank the family members and close personal friends who have suffered through my groussing when the story didn't flow or unfold the way I wanted it to.

His Perfect Submissive

Kara hated waiting.

She perched nervously on the edge of the gray leather chair in the tastefully decorated reception area and waited for Slade Westin to return to his office. The spacious waiting area was decorated in shades of cream, teal, and gray. Watercolor paintings of skyscrapers, malls, and office buildings complete with perfect landscapes and glass vestibules graced the walls. The décor was rich, pleasing, and designed to impress.

Coming up with a way to raise the money her brother had embezzled hadn't been easy. She'd spent half the night crunching numbers and calculating. The figures hadn't lied. If she took the maximum cash advances on her credit cards and borrowed against every cent in her 401k, she'd be able to come up with exactly fifteen thousand, half of what her brother had stolen from Mr. Westin.

She'd taken the day off work and come to his office without an appointment. She planned to sit in his office until he gave up and saw her, or had her arrested for trespassing, whichever came first.

Whether she made any headway or not she had to try one last time to make him see that he would gain nothing by going to the police. She hoped coming in person and having some cash, as a down payment, would go a ways in changing his mind.

If it didn't? She wouldn't let herself go there. She couldn't. The ramifications of failure were too great. Her mother would be beside herself. The stress of having her son on trial and then having him in jail would be a lethal blow to her mother's already failing health. While she knew her brother was spoiled, immature, and way too impulsive for his own good, she loved him. No matter how much he might deserve whatever he got from Mr. Westin or the police, she just couldn't stand by and let him go to prison. Especially, if she could do something, anything, that would help.

Slade exited his private elevator and strode into the reception area of his office. His receptionist, Leanne, had died her hair a shocking red today. He smothered a grin. Changing her hair color was her latest form of rebellion against the corporate dress code, and he secretly enjoyed her mutinous protest.

Leanne looked up and reached for a stack of messages. "Ms Hastings is here to see you, Mr. Westin," she said, handing him the messages.

God, deliver me, Slade thought with a sigh. He knew what she wanted. He didn't want to play. He'd already made it abundantly clear that he intended to turn the matter over to the police and let them sort out the details.

He thumbed through the stack of messages, knowing he didn't have much choice about seeing her. She was sitting in the reception area and had probably overheard Leanne tell him she was waiting. Still, he wanted to put off the inevitable as long as possible.

He turned and headed toward his office, hoping for a smooth getaway. "Mr. Westin?" a soft female voice asked.

"That's me," Slade answered turning toward the voice with a resigned sigh.

"I'm Kara Hastings. We talked on the phone yesterday. I can't tell you how sorry I am about this."

He lifted his gaze from the stack of messages he'd been sorting. His annoyance at her intrusion dissolved as he allowed his gaze to glide over her.

Innocent. The single word echoed in his brain, reverberating like a sharp kick to some buried part of his soul. The descriptive encompassed her and described her perfectly, yet left plenty of room for expansion into the many layers he sensed buried beneath her surface.

He let his eyes linger on the soft waves of dark hair that hung loose around a pretty face with a pert nose. Her peaches and cream skin glowed softly making his fingers itch to touch the soft line of her cheek and the full swell of her lip.

Her soft musky perfume teased his nostrils as her wide brown eyes skittered away from his. They echoed a hint of shyness and sadness that didn't quite detract from her attractiveness.

She was dressed simply in black slacks and a white sweater that hung off her shoulders. The soft folds of the sweater brushed the full softness of her breasts before drifting downward to skim full rounded hips. The thick folds ended precisely at her knees.

Some would consider her overweight but he found her softness perfect. She was rounded and soft in a way that had him reining in thoughts of plunging hard maleness into female softness.

The shy way she waited for him to take the lead stirred the sensation of deep protectiveness in him.

"Come on back Kara," he sighed, going against his own better judgment, which clamored distantly in his mind.

"Thank you for seeing me Mr. Westin," she said softly as she followed him down the hallway toward his office. Her voice was smooth as caramel and just as sweet, he thought as he paused to open the door before ushering her inside.

Sexy. The word hung in his mind baffling him. It'd been three years since he'd allowed himself to think of sex or of anything remotely connected to it.

"Have a seat Kara," he offered as he sat down behind his desk.

He rested his elbows on the desk, heaved a sigh and tented his fingers as he studied her. His first inclination had been to reiterate his plan to turn her brother's case over to the police and send her on her way but something about her, the sweetness, and the buried sadness in her eyes tugged at him, and God help him he wanted to help her.

"I told you yesterday that your brother's case was a matter for the police. So far I haven't heard anything that has changed my mind about that," he said.

Her expression tightened, and she bowed her head. "I know you said you weren't interested in taking payments but— Is there any chance you might change your mind about it?"

He felt a jolt of sympathy. She was sweet and innocent. He knew it hadn't been her that had inflated expenses and pocketed the difference. It bothered him to see her cowed in shame.

"It will take me a few weeks but I can get advances from my credit cards and borrow against my 401k. I can give you fifteen thousand as a down payment on what my brother stole and pay the rest in payments."

"Kara," he sighed, wanting to punch her brother's lights out for bringing shame on her. "My problem with taking payments isn't the money itself. I could afford to forgive the money entirely and it wouldn't change my standard of living even a little bit."

"If it's not the money then why not take the payments and move on?"

"It is not the damned money; I won't get the money back by going to the police, at least not for a long time." His voice came out harsher than he intended and laced with the frustration he felt toward her brother. Ted was talented, and up until the accounting department had brought the questionable numbers to his attention he had planned to promote him.

"What did Ted do with the money?" he asked his voice softening. "Any chance he still has any of it? "

Kara shook her head and dipped her chin. There's that shame again, he thought. "He got caught up in gambling again. He's had problems before and I should have known he was in trouble when he had money, but I didn't." She shrugged, her voice small and filled with guilt. "Things were really tight financially and I was just glad he was finally getting things together and was able to help out a little."

Damn it to hell. He hated gambling and the pain it caused its innocent victims. Remembered sadness filled him as he recalled his fourth birthday and the excitement that had fired his blood as he'd looked forward to a real party with friends from Sunday school and balloons and everything. In the end the party hadn't happened. The sheriff had shown up and hauled the family's meager belongings to the curb and in the struggle to find another place to live his birthday party had been forgotten. It hadn't been the first or the last time his family had been evicted due to his father's gambling the rent money on a horse that couldn't lose or a football game that was a sure thing.

Slade leaned back in his chair and sighed. He wondered what financial obligations Kara was struggling under that her brother was shirking.

He felt the stirring of dominance he'd worked to bury and an irrational desire to protect her from the pain gamblers brought on their families.

He studied the blunt tips of his tented fingers. He could take the worry of her brother going to jail off her shoulders. He didn't have to go to the police. Helping her would cost him thirty thousand dollars, but it was a doable solution. He could afford the loss. Not going public with the embezzlement scandal would save a lot of negative press and questions around how her brother had managed to skim thirty thousand dollars without being immediately caught.

Financially it was probably a wash. If the negative press cost him even one contract it could easily cost him hundreds of thousands more than the thirty thousand her brother had taken.

He liked Kara. She stirred his protective instincts and made him feel alive in a way he hadn't in a long, long time.

Still, gambling was an addiction. If her brother was addicted he probably needed to be allowed to hit bottom. He worried that without the threat of jail Ted would continue to gamble until he was in so deep he couldn't get out and that would be worse for Kara in the long run.

"What about your parents Kara?"

"My dad is dead. Her head was tipped forward; her eyes focused on her lap. "Mom has heart disease and emphysema. She doesn't know about Ted's—problems. I don't want to tell her if I don't have to. Sh-she is not well and I'm afraid that the stress of a trial would j-just be the end. The doctors say she doesn't have l-long and I don't want her last to be—" She sucked in an audible breath and bit her lip before rushing on. "Well—you know what I mean—"

Slade thought for a minute she was going to cry and didn't know what he'd do if she did.

He was spared from further consideration on the matter when the intercom on his desk buzzed. "Mr. Westin, Mr. Blake is here."

"Put him in the conference room, I'll be finished in a minute."

"I'm sorry to intrude on your day," Kara said softly.

"It's not a problem Kara," he said and meant it. "Ted has created one hell of a big mess. I don't know yet what I'm going to do about it, but you've given me a lot to think about. When I've made a decision I'll let you know."

He stood and Kara followed suit. "Thank you Mr. Westin. I appreciate your kindness and your willingness to at least think about meeting me half way."

"You're welcome Kara, but don't thank me yet. I'm not guaranteeing you any outcome at this point."

Chapter 2

Slade stirred and woke with a start. He'd been dreaming of Kara. The musky floral scent she wore still teased the sleep-tinged corners of his mind and the soft, husky tenor of her voice still filled his ears.

Between the cobwebs of remembered sleep and the scattered pieces of dreams he'd dislodged when he woke there was the solid knowledge that he wanted her.

Through no intention of her own, Kara's sweet, innocent, nature had breathed life into long forgotten places. After she'd left his office he'd felt a sexual tug toward the natural dominance he'd buried. In one short meeting she'd managed to nudge to life all the dominant feelings he'd buried after Susan walked out.

He propped one arm behind his head, completely awake now. Kara's untapped submissive quality mystified him and left him wondering how he'd managed to miss it at first. The signs were obvious in retrospect. It had been plain in the way she'd waited for him to take the lead in his office and again in the way her gaze had kept scooting away from his.

Kara didn't ooze sexual confidence. Certainly not the blatant form of tie me up, beat me, and make me suck your cock submission that Susan had. Kara's passive quality ran deeper than that and seemed more a part of her true nature than Susan's had ever been. Susan had played a role, always trying to realize what she perceived dominance and submission to be while Kara was submissive at her core.

It was odd to realize after so many years of carrying around bitter disillusionment, that what he'd thought was real with Susan had been little more than wishful thinking on his part.

Susan had been a scorcher, a candle burning at both ends. She had never wanted love or protection. She'd wanted only dominance. To her domination wasn't a combination of give and take. She wanted only the limit pushing extremes of pain and humiliation. Even when they'd made love she'd always wanted it rough.

The more he'd given in to her desire for the rougher side of dominance the more she'd wanted. Finally he'd bumped up against his own hard limits. They'd come to an impasse in the relationship when she'd wanted him to cut her and he'd refused. The relationship had deteriorated after that and she'd ended things within a few weeks.

The end of the relationship had left him disillusioned. He'd dated for awhile after Susan, but the women he'd met had either not been submissive at all or had been into playing at submissiveness, or they had been seeking the extremes like Susan. He'd dated a few that were more interested in his wallet than in him and that had gotten old too. There had been no one that had aroused the desire to protect and dominate that Kara had incited within just a few minutes.

The whole dating game had left him disheartened. After awhile he'd stopped believing that there was anyone who wanted the same things he wanted.

Meeting Kara had stirred hope within him. He'd noticed the difference within himself right away. Susan's desire for rough sex had made him want to push limits and force her submission. Kara's sweet, sexy innocence made him want to wrap her in pleasure and shelter her from ugliness.

He let his mind wander as he thought about what he wanted. An image of Kara in his kitchen, wearing pink fuzzy slippers and his terry robe came to mind. Her hair was tangled and tumbled around her face as she stirred cream into his morning coffee.

As that image receded he saw her lying on the couch in front of a blazing fire. Her head rested on a pillow in his lap, the rest of her stretched out on the couch. The firelight cast dancing shadows across the soft planes of her face. The woodsy smell of the fire mingled with the musky woman scent of her, teasing his nostrils. She stretched, pulling silk pajamas taut across her hips and breasts as she turned to look up at him. Her gaze was filled with such trust and adoration that it left him reeling.

He looked down at her, his expression a combination of indulgence and dominance as he stroked her soft breasts that swelled against the peach silk of her pajamas. She moaned, softly, her dark eyes fixed on his, as she arched into his palm. "Oh god, that feels so good" she moaned in a soft husky voice that made his cock twitch. Her soft whimper of pleasure when his fingers found and stroked her hardening nipples made him feel powerful and protective.

He imagined her beneath him then, her soft brown eyes fixed on his as he fucked her. In his mind's eye each deep, hard thrust of his powerful body drove them both toward a crescendo of pleasure and onward to shattering orgasm. She clung to him; her eyes open as she willfully submitted her body and her soul to his mastery.

He wanted her. The knowledge struck him hard, then settled into him with a sensation of rightness that he couldn't ignore.

He didn't want to wait to have her, didn't want to waste time playing dating games. He didn't need to date her to know that he wanted her, not as a one-time deal, not temporarily, but forever.

As he thought about the situation with Kara and her brother an idea began to form. He could use Ted to force her to marry him. He was almost certain she would agree to marriage, even one that seemed strange to her, if it meant her brother wouldn't face the threat of prosecution.

He sighed as the plan formed in his mind. He would offer to forgive her brother's theft and not turn over the evidence he held against him if she agreed to marry him. He would make forgiveness of the money dependent on her staying married to him for one year and on Ted getting treatment for his gambling addiction.

He needed the year to show Kara that a relationship based on his control and her willing surrender was what she wanted too. He wanted her brother to get help with his gambling problem. The last thing he needed was for him to get in more trouble with the law. He knew that if Ted continued on the same course, at some point neither he nor Kara would be able to drag him out of trouble. He wouldn't stand by doing nothing and see Kara hurt again.

He didn't feel particularly good about using the situation with her brother to force her into a marriage she wasn't ready for, but he believed that in the end the marriage would be good for everyone concerned. He would have Kara in his life and eventually in his bed. She would be protected from her brother and would be well loved and cared for. Ted would escape prison and be forced to get the help he needed. All in all it wasn't a bad solution to the mess that had been dropped in his lap.

The big question looming in his mind was how Kara would react to his proposal. He knew she was inexperienced with men and he expected her inexperience to give her serious misgivings, especially considering he was almost a stranger. He knew too that if he were to be fair to her he would have to explain that their relationship would be based on dominance and submission.

* * * *

She picked up the phone on the second ring, swallowing a mouth full of hot coffee before she muttered hello.

"Kara?"

"Yes." She put her mug on the counter as her mind

scrambled to place the voice on the other end of the line. The deep voice was familiar, yet she couldn't immediately place it.

"This is Slade Westin. I hope I'm not waking you."

"No, Mr. Westin. I'm awake. I have to get up early for work." She hadn't expected him to call quite so soon and now that he had, she didn't know whether to be glad to hear from him or worried. His voice gave her no clue as to what his call meant for her brother.

"Good, I'm glad I didn't wake you." She thought she detected a smile in his deep throaty voice and felt a tendril of relief wash through her. "I think I have a solution that will be acceptable to both of us."

"You do? Really? That's wonderful." She felt truly happy for the first time in the weeks since her brother had told her about the trouble he was in. "What is it?"

"It's rather—involved. I'd rather go over it with you in person. Can you meet me at my office this morning?"

Kara glanced at her watch. "I think so, but I'm supposed to be at work this morning and I'll have to call and get someone to cover for me."

"No, don't go to the trouble. Can you get away for lunch?"

"I usually get lunch at eleven-thirty."

"That works." His voice carried a hint of mastery, as if he'd set out on a mission and had accomplished it. She realized taking charge of situations was probably something he did all the time. She knew most people didn't get to the top of their professions by taking a back seat, letting others make decisions for them.

She didn't mind that he seemed comfortable taking control. In fact, she liked it. It was nice to not have to make the decisions and chart the course for everyone else for a change.

"I'll take you to lunch and we can talk," he said.

"Thank you—for everything, Mr. Westin." She let her voice trail off conveying the smile she felt.

"You're welcome Kara. I hope you feel the same after we've talked." His voice carried a certain softness she hadn't sensed in it before. "Now, where do you work?"

She gave him the name of the vet clinic and directions. He told her he was familiar with the area and that he'd be there by eleven thirty.

Kara spent the morning wondering what sort of solution Slade had come up with and hoping that it was a workable one. But then, she knew she'd do anything to keep her baby brother out of jail.

Kara was busy holding a cat for a blood draw when she heard the chime that announced that someone had entered the clinic. She recognized Slade's deep rich voice as he asked for her at the reception desk. She heard the receptionist tell him she was with a patient, and that she'd be with him in a minute.

Her heart kicked up a notch. Her stomach felt queasy with pent up nerves.

The vet finished drawing blood and Kara returned the angry cat to its carrier before heading for the waiting room.

"Sorry to keep you waiting. Things are always busy and unpredictable around here." He stood near the bulletin board with his hands in his pockets, looking as if he belonged in the office.

"Interested in a kitty?" she asked noticing that he was looking at the free cat to good home flyer tacked to the bulletin board.

He shrugged broad shoulders. "I like cats, but I'm not exactly jumping over myself to get one," He quirked a smile, "although I don't doubt that I could be talked into it if the right person was doing the talking."

Is he flirting with me? She wondered. She felt off balance by the prospect. She never flirted, didn't even know how really. What had happened when she was seven had made her distrustful and uneasy around men and she avoided them as much as she could.

If she hadn't needed Slade's help with her brother's situation she wouldn't have agreed to see him. She was going to lunch with him only because they needed to talk about Ted and resolving his mess.

"We've got a couple nice cats in the back that are looking for homes," she offered. She felt completely confused. She wasn't sure if he had been flirting, and if he had been, she didn't know what she should do about it." Maybe someday," he allowed. Where would you like to go for lunch?"

"There's a nice sandwich shop around the corner from here. They have good soups too. Otherwise it's pretty much fast food alley."

"The sandwich shop sounds fine. You direct and I'll drive."

Once they were seated in the comfortable gray leather seats of his Cadillac Escalade she gave him directions to the nearby sandwich shop.

"So, what's your plan?" she asked as soon as he had maneuvered the Big SUV onto the road.

"Patience Kara," he smiled. "I'll tell you everything in good time."

She shrugged and fell silent. He sensed the distance immediately. He'd hurt her feelings, made her uncomfortable, he realized. "So, what do you do at the vet clinic, besides try to give away cats?" he teased, trying to smooth over the hurt feelings.

"I'm a vet tech," she answered softly as he turned into the parking lot and found a parking space near the front of the restaurant.

God she's shy and skittish. She'll never agree to this, he thought.

"Do you like being a vet tech?"

She smiled glancing down at her hands. "I love animals so it's almost a perfect job for me."

"Almost?"

"The times when we lose a patient or have to put one to sleep are hard. I hate that part of it."

"What about the cats you have at the office. Will you have to put them to sleep if you don't find homes for them?" he asked. No wonder she's trying to give cats away, he thought, already contemplating taking the cats to keep them from having to be put to sleep, and more honestly, to spare Kara from that part of her job.

"No, we work with a couple no kill shelters in the area. If we can't find homes for them we can place them with a shelter."

"That sounds like a good solution."

He turned off the ignition and took the keys. Their conversation was forgotten as they climbed out of the SUV.

Kara got out quickly, not waiting for him to come around and open her door. He waited for her at the front of his vehicle and held the restaurant door open for her.

They stood at the counter, reading the overhead menu. "What do you recommend?" he asked.

"The turkey melt on rye is my favorite, but the pastrami is also very good."

Once they had given their order and found a seat in a quiet corner Slade slipped into the role of negotiator. It was a role he played often and one he was good at.

"I suppose you're dying to know the particulars of the plan I've come up with." He offered her what he hoped was a disarming smile.

She nodded, taking a sip of her drink.

"Well, it's unconventional but it meets my needs and," he drew in a deep breath, "I think it meets yours too."

Kara nodded, and a strand of dark hair fell over her shoulder. Her dark eyes were fixed on his. She looked fragile, practically swallowed by the navy blue surgical scrub pants and top she wore.

"I don't like the idea of you borrowing against your credit cards and your 401k. It's not sound financially. It would put you in debt and you told me last time we met that you've already had a hard time financially. It's also not fair to you. Your brother should pay back the money he stole. But, even if I did agree to it, it would only take care of half the problem. You'd still have monthly payments on the balance. With payments on the 401k loan and the credit cards and payments to me I'm afraid it would only make it difficult for you. It's not an acceptable solution."

"Mr. Westin, things have been hard because of my mom's medicines, they cost a lot. But I assure you that I will pay you. I'll get another job if that's what it takes. I'll do what I need to in order to keep my brother out of jail."

"Your brother should be the one who pays the money back. I know you think it's a good thing to help him out, but rescuing him isn't teaching him anything. It's allowing him to continue his behavior. Even if I was willing to take payments from Ted, payments and interest on thirty thousand would be pushing it for him, especially now that he doesn't have a job."

The look on her face told him that her brother's unemployed status was news to her. But he plunged on. "I've decided to forget about the money, but there are a couple conditions."

"Oh Mr. Westin that's wonderful, but it doesn't seem fair to you." She was looking at him, her deep brown eyes shadowed with regret.

"I'm happy with the solution," he assured.

"Well—what are the conditions?" she asked hesitantly.

"First, that you stay out of my way and let me deal with your brother on my own terms. He won't get around me as easily as he does you. Second, your brother goes to regular gambler's anonymous meetings. And third, you marry me."

Kara shook her head as if she wasn't sure she'd heard him correctly. "What?"

He covered her small hand with his much larger one, ignoring her attempt to pull away. He rubbed the soft skin where her thumb joined her palm. "You heard me correctly. I want you to marry me, Kara. It's the price for forgiving your brother's theft and for not turning it over to the authorities."

"You're serious?"

"Yes, Kara. I'm serious. If you agree to marry me and your brother agrees to treatment for his gambling I'll rehire him into a position where he can't get his hands on any money.

He'll be getting the help he needs, avoid jail, and have a job. You won't be trying to pull everything together by yourself anymore. I'll take care of you. I won't be alone and that'll make me happy."

"Why? I don't understand."

"I like you, Kara. You have an aura of sweetness and innocence that lights my fire."

"Mr. Westin!" she hissed. The way she looked around to see if anyone else had overheard and the pink that tinged her cheeks made him smile.

"Call me Slade, Kara."

"Slade then." He heard her deeply inhaled breath. "I don't understand what you'd get out of this. I'm fat, I'm not rich, and I'm afraid I don't know what to do with a fire once it's lighted. I-uhm, I've never—uhm."

She blushed a deeper red and looked at the table as if she was thinking about crawling under it.

"You're not fat. You're beautifully proportioned, besides I like my women to have something to hold onto." He let his eyes wander, taking in the smoothness of her skin, the squared shoulders, and the soft rise of her breasts, barely discernable beneath the scrub top she wore. I don't care that you're not wealthy. And I know you've never been with a man." He caressed her hand again, "I knew when I looked up from the messages and saw you standing there in my office yesterday."

"You did?" Her voice was tinged with horror. "Is it that obvious?"

"Not to everyone probably, but it was to me." He let his eyes caress her, wishing he could pass some of the certainty he felt about the marriage on to her. "Don't worry Kara, I'll teach you everything you need to know about tamping my fires."

"It's—uhm—it's not just not knowing—uhm—what to do."

Given the way she was hemming and hawing and the bright red of her cheeks, he figured she was glad to be saved from further explanation by the arrival of their sandwiches. He waited for the waitress to leave before continuing.

He left his sandwich untouched and plunged on. "There are a few things you need to know about me before you make your decision."

He watched the uncertainty that flitted across her face as he searched for the right words to describe what he wanted.

"I know it's not politically correct, but what I want is an old fashioned marriage, one in which I take the lead.

"It's important that you understand that if you agree to become my wife our marriage will be built on my control and your submission to my authority. That doesn't mean I won't discuss things or that I won't take your opinions into account, but it does mean I'll make the final decisions.

"I've dated spoiled, obstinate women in the past and there's no room in my life for that. I won't do daily battle with my wife about who is going to make which decisions, nor will I put up with sullenness and temper tantrums. I'm laying it out from the beginning. I wear the pants and I make the decisions."

He watched her face; unable to tell what she was thinking from the closed expression she wore. He continued on, taking it as a positive sign that she hadn't gotten up and walked out.

"One of the reasons I think it could be good between us is that you don't seem willful or spoiled. You seem submissive and I like that. A lot. But even so, I don't want there to be any misunderstanding later. If you were to marry me and behave like some of the women I've dated," he sighed, "you probably wouldn't like the outcome much."

She shifted uneasily in her seat and avoided his gaze. "Exactly what do you mean, by that?" she asked, her attention focused on the straw wrapper she was twisting into a tight coil.

"I know it's not politically correct but what I mean is that if the situation warranted it I would use physical discipline, like spanking or bondage, to keep you in line. I won't put up with a spoiled wife."

He watched her abuse of the straw wrapper intensify. "You

don't need to be afraid of me. I'm not a crazy and I'm not into abuse. I would never physically injure you, but I am capable and would not hesitate to put limits on undesirable behavior."

He searched her pale face, wondering if his honesty had scared her away. From her death grip on the straw wrapper and the tight line of her jaw as she fixed her gaze on the table, he figured he was pretty close. Much as he would have preferred to stick to white picket fences and rose gardens, his own sense of decency had required him to be upfront and honest with her about his expectations for their marriage.

"If you agree to become my wife I'd expect you to quit your job. I'd want you to be able to devote your time and energy to taking care of our home and me."

"I couldn't just quit my job, even if I wanted to. I pay part of my mother's medical expenses, and if I didn't she'd have to do without some of her medicines, and she can't do that. I can't quit my job even to save my brother, Mr. Westin." She bowed her head and he sensed her defeat in the sudden droop of her shoulders. "I'm sorry."

"Kara," he dropped his hands over hers. "I wouldn't expect you to quit your job and leave your mom in the lurch or do without yourself. If you were my wife I'd take care of you and that would include taking care of your mother's medical expenses. God knows I have enough money. You wouldn't want for much. Neither would your mother."

"It sounds like you'd be getting the bad end of the stick on this whole arrangement," she said. He watched as she shifted in her seat and raised her gaze, pinning him, her expression watchful as she continued. "You're suggesting all this because my brother stole money from you, but you're not going to recover any of the money and in fact you're going to spend even more money taking care of me and my mother. From a financial standpoint it doesn't make any sense Mr. Westin."

"Slade," he corrected. "It makes perfect sense Kara. I have simple needs. I've already told you, I want an old fashioned marriage and an obedient and submissive wife. I want an enthusiastic partner in my bed and someone to explore sexually with me. Truthfully, I'm tired of being alone, and I'm willing to turn loose of some money to get the kind of wife and marriage I want. There isn't anything shady or behind the scenes going on. I've told you what I want and relinquishing some money to get it makes perfect sense."

Kara stared at him, unseeing, her blood cold, her sandwich forgotten in front of her. She opened her mouth to speak several times but closed it again without having uttered a single sound.

"You don't need to be afraid of me or of marrying me. I know you are inexperienced and I'll be patient with you. I'm not selfish Kara. I've been around the block and I know how to make a woman feel good in bed."

"Slade," the single word squeaked out after a false start. Her stomach churned and her brain raced through everything he'd just said. She felt as if her emotions had been stripped bare and left ragged. She knew that all the patience he could muster wouldn't be enough.

"Yes Kara," his voice was gentle, prompting.

The idea of agreeing to surrender herself to him was overwhelming. He'd said she didn't need to be afraid of him that he'd be patient but he didn't know she was damaged.

Misery swelled within her. She needed to come clean, to tell him the truth about her past. She needed him to understand that the unreasonable panic that overtook her, when a man stood too close or when an unexpected whiff of familiar aftershave caught her off guard was a part of her, and was something she could not escape or predict.

It was too much to expect anyone to understand the sudden panic that could wash over her or the mortification that followed, yet she knew he had a right to know. She swallowed hard and tried to gather enough saliva to wet her dry mouth. She still couldn't force the words past the shame that lodged in her throat. She knew intellectually that she bore no blame for what had happened to her when she was a child but the knowledge did nothing to stop the intensity of the shame, or the pain that lived deep within her.

"Kara, are you okay?" he asked. His voice nudged her back to the present, to the reality of the situation in front of her, to the necessity of keeping Ted out of jail.

She nodded, not trusting her voice. She felt completely overwhelmed, empty.

She could promise to be obedient, to clean his house, to be there when he came home from work. She could even quit her job if he insisted, but there was absolutely no way she would ever be the enthusiastic uninhibited partner he wanted in bed. She was too damaged. There was nothing about sex that even mildly intrigued her. That part of her didn't exist; it had been snuffed out before it had had a chance to develop.

If she agreed to marry him without telling him the truth she'd be deceiving him, purposely making a promise she knew she could never keep. It would be the height of dishonesty and she despised deceit.

He'd gone out of his way to help her and she hated herself for the deception she was going to commit. But more than she needed to be honest with Slade, she needed to keep Ted out of jail. Tears clogged her throat and threatened to spill. She felt bleak and hollow. She wanted to cry lonely, sad, shame filled tears, yet she knew she wouldn't, couldn't. She picked up her sandwich, more to distract herself from the intensity of her emotions than because she wanted to eat.

She took a bite and chewed methodically, not even tasting the turkey on rye. Swallowing helped push the hard ball of tears down and made her feel a little more in control of her ragged emotions.

Guilt kicked at Slade's chest as he watched the tangle of emotions that chased across her pale face. She seemed lost in some deep, sad place and he ached to take back every word that had caused her pain.

After a few bites of her sandwich she seemed to draw on

some inner reserve. She looked at him. Her gaze was solid and unwavering as it found and held his. "Mr. Westin—Slade, I appreciate everything you've done for me and my brother."

Here it comes, she's going to turn me down, he thought as her gaze skittered away.

"I know you could have turned everything over to the police and we could be looking at a trial and lawyers. If marrying you is what I have to do to keep my brother out of jail then I'll do it." She sucked in a deep breath.

"I would like your word that the details of our marriage and Ted's part in it will not be disclosed to anyone. I also want your word that the—uhm—nature of our marriage will remain private."

"You have my word Kara."

"And you have mine that I'll do my best to be the kind of wife you want. But I really don't know how this can be what you want."

Her words socked him hard. This quiet resolved reaction wasn't what he wanted. What he wanted was her to be happy about marrying him. He didn't like making her unhappy, but then again he hadn't expected her to be excited about marrying him. He'd known from the beginning that making her happy would come later, after they were married. Once Kara trusted him, knew him, he'd teach her the joy to be found in surrendering herself to him.

"You're right. It's not what I really want. But it's a start, and I'll settle for it."

Chapter 3

Panic rose clawing through her as the first notes of "Here Comes the Bride" filtered through the church.

"Are you ready?" Ted asked.

She swallowed hard and nodded her head, not trusting her voice. She wasn't ready. Not by a long shot.

Her stomach churned and dizziness circled her like a hungry lion as she let Ted lead her toward the back of the sanctuary. She felt the frantic beating of her heart in her head and in her ears. Each beat brought a woosh of sound that echoed drowning out the other sounds around her.

Ted urged her forward. She tried to keep her mind focused on just the simple act of putting one foot in front of the other as blackness swiped at the outside edges of her vision. She tried to close her mind to everything except the immediacy of what she needed to do to guarantee Ted's freedom.

She swallowed hard attempting to generate some saliva to wet her mouth but came up dry. Panic clawed in her chest. Unshed tears and heated breath mingled and caught in the back of her throat. She was hyperventilating she knew, but felt helpless to stop even as the darkness encroached.

She hadn't known exactly what dominance and submission was when Slade had mentioned it and she had accepted his proposal. She knew now, and the shadow his demands cast over her future obliterated everything safe and familiar. She blinked back tears of fear and loneliness. Dread coursed through her bringing images of force and pain that twisted and turned in her mind superimposing themselves onto her future.

Run! Run! Run! Her mind screamed as she stopped beside Slade. Each thump of her heart echoed in her ears and shrunk her area of vision. Darkness crept inward from the edges and hovered threatening to enclose her in a murky cocoon of darkness.

Slade's clean male scent engulfed her as he took her small trembling hand in his large steady one. His touch was gentle as his thumb caressed the soft skin where her thumb joined her palm. For a reason Kara didn't understand the familiar touch provided a small measure of calm. She used the calm to help her focus on taking the deep slow breaths that she hoped would keep the hovering blackness away.

She breathed deep and slow purposely slowing down everything in her mind. As if in slow motion she noticed the long white wedding dress she wore felt sticky where it touched her sweaty legs. She sucked in the scent of roses that filled the air. She heard the rustle in the pews behind her as people shifted in their seats. She felt the gentleness in Slade's touch as he continued to caress her hand.

She heard the preacher's voice and Slade's calm, assured responses as if they came from a great distance. She noticed but didn't focus on the nausea that rose in the back of her throat.

Somehow she managed to murmur, "I do" at the right times, yet when the ceremony ended Kara scarcely knew what she had promised. She felt sick and shaky and alone.

Breathe.

Slowly.

Deeply.

In.

Out.

Relax.

She coached herself through the familiar breathing ritual again and again as she fought the tide of painful memories and the frightening images from the internet that painted themselves on the future.

The words, "You may kiss the bride," penetrated the heavy cloak of wooziness and spiraling memories. Her mind screamed at her to run; yet she was absolutely numb as if her being was held in distant limbo, unable to move of its own accord.

She was only marginally aware as Slade tilted her chin and kissed her. The kiss was soft. Gentle, she observed from some distant other worldly place. He smelled of some spicy brand of soap she couldn't place and tasted of mint.

She was vaguely aware of turning, of Slade's hand settling at the small of her back as they turned to walk back up the aisle. Mostly though, she focused on containing the roiling waves of nausea that expanded within her threatening to break through her iron control at any second.

"Are you okay?" Slade asked in a whisper as they reached the rear of the sanctuary.

"I think I'm going to be sick," she muttered miserably as she swallowed back another tide of nausea. "I need a restroom."

Kara was barely aware of being hustled along the tiled hallway. "Will you be okay in there by yourself? You're not going to pass out on me are you?" Slade asked as he pushed open a door marked women.

Yes. No. She didn't know. Kara nodded. She'd be okay. She didn't know about passing out, but she knew the last thing she needed was for Slade to hover over her as she heaved.

In the end, she didn't throw up. She stood with her head pressed against the coolness of the wall as roils of nausea rose and fell in giant waves. She gagged, swallowing back the hollowness as she tried to rein in the nausea. She took deep breaths, counting slowly to four as she gulped in air and counting to four again as she released it. The familiar exercise helped her focus and push through the nausea.

"Kara, are you okay?" Slade asked through the door.

"Yes," she answered. "I just need a minute more."

"Take your time," he answered.

His voice was gentle. Patient. Kind, she marveled.

She dampened a paper towel with cool water and sponged off her face. She was feeling better, though not a lot. She hadn't slept much since she had agreed to marry Slade. The nightmares that had troubled her when she was younger had returned, sharper, more sinister, the danger seeming more real than it had before. She hadn't eaten breakfast or lunch. She felt woozy and her head was pounding but at least the nausea had receded.

At last she opened the door and feeling shy and weak rejoined Slade.

"Better?" he asked as she left the restroom. He eyed her carefully, taking in her pale complexion and the dark circles just visible under what remained of her makeup. He wished not for the first time that day, that he had taken things more slowly and that he had made time for them to become better acquainted before the wedding.

She nodded. "I'm better but I'd kill for some Tylenol."

"Headache?"

She nodded again. "Thank you for helping me find the restroom."

"Not a problem Kara." He took her hand. She looked at the floor, her eyes vacant as if she had slipped into some distant place he couldn't see. "Kara, look at me please," he used his Master voice, purposely lacing the commanding tone with the concern he felt.

She raised her gaze gradually, her eyes slowly climbing his chest until her gaze locked with his. She was afraid of him, he could sense it in the slow testing way she met his gaze, yet she was doing what he'd asked.

"Try to relax. I'm sure you're scared shitless marrying someone you don't know very well but your life with me will be good. I promise."

She dropped her gaze from his. He felt sure she didn't believe him, although he didn't understand why she found it so difficult to trust him.

The idea of marrying her in exchange for not filing charges against her brother had sprung into his mind and he'd acted on it. He'd seen something he wanted intensely when he'd met Kara and he'd pushed her, not taking time to consider what she might want or need. As uncharacteristically selfish as the move had been he had been up front and straight with her about what he wanted in a wife and she had agreed to the marriage.

He didn't understand why she found it impossible to trust him, but he blamed himself for her distrust and the unhappiness that clung to her. He hoped once the reception was over and they were alone together he'd be able to begin to repair some of the damage his selfish manipulation had caused.

Chapter 4

The wedding was over. The reception was over. All that remained to get through was the honeymoon and a year of being his wife.

Slade opened the SUV's door for her and waited until she was inside and had her seat belt fastened before he shut it.

The thought of being alone with him terrified her. She had barely gotten through the wedding and being alone in the cabin would be far worse. There would be nothing to provide a buffer between her and his desire for sex.

She closed her eyes, the images she'd pulled up on the internet when she'd searched for information on dominance and submission taunting her. She was trapped. Either she had to open her soul and share the horror of her past, and hope he'd leave her alone, or she had to find a way to endure his sexual demands.

Both options filled her with despair. She didn't want to talk about what had happened to her, didn't want to open herself to the pity that was always there when people knew her history. She didn't want to hear again how she should get counseling, as if somehow the horror she had been through could be erased with a little talk therapy.

As much as she detested talking about what had happened to her the panic attacks were worse. She hated the thundering of her heart, the dizziness, the puking. She detested being weak and feeling helpless. It was bad enough she had to endure the attacks when she was alone but she absolutely loathed having other people see her in that defenseless pathetic state.

The slamming of the driver's side door startled her from her thoughts. "How's your headache?" Slade asked when he was seated in the driver's seat with the engine running.

"It still hurts," she answered, thinking that hurt was an understatement. It pounded, the pain almost blinding in its intensity. She needed caffeine and food and probably sleep too.

"I'll stop and get you some Tylenol before we get on the highway."

"Thank you," she sighed leaning her head back against the headrest and closing her eyes against the pain in her temples. "Thank you for being nice to me today."

"Of course, I've been nice to you. I take good care of what belongs to me." He maneuvered the car into the traffic.

His voice was calm, matter of fact. Her head spun and she felt nauseous. She didn't want to belong to him, or to anyone else. She wanted her nice, safe, lonely little life back. She wanted to work at the vet clinic and come home in the evening and decide what to fix for dinner.

She didn't want to belong to him. She didn't want to have to try to be obedient when everything in her cried out that she should run.

He drove into the convenience store parking lot, brought the car to a stop, and killed the engine. Turning toward her he traced the line of her cheek with a gentle hand. She fought the urge to draw away.

"Why don't you forget about everything else and for now; just work on trusting me? I promise you that everything else is going to fall into place."

"I'll try," she said softly, doubting that things would fall into place as smoothly as he thought they would. There were too many skeletons in her closet and too much in her past that rendered her incapable of being a wife.

"I guess that's all I can ask," he said stroking her cheek again. "Do you want something to drink with the Tylenol?"

Kara nodded. Caffeine, she thought greedily. "A Mountain Dew would be really nice."

"In a bottle or from the fountain?"

The question threw her for a moment. No one had ever asked her if she wanted a drink from the fountain or from a bottle before. "From the fountain, with lots of ice?" she asked hopefully.

He quirked a smile. "Done, if that's what you want."

She watched his long-legged, self-assured saunter as he walked into the store. He was tall and broad shouldered. Strong, she realized. His size and strength should have made her feel vulnerable yet his attentiveness had made her feel cared for and safe.

The kindness with which he had treated her during the day had left her feeling strangely confused. That he cared what she wanted, especially about something as minor as whether her drink came from the fountain or from a bottle, only added another layer of confusion.

He'd talked to her about dominance and obedience the day he'd asked her to marry him. He'd told her what he wanted in a wife. He'd been gentle enough and understanding enough of her uncertainty but he'd not asked her what she wanted in a husband or from marriage in general.

His behavior had left her convinced that he would be the one in charge, the one who would make the decisions and she would be expected to acquiesce. He'd left little doubt that there would be consequences if she didn't bend to his will. Though he hadn't been specific about the consequences the internet had filled in the gaps.

She watched him through the store window as he took out his wallet and paid for the purchases. Her gaze followed as he ambled back to the SUV, stuffing his wallet into his back pocket as he walked.

He opened the door. "Mountain Dew, lots of ice, and

Tylenol," he said handing the items to her. He climbed into the driver's seat and waited while she opened the bottle and tapped four tablets into her palm.

"Thank you," she breathed feeling inexplicably warm and temporarily safe as she swallowed the medicine.

They had been back on the highway for several minutes before Slade spoke again. "What do you know about the lifestyle of dominance and submission, Kara?" he asked.

The question threw her and she debated momentarily whether to tell him what she'd learned about it on the internet. For some reason she couldn't really identify she decided to keep her internet research to herself. "Uu—h not much really, except for what you said the day you asked me to marry you. I know what the words mean generally but I don't have any— experience. I told you that before."

"I know you did," he glanced at her, "but you seem... surprised... every time I do something nice. I'm just trying to figure out if you're expecting me to behave like a jerk because of the dominance and submission or if there's something else."

He glanced at her, taking in the soft waves of dark hair that fell around her face and the soft doe brown eyes that avoided him.

"I-I don't know really. You never said anything about being nice, except for taking care of me financially."

Damn. He thought he'd painted a clearer picture.

"You talked about wanting me to be submissive and obedient and—h-hitting me if I wasn't."

He winced, His jaw clenching. No wonder she was jumpy and skittish if she was constantly expecting him to haul off and hit her if she wasn't suitably submissive.

"I—uhm—I don't really know what to expect. You've been nice, but—" Her voice was laced with weariness. She sounded sad. Defeated.

"God, Kara, I did not talk about hitting you. I talked about spanking you. They're two very different things." His voice was sharper than he intended, and the level of frustration he felt surprised him.

She shrugged, her gaze glued to her hands. He supposed she was afraid to get into it with him. She was probably afraid he'd backhand her for disagreeing with him.

"I'm a dominant, not a damned sadist. And definitely not a wife beater."

"What—umm—what's the difference?" She had sunk into the corner of the seat as far from him as possible. Her voice was tiny, little more than a whisper, and he thought it contained more than a hint of fear.

What a friggin mess, he thought. He drew a deep breath and slid his hand across the seat, taking Kara's hand in his. It felt important to have her hand nestled in his as he sorted out the misunderstanding and tried to work his way through the lingering distrust his bungled proposal had left her with.

"A sadist is someone who enjoys inflicting pain on someone else. Being dominant is more about enjoying being in control and sometimes the knowledge that you have the power to inflict pain if you wanted to," he explained.

"But you don't want to? Inflict pain I mean."

"Not just for pain's sake, no Kara, I don't." He sighed, feeling weary of her distrust.

She looked at him. Her gaze still filled with doubt. He took a deep breath. "If I were a sadist I would spank you just because I enjoyed hurting you." He paused, choosing his words carefully. "As a dominant, choosing to spank you would have other reasons behind it. I would still likely intend for it to hurt, and it might even make you cry but my goal would be to help you submit to my authority. It wouldn't be just about hurting you. Does that make sense?"

She shrugged. "Sort of. What you're saying is you want to be in control and you're willing to hit me to make me do what you want me to?"

"No Kara, I'm not a control freak. Think about it a little bit." He struggled for patience, frustrated that she continued to think the worst of him. "If I were a control freak I wouldn't have asked you what you wanted to drink. I would have brought you what I wanted you to have." He paused letting his words sink in. "I wouldn't have called you practically every day to find out your preferences for wedding flowers and cake and everything else. If I was a control freak I would have made the damned decisions and left you to put up with them."

Kara shrank further against the passenger door tugging her hand free of his. He immediately regretted the rough edges of frustration that had entered his voice. He remained silent. He needed time to regain his patience and his equilibrium. He needed to stay calm if he was going to work through her vision of him as a control freak and a batterer. Hell.

"I'm sorry." Her voice was soft and delicate and almost inaudible from her corner of the car.

"There's nothing for you to be sorry about Kara. You took what you took from what I said. It's an honest mistake. It's not your fault I behaved like a selfish bastard rushing you into marriage because it's what I wanted." He drew a deep breath and reached for her hand again. He twined his fingers with hers. "If I had it to do over again I would take more time and not rush you quite so much."

The words sat between them in the silence that descended over the car. Several minutes passed before Slade spoke again, and when he did his voice was soft and without the rough edges of frustration. "I don't know where you got the idea that I would ever hit you for any reason or under any circumstance. I wouldn't. Ever."

"But you said—" her voice trailed off.

"I said that if the situation warranted it I would paddle your backside to keep you in line. At least from my perspective there's a big difference between hitting someone and spanking them."

She shrugged. "It seems like pretty much the same thing to me."

"They're different Kara." He sighed, squeezing her hand.

"Hitting is an out of control; impulsive act intended to physically hurt someone. It's used to bully someone and make them comply when they don't really want to. It's about a bigger person picking on a smaller one." He cast her a sidelong glance. "Spanking is very controlled and purposeful. It's an intimate expression of a dominant's control and a submissive's desire to submit to his control."

He glanced toward Kara. She was so innocent it made him ache. He couldn't imagine ever wanting to force her to do anything she didn't want to do. And if he did want to compel her to do something spanking her would be the last method he'd choose. "It's not something I would ever do to you without your consent."

Kara was quiet. Still. He maneuvered the car in and out of traffic and cast the occasional sideways glance at her as she sat silently. She was probably trying to work out what all of this meant for her. He wished he could help her but he knew there were some things she wouldn't understand until she experienced them for herself.

"Are you hungry?" he asked after awhile.

She nodded.

"It's about two hours to the cabin. Would you rather stop now or wait till we are closer to the cabin where we can find somewhere fancier?"

"Can we stop now? I haven't eaten today and I am really hungry."

"Kara," he sighed, hoping his exasperation was clear in his voice. "It's 4:30 in the afternoon and you haven't eaten. It's no wonder you have a headache."

"I know." She sighed deeply. "I was too nervous to eat this morning and I didn't want to be sick so I didn't eat at the reception."

He decided it was a good thing for her backside that he was committed to taking his time and introducing her to discipline gradually, otherwise he would be sorely tempted to spank her sweet little bottom for not eating.

"Are you feeling better? Is talking helping?" he asked as he maneuvered the SUV off the exit ramp.

At the bottom of the ramp he turned right and followed the sign that advertised several restaurants in that direction.

"Yes it's helping. I don't feel quite as scared. I still feel—" he cast a sideways glance at her, mesmerized by the tangle of emotions that played over her expressive face as she searched for the right word.

"Uncertain?" he supplied. "Steak okay?" he asked as he turned the car onto the frontage road that served several fast food restaurants and a steak house.

"Steak sounds wonderful. No, not really uncertain, although that's part of it I guess."

He pulled the SUV into the Ned's Steakhouse parking lot and parked.

"So, if it's not uncertain?"

"More like—lost—."

"Uhm—Lost huh?" He pondered her choice of words, wondering what she meant by lost, what she still needed from him that he hadn't given her. He killed the engine and turned in the seat so he could give her his full attention. "Talk to me about feeling lost Kara."

She sucked in a deep breath and dropped her gaze to her hand that was still enclosed in his. He stroked her with his thumb.

"I feel like I don't know anything." Her voice was earnest. "I don't know where I fit in this whole dominant submission thing. I don't know anything about being submissive or what that means to you." Her voice rose and caught and he thought for a moment she was going to cry.

He longed to pull her against his chest and wrap her in his arms but she was too tense, her breathing too ragged and he knew that such a move would only make her pull away.

He knew she was used to knowing where she fit and that she was probably also used to feeling confident of her abilities. He hadn't meant to, but he had taken that away and left her feeling uncertain and inadequate.

He wished he had it to do over again, and could take the time to make things right between them instead of rushing her into the marriage as he had, but he didn't have that luxury.

"Dominance and submission is complex Kara. It's different for every couple that does it. I cannot explain what it will become for us, partly because it will depend some on what you want it to be too. It's the kind of thing you'll have to experience to really understand."

"Yes, but I'm afraid I'm going to mess everything up before I get there," she sighed.

Her voice was so solemn that it cut at him. He stroked her cheek. "There is nothing to mess up Kara. I know I dumped a lot in your lap the day I asked you to marry me but really all I want from you right now is to earn your trust and get to know you better. The rest of it will fall into place over time. Okay?"

She didn't know how it happened or when she had stopped fearing him and had started trusting him, at least a little but his reassurance soothed her.

He stroked her cheek and she nodded her understanding. Then his mouth pressed against hers. She tensed, anticipating the breathlessness and the terror as the memory of being held down, her breath cut off by someone larger and stronger teased the edges of her consciousness.

The kiss wasn't like the ones that she remembered. This one was a gentle caress that coaxed more than it demanded. Slade's mouth didn't hamper her ability to breathe, didn't cause her to feel dizzy or to black out.

She relaxed a little, bemused by the gentle stroke of Slade's tongue along her lip and the command to open her mouth that he whispered against her lip.

She opened her mouth, unprepared for the soft stroke of Slade's tongue as it teased her mouth. The unfamiliar intimacy sent a stab of heat to her center.

She was shocked by the warmth that filled her and by the

lack of terror. There was no fear, no dizziness, no nausea, no panic attack. Only sweetness and the sense that she was okay, that Slade wasn't going to hurt her.

She lifted her hands to his broad shoulders, liking the solidness of him beneath her hands.

She didn't protest as his tongue slid into her mouth, teasing an intimate dance of liquid warmth in its wake.

Her mind raced. He'd been kind and gentle and matter of fact when he'd explained his feelings about dominance and submission and what he wanted from her. The whole day he'd treated her with kindness and respect. He hadn't belittled her when he could have. He'd remembered her headache and gotten her medicine, he'd cared that she preferred Mountain Dew from the fountain rather than a bottle.

It all combined making her feel soft and warm, cared for, and taken care of in a way that was completely new to her. She clung to him feeling grateful to him for helping her brother and for trying to make her feel comfortable in this new marriage. His kiss deepened, his mouth urging hers to open more as one large hand slid up her back and beneath the curtain of her hair to caress the tight spot at the base of her neck. She opened her mouth, allowing his tongue to find hers again.

His hand kneaded her tight muscles, easing the strain that had overwhelmed her. His tongue explored her mouth engulfing her in unfamiliar pleasure that made her open to him, admitting him, like a flower opens to admit the sunshine.

She felt his hand move as it slipped beneath her sweater. She shifted slightly, moaning a protest that was swallowed up by his mouth. "Um—please. Slade—no—" she murmured, twisting to avoid the touch of his palm as it slid up her rib cage toward her breast.

"Shhh Kara, I just want to make you feel good," he whispered against her neck as his hand stilled. His other hand stroked her hair and her neck.

She heaved a sigh of relief, the knowledge that the hand beneath her sweater had paused that he was waiting for her permission to go forward eased her fear and made her feel more comfortable. The knowledge that he would stop if she insisted made her feel safe. His hand felt good where it rested against her rib cage. She both wanted him to touch her and wanted him to stop.

"Relax and let me make you feel good Kara," he whispered in her ear as his hand began to slip slowly up her rib cage toward her breast.

She wanted to protest but her breath caught in her throat as his large, warm hand closed over her breast. The sensation was hot and bold and completely new. She'd never experienced anything like it before.

His fingers caressed her breasts and then her nipples through the lacy fabric of her bra. She felt dizzy with pleasure. Heat pooled in her midsection and lower in her pelvis as He pushed her bra up shifting it so that her breasts were free and bare to his touch. A tremor ran from her nipples to the heated core between her legs and she moaned as Slade eased her back slightly. His mouth slipped from hers, his eyes intent on her face, watching her, as he continued to stroke her now bare nipples, teasing them, making her want the next gentle brush of his fingers on the hard peaks. She was aware of him watching her, of him enjoying her pleasure.

She closed her eyes, whimpering her satisfaction. As she whimpered Slade began to pinch her nipples, not hard, but just enough that the sensation alternated between intense bliss and pain that hovered on the edge of pleasure. Kara was lost in the sensation, arching her back and offering her breasts to him.

She felt as if her entire being was on fire, consumed, and all she wanted was more of the exquisite pleasure-pain he was giving her.

His touch was like sweet magic. She was tight with pleasure as she moaned, arching her tender nipples into his hands not understanding the urgency to have him tease them or why it was happening now. She only knew that his touch felt good and she wanted it to continue.

"Kara, Honey," he whispered throatily against her mouth. "We have to stop."

She whined in protest, the magic that had taken over beginning to dissipate as his hand on her nipples gentled, and he stroked her tenderly.

She didn't want him to stop. The knowledge shocked her.

Disappointment swelled within her as Slade's touch gentled and the pleasure pain sensation he'd been building began to wane.

He pulled her tight against him flattening her breasts against his chest as he settled his mouth on hers. "We have to stop," he whispered as he lifted his lips from hers. He pressed her face against his chest and tugged her bra back in place. "I don't want your first time to be here in a parking lot."

She hid her face in his chest feeling a flush of embarrassment at the way she had whined and whimpered as he'd pinched and teased her.

She felt lost in the aftermath of the passion he had ignited. She had never imagined that she could actually like being held or kissed or God forbid, touched. The knowledge that she had enjoyed it stunned her and left her reeling.

She could not even begin to understand why she had dissolved in Slade's arms or how she could have actually enjoyed the feel of his mouth and the touch of his hands on her breasts.

Slade held her, his hand idly stroking her back as she snuggled against his chest, marveling at the contentment she felt.

Confusion tugged at her mind. She'd always thought her ability to enjoy intimacy with a man had been taken from her when she was seven. Yet she couldn't deny what she'd felt with Slade.

The thought that it had something to do with trust crossed her mind and began to take root. She'd never feared her father or her brother and they were both male. Of course they had never touched her intimately either. But she thought it went beyond that. Maybe she hadn't feared them because she had trusted them not to hurt her.

Maybe Slade didn't frighten her because she trusted him not to hurt her. The knowledge both bewildered and thrilled her.

He felt her stir against him and finally pull away as she sat up. She looked up at him with a soft bemused smile that sparkled in her eyes and warmed her face.

A soft blush crept across her cheeks surprising him after her heated response. "You're not feeling embarrassed, are you?" he asked.

"Yes." Her single word response was something between a whisper and a croak.

The knowledge that she was embarrassed by her response stabbed him in the gut and made him want to protect her. "Kara, there's no reason for you to be shy with me." He stroked his knuckles along her cheekbone. "I like making you feel good and I love the way you responded to me. It was like having liquid fire beneath my hands." He nuzzled the top of her head, drawing in the soft floral scent of her hair. "It's beautiful. You're beautiful. There's nothing to be ashamed or embarrassed about."

He snuggled her against him, resting his chin against the top of her head.

She intrigued him. She was so painfully shy, in some ways so repressed, and yet she had been so responsive she had made his head spin with desire.

Finally he drew a deep breath. "How about we get some dinner, before my good intentions fly out the window?"

Chapter 5

Kara was suffused in the warm tingle of pleasure as Slade helped her down from the SUV. Everything felt fuzzy, as if a fog of bliss surrounded her. Although she knew that eventually the pleasant mist would lift, and like Cinderella, she would revert to her damaged self, she was in no hurry for that to happen.

She didn't know how he'd managed it, without the terror filled memories raising their ugly heads, but Slade had given her a taste of sexual pleasure and an awareness of herself as feminine and desirable that was pleasant and exciting and completely new to her. She felt almost whole for the first time in her adult life and she was loath to break the magical spell he had cast.

She didn't pull away, didn't even think of pulling away, as he tugged her against his side and wrapped one strong arm around her, anchoring her to him. She went smoothly, surprised at how well she fit into the spot against his side and by how well they moved together, almost as if they had been friends for years.

Slade was tall and lithe, a contrast to her softer, rounder form and yet, as they walked his muscles rippled against her hinting at a controlled power that made her feel dainty in comparison. The heat of his body radiated into her, warming her against the nip in the December air.

She felt strangely lighthearted, almost giddy as Slade

opened the heavy restaurant door and urged her inside. He released her from his side, taking her hand, as he led the way to the back of the empty restaurant.

Kara glanced around enjoying the homey atmosphere created by a combination of stucco and rustic wood walls. The stucco was a pretty off white, with vines and morning glories painted on it. The wood walls were adorned with shelves that held collections of old cups and saucers, teapots, and salt and pepper shakers.

"This okay with you?" Slade asked as he stopped near a corner booth.

"It's fine," Kara answered, sliding into the booth while Slade sat down opposite her.

Kara's gaze was drawn to the collection of miniature teapots on the shelf above their table. The teapots were some kind of china. Each piece had a detailed flower motif painted on its side and a narrow band of gold along the top. The craftsmanship was detailed, making her want to look at the pieces more closely.

When her attention drifted back to Slade his gaze was resting on her. His expression was relaxed, almost indulgent. "How's your head?" he asked.

"Much better," she sighed.

Their attention was drawn to the waitress, an older woman wearing a paisley dress who trudged out of the back carrying menus and water.

She recited the daily specials and left them to look over the menus. "What sounds good?" Slade asked after a few minutes spent studying the menu.

"Everything sounds good. I'm starving." Kara smiled; surprised by how easy the words came to her now that she was no longer afraid.

"I'm going back and forth between the steak and the turkey Manhattan. But I think I'm going to have the turkey. It's hard to beat mashed potatoes and gravy for comfort food."

"You're probably right, but I'm going for the steak," Slade

responded with a lopsided smile.

Kara leaned back against the booth, feeling relaxed and comfortable. Mellow. She watched; fascinated by Slade's hands as he folded his menu and slid it toward the center of the table, where he placed it atop hers.

He had nice hands, large palms, with long fingers and just a smattering of dark hairs on the backs of his hands and around his knuckles. She remembered the way his large calloused hand had engulfed hers and the tender way his thumb had caressed her hand during their wedding. She still didn't understand why the simple touch had imparted comfort. She wondered if he'd known how close she was to passing out, and if he'd intended his caress to give her reassurance.

She looked up to find his gaze resting on her; his intense blue gray eyes seemed to take a quiet analytical inventory. He opened his mouth as if to speak but the waitress bustled through the swinging doors that separated the dining room from the kitchen at just that moment leaving whatever he'd been about to say unsaid.

Kara relaxed and enjoyed the deep timber of his voice and the slight edge of buried humor that stroked and soothed her as he chatted with the waitress about the weather and their shared hope that the coming winter would be a mild one.

He ordered for both of them, sending a smile in Kara's direction as he ordered her a turkey Manhattan and a Mountain Dew with lots of ice.

When the waitress left Slade slid his hands across the table, capturing both of Kara's hands in his. She looked up, making no effort to free her hands as it hit her that she was beginning to like him. A lot.

She thought back over the brief time she'd known him and wondered about him, how he'd come to own the company her brother had worked for. "Are the paintings at your office the buildings you've built?" Kara asked, wanting to know more about him.

"Yes, they are." He smiled at her. His smile was slow and

lazy, almost an invitation to ask more questions.

"They all seemed to have sections with a lot of glass. They seem—different. They're not typical run of the mill boxy skyscrapers."

He smiled squeezing her hands. "It's my philosophy that people function better when they can see the outdoors. As a consequence most of the buildings I've worked on in the past five years have had a lot of glasswork and a lot of plants in courtyards and things, as a central part of the design."

Kara relaxed, enjoying the warmth of his hands on hers and the twinge of pride not quite buried in his deep voice.

"What about the heart center you were working on when you were making the wedding arrangements? Does it have the glasswork too?"

"The heart center." He sighed deeply. "Now that was the project from hell." He squeezed her hands and smiled. "I really am sorry about that, Kara."

"Sorry—for what?" she asked feeling as if she'd missed some vital piece of the conversation.

"For not being there, for starters." He sighed, his thumb caressing her hand. "When I asked you to marry me I had every intention of wining and dining you. I planned on us spending some time together and getting to know each other before today." He sighed, his gray blue gaze meeting hers. "I know today was rough for you and it might not have been if we'd had some time together the past couple weeks."

Warmth settled in her middle. It made her feel good to know that he had wanted to take her out and get to know her, that his desire was not just to possess her sexually.

"My good intentions sure went to hell in a hurry."

"What happened?" she asked.

"Issues," His lips twitched into the lopsided smile that was beginning to feel familiar to her. "Are you sure you care about this? It can't be very interesting."

She shrugged. "I'm curious about your work."

"Well, the condensed version is that everything that could

go wrong with the project went wrong. We had weather delays. Then the bricklayers were on strike. We had trouble getting materials because of the tornados in the south. Then the project manager got into trouble and had to be fired. The man who replaced him had a heart attack."

"Ted was the one who had to be fired?"

He nodded, just one short bob of his head.

The knowledge that her brother's theft had made a bad situation worse for him was like a kick to her midsection.

He gave her hand a reassuring squeeze.

"There is always some wiggle room built into a contract but there were so many problems with this one, that it made pretty clean work of the wiggle room. To make matters worse, there was a late completion clause in the contract."

"What's—a late completion clause?" Kara asked.

"It's part of a contract that specifies charges to a construction company if they don't finish a project on time. In this case the charge was a hundred thousand dollars a day."

A hundred thousand a day. Ten days—a million dollars. "God, Slade," her eyes flew to his. "Did you get it finished on time?"

"We were a couple days late."

He smiled at the expression as her eyes widened and her mouth gaped.

"It was still a profitable project." He winked as if he was letting her in on a secret. "We ended up okay financially, but I imagine you can see why I had to work—and why I didn't take you out."

"I do understand," she said softly, thinking back to the times he'd called to ask what colors she wanted for the wedding, what kind of cake, what kind of flowers. She hadn't understood at the time how busy he had been. At the time she'd been mildly irritated that he was acting as if their marriage was something she wanted, when he had forced her capitulation.

He smiled, drawing circles on the tender skin of her wrist with his thumb. "You didn't miss much. I wouldn't have been very good company. I was feeling pretty—stressed."

"I'm surprised you even talked to me after what Ted did and the extra problems it caused," she said feeling the familiar kick of guilt.

"To be honest, I wasn't looking forward to it, when my secretary said you were waiting for me." He sighed. "Then I actually saw you and I didn't mind so much." His smile was gentle and reflective, and softened his jaw and the area around his eyes. "I still didn't plan to let Ted off. But then I couldn't get you out of my system," He looked down at where their hands were joined on the table. "And as they say, the rest is history."

He watched the shy dip of her head, wondering how this strong, intelligent, beautiful woman had managed to evade other men for all of her twenty-seven years. He wondered too why she was so painfully shy about some things and so matter-of-fact about others.

"Here comes our food," Kara said as the waitress backed through the swinging doors carrying an armload of plates.

Slade reluctantly released her hands as the waitress neared the table. He'd enjoyed the simple conversation about his work more than he could remember enjoying any of the conversations he'd had with Susan or any of the dates that had come after her.

He knew if he had told Susan or any of the other women he'd dated about the difficulties with the project they would have either dozed off in boredom or immediately begun calculating how much he must be worth to be able to afford to have hundred thousand dollar a day late completion clauses in his contracts.

With Kara it was different. There had been an aura of concern as her gaze had flown to his and she'd asked if he'd finished on time. He didn't think it had even dawned on her that her financial life was now tied to his. He didn't think she even realized that his gain, and it had been a substantial one even with the late completion charges, was her gain too.

He watched her as she cut into her turkey and swirled it through the mashed potatoes and gravy before carrying a fork full to her mouth. He was fascinated, his attention held by the simplest movements as she trailed turkey through gravy. He was captivated by the velvet softness of dark brown eyes that for the moment avoided his. His eyes rested on the dainty hands enjoying the glint of the diamond that glimmered from her ring finger catching the light as she moved.

He cut into his steak, freeing juices that ran onto his plate. He'd wanted her from the moment he'd laid eyes on her that first day at the office when his awareness of her had edged over into hunger.

He speared a piece of steak and allowed his thoughts to drift to the day he'd proposed. He'd been out to acquire her then; the way people acquired other things they wanted. He hadn't seen her then, not really, not completely, not as a real person. He'd seen instead a vision of what he'd wanted her to be. He'd been immediately aware of the submissive quality and the innocence that clung to her and he'd glimpsed in her a depth of loyalty toward her brother and her mother that made him want the same kind of loyalty for himself.

He had been smitten, overwhelmed with the desire to have someone who shared his desire for the softer more romantic side of dominance and submission. Even when she'd been hesitant and seemed to not know the first thing about D/s, he'd seen only the loyal, obedient, submissive wife he imagined she could be and he'd forced her into marriage.

The selfishness with which he'd approached her had hit him full in the face that afternoon. He remembered her standing next to him, fragile, pale, and trembling. The misery etched on her face when she'd muttered that she was going to be sick reminded him that he had hurt her.

He speared a piece of steak and carried it to his mouth. His guilt wouldn't do anyone any good. What he needed to do was make things right with Kara. He needed to reel himself in and focus on giving her time and space and gentle dominance so she could discover what he already knew, that she could be happy with him.

He watched as she speared another piece of turkey and swirled it through the mashed potatoes and gravy. It stunned him that as much as he'd bullied her and as selfish as he'd been, she still felt anything positive toward him.

She glanced up from her plate and caught his eyes resting on her. His expression was relaxed and intimate, like a gentle touch. It made her feel toasty and a little tipsy, sort of like the feeling she got at New Years when she drank champagne.

She smiled self-consciously and glanced away from the intensity of his gaze.

"I know I've told you what I want from marriage, but I never slowed down enough to ask what you want. I'm sorry I didn't ask sooner." He cast her a half smile, just a twitch of his lips, and a softening of his features. "Are there things you want to be part of our marriage?"

She nearly choked on her turkey and had to take a drink of her Mountain Dew to wash it all down.

"I've never really thought about it," she said when she recovered. "I never planned to marry."

The words reminded her how hopeless their marriage was and how dishonest she had been in not telling him about her past. She sucked in a deep breath and let it out again. Slade had managed to touch some sensual part of her without waking the demons inside her, but she couldn't imagine she'd feel anything but claustrophobic desperation when his weight was on top of her pushing her into the bed.

"Even so, you are married. There must be things you want from marriage," he coaxed, drawing her mind back to the conversation. "I can't make you happy if I don't know what you want or what you need."

She looked across the table feeling lost in the question and in his unflinchingly steady gaze. The earnestness in his words and in his gaze made her believe he did want her to be happy.

She struggled with what she needed, what she wanted and

whether she wanted any part of the marriage at all.

She'd been forced into it in the first place. She never would have chosen to marry at all if it hadn't been the only way to keep her brother out of jail. Yet, now that she was married…she couldn't envision enjoying sex, with anyone, and yet she liked Slade.

She dipped her head, shying away from the power of his gaze and then stealing a glance at him as she started to speak. "Trust isn't easy for me," she said in a small voice.

Slade nodded.

"I need to be able to trust you Slade." Her voice sounded pleading and she hated the weakness in it, the beseeching quality.

"You can Kara. Always."

She sighed.

"What else do you need? Kara?" His voice was soft, a whisper of sensation that affected her almost like a touch. Her tummy tightened as if he had touched her.

She glanced at her hands knotted against the Formica table. "I would like to—" she swallowed hard and blinked back tears that rose in her eyes, hating the fact that she felt teary all of a sudden.

She looked at him through the glimmer of unshed tears and read in his expression only an honest desire to understand what she wanted. "I would like to feel at least cared for." The admission left her feeling cold and alone, as if she was begging for scraps of affection that she was not entitled to. "I know that wasn't part of our agreement but——the idea of having— of—" She sucked in a deep breath and closed her eyes fighting the tide of embarrassment that washed over her.

"The idea of making love with me——I get that part of it- —now go on—"

She opened her eyes feeling utterly embarrassed. His knowing smile loosed a tingle of awareness that shot through her making her feel cared for and protected in spite of her embarrassment.

"The idea of doing—that—without you at least liking me a little bit makes me feel——really empty."

"Kara," he said in a deep husky voice, "I'm not going to lie to you and tell you I'm head over heels madly in love with you. I'm not. Yet." He reached across the table and took her hand in his. His gaze met and held hers, solid, unwavering.

He stroked her hand absently. "Someday when I do tell you that I love you I want it to mean something and it won't if I throw the word around now."

He sighed.

Her stomach did summersaults. Did he mean that he thought he could fall in love with her someday? Her mind raced as she tried to sort out her own feelings. She liked him, but did she want him to love her? Did she want to love him?

She felt dizzy as she thought about loving and being loved. She'd never even let herself think about those subjects before because she'd always known those possibilities were out of her reach. What was it about Slade that made her want to allow a sliver of hope?

Slade stroked the soft skin on the underside of her wrist and she raised her gaze to meet the frank candor that stared back at her. "When you came into my office to plead your brother's case I hadn't wanted a woman in over three years. I really thought that part of me was dead." He squeezed her hand.

"I've done my share of playing around the edges of bdsm and dominance and submission and there are certain feelings that go with that kind of play, but what I feel for you is different. I didn't marry you just to play sex games with you Kara. You're too special for that. What I feel goes deeper than just liking you."

Her chest felt tight and full. She was dumfounded. Her emotions felt scattered and she didn't know what to say. She wondered why he had sworn off women but bit down on her lip, afraid to ask. "I like you too. A lot." She smiled shyly. "I wouldn't have married you if I didn't have to, because——," she drew a breath so deep she ached, "—because of some things that happened a long time ago—but now that we are married I really want it to be good between us."

He smiled, a gentle softening of his features that made Kara feel melted inside. "I'm glad you want it to be good. I'll do my best to see that it is."

She glanced up, feeling hopeful and optimistic about their marriage and less worried about their wedding night than she had before. She was beginning to hope that she would be able to be intimate with Slade without the ugly memories resurfacing.

The waitress walked toward them snaring her attention. "Did you two save room for dessert?" the waitress asked as she stopped near their table.

"No, not me," Kara answered with a smile.

"What do you have?" Slade asked, giving the waitress a smile that said he was willing to let her tempt him.

"We have peach, cherry, and apple pie, chocolate cake, strawberry shortcake, ice cream——"

"Strawberry shortcake sounds good."

"Strawberry shortcake it is then," the waitress said moving away from the table.

"Share with me Kara?" Slade asked.

The request startled her. She'd never shared a dessert with anyone before. The idea of sharing with him, eating from the same bowl, their spoons touching, felt intimate.

"Okay, but just a little."

Slade studied her. She looked more relaxed and happy than he'd seen her look before. Her velvety soft brown eyes seemed to sparkle with life and her skin glowed with health. The peach undertones of her complexion complimented the soft waves of shiny dark brown hair that cascaded around her face. She seemed relaxed, not huddling in her oversized sweater as she'd done earlier in the day.

He had been trying to gain her trust and ease her fears. He was pleased that she seemed to be softening toward him. The shy innocence still clung to her like a glove, but he liked it as long as it didn't stem from fear. "You look like you're feeling better," he said after a moment.

She nodded her head and laid her hand atop his. The simple gesture shocked and pleased him. It was the first physical intimacy she'd instigated and though it was only a touch he was elated that she felt safe enough with him to instigate it. He smiled at her and rolled his hand as he took her hand in his, twining his fingers with hers.

He found it odd that such a straightforward touch; such a simple move from Kara had given him such a jolt of pleasure and satisfaction. He was sexually experienced, his sexual tastes running the gamut, and yet, none of his sexual exploits had given him the sharp jolt of deep down contentment that Kara's hand landing trustingly on his had just given him.

"Are you feeling less lost?" he asked.

She smiled. "I feel lots less lost. Thanks to you."

He squeezed her hand and his heart soared. He felt warmed by her appreciation and by the growing trust he could tell she felt.

He sighed deeply, tranquility settling over him. It hadn't been an easy day for him and he knew it had been a heck of a lot worse for Kara, but there was reason to hope it would work out alright.

He was profoundly grateful that Kara wasn't sharp and resentful or distant toward him. He knew she had every reason to be. He'd run rough shod over her, forcing her into a marriage that had clearly made her more than a little uneasy. He sighed. He'd never seen her angry, even when she'd had every reason to be spitting mad at her brother she'd shown only an even keeled determination to help him.

He glanced up as the waitress came out of the back carrying a large dessert dish filled with strawberries and ice cream topped with whipped cream. "Here comes dessert," he told Kara as the waitress approached.

The waitress placed the bowl on the table between them

and handed him two spoons. "Anything else I can get you? Refills on the drinks?"

"No, we're fine. Thanks." Slade responded.

After the waitress had gone he handed Kara one of the spoons and nudged the dish toward her. She eyed the massive concoction but didn't dig in.

He steered the topic of conversation toward Christmas and their differing Christmas traditions as he slid the ice cream closer to her and urged her to eat. He smiled inwardly as she shyly dipped her spoon into the melted ice cream and strawberries that had dripped down the side of the sundae. He liked the intimacy of sharing dessert with her.

Their conversation drifted into a discussion of how they could merge the traditions of their two families. That led to the rather obvious solution of them having the Christmas celebrations at their house.

After inquiring whether the house was big enough to house so many people Kara enthusiastically agreed to host the dinner. He enjoyed the sparkle in her eyes as she savored the ice cream and talked about fixing some of the traditional family recipes she'd stopped making as her own family had shrunk. The happiness she seemed to feel helped ease the lump of regret that had risen in his chest when he realized she had never seen his house, their house, not even a picture.

His heart swelled with admiration that tangled with the heartfelt wish that he had been able to spend more time with her before the wedding. Rushing into the marriage had caused her distress and cheated her out of the pleasure that should have been present on her wedding day. That she was still open and warm, trusting, rather than resentful and angry amazed him.

She dipped her spoon into the strawberries and melted ice cream that had run down the side of the frozen creation. He watched as she carried the melted mixture to her mouth.

Watching her eat was a sensual affair that stirred his fantasies. In his minds eye he imagined her as he anticipated she would be when they knew each other better and he had earned her complete trust.

In his fantasy she was naked, kneeling submissively next to him as he lifted spoonfuls of strawberry sundae to her lips. She was comfortable with her nudity, content with the nice curves of her body. She opened her mouth, obediently swallowing each spoonful of sweet concoction.

In his imagination he let the cold mixture spill so that it dripped between her breasts and onto the soft skin of her belly below. He imagined her response, watched in his minds eye as her nipples puckered in reaction to the cold ice cream. He continued to feed her, occasionally spilling little streams of ice cream that dripped onto her puckered nipples and onto the sensitive skin of her tummy trickling down like miniature streams to disappear into the dark triangle nestled between her legs. When he had her drizzled in melted ice cream he laid her back and slowly licked the melted delicacy from her.

He started with her mouth, sucking and kissing, licking every trace of ice cream from her. Her mouth was open, her tongue mating with his as she sighed deeply, enjoying his kisses but impatient for his mouth to move lower where he'd feast on her breasts and the hard peaks of her nipples. He'd draw her pleasure out there, alternating between little love nibbles that made her gasp and soothing caresses of his tongue that made her moan with pleasure. He already knew how sensitive her nipples were and how he could carry her along with the alternating sensations of sharp and soft.

He could almost hear the whimpers as his mouth slid lower, his tongue teasing the soft feminine arch of her belly, enjoying the tender responsive skin there.

He went slowly so that each touch of his tongue made her ache for more. He built her passion with breathtaking slowness. The zig-zag pattern of the ice cream that he followed lower heightened her awareness of him and prepared her for the eventual destination of his tongue as he slowly followed the line of melted ice cream to where it disappeared in the dark patch of curls that nestled between her legs.

He inhaled the sexy female scent of her as he continued, his tongue swirling through the dark hair, his mouth making slurping noises as he sucked at her fur covered mound licking the ice cream from her. He enjoyed the bucking of her hips and the ferocity of her desire as his tongue circled, teasing, just barely missing her clit as he licked at the channels of melted ice cream that disappeared into her female softness.

"What's Christmas like with your family?" The question jerked him from the fantasy.

He swallowed hard and reined in his wayward thoughts. Christmas! He reminded himself, as his thoughts would have gone off in pursuit of the fantasy ice cream that had disappeared into Kara's feminine folds.

"It's pretty traditional. Most things with my family are pretty traditional." He smiled, his mind drifting just briefly to the fantasy ice cream. "Since my mom has gotten older, my sisters have started having dinner at their houses. Everyone else brings stuff. There's more food than you can imagine." He grinned. "The women cook and talk and the men watch football and drink beer. The house is full of kids and noise." He smiled at her. "It's nice. Laid back. You'll like it."

He scraped the last bits of ice cream and cake from the bottom of the bowl and extended his spoon to Kara, the fantasy resurfacing as she lowered her lashes and opened her mouth for the bite he offered.

Pull yourself together, he thought as he pushed away thoughts of melting ice cream trailing down Kara's front and tugged his wayward thoughts back to the drive that lay ahead.

"Shall we get back on the road?" he asked pushing the bowl to the side.

Kara nodded, surprised to find herself looking forward to being in the SUV with him. His sexual knowledge and candor, which had embarrassed her at first, now seemed more reassuring than frightening and she no longer feared him in the same way she had before.

Slade stood, and dug his wallet from his hip pocket. He pulled several bills from it and left them on the table.

"Next stop cabin?" he asked taking her hand in his and pulling her against the warm hollow at his side where she fit so well.

She nodded, feeling safe in his embrace. She released a deep breath, marveling that she'd been able to leave the panic attacks behind...at least temporarily.

She owed Slade for that, she realized. It was his confidence, his experience, and the calm direct way he'd tackled her fears that made her trust him. And it was the trust that had short-circuited the panic attacks. The more she thought about it the more sure she was.

Slade pushed the heavy restaurant door open and maneuvered himself and Kara through it. She snuggled closer against him as they stepped into the darkened parking lot.

"Cold?" he asked pulling her closer and wrapping his arm more tightly around her.

"No, just appreciative," she sighed.

Chapter 6

"Wait here. I'll get the lights," Slade said as he pushed the cabin door open.

Kara waited on the plank porch as he stepped into the darkness inside. She wrapped her arms around herself as the cold winter breeze licked at her, chilling her even through her thick sweater. She stepped toward the cabin door and would have stepped inside if she hadn't slammed into Slade's tall body just as light flooded the porch. "I asked you to wait till I had the lights on," he said, as his hands grasped her upper arms.

His voice contained an edge that sent a tingle of alarm up her back. His voice was calm. His eyes were dark, more gray now than blue and they held her as surely as his hands. "From now on you need to do what I ask," he said. He didn't seem angry, just firm, but she knew he wasn't happy that she'd started into the cabin without waiting for him.

His attitude annoyed her. She knew she'd agreed to be an obedient wife, but surely that had some reasonable limits associated with it. It wasn't like she had disobeyed him just to be disobedient; she'd only wanted to get inside where it was warmer. She sucked in a breath to explain but the thought abandoned her in a startled yelp as Slade bent and scooped her up in one fluid movement.

Panic shot through her as he straightened with her grasped in his arms. The memory of him telling her he'd be willing to spank her to keep her in line exploded in her mind. The images she'd seen during her internet research into dominance and submission, domestic discipline, and BDSM, which all seemed somehow connected, sprang to her mind. Fear exploded making her heart pound.

The memory of him promising that he would never spank her without her consent followed, slowly expanding within her.

Her mind spun as he turned and carried her into the cabin, pausing to kick the door closed behind them. He had been disgruntled. His voice had conveyed displeasure, yet she knew she was in no physical danger from him. He had promised that he wouldn't spank her without her consent, and when she stopped to consider it she believed him.

Even so, the sudden kick of adrenaline that had surged through her during the seconds she'd thought he might intend to spank her had released a swarm of unhappy memories. Dizzy nausea tore through her. Thoughts tumbled one over the other, fragmented, disconnected.

Defenselessness. Darkness. The damp moldy smell of a basement combined with the odor of death. She remembered being lifted, even as she kicked and fought. She knew in a kind of distant way that they were the stray memories of a seven year old fighting a much stronger, more powerful adult. But in that moment they were real. The memories were real, the images that would have been better left buried were real.

She scrambled against Slade's grip. She didn't want to be picked up. She didn't want to be helpless or defenseless, not now, not ever again.

"Put me down!" She kicked her legs. Slade's grasp was strong and her kicks were little more than ineffectual wiggles.

On their own the kicks wouldn't have been enough to stop him, but the panic that edged her voice stopped him dead in his tracks. He loosened his hold, letting her slide to the floor. He held onto her steadying her until she was settled on her feet, then he let her go. As soon as he released her she backed away, her chest rising and falling with each agitated breath.

He stood rooted to the spot where he'd stopped with her in his arms. He didn't move toward her or make any effort to touch her as his gaze rested on her, studying her.

His confusion at her reaction fell away as recognition hit him. Fear. He knew it when he saw it, even if he didn't understand its origins.

It hadn't been his intent to frighten her as he'd lifted her, intending to carry her over the threshold. He'd hoped she would find his adherence to the tradition romantic. While he had expected her to protest that she was too heavy or that theirs wasn't a traditional marriage he hadn't expected it to frighten her.

He waited, patient, quiet, allowing her to regain her composure without his interference. He made a mental note to move more slowly with her, to warn her before he picked her up in the future.

He let his gaze wander the living room of the cabin. He gave Kara space, not wanting to add to her discomfort by focusing on her fear.

The room was nice. It smelled of lemon and furniture polish and was decorated in dark shades of green and cream. Natural stone and wood gave the room a rustic country look. It sported a massive stone fireplace that took up an entire wall. The furniture, a loveseat with built in recliners and a large overstuffed rocker, looked like they would be comfortable. The pieces were arranged to provide a nice space for an intimate conversation or a romantic snuggle in front of the fireplace. A big screen television sat in the corner, easily viewable from either the chair or the loveseat.

When he sensed Kara had regained a measure of calm he extended his hand to her. "Care to have a look around our home away from home?" he asked.

She looked shy and embarrassed, but she placed her hand in his outstretched palm and moved closer. Hand in hand they wandered through the small cabin. They poked into the cupboards and the refrigerator in the nicely equipped kitchen commenting over the generous stash of snacks stowed in the cupboards and the variety of sodas in the refrigerator.

Slade tugged Kara into the bedroom mentally holding his breath as he awaited her reaction to the king-sized bed made of yellow pine logs that dominated the room. He half expected her to bolt for the door as the intimacy of their situation closed in on her.

"I love the fireplace," she said, her eyes resting on the massive stone fireplace that took up most of the bedroom wall.

"I thought you might like the fireplaces," he said. "They're one of the reasons I chose this cabin over some of the others I saw."

"You picked it——because——because you thought I might like fireplaces?"

He nodded. "I wasn't able to spend time with you before the wedding, but I didn't totally shirk my responsibilities as a husband." He smiled down into her upturned face. He caressed her cheek, gazing directly into her deep brown eyes. "I do want to make you happy Kara."

Trust and something else he couldn't put his finger on warred in her eyes. He watched the mingling expressions that chased across her face, wanting her with an ache that started deep within him. He slid his hand from her cheek, slipping it under the curtain of dark brown hair that cascaded down to her shoulders and rested his palm on the nape of her neck as he bent and kissed her.

He kept the kiss purposefully gentle and slow. He teased her mouth with his, his tongue flicking her lips, and urging them apart. When her mouth opened beneath the lazy urging of his he savored the sweet vanilla taste of her.

His mouth still plundering her sweetness, he wrapped his arms around her and drew her close, liking the soft warm pressure of her breasts as they molded themselves against the hard wall of his chest.

He lifted his head slowly, his breath ragged from the kiss and the pent up desire that raged through him. He wanted to kiss her again.

Hell, he wanted to do a lot more than just kiss her. He wanted to lay her down on the quilt-covered bed and touch her with his hands and his mouth. He wanted to feel the weight of her breasts in his palms. He wanted to tease her nipples until they were hard pebbles against him. He wanted to explore the soft indentation at her waist and the smooth swell of her backside. He wanted her soft body naked beneath him so that he could touch and taste and savor every part of her.

He drew a deep breath and struggled to rein in his need. He knew instinctively that it was too soon for her, that he needed to give her time to get used to him touching her and kissing her without it going anywhere near the bed.

He couldn't unleash the full maelstrom of his desire now. If he did she'd shrink from it and from him and he'd lose much of the trust he'd built with her. For now he would keep things light and comfortable and let her find her footing.

He caressed her arms and shoulders, feeling the tension melt beneath his hands. "The bed looks comfortable," he said softly, wanting to draw her attention to it now so that she would have time to get used to the idea of sharing it with him before that intimacy became a reality.

She stepped back, turning, her gaze skittering to rest on the massive bed. He watched as she worried her lower lip with the sharp edges of her perfect white teeth.

She didn't say anything but he had the strong sense that she was trying to figure out a way to get out of sharing the big bed with him. Hell, she'd probably offer to sleep on the loveseat in the living room if she thought he'd let her get away with it.

He'd already decided there was no chance of that. He would wait for sex if she wasn't ready. He'd wait for her submission if she needed more time to make sense of the intricacies of dominance and submission. He wouldn't bully her on those things but she was not going to sleep anywhere but next to him.

His eyes rested on the massive wood framed bed as he contemplated how many ways he could tie Kara to it. He wondered idly how long it would be before she'd trust him enough that she'd let him tie her up.

He drew his mind from the fantasy stirring to life in his mind and focused on Kara instead. "Want to look at the bathroom?" he asked. "From the pictures on the internet it looked nice."

She nodded; and Slade was sure she was happy to escape the intimacy of the bedroom and the imposing presence of the bed.

He ushered her into the bathroom ahead of him, bumping into her when she came to an abrupt stop just inside the bathroom door. "There's a fireplace in here too," she said with astonishment in her voice as she looked back at him. The expression of surprise and pleasure that filled her face jolted him.

"I know," Slade murmured. "I chose this cabin because I thought you might like taking a bath in front of the fire. I've heard women go for that sort of thing."

Kara looked back over her shoulder and smiled up at him feeling suffused with warmth. The knowledge that he'd specifically chosen this cabin because it had several fireplaces, and because he'd thought she might like bathing in front of the fireplace, made her feel treasured.

"Why are you so nice to me, Slade?" she asked softly. "My brother stole your money—— I don't deserve——"

"Shhh-shh, Kara," Slade whispered in her ear as he pulled her against him. She didn't resist, didn't even want to as he wrapped his arms around her and pulled her back against him so that his chest pressed against her back, warming her even through her thick sweater. She felt the puff of his breath as he nuzzled the top of her head and planted kisses there.

The bathroom doorway was not the most romantic spot

but Kara hardly noticed where they were as Slade's deep voice smoothed her jangled nerves. "You deserve to be cherished Kara. I knew that right from the very beginning, when you came into my office all ready to fight for your brother."

"You knew? How?"

She felt him shrug.

"I'm not sure how I knew, but I did. Instinct I guess."

His arms tightened around her. "The very first thing I felt, aside from physical attraction, was a desire to protect you."

She snuggled her back into his chest, liking the feel of his warm breath stirring her hair and the soft rumble of his voice in her ear. She was beginning to like him. She was beginning to like the way he thought about her wants and pandered to them, treating her like she was someone to be spoiled and cherished rather than the sister of the man who had stolen thirty thousand of his dollars.

She sighed. It would be nice if she could melt into Slade and let him protect her.

"You looked sad and I had the sense that you had the whole weight of the world on your shoulders." He tightened his arms around her and she nestled closer.

"I did. I was terrified that my brother would go to prison and that the stress of a trial and everything would kill my mother."

"I know, you told me when you were in my office, remember?"

She nodded.

"You haunted me Kara. I wasn't good for anything else the rest of the day. I kept thinking about you, remembering what you looked like. I couldn't forget how scared and unhappy you looked and I kept thinking about how I wanted to take the load off your shoulders and see you smile."

She still didn't understand why he'd insisted she marry him. He could have helped her without marrying her, but she felt soft toward him, and trusting in a way she had never expected to feel toward anyone, especially not a man she'd expected to dominate and bully her.

He tightened his arms around her pulling her more snugly against him. "Now that I've seen you smile I know that it makes me very happy."

She felt the protective walls she'd begun erecting around herself when she was seven beginning to melt. Slade was a good man. He was honorable and dependable. He might have forced her into a marriage she hadn't wanted but he hadn't abused his power as her husband.

He deserved to have a wife who was as honorable and direct as he was, someone who was not damaged, whose family hadn't stolen from him. He deserved more than a wife with a closet full of skeletons she couldn't even bring herself to talk about.

Yet, he'd married her and she liked him, really liked him. In some deep primal part of herself she wanted to throw caution to the wind and take the chance that she could actually become the submissive wife he'd described the day he'd proposed. Part of her wanted to believe that they could share a happy life together.

She remembered he'd said he wanted an obedient wife, someone he didn't have to argue with about every decision. She thought she could learn to be obedient. Still, she doubted she'd ever measure up in the sexual department. He'd said he wanted an enthusiastic sexual partner and she was not enthusiastic about sex. The whole idea made her break out in a cold sweat.

Still she left a little room for hope. Given time there was a very small chance that she could tell him about her past and somehow trust him enough that she could learn to like sex, at least a little bit. The fact that she had enjoyed making out with him in the SUV at the restaurant gave her room for hope.

She snuggled against his chest enjoying the security she felt there. He was strong and stable. Trustworthy. She knew instinctively that he would protect her, that he would never purposely hurt her and that he wouldn't let anyone else hurt her either.

"Do you need to call and check on your mom before it gets late?" Slade asked nuzzling the top of her head.

"I probably should, yes." She said as she shifted away from the warmth of his embrace.

"I didn't mean this minute," he said softly, his breath brushing her ear as he pulled her back against his chest. "I like holding you and I'm not quite ready to let you go."

She smiled and snuggled back into his arms, content to stay nestled against him until he was ready to let her go. He held her for several minutes before he spoke again.

"You can use my cell phone, to talk to your mom. I've got a few groceries to bring in and I'll get fires going in the fireplaces while you're talking."

When I'm done talking, what then? The thought broadsided her. The peace that had settled over her as she'd relaxed against his chest seemed shattered as they shifted apart.

Chapter 7

Slade withdrew his cell phone from a case on his belt, pressed a few keys to unlock the keypad and handed it to her. "Take your time with your mom," he said softly as he bent and kissed her.

"Thanks Slade," she said as she looked up meeting his blue gray gaze.

"You're welcome honey," he said caressing her cheek gently before he turned and walked back through the bedroom and back into the living room.

Kara looked for a place where she could sit to talk to her mom. The bed seemed too intimate so she ambled into the living room and curled up at one end of the love seat. She dialed her number and tucked the phone under her ear.

Slade only caught glimpses of Kara and stray bits of her end of the conversation as he puttered around the kitchen stowing the groceries he'd brought along. He hadn't realized before how dependent Kara's mom was on her. He listened as Kara asked about her blood sugar and her blood pressure and reminded her of which medications she needed to take.

He smiled as he heard Kara describing the cabin and telling her mom that he'd picked it because he'd thought she'd like all the fireplaces. He warmed at the appreciation in her voice but then he knew Kara appreciated even the smallest things. That had been one of the first things he had noticed about her and it was one of the reasons he'd gone to the extra trouble to look for a cabin he thought she would really like.

Seeing her light up with pleasure the way she had when she'd seen the bathroom fireplace had made it worth the extra effort it had taken to spoil her, and it made him determined to continue spoiling her every chance he got.

He drifted with her end of the conversation, glad to hear in her voice and in her words that she was beginning to trust him. He had definitely tried to show her, both with words and with his actions that he was trustworthy. He wasn't sure exactly when she'd begun to relax and trust him and he wasn't sure how strong her trust was, even yet, but she did know she trusted him more than she had at the wedding, and that was enough for now.

With the groceries put away he carried wood in from the stack on the porch and began to build fires in the fireplaces. He'd just finished stoking the fire in the living room when he heard Kara tell her mom she'd call her the next day.

Slade rose from his squatted position in front of the fire and moved toward the loveseat where Kara was seated with her legs curled beneath her, the phone resting in her lap, a worried frown marring her otherwise perfect features. "How's your mom?" he asked.

"Her sugar and blood pressure are both a little high, but otherwise she seems okay."

He could detect a trace of worry in her voice. "You're worried about her though?" he asked as he sat down next to her.

"I'm always a little worried about her," she answered with a sigh.

He felt a stab of sympathy but didn't know how to help. "I gave her the cell number and the cabin number when you were changing at the church. She'll be able to reach you if she needs to."

"Thanks for doing that." She smiled up at him. "It was nice of you to think about it." Her voice was soft and husky with appreciation but there was also an undercurrent of apprehension that drew his attention.

"Honey, what is it? It's not just your mom is it?"

No, it wasn't just her mom, and it wasn't just sex either. She felt uncertain, stressed, her nerves jangled. She felt on edge and there was no one thing she could point to as the cause. It was more that she felt overwhelmed by the combination of all of it.

She had only horrendous memories of sex, memories she had kept locked away and had never allowed to surface. While she trusted Slade not to make the experience unbearable she was still afraid that the experience itself would let loose all the demons she'd fought so hard to lock away all those years ago. She feared that all of the ugliness would come rushing back too strong and too powerful for her to be able to make it go away again.

She felt as lost and alone as she had at seven when doctors, police, psychiatrists and her parents had all questioned her, all wanting to know what had happened to her and Kayla. She hadn't given specifics then. She'd buried the sex, the brutality, and the ugliness deep in her seven-year-old psyche, and she'd never let it out in all the years since. She swallowed back the bitter taste of fear. She didn't want to let it out now any more than she had then.

"Come here, Kara," Slade said softly.

She pushed away the ugliness of her thoughts and scooted closer to him. She still felt icy in spite of the fire that roared in the fireplace. Slade turned toward her, wrapping his arms around her.

"Why so uptight all of a sudden? You can trust me. I'm not going to push you to do anything you don't want to do. Okay?"

She nodded. She could trust him. Did trust him. Still she felt scattered and unfocused inside like shards of shattered glass.

"We can snuggle in front of the fire, kiss like we did at the restaurant." Slade drew her against his chest, his fingers stroking her hair and her face.

She snuggled into his arms, burying her face against his chest, inhaling his strength and stability as his warmth ebbed into her chasing away some of the chill and the doubts that had overtaken her.

"You can relax honey, absolutely nothing is going to happen that you don't want to happen," he whispered as he kissed her forehead.

He watched as she looked up at him, her eyes huge in her face. He bent his head and kissed her gently on the forehead. Then he dropped a playful kiss on her nose. He could feel her apprehension waning as he spread playful kisses over nose, her cheeks, her chin.

He kept his kisses gentle, almost playful as he smiled down at her between them. He'd spent most of the day trying to get her to relax and trust him and he'd be dammed if he would send her into an emotional tailspin by rushing her at this point, no matter how hard his cock was or how badly it ached to be inside her.

He continued to kiss her, gently, leisurely, the kisses not building in intensity or designed to take them anywhere. He could feel the last traces of her apprehension dissolving as he kissed and caressed her.

"Feeling better?" he asked after a lengthy silence.

He felt her nod against his shoulder as her eyes rose to meet his. He thought that the pure unadulterated trust he saw in her gaze was worth just about any price. "I just felt overwhelmed I've never done this before. I don't know what to expect or whether I will even like it. What if I hate it?"

He caught the edge of panic in her voice. "Shhh Kara, you won't hate sex," he soothed. "The capacity to enjoy sex is wired into all of us I think. It might hurt a little at first; it does sometimes for women. Is that what you're worried about?"

"Some."

"Then I'll just have to be careful and slow. There's a lot I can do to make it better the first time." Like keep my cock out of you while I'm this hard and this ready, he thought to himself.

"Really?" Her surprise coated her voice. She eased away from him looking up into his face, her eyes questioning the truth of what he'd said.

"Yes, really," he chuckled tugging her against him.

She still looked painfully shy and timid as her tongue darted out to moisten her lips.

"We don't have to do anything. We can stop or slow down. Whatever you need." Her soulful brown gaze climbed his chest, till her gaze had connected with his. He studied her eyes, trying to decipher the cacophony of emotions that stared at him from their depths. He saw shadows of sadness and fear which he didn't really understand but the trust that also shone from her eyes made his heart swell with pride and the need to make this first time good for her.

He bent his head to nibble her full lower lip, teasing her mouth with his tongue and teeth. "So serious Kara," he whispered. "I will make it good. I will make you feel good. I promise."

She sighed, a soft almost resigned sound that niggled at his conscience. He should slow down, stop, give her more time to get used to him.

"I can talk you through it," he teased in an effort to lighten the mood.

"Yes. Please." The breathy request and the way her brown eyes held his was almost his undoing.

He stroked her shoulder, watched her swallow. "Please?" She reiterated her request.

He nodded, just one short bob of his head as he pulled her toward him.

"I like it when you talk about sex—you seem to—-know what you're talking about, and—-um, that makes me feel better," she dipped her head resting her forehead on his chest.

He felt a stab of affection zip through him as his heart missed a beat. She was very shy and very inexperienced, yet she seemed completely without pretense, baldly telling him that she liked it when he talked dirty.

Still, she'd looked so worried that he toyed with the idea of just taking her to bed and holding her until she fell asleep. Only the knowledge that if he did that she'd still have whatever fears had lurked in the shadows of her gaze stopped him. There was something to be said for plowing through her fear and showing her the pleasure.

"I'm going to carry you to our bed," he said, caressing the line of her cheekbone with his knuckles.

"I'm going to kiss you and I'm going to make you feel good Kara, really good, like in the SUV earlier, except I won't have to stop unless you want me to." He stroked her hair. Loving the soft trusting way she relaxed against him.

She didn't raise her gaze but he watched as a blush stole up her cheeks. He felt protectiveness swell inside him. More than anything else he wanted to make her first sexual experience mind-blowingly good for her.

"I don't want you to do anything but just relax and trust me. Let me know if anything hurts in a bad way or makes you uncomfortable, okay?"

She nodded her head unable to find her voice. She felt vulnerable and afraid, and yet she trusted Slade. She knew if she was ever going to have a first sexual experience she wanted it to be with him.

He pulled her against him and kissed her deeply, his mouth stroking hers as he caressed her shoulders and her back. When he ended the kiss he stood and lifted her in his arms, loving the way she nuzzled her face against his chest as he carried her.

Kara liked the clean spicy scent that clung to him and the solidness and strength that emanated from him. She liked the way he carried her, lifting her in his powerful arms and carrying her as if she weighed nothing at all.

The bed was soft beneath her, as he settled her on it. She looked up, her eyes meeting his as he stood beside the bed looking down at her.

"Okay so far?" he asked as he bent to remove his shoes.

"Yes," the single word slipped through her suddenly dry throat. She moistened her lips as she watched him, her gaze fixed on him as he straightened and tugged his sweater off over his head. Her gaze was drawn to his broad shoulders and the muscles that bunched beneath his smooth skin as he tossed the sweater aside. She eyed the broad expanse of his chest and the covering of fine black hair that grew there and wondered idly if the hairs would tickle her nose if she pressed her face against his bare chest as she had pressed her face against his chest earlier.

Her breath seemed to stall as his hands went to his belt. Her eyes followed the deft movements of his large hands as he unfastened the belt and tugged it free of the waistband of his jeans and dropped it into the pile with his shoes and sweater.

Her heart hammered in her chest and echoed in her ears as she watched in breathless anticipation. "Still doing okay?" he asked as he lowered himself onto the bed beside her.

She nodded.

The noise in her head and in her ears intensified as he stretched beside her, pulling her against him. Fear and growing excitement warred for dominance as she snuggled against him. He kissed her, gently at first, but with growing passion, as his hands stroked her face and her hair, before they lowered to her bottom where he cupped the cheeks of her bottom as he tugged her lower body into closer contact with his.

She felt the hard line of his penis press against her thigh and was surprised that his hardness fascinated her. Her only other experience with a man's cock had been ugly and brutal and she couldn't fathom why she felt excited rather than repulsed as Slade's erection grazed her thigh.

The image of the other man, his cock standing rigid in front of him as he stood menacingly over her spilled slowly into her mind. She squeezed her eyes shut and willed the ugly memories of the other man and his cock away.

She could hear the rapid thud thud thud of her own heart in her ears as Slade shifted so that he was partially above her. He kissed her lightly, teasing a string of little kisses around the edge of her mouth. He used his tongue to trace a line around her bottom lip, retracing the line again and again until the ugly images receded and she was pressing against him, her whimpers caught beneath his mouth.

He nibbled her lower lip with teeth that promised just a hint of pain. Then he eased the slight sting away with a gentle stroke of his tongue. She moaned, opening her mouth beneath his and kissing him back.

She felt shy and uncertain at first but Slade's mouth led hers in an intimate dance that soon gave way to the need for more than just mouths and tongues and the teasing nibble of teeth on lips and tongues.

She clung to him barely recognizing the mewling begging sounds that came from her. She desperately wanted his hands on her breasts, his fingers pinching her nipples as they had when they had stopped at the restaurant.

The more needy she became the more obstinate Slade seemed. He possessed her mouth, urging it open for the bold exploration of his tongue.

She clung to him, opening her mouth at his urging, moaning against his insurgence, as she tried to communicate her need for his hands on her breasts.

Her desire loosened her inhibitions and she snaked her hand timidly down Slade's chest, to his belly and lower so that she could stroke her palm tentatively along the length of his erection that strained against his jeans.

She felt rather than heard his sharply indrawn breath as she touched him. She drew her hand back as if she'd been stung. She wondered if she'd been too forward. "Don't get shy now," he whispered throatily. "It feels good. You just surprised me."

He moved his hips, pressing his jeans covered hardness against her palm. She cupped him with her hand, stroking from the base of his cock to the tip and back down again. She enjoyed the tremors she felt work through his hard member as she continued to stroke him through the worn denim of his jeans. She delighted in drawing strangled sounds of pleasure from him.

Slade slid his hand beneath the hem of her sweater. She jerked at the unexpected touch of his palm against the soft flesh of her tummy. She looked up feeling shy and small as she met the intensity of his gaze. His gaze touched her, stroking her as surely and as intimately as the calloused hand that slid over the soft skin of her belly sending a flurry of excitement deep into her core.

Unable to pull away from the depth of his gaze she stared up at him. She arched against his touch, only barely conscious of the wanting sounds that came from her.

Unable to be still beneath the onslaught of deepening sensation she arched toward him longing for his gentle calloused hands to move upward to claim her breasts. She continued to stroke him through his jeans. She varied her touches, experimenting to see what drew the most response.

She could feel his passion growing, it was evident in the way his mouth plundered hers and in the way he rocked his hips thrusting his hard cock against her palm with greater and greater urgency. His movements were fast, and she could sense the tension within him, growing, spiraling, hot, tight and a little dangerous.

He trailed his hand over the soft flesh of her belly again except now the touch was gentle almost a tickle. She arched against his palm, her body on fire and wanting more.

She whimpered and moaned clinging to him, as he caressed his way up her rib cage. He circled her breasts, first one and then the other with his finger. His mouth absorbed the gasp that shook her as he circled her nipple, teasing her with the promise of the exquisite pleasure he dangled just outside her reach.

He palmed her breasts, lifting them, teasing the nipples

with his palms. He circled the flats of his hands over the hard beads. She was lost in the sensation, wanting more of his touch, wanting the divine combination of pleasure and pain he'd given her before.

She was so lost in the passion he'd ignited that she didn't even think to protest when he urged her up, pulling off her sweater and unsnapping her bra. "I want to watch your nipples harden when I touch them," he groaned into her hair as he pressed her back against the bed.

When her hand would have slid back down his belly to the hard bulge in his jeans he captured both her hands in one of his and pinned them over her head. She stared up at him feeling confused. Hadn't he liked the way she'd touched him?

"This time is just for you. I want to make it good for you." He peered down into her face, his expression a mingling of intensity and gentleness that stole her breath. "You'll get your chance to take care of me in a little while," he whispered as he bent to nibble at her lips.

He dragged his thumbnail over the hardened tip of her nipple. She gasped at the sharpness of the unfamiliar sensation and moaned from somewhere deep in her chest.

It was pleasure and something sharper, not quite pain. It was like a thousand miniature lights that exploded in her mind's eye carrying her deeper into the storm of passion. She shuddered, arching upward for more but gasped when Slade drew his thumbnail across her other nipple.

He smiled indulgently as he gazed down into her face. Slowly, his gaze never drifting from her he reached out tweaking first one nipple and then the other as he drew deep gasps of pleasure from her. Dipping his head he sucked her left nipple into his mouth, holding it in the gentle grip of his teeth as he licked it loosening a tide of sensation that started in her breasts and ended in a tight coil between her legs. "You like that don't you sweetheart?" he asked doing it again to the other breast.

"Y-y-yes," she moaned, arching her breasts upward, hungry

for his touch.

"Beautiful." He breathed the word reverently as he dipped his head spreading slow kisses from the closed waistband of her jeans, across her tummy. His warm breath curled over her skin as his kisses returned to the soft skin just above the snap of her jeans. He licked her there, nibbling, teasing, making her want.

Her stomach tightened, the hollow core between her legs feeling molten as she arched toward Slade's mouth, loving the light touch of his mouth as he alternately tongued and nibbled her belly.

"I'm going to release your hands. Keep them where they are," he said.

The deep rumble of his voice near her ear echoed within her, stroking her as effectively as his hands. She realized in some fevered place that she had liked the authority in his voice.

He smoothed the flat of his hand over the arch of her belly, sliding up her rib cage till he had both her breasts beneath his palms. He took her nipples, one in each hand, alternately pleasuring and punishing the hard nubs as he looked down into her face.

She looked up at him feeling sucked into his depths by the intensity of his gaze. It was as if his expression, a mingling of heat and ardor and something softer, affection maybe, held her firmly in its grasp as he alternately pinched and stroked her nipples. He was purposely moderating the pleasure and pain to keep her at a fever pitch.

"Slade," she whimpered, whining, begging.

She felt so fevered, her body so taut, that she found it impossible to be still. She bucked, arching her body toward him, aware but uncaring that he was watching her, his eyes filled with something deep and warm.

She loved the harsh pain followed by the intense pleasure that followed as he led her through the rise of pain and the crash of pleasure over and over again.

She was beside herself, her hands gripped in the quilt, above her head where he had told her to keep them. Her body was covered in a fine sheen of sweat, her feminine center feeling hot as it clasped involuntarily. She whimpered and whined, twisting toward him, wanting more but not being able to identify what it was she wanted.

Slade released one nipple and used his hand to tug the zipper of her jeans down. He slid his hand into the opening, and tunneled beneath her panties to find the warm, wet center of her sex. She whimpered, the pleasure-pain on her nipples forgotten as he placed his hand against her. He rocked his palm against her, loosening tendrils of pure pleasure that gathered in her midsection spilling into the hollow between her legs. She felt as if her body was stretching, tightening, as if it was reaching higher and higher for something held just out of reach.

She whimpered unable to keep herself from thrusting against his hand as he stroked her. "Lift your bottom Kara, I want to be able to touch you without your clothes in the way."

She lifted her behind, missing his touch as he shifted and quickly divested her of what remained of her clothing.

"Much better," he said.

He placed his hand between her legs stroking her slowly and more intimately than he had when she'd been wearing her jeans. His fingers slid over her outer lips, parting her just enough that he brushed her tender center with each pass of his fingers.

That he was only brushing her sensitive middle seemed to heighten her awareness of the pleasure building in the deep dark place between her legs. She lifted, arching toward him, rotating her hips in a silent plea for more of his touch.

"I want to kiss you here," he said, covering her with one large possessive hand. She felt herself stiffen at the thought of such intimacy. "Just relax sweetheart, it's all about making you feel good."

His voice was a deep sexy rumble that released a tide of tingles deep in her center. She liked the way he talked to her.

The endearments that stroked her senses made her feel protected and safe.

"I didn't know I could feel this good," she whispered, looking at him through eyes that seemed clouded by the passion coursing through her.

"It's about to get a whole lot better," he murmured as he settled at the bottom of the bed between her splayed legs and his mouth slowly lowered to take possession of her. His kiss was neither hard nor soft as it settled on her.

It was intimate. More intimate than she could have imagined. She tensed when he spread her lips apart with his fingers and tongued her clit. She wasn't prepared for the sharp suddenness of the sensation or for the tingle that quickly became a throb as he continued to lick her.

When Slade increased the tempo of his strokes she drew a sharp breath and closed her eyes, basking in the heat and sensations that pooled at her center. "Just relax and let me make you feel good," he whispered, his breath fanning her heated center. She felt his fingers on her, parting her and then easing slowly inside. She gasped at the intrusion, then moaned softly, as her body opened to the pleasure of it.

It had been a very long time since her body had been spread and opened and even then it had not happened with gentleness or intimacy. The other time had been rough and painful. It had been ugly and crude and yet, the memories of that other time and place wouldn't be denied. They began to escape from their prison to crowd her consciousness, crowding into the circle of pleasure Slade was creating.

She felt sickness swelling, nearly clogging the back of her throat. She closed her mind to everything except willing the ugliness back into its prison.

This is Slade. Not that other man, she told herself.

This is Slade. I trust him. He won't hurt me. He isn't hurting me.

Breathe.

In.

Out.

She repeated the mantra over and over again in her mind until gradually the sickness receded and her mind centered again on the pleasurable sensations overtaking her body.

Slade drew back a little, easing his finger deeper. Kara's muscles tightened, clamping down against his finger. He stroked her slowly, rhythmically as his tongue approximated the same rhythm against her clit.

"Relax, I'm going to add another finger," Slade said softly. His breath was warm as it wafted across her heated pulsating womanhood. She was thankful for the warning, although she didn't think it helped her to relax. She stilled, her body tense, waiting, wondering what this new sensation would feel like as she felt the broader intrusion of another digit at the opening of her body. He slid into her, pausing, giving her time to adjust to his presence.

"Okay honey?" he asked as her body stretched to accommodate his fingers.

"Um-huh," she moaned softly. Her body felt stretched and tight, and yet it was a good sensation, one that made her feel whole and complete. He dipped his head kissing her pussy and lapping at her clit as he began to rotate his fingers inside her.

The duality of his motions and the tightness within her released showers of sensation that splintered from her core and scattered upward like fireworks across a darkened sky. She arched, unable to keep her body still as she sought more. The pleasure intensified, sharpened and tightened heating her center.

She stretched her body upward, her being held in an unfamiliar and desperate state of wanting. She strained against Slade's fingers and his mouth whimpering, whining, wanting more of the exquisite pleasure that was taking her higher and higher with each deliberate thrust of his fingers.

"Please. Slade. Please." Her voice was little more than a ragged moan. She was consumed with passion and with helplessness and frustration. She wanted to go higher, reach that place that dangled just outside her reach.

"Shh-shh, I'll give you everything you need honey," he said, pausing to press another finger deeply into her spasming pussy. The third finger stretched her and yet it was not a painful stretching.

He swirled her clit with his tongue as he thrust his fingers slowly and deeply into her writhing heat. She moaned, her breath coming from deep in her chest. He cast his arm across her thighs so that he was holding her open and helpless with just that one arm splayed across her spread thighs. With her legs held open she was helpless to avoid the heightening sensation as his tongue prodded her clit. She could not avoid the tightening, spiraling, splintering of her body as he thrust his fingers deep into her. She began to whimper, soft, little mewling whines as the tension heightened and her body began to throb and as something intangible coalesced deep inside, where his fingers were stroking.

"Oh, Slade," she moaned, tossing her head to one side and then the other as he held her open beneath his mouth. He plundered her femininity, his mouth taking her clit inside his warmth, pushing her toward some imperceptible barrier.

"Relax and let go," he coached, his words muffled against her. She squeezed her eyes closed, knotting her hands in the quilt over her head as she began to quiver and cry out his name.

"Good girl, let go," he urged, as he licked her, suckling her pussy. She was aware of his arm as it shifted from her thighs and moved upward where he pinched her nipples, giving her the pleasure-pain she liked.

She was lost in the onslaught. She whimpered, moaning, as she exploded into a million diamond bright splinters of brightly colored glass that spasmed beneath his touch.

His mouth on her gentled as she shattered. She whimpered, her body arching helplessly as each touch of his tongue, each press of his mouth against her tender pussy sent a flurry of delicate sensations that careened through her, pooling deep in the hollow between her legs. She writhed on the bed beneath his mouth, her mind and body one in the place with the splintering shards of multi-colored glass.

Gradually he allowed her body to quiet and descend. She was still breathing hard, her breath still coming in sharp gasps as he moved to lie beside her. He stroked her hair with gentle fingers. She yielded to him reveling in his touch and molding herself to him.

His mouth found hers, and he kissed her gently, slowly. She tasted herself on his tongue as they kissed. He stroked her, helping her to relax as he eased her into a blissful resting place after the mind-shattering climax she had enjoyed.

She basked in the touch of his hands on her body. She enjoyed the smoothness of the sensation as his hands slid down her body till he held her bottom cheeks one in each hand. He pulled her closer so that she was pressed against the length of him.

Then he stroked her bottom. She pulled back just a tiny bit, enough to allow her hand to slip between them as she began her own tentative explorations of his body. She stroked the hard plane of his chest, enjoying the soft tickle of his chest hair as she slid her palms over the hardness of his chest. She ran her finger over the hollow at the base of his throat, and over one hard, male nipple.

Slade's gaze rested on her. His expression was filled with indulgence as he allowed her the freedom to explore his body. Her hand dropped lower, sliding across the flatness of his belly and lower to his cock still trapped within his worn jeans.

She stroked him, frustration growing as the warm denim impeded her touch. She grunted in frustration as she slid her palm along his length.

"Let me help," Slade said as he slid off the bed, tugging his jeans open and pulling jeans and briefs down his legs in one smooth motion.

Kara watched transfixed, her eyes drawn to the length and

width of his erect cock. It strained toward her as he rejoined her on the bed.

For just an instant another man and another cock, one that had been menacing intruded, but she pushed the ugly memory aside and reached for Slade stroking him, enjoying the way his hard manhood arched toward her touch. Her hand traveled the length of his cock, slowly, sensuously.

"Oh God honey," Slade said against her ear as she used a single finger to circle the tip of him.

She repeated the touch again, thrilled that it drew another deep ripple of pleasure that emanated from his large hard body into her softer one.

She loved the sensation, loved that she could give him pleasure. He had been nice to her, patient and kind. He had made her first real sexual experience good beyond anything she could have imagined and she wanted to give him the same kind of pleasure.

She experimented with him, her hands tentative as she tried different strokes. When she found one that caused him to moan or arch toward her she repeated it and tucked it away in her mind for later use.

She stroked the head of his cock with her palm, drawing tremors and gasps as he moaned and arched toward her. She watched the hard, glistening tip of his cock as she stroked him. She could tell Slade was enjoying her touch, but she knew he needed more.

She felt uncertain and shy as she scooted down in the bed and found the tip of his cock with her mouth. She had done this before, but not since she was seven and the situation had been so different as to render the experiences not the same at all.

She looked up at him her gaze locking with his as she sought his approval. He arched toward her, his eyes a combination of hard and soft as she tasted him tentatively. Enthralled by the passion and fascinated by his unconscious responses she sucked him into her mouth, circling the tip of his penis with her tongue, duplicating the stroke that had drawn deep guttural gasps when she'd done it with her hand.

"Oh God, Kara," he uttered as he lifted his hips toward her. She sucked him deeper into her mouth, liking the feel of his hardness thrusting against the back of her mouth.

It had been a long, long time since she'd had a man's cock in her mouth. That first experience when she was a child had been nothing like this. There had been nothing good then. It had been hard, ugly, violent. She remembered the force with which he had shoved himself into her mouth and down her throat. He had made her gag and then had smacked her for gagging.

She pushed the ugly memories aside as she concentrated on Slade.

She circled him again, her tongue trailing the underside of his cock. He began to thrust against her mouth, driving himself deeper with each pumping motion of his hips. "Oh, God baby, that's it."

Kara slid her mouth up and down his length, taking most of him into her mouth with each pass. She could feel his body tightening, the tension seeming to grow as each touch of her tongue on the head of his cock pushed him further toward that place where he would explode as she herself had exploded.

Slade moaned, his body thrusting hard against her face as his passion mounted. The hard thrust of his hips and the pressure of his cock against the back of her throat, and the strength and fervor frightened her. The memory of a man's cock cutting off her ability to breathe exploded within her and she prayed she wouldn't gag as she had when she was seven.

She tried to push the ugly memories aside, determined to give Slade the same pleasure he had given her. She could feel him straining for his own release, the same release he had given her and she struggled to close out the memories that grew stronger with each powerful thrust.

As his passion intensified he grasped her head, holding

her in place as he thrust upward, his hard cock slamming against the back of her throat. She nearly gagged but he withdrew a fraction. She scrunched her eyes closed and tried to move away but his hands held her as he thrust into her mouth again.

Without warning the memories she'd kept trapped were free, tearing through her. Buried images slammed into her consciousness. The pervading smell of damp that had filled the basement where she had been kept and the frequent sounds of sirens that came close but were still too far away to offer help exploded in her mind.

She was no longer with Slade. It was no longer his cock in her mouth. Instead she was seven, her head held immobile while the vile stranger thrust his huge smelly dick into her mouth. Her mouth ached more with each thrust and she gagged gasping for breath with each powerful surge.

The memory receded leaving her aware of reality but it was too late. She scrambled from the bed and dashed for the bathroom as she gagged. The contents of her stomach rose into the back of her throat as she slid to the floor in front of the toilet. She lifted the lid and hung her head over the bowl as desperation and embarrassment clawed through her.

Her head spun as she gagged into the toilet. The memory of Slade holding her head still as he'd thrust his cock into her helpless mouth brought fresh tears and fresh embarrassment.

She'd wanted his cock, wanted to please him but once he'd grasped her head everything had happened too quickly. In that split second she'd been back in the basement prison where she'd been kept. She'd been seven. Helpless. Alone. Afraid.

By the time the ugliness had started to recede it was too late to stop the panic attack. She trembled, shivering. She gagged, her stomach lurching as she vomited into the toilet. Wet tears cascaded down her face.

Chapter 8

What in the hell? Slade asked the question of himself as Kara tumbled backward off the bed, retching as she dashed toward the bathroom.

He didn't know what had happened but he was damn sure going to find out. He climbed out of the bed and not bothering to pull on his jeans strode into the bathroom all set to demand answers.

The sight that met his eyes made his gut clench. Kara sat hunched on the floor, her head hanging over the toilet, her hair dangling in the way as she vomited. The repetitive sounds of her gagging and the contents of her stomach filling the toilet bowl kicked at his conscience.

He'd known she was a virgin but he'd thought that by the time he'd carried her to their bed she was as into it as he was. She'd been so sweet, so responsive, so wet. It had been her that had reached for his cock, touching him shyly, with her hands, making him ache before she ever took him into her mouth. Hell, he'd have bet his entire business that she'd been as into it as he was.

Even so, guilt tore at him. Something had happened. It couldn't have been the taste of him. She'd pulled away and tumbled off the bed before he'd made it all the way to climax.

"I'm sorry." She gagged. "So sorry. I didn't mean to—" she lost some more of her dinner into the toilet. "I—oh God!," she gagged again.

The sight of her hunched, alternately puking and apologizing made him feel protective. He didn't care what had happened, he wanted to comfort her and make whatever was wrong right. "Sh—shhh. Just relax honey. You can tell me what happened when you feel better." He stepped toward her reaching forward to rescue the long strands of bed-tousled hair from the toilet.

"I'm sorry." She was sobbing, her breath coming in choppy little gasps as she hung her head over the toilet.

"I know you didn't mean for this to happen sweetheart," he said. "Are you done throwing up do you think?"

"Maybe. I think. That part doesn't usually last long." She hiccupped.

Usually? This had happened before? His mind raced. "Whoa Kara. You lost me. That part of what?" he asked as his mind groped to make sense of the sudden turn of events.

As he waited for her answer he turned to the sink and grabbed a washcloth from the towel rack. He turned on the cold-water and ran the rag under it. "This has happened before?"

"I h-h-" she hiccupped. He squeezed out the excess water from the rag before settling on his knees on the floor in front of her.

He tilted her chin, gazing down into her face. His concern grew as she shivered, her teeth chattering. Sadness surrounded her.

"I h—have panic attacks," she said through chattering teeth.

She dipped her head, closing her eyes. He sensed her shame but didn't comment.

He tilted her chin and began to wipe her face free of the tears and vomit.

She began to cry again. Not the short choppy little gasps of before, but a silent trickle of tears that wound their way down her face.

Her silent tears touched him deeply. He'd never seen her

cry. Even when she'd come to his office afraid that her brother would end up in prison and the stress of his trial would kill her mother she hadn't cried.

He finished cleaning her face, then tossed the rag in the sink and pulled her against his chest, wanting to make whatever was wrong better. He held her, rocking her as if she were a child. Still she couldn't seem to get a grip. Her tears continued to trickle down her face dripping onto his bare chest.

"Shhhh honey, it's okay," he whispered softly as his body absorbed another of the violent shivers. He rocked her back and forth and stroked her hair back away from her face. She didn't open her eyes, didn't look at him, and didn't raise her face as he stroked her.

She trembled, her teeth chattering as she shivered. "Listen sweetheart, look at me," he said softly wondering if he could even reach her where she was. She seemed disconnected, as if she were only partially aware of where she was. That and the nearly constant shivers worried him.

Very slowly she opened her eyes. Her gaze climbed his chest until her gaze met his. Deep, misery stared back at him but at least there seemed to be some awareness of where she was and what was going on. "Listen to me honey."

Her attention seemed to wander and he snapped his fingers in front of her face drawing her focus back to him. "I'm going to carry you into the living room. We're going to sit by the fire until you are warm and until you feel better. Okay?"

She nodded her brain feeling fuzzy and overwhelmed. She knew that the freezing, the nausea, the dizziness, the weakness that sapped every drop of her energy was part of the panic attack. They always left her feeling as if she'd been kicked to her knees.

She closed her eyes shutting out everything around her as Slade lifted her. She didn't have the energy to argue. Instead she savored his strength, needing it and his kindness for just a little while till her own strength returned.

He paused by the bed standing her on her feet but steadying

her with one hand while he tugged the quilt off the bed and wrapped it around her with the other. When he had her enclosed in the soft folds of the blanket he lifted her again.

She lulled her head against his shoulder feeling dizzy and sick to her stomach and more miserable than she could remember feeling. She closed her eyes and swallowed hard, hoping she wouldn't be sick again.

Slade carried her down with him as he eased into the big rocker in the living room. Once he was seated he shifted her, positioning her so that she sat across his lap with her head nestled against his shoulder.

She was a pool of conflicting emotions as she waited, dreading the moment when he demanded to know what had happened and why she had fallen apart. She didn't know how she could explain why she had gone from enthusiastically sucking his cock to a blubbering heap on the bathroom floor without telling him about the stranger that had kidnapped her and her twin sister.

Her skin crawled as she contemplated what she'd tell him. She knew he wouldn't understand her panic unless she told him how the man had held her face, nearly smothering her as he slammed his dick into her mouth again and again. She heaved a sigh, reaching a decision. She'd tell Slade what she needed to to make him understand why she'd fallen apart but she couldn't give him more.

She had never disclosed what had happened between being kidnapped and being found even when the psychiatrists, detectives, and doctors had tried to badger it out of her.

Nothing had changed to make her want to relive the gruesome ordeal. She didn't want to face the pain that lived in her heart when she thought about the events that had happened during the nightmare of her captivity.

She couldn't explain what she herself didn't understand. She couldn't tell Slade, or the police, or the psychiatrists or her parents why she was alive and Kayla was dead. It made no sense.

Kara leaned against him, needing to absorb his strength. He was silent, stroking her arms and her back. His touches and his silence soothed her scattered nerves but did nothing to alleviate the guilt and pain that went clear through her.

Slade took care of her. When the misery overwhelmed her clogging her throat he drew the quilt closer and wordlessly wrapped his arms more tightly around her, not saying anything, just giving her warmth and closeness she desperately needed.

The gentle way he cared for her intensified the anguish that ate at her. She didn't deserve his care. Her brother had stolen from him and she'd lied to him when she'd let him think she could be an obedient and passionate wife.

Slade's body absorbed the shiver as her teeth rattled. She sniffed and stirred on his lap, her bottom grinding against the ache in his groin.

"How're you doing, honey?" he asked gently, ignoring the ache.

She sniffed again and pressed her face into his chest. "I'm so sorry—" she sucked in a deep breath. "I—I Kn-know you want to d-div-divorce me." Hot wet tears leaked onto his chest and her shudder echoed through him.

He didn't want to divorce her. He wanted to protect her, to erase whatever had hurt her and make her whole again. He nuzzled the top of her head placing a series of little kisses there. "I don't want to divorce you. Not now. Not ever." He pulled her closer, wrapping the quilt more snugly around her as he rocked her.

"I just want to understand what hurt you."

She buried her face more deeply in his chest and he could feel the tremor that worked through her, even as her tears, the silent ones that tore at him the most ran down his chest.

He stroked her back as she drew a deep breath. "When I was seven—" She stopped. He waited.

She sucked in another breath and let it go.

His heart felt bruised. He knew without any doubt that

whatever had happened when she was seven had wounded her profoundly. His arms tightened around her, as he willed her to go on.

"When I was seven," she started again. "I was—I was—kidnapped."

Seven. His niece Nicole was seven. He pictured her. She was small for her age and had dark hair that just brushed the bottoms of her ears and deep brown eyes that sparkled when she laughed. She was innocent, a child.

His body tensed as he imagined Kara at Nicole's age.

He stroked Kara's hair and her back, comforting her as best he could. He thought about Nicole and what she would need if something this awful were to happen to her. "He asked me to help him look for his p-p-puppy." She choked up, her voice ending on a sob.

He felt her hands twisting in the quilt.

"When I got c-close to his truck he picked me up and threw me in. H-h-he had a knife." She sucked a deep breath and burrowed her head into his shoulder sucking in another gulp of air.

Slade held her against his shoulder, his hand splayed over the back of her head. He wished he knew what to say or do that would make this easier for her.

There was nothing he could do but hold her. He remained silent giving her time.

She sniffed against his shoulder. "H-he said he would k-kill me if I tried to get away, s-so I didn't t-try."

"He...molested you?" Slade asked, kissing the top of her head and holding her tighter. He'd offered the word, wanting to spare her having to drudge up the words to explain her ordeal.

"Y—yes. N—n-no. I-it was quite a bit worse. H-he...um..." She sucked in a breath and tried again. "Hhh...h-he—"

"Raped you?" he asked, vile hatred for the man rising in his chest as he dreaded her answer.

"Yes." The word came out on a big gush of air that broke

apart on a sob.

Not since he'd been four and watched the sheriff haul his family's belongings to the curb had Slade felt more helpless.

"Shh——shh baby. I'm sorry. So sorry that happened," he said as he rocked them.

After several minutes he urged her chin up and wiped tender fingers over the tears that still ran like silent rivers down her cheeks.

"Did I do something? Before? Did something happen that made this all real for you again?"

She blinked up at him her eyes large and filled with tears. She was the picture of misery and it made his heart buckle. He could see indecision in her expression.

"Tell me the truth Kara. I need to know." He stroked her hair back from her face, his eyes searching for the answers on her face and in her expression, even as she twisted on his lap, closing her expression and attempting to hide the depths of her misery from him.

She tipped her head downward. He sensed that she was hiding from him, hiding her shame. He wrapped his arms around her offering what comfort and support he could. He felt her short choppy breaths lengthen as she tried to regain the control she'd lost. "When he—p-put his—p-penis in m-my mouth," she scrunched her eyes shut and drew a deep breath. "H-he held m-my h-head still. I couldn't b-breathe."

Understanding and the implications of what she said hit Slade with the force of an avalanche. He remembered how he'd held her head as he'd driven himself into her mouth.

Shame and regret filled him. Sickness settled in the pit of his stomach.

"I'm so sorry sweetheart. I didn't know." The apology seemed inadequate and yet he didn't know what more to say. He pulled her tighter, wrapping his arms around her as he kissed her, his mouth gently following the salty trails her tears had left.

"It's not your fault. It's just—" She sucked in air. "It's just

I can't—"

He lifted his head, his attention drawn to her pale features and the dark eyes that remained fixed on her lap where they avoided the lure of his gaze. "You lost me. You can't what Kara?" he asked feeling like he'd been caught in a vortex he couldn't break free of.

Her lip trembled and she clenched her hands in her lap as she raised her eyes to meet his gaze. "I lied when I let you think I could be a—g—good sex partner. I can't."

"Kara, honey," He tipped her chin up so he could meet her gaze. "You're a great sex partner. You're sweet and passionate and responsive." He stroked her cheek. "This is one experience that ended badly because I didn't know—" he sucked in a deep breath, "about what happened to you and how it would effect you."

He watched as she dipped her gaze, drawing away, putting distance between them. "I left you—um—unfulfilled."

"And I'll live. It's not the end of the world." He stroked her hair back away from her face tilting her chin so he could read her expression.

"I can't do this again. Please—please don't make me."

He understood. He'd seen her anguish, heard it in her voice, felt it in the tremors that had shaken her long after they'd settled into the chair. Yet he wasn't willing to release her from their marriage.

"So where are you thinking this leaves our marriage Kara? I don't want a divorce."

"I don't know where it leaves it." Her voice was soft and hollow. Empty. "I don't have anything to offer you. I can't— I don't want to—" She bit down on her lip and he had the impression she was fighting back tears. "It wasn't fair of me to marry you and I'm sorry I got you into this."

He felt her breaths deepen and become short. She bit her lip hard enough he expected he'd taste blood if he were to kiss her. She was putting up a hard fight against the tears, but he sensed they were going to fall in spite of her efforts to control them.

"You could lean on me Kara. You could take what I'm offering and trust me," he said as he wrapped her in his arms just before the first of her tears slid down her nose and onto his chest.

Kara let him hold her while she cried. She was too tired, too emotionally drained to do anything else. She didn't want a divorce but she didn't deserve his patience or his understanding. She had lied to him, and was still lying to him to some extent.

His words echoed in her mind as he held her, wiping her tears and rocking her in the stillness of the cabin's living room while the fire died down to embers in the grate.

She did trust him, she'd told him more than she'd ever told anyone, including her parents about what had happened during her imprisonment. She knew she could get used to him cradling her against his chest, giving her the understanding her soul thirsted for.

If only she deserved what he offered. But she didn't. She'd lied to him. She was still lying to him.

It wouldn't be fair to take his gentleness and understanding without being able to reciprocate. And she couldn't. Even if by some miracle she was able to get through the sex act without a panic attack the threat of one coming out of the blue because of some scent, some seemingly minor action, would always be there. Slade deserved better than what she could offer.

She drifted on the bleakness of her thoughts, wondering how she could make Slade understand that he needed to let her go, that she couldn't give him what he wanted, what he deserved.

Eventually, exhaustion overwhelmed her worry and a fitful sleep claimed her.

* * * *

"Kara, sweetheart, it's time to go to bed." She heard Slade's voice, a soft reassuring rumble close to her ear. The sound of her own whimpers and the dark images that had filled her dreams dissolved as she sat up feeling groggy and disoriented.

"You okay? You were having a bad dream," Slade said as he shifted beneath her, pushing her hair back away from her face.

She yawned and sighed sleepily. She was so tired her bones ached and she felt sadness clear to the center of her being. She didn't feel okay. She didn't think she'd ever feel okay again, but that was how the panic attacks and the aftermath of the nightmares usually left her.

Slade urged her off his lap, and stood up behind her as soon as she was upright. "Come on, to bed with you," he said putting his hands on her shoulders and urging her toward the darkened bedroom. If he'd left her on her own she'd have sunk back into the recently vacated chair and gone back to sleep.

She was barely aware of walking to the bedroom and only vaguely aware of stopping near the bedside as Slade released her shoulders and moved around beside her. She was dimly aware of the play of fire that still glowed in the fireplace grate casting dancing shadows and light over him. The light cast him in a warm glow that illuminated a strong muscular hip and rippling shoulders as he shifted to draw the blanket and the sheet back.

She watched spellbound as he turned toward her, the firelight casting shadows across the hard planes of his chest. Her gaze dipped lower caressing the flatness of his belly and his cock that rested flacid in a thatch of curly pubic hair.

She caught her breath, embarrassment sweeping her. She felt suddenly intimidated by the bed and by Slade's large, solid body next to her and by her own nudity beneath the folds of the quilt that covered her.

"In you get," Slade said, seemingly completely undisturbed by his own nudity or hers as he raised the sheet and blanket so that she could crawl into the bed beneath them.

She turned toward him, her teeth embedded in her lower lip as she lifted her gaze to his face and kept it fixed there.

Shyness and confusion mingled, stretching her nerves tighter as she stood eying him hesitantly while he waited for her to climb into the bed.

It was silly she knew, given the way she had opened her legs and writhed beneath his mouth as he had taken intimate control of her body giving her the ultimate pleasure. Still, she felt shy about dropping the quilt and climbing naked into bed. She wasn't used to being naked. Even when she was alone she wore a nightgown or a robe.

She nibbled her lip. She wanted to avoid the big bed all together, and she especially wanted to avoid it when they were both naked. She opened her mouth to tell him she'd sleep on the couch.

"If you're thinking of suggesting you sleep on the loveseat or in the recliner, don't," Slade said. One look at the determination that marked his expression had her dropping the quilt and climbing into the bed like an obedient child.

"I'll get you something to help you sleep," he said, smoothing the covers down around her as she settled into the softness of the big bed.

She watched the play of firelight over the tight muscles of his perfectly rounded ass as he padded naked into the bathroom.

He returned a moment later with a paper cup filled with water. "What is this?" she asked as she sat up in the bed, holding the sheet and blanket to her chest as she took the tablet he held out to her.

"Tylenol PM. It'll help you sleep and help keep the nightmares away." How does he know about the nightmares, she wondered as she swallowed the tablet and handed him back the empty cup. She was thankful for his caring treatment even if she knew she didn't deserve it and couldn't give back anything even close.

"Thanks," she said softly as she settled back in the bed, moving to the far side, as far away from him and the embarrassing memories of their sexual encounter as the bed would allow.

New embarrassment coursed through her as he turned away with the cup. She needed him to leave a light on in the bathroom so that if she woke up in the night she would see some light, so her first thought on waking wasn't the panic that stemmed from believing she was back in the pitch black of the basement where she'd been kept.

She rolled words around in her mind, struggling with how to ask him for the little bit of light she needed but shame and mortification washed through her. How could she admit that at twenty-seven she was still afraid to sleep in the dark?

She left the question of the light and how to ask him to leave one on dangling as his deep voice cut into her thoughts.

"Roll onto your tummy and I'll rub your back till you fall asleep," Slade said softly.

She rolled to her belly, propping her head on her folded arms as Slade moved into the bed beside her.

"You're too nice to me," she said softly as his warm, gentle hands began to caress her back.

"It assuages my guilt a little," he said as his hands made smaller and then larger circles on her back.

"You don't have any reason to feel guilty," she murmured.

"If I hadn't pushed you into marriage so quickly we would have gotten to know each other better before things got sexual. With a little more time you might have felt comfortable telling me about...what happened. If I'd known I would have been more careful and I wouldn't have hurt you."

She felt sadness and guilt settle into her belly. "It's my fault, I should have told you."

"There's enough blame for both of us," Slade said as he slid his hands up between her shoulder blades, and across her shoulders. She marveled that he wasn't angry, that he wasn't blaming her for ruining their honeymoon, that he wasn't shouting at her for being a fraud, that he was rubbing her back, giving her pleasure when he had every reason to be angry.

She felt her tension easing, slipping away as he slid warm hands down her back and back up again. His strokes were slow, purposeful, calming. She relaxed beneath the comforting caress as she let her mind and body drift toward drug induced sleep.

"Slade?" she asked sleepily after a long silence.

"What honey?" he answered softly.

"When you said I could trust you and take what you were offering, what did you mean?" she slurred her words as the calming strokes on her back and the sleeping pill he had given her combined to ease her toward sleep.

Chapter 9

The cloying, pungent smell of aftershave mingled with the smell of death assaulted Kara. She sank back against the cold cement blocks, trying in vain to make herself invisible against the basement wall. She prayed he would leave her alone, but of course he didn't. He never left her alone.

He leaned over her, leering, his intent to do it again clear in his expression. She drew her knees up to her chin and wrapped trembling arms tight around them to hold them there in a feeble attempt to protect herself.

She hated him. She despised what he had done to her and loathed him even more for what he'd done to Kayla.

He knocked her to the side with one large open palm that connected with the side of her already badly bruised face. He pried her legs apart. She cried, and kicked as hard as she could as she screamed at him to leave her alone. She felt herself smothering, losing her breath as she wondered if he was going to kill her like he'd killed Kayla.

"Shh—Kara honey, you're having another bad dream."

Slade. Just as she recognized the touch and the voice the nightmare broke apart and fell away leaving only the scattered remnants of the dream.

"You're okay sweetheart. You were having another bad dream." He pulled her into the curve of his body, so that her back pressed against his chest as he wrapped his arms around her and anchored her against the warmth and safety of his body.

"Relax honey, you're okay. I have you." He whispered the soft words as he nuzzled the back of her neck, his lips grazing her shoulder.

"You're okay. Nobody's going to hurt you. You're safe."

His mouth continued to spread little kisses over her shoulders.

She ached with exhaustion and she knew he had to be tired too. This wasn't the first time she'd woken him during this night that seemed a thousand hours long. She remembered waking to find him pulling her close, whispering sweet gentle things in her ear and against her skin as he'd kissed her earlier in the night. "I'm sorry Slade. I should go sleep in the other room so I won't keep waking you."

"I want you here with me Kara."

"You'll never get any sleep if I stay here," she said softly. "I always have a string of nightmares after I have a panic attack. It's like the attack opens the gates of hell and all the bad stuff that happened comes out." She drew a deep breath. "I can't help it. It just happens. Let me sleep on the love seat, please."

"No, Kara." His voice was firm as it had been when he'd ordered her to get into the bed what seemed like hours before.

"Then will you let me turn on the light in the bathroom? I——um——I need to sleep with a light on." Embarrassment cut through her.

"I'll turn on the light, you stay put," he ordered as he shifted away from her and climbed out of bed. He turned on the light in the bathroom and adjusted the door so that it provided a reassuring shaft of light without glaring into the room.

"Thanks Slade," she sighed as he got back into bed and pulled her against him. She put herself through the exercises that usually helped ease the tension left from a nightmare. She started at her feet, reminding herself to relax each part of her body as she moved mentally up from her feet to focus on her calves and then her thighs. She moved her attention upward through the rest of her body, reminding each part to loosen and release its tension. By the time she finished the mental exercise she was relaxed against Slade but feeling wide-awake.

"How often do you have panic attacks?" he asked, his voice soft against the back of her ear.

"Not very often, but I hate having them so any is too many."

He held her in the silence, not saying anything. "Why didn't you tell me about them Kara?" he asked after awhile.

She shrugged, thinking back to why she hadn't told him when they were in the SUV, or later when they'd been on the loveseat, before he carried her to the bed. "After you——we—— " She sighed, took a deep breath and started again. "After we stopped at the restaurant I thought maybe I'd be able to——I thought maybe I could get through sex without having one. I thought maybe I wouldn't have to tell you."

Slade was silent awhile, his breath slow as it ruffled the hair near her ear.

"I'm sorry. I know I should have told you, but they're embarrassing. They make me feel weak and sick and——and I didn't want you to know."

He was quiet for a while, as his breath brushed the back of her neck. "I understand why you didn't tell me." His voice was quiet and without judgment.

She was silent, absorbing his calmness, marveling that he wasn't angry with her and that he didn't seem hurt that she had chosen not to tell him.

She frowned into the pre-dawn darkness. She liked him, and was beginning to trust him and to count on him for little bits of tenderness that soothed the tattered places in her soul.

She liked him enough that it caused a physical ache when she thought about asking him to release her from their marriage. Still she knew she couldn't keep absorbing his warmth and kindness while she had nothing to give back.

It wouldn't be fair, but even if that didn't stop her she

knew that eventually he would become frustrated by her inability to meet him half way.

"Slade?" Her voice was soft and tentative.

"What honey?" His arm tightened around her.

"Last night, when you said I could take what you were offering, what did you mean?"

"You asked me that last night, just before you fell asleep, remember?" Slade asked softly.

He felt the nod of her head and the silky stir of her hair as it shifted against his shoulder.

"I know I said we'd wait until you were ready before we addressed dominance and submission but there are aspects of that lifestyle that I think would help us deal with your fears about sex."

"I don't want to have sex again Slade. I can't——I know I promised——but I just can't." She sucked a deep breath. "Don't make me. Please."

He heard the raw ragged fear that laced her voice and wanted to pull her closer, to tell her it would be okay, that he wouldn't make her do anything she didn't want to do.

It was true. He would never force her, but he would certainly push her to the very edges of her comfort zone, and then he'd pause there to stretch and expand that zone of comfort. It wouldn't always be comfortable. In fact, it might get damned uncomfortable, but he thought that dismantling the fear which had held her captive since she was seven would be worth a degree of discomfort.

The problem was he didn't expect her to understand or to see the wisdom in approaching the fear his way. So he would need to build a deep trust, the kind that came from consciously building and testing her confidence in him. He knew how to do that within a relationship built on a framework of dominance and submission. He wasn't sure how to do it without the framework.

Slade was silent for a long time. "I know you believe that you don't ever want to have sex again," Slade said very quietly.

"I know you're afraid. I can understand why after what happened to you when you were a child, but Kara, the fear has held you in its grip and limited your life for twenty years. Don't you want to be free of it?"

She rolled over so that she was lying on her back looking up at the ceiling with an expression that said she wanted to trust him but wasn't sure she could.

"I am afraid Slade. I live with the knowledge that one whiff of the aftershave he wore, or a familiar phrase, will trigger a panic attack. I don't know how to stop being afraid. If I did-." Slade heard the frustration and the fear that edged her voice and wished he could instantly ease both. He couldn't. Healing, like her trust, would take time and patience.

"I know you don't see how Kara." He sighed deeply, rolling to his side and lifting his hand to trace the line of her cheek and jaw, meeting the mingled fear and trust in her eyes as she turned her gaze toward him.

"You don't need to understand how it all works honey. All you need to do is trust me to figure out the pieces. Submit. Do what I tell you because you trust me. It really is as simple as that."

She drew a deep breath, her brain spinning dizzily. "I don't understand. If I—do what you tell me, you think I'll stop being afraid? I don't understand how that would work." She drew a deep breath. "I think I would be even more afraid if I had no control than I am now."

Slade drew a deep breath. "Choosing to submit to me doesn't take your control away. If you were to decide to give me your power today you could change your mind and take it back tomorrow. It's at your discretion, a kind of continuous ongoing decision. It's not an all or nothing kind of thing."

He stroked her arm lightly. "It is something you will have to give me willingly. I won't take it if you don't want to give it."

"But then, what's the point if I can change my mind back and forth?"

"The dominance and submission aspects of a relationship add—a kind of foundation—on which everything else is built. It's a commitment like deciding to be faithful to one partner. You always have the power to change your mind but you probably wouldn't."

He sighed searching for the proper words to explain the depth of trust inherent in D/s relationships and the reasons he didn't think she would ever want to take back her power once she had given it to him.

"It's not a decision to make lightly," he said stroking her shoulder idly. "But I think the foundation of that kind of lifestyle and the relationship that we would build would help. For one thing, you wouldn't be facing the panic attacks alone. I would be there with you, supporting you through the aftermath, just like I was this time."

He was quiet for a minute remembering what she had said about living with the fear of something triggering a panic attack and her frustration at not knowing how to get beyond the fear of the attacks.

"I think that knowing that you would not be alone might in and of itself diffuse the power the threat of them has."

Kara thought about his words. The panic attack had been ugly. It had left her feeling as if someone had sucked every drop of energy from her, and yet, as bad as the attack had been and as weak as she had been after it, she had not reached the same low level she had reached with other attacks she'd had. She was sure that was because he had been there with her, holding her, stroking her, whispering reassuring words when she woke fresh from the violence of yet another nightmare.

Kara felt the stirring of hope like the brush of butterfly wings deep in her soul. Was it possible that something about dominance and submission, giving her power to Slade, could help her get beyond what had happened to her? If she took this chance, grasped this opportunity would she someday be able to meet Slade half way as a whole person, unafraid of sex, able to give and receive physical love without fear and panic making her feel like she was suffocating?

"So, you think there is hope for me to stop being afraid of sex and the panic attacks it causes?" Kara asked.

"There isn't a magic bullet. I don't think your fear would disappear instantly. It's too deep and too old. The fear going away would be the by-product of time, training, and trust."

He studied her. She could feel his eyes sweeping over her face, as if he were quietly gauging her reaction. "The cornerstone of dominance and submission is trust. We would start by building your trust in me. When you trusted me sufficiently I would start teaching you to obey me. We'd start with easy things that didn't cause you great distress and eventually when you had the foundation of trust and obedience to support you, move into more difficult areas. Hope rose within her. She already trusted Slade and she'd only known him for a couple weeks, most of which they'd spent separate. "The focus on trust and obedience would make it easier for you to do the hard things that I would ask you to do to help you get beyond the fear."

Excitement swelled in her chest. If there really was a way to get rid of the fear that had haunted her, that had stalked every waking moment for twenty years she wanted to take the risk. "Are you sure it will work? Have you—have you done this kind of thing before?"

"Trained a sub? Yes, I've done that before."

She sensed a smile in the softness of his voice but couldn't see his expression in the darkened room. She wondered if he was remembering the sub he'd trained and felt an irrational stirring of jealousy.

"I have never personally used dominance to help a sub deal with fears as deep as yours, but I know several people who have. It's not unusual to use certain aspects of dominance and submission to help someone overcome a fear or to expand their comfort zone."

Her excitement soared, tethered only by her uncertainty.

She wanted to be free of the fear and the panic attacks more than she had ever wanted anything else in her life.

The promise of being free of the constant fear of someone getting too close or of an unexpected scent catching her off guard and triggering a panic attack, was like being offered a chance at wholeness when she'd lived most of her life in a shell. "It will work? You're sure?"

"Yes, Kara, I'm sure it will work. I wouldn't suggest it if I wasn't."

"If I say yes, then what?"

"If you say yes, then there will be some ground rules, simple easy ones at the beginning. More difficult ones later," Slade answered.

"Like—like what kind of ground rules? Do I get a sneak preview?"

"If having one makes you more comfortable," Slade responded.

Kara waited anxiously for the other shoe to drop as she wondered what it would take to be free of her fear once and for all.

He propped himself on one arm so that he loomed over her, with his face only inches above hers as his unflinching gaze met hers in the predawn darkness. "First, there will be no more hiding from me. That means no more half-truths, no more looking down and avoiding meeting my gaze, no more big bulky sweaters to hide beneath. You will need to be completely open and honest about everything you're thinking and feeling. I need to understand what's going on with you emotionally and physically so I don't hurt you."

She shifted to face him more fully. She gazed up into his face, her eyes deciphering the determination and the affection that warred for dominance on his face.

Fear clawed at her. She hadn't said yes and already he was disrupting her world. "I don't have anything but big bulky sweaters."

"Buy some other things honey, I'll go with you if you want,

but it's not negotiable."

She felt as if she were folding in on herself, as if everything was suddenly upended and she didn't know where anything fit anymore.

"What else?" Her voice was dry, flat, just a hoarse whisper as she looked up at him, her heart pounding in her chest. She felt fearful of the spell he was weaving around her, and yet she didn't want to be free of it.

"I want you to trust me implicitly. I know that takes time and I don't expect you to trust me completely overnight but I want you to work toward trusting me that much. I want you to submit to being my wife and accept me as your husband and eventually as your master. I want you to stop trying to figure out ways to wiggle out of our marriage."

She raised her gaze to his, sensing his gaze in the murkiness of dawn light that was just shifting through the shades on the window. It surprised her that he knew she'd been thinking about asking him to release her from the marriage.

"I know you were thinking about it Kara." He smiled at her. His smile was comforting in its familiarity. It made her want to cling to him and the unique combination of strength and tenderness he was offering. She wanted the connection, the stability, and the safety he offered, yet she couldn't really even imagine having that kind of stability in her life. There had never been anyone in her life that she could trust completely, and those she'd thought she could count on had abandoned her at the worst possible time.

In the aftermath of her victimization her family had fallen apart. In the end she had been left to fend for herself and her brother. It had made her strong, but had scarred her in ways she couldn't even begin to understand.

She wanted to trust Slade implicitly as he had asked her to. She wanted to be able to lean on him and count on him to be there when she felt the familiar suffocating panic, the way he had been there the night before but she desperately needed to be able to give back. It wasn't enough to just take from him.

Her mind spun on the precipice of decision. She did trust him. She had told him more about her kidnapping than she had ever told anyone else, even her parents. She hadn't told him everything but she'd told him some of the worst and he hadn't left her. In fact, he'd drawn her closer and become if anything stronger, more stable, and more nurturing.

"I do trust you Slade. A lot," she murmured. "Thinking about getting out of our marriage has nothing to do with trusting you."

"What does it have to do with, honey?" he asked. She felt his eyes on her, studying her expression as she shifted next to him, her eyes focused on his chest.

"I was thinking about asking you to let me out of the marriage because I can't...meet you half way. I can't give you anything close to what you give me. You've been patient and gentle and I'm just...scared...and broken." She sucked in a deep breath. "It's not fair to you—"

"Kara honey, you give me plenty. You trusted me enough to marry me, that's a huge gift all by itself, especially when I know how scared you were." He nuzzled the top of her head, spreading little kisses over her crown. "I don't take that as a little thing at all."

"But I didn't have much choice—"

"It's true I didn't leave you much choice about marrying me but you had a lot of choices about how you dealt with the marriage after the fact. You could have been distant and cold and angry. You could have met me with stony silence. You could have used coldness and anger to keep me at arm's length. You could have been difficult; bitchy. You weren't any of those things. Instead you were open. You trusted me with your feelings after the wedding. You trusted me with your body last night. Those are not little things, honey."

"It doesn't feel like much compared to the way you took care of me last night." She swallowed hard, fighting back tears that sprang to her eyes. "No one else has ever...taken care of me like that before."

He stroked her cheek and kissed her gently as she fought to control the swell of loneliness her words had expressed. "Your parents didn't?"

She shook her head.

"They should have."

"They weren't in very good shape after——" She drew a deep breath and swallowed hard. She didn't want to cry, not now, not again.

"You can relax and trust me honey. I'm going to take care of you from now on. It's part of being your husband. I care about you. I want to see you happy."

She was quiet, trying to wrap her mind around what he was saying. Everything he was offering seemed bigger and deeper than anything she had contemplated before.

"You're considering intensifying your gift to me by becoming my submissive as well as my wife. That's giving me a whole lot, baby, more than I deserve."

"If I do——become your submissive——are there other— um—expectations?"

"Yes." He used his finger to tilt her face so that her gaze was meeting the full steady flicker of dominance from his. "When we're alone together I'll want you to call me Sir or Master. Either one works as a way of remembering that you are mine. I want you to begin to get used to thinking of me as your dominant, not just your husband."

"I want you to be both. I need you to be both." The words startled Kara. She hadn't realized she intended to speak them until they were out.

He stroked her shoulder lightly. "Talk to me honey, I can see you're afraid," he said.

She dipped her gaze, avoiding the intensity of his expression. "I don't want to lose the husband I trust in exchange for a Master or a dominant I don't know."

"You don't need to worry. We're one in the same. A Master is just a more potent form of a husband. In a dominance and submission sense a Master is someone who takes care of you, emotionally, physically, spiritually, the way a husband does in vanilla relationships. Dominance and submission just adds another deeper layer and kind of a foundation on which the marriage is built. I want you to begin to understand that I care for you. I want you to begin to feel worthy of my care and attention. Calling me Master or Sir will help you do that. But the husband part is still right here and isn't going anywhere."

She gazed up at him in the pale light of dawn that was beginning to streak in through the shade covered windows. Her eyes traced the hard lines of determination that marked his jaw line and his brow before softening at his mouth.

"Okay so far?" Slade asked studying her intently.

She nodded although she felt far from certain. She was okay with the half-truths about her captivity for now. She knew that eventually she would tell Slade about Kayla's death and the more complete story of what had happened to her during her captivity.

Her real worry was that she would probably never be able to get pregnant or have children. The doctors who had repaired her after she was raped had said there was so much scar tissue it was unlikely that she'd ever be able to get pregnant or carry a child to term. It hadn't seemed important when she was seven, and she hadn't asked her doctor about it since. It hadn't seemed important at first, but now it did. Slade would want children, children she wouldn't be able to give him. That knowledge, and the knowledge she was keeping it from him added another link in the chain of deceit that weighed upon her.

His voice drew her attention back to him. "I'll want your obedience. That means if I ask you to do something I'll expect you to do it, even if it feels strange at first."

"What if I can't do it?" Fear caught in her throat as she contemplated the number of things he could ask her to do that she wouldn't be able to force herself to do.

"Then I would expect you to tell me, Kara. Nothing in our

dominant and submissive roles goes against either of us using good common sense. Nothing in our roles takes away from the fact that I care about you and I want to help you. If I'm asking you to do something you're uncomfortable with I want you to tell me. I don't want to hurt you. I don't plan to ask you to do anything that would hurt you, although it might embarrass you a little. It's all supposed to be good in the long run."

"Why would it embarrass me?" she asked thinking that he'd already seen her naked, already kissed her most intimate places. He'd already seen her in full melt-down after a panic attack. What more could there be that would embarrass her?

"Because every part of your body would belong to me and you might find my claiming certain parts—embarrassing."

"Oh." She wasn't sure what he meant but her mind spiraled around the thought that he might be talking about claiming her anally. She wasn't sure how she felt about that. It was the one part of her body that hadn't been sullied by the rape. Still, she felt uncertain about Slade touching her there.

"There's a difference between something being out of your comfort zone, and it being so far outside it that you can't do it or don't want to. I want you to tell me how you're feeling about everything we're doing. I need to know how you feel so I know when to expand your comfort zone and when to help you bask in where you are."

"What if I have another panic attack?"

"I can't promise you won't. I can promise that I'll be careful not to push you so far or so fast that you have one. But if you have one I'll stay with you and hold you and we'll talk our way through it just like we have this time."

Kara thought about the way Slade had taken care of her after the panic attack. At the beginning she'd been so mortified at the thought of having one and embarrassing herself, and yet, when it had happened he'd been there, warm and solid, calm and nurturing.

She thought over his words. She'd been afraid of dominance

and submission at the outset of their marriage largely because of the pictures and descriptions she'd seen on internet websites. But his words in the car and his words just now had reduced her fears. It all boiled down to trust and whether she trusted him enough to do what he asked of her.

"If I say yes, can we talk about the sweaters? I really don't like clothes that make me feel...exposed and vulnerable."

"Kara," he sighed. "You're making too much of what I said about your sweaters. You can wear sweaters, just not ones that hang past your knees and four inches off each shoulder."

"Oh," she whispered, feeling stung by his description of her clothes.

"I'm sorry. I didn't mean to hurt your feelings, honey." He snuggled her against him. "They're not bad. Just a little too big for you. Besides," he arched a teasing eyebrow; "I like you much better like you are now, without any clothes at all." He leaned over her, his mouth hovering above hers.

She gazed up at him feeling lighter than she could ever remember feeling. The knowledge that he knew what had happened to her and that it hadn't changed his feelings about her made her feel warm and cozy inside.

"So? Is this yes?" Slade asked, his mouth still hovering above hers as he gazed intently into her face.

Her mind raced. He wanted an answer. A simple yes or no.

Chapter 10

Kara's mind groped for an answer. He wanted an answer, he wanted her to boil her feelings into a simple yes she trusted him enough or no she didn't. Either she would submit to him or she wouldn't. How did she distill everything she felt into a simple yes or no?

She struggled for an answer, wondering if she trusted him enough to let him call the shots in their relationship, if she trusted him enough to defer to his judgment and accept his decisions about things that affected her intimately. Did she know him well enough for that?

Even more importantly, she questioned whether she could trust him not to be repulsed by the things she would eventually have to tell.

She knew he was a good man. He was above everything else dependable. He'd been unshakable when she'd been lost in the panic attack and its aftermath. He'd stayed with her anchoring her when she'd felt traumatized all over again by the nightmares that had come one after the other. He hadn't wavered. He'd just been there, strong, stable, comforting, whispering gentle things that had made her feel safe and protected. He'd given her what she needed, no questions asked.

She knew he wanted her submission, that it mattered to him, that her submission was something she could give him that would even the score a little between them.

"Yes Slade, it's yes. I want to try to...to be submissive,"

Kara answered.

Slade caught the undercurrent of uncertainty that ran through the soft lilt of her voice. He understood. It wasn't an easy decision to choose to give up control, to trust another to care for you, especially when you hadn't known them for very long.

"Open your mouth for me baby," he said as he lowered his mouth to hers.

She parted her lips as his mouth descended. He teased her lips with his teeth, nibbling first her full lower lip and then her thinner upper one. He urged her mouth open further and sucked her lower lip into his mouth where he flicked it with his tongue.

She moaned softly. He knew she enjoyed the sharp thrill of pain with pleasure and he gave her what she wanted, alternately worrying her lip with his teeth and soothing the minor discomfort with his tongue.

Eventually he released her lip to trail his mouth down her neck alternately nipping and soothing the sting of his teeth with the gentle swipe of his tongue.

Slade enjoyed her pleasure as she arched the sweet softness of her body toward him. Her short, rapid breaths made her breasts heave and fall in quick succession, which made her pretty rose, tipped nipples dance temptingly before him.

He knew that she was subconsciously enticing him to take her nipples but he held back, feeling compelled to make her tell him what she wanted this time.

She needed to get used to voicing her wants and needs, besides; he would enjoy hearing her soft silky voice asking him for all the things he wanted to give her anyway.

"Tell me what you want honey," Slade said as he nibbled at her neck alternately sending a scattering of pain shafts through her and soothing them away with a gentle tongue.

She arched her body upward. He understood the wordless begging of her body but he held back. "What do you want baby?" he asked ignoring the frantic push of her breasts against his chest. "Do you want my hands on your breasts, my hands teasing your nipples?"

She nodded, arching toward him, consumed with passion she couldn't deny even though she feared it would lead to another panic attack.

"No Kara, tell Me. Use words," he said against her neck as he sucked her earlobe into his mouth and nibbled it with the sharp edges of his teeth.

"Yes, I want," she arched against him. He released her ear lobe and moved so that he could watch the expressions that flitted across her face as he awaited her answer. "I want your hands on my breasts, um—pinching my—um nipples."

He slid his hands to her breasts, sliding his palms over her round full breasts caressing the pink tips with the flats of his hands as she arched against them, moaning in protest because he hadn't yet begun to pinch the tender peaks. "Like this?" he asked alternately caressing the pink buds and pinching them.

"Y-yyyyyes," she said on a long exhaled breath.

"Yes who, honey?"

She looked up at him for a moment, seeming confused. He stilled his hands, waiting for her answer. Slow understanding of what he wanted came into her expression. "Yes. Master," she said on a sigh that was like sweet music to his ears.

He pleasured her breasts with his hands and then his mouth, purposely building her pleasure with each touch. He slid his hand down over her chest and belly till his fingers dipped between her legs. She was ready for him. Her body was wet and slick with her need. "Kara, honey, I want my cock buried inside you," he whispered against her ear.

He felt her stiffen. "I don't know if—if I can."

"You can honey. Focus on me. Don't think about anything else except you and me, here and now."

"I'll try," she said softly.

"I'll try. Who," he corrected.

"I'll try, Master."

"Good girl," he whispered against her neck. "Come over

me, like you are going to sit down straddle of my cock," he said softly.

She stared at him, uncertainty casting harsh lines on her brow as she moved awkwardly, until she was sitting astride him, just below his cock. He lifted her, shifting her so that her pussy was against his straining cock. "When you're ready lift up and, lower yourself onto me," he said in a passion roughened voice as she stared down at him, her eyes wide with indecision.

He stroked her breasts, watching as she waged a silent war with herself. He couldn't help wondering if he'd pushed her too far too fast or if she'd succumb to her own rising passion. Her teeth nibbled her lower lip as his hands stroked the tender skin at the insides of her thighs before feathering upward to stroke the pink nub that peeked between the lips of her sex.

She whimpered as he stroked her. He knew her desire heightened with each gentle flick of his finger. He moved his finger, arching his body toward her so that his hard cock pressed and stroked where his finger had been. She moaned, tossing her head back so that her bed-tousled hair tumbled back over her shoulders.

He slid his hand up the soft thrust of her belly toward her breasts as he continued to rock his straining body beneath her so that he stroked between her labia, spreading her slickness with his cock. He stroked his hands over her breasts and down her sides, learning her body, enjoying the soft smooth texture of her beneath his hands. Her breath was coming in short little gasps as she moved her body against him, whimpering her need as he squeezed her nipples hard, giving her the pain he knew she enjoyed.

"Oh Master," she whimpered.

"What do you want honey?" he asked as he stroked her with his body, and tightened his fingers on her nipples.

"More. You." She moaned.

"Do you want me inside you Kara?" he asked?

She nodded, silently, her eyes closed on a wave of pure pleasure.

He lifted her soft round hips, shifting her so that her pussy was above his cock. "Lower yourself onto me honey. Slow or fast. Hard or easy. However you want it. I want you to control things this first time."

He watched as she sunk her teeth into the soft kiss swollen fullness of her bottom lip and lowered herself slowly onto his throbbing member. Her descent was like slow torture as he felt the slow enveloping pressure and wetness of her body slowly swallowing his. He watched, spellbound as his body disappeared into hers.

Watching their bodies meld like that was incredibly hot and sweet and made him ache to come inside her. He felt her body stretch and spasm around his as she adjusted to his width and length.

She settled herself astride him, his body completely encased in her heat. "I did it," she said her eyes filled with such pride and mastery that it made his heart pick up speed. "No panic attack. I can't believe I did it."

He smiled up at her, catching her excitement. It thrilled him that he'd been able to help her feel a level of sexual confidence he knew she'd never expected. "I told you you could do it," he said softly.

His hands stroked the soft skin at the inside of her thighs and feathered upward to her center. "You ready for a little more pleasure sweetheart?" he asked as he stroked the insides of her thighs, trailing his fingers nearer her heated center with each stroke.

"Yes Master." He basked in her submission, loving her softness and the gentle smile that lit her face from the inside out. She was everything he'd ever wanted in a submissive and he hadn't yet lifted a finger to enhance her naturally submissive nature with training. When she finally got beyond the memories of being raped and the fear of the panic attacks she'd be a walking inferno.

He settled his hands on her hips, steadying her body as he arched upward, his powerful thrust stroking her deeply and slowly. He loved the deep gasp that whispered out of her and the way her body squeezed his as he surged within her.

She moaned softly. He felt her body tightening against his as he slid deep, holding himself still against the grasping walls of her pussy.

"God baby that's good," he whispered as her body clenched against his. He continued to stroke her slowly and deeply, maintaining rigid control over himself, controlling his raging desire to thrust into her hard and fast. He enjoyed the expression of wonder and delight that filled her face as he moved slowly within her.

"You are beautiful, Kara." He sighed reverently as he raised his hands to cup her soft warm breasts, testing the weight of them against his palms. He slid his hands over the globes, caressing and teasing the flats of his hands over her nipples again and again as he thrust his body slowly into hers.

She moaned softly, her breasts aching as she arched more firmly into his palms and rocked her body against his, matching his rhythm as smoothly as if she'd been born to it.

"That's it baby, lift your bottom a little and come back down," he whispered as his hands on her hips guided her motions. Once she had the rhythm she drove herself hard and deep onto his cock, meeting him thrust for thrust. His eyes feasted on the deeply sexual view of his body disappearing slowly into hers as she slid down his length and settled herself upon him, rocking gently before she lifted again.

His mind spun, his balls tightening. He found the tender nub between the lips of her sex and began to stroke her as she moved downward onto him.

She moaned, throwing her head back so that her hair cascaded down her back like a sexy cloud. She slid slowly up his cock and down again, her pussy clenching against his erection as she moved. She began to make soft panting, moaning noises that made his cock throb and his balls ache with the need to cum as he thrust deep into her.

As the moans solidified on one long drawn out wail that was punctuated only by the spasms of her pussy, he released his control, bucking against her as his body erupted, filling her with his ejaculate.

He shuddered hard against her and wrapped his arms around her, pulling her down on top of him while his cock nestled inside her. She collapsed against him warm and relaxed as if she had always belonged there.

He felt his heart swell with admiration and affection. He'd never felt as warm and protective toward a woman. He'd never felt quite the same stir of emotional connectedness from the sexual act as he'd felt as he'd watched his body join with hers. He stroked her hair and her back, loving the solid softness of her atop him as their breathing slowed.

"How are you doing baby?" he asked when their breathing had evened.

"I didn't know it could be like that." Her voice was soft around the edges and filled with wonder and sated sleepiness.

"It should always be like that honey," he said thinking how sweet and sexy and warm it had been and how much he liked that aspect of making love with her.

Slade relaxed; letting his thoughts wander as Kara dozed on his chest. She was soft and pliant against him, her body nestled atop his, as his erection gradually softened and eased from her body. The hushed rasp of her delicate snores ruffled his chest hair. He let her doze, contentment filling him. Everything he'd always intuitively known he wanted in a wife seemed wrapped up in Kara.

It was as his mind drifted that he realized with an emotional thud that they hadn't talked about birth control, and he hadn't used any. He wondered if she was on the pill, and hoped she was, even though he wouldn't mind her getting pregnant.

His mind drifted to the things he wanted to share with her. There with the intricacies of dominance and submission and the exquisite sexual and emotional bond that would come from that aspect of their relationship was the knowledge that he also wanted to share the everyday trivial things. He wanted to eat breakfast with her, and talk about his work. He wanted her with him when he babysat his nieces and nephews on Friday nights. He wanted to share his amusement with her when one of the kids said something funny.

Someday, when she was ready for motherhood he wanted to share parenthood with her. He wanted to watch her belly swell with his baby. He wanted to go to the doctor with her and be there with her when she gave birth to their son or daughter. He wanted to decorate a nursery and share the intimacy of late night feedings and diaper changes.

The sensation of wanting it all, and believing he could have it with Kara now seemed alien to him. He'd had relationships with women who had fully understood the roles of dominance and submission. They'd submitted to him without limitation and the emotional and sexual connection had been mind-boggling but there had been no depth of sharing beyond the sexual components of dominance and submission. They had been play partners. He hadn't been able to imagine sharing his life with them or raising children with them as he could so easily imagine with Kara.

He'd also been with women who were everything he wanted in a friend but who were simply not wired the same way he was and so, although he had tried with some of them, sex between them had been lacking. Kara was the first who was both everything he wanted as a submissive sex partner and everything he wanted in a friend and a life partner.

There was so much he wanted to do with her, so much he wanted to teach her, so much he wanted to share with her that he felt suddenly overwhelmed by the role of husband and master.

He thought back over the night before. He hadn't slept much during the night. Kara had been restless, her sleep seeming to be disturbed by one dream after another throughout the night. He'd kept her close, gently waking her and urging her back to sleep as each nightmare broke over her.

He'd started their marriage wanting to introduce her to the pleasures of dominance and submission and the raw pleasure of sex, yet, when she'd had the panic attack his focus had changed. It hadn't been about sex or dominance or submission. It had been simply about caring for her, giving her the comfort she needed.

Sometime during the night as his brain had followed a thousand different paths of thought it had become clear to him that he wanted more than just sexual pleasure, or even dominance and submission with Kara. He wanted to really know her. He wanted to know what she thought about things and how she felt. He wanted to understand what made her tick, and why it did. He wanted to learn her favorite color, and her favorite food and know what she liked on television and a hundred other insignificant things.

She shifted and muttered something he couldn't make out against his chest. "You awake sweetheart?" he asked as he stroked her back.

"Um huh. I'm awake. I need to move. I'm too heavy," she mumbled, sleep still clouding her voice.

"You are perfect." He tightened his arms around her, holding her when she would have slipped off him. "I like it that you fell asleep on me, with your body still holding mine like that. Making love with you was warm and sexy. It's never been quite like that with anyone else, ever."

He stroked her hair, and her back.

"You liked it? Really?"

"Yes, I did. And if I didn't need breakfast and coffee I'd turn you over and show you just how much I liked it."

"I liked it too," she said shyly.

He held her for awhile, stroking her back and her hair, pressing her head against his shoulder when she would have risen. He enjoyed her small sigh of submission as she relaxed beneath the pressure of his palm and rested her cheek against his chest.

"Do you want to have a shower and go into town for some breakfast? We can decide what to do with the rest of the day while we eat?"

"That sounds nice. Do you want the first shower?" she asked pushing away the last dregs of sleep to fully realize that she was still pooled atop Slade. His now soft cock still nestled against her.

"I was thinking more of a joint shower."

Chapter 11

Kara felt as if she was walking on sunshine as she stepped onto the cabin's plank porch and waited for Slade to lock the cabin door behind them. When he finished with the door he put his arm around her waist, stopping to draw her closer and drop a gentle kiss on her mouth before leading them toward the SUV.

She could still hardly believe their lovemaking that morning had been real. Her mind drifted lazily over their mating and the intimate shower they had shared afterward. She remembered how Slade had lathered her body and tenderly washed her hair. It had left her feeling utterly safe and protected, in a way that was wonderfully new and completely unexpected.

Appreciation swelled within her as she remembered the gentle way he had eased her into lovemaking. He had understood her fear and had urged her on top because he had known that being there would give her a sense of control that would make it less scary for her.

She had submitted to him, given him her promise of obedience. He had taken her surrender and used it to make her feel safe and protected.

The knowledge made her feel soft inside and compliant in a way that she had never expected to feel toward any man. Far from being scary, his treatment of her had made her want to surrender to his authority and the sense of safety it gave her.

Slade opened the passenger door for her. She moved reluctantly from the warm hollow at his side and climbed into the SUV. He waited till she had fastened her seatbelt before he closed the door and ambled around to the driver's side.

She watched surreptitiously as he started the SUV and pointed it down the gravel lane that led to the main road.

They were both quiet and peacefully introspective as they took the narrow road toward town.

Slade's hand rested possessively on Kara's knee, his touch reminding her of the slow deliberate way his body had thrust into hers and the way her body had responded. It had been exquisitely beautiful, nothing like the painful revolting experiences when she was a child. She marveled at the difference, her mind grappling to make sense of everything that had happened since their marriage.

In town, Slade parked in front of a small café on the town square and helped Kara out of the SUV. "After breakfast do you want to walk around and explore the shops for awhile?" he asked, taking her hand and tugging her up against his side as they walked toward the door of the diner.

"That would be fun," she said softly. Just the thought of being with Slade, her hand nestled in his as they strolled around the square caused her heart to pick up speed.

The restaurant was busy and loud. Men in overhauls and John Deere caps sat at tables near tables of men wearing worn camouflage coveralls and bright orange caps. They all laughed and guffawed back and forth between tables as if they'd known each other forever.

Slade urged her toward a table near the back of the restaurant and far away from the tables of men gathered for coffee and conversation. They had just sat down when the waitress, a young woman in blue jeans, came to the table with coffee.

"Coffee?" she asked as she turned their cups over.

"Not for me, thanks," Kara said.

"Yes, please." Slade answered on a pleasant sigh that made Kara wonder if he was addicted to his morning coffee or if he just enjoyed it on occasion.

"What can I get you?" the waitress asked, setting the coffee pot on the table and taking a pen and pad of paper out of her apron pocket.

"Menus, for a start?" Slade asked.

"Sorry," she said, turning to reach around a half wall that separated the seating area of the restaurant from the kitchen. She turned back around with menus. "Most people that come here live around here and have forever. They all know the menu."

"Not a problem," Slade said smoothly.

"What brings you to Redfalls?" she asked as she laid menus in front of them.

"We're on our honeymoon," Slade answered with a smile as he opened the menu she'd handed him.

"How nice," she responded. "You should think about attending the Christmas by candlelight festival tonight. The shops stay open late and many of them put out luminaries. There are sleigh rides and carolers. It's festive and pretty, and romantic."

"It sounds wonderful," Kara said softly.

"It is," the waitress said with a smile. "I'll let you two look over the menu. I'll be back to take your order."

Kara's soft-spoken enthusiasm had drawn Slade's attention. "Do you want to do Christmas by candlelight tonight?" he asked as he lifted his gaze from the menu he'd been studying.

"It sounds like fun. Sleigh rides. Carolers. Christmas shopping. What's not to like?"

Slade thought she looked like a child who had just found her stocking filled with Christmas goodies. Her dark eyes, which had always attracted him, twinkled with an inner happiness that made him feel caught up in her enthusiasm.

He found himself feeling content as he studied her. It made

him feel good to see her looking happy and relaxed.

"You like Christmas." He smiled, and took her hand, enclosing it in his. He liked the way her fingers curved trustingly around his.

"Yes, I do. It's magical." Her voice was soft with contentment. "What about you? Do you like Christmas?"

He nodded, and smiled. "It's my favorite time of year. I like snow and cold weather...and the old Christmas carols." He met her gaze and stroked her thumb, which made her heart race. "And just the general gaiety of the season, I guess." He met her gaze levelly.

She smiled up at him, glad that he liked Christmas too. Neither her mom nor her brother cared much for the season and most years when she hung the Christmas lights and put up the tree she felt as if she was doing the celebrating for all of them.

"Do you put up decorations? Lights? A tree?" she asked, surprised to realize that she was waiting anxiously for his answer.

"Yes." He smiled. "Even though the house sits back from the road and isn't visible from the street, it's still nice to see the lights when I come home, and it's nice for my nieces and nephews when they visit."

She smiled. Her mind wandered, imagining them laughing and drinking eggnog as they hung Christmas ornaments on the tree while the familiar strains of "Silent Night" played in the background. Maybe this year Christmas would finally live up to the magic she had always envisioned it having. Maybe this year the magic of the season would finally swallow up the ugliness of the past.

He smiled but his eyes studied her, making her feel as if he were taking her apart piece by piece, learning her little by little. "Having lights and a tree are important to you."

She nodded, surprised that he'd been able to get that from what little she'd said.

"It's more than just liking the lights though." It was a

statement, not a question, and yet she knew he was questioning.

She nodded. "Yes. It's more than liking the lights." She smiled, but her voice sounded sad even to her own ears.

The waitress arrived at their table to take their order. They both glanced quickly at the menu and made selections as the waitress wrote down their orders.

"You were going to tell me why Christmas trees and lights are important to you," Slade reminded her when the waitress moved away.

She hadn't been going to tell him, she thought as she looked down at the tabletop and at their hands joined atop it. She could feel his steady gaze from across the table but could not bring herself to look at him. She wanted to avoid the conversation, and the heavy feelings it carried. She'd rather bask in the remembered haze of their lovemaking and the thrill of Slade's gentle touch for a while longer.

If she hadn't promised Slade she wouldn't hide from him— if she hadn't promised him honesty she would have been tempted to change the subject. But as it was she drew a deep breath and plunged in.

"When—after—when they found me after—" She looked up, as Slade's other hand found her free hand and curled around it, wordlessly offering comfort.

Her gaze dropped to the table and her voice became little more than a subdued whisper. "A-after they found me was a really terrible time for everyone. I was in the hospital f-for a-a while. When I finally got to go home it was close to Christmas and the Christmas lights were on in our neighborhood and everything was bright and twinkling and happy. It was so cheerful and such a stark contrast to the dreariness of the hospital and everything I'd been through—"

She glanced up. Slade's gaze rested on her, the familiar intense, analytical expression in his gray eyes as he studied her face.

"Anyway—it gave me hope that I could be happy again, that my family could be happy again, in spite of—in spite of— everything." Her voice broke apart. She drew a deep steadying breath. "I still see Christmas lights and it makes me feel— hopeful."

Slade's chest felt tight. She'd been through so much when she'd still been too young to even understand it all. Still, she'd coped miraculously well. When he met her she'd had a stable job, responsibility at work and at home with the care of her mother. She'd sprung to her brother's defense, meeting him at his office and offering well thought out solutions to keep her brother out of jail. She was shy, and sexually repressed, but she had an internal strength he admired.

He knew from the tenor of her voice and the way she stared at the Formica topped table that she'd only scratched the surface, that there was more he needed to know about what had happened to her and more she needed to tell. If they hadn't just ordered breakfast he would have shepherded her out of the restaurant and taken her somewhere quiet where he would have drawn the rest of the past out of her one piece at a time until he knew it all and none of it was left to fester and hurt her.

As it was he let her withdraw from the painful place she'd allowed him to glimpse, feeling honored by the gift of honesty. He ached with the knowledge that her reprieve was temporary, that they'd have to revisit it. To be any good as her husband or her master he needed to know and understand it all, so that there wasn't anything left unsaid that would come up to hurt her later.

"Didn't you have counseling? Help? Someone to talk to about what happened?" he asked, stroking her palm.

"No. I didn't want counseling. I didn't want to talk about it. I still don't—"

She tugged her hand from his caress, and lowered it to her lap. Her voice was flat. Unemotional. It was as if an invisible wall had come up between them. He was bewildered by her reaction.

For a moment they had been close, touching in a way that had nothing to do with their hands nestled together atop the table. He'd been with her as a child, understanding what the overwhelming loneliness that had gripped her must have been like and how magical the Christmas lights must have seemed and what hope they must have given her after everything that had happened to her.

He'd been there, fully immersed, empathizing with what it must have been like for her, then suddenly she'd darted away, behind an impenetrable wall, leaving him alone with the feelings.

He was dubious about the lack of help she'd received in the aftermath of being raped and he thought it would be a good idea for her to see someone. Not just anyone but someone good—someone who specialized in childhood sexual trauma—someone who could help her exorcise the parts of her past that still caused her pain.

Kara felt herself close down emotionally as the closeness between them shattered. She had shared a piece of her past that she had never shared with anyone and she would have sworn he was there with her, understanding why Christmas lights meant eternal hope. Then suddenly, with the intrusion of counseling into their conversation, the magical bonding had shattered. Her desire to surrender herself to him wavered like a candle in the wind in the face of the knowledge that he believed in counseling.

The fear that he thought going to counseling and rehashing everything that had happened to her would somehow heal the pain of being raped made her angry in spite of the knowledge that her feeling was illogical. More than making her angry, it frightened her. She didn't want to go to counseling. Ever.

There was no cure for what had happened. There was no amount of talking or wishing things had been different that would change them. There would always be a big pocket of pain in her past. She could wallow in it and let it overcome her or she could choose to accept its presence and move on.

From the very beginning, she'd chosen to accept it and move on. Even as a child she hadn't wanted to look back, and except for the panic attacks, she had pretty much managed not to look back, most of the time.

Kara felt detached and distant as they ate their breakfasts. Slade talked about his family's Christmas traditions and asked her about hers. She responded appropriately but the magical aftermath of their lovemaking had dwindled in the face of her worry that he'd want her to go to counseling. The burgeoning trust that had blossomed earlier was scattered and she felt cold, alone, and unsettled.

She stood next to him at the cash register as he fished his wallet from the hip pocket of his jeans. She wished she could nudge herself out of the dark mood and the distrustful, lonely space his words had put her in.

She didn't want to distrust him. She wanted to go back to the wonder of trusting him and to the appreciation she had felt that morning when she'd realized that he'd purposely structured their lovemaking to give her control so that she could feel pleasure rather than fear.

She wanted the soft warm glow that trusting him and accepting his care and his authority gave her. She wanted back the feelings that had come with her submission, yet she felt emotionally scattered, alone, and afraid.

Slade paid the bill and returned his wallet to his pocket. He ushered her from the restaurant with a slight touch at the small of her back. When they reached the sidewalk he turned her slowly to face him.

"Are you okay? You seem a little—distant," he said tipping her chin to gaze down into her face.

"Talking about the past makes me sad. But I'm okay." She wasn't lying—not really, she told herself. Talking about the past did make her sad. She just didn't mention that it had been the intrusion of counseling into their conversation that had turned her feelings inside out, leaving her uncertain about her submission and what it meant if he wanted her to see a therapist.

"I didn't mean to bring up an unhappy subject," Slade said.

"I know," she sighed, finding his hand and curling hers into it.

"I don't know you well enough yet to know what's painful and what's safe," he sighed. "I don't ever want to hurt you."

"I know."

He lifted their joined hands to his lips and kissed the back of her hand. "So we're okay then?"

"Yes Sir, we're fine," she answered. His gentleness with her reawakened her desire to submit to him, and she found the use of the word Sir made her feel connected and safe. He tilted her chin, peered into her face, his blue gray gaze intent on her as he studied her expression.

She watched spellbound as his head descended. His mouth found hers, just barely brushing her lips as she parted them beneath the first intimate touch. Slivers of sensation shafted through her, the memories of the pleasure he had given her and the ways he had taken care of her filling her mind as she leaned against him.

Her hands found his shoulders, and she clung to him steadying herself as his kiss deepened. She felt molten and slightly dizzy, as if she were melting from the inside out, as if she was letting his essence inside her where it warmed the cold lonely places in her soul. A coil of heat swelled within her center and she longed to melt beneath him. She was suffused with pleasure and the desire to surrender her body, her will, everything she was to him. Longing to belong to him, to be cherished by him, to deserve the attention, affection and patience he'd already shown her swirled within her in a cacophony of sensation, she felt light and heavy, safe and nervous all at the same time. She wanted to sink into him, have him sink into her, she wanted to meld, to belong. She moaned an involuntary protest as he lifted his mouth from hers and stood looking down at her with passion raging in his gaze.

She swayed against him, feeling flushed as she met the intensity expressed in his face, feeling the coiled power in every muscle of his body that still pressed against her, amazed that far from frightening her, his power enthralled her, making her want to curl up, safe in the circle of his power.

She shook her head, dazed by the potency of the longing to surrender herself to Slade, to give him her body, her will, everything he wanted.

She stood pressed against him, dazzled by the knowledge that though she had promised him her submission, the things he had asked were a small measure of what she could give him, what she now realized she wanted to give him.

Slade drew a deep breath, struggling to corral the sexual hunger that raged through him. God, she set him on fire. Every time he touched her he wanted to consume her, own her, take her to a deeper level, where he could show her the beauty and joy of giving herself completely.

He looked down at her, smiling inwardly at the bemused expression on her face and the flush that colored her cheeks. "You okay?" Slade asked stroking her hair back away from her face.

"Fine. I – I just never expected it to feel like this."

Her words made him want to pull her closer, they made him want to show her just how good it could be, how deep the pleasure would be when she held nothing back, when she submitted everything she was to his control. But even more than he wanted that, he needed to understand where she was, what she wanted, what she needed.

"It?" He cocked an eyebrow. "You mean kissing? Sex? Submission?"

Her gaze lifted, her eyes meeting his, their velvety brown depths threatening to pull him in. "Submission." Her brow furrowed as if she were considering. "I think." She nibbled her lip. "It's just... I thought I had experienced submission this morning, but just now, it felt like there was more...like I wanted to give you more."

Joy, pleasure, and an indescribable headiness bubbled up inside Slade. She'd been so shy, so fearful, so skittish he'd expected it would take weeks for her to get comfortable with the idea of submission, even the limited amount he'd asked for.

He kissed her softly, gently, his thumb stroking her neck as he basked in the heady combination of her trust and his power which filtered through him. "Yes honey, there is more. The feeling is deeper, harder, more encompassing the more control you give." He drew a deep breath, wondering if it was too soon, if he was pushing her too much. "I would love to show you when you are ready. Do you think you are ready to deepen your submission to the next level?"

She stared up at him her mouth feeling dry and her brain scrambling for words that wouldn't come. She didn't know how to answer. All she knew was that when he held her and kissed her she felt safe and warm and when he made love to her she wanted to melt into him and give him anything he asked for. But was she ready to deepen her submission? Wouldn't submitting more mean doing whatever he asked, even going to see a counselor if he asked her to?

Her blood ran cold at the thought of having to see a psychiatrist. She'd had enough of them when she was seven to last an entire lifetime.

Chapter 12

Slade stared down into Kara's upturned face. He watched, his cock aching and his hands itching to draw her closer, as her tongue darted out to moisten her lips. Her eyes were that soft deep brown that made him feel as if he could drown in their magnetic pull as they studied him from beneath long strands of dark hair that blew forward in the breeze. He could feel her internal struggle and knew he was rushing her, probably pushing her too damned fast and too damned hard.

As much as he wanted to kiss her again, to strip away her hesitancy, to reassure her, he didn't move his head the few inches it would have taken to bring his lips into contact with the soft yielding warmth of her mouth.

She needed to take this step on her own. The decision to trust him enough to put herself in his power with nothing held back was hers and hers alone and he would not push her to make it.

He didn't want her to submit to save her brother or to deliver on her wedding vows, or because he was kissing her and making her want more than hot kisses. He wanted her to give him the gift of her submission because surrendering to him, yielding to his dominance made her whole, the same way dominating her, caring for her, cherishing her completed him.

The silence was long, time seeming to lose meaning as cars passed on the town square. Some of them parked and people got out and went into the shops.

"Do you need to think about it?" he asked after several minutes of silence.

She nodded but drooped under the admission. "I'm sorry," she said softly. She looked sad. Ashamed.

"It's all right Kara, there's no shame in needing to think about things before making an important decision," he said softly.

She bowed her head, her gaze intent on the bricks at her feet.

"This is a very important decision, honey. I'm pleased you are even considering it at this point." He squeezed her shoulder. "If you do decide to submit to me more than you already have it will change things between us. So far I've treated you as an equal. If you decide to submit to me that will change. I will still treat you with care and respect but you will be my submissive. I will push you and challenge you when I think you need that. Sometimes, when your behavior warrants it, I'll punish you to help you become an even better submissive." He stroked back the hair that the wind had blown into her face, his fingers caressing her cheek.

"I will also take care of you. I'll cherish you and protect you. You will belong to me."

His finger traced her cheek and her lips. He willed her to lift her eyes, to allow him to see at least a hint of the feelings she kept trapped beneath the lowered gaze. He knew he could simply order her to look at him, but he wanted her to raise her gaze on her own.

His heart picked up speed as her gaze lifted slowly, her eyes resting somewhere near the top button of his shirt before they climbed the last few inches to meet his own.

He glimpsed turbulence and uncertainty in her expression. "I'm patient Kara. I want your complete submission but I won't rush you into it before you're ready."

She nodded, her gaze skittering to the ground. He watched the soft skin of her throat tauten as she swallowed. Under other circumstances he would have found her down turned gaze, and the nervous swallowing utterly submissive and beautiful but now it only expressed confusion and uncertainty.

He was marginally disappointed that she wasn't ready to go to the next level. After their morning lovemaking and the shower they'd shared he'd thought that she'd taken to dominance and submission like a duck to water. He'd thought after she'd admitted to wanting to give him more that she was ready and yet he hadn't expected her to realize that there even was another level at this point.

He stifled a deep sigh. Maybe he should have been more specific, spelled out specifically what the next level would entail. Maybe he should have told her that his control would tighten gradually over time, that it wouldn't happen all at once. She had asked him for specifics that morning before she'd agreed to give him her limited submission. Maybe she needed the same kind of assurances in order to go to the next level.

He schooled his features and softened his voice to hide his disappointment. "Come on," he said wrapping a loose arm around her waist and drawing her toward him, tugging her along as he ambled up the quaint brick sidewalk past old storefronts with picture windows that were decked out in Christmas decorations.

He wanted her complete submission more than he had ever wanted anything in any relationship he'd ever been in, but she was different from other submissives he had trained and dominated.

Others he trained had flourished under the harsh inflexibility of his dominance. They had come to him wanting strict control and he had given it. They had recognized their need to submit and had yielded to his rigid demands willfully.

Kara, however, was not like anyone else he had known. With her he hadn't been inflexible and he hadn't issued demands. With her he couldn't.

She had that demure air of innocence and was wounded in ways he was only beginning to understand. He knew instinctively that she would shrivel under the kind of harsh dominance he had practiced in the past. She was sweet. Innocent. She needed tenderness and coaxing more than she needed severity.

He took a deep breath pushing away his impatience to deepen her submission. She was afraid, he knew that, understood it. He realized the need to be patient.

He knew that for all effects and purposes she'd already given herself to him, her verbal acquiescence was just frosting on the cake. He'd had plenty of time as she'd drifted between sleep and bad dreams to remember how sweetly she had yielded to him before the panic attack.

As he'd lain awake watching over her as she'd slept he'd wondered how she'd been able to relinquish herself to his sexual control when the only experiences she'd had of sex were bad. The knowledge that she had trusted him enough to let him touch her, when she'd been terrified his touch would bring on a panic attack still shocked him.

She'd already given him a level of trust that had taken more experienced submissives months to master. He knew he should be satisfied with what she'd already given him, but remembering her sweetness and her innocence as she had kissed and licked his cock only made him hungry for more. He wanted to possess her, to own her, to have her knowingly submit to his ownership. In exchange he wanted to cherish her. Protect her. Love her.

The thought that he was falling in love with her caught him off guard, setting him back like a strong kick to the chest. But as the initial shock wore off the knowledge that it was true settled into him.

Sometime during the night as he'd watched over her, easing her from nightmares and coaxing her back to sleep he'd felt a sense of completeness invade him.

The sense of being content in his masculinity and at peace with his dominance had deepened as dawn had arrived and the first rays of morning sunshine had squeezed through the blinds of the cabin's windows.

Tranquility surrounding his dominance had always been elusive. But Kara's innocence brought out the best in him. It made him temper his dominance with tenderness and made him consider her feelings before he issued demands. He liked the protective feelings that filled him when he was with her and he liked the knowledge that she appreciated his care. She didn't take him for granted.

Knowing the way she'd been brutalized and the way she still hurt from it made him cherish her submission all the more. That she had trusted him when she'd had no real reason to do so made him want to wrap her up and protect her from anything or anyone that could hurt her.

He stroked her waist through her bulky sweater, his fingers tingling as they touched bare skin through the open weave.

They strolled up the wide brick sidewalk past an antique shop with a closed sign in its window. They took their time, pausing to window shop.

"There's a clothing shop up the street," he said as the sweet scent of her hair combined with the brisk wind to tease his nostrils. "You did promise to replace your baggy sweaters. We could stop and look for some new ones while we're here."

Panic shot through her. She recognized it as unreasonable, and yet the feeling persisted. "I guess we could," she answered, her voice sounding hollow and unenthusiastic even to her own ears.

"You're still worried about the new clothes?" Slade guessed.

She nodded, her chest feeling as if someone had squeezed it in a vice. "I haven't worn anything but big sweaters and big scrubs since—"

"Since you were raped," Slade filled in for her.

She nodded again, biting her bottom lip, drawing blood.

"I understand that this is difficult for you," he said turning her and lifting her chin so that she had no alternative but to meet his piercing gaze. She wanted to pull her chin away, to avoid the intensity of his eyes that felt as if they were digging into her very soul, unearthing things she'd buried deep. "You promised to stop hiding in the baggy clothes. Have you changed your mind?"

His voice was gentle, but firm, as it stroked along her back making her nerves jump. She shook her head. She hadn't changed her mind but that didn't mean she in any way wanted new clothes. The whole idea of wearing anything that drew attention to her filled her with dread and a thick sense of foreboding.

"You've trusted me on other things that were difficult for you at the time you did them. How did those things work out?"

"They worked out okay, better than okay," she admitted. "But this is—different." Her voice felt tight as she squeezed it past the large lump in her throat.

He was facing her, his fingers still holding her chin at that angle that compelled her to meet his gaze. "Tell me how it's different honey," he said softly.

She licked her lips nervously and tasted the blood that lingered where she'd bit her lip. She felt cold inside. Hollow.

He stroked her arm through her sweater. His dark eyes were patient as she switched her weight from foot to foot and drew a deep breath. "The truth Kara, just spit it out, don't make it harder than it is, honey."

"The other things you asked me to do—" she squirmed beneath the intensity of his gaze. "All I had to do was trust you. Wearing clothes that leave me—" She swallowed hard. "—uncovered—is like trusting everyone else too. I— don't." She twisted her hands together. "I don't trust anyone really, except you. I don't even know why I trust you."

Regretting her words even before they were completely out of her mouth she tugged her face free of Slade's grip and prayed for the ground to swallow her. She didn't want to see pity in his eyes. Embarrassment swelled within her.

They were married, had shared a bed. He'd been with her through a panic attack and he'd held her through the nightmares that had followed, but telling him outright that she trusted him, and admitting that she didn't understand why made her feel emotionally vulnerable.

She raised her gaze slowly, letting it linger as it followed the line of buttons that ran up his chest. When at last she met his gaze she was surprised by the softness that filled his expression. "Thanks honey," he said softly. "I'm honored that you trust me. There is no more important gift you could give me."

His voice was soft and his gaze gentle as it rested on her. "About the clothes though, I'm not talking about buying things that would leave you bare to the world. Just normal clothes. Sweaters. Blouses. Slacks. Jeans. Dresses."

Images of normal clothes swam in her mind. She imagined stylish jeans, sweaters that would accentuate her breasts and cleavage and soft flowing dresses that would breeze around her legs when she walked. She imagined pretty colors, and soft fabrics. She closed her eyes wishing she could imagine herself wearing clothes like that but even when she imagined the clothes she imagined them hanging on hangers. She didn't wear pretty clothes—not since—

She wore black, white, and navy blue. Baggy jeans. Baggy sweaters. Scrubs. Big, baggy scrubs.

"I feel n-naked in clothes like that." Her voice was little more than a hoarse, pain-filled whisper carried along on the swift breeze that tossed her hair around her face.

Slade closed his eyes as the knowledge hit him square in the face. He finally understood why the idea of wearing stylish clothes made her uncomfortable. She'd been hiding beneath the big sweaters, maybe blaming herself for the rape, afraid that if she showed a glimpse of her body she'd be inviting it again. And here he was taking away the shapeless clothes that made her feel safe.

"Twenty years is a long time to hide out under baggy sweaters," he sighed.

She closed her eyes. "I know." Her voice was small. Tired.

He wanted her out of hiding but he understood why she

wanted to stay safe beneath sagging folds of sweaters that hid her from view. He wanted her ugly baggy sweaters replaced but he wanted to accomplish it without hurting her.

He sucked in a deep breath. "You do know that your clothes had nothing to do with what happened?"

She didn't answer.

He drew an exasperated breath. "What you were wearing that day didn't make a molehill's bit of difference to what happened. Men don't rape women or little girls because of what they're wearing although some of them use it as a way to justify their behavior."

"I know." She sighed, closing her eyes, shutting him out. "But I don't want men to look at me." Her voice was so soft he had to strain to hear but the fear in it cut through him like a knife and made him want to protect her.

"I can understand why honey." He lifted his hand and rested it against her cheek."

She nuzzled into his palm. His heart surged delighting in the fact that she was drawing comfort from his touch. The miracle of her trust, that she trusted him, even in the face of him asking her to do something that was difficult and painful for her reached him at a deep level.

"We need to do this more slowly."

"I'm sorry. I don't mean to be..." Her voice was soft and filled with pain.

"I know you're afraid honey. I knew you were afraid when we talked about it this morning but I didn't understand all the implications then."

She was silent, her eyes fixed on the brick sidewalk at her feet.

His mind was spinning, the analytical, problem solving wheels he used in business turning as he tried to figure out how to push Kara beyond her fears without causing her more emotional distress. God knows she'd had enough emotional distress in the past twenty-four hours.

"You know I'm not going to hurt you or allow anyone else

to hurt you?" he asked as she lifted her gaze.

"Yes," she answered softly.

"Good," he praised, his thumb stroking her cheek. "We're going to find some casual, comfortable things that fit you. For right now you'll just wear them when you're with me. If any other man even looks at you in a way that makes you uncomfortable I'll take him apart, okay?"

"Will you really?" A soft warm smile filled her face.

He shrugged. "Of course, if it makes you feel better." He knew she wouldn't really want him to take some guy apart just for looking at her but he wanted her to know she was safe, that he'd protect her from lecherous advances.

She smiled up at him. She was surprised at just how much better it made her feel to know he would take care of her, that he wouldn't let anyone bother her.

"So this is workable for you then? Not too difficult or too scary?"

"It's—in theory it's okay. I don't know how I'll feel when I'm actually—wearing—."

"You'll be fine Kara. If you're not we'll talk about it and we'll work it out. You have my promise on that." His confidence radiated outward and began to sink into her. "Just trust me, honey, none of this is meant to hurt you, remember?"

He took her hand, engulfing it in his much larger one. He squeezed her fingers reassuringly as he led her toward the clothing store on the corner.

Maybe he was right. Maybe she would be fine. She wondered if it was possible to leave the past with its darkness, death and pain behind. He kept asking her to trust him, dangling the unspoken promise that she would feel better if she submitted completely, trusted completely. But the idea of blind trust, of complete submission petrified her, even as a return to the feelings she'd had when she'd submitted to him that morning beckoned.

She'd trusted him that morning when he'd promised to help her get beyond her fear of sex. He'd taken the lead, telling her with perfect candor and easy confidence what he wanted from her. Then with his own special mix of bossiness and tenderness he'd urged her astride him. She'd given him the implicit trust he'd asked for.

She'd trusted him and he'd rewarded her with his understanding and knowledge of what she needed. He had taken the cruelty, degradation, and pain that she had always associated with sex and given her an experience that was in sharp contrast. She'd walked away with the knowledge that sex wasn't always excruciating, revolting, and degrading. In fact, he'd shown her that sometimes it could be downright beautiful.

As she sauntered up the wide sidewalk beside him, Kara was disappointed in herself. Slade had been beyond patient and considerate. All he'd asked was if she was ready to deepen her submission. She'd responded by holding him at arms length and stubbornly refusing him an answer.

She wasn't sure what would happen if she told him she was ready. He'd mentioned that he would make more demands, challenge her, punish her if her behavior warranted it.

She wondered what kind of demands he'd make, feeling fearful that he'd ask her to go to counseling. If only she knew that counseling was off the table—

She was still pondering whether she should agree to deepen her submission when Slade swung the heavy door of the clothing store open. The hinge whined as the door opened and scratched against the rough floor of the shop. Kara wondered what she was getting herself into as he propelled her into the store with its dim lighting and hard wood floors that had long since seen the last of the varnish that might have one day protected their surfaces. Now the store smelled of wax and new clothes.

"Can I help you find something?" an old man with white hair, stooped shoulders and gold-rimmed glasses asked as he looked up at them from behind an old cash register where he was counting money into the till.

"We're okay on our own. If you could point us to ladies wear," Slade said.

"Ladies wear is back that way," the old man said gesturing to the far corner of the store as he dropped his gaze back to the money he was counting into the cash drawer.

Kara's heart was beating triple time by the time they reached the ladies wear department. Her stomach churned. She didn't shop for clothes very often, and when she did she picked them up at the local Goodwill store. She bought big and bigger, white, black and navy blue. Never anything that attracted attention.

She looked around feeling overwhelmed. She didn't know what to look at first as her eyes drifted from rack to rack of pretty clothes. Was there nothing in black or navy, she wondered in panic.

Slade's eyes settled on Kara as she looked from rack to rack seeming frightened by the simple task of finding some sweaters to replace the ones that were too big. She certainly didn't shop like his sisters. On the very few occasions he'd been roped into shopping with them, the scene had reminded him of a school of sharks at feeding time. All five of his sisters attacked the racks, all of them grabbing things and holding them aloft for the approval or disapproval of the others as they laughed and joked.

He sucked in a deep breath silently thanking God and his parents that he had been raised with sisters and knew how to shop. "What size do you wear Kara?" he asked as he skimmed through the rack in front of him.

"Ummm——twenty," Kara answered.

Slade knew she didn't wear a twenty. His mom wore a twenty, and Kara was quite a bit smaller. He kept his mouth shut, knowing from experience how sensitive women were about the sizes sewn into their clothes. "These are nice," he said holding a dusty rose and a teal green sweater up for her inspection.

She lifted her eyes to study the garments. "They're pretty

but they look too small for me. Do they have a larger size?"

Slade bit his lip to keep himself quiet. The teal was a twenty and the rose was an eighteen. He'd lay odds the eighteen was too big, unless she intended to wear it hanging off her shoulders like she'd worn her other sweaters. The sixteen would probably fit.

He didn't argue. He wanted to ease her into the idea of buying new clothes not get lost in a debate about what size she wore. He held a twenty aloft. "How about this one?" he asked. "Want to try it on?" he urged.

"I—um—yeah. I'll try it on."

He handed her the sweater, fighting hard to keep his smile hidden. Kara was so far out of her element even in this backwoods shop that he had no idea how she would keep pace with his sisters who would undoubtedly be inviting her to join them on one of their shopping expeditions as soon as they got home from their honeymoon.

"Let me see when you get it on," Slade called after her as she wound her way toward the fitting room.

"I will," she answered softly. He liked her easy compliance, her obedience. He made a mental note to mention it and compliment her later.

Kara emerged from the dressing room a few minutes later. The sweater hung on her as he'd expected it would. "Too big," he said looking up from a rack near the fitting room door. "Want to try on one of the others?"

"I like them big," she sighed.

"I don't," he responded. His voice was clipped and brooked no argument. "Try this one," he said handing her the sixteen.

Obediently she disappeared into the dressing room with the sweater. She reappeared a few moments later wearing it. "That looks nice honey, what do you think of it?" he asked.

"I like it." Her answer was simple, but her soft gentle smile sent his heart into overdrive.

He felt hopeful. Maybe one baby step at a time he could build her confidence and drag her beyond the fear that held her hostage. "You look nice."

She did look nice, except for the baggy jeans that drooped at her waist and hung at the crotch. "Hang on a minute. Don't take that sweater off yet."

Her glance was quizzical but he didn't respond to the questions in her expression as he weaved through the racks. "Here, try these with the sweater," he said extending a pair of black jeans he'd pulled from a kiosk near the center of the ladies wear department

"I didn't think men were into shopping," she said taking the jeans.

"Did you forget? I have five sisters? I had to learn how to shop just to keep up."

She disappeared into the fitting room. He watched her socked feet beneath the fitting room door, imagining her skimming the baggy jeans down past the soft round swell of her bottom and off her legs at the bottom.

"What do you think?" she asked as she stepped out of the dressing room.

He wolf whistled. Delighting in the bright blush that crept up her face. "I think you look really nice," he said softening his voice and using it as a caress. "Very pretty Kara."

When they trudged out of the store, more than an hour later they were both loaded down with packages. Kara felt light-hearted and happy.

Slade was good for her she realized. He'd talked her into the clothes, then teased and played until she'd given up and agreed to let him buy her everything he'd liked on her, which was pretty much everything as long as it didn't sag and bag too much.

"Slade?" she said softly when they were ensconced in the SUV with the packages stowed in the rear seat.

"Yeah honey?" he asked absently.

"Thanks," she answered. "I wasn't looking forward to that, and you made it fun."

"You're welcome honey."

He pulled the SUV out of its parking spot and onto the road that circled the town square.

"Slade?" she asked again.

"Yeah?" he asked dropping his hand onto her knee.

"What we were talking about earlier— I've thought about it. I'm ready to—uhm—to—to be—your submissive." There, I did it. I got it out, she thought as she twisted her hands in her lap wondering if she really could comply with Slade's demands. She wanted to—but—

Chapter 13

Slade's heart stopped, stock-still. She had shocked him. Again. *She's ready to submit to me? Fully? Completely? No questions, no limits?* His mind raced scrambling over one thought and then another as his body swelled and hardened. Sharp shafts of pleasure shot through him.

God I want her—but not just sexually. What I want is...deeper. More like an unfathomable level of intimacy and love. His mind raced. He'd wanted her submission more than he'd ever wanted anything and she'd given it to him without playing games, and without asking for anything in return.

He felt as if the ground had been snatched from beneath him. He couldn't breathe. He couldn't find his voice. He struggled for coherent words and stole a quick glance in her direction as he eased the car onto the main road that led away from town.

Her deep brown eyes were fixed on him and he had the sudden feeling that the scales were tipped. Where before he had studied her, gauging every nuance that floated across her pretty face their roles had reversed and it was she who was studying him.

He squeezed her knee gently. "I'm glad, you decided in my favor," he said softly, still feeling awed by her level of trust and the nearly blind faith she was putting in him.

She blushed. He pretended not to notice.

"There's a park up ahead. I'll park there and we can take a

walk by the lake and talk. I need to know about your limits. We need to give you a safe word."

He felt as if he was blathering, still only partially coherent. He glanced in her direction and realized from her confused expression that she didn't know what he was talking about.

He drew a deep breath. He should have known discussing limits and safe words would be beyond her level of experience.

Protectiveness swelled within him. She was completely new to dominance and submission. The knowledge that she was probably feeling vulnerable and unsure of herself made him want to hold her gently and reassure her of his ability to live up to the trust she was placing in him.

He knew he was going to have to go slowly with her so that he could communicate her worth and the value of her submission through his actions and not just his words. He wanted to show her how much he cherished the trust she had placed in him and how highly he prized her submission.

He wanted to nurture the bond of trust and grow it until their relationship was based on an intense give and take of intimacy so deep and rich there was nothing that they didn't share. He wanted to know her inside out, to understand everything about her.

He would know her, but it would be a slow learning process. It would take time to slowly, patiently topple each of her boundaries until there was no part of her he didn't know and understand and no part of her he didn't know how to nurture and care for.

"How are you doing?" he asked as he slipped the SUV into a parking space near a lookout that overlooked the lake and the valley below.

"O-Okay," she answered, her voice so soft he had to strain to hear it.

"Are you really okay or are you just saying that because you think it's what I want to hear?" he asked.

He cut the engine and turned in the seat so he could study her expression. She was nibbling her lower lip and her hands were fiddling in her lap. "Nervous?" he asked.

She raised her gaze, her deep brown eyes meeting and holding his. "Nervous doesn't even begin to cover it. Scared, stiff is more like it," she breathed.

"There's nothing to be scared of. The last thing I want to do is hurt you."

Her eyes as she looked up at him were huge in her pale face. "Submission isn't just sexual. It's emotional and psychological and in an ideal situation spiritual." He took a deep breath trying to put into words everything he felt, everything he hoped for and wanted to build with her.

"I don't just want sexual submission Kara." He stroked her fingers with his thumb as he glanced down at her knee where their clasped hands rested. "I want it all, every thought...every feeling...every fantasy—everything you've been afraid to tell anyone else. I want to know and understand everything about you. I want to take care of every need you have."

He felt the tremor that worked through her. It was too much, too damned soon but he wanted her to understand that what he wanted was not just her sexual submission.

He opened his mouth to suggest they take a walk.

She looked up at him pinning him with almond shaped eyes the deep rich color of ground coffee. He felt his breath catch in his chest and hold there as she glanced back at her lap.

"I—I want to give you everything Slade. I will give you as much as I can—at least as much as I know how." She looked to her lap, he could feel her confusion and uncertainty as clearly as if it was his.

"I—" She took a deep breath and seemed to steady herself. "What you want—the obedience part I understand. The rest——I'm confused how it all fits together—"

Once again she had shocked him, left him reeling as surely as if she'd hauled back and socked him in the gut. Her words, stumbled over and imprecise as they were, were filled with the essence of who she was and what she felt at the most basic primal level. He thrilled to the openness and the honesty. She might be confused about the parameters of dominance and submission but she had laid her emotions open for him to see.

Chapter 14

"Let's take a walk and talk," Slade said opening his door.

Kara's emotions felt scrambled as she unfastened her seatbelt with fingers that trembled on the latch. Her heart hammered in her chest and her throat felt as dry as sandpaper.

Her stomach churned with uncertainty about what Slade would expect now that she had decided to submit herself completely to his authority.

Her brain tussled with the memory of the serious tone in his voice when he'd told her that their relationship would change if she decided to submit more fully. He had sounded completely serious when he'd told her that he would push her and challenge her and that he might spank her if he thought it would help her become a better submissive.

A shiver of dread ran through her. She didn't want him to spank her—ever. But then, she didn't ever want to displease him.

In truth she'd agreed to deepen her submission because she wanted his approval. She couldn't remember exactly when she had started to be attracted to him rather than frightened by him. It had all happened so quickly. But the fact was she liked him. She liked the matter of fact way he addressed things and the way he took the lead in their relationship. She liked the way he praised her and the way he encouraged her.

She watched, her mouth dry, as he walked around the front of the SUV. She watched the play of his thigh muscles beneath his well-worn jeans as his long strides carried him toward her. Her tongue darted out to moisten her parched lips as she remembered the feel of his mouth against hers.

Even now, her body still heated and moistened with the memory of the strength and tenderness with which he'd taken her that morning. He had told her what he wanted her to do and she had complied, in spite of her fear and awkwardness.

Even with nervousness and uncertainty making her stomach churn she didn't doubt her decision to submit to him. She'd submitted to him that morning and he'd used the power she'd given him to give her pleasure and the first real peace she'd felt since the innocence of childhood had been snatched away.

She had felt utter tranquility that morning when she'd finally allowed herself to trust him and to submit her will to his. She wanted to hang on to the serenity that had existed in that brief magical time before her doubts had resurfaced.

She nibbled her lip as tension curled in her belly and twisted images of herself kneeling at his feet as he struck her with a thick leather belt exploded in her minds eye.

She didn't really believe he would beat her like that. He had been consistently patient, consistently gentle, yet doubts and memories clouded her mind and cut through her desire for submission and the accompanying peace and tranquility making her feel isolated and alone.

Sickness churned as her mind flashed to the man who had kidnapped her. He had stood over her bared back, his thick, black belt doubled in his large fist. He had snapped the leather menacingly, making her cringe before he hit her. She shivered as she remembered the heat of the stokes he had placed one on top of the other all up and down her back and legs. She remembered biting her lip to keep from screaming her agony, because even then she had understood that he liked hurting her and the more she screamed the harder he would hit.

She shoved the ugly thoughts away and tried to gather her confidence.

She jumped, startled as the door slid open. "You okay?" Slade asked.

She swallowed hard, the confidence she'd felt as she'd promised her submission shattered. "I-I'm okay."

He took her hand and helped her from the vehicle. She looked down at his hand, so large, so powerful where it clasped her much smaller, paler one. One hard squeeze and he could easily break every bone in her hand, she thought.

"Are you really okay Kara, or are you just telling me that because you think it's what I want to hear?" Slade asked as they ambled hand in hand down a winding dirt path that meandered between trees and boulders.

She sucked a deep breath and held it. Was she okay? Would she be okay if Slade decided to spank her?

"Nervous about submitting?" Slade asked.

"Yes—" The single word whispered out of her.

"What worries you the most?" His voice was soft, gentle, probing, soliciting her response.

He stopped, and pulled her around to face him when she didn't immediately answer. "What scares you honey?"

"Th-that you will—s-spank me," she muttered softly.

He pulled her close. "God knows I don't want to scare you Kara," he sighed, his breath fanning her hair. "But if you submit to me I will spank you if you are disobedient. Spanking you when you need it is part of my dominance over you." She felt his hand tighten on her back. "I purposely give you praise, don't you think you'd want me to give you punishment too if you needed it?" he asked.

She shook her head trying to imagine a scenario in which she could imagine Slade spanking her. She shivered involuntarily as she remembered the beatings the man who had raped her had inflicted. He'd forced her to kneel with her face on the dirty floor as he striped her back with his belt. Remembered humiliation crawled through her.

She cringed involuntarily. "I wouldn't want to make you that angry."

He pulled her against his chest and stroked her hair. Shyness and embarrassment crawling through her midsection, she shifted and lifted her gaze to his. "I don't think I could— I'd be—" Mortified. Embarrassed. *Crying my eyes out before you ever touched me*, her mind raced on, leaving her voice in the dust.

He tightened his arms around her. "Haven't I told you before, spanking is not about anger?" He sighed. "I wouldn't spank you when I was angry. If you needed to be spanked and I was angry I would cool down first. I wouldn't take a chance on hurting you Kara, emotionally or physically. Ever."

She felt more confused than ever. It was good he wouldn't hit her in anger, but why did he have to hit her at all? How could he say he wouldn't hurt her in the same sentence he was talking about spanking her? Didn't spanking, by definition, hurt?

Her head spun. She still couldn't imagine Slade spanking her. He'd held her all night, tenderly wiping her tears away when she woke from bad dreams drenched in sweat and trembling with memories she couldn't push away. She couldn't imagine him hitting her, purposely inflicting pain after he'd displayed such tenderness.

She shivered involuntarily, the bleakness of the sky and the crispness of the wind adding to the sense of desolation she felt. "I—I don't understand wh—why you would want to spank me, o—or why I would let you."

He tilted her chin so she was helpless to avoid his pinning gaze. "Why you would let me spank you, Kara, is that agreeing to accept the discipline I think is appropriate for you is part of your submission to me. When you agree to submit to me you agree to accept my decisions about what is best for you. Do you understand?"

The air gushed out of her lungs leaving her dizzy. She swallowed gasping like a dying fish.

His gaze stroked her face. She could sense him studying her and could sense compassion in his expression.

"Trust me Kara. I know the idea of being spanked is strange to you. Hell, it probably seems perverse as hell. Why would someone show affection through spanking, right?" He shoved his hand through his hair and rocked back on his heels. "I know right now you think you don't need or want discipline but someday you will and it's best that we have it as part of the framework of our relationship from the beginning."

She thought of the man and the belt and the stinging welts that turned to blue and black marks that had criss-crossed her back and legs. The bruises had remained for a week after she'd been found. She doubted there would ever be a time when she'd want Slade to hit her, discipline or not.

She opened her mouth to tell him that she wouldn't disappoint him and even if she did she wouldn't want him to beat her but he slid a finger over her lips. "Sh—- just trust me," he said softly. "We'll take it slowly. It'll be right for you when it happens or it won't happen at all. You can trust me on that Kara."

Silenced, she gazed up at him. Her mind scrambled to reconcile the conflicting images of being whipped with a belt as she curled in the dirt with the image of Slade striking her bottom as he pressed her across his lap. The conflicting images in her mind were not the same. One was ugly with cruelty. The other was controlled and made her feel safe and loved in a way that she didn't understand. Yet neither image squared with the memory of Slade holding her, wiping away her tears the night before.

"When the time comes, spanking is something I will do for you honey. I'm not going to lie to you, if it's a punishment spanking it will hurt, probably quite a lot. But in the end the physical pain I give you will help take away emotional pain. That's its job. When it's over there will be forgiveness and you'll feel safe and loved."

He drew her toward him "Spanking a submissive is something a dominant does for her as much as to her." He sighed. "Every couple has their own way of looking at it I expect, but the way I see it, spanking you when you are disobedient is part of how I show my dominance over you. It's part of how I take care of you, how I keep you safe in my care. Submitting to being spanked is part of how you demonstrate your submission to me."

He stroked her hair. "It's all about taking care of you and taking care of our relationship. It's not all that different from rubbing your back to help you relax last night." He drew a deep breath. "I did that because I knew you needed to relax and because I knew it would help you. When I spank you it will be for the same reasons. I might spank you playfully just because I want to or because you want me to. But if I spank you seriously it will be because you need it and because it will help you."

She sighed enjoying the warmth of his chest. The way he described it didn't sound as painful and humiliating as she'd first imagined. Still, though she could imagine him spanking her, she couldn't imagine herself finding it anything but painful and humiliating.

"Think about it this way," he said after a few minutes of silence. "Sometimes what someone needs to make them feel good is pleasure. Other times, they need boundaries because the boundaries make them feel safe and protected. As your dominant it's my responsibility to know what you need and provide it for you.

"Right now you feel uncertain and insecure," he said lowering his lips until they brushed hers. "You need a little tenderness to help you feel better."

His mouth lingered, his lips brushing hers until the tension coiled tightly in her midsection began to melt only to be replaced by a deeper tightening that centered deep inside her. His tongue teased the edges of her lips until the caress of his mouth eased her desire to argue with him about spankings and she relaxed against him.

She whimpered against the warmth of his mouth, remembering how gentle he had been the night before when he'd scooped her up and carried her to the chair. Not once that night or since had he expressed anger or frustration. Not once had he blamed her for not telling him about the rape and the panic attacks. Instead he had held her, rocking her, seeming to understand intuitively exactly what she needed and giving it to her without reservation and without asking anything in return.

Maybe he was right. Maybe she did need to trust him to know what she needed.

She parted her lips on a sigh, allowing his tongue access to her mouth as his hands slid beneath her hair and blazed a path of warmth up her neck and over her shoulders. He massaged away the tension that pooled at the base of her skull and between her shoulder blades.

Finally he lifted his mouth from hers. "Trust me Kara?" he asked softly as he gazed into her eyes.

"S-Slade——" She sighed, dipping her chin to avoid the heat and sexual knowledge that blazed in his eyes.

He took her chin and gently raised it until she was forced to meet his gaze. "You were going to stop hiding from me, remember?" he asked.

She raised her gaze and nodded slowly. "I do trust you, more than I've trusted anyone in a long time." She swallowed hard as a lump swelled in her throat. "I just——" She sighed. "The idea of being spanked——" She drew a deep breath. "It really scares me."

"I know it does, honey. And I know you're still having a hard time trusting me about it."

She nodded. "I don't understand why you can't not——" She sucked air, her head swimming. "What I mean is if—if—um— Why can't you just agree not to s-spank me. Unless—unless spanking is something you need—um—sexually." She swallowed hard and stared over his shoulder at the rocky ground as nervousness gnawed in her gut. "Is it—sexual for you?"

Slade sighed. "That's a pretty loaded question honey. Are

you sure you are really ready for the answer?"

Kara was silent, indecision gnawing at her gut. She wasn't sure about anything, except that she wanted him to take care of her, to protect her, to continue to treat her with gentleness and tenderness. She wanted to bend to his will, to yield to him, to submit, but she wanted to do it because she trusted him, not because he would spank her if she didn't.

Slade could feel the tension coiled in her body as he stroked her shoulders.

"Dominance is sexual for me Kara." He sighed wondering if she had enough experience to understand. "Your submission and your obedience is important. When I ask you to do something and you do it for no reason other than because I have asked you I respond sexually. I've never been anything but up front with you about wanting your submission and obedience."

"I know." The words whispered out of her carrying an almost tangible thread of shame that cut him to the quick. He hadn't intended to shame her.

He sighed. He'd been a dominant for a long time and had played with several experienced submissives over the years. In all that time he'd never been caught so flat-footed with a submissive. Normally he could read a woman's expression and know whether she needed more or less, whether he needed to demand more or whether he needed to pull back.

Kara left him uncertain what she needed from him. She was such a mass of contradictions that reading her proved nearly impossible. She wanted to submit to him, had offered her submission, yet the idea of him spanking her as part of that submission had frightened her to the point that she had fallen back into the nervous habit of speaking in broken sentences and had nearly begged him to promise not to spank her.

She had asked him whether spanking was sexual for him. From another submissive that question would have been a request for information that he would have answered with brutal candor. But with Kara, he wasn't sure whether the truth would be helpful or whether it would make her more nervous and more afraid.

In the end he opted for honesty, believing in his gut that honest communication was the crucial foundation between a dominant and a submissive.

"Having the right to spank you when you've messed up is a sexual turn on for me. Actually spanking you would be more like sexual intoxication."

She heaved a frustrated sigh. "I don't understand, what's so great about it."

Slade smiled at the tone of frustration and stroked her cheek as he tipped her face upward so he could read her expressions more easily. "To begin with you have a beautiful round bottom that's perfect for spanking." He launched the words and watched her face for reaction. He was rewarded as a soft blush crept up her cheeks. "I would enjoy turning it a nice bright pink. I would enjoy hearing the sounds you made as I spanked you and I'd like hearing you plead with me to stop."

He watched her blush deepen and noted the increase in her respirations as he stroked the pad of his thumb over her lips. He watched as her eyes took on a glazed dreamy expression and her lips parted to admit the tip of his thumb which she moistened with a swirl of her tongue.

A sharp shaft of desire shot through him and his body hardened as he imagined the swirl of her tongue on his cock instead. He calmed his breathing and pulled his thumb from the gentle suction of her mouth.

Hmmm—so she's afraid of being spanked, but not immune to the sensuality of the act he surmised.

"More than any of that I would love teaching you, honey."

He leaned forward and pressed a gentle kiss to the frown line that marred her otherwise perfect forehead. "If I were to spank you I would show you how blurry the line between pain and pleasure can be. He kissed her, nibbling at her lips until she sighed and kissed him back.

She shivered.

"For now I know you are afraid of me spanking you so, for the time being, unless you completely disregard an order I won't spank you—deal?"

A sigh whispered past her lips as she nodded. Slade felt the tension she'd been holding onto slowly melt. He wrapped his arms around her, sheltering her against the brisk wind that had picked up so that it blew cold lashes across the lake. "Feel better?" he asked.

She nodded.

He held her for a long time, letting peace and quiet lull him as his palm slid silently up and down the length of her back. She felt like heaven nestled against him, her face resting trustingly against his chest, the sweet smell of her hair teasing his senses.

After a long time he drew a deep breath hating himself for the question even before he uttered it. "Kara?" He made his voice soft and non-threatening.

"Hmm?" Her voice was soft and sweet against his chest.

His gut twisted. "Will you tell me about the rape?"

Chapter 15

His request sounded stark and cold with her warmth pooled against him yet he knew he needed to know the specifics of what had happened to her, otherwise he risked saying or doing something that would hurt her.

She shivered, burying her face more deeply against him.

"Kara? Honey? It's important that I know what happened. You've promised your submission. That means I need to know anything that could potentially hurt you so I don't ask you to do something that would be painful for you." He stroked her back and pulled her closer, dropping kisses on the top of her head.

He felt her emotional distance in spite of the fact that she remained huddled against him seeming needier than he'd ever seen her.

He wished there was enough physical closeness and enough emotional support to make the retelling not hurt, but deep down he knew that it would be painful for her. It would probably always be painful for her, but he wanted the pain of it out of the way.

He wished again that he had taken more time to get to know her before their relationship became intimate. He would have liked the luxury of spreading his questions over weeks and months as he got to know her, as their intimacy deepened but their relationship had deepened dramatically in the aftermath of her panic attack.

Her submission made it imperative that he know the details of the attack. His gut cringed. She had gifted him with sweetness and innocence and instead of showing her the pleasures of being his submissive he was going to make her recount the most painful and degrading moments of her life. It seemed ugly and unfair, yet, there was no way around it. He needed to know what had happened.

He softened his voice "Baby, I need to know what happened so I don't hurt you again."

"Please Slade. I don't want to remember." Her voice was edged with fear and she clung to him.

The memory of her fleeing from their bed, retching over the toilet as tears streaked her face, lashed at him like a knife. "You do remember though. You remembered last night and it caused a panic attack." He made his voice soft. Gentle. Purposely cajoling.

She quivered. His body absorbed the tremor. He pulled her closer, and wrapped his arms more tightly around her, willing his body to comfort her.

She was quiet, her face burrowed into his chest as if she could avoid the conversation by hiding her face. He continued to stroke her back and her hair, hoping his touch and his quiet gave her the comfort and security she needed.

She was taut against him, her breaths even and measured as if she were mentally counting her way through each inhale and exhale.

"He had a knife," she said finally. Her voice was ragged with tension.

He stroked her back but didn't urge her to say any more. He'd be patient, give her all the time she needed, the whole damned day if it took that long to help her get through it.

"He took me to an abandoned house."

"He was a stranger?"

She nodded against his chest.

"He kept me in the cellar. It was dark and I couldn't see anything." She trembled against him.

Sudden knowledge ricocheted through him carving a painful gash in his heart. She'd needed to have the light in the bathroom on because waking up in the darkness reminded her of her captivity.

He rubbed her back, allowing her to fall into silence, not pushing her for more but giving her as much comfort and patience as he could.

"It was completely dark, except for when he was there. When he came he brought a lantern and food. It was such a relief to have light and I was so hungry."

She gulped in air. "He would force me to kiss—to—uhm—to kiss his—-" Slade squeezed his eyes shut. "—His private parts." His arms tightened protectively around her. He nuzzled the top of her head and dropped kisses on the fragrant cloud of hair that tickled his nose. It wasn't enough to take away her pain, but he hoped she understood that he cared, that he wanted to make it better.

She burrowed into his chest. "He made me—" He heard her audible intake of breath. "He made me suck—uhm—his—"

"It's okay, I understand." The image of smashing every bone in the bastard's face flashed in Slade's mind's eye. "Ii-if I had done it g-good enough he'd let me eat."

She sucked air in deep gasps. He held her, rocking her silently. He felt the tears that oozed from her eyes and leaked onto his jacket.

"The really dumb thing is, I almost looked forward to him coming." Her voice was sad and tinged with shame.

"There's nothing dumb about it. You were a child, alone in the dark and you were hungry. He brought light and food. You did what you needed to do to stay alive and get out." He held her, stroking her back and shoulders.

He allowed the silence to lengthen.

"There was no way to even tell how much time passed," she whispered after several minutes of silence.

Slade's chest ached. He could only imagine what it must

have been like for her. She'd been seven. He thought of his niece and imagined Kara at her age. At seven his niece was still afraid of the dark and needed to sleep with the door cracked and the hall light on when she stayed overnight.

"It was eight days."

Eight days. His stomach rolled at the thought of her in the basement prison for eight days. Just the thought of her alone in the dark made his skin crawl. The knowledge that the bastard had done more than just keep her locked in made his chest hurt.

He stroked her hair and her back. "Were you blindfolded? Bound?"

She shook her head pressing her face against his chest as she took a deep shuddering breath. "We—I was locked in. There weren't any windows and he locked the door. There was no way out."

She sucked a deep breath. "I hated hearing the key scrape in the lock. I hated—" She shuddered against him. "I hated what he did. I hated..." She sucked a deep breath and continued in a rush, as if she couldn't wait to be finished. "I hated his weight on me, the way he pried my knees apart, the pain." She sniffed against his chest, her body tense.

Slade held her, hating the bastard who'd terrorized her and hating himself for making her revisit the whole ugly ordeal. He wished to God he knew how to go back and undo all the pain she'd endured during the eight days of hell.

His heart ached. He had failed in his role as her dominant. Hadn't he just told her it was his job to figure out what she needed and give it to her? She'd been through hell and if he was honest he knew he'd put her through more. And for what? He didn't know what she needed and he didn't know how to give it to her.

Guilt seeped through him. She'd begged him to not make her have sex that morning and he'd responded as if he'd known better than she what she needed. He'd insisted that he could make it better, that he could help her, heal her fear.

He shuddered, remembering with self-contempt the way he'd played her body. He'd given her an orgasm. Big fucking deal, so I know what buttons to push to draw a physical response, he thought, remembering with disdain the pride he'd felt in his ability to pleasure her.

He remembered the joy on her face when she'd realized she'd made love without having a panic attack and felt scorn for himself. No matter what else had happened, he'd taken advantage of her, pushed her, sweet-talked her into giving in without stopping to think of the emotional price she'd have to pay. He couldn't even claim he hadn't known about the rape then. He'd known.

It hadn't seemed as real or as concrete then. He'd known it had happened and he'd known she was still emotionally fragile, but he hadn't really understood, what she'd been through.

"He was big and heavy. I could hardly breathe when he was on top of me."

She drew a shuddery breath. He felt the dampness of her tears through his jacket and knew his insistence that she tell him about the rape had ripped open old wounds. He'd made her cry. Again. She wasn't crying deep racking sobs, like the night before. Those he could have handled easier than the silent tears that worked their way through his coat and into his heart filling him with guilt and remorse at the way he had treated her.

Sickness coiled in his gut. God, I've done nothing but hurt her. I've been hurting her from the beginning.

"I fought and cried but it didn't matter, he just f-forced my legs apart and—and—" She sucked a deep breath and then another. "It didn't matter how much it hurt or how hard I fought." She sighed.

Bitterness rose in Slade's throat. "Shhh baby, it's alright." His chest ached for what she had endured, both back then and at his own hands. The degradation and humiliation she must have felt when he'd held her head steady and thrust himself into her mouth gnawed at him, filling him with shame.

"I wasn't strong enough—" Her voice was sad and thick with tears.

"It wasn't your fault Kara," he said stroking the back of her head and pressing her face against his chest.

"I wasn't strong enough. I couldn't kick him hard enough to make him stop."

"You were a child, honey." He stroked her hair. "You couldn't be expected to fight off a grown man."

Slade swallowed hard, his jaw aching from being clenched so tight. Sickness churned in his gut as he imagined her cowering in the dark on the smelly dirt floor. He imagined her alternately dreading the sadistic bastard's arrival and needing light and something to eat.

The viciousness of what she'd been through chewed at him, stealing the air from his lungs and making him ache with pent up rage and the knowledge that his own behavior had added a level of pain he hadn't even begun to understand at the time.

He squeezed his eyes shut, praying he was wrong, but betting he wasn't as a sudden insight crashed through his brain. "Kara baby, did he—hit you—spank you?"

She nodded wordlessly, her breath coming in shallow gasps as a new wave of tears trickled silently down her face.

"God Kara—why didn't you tell me?" The words exited him in a half whisper half groan. He stroked her head, her back, and her shoulders, needing to ease the pain his lack of understanding had caused. "Is that why you were so worried about the spankings, honey?" He sighed. "Why didn't you just tell me. I would have understood. We would have dealt with it."

"What he did wasn't spanking, at least not spanking like— like you talked about it." She sucked in a deep breath. "He hit me as hard as he could with his belt. He wanted to hurt me. I know it's not the same thing." She looked up at him her eyelashes still wet with tears, the paths of her tears still wet on her face.

He held her tightly, amazement coursing through him. She had every reason to hate him, and yet she trusted him, trusted his description of spanking more than she trusted her own experience of what it had been like. The knowledge shook him to his core, making him feel at once utterly dominant and unworthy of the submission she had granted him.

In spite of all his talk of a dominant knowing what a submissive needed and providing it he knew he had failed her. Her despair the night before had been so deep and so raw that it had taken her most of the night to shake free of the grip it had held on her. Then he'd urged her into making love in the morning; never stopping to think it might actually add pain rather than relieve it.

What a jerk. What a fucking jackass, he swore at himself.

His hand knotted in her hair holding her against his chest as he silently went over the ways he'd hurt her and made silent amends for his bullish behavior.

He wished there was some way to go back and start over. If he could do it again he would do everything so damn differently. He would not force her into marriage. He would not tell her he wanted an obedient wife and he damn sure wouldn't have mentioned the possibility of punishing her.

If he could start over he'd ease her into his lifestyle slowly, introducing her to dominance and submission gradually as she got to know him and as he got to know her.

Hell. It was no wonder she'd been terrified of him. He hadn't done anything to make his desires palatable to someone like her who had suffered pain and degradation at the hands of a man who had used his strength to overwhelm her meager resistance.

He remembered the fear in her expression, the tremors that had worked through her as they'd recited their vows.

Guilt stabbed at him. She'd been sick with fear, probably imagining that marriage to him would be little better than a year long continuation of the rape she'd already endured.

Shame washed over him as he realized how close to the

truth that had been. Although he had not intended it to be painful her first intimate encounter with him had ended in disaster.

He despised himself for what he'd done. Before Kara he'd prided himself on the fact that he'd never, ever, injured a submissive in his care. The knowledge that he'd carved emotional wounds into Kara cut him to the core.

Shit. Hell. Damnation. He swore silently at himself, as he wondered how he was ever going to make amends for the emotional wounds he'd added to those she already carried.

He nuzzled against her, enjoying the sweet musky fragrance of her hair. If he could do it again he'd be so damned slow, so damned careful with her. If he could start over he'd make sure he didn't hurt her, didn't scare her, and didn't give her any reasons to fear him.

His mind drifted to the night before and the way she'd wrenched herself out of his grasp as she'd scrambled from their bed.

Sickness pooled in his gut as he remembered the sound of her retching. The image of her hunched on the bathroom floor with tears streaming down her face tortured him. It had been his fault that things had gotten so damned out of hand. He was to blame.

Guilt, bleak, dark, inescapable swelled inside him.

His behavior had been inexcusable. He'd behaved like a first rate jackass, forcing her to marry him, ignoring her fears and rolling past them as if they'd been the overreactions of a nervous virgin.

Even after she'd told him about the rape he'd pushed her. He'd been so desperate to heal the visible wounds he'd insisted she buy clothes that showed her figure, even after she'd told him that form-fitting clothes made her feel vulnerable.

Jesus. Even then, when I knew she'd been raped, I pushed her and cajoled her and forced her into submission.

The guilt that washed over him cancelled out any hope that she would willingly choose to stay married to him once he gave her another choice. He couldn't blame her. He had heaped hurt upon hurt on her in the short period of time he had known her.

Even then, when she'd been lost in misery that he had caused she hadn't lashed out at him, she hadn't blamed him. In fact, she'd found reasons to absolve him of any guilt, taking the blame for not telling him about the rape instead of blaming him for forcing her into a marriage she hadn't wanted in the first place. That she hadn't been angry and emotional or cold and aloof with him amazed him.

He thought back on the day he'd proposed. She'd looked small and fragile in the voluptuous scrubs, her paleness when he gave her the details of the marriage he wanted had only added to her air of fragility. He'd known she was afraid, and yet aside from stating she couldn't quit her job because her mother depended on her for help with medications and requesting that the details of their marriage be kept private she had agreed to the marriage without much fuss.

Now that he knew what the marriage and her loyalty to her brother had cost her he admired her even more. It wasn't only her willingness to make the best of the screwed up situation he had placed her in, but her ability to do it without animosity that he admired. He doubted if the situation were reversed he would be so generous.

As much as he wanted her, as much as he admired her; maybe because he admired her so much, he could not allow himself to continue to force her to remain married to him now that he understood what their marriage was costing her emotionally. He would not force her to submit to his touch knowing as he now did that every touch, every intimacy had to remind her of the rape.

Forcing her to remain with him would be akin to torturing her and he would not allow himself to do that no matter how much losing her would hurt.

His decision made, he stood holding her, remembering the sweet way she'd promised her submission less than an hour before. The pleasure that had shot through him as she'd offered herself to him, not really knowing even what that entailed had swelled and grown as they'd talked through her fear of being spanked.

He now knew the deepening affection he'd felt was love. Yet gaping emptiness took over where love had been as he faced the knowledge that he had to release her from the promises she'd made. He didn't want to release her, didn't want to let her out of his life but he knew once he allowed her the option of returning to her old life she would be gone.

He couldn't blame her for leaving him. He'd done nothing except heap pain upon pain from the beginning.

He held her, wondering how he was going to make up for the pain he'd given her. He would forgive her brother's debt, but it hardly made up for the emotional pain he'd inflicted or the wounds he'd forced her to reopen.

He wished there was a way to keep her that wouldn't cause her more harm. His heart shuddered in his chest as he thought about the shy way she smiled up at him and the nervous way she repeated the first words in sentences when she was nervous. His heart was already filled with her absence as he dreaded the letting go.

Chapter 16

"Kara?"

"Slade?" she answered softly.

"I've made a huge mistake and I've hurt you because of it." His words drew her gaze. She looked up at him noting the mingled regret and guilt that clouded his features. "I never meant for our marriage to be like this. I never meant for it to be painful for you at all." His sigh brushed the hair at her temple and she savored the gentle whisper of his breath.

"You didn't know—"

"No, I didn't know." His voice was soft, and rough, and a muscle jumped along his jaw. "Still, I never should have forced you to marry me. Using your brother's theft to make you marry me, on my own selfish terms—" he sighed. "I knew the day I offered to forgive your brother's debt in exchange for marriage that you were scared of what I was offering. I chose to ignore what you were feeling in the hope that I'd be able to show you it wasn't so bad after we were married."

He paused. "It would have been bad enough if you'd had some experience and had known the score, but with everything that happened when you were a child—your—innocence—"

He shook his head as if to clear it. "I realize now how painful it is for you and I know it can't work the way I had hoped it would. It's completely my fault we're in this mess—"

His sigh hissed in her ears but she couldn't find her voice.

"Kara, if you want to leave me, leave our marriage, I won't stand in your way." His expression was hard, his stance stiff, but his voice soft with regret.

She felt her shoulders slump and her insides go numb. After everything he was he dumping her.

She balled her fists, her head feeling as if it was going to explode. She should have known better than to tell him so much. She'd told her parents less and they hadn't been able to deal with it. In hindsight she didn't know what had made her think that Slade would be able to deal with what had happened to her any better than her parents had.

She backed away, avoiding his gaze, closing out his voice. She retreated into herself, feeling as if she was crumbling from the inside out. The warmth and safety she'd felt with him disintegrated into deep emptiness that left her desperately fragile and frantic to protect herself from the anguish and loneliness that closed in on her.

If he'd yelled at her with anger, hatred, venom, blame or a hundred other things she could have dealt with it better than she could deal with the quiet finality in his voice.

Her heart hammered and her chest burned with the need to breathe but she couldn't seem to get a breath past the tightness in her chest.

The pain bubbled up inside her and she closed her mind to any more of the painful words. She knew he wanted to be free of her, nothing else mattered.

Everything around her seemed to slow to a crawl as if it were happening in slow motion. She raised her eyes and sought his gaze. She searched his expression for the gentleness she'd come to expect from him. It was gone. In its place were guilt and remorse and inflexible determination that made her feel helpless to sway his decision.

"You can relax Kara. There aren't any strings attached. I'm not going to the police about your brother."

Kara hunched her shoulders against the cold wind and turned away from him.

Fighting back hot tears that stung her throat and chest she trudged up the hill toward the turn out where they had parked. The hurt was immense when she realized how little importance he had placed on her submission. He'd walked away from her, from her gift without a backward glance.

She was aware of Slade beside her and was painfully aware that he didn't attempt to touch her or stop her retreat. Bitter agony filled her.

She gulped deep breaths of air as she fought back the tide of despair that closed in on her. Slade was right, their brief union hadn't been without pain. She had cried more in the handful of hours they'd been married than she had in the entire past year. But for the first time she could remember, she hadn't felt alone in her misery. Slade had been there with her, listening, cajoling, and trying to make her feel better.

When she had been afraid of his dominance, he had matter-of-factly talked her through the fear. When she'd been frightened of lovemaking, he had been understanding and patient, coaching her until she was able to relax. When she'd been consumed by shame and embarrassment, he'd been there, quiet, and solid, holding her, giving her the tenderness she needed most.

She swallowed hard against the lump that filled her throat. For reasons she didn't completely understand she had trusted him and had counted on his stable, reassuring presence way more than was reasonable given the brief time they'd known each other.

Pain filled her chest. The prospect of a future without him stretched out bleakly in every direction.

When he'd asked her to tell him about the rape she had complied, trusting him with details she had never shared with anyone. In spite of the fact that she'd never met anyone who had been able to handle the truth She'd trusted Slade. Blindly. Stupidly.

She cursed herself for being a fool. Even her own parents, who she was sure had loved her, had not been able to deal with the aftermath of the attack. She shivered as the tide of memories began to topple in on her even as she tried in vain to hold them back.

She jerked as she heard it again, the loud pop that carried from the park at the corner where she and Kayla had been abducted. Even at seven she had recognized the sound and she'd known what it meant. When the police had come, their cars flashing red and blue and clogging the street it had confirmed what she had already known. Her daddy was dead.

Her mother collapsed when she opened the door to flashing lights and a solemn policeman. For Kara her father's suicide and her mother's descent into alcoholism and addiction to prescription drugs had marked an escalation in the darkness that had never really lifted.

"Kara? Are you okay?" Slade's voice and touch startled her from her thoughts.

"Yes—no—I don't know. Bad memories," she choked out as she looked up and realized they were standing next to the SUV.

"Want to talk about it?" he asked, his finger caressing her elbow through her jacket.

She shook her head wordlessly.

Slade sighed and unlocked her door. "Are you hungry?"

She shook her head. The last thing she wanted to think about was food.

Slade opened her door and waited while she settled into the seat. She felt battered and raw and overwhelmingly tired. She needed to be alone to get a grip on her emotions before they ripped her apart.

Slade was silent, she hadn't offered any plans when he'd told her he wouldn't stand in her way if she wanted to leave their marriage. In fact, she hadn't said anything at all since his announcement and apology. She had been cold and distant, completely aloof.

Resolved to accept her decision he climbed in behind the wheel and started the engine.

It wasn't until they were leaving the park that he spoke. "I'm guessing you're eager to get home and get back to your own life but I'd rather not drive back tonight if it's okay with you. Neither of us slept much last night, and if we leave now it will be well after midnight before we get back."

Kara shrugged. "It's okay. It's not like I have a job or anything." It was the first bitterness she had ever expressed and it sliced at him.

He glanced sharply in her direction and heaved a sigh. "Look Kara, I know I messed up your life. I'm sorry. I'll give you support, whatever you need, till you are back on your feet."

Kara leaned back against the seat and closed her eyes. It was too painful and her feelings were too raw. She wasn't emotionally strong enough to talk about her brother or the prospect of taking support from Slade. She needed to regain her equilibrium first.

She breathed in deep slow breaths counting slowly to four before she exhaled and counting to four again before she inhaled. Her nerves were frayed and she knew she was hanging onto her composure by a thread. She desperately needed to be alone. She needed to release the tears and pent up emotion that clogged her throat before they spilled out.

"What's next?" She asked softly without opening her eyes.

"What do you want to be next Kara?" Slade asked.

She shrugged. Numb except for the pain that filled her. What she wanted was to stay married to him, to give their marriage a real chance, but she couldn't say that. She wouldn't use Slade's sense of honor to keep him in a marriage he no longer wanted. "I could use a nap. I didn't get much sleep last night."

"Take a nap then. I'll leave you alone. When you wake up we'll get some dinner and do the Christmas festival."

Her heart squeezed. She didn't want to go to the Christmas festival, not now, not when her heart felt as if it had been shredded into a million pieces.

She couldn't handle twinkling lights and cheerful music. The magic and hope she usually equated with the season had died with the knowledge that Slade was sending her back to her own life.

* * * *

It was dusk and a thick carpet of snow had coated the landscape by the time Slade heard Kara stirring in the bedroom they had shared just that morning. So much had changed that it seemed as if a lifetime had passed since he had urged her atop him and they had made love in the predawn darkness. It seemed eons since she'd looked down at him, her eyes still glazed with passion, her expression triumphant.

He sighed deeply. The clean, crisp, joy he'd felt when they'd made love without the reoccurrence of a panic attack was forever tarnished by the violence that had been done to her and his knowledge of it. He almost wished he'd let sleeping dogs sleep and not asked her about the details. Almost, except then he would have continued to hurt her without really knowing it.

The afternoon hadn't been easy for him. Kara had spent the afternoon in the bedroom. He'd stayed in the living room in the rocking recliner where he had held her the night before. Her feminine musky scent still clung to the chair and had taunted him as he'd brooded about her and the emotional damage he'd done. By mid-afternoon it had started to snow, big flakes of white fluff that had gradually covered the landscape in a thick coat of white.

Snow usually made him feel lighthearted but tonight it only served to underscore his bleak mood. Memories of Kara looking at him with fear and distrust at their wedding and crying into his shoulder after he'd caused the panic attack the night before tormented him. He still couldn't get past the knowledge that he had hurt her.

He sucked in a deep breath and squared his shoulders, fighting the sense of looming loss that filled him whenever he thought of facing the future without her. He had known her a very short time but even so he'd known instinctually that she was the one he wanted to spend the rest of his life with.

She had a sweet naturally submissive quality that made him want to protect and cherish her. She brought out his natural dominance but did not make him want to be severe in his dominance as he had been with Susan. Kara made him feel protective and gentle.

He treasured the soft and mellow parts of her and the way she allowed him to take the lead in their relationship. Even more he treasured the times when she opened herself emotionally and allowed him to touch the depths of her being, to see her at a sublime, almost spiritual level. He liked the way she sometimes caught him off guard with some zinger that made his breath catch. He liked the fact that she filled him with the desire to give her so much pleasure that the pleasure obliterated any memory of the brutality that marred her past.

He shoved a shaky hand through his hair, and pushed the thought away, knowing he would never be able to give her enough pleasure to wipe out the ugliness. He'd tried, and all he'd done was deepen her pain.

He sighed, wishing he could be what she needed, but after what she'd been through, she needed a placid husband, someone who would be calm and non-demanding in bed. She sure as hell didn't need someone like him, a dominant with an overpowered sex drive and kinky fantasies. He would never be able to settle for having lukewarm sex in the dark and pretending it hadn't happened when morning came.

He wanted so much more than simple sex, more even than her willing submission. He wanted her to open herself, to surrender herself to him completely so that there was no part of her he didn't know intimately and understand just as intimately.

The hopelessness of the situation frustrated him. He loved her. He wanted her. He chewed his lip, trying to piece together the fragmented pieces of what they'd been building together.

If he thought there was a snowball's chance in hell of it working he would happily step back from demanding the physical expressions of her submission and give her time to grow into that part of the relationship.

But even if he didn't require any physical expression of her submission, he could not imagine her wanting a relationship that included making love on a regular basis. Even if she enjoyed lovemaking in the physical sense, which she had seemed to, how could she stand it in an emotional sense when every act that was supposed to convey love and affection instead brought memories of vicious brutality?

He heaved a sigh and pushed the thoughts away. It didn't matter how many ways he looked at their situation, or how many ways he turned the details around in his mind. The simple fact that he had forced her into a marriage that would always be painful for her still remained.

Allowing her to leave their marriage was the only way he knew to give her the peace she deserved. Much as he hated the thought he knew that what he needed to do was back slowly out of her life and release her without inflicting any more damage than he'd already inflicted.

He heard her moving around in the bathroom and wished for the thousandth time that he knew how to heal the emotional injuries the bastard who had raped her had inflicted. He wished he could make himself believe it was even possible for her to be free of the memories. The knowledge that she was still so wounded she needed to sleep with a light on sucked any remnants of hope out of him.

"Did you have a good sleep?" he asked when she finally emerged from the bedroom looking rumpled and bed tousled a few minutes later.

"I slept like a rock," she answered. "Did you sleep?"

He shook his head. "No, I watched football and watched the snow fall."

"It snowed?" she asked her face brightening for a split second before the twinkle in her eyes flickered and died.

"It was still snowing the last time I looked," he answered. "Are you hungry? Want to go get some dinner?"

She nodded. "Will you give me a minute to get presentable?"

"You're well past presentable. You're beautiful Kara, inside and out. You always have been." He said the words softly, more to himself than her.

She raised her gaze to his, as her heart gave a painful shudder. *Beautiful no. I'm used, injured, permanently fearful.* She was confused. Why would he call her beautiful when he knew about the rape, when he was sending her home because he no longer wanted her?

She felt his impending absence acutely. Bleakness swelled and overwhelmed her as she contemplated her life without him.

I like him. I like being with him. I like the way he makes me feel safe, protected, honored. Maybe I even love him. The knowledge that there wasn't any maybe about it hit her hard and heavy, stealing her breath like a sudden unexpected jab to the chest.

Overwhelmed by the sudden knowledge that she loved him she turned and fled toward the bathroom before she lost control and gave in to the helpless tears that still clogged her throat in spite of an afternoon spent trying to push them aside.

She ran a comb through her hair and changed her mussed clothes before rejoining Slade.

"Ready?" he asked?

She nodded, and took the hand he offered. Her heart clenched at the warmth that shot through her as his large hand engulfed her smaller one.

The knowledge that she would miss him tightened the noose around her heart intensifying the ache that filled her chest.

* * * *

Slade hated the awkwardness and distance between them.

He had tried several times to start a conversation but Kara was quiet and withdrawn. She was more withdrawn than she'd been even after their wedding when she'd been terrified of him. At least then she'd been willing to let him in, willing to talk about why she was so afraid.

Tonight she kept to her side of the vehicle, responding only when she had to. She had left him and mentally was already back home with her mother, he supposed.

Dinner was a nearly silent affair and he wished for the warm conversation they had enjoyed the night before. Then he had been cognizant that they were both engaged in trying to build something. Tonight he was aware only of the crumbling of even the barest of friendship and the weight of impending loss.

He sighed as he paid for their dinners, wishing he hadn't promised Kara they would stay in town for the Christmas festival. The prospect of Christmas carols, and jostling amongst a crowd of excited shoppers and animated children only served to remind him of the future he'd envisioned sharing with Kara, and the profound knowledge that she was leaving and he would miss her.

He did his best to push thoughts of missing her out of his mind as he shoved his wallet back into his pocket and wished the waitress a happy holiday.

He couldn't heal Kara's past. He couldn't take away the memories that caused her panic attacks, but he could damn well let her enjoy the Christmas festival without allowing his bleak mood to ruin it for her.

He offered his hand, his body heating when she slid her smaller hand trustingly into his. Once on the sidewalk, they were greeted by the familiar strains of "Silent Night" being sung by a band of roving carolers.

He and Kara wandered hand in hand up the brick sidewalk. He noticed a smiling couple peering into a display of engagement rings in the window of the jewelry store and felt a stab of regret. He wished he'd taken time to take Kara shopping for an engagement ring before their marriage instead of settling for a simple wedding band with a single diamond. He wished he'd taken enough time to make her happy about their engagement instead of forcing her into it. If he had had more time to date her she might have told him about the rape and he might have been able to avoid hurting her.

Another couple passed, their eyes bright, their voices low as they whispered conspiratorially over the heads of two blonde haired little girls who danced along the sidewalk in front of them.

A younger couple shuffled by them. The husband labored under an armload of packages and the woman waddled, her pregnant tummy shifting from side to side as she trudged through the snow. Their evident happiness cut at Slade. He'd hoped he and Kara would have children together someday.

The breath shuddered in his chest. It was possible that they could still have a child together. They hadn't taken precautions that morning. Kara could have become pregnant.

The thought jarred him. He had wanted a baby with her, had even fantasized about watching her tummy grow large and going to the doctor with her, listening to their baby's heartbeat together.

The images in his mind died a slow death. Although a pregnancy would tie her to him, and perhaps give him another chance to make their marriage work he did not want her to be pregnant. He could not think of anything that would be worse for her than to be tied to him and to their marriage because she was carrying his baby.

The loss of their future and everything he'd hoped to build with her filled him with heavy grief. He sighed, and cleared his throat; eager to be away from the glitter of Christmas and the joyous atmosphere that was so at odds with his own bleak mood.

"Did you say something?" Kara asked, her eyes lifting.

Slade stared down at her, mesmerized as big fluffy snowflakes kissed her cheeks and clung to her eyelashes. Her eyes twinkled in the light cast from the street lamps that lined the street. She was beautiful; so damned soft, so gentle, so seductively submissive. Just looking at her made him want to take her in his arms and make slow passionate love to her.

But something about her expression stopped his wayward thoughts. Something wasn't right. What he'd at first thought was merriment making her eyes sparkle couldn't be merriment because she didn't look happy. In fact when he looked closely everything about her seemed stiff and tight.

Kara turned away quickly, as she felt her control over her emotions begin to crumble. She did not want to cry. She didn't want Slade to know how much his rejection hurt, nor did she want him to feel as if he had to stay married to her out of some misplaced sense of integrity.

I am not going to cry, she told herself as she stared unseeing into the window of the dime store. She willed the sobs to stay lodged in her throat and prayed Slade would remain oblivious to the dampness that moistened her cheeks.

She felt his hands on her shoulders, felt him turning her toward him and gulped back a sob. "Are you crying?" he asked suspiciously.

"No, I have something in my eye." She choked out the lie.

Slade's eyes narrowed as he peered down at her. "No you're crying," he said softly as he continued to stare down at her.

She remained silent, the band around her chest tightening as she struggled to keep her sobs from breaking loose.

"Talk to me honey, what's wrong? Are you that eager to be home?"

She bit her lip, swallowing a new tide of tears that swelled in her chest. She shook her head side-to-side and wished she could melt into the snow near their feet.

Chapter 17

Slade backed her into the alley and moved so that his body shielded her from the curious stares of passers by. "Kara? Honey? Tell me what's wrong." His voice was gentle, beseeching.

She kept her gaze pinned to the ground as she shook her head, and bit her lip in an effort to hold back the tide of emotion that had been building all day. How could she tell him she didn't want to go home, that she wanted to stay married to him when their entire marriage had been a farce? What kind of person was she to want to be with someone that didn't want to be with her?

"Bad memories?"

She shook her head.

"Then what?"

She turned her face away from his searching gaze as fresh tears leaked from her eyes and trickled in icy rivulets down her cheeks. He reached out, his hand gentle on her cheek as he turned her face back toward him, not allowing her to avoid his gaze as her misery choked her. "Talk to me baby. What's going on? Why are you so unhappy?"

She drew a deep breath, wanting more than anything else to be wrapped in the comforting warmth of his arms, and to have that reassuring warmth mean that he still wanted her.

"I won't touch you tonight. I'll sleep on the couch if that's what you're afraid of." His voice was gentle as he wiped his palms gently over her damp cheeks then wiped her tears on his jeans.

She swallowed back a tide of fresh pain. "N-no, that's not it." She sighed.

"Then what is?"

She stared at the ground, feeling trapped by his unwavering scrutiny and his persistent questioning. The knowledge that he wasn't going to stop badgering her until she told him why she was upset settled into her. She drew a deep breath and said, "You're sending me—h-home." The pain she'd wanted to hide from him was thick in her voice.

He stared at her, his expression perplexed. "I thought——" He sighed, his brow furrowing in confusion. "Don't you want to go home Kara?"

She burrowed deeper into her coat but found the layers of wool poor protection against the shame that swept her. "I should be happy to go b-back to my own life b-but I'm not." She choked back a strangled sob and dashed at her tears with the back of her hand.

"Are you trying to say you want to stay——married?"

Fresh tears trickled down her face. She shook her head helplessly. She wanted to stay married, but not if he didn't want it too.

"Kara?" His voice was gentle but had taken on that edge that said he wouldn't be dissuaded.

She swallowed hard, her chest aching with despair. "Not when you don't want me."

"Not want you?" His sigh was deep and harsh but when he spoke again his voice was so soft it made her heart catch. "Honey it's not like that. I want you more than I've ever wanted any woman in my life." He sighed and reached out to stroke a tender hand over her damp cheek.

"I don't understand—then why?" The words exited on a shaky breath as she raised her gaze, searching his expression in order to make sense of the confusion in her mind.

He sighed deeply. "Because, being married to me is painful

for you, Kara." His voice was hard. "I hurt you—— I knew there would be a period of adjustment. I didn't expect you to be happy right away but I didn't expect to make you miserable. I didn't expect to hurt you at every turn." He sighed. "I won't keep torturing you while I hope it gets better."

"Slade," she sighed raising her gaze to meet his. "I'm okay. I'm emotionally fried but it's not your fault."

"The hell its not." His voice was little more than a soft hiss. "I took advantage of your brother's situation to force you into a marriage any idiot should have been able to see you were terrified of. I thought that if I gave you enough time it would work out."

She kept her gaze focused on him, her heart thudding heavily in her chest.

"I hadn't intended to initiate sex until you were comfortable with me but you seemed resigned. I thought if I made it good for you it would help." He sighed. "If I'd known about the rape then—" He sighed his brow furrowing.

"I should have told you about—about what happened sooner—"

"Yes, you should have." His gaze met hers with unflinching candor. "Telling would have saved you an awful lot of distress. But I understand why you didn't. You didn't have any reason to trust me at that point."

She dipped her head. "I was terrified it would be like being raped again."

"I'm sorry honey." His words were soft, like a caress that swirled over her. "It shouldn't have been like that. I would give anything if I could go back and make it better."

"I couldn't tell you." She took a deep breath. "I was afraid if I told you——you wouldn't want me and you'd go to the police about Ted."

"Honey, there is nothing, nothing at all, about what happened to you that makes me want you any less," he said meeting her gaze with unwavering seriousness.

"Even the panic attack?"

He shook his head as he met her gaze. "Did I treat you like I wanted to get rid of you?"

Slade watched the emotions that played across her face and the softening of her features as she considered his question. "No," she answered slowly, "you didn't treat me like you wanted to be rid of me." She drew a deep breath and let it out on a sigh. "I'm sorry about——um——" her gaze shied away from his. "I'm sorry about——the way——um——the panic attack happened. I didn't know it was going to happen when it did. I expected it—early—when you first started———" She looked up, her gaze skittish and shy. "I didn't feel the fear and revulsion I'd expected to feel."

The jagged edges of guilt he'd felt since she'd told him the details of the rape began to smooth. He swallowed feeling the lessening of tension that had been balled in his chest since early that afternoon. "I'm glad honey."

He stroked her hair back away from her damp cheeks and drew a deep breath. It was important that she understand why he had offered to let her go. "After you told me about the rape this afternoon—I—" he shook his head and took a deep breath. "I kept imagining how it must have been for you— how every time I touched you it must have reminded you of being raped. I couldn't stop imagining how that must have felt. I couldn't justify continuing to do something that would hurt you that much."

She shook her head fixing him with her gaze. "It wasn't anything like——" He watched her, his gaze taking in the nuances of emotion that flitted across her face as she moistened her lips. "I wasn't afraid once you started talking to me. I trusted you and what you were doing felt—good. It was nothing like being raped, Slade. Nothing at all."

"But—something happened to cause the panic attack—" He raised a quizzical eyebrow.

She dipped her head, unable to meet his gaze as remembered shame washed over her. "When you——when you——held my head." She squeezed her eyes shut, and shook her head as if to dislodge the memory. "He did th-that—when—when—he made me—" She swallowed back her revulsion and shame and the rising nausea that came with it. "Wh-When you held my head like that there was no warning. It—it was like falling into a slow motion flashback and not being able to get out. By the time I knew where I was it was too late. I was already in the bathroom being sick and you were there."

He took her hands, drawing her toward him and easing her against his length. "I'm sorry honey," he said pulling her head against the hollow of his shoulder and cradling it there.

She relaxed against him, thankful to be in the safe harbor of his arms again. She didn't want to think about anything except how safe she felt as he folded her against him.

Slade loved the soft sigh of contentment that eased from her body as she pressed her face against his chest and relaxed in his arms.

"It wasn't your fault. You had no way to know it would trigger anything," she whispered.

The deep remorse that had filled him when he'd listened to her describe her victimization that afternoon began to ease. Tendrils of hope began to work through him.

He closed his eyes, savoring the simple pleasure of having her safe and snug in his arms. He inhaled the delicate musky scent that wafted upward, taking pleasure in the way her curves pressed against him.

Her softness sent his mind spiraling with visions of making the slowest, sweetest, most gentle love to her. He wanted to show her with his mouth, his hands, and his body how much he loved her, how much he desired and wanted her. He ached with the need to make her feel safe. He wanted to see her smile without there being any unhappiness to mar her beauty.

He didn't want to let her go, not now, not ever. "Kara honey," he sighed as he stroked her cheek and rocked her gently. "I know our marriage got off to a rocky start. I know it has been painful for you, but I believe that if we both want to we can make it work. Will you stay with me and let me try to make things right between us?"

Her head lifted and she gazed at him, her expression soft as she met his gaze. "There won't be any pressure. We'll take whatever time you need."

The warmth in her eyes touched him, filling him with tenderness and the need to give her everything she needed to be happy in their marriage.

"There are no strings. I won't go to the police if you say no. You don't have to submit or have sex or do anything else you don't want to do. I just want to start over, to see if we can make our marriage work. I want to make you happy honey."

She sighed. "You don't need another chance, you haven't done anything wrong. You gave me a chance to keep my brother out of jail, and I appreciated that. You told me what you wanted. If anyone's at fault it's me. I'm the one that's having trouble living up to my end of the bargain."

"Agreement or not, you've been miserable honey. Making you unhappy wasn't ever part of the bargain."

"Me not being happy—it's—" she drew a deep breath and started again. "Me not being happy—," she sighed. "It's not your fault. I haven't been really happy since before—the rape."

The admission knocked the breath out of him. He gazed down at her head nestled trustingly against his chest as the desire to make everything right for her overwhelmed him.

He tightened his arms around her, understanding her pain but not knowing how else to help.

"The rape—destroyed my family. My dad—died. My mom anesthetized herself with prescription drugs and booze. I did my best to pretend it hadn't happened then and I don't want to talk about it now."

"I understand, honey," he said through the wave of protectiveness that swept him. The knowledge that she'd been abandoned with her pain intensified his desire to see her smile.

"I cried because the memories hurt. They always hurt."

"I get it now," he said softly. "I'm sorry, I didn't understand before." He stroked her hair. "I didn't know how traumatic the rape was or how painful it would still be to talk about. It happened a long time ago, and I thought maybe it would have mellowed some." He sighed. "If I could go back and not hurt you I would, but I can't go back."

He stroked his fingers over her cheekbones, his attention snared by the strength of the bone structure beneath the softness of her skin. Her appearance and demeanor were misleading, he decided as he contemplated her. She looked soft, sweet, but he knew there was an underlying toughness to her that he admired.

He could only imagine the pain and loneliness she would have felt when, at seven, she'd essentially been left alone to figure out how to cope with the brutality of an attack that would have made even less sense to her then. He let his gaze meet and hold hers, as the love and the protectiveness he felt for her surged within him.

"I will understand if being married is too painful or if sexual intimacy hurts too much and you want out. I will let you go if it's what you want, but it's not what I want Kara." He stroked her hair and gazed down into her upturned face, finding himself mesmerized by the eyes that looked up, meeting his with an openness that hadn't been there before.

"I love you honey." He let his words sink in as he let his gaze caress her with the love he felt. He wanted her to know that he wanted her to stay because he loved her. "If you stay you have my word, I won't ask for sex or your submission until you tell me you want it."

Kara sighed and closed her eyes. He could feel the tightness that had never really left her, easing from her body. For a minute he wondered if he'd misread the situation. Maybe she did want to be free of him and she was relaxing because he had said he'd let her go if that's what she wanted. Maybe marriage would be too painful, too filled with unhappy reminders.

"Our marriage doesn't make me unhappy Slade," she began

slowly. "Making love doesn't either. At first I thought it would feel like being raped again——but it wasn't like that. It didn't feel anything like that—"

She lifted her face and looked up at him. "Being with you is the first time since—" He watched her swallow, noticing how her gaze dropped to his chest and then traveled upward again. "It's the first time since I was raped that I haven't felt completely alone." She met his gaze fully and for the first time since he'd known her and didn't flinch away.

"Even last night, when I was at my absolute worst you didn't leave me. You stayed. You held me. You don't know how much you being there, holding me helped." She swallowed hard. "I cried, but not because you hurt me, more because the memory of the rape was so overwhelming.

Kara's heart expanded with joy as he held her. She found it hard to believe he loved her. He was so much stronger than she was that she felt fragile by comparison. Yet when she stood next to him, and he cradled her against his length she felt whole and complete.

More than anything else, he made her feel safe. Even when he refused to allow her to skirt painful issues his presence made her feel safe.

"I love you," she whispered as she burrowed closer to him, loving the sensation of warmth and safety as his arms closed tightly around her, anchoring her to his strength.

"I don't want to leave and we don't have to give up sex. All I really need is you to love me and I'll be okay."

"Shhh—that's a sweet sentiment," he said softly, "but I want you to take some time and really think about what you need. We have all the time in the world to figure out sex."

A sharp shaft of love stabbed her heart and seeped through her, spreading a tide of warmth and contentment. She gazed past Slade's shoulder toward the snow-covered town.

For the first time in twenty years she felt as if everything would be okay, as if this year, Christmas would finally live up to its promise.

"The town is beautiful isn't it?" Kara asked her voice filled with awe as she watched the snow fall past the street lights that illuminated the heavy flakes. Christmas lights twinkled in shop windows and the sounds of Christmas music filled the night adding to the beauty she saw.

Slade followed her line of vision and gazed at the picturesque town spread out before them. He watched as large flakes of snow cascaded down, their frothy edges catching and reflecting the light cast by the street lamps. "It's like something off a Christmas card."

He turned his gaze back to Kara, watching as flakes of snow brushed her cheeks and clung momentarily to her eyelashes before being blinked away. He had always thought she was pretty but she was strikingly beautiful with the sadness that had clung to her replaced with something brighter, happiness maybe—or hope. He wasn't sure, except that her eyes seemed brighter, her skin more radiant.

"It is very pretty, but it's not even close to how beautiful you are right now." He brushed a thumb over the softness of her cheek. "You look happier than I've ever seen you."

"I am happy," she whispered.

"Good. I want you to be happy honey," he said as he bent to kiss her.

He kissed her slowly, without hurry. The leisurely caress of his mouth reiterated his promise that he wouldn't demand more than she was ready to give. His mouth explored the line and texture of her lips, his tongue touching, tasting, and teasing its way around her mouth at a deliberate snail's pace. He moved his mouth slowly, not wanting to give her any cause for alarm.

He'd meant what he'd said. He'd give her all the time she wanted. He wouldn't hurry her.

The leisurely tenderness of his kiss mirrored the gentleness and patience he intended to show her in their marriage. His tongue stroked her lips with unhurried deliberation as it coaxed admittance from them. Finally she opened her mouth for him, accepting the caress of his tongue inside her mouth as well as outside. Passion coursed through him, heating him, making him think of tangled sheets and entwined legs, but he held himself in check. He might want to hustle her to the cabin and make love to her, but he wouldn't. He kept his promises.

He deepened the kiss, the strokes of his tongue becoming slower and more languid as he savored the warm slickness of her mouth and the sweet cocoa flavor that remained from the hot chocolate she'd had with dinner.

Kara was awed by the gentleness of Slade's kisses. He'd kissed her before, always with respect, and tenderness but never like this, never with so much reverence that her knees felt weak.

This kiss was like gentle, patient, lovemaking that involved nothing more than the mating of their mouths.

The kiss made her breasts ache. She trembled within the circle of his arms feeling overwhelmed by his tenderness.

His tongue stroked her mouth slowly, the touch strangely reassuring even as it ignited desire that pooled warm and tight within her belly. The press of his mouth against hers sought her acquiescence to his tender domination.

She surrendered to his gentle possession. She rose to her tiptoes, opening her mouth to the probing strokes of his tongue. He responded to her capitulation by engaging her tongue in an erotic slow dance that made her center quiver and her breasts throb.

He was excruciatingly patient, his tongue flicking hers, in silent invitation. Hers answered, brushing shyly against his. She melted under the reverent gentleness of the kiss, surrendering her anxiety, to the stronger bond of trust that bound her to him.

When at last their eager mouths shifted apart Slade lifted his head and gazed down at Kara. Her lips were puffy and pink where his mouth had brushed hers. The sense of trepidation that had always shadowed her eyes before was gone and her gaze was filled with a new warmth that heightened his spirits and made him want to kiss her again.

Nothing in his sexual repertoire had prepared him for the power of the kiss or for the warm contentment that filled him in its aftermath. He'd never kissed in a way that combined poignant emotion and the need to dominate with exquisite tenderness.

"That was some kiss," he said, softly.

Kara snuggled against him. "I didn't know it could be like that—so gentle—"

Slade drew her closer, pulling her into tighter contact, giving her the tenderness he knew she needed. He knew the brutality of the rape followed by the emotional abandonment of her family had left her emotionally destitute and that it would take a lot of affectionate gentle moments to even begin to compensate for what had been denied in childhood. Yet, he swore that over the weeks, months, and years of their marriage he would find and fill all the spaces that had been left empty when she was a child.

He knew she would need massive amounts of patience and commitment to build even her ability to trust. Even then, he knew it might be a long time before she trusted him enough to submit completely.

Even when he'd earned her trust and earned her submission she'd continue to need a lot from him. Her background had left her wounded and emotionally needy. He'd need to give her steady affection, unwavering commitment, and a tender, loving form of dominance.

Her submission, when she was ready to give it, would be all the more sweet because it would be born of a deep trust, painstakingly built and nurtured. It wouldn't be the submission of someone wanting to play a role for a time, but would be real submission born of her trust and devotion to him.

Chapter 18

"Thanks for a great evening," Kara said softly as Slade opened the cabin door, flicking on the light as he allowed her to precede him into the welcome warmth of the cabin.

"You're welcome, honey," he answered smiling down at her. "I had a nice time too." She thought for a moment he intended to kiss her. His eyes were focused on her mouth and he was close enough, his body almost touching hers, but the moment passed leaving her disappointed.

The silence in the cabin and the untried changes in their relationship left Kara feeling awkward and strangely melancholy. She shrugged out of her coat and hung it on a hook near the door.

She was jittery and unsettled as she stood in the center of the cabin's small living room, her arms wrapped around her middle. "Still cold Honey?" Slade asked as he toed his shoes off and kicked them into line beside hers atop the rug near the door. "I'm still a little cold from being outside but I'll warm up."

"Would you like me to light a fire?" he asked looking down at her with a gaze that had her mind spinning with images of them making love on the large pine bed.

She smiled. "A fire would be perfect. I'd love it."

"There's a bottle of blackberry brandy in the refrigerator. Would you mind fixing us a couple glasses while I light the fire?" Slade asked.

"I wouldn't mind at all," she answered as he knelt and began laying kindling in the fireplace grate.

Her thoughts spun as she opened the refrigerator and sought out the brandy. She had enjoyed the Christmas festival and the evening spent more as friends than lovers. Their exchanges had been warm, friendly, and even subtly romantic but true to his word, Slade had not pushed the issue of sex or brought up his desire for her submission. He'd kissed her a few times. He'd held her hand, held her close when she'd shivered, but his touches had been friendly, not demanding or sexual.

She mentally reviewed the events of the evening, trying to figure out why she felt disappointed and distant when she'd so thoroughly enjoyed their evening together.

She'd loved everything about the sleigh ride they'd taken around the town square. She'd been delighted by the jingle of the bells on the horse's harness and the slight woosh as the sleigh glided through the newly accumulated snow. The snowflakes that drifted down, sticking to their faces had only added to her enjoyment. She'd been charmed by the glow of Christmas lights that hung from roofs, trees, and windows creating a virtual fairyland of lights.

She'd felt treasured by Slade. He'd held her close to him, and when she'd shivered he'd taken a quilt from a box in the sleigh and unfolded it, bundling it around her.

After their sleigh ride he'd suggested they head into the shops to warm up. She'd had a good time helping him shop for Christmas gifts. She'd enjoyed watching his brow furrow in concentration as he tried to decide whether Tinker Toys or Legos would make the better gift for his youngest nephew Theo. Her mind had been snared by the imagined images of Slade and Theo, lying on the carpet, their heads together as they built Tinker Toy Skyscrapers and Lego trains.

She'd enjoyed the small yarn shop where she'd purchased several skeins of deep burgundy and cream yarn. She'd appreciated Slade's patience as she'd wandered the narrow passages comparing various types and colors of yarn, touching practically every skein in the store, and selecting and putting back no less than six times before she'd finally made her purchase.

Slade had been attentive, polite, and warm, but hadn't mentioned sex or treated her in any way that would make her think that sex was on his agenda anytime soon. As she poured generous tumblers of the sweet smelling brandy the only explanation she could come up with for the disconnection and melancholy she felt was that she missed the sexual pull that had existed between them before Slade had decided she needed more time.

She sighed deeply as she recapped the brandy and returned it to the refrigerator. Frustration curled deep in her center. She didn't need time to come to terms with sex, or to learn that she liked feeling submissive to Slade. She'd discovered that morning that she could enjoy making love. She also knew that there had been a deep sense of well being associated with submission. She'd been astounded by the near euphoria she'd felt when she'd finally given in and trusted Slade, focusing on following his instructions, letting the sound of his voice and his directions drown out her own fears.

She wanted to feel the deep tranquility again, and to hold onto it longer this time. Since he'd decided to be patient and give her time to get her mind wrapped around the idea of having sex he'd been protective and attentive to her needs but there hadn't been even a hint of dominance. She realized she missed the part of him he'd pushed into hiding for her benefit.

She appreciated him giving her time and being patient but she wanted sex, she wanted to experience the wonder of surrendering herself to Slade and the passion he ignited. She wanted to feel again the sensation of cresting tension and the explosion of ecstasy that had followed it. She wanted to savor the rush when color and sensation erupted and cascaded over her, showering her in bliss.

More than sex she wanted to experience the deep sense of well being that had come with surrendering to Slade. Yet, when she thought of some of the internet sites she'd seen when she was looking for information on dominance and submission her chest constricted.

She wanted Slade's dominance but she didn't want the rough treatment she'd seen on some of the sites and in some of the groups that were devoted to dominance and submission and bdsm. She didn't know whether bdsm and dominance and submission were the same thing or whether they were all parts of something different.

She wanted to submit to Slade but she didn't want the torture and humiliation that had been depicted on some of the sites she'd seen. Slade had said there was no submission without her accepting spankings. Did that mean—?

She blanched at remembered images of cowed women with angry red welts criss-crossing their bottoms and legs and others with needles jutting out of various parts of their bodies. She didn't want torture and humiliation. She wanted love, protection, safety, and warmth.

She sighed, her head beginning to ache. The new parameters of their relationship had helped her relax and had allowed her time to sort out some of her feelings, but she remained confused.

She missed the intimacy of their old relationship. She wanted to submit to Slade's control again, to test the feelings to see if she felt the same deep sense of well being she'd felt the first time she'd surrendered to him.

Shrugging off the strange feelings she picked up the tumblers of brandy and carried them back to the living room. Slade had just lit the kindling and was carefully arranging logs on the grate when she sat down on the loveseat in front of the fire.

She set the glasses of brandy on the coffee table in front of her and pulled her legs up beneath her. She felt tense and slightly nervous as she watched the rhythmic play of muscles across Slade's broad back and shoulders as he positioned the last few pieces of wood. Just the sight of his broad shoulders and the hint of male power she knew hid beneath the thick folds of his sweater made her body tighten and moisten with awareness.

At last he pulled the screen across in front of the fire and straightened. She watched his movements, feeling her chest constrict in mingled anticipation and anxiety as he ambled toward the loveseat.

Unfamiliar yearning combined with edginess making her tingle with awareness as Slade sat down next to her. His thigh brushed hers as he sat.

She jerked at the unexpected contact and the deep and unanticipated stab of sexual desire that ricocheted through her. Slade slipped his arm along the back of the seat, behind her head. She felt the tender stroke of his fingers on the side of her neck and turned her face toward him.

She raised her gaze to his, her gaze seeking the familiar solidness as a tide of unfamiliar and confusing feelings tumbled through her. She swallowed hard trying to make sense out of the confusing mass. It seemed inconceivable that after so many years spent avoiding men she wanted to be atop Slade, his body joined intimately with hers. Yet that is precisely what she wanted.

Tangled feelings and images unfolded in picture form in her mind's eye. She imagined herself atop Slade's powerful body, as she'd been that morning. Her head was thrown back, her hair hanging loose around her shoulders and partially covering her breasts as she alternately rose and sank burying Slade's shaft deep within her with each downward thrust of her body.

If the images in her mind were confusing, the feelings associated with them were far more so. The feelings were deep and intimate. In her fantasy she was not afraid, in fact, she was savoring each thrust of Slade's hard body, luxuriating in the sensations that spiraled and built deep in her core.

Emotionally she was grasping for something...an openness a depth of connection she'd only brushed against before. There was a sense of wanting to peel away layers of self-protection; to open herself to Slade, so that there was nothing separating them. In her mind's eye she was open and vulnerable, her soul lay bare before him, and yet, she was not afraid or even anxious. She trusted him completely.

The bond that stretched between them seemed pure and deep. There was an awareness that she didn't want to leave the sensation of oneness behind when their mating ended.

He stroked her neck again, the light touch of his fingers halfway between a caress and a tickle drawing her back to the cabin and the fire. The desire to give herself to his control, to experience again the rush of profound tranquility she had experienced when she had submitted to him that morning remained strong as he continued to stroke her neck with fingers that made her nerve endings dance with pleasure.

"Honestly, Kara, how are you doing? Are you feeling more relaxed? More comfortable with me? With our relationship?" he asked.

She could feel his gaze on her, sense his perceptive study of her, almost feel him mentally stripping away superficial layers as he searched out feelings and desires. His insightfulness and his patience added to her desire to be completely honest, to reach for that level of vulnerability she'd only grasped at before. She swallowed hard and brought her gaze up to meet his. "I feel better—more relaxed in some ways." She sighed. "But I feel— confused too," she answered.

"About what sweetheart?" His voice was soft, probing.

She sighed and dropped her gaze as her mind sought frantically for where to begin. "I enjoyed our evening. I appreciate you giving me time, being patient. It was nice not to feel—-pressure."

Slade met her gaze levelly. "I meant what I said. I want you to have the time you need to be comfortable with me—with our relationship. No strings. No pressure. My main concern right now is for you to be happy, to be comfortable."

"I am happy, generally."

"But—?" He stroked her neck again spreading tendrils of desire that shot through her.

She dipped her head. "I know you said I didn't have to submit until I'm ready—but—" she gnawed her lip as she sought the right words. "How am I supposed to know if I'm ready?" She sucked in a deep breath and let it out slowly in an effort to slow her racing thoughts.

"You'll know honey. You'll think about it, dream about it. Thoughts of submitting, of being dominated will drive your fantasies." He stroked her neck. "It's pretty compelling; it's not something you'll miss."

"But I—" she swallowed hard as the emotions bubbled to the surface. "I—liked what we did this morning. When you were telling me what you wanted me to do and I wasn't thinking about anything except doing it. I felt—complete—peace. I want to feel that again, Slade. I want to submit again."

He pulled her to him and kissed her forehead gently. "You will feel all that and much more, but not yet," he said softly.

Disappointment stabbed her. "Why?" she asked, frustration and sadness edging her voice. She'd expected him to be happy that she wanted to submit to him. She hadn't expected him to throw bricks in her path.

"Because, Kara the concept of submission still worries you," he stated looking down at her, his eyes deep with understanding. "And because I'm not willing to risk hurting you again to give you a little short term pleasure."

"Some of it worries me but not all of it," she sighed.

She sucked in a deep breath and let it out in an effort to ease the hollow disappointment that squeezed her chest. She felt her eyes shift away from his steady penetrating gaze. "It's—-the irrevocable nature that scares me."

"How did you come by the notion that submission is somehow irrevocable?" he asked. "I've never thought of it that way."

She shrugged. "I don't know, the internet maybe." She studied her hands. She felt despondent. Alone. Rejected.

"The internet honey?" he asked tipping her chin so that she was forced to look at him. He raised a quizzical eyebrow.

"I looked at the internet—before we were married, after you proposed. I looked up dominance and submission and some of those sites mentioned bdsm. I wasn't sure what any of it meant—or what you wanted. There were sites about—-" she swallowed hard, "all kinds of things. It made me feel worse, not better, so I stopped looking."

"God, honey." He sighed. "I wish you'd asked me. I would have told you anything you wanted to know."

"I didn't feel comfortable asking you then."

"I suppose not, I was the cause of your discomfort," he answered. "But you feel okay about asking me now?"

She nodded.

"So…ask away." He smiled into her eyes and stroked the sensitive hollow of her neck making her stomach tighten with desire. The deep baritone of his voice skittered along her nerve endings and seeped through her. She savored the sweetness of his approval and enjoyed the pleasure that came from knowing she had pleased him, at least a little.

He stroked her hair back from her cheeks, his eyes intent upon her face. "Are you comfortable telling me what scares you about submitting to me?" he asked softly, his eyes never leaving her face.

She nodded slowly. She was tired of wondering what he would demand—what the similarities between dominance and submission and bdsm were. She needed to know specifically what he wanted even if in the end, she didn't like what she heard.

Her hands twisted idly in her lap, and she gnawed at her lip as she tried to decide where to begin. Slade gathered her hands into his, and held them securely within his large palms. "Let me have it Kara. What worries you?"

The measured control he exerted over her fidgeting hands calmed her. She raised her gaze to his, and found his expression filled with empathy. "One of the sites I visited on the internet dealt with something called," she struggled to remember the term, "total power exchange, or something like that I think."

"You didn't like what you saw at the site?" he guessed.

She shook her head sharply. "Being treated like that—" she drew a deep breath and let it go. "It would be too much like—"

Slade watched as her eyes took on the sad, far away look they sometimes got when she was thinking about the past. He understood. Surrendering all her power and being treated like a slave would be too much like what had been done to her when she was a child, when what little power she'd had as a child had been taken against her will.

He lifted his hand and stroked her neck gently, drawing her gaze and her attention back to him. "What did you see that upset you?"

Her eyes held his. "There were people who had cuts from being hit with canes and things. Some were being held down and burned—branded. Some were being stuck—um—all over with needles—"

Slade drew a deep breath. "I think you're misinterpreting what you saw honey. I know it seemed extreme to you. It seems that way to me too—" He sighed as he stroked her neck. "The truth is things aren't always the way they seem. Not everyone that embraces total power exchange enjoys those extremes. In fact, most don't."

"You're sure?"

He smiled down at her, loving her innocence and the gentleness of her spirit. "Yes, I'm pretty sure.

"What you wandered into on the internet was at the extreme end of things, but even so, the people you saw were enjoying what they were doing. There are people who derive pleasure from pain, the same as there are people who derive pleasure from inflicting pain."

"It's hard to imagine someone enjoying being burned or beaten to the point that they have cuts all over," Kara said softly.

"Some people find it hard to believe that anyone could enjoy giving their power to another person. But you enjoyed surrendering to me this morning." He arched an eyebrow, and stroked her cheek. "Some people would have felt out of control and anxious, yet you felt peace. People experience things differently."

She swallowed hard. "Is total power exchange what you want?" He watched her gaze shift down till it rested somewhere in the vicinity of her lap. She was nibbling her lip again, her hands fidgeting in her lap.

He turned the question around in his mind. Was total power exchange what he wanted? If he was honest, he did want that kind of power over Kara. More because he wanted the total absolute trust that went with it than for any other reason.

He wasn't a stranger to the sharper edges of dominance and submission. He enjoyed rough play, pushing his submissive to the edge with the extremes of pain and pleasure. He found the power erotic and exhilarating, but with Kara his dominance was different. It was softer. He didn't want to push her to the rougher edges between pleasure and pain he wanted to wrap her up in softness and warmth and give her peace, contentment, joy. As he thought about it he realized he hadn't missed the harsher edges where he'd played before.

He stroked her cheek and urged her chin upward until she was looking up at him. "Maybe someday when we've been married a long time and you have complete and total confidence in my ability to live up to the amount of trust that kind of submission would require, but that's a long time in the future." He met her gaze steadily. "It's a deep commitment honey, a lot different in reality than it is on the internet."

"If someday we did that, would you—" She sucked a deep breath.

"No honey, even then I wouldn't whip you to the point of

leaving cuts. I don't want to hurt you, physically or mentally. I'd rather use your submission to give you pleasure."

He reached for the glass of brandy she'd placed on the coffee table and took a drink. "Want some?" he offered.

She took the glass he extended toward her and took a tentative taste. "Um, it's sweet," she said taking another sip.

"It'll warm you up if you're still cold."

"I can tell," she practically purred. "I feel warm inside."

He stroked her neck. She shifted toward him, raising her gaze to his. "Are you feeling better? Anything else you want to ask me?" he asked gently.

He knew from the way her gaze dropped to her lap that there was more she wanted to know. He watched as she shifted under his watchful gaze, twisting her hands in her lap and as her gaze climbed his shirt front. He itched to question her, to probe in ways that would make it easier for her to ask what she wanted to know, but he held back. She needed to learn to come to him with things that worried her. She would never learn if he made it easy every time.

He remained patient while she took another sip of brandy.

"I know submission is important to you, that it's something you want. You told me that from the beginning." She paused for breath, seemed to gather her thoughts, then went on. "You're a nice man Slade. You are honorable and dependable and trustworthy—all things I needed for a long time without really knowing it—" She sucked a deep breath. "When you suggested we go our own ways I realized I didn't want to go." She lifted her eyes, gifting him with a glimpse of deep brown. "Sometimes I feel like I just take from you and don't give anything back." She sighed. "I want to be able to make you happy and I'm afraid you will want more than I am able to give."

"You worry too damned much," he growled. You need to relax and trust me," he said softly. "In the first place, I know about the rape, I'm not going to ask you to do anything that I think will hurt you." He stroked her cheek. "I also know you're not very experienced. If I ask you to do something I don't think you know how to do I'll explain it or show you."

She leaned her cheek into his palm. "It seems like such a big step, such a serious step."

"It is and it isn't," he sighed. "It's serious in that once we agree on something I will hold you to it. I don't think you will find it any more difficult to comply with my requests than you found it this morning. You can trust me to take care of you Kara. That one thing is at the heart of all of it." He stroked her cheek, his gaze intense as it rested on her. "I understand that you're nervous and a little afraid but I'll go very slowly." He stroked the hair away from her cheeks. "I don't want to hurt you any more than you want to be hurt."

Kara pressed her cheek into his palm and looked up at him, her eyes dark against her face. He loved being the recipient of her trust and would do nothing to damage that fragile bond.

They fell into a companionable silence. He stroked her hair, enjoying the softness of it as it glided through his fingers. He felt the remaining tendrils of tension ease from her.

"I want to submit Slade," she said. Her voice was so soft he had to strain to hear it over the pop and crackle of the fire. "There are parts of it that I don't understand, but I trust you and…" she let out a deep shuddering breath. "I want you to…um…help me learn what I need to do to be a good submissive."

He sighed deeply and pulled her closer, cradling her head against his chest, absorbing her sweetness and the pleasure that coursed through him at her simple declaration of trust and submission. "For now you don't need to do anything other than what you're doing. I want you to sleep on this decision. Be sure this is what you want. Sometimes—when people get caught up in something and they want something very badly it clouds their decision making ability. Sleep on it tonight. If you still want to submit to me in the morning we'll talk about it some more."

"I am sure. I don't need to sleep on it."

"Shhh," he said softly. "Do it anyway."

Chapter 19

Kara awoke to the dusty fingers of dawn that crept through the shades streaking the room with shafts of pink and purple. She glanced toward the bathroom. The light was still on, the bathroom door still slightly ajar to allow the reassuring pool of light just the way Slade had arranged it before he'd followed her into bed the night before.

She sighed contentedly. He was such a nice man. He'd been constantly protective and considerate. She smiled feeling soft inside, utterly cared for, as she remembered how he'd turned on the bathroom light and adjusted the door so that the pool of light that fell in a comforting circle advanced far enough into the room to provide her relief from the terror of waking in the dark.

He was so strong. Dependable. She snuggled closer to him, enjoying the clean male scent of him and the safety she felt as he shifted toward her, his arm tightening around her, safeguarding her even in his sleep.

She forced herself to relax, although she felt jittery and tense. "Good morning Master." She practiced the words in her mind, repeating them again and again until she was sure she had them down pat and wouldn't falter when the time came to greet him. He had asked her to sleep on her decision the night before, but she believed that the simple greeting would let him know she wanted to give her submission, that she was serious about the commitment.

Her thoughts drifted. With those words she would relinquish her control and welcome his control over her. Did she know him well enough? Did she trust him enough to agree to promise to bend her will to his?

She knew he wasn't selfish. He hadn't shown himself to be the kind of man to put his own wants and needs ahead of her feelings. In fact, quite to the contrary, he had proven himself to put her feelings first even to his own detriment.

The few times she had surrendered, bending her will to his still resonated in her mind, drawing her back and making her want to feel again the spiral of physical pleasure and the sensation of being safe that had come with her surrender. She thought it strange that the sense of utter contentment and safety had come not with maintaining a death grip on her own power but on giving up control and trusting Slade.

She yearned to experience again the strange sensation of giving up her power only to have her physical and emotional needs so completely met that she longed for nothing.

She knew the experience of surrendering her will had fundamentally changed her. Perhaps it was that she realized that Slade hadn't taken her power and used it to weaken her. When he had used his power over her he had used it to ferret out her needs, and then to meet each one. The sensation of being so completely cared for was like an addictive drug that she yearned for more of.

Her thoughts wandered. She thought about all the things he could ask of her, some of them things she would enjoy, and others things she might not enjoy. Still, she resolved to obey the instructions he gave her. He had been understanding and patient, surely that would continue when she promised her submission.

She rolled over and watched Slade as he slept. His dark hair was tousled against the pillow, the arm that wasn't across her midsection held his pillow, his plain gold wedding ring a dull pink gold in the morning light. The dark shadow of his morning beard added a rakish appearance to his otherwise smooth features.

The truth was she wanted more than just the security and pleasure that had come with her submission to Slade. She wanted to submit to him because he wanted her submission, because he valued it. She wanted to submit because she was falling in love with him and she wanted to please him. She wanted to make him smile, make him laugh.

In just a few short hours she'd come to depend on his patience, his understanding, but also his direction and the steady pressure he wasn't afraid to assert when the situation required it. He'd made her do things she hadn't had the nerve to do since she was kidnapped.

Her mind drifted to the clothes that filled the closet. Although it had been difficult for her to even consider clothing in colors that would draw attention to her, he'd urged her to try on sweaters in soft fabrics and pretty colors. Then he'd teased and cajoled until she gave in and let him buy them for her. Having the blouses and sweaters and jeans that didn't bag on her was like getting a piece of her life back. In some ways it felt like she was slowly coming out of the dark abyss where she had hidden, afraid to come out, since she was seven.

She would never have purchased the clothes on her own. Doing something that brought attention to her, without him compelling her to do it would have been too difficult. But Slade had asserted just enough pressure to persuade her to move beyond her established comfort zone of baggy pants and baggier sweaters in dull, boring colors. He hadn't forced her to take the step. He'd exerted steady pressure and expectation, then he'd encouraged her to take the step. Then he'd been there offering steady support while she'd taken it.

She wanted to give her submission to show her gratitude and her growing affection but it was even more than that. She wanted to submit to Slade because she trusted him and because she felt safe and sheltered within his power, within his control. He was good for her, his power in her life was good for her.

She knew it would not always be easy. She knew he was

not above making her do the difficult things she needed to do to regain the pieces of her self that had been stolen from her when she was still a child. Yet, she knew even though he would compel her to take the steps she needed to take he would take her feelings into account, and he'd give her the support she needed. Not once since she had known him had he fled from her emotions or abandoned her to them. For the first time in a long, long, time she didn't feel as if she was facing everything that had happened to her alone.

She felt Slade stir against her and turned her head so she could watch as he woke. She marveled at the warmth that unfurled in her chest as he came slowly awake. She watched as his eyes blinked open and adjusted gradually to the slightly brightening shafts of pink and purple that filtered into the room. She smiled at him as his eyes focused on her.

He rolled and captured her, his arms trapping her as his chest loomed over her. "Good morning Kara," he said, smiling down at her.

Her heart pounded and affection swelled. She drew a deep breath and let it out. "Good morning——Master," she said softly, stumbling over the word just a little. She liked the sound of it in her ears and the way it resonated into her being making her feel sheltered. Safe.

She looked up at him, wanting to be his, wanting to belong to him, wanting to be worthy of the care he gave her.

He smiled softly. "So you still want to submit to me even after sleeping on it?" His eyes were intent as he looked down into her face.

"Yes Sir."

He caressed a tousle of hair away from her face, his gaze making a slow sweeping study of her facial features. The intensity of his inspection unnerved her but she remained still, and willed herself to remain open to him, rather than to withdraw into herself and away from his probing gaze. She had in effect given herself to him when she'd called him Master. He owned her now. It was what he wanted, it was what she wanted.

He stroked her cheek as his eyes continued to make a thorough appraisal. His hand was gentle but its effect on her equilibrium was powerful. She leaned her face into his hand and spread a series of kisses over his palm and wrist, desperate to express the profound appreciation and devotion she felt.

His chest expanded with affection as she scattered kisses over his hand. He loved the submissive nature of the act and the softness of the expression that filled her eyes as she looked up at him. The profundity of the trust she was willing to grant him filled her eyes, awakening a deep reverence within him. He was honored by the gift. In spite of what she'd said, he knew it hadn't been easy for her.

The reverence he felt toward her submission and his enchantment with her, fueled an intense desire to protect her from anything that could possibly hurt her. Her willingness to trust him so completely after so short a time increased his resolve to treat her with the gentleness he knew she still needed, and would probably continue to need for a long time.

His hand stroked her neck and shoulder. His cock swelled and strained toward her in response to the knowledge that she had given herself to him, that she wanted his mastery over her.

Pure pleasure filled him. She was everything he wanted in a wife, in a submissive, in a life partner. That she had given herself to him, not in fear but in absolute trust shook him. He found it hard to believe that the union which had started out so rough, with her so frightened of him had turned out so well.

He shifted slightly bringing her with him so that he was on his back with her head pillowed on his shoulder. His eyes were drawn to the tent in the quilt spread haphazardly over his lower body. He wanted her, yet he held himself in check. There would be time to show her more of the baser delights, but for right now he wanted to savor the moment with her. He wanted to shower her in all the patience and gentleness and love he could muster.

"Comfortable Little One," Slade asked ignoring the discomfort radiating from his own pelvic region.

She rolled to her side and looked up at him from her vantage point where her head rested on his shoulder. Her eyes were clear and bright this morning. The shadows of the previous day were gone. "Comfortable?" he asked again.

"Y-yes Master," she responded softly. "But you don't— look very comfortable. Does it—hurt?"

He glanced down, following her gaze to where it rested on the tented quilt strewn across him.

He smiled at her concern. "It's more—sensitive—than all out painful, though there is an achey quality."

"W-would you like me to—do something about it?" she asked.

He smiled at her, feeling his love for her growing exponentially as he studied her knitted brow. "That depends on what you'd like to do about it honey."

"I—I—um don't know very much about—-what—-" she sucked a deep breath. "But I could—-um—be on top like yesterday."

He gazed down at her head pillowed on his shoulder and felt a smile tug at his mouth as he noted the pink that tinged her cheeks and the frown that drew lines across her forehead.

He stroked a finger over the frown. "Did you like that position Honey? Do you like being on top?"

Her frown deepened and she worried her lip with the sharp edges of her teeth as she nodded. "I—I didn't feel any sense of claustrophobia—-it didn't remind me of —anything bad."

An ache erupted in his chest. The ache was followed quickly by doubts that began to cloud his mind, and then by anger that was directed fully at himself. He knew it wasn't fair to expect sex from her when her biggest concern was whether the event would remind her of being raped.

She did offer her submission to me damn it, he reminded himself. He swallowed hard. Is she submitting because she wants to or out of fear I'm going to turn her damned brother in, he wondered. Perplexed and bewildered he looked down at her nestled upon his shoulder.

She smiled as she gazed up at him. The smile and the warmth that shone in her eyes warred with the doubt that gnawed at his gut.

"The position," she began then faltered, as her tongue darted out to moisten her lips. Her gaze drifted away from his and he had the feeling she'd pulled the shutters closed against him.

He stroked her shoulder and waited for her to finish.

"The position——it——you let me have control over how——-it happened. You knew it would be better for me that way." Her gaze rose and held his.

Yes, he'd known it would be better for her that way. He hadn't expected her to realize he'd chosen the position because it would be better for her if she controlled the cadence of their mating but pleasure shot through him at the innocence of her admission. It thrilled him to know that she knew he had considered her feelings, that he wanted it to be good for her too.

He nodded. "That's how it should be honey. I'm not selfish. I wanted you to enjoy making love too."

She grinned up at him. "I did enjoy it." He watched as her cheeks pinkened and her gaze dropped lower.

"Do you think we could—do it again?" she asked shyly against his shoulder.

Elation zipped through him. She wanted to make love again! He was filled with joy at the knowledge that she wasn't dreading it, that in fact she was asking him to make love to her.

His response was instantaneous. He rolled, shifting her so that she was beneath him and he loomed over her. "Your choice Baby, the position you know or a new one."

Kara nibbled her lip. "What's the new position?"

"That's for me to know and you to find out. You will have

to get out of bed for the new one though," he teased, tossing the blanket off them as he rolled off the bed. He turned as she made a wild grab for the blanket.

"No you don't," he teased. "No blankets allowed." He lifted the blanket and held it out of reach.

She rolled to a sitting position on the side of the bed and sat looking up at him with a delightful pout on her face. "I don't have any clothes on," she said, stating the obvious.

"Yeah, I'd kinda noticed that," he teased raising an eyebrow as he allowed his gaze to linger on her breasts, before dropping lower. Her skin was all pale milky softness, the hard dusky pink of her nipples a sharp contrast against the softness of her breasts.

He watched her expression. He was having fun teasing her, dangling the blankets out of her reach but he would halt their game in a heartbeat if her expression gave any indication that she was not enjoying the game. He didn't want to hurt her or harm the fragile sexual self-confidence that he could see was gradually emerging.

"Slade—Master," she corrected. He watched her expression waver between frustration and something else he couldn't easily identify.

"Come on honey, I thought you were going to help me out," he whined.

"I didn't know it was going to require me to be—naked."

He sighed wondering why every woman he'd ever met had some kind of a hang up about her body. He couldn't help wondering why nudity was such a big deal. It wasn't like he hadn't seen her naked before. "Hey, it's not my fault you're beautiful naked," he teased as he bent and tugged her from the bed.

She stood and he pulled her into his arms, wrapping her in a tight embrace. "I love looking at you naked," he whispered against her ear. "You are beautiful. I love looking at you."

She used her hands and pressed against his chest leaning back in his embrace and gazing up at him with a puzzled expression as if she was trying to determine if he was telling the truth. Her expression was shadowed, and the words she'd said when he'd proposed slammed into his brain. Did she really think she was fat? Hell, she was perfect in his book. He thought for a minute, wanting her to know what he saw when he looked at her.

"I love these breasts with their pretty pink tips," he whispered, trailing his hand lightly over her breasts. "They're so soft, so responsive." He chuckled as he watched her nipples peak as if they operated totally on his cue.

"I like this little dip at your waist." He skimmed his hand over her side, following the natural contour where her waist dipped before flaring out toward softly padded womanly hips. "I love this soft part of your tummy." He traced his palm over the feminine swell of her belly. He'd never understand why women hated the extra pound or two carried there. He liked the extra softness and thought, not for the first time, that washboard abs were highly overrated. He knelt, and blew a soft breath over her belly, following his breath with the gentle touch of his tongue which outlined her navel.

He loved the way she caught her breath and swayed against him as he kissed her tummy.

"And this," he whispered throatily as he dipped his palm lower, sliding his fingers through the tangle of curls that covered her pubic mound. "You're so feminine and dainty here. So pretty. To think this is all for me, that you're willingly giving all of this to me." He sighed.

She shivered at the intimate touch but swayed toward him.

"I'm planning to keep you naked a lot honey so you're going to need to get used to it."

He stood and pulled her against him. He loved her sweetness, her innocence.

"You're beautiful too," she whispered her eyes luminous as she lifted her gaze to his, then dropped it again. His eyes followed her gaze to where it rested on his throbbing erection. Her expression was an intoxicating mixture of shyness and boldness that made his cock ache. "Can I——" She shifted her feet, raising her gaze to his as shyness battled boldness. "Umm—Can I touch?" she asked.

"Any time you like honey," he responded on a strangled breath that came from somewhere deep within him. He planted his feet and struggled to maintain control as he realized she had probably never had the opportunity to explore a man's erection before, at least not as an adult in a setting in which she controlled the pace of the touching.

He stood steady beneath the shy touches of her finger that shot shock waves of sensation through his penis. He loved the light, tentative touch. It made him ache to be held more firmly in her small hand. His cock arched toward the tender finger that stroked it, drawing a shy smile from her.

He groaned audibly but allowed her to explore his length while he fought for control. The timid brush of her finger as she drew it down his length was nearly his undoing. He closed his eyes, clenching his jaw as he allowed her continued exploration.

"That…feels…so…good," he said huskily as he pressed his cock toward her tentative finger, wanting her hand wrapped around him, stroking him.

She looked up at him, her eyes locked to his, her expression filled with both boldness and confusion as she slowly lowered her hand, cupping his balls.

He clenched his jaw, enjoying her curiosity but desperately wanting her soft little hand wrapped around his cock.

He growled low in his throat as she eased her hand back up his shaft, before slowly enclosing him in her hand. "That's so good," he moaned as he placed his hand over hers. There was no timidity as his hand guided hers, and he showed her how to stroke him to bring him to orgasm.

He groaned against her ear as he rocked his hips, thrusting himself into their joined hands. "Baby—it's so damned good," he groaned, his body tight. He breathed her name against her neck as his control shattered and he jerked spilling his semen over their joined hands.

Slade came back to earth slowly, the fuzziness in his brain beginning to clear. Kara was smiling up at him, the softness in her eyes and the pride that filled her face filled him with pleasure. He buried his face in her neck and tantalized her with his teeth and his tongue. He tongued a line from her earlobe to her shoulder then scattered a series of nips along the invisible line he'd tongued before soothing them with his kisses.

"See what you do to me?" he whispered huskily against her neck.

She smiled up at him, looking proud, confident. He wrapped his arms around her, holding her to him, allowing his mouth to make its way to hers. He feasted on her enjoying the slick warmth of her mouth.

Although he had just enjoyed a powerful orgasm he was still hard, still hungry. "I'm going to lift you. When I do, wrap your legs around my waist," he whispered against the shell of her ear.

She didn't respond but when he lifted her she wrapped her legs around him, and wrapped her arms around his neck. "Is that what you were going to show me?" Kara asked as she kissed his shoulders, first one and then the other.

"No. That was an unscheduled stop," Slade muttered teasing the shell of her ear with his tongue. She gasped in pleasure as he sucked the lobe of her ear into his mouth and swirled it with his tongue. His warm breath fanned across her neck inciting a riot of sensations that made her nipples pucker where they pressed against his chest.

He carried her to the bathroom, and with her legs still wrapped around his waist reached into the shower to turn on the water.

"What—? What are you going to do?" Kara asked looking up at him with puzzlement.

"I'm going to get us good and wet, and a little soapy and then I'm going to teach you another way to make love, Slade answered moving them into the path of the warm jets of water.

"Another way?" she asked her voice conveying surprise. "How many ways are there?"

"Quite a few." He chuckled.

She welcomed the strokes of Slade's large hands as he spread lather over her breasts and down her belly where he allowed some of the lather to drop lower so that it lingered at the juncture where their bodies melded. She reveled in the pleasure soaring within her as his hands slid over her.

She arched against his palms, her body already relaxing at his touch, already seeking the pleasure she knew he could give. She sighed deeply, inviting his large work roughened hands to stroke down her sides, over her rib cage.

He ran his palms over her breasts, circling her nipples but studiously avoiding contact with them. She bit her lip, her mind focused on the sensations as his hands slid over her back and chest again before sliding past the puckered tips that begged his attention. Desire shot through her and she squirmed against him, whining in protest as his hands slid past her quivering nipples once again.

She needed him to touch her, to pinch her nipples. Hard, gentle, she didn't care; she just needed him to soothe the throbbing ache that had taken up residence in her center. She shifted trying to bring the aching tips into the path of his marauding hands giving up the hope of understanding what made her want Slade's touch so much.

She whimpered brokenly. Her body was tense and tight. She felt fevered. All she could think of was the path of his hands as they disappointed her by sliding past her aching nipples one more time. "You could always ask me for what you want," Slade whispered near here ear.

"Please Slade," she begged. "You know what I want."

"Yes, I do." He lifted his face, his slate colored eyes holding her with the intensity of the passion that filled his gaze. "I still enjoy hearing you ask. And by the way, what happened to

Sir?"

His palm slid slowly up the curve of her breast, his palm just brushing her areola as his gaze held her immobile. She drew a deep breath, the frustration of his palms just barely missing the hard thrust of her nipples more than she could stand.

"Please Sir, I need your hands." Her voice came out tight, her frustration evident in the tears that caught in the edges of her voice.

Her breasts ached. She wanted him to touch her breasts, she wanted pleasure with a jagged edged need that made her feel at once lost and consumed.

Slade relented, his palms gliding smoothly over her breasts and nipples. Her breath caught at the intensity of the pleasure that shot through her as she arched into his hands, feeling as if she had come home, as if in his hands was the most perfect place to be. She moaned as his mouth found hers. His hands and mouth worked in tandem to soothe away the frustration.

His mouth pushed hers open, his tongue sliding inside. She whimpered softly. The frustration she'd felt when he was teasing her grew as she pressed against him. She needed him. She wanted him. She wanted his touch with a desperation she hadn't thought possible. She writhed against him, the need coiled deep within her feminine core constricting and overcoming her shyness.

"Please Sir," she begged as she tightened her legs around him.

"Easy Baby," he whispered as he grasped her hips, lifting her upward then slowly, gradually impaling her on his hard shaft.

Pleasure suffused her as she slowly sank upon him, taking all of his length inside her. She arched, her body slowly adjusting as he filled her. She shifted, accepting him as her body contracted around his. Pleasure coalesced in vibrant shades of magenta, purple, and fuchsia that teased the outside edges of her vision. She closed her eyes, her mind focused on the delicious sensation as his cock stroked her depths sending deep tendrils of pleasure ricocheting through her. She rocked against him, her body straining to bring more of him into her with each thrust of his powerful body.

He carried her toward the invisible peak of pleasure that danced just outside her reach. Each movement of their joined bodies took her higher, spiraling her closer to ecstasy. Her body contracted and waves of pleasure gathered as she felt the first edges of her release. "Cum baby. Let go. Cum for your master." His deep voice against her ear urged her on as he thrust himself deep within her. She vaguely registered the sound, half between a moan and a wail as it broke free from her. Magenta, purple and fuchsia light exploded in her mind's eye. She could no more stop the deep moans that exited her body than she could stop the tremors that shook her.

She panted, her body still convulsing in rhythm with Slade's straining thrusts. "Cum again honey, cum again for me," he urged as he drove into her

Master. The word made her feel compliant and docile, eager to surrender completely to Slade's dominance. She tightened her legs around his waist, pulling him deeper into her as pleasure soared. She shuddered, her body contracting, squeezing as she climbed toward the peak of final satisfaction. She clenched her legs around Slade's waist. He thrust deep, his power ricocheting through her as her pleasure broke in a sharp crest. He held her tight, his body shuddering, his cock spasming within her.

Slade wrapped his arms around her, his breath still coming in gasps that matched her own. He held her to him as water sprayed down on them wetting their hair and running down their faces in rivulets.

Slade turned her face gently so that his back shielded her from most of the water as his water drenched lips found hers. Their faces were slick and wet from the shower but his mouth was tender as it slid over her lips, his tongue stroking with exquisite care over the places he had nipped earlier. "Did I hurt you honey?" he asked against the side of her neck where his teeth had grazed earlier. "Are you okay?"

"I'm way beyond okay," Kara answered dreamily.

She shivered with pleasure at the roughness of his chin and the contrasting tenderness of his mouth as he pressed kisses to the sensitive hollow of her neck. She trembled as he tongued her earlobe.

"And you thought you wouldn't be able to please me," he sighed against her ear. "Do you have any lingering doubts?"

She shook her head. She didn't know anything except that she was happy. Truly, truly happy.

She had pleased him. The knowledge settled into her filling her with contentment.

After a long time Slade eased her down his length settling her on her feet before reaching past her to turn off the water which had cooled from hot to barely tepid. She'd barely registered the change in water temperature her brain was so fuzzy.

She watched as he reached past her for a towel which he wrapped around her before he lifted her and carried her to their bed.

She looked up at him her body languid, her mind soft as he stroked her cheek. "Master," she sighed.

"Sweetheart?" he responded.

"Nothing. I just like calling you that." He smiled down at her, his heart swelling with a mingling of love, pride and protectiveness. "You make me feel safe," she continued, her voice filled with awe.

He gazed at her enjoying her flushed features. Her expression was soft and warm, her eyes like melted chocolate as they rested on him. He'd gained her trust. He knew. It was there in her eyes, open and unobstructed.

He enjoyed her bemused state and reveled in the knowledge that he had given her the pleasure that had led to the dazed smile and the heightened submissiveness.

He stroked her cheek and studied the sweet wonderstruck

expression that filled her face. "I hope you'll always like calling me that." His voice was soft, but he hoped it conveyed his seriousness.

"Why wouldn't I?"

"Because sweetheart," he stroked the tangles away from her face, "submission isn't just pleasure. There will be times when I will ask you to do things you don't want to do and I'll expect your obedience then too."

Chapter 20

Excitement and nervousness churned in the pit of Kara's stomach as she glanced at the clock for the third time in as many minutes. Five twenty. Slade would be home any minute. She tugged at the lower edge of her pink lace bra, hoping for the umpteenth time that he liked her surprise.

Though he'd shown her more ways to make love than she had thought existed, meeting him at the door in nothing but her bra and panties was not something she'd done before.

She drew a deep breath. It was one thing to follow his instructions, to give up her power in the immediacy of his request. That required only a willingness to yield her authority to him. To take the initiative, to do something she thought would please him, in the absence of him asking her to do it was much more difficult.

Nervousness unfurled in her stomach. She nibbled her lip, reminding herself that she still had time to put her clothes back on. Slade didn't know she was planning to meet him in nothing but her skivvies so he'd be none the wiser if she chickened out now.

She drew a deep breath. She didn't want to chicken out though, not really. She shook her head as if to dislodge the flurry of doubts that kept surfacing in her mind. Doubts and all, she wanted to do this for him.

She knew that having her meet him at the door in sexy lingerie was a fantasy of his. He'd shared the fantasy as part of a larger more involved fantasy a few nights before as they'd snuggled together trading fantasies in the warm afterglow of making love.

He would like it, she told herself. It was after all his fantasy that had given her the idea in the first place.

She relaxed a little. Excitement mingled with nervousness and apprehension as she wondered whether he would take her meeting him at the door in lacy lingerie as a signal that she was ready for the rest of the fantasy he'd shared.

She sucked a deep breath remembering the story he'd weaved. Was she ready?

A sliver of fear chased up her spine at the thought of Slade possessing her the way he'd described in the fantasy. Surely, him entering her anally would be painful, even if he was as slow and careful as he'd been in the story he'd told. She closed her eyes. She couldn't really imagine it being other than painful even if he took as much time and used as much care as he had in the fantasy. He was large and she had never been penetrated that way before. It would have to hurt.

Her mind spun. Even with the expectation of physical pain heavy on her mind, she wanted to surrender to him. She wanted to give him dominion over every part of her.

She saw welcoming the discomfort of his possession as part of her submission. Uneasiness crawled up her spine as she wondered whether she would actually be able to surrender so completely that she'd welcome the pain.

She knew she wanted to feel again the intense trust she felt when she ceded her authority to him, but was it possible to feel trust and love even in the midst of pain? She thought back to the morning after their disastrous wedding night, remembering the way Slade had orchestrated their lovemaking so that she was on top, in control of the pace and power of it, because he knew it would be better for her that way.

A smile tugged at her mouth as the memory chased through her mind. She felt herself relaxing a little. She knew that even if his possession was physically painful he would do everything he could to mitigate her discomfort. He watched out for her, took care of her. He always had. She knew he wouldn't want it to be any more painful than it absolutely had to be.

A tight, heavy sensation invaded her center. The thought of Slade claiming her that way excited her in spite of the uneasiness she felt. She could already feel the tell-tale moistness seeping into the lace of her panties and dampening her thigh.

She sighed. She wanted the feeling of belonging to him completely, of being his to command. The desire for his ownership, his care, and his praise was strong, and it helped drown out the fear.

She released a pent up breath. She knew he'd been purposely stretching her boundaries, gradually easing her beyond her comfort zones, slowly preparing her to surrender herself in this way and in others. He'd been introducing fantasies and topics that she felt certain were intended to ease her beyond the strictures of her current comfort zone.

His approach had worked. Their discussions and the sharing of their fantasies had both incited her curiosity and made her feel more comfortable with things she had initially found unsettling.

Slade had been constant in his attention, alternating between challenging her to try new things that were beyond her comfort zone and nurturing her where she was. She loved him for both the challenges he set before her and the warm, loving care he gave her.

With the challenges he had slowly opened a new world of sexual pleasure to her. She enjoyed the excitement of never knowing what he would ask of her or what he would do to increase her pleasure or his own. In between the challenges they basked inside her comfort zone. He often just held her, telling how much he loved her and how proud he was of her, which made her want to please him all the more. Other times, his lovemaking was exquisitely tender, an expression of the depth of his love for her.

She drew her gaze back to the clock. Five-thirty.

Just as she glanced at the clock she heard the familiar sound of Slade's SUV in the gravel drive. Excitement and nervousness warred for control.

She had missed him. She wanted to see him, wrap her arms around him and have him wrap his around her. Would her choice of clothing get in the way, mess that up, she wondered?

The doubts returned, chasing one after the other through her mind. She wanted to run to the bedroom to put on her clothes, but she stood rooted to the spot waiting as she heard his footsteps approaching the door, and then the sound of his key scraping the lock.

She watched, her breath suspended in her chest as the doorknob turned and the door pushed open. "Hello Master," she said breathily, feeling at once excited, scared, and a little silly wearing such scanty bedroom attire in the middle of the afternoon

He stopped stock still in the doorway. She felt a surge of adrenaline as she tried to decipher the expressions that chased across his face.

The expressions slowly morphed from shock to surprise to something she couldn't immediately decipher. Her breathing returned to normal, her heart rate slowed. He looked surprised, but happy. His surprised expression slowly melted into one of lust. She watched as his gaze slid over her, lingering on the swell of her breasts and bottom, his eyes telegraphing his desire.

He shook his head, whistling softly between his teeth as if he'd been knocked off his feet and was just now finding solid ground. Silently he motioned for her to turn around.

Once she'd made a full circle she raised her gaze to his. She could feel the warmth of a blush that suffused her cheeks. "I missed you," she said softly.

"I missed you too, sweetheart. You look beautiful and I love the outfit," he said opening his arms to her.

"I'm glad you liked it," she answered moving smoothly into

his embrace. She sank against the warmth of his hard body, luxuriating in the pleasure she felt there in the safe circle of his arms. She absorbed the sensation.

Warmth, submission, and servitude were soft as butterfly wings spreading a feeling of wellbeing through her as she thought about their relationship, and the role she had given him. The roles of master, friend, and husband had merged into one role that encompassed them all in the brief time since their wedding.

"It's not Valentine's Day, Christmas, or my birthday, to what do I owe this stunning greeting?" he asked as he held her, stroking her back, his hands skimming lower so that they brushed teasingly over the curve of her bottom, his fingers lightly skimming the lace clad cleft between the cheeks of her ass.

"Um…" She swallowed hard, feeling nervous, looking for the right words to express herself. Once she found them they poured forth in a rush. "There's no occasion really. I love you and I like making you happy. The fantasy you told me the other night, gave me the idea." She shrugged. "I just thought you would like it."

Slade moved back slightly his gaze resting on her face, "I way more than like it, honey."

She smiled up at him basking in the knowledge that she had pleased him.

"Do you have anything cooking that can't wait till later?"

She smiled and shook her head. "We're having your favorite, sirloin tips, but I haven't started cooking them yet."

"Umm—you're good to me," he whispered.

"It's easy. I love you," she whispered softly.

"I love you too honey. More than I thought possible."

She smiled and snuggled into his arms, enjoying the simple pleasure of being held warm and tight against his chest, secure in the knowledge that she loved him and he loved her. At that moment she couldn't envision life being any better than it already was.

Slade nuzzled the top of her head, intoxicated by the sweet smell of her hair and the warmth of her nearly naked body pressed against him. God he loved her.

He held her, his finger lightly teasing the edge of her lace panties, delighting at the way she responded to the light touch, her skin seeming almost to hum beneath the soft teasing stroke of his finger.

He'd loved her surprise though finding her waiting for him in nothing more than a couple strips of pink lace had almost been his undoing. His cock still throbbed, aching for release, but his joy at her surprise was deeper than the physical ache to possess her.

He was warmed by the knowledge that she had felt safe enough in their relationship to take the initiative to step beyond his requests, to do something he hadn't specifically asked her to do. It made him feel warm inside, to know she'd done it just because she had wanted to please him.

As he held her, his hands skimming her back and bottom his mind drifted to the fantasy he'd shared with her. It had begun with her meeting him at the door in her bra and panties but it hadn't ended there.

He wondered if her greeting was intended to let him know that she was ready to explore the rest of the fantasy he'd shared. He toyed with the question, wondering if it was too soon to introduce her to the reality of bondage and anal sex.

"Kara," he said softly as he teased her thigh where the pink lace of her panties met her soft skin.

"Hmm?"

"I love the way you met me today, love that you wanted to please me."

She snuggled closer and he pulled her tighter against him, loving the way the soft contours of her body fit against the more angular planes of his.

"You said you'd been thinking about my fantasy. Were there any other...parts...you thought about?"

She squirmed in his arms and eased back enough that she

could look up at him. "I've thought about all of it," she said, her gaze slowly traveling downward till it rested on his chest.

"And?" he asked gently tipping her chin so that he could look into her eyes.

"And…" She sucked in a big gulp of air. "And… I'm a…" She nibbled her lip. "I'm — ready."

Pleasure shot through him. He was blown away once again by the level of trust she placed in him. It surprised him that she was ready to submit in spite of the tension he could feel coiling in places that had just moments before been supple beneath his hands.

"Kara honey, there's nothing to be afraid of. It'll be good for you or I will stop, simple as that." He stroked her back just above the lace edge of her panties. "You know I don't ever want to hurt you."

She trembled delicately and looked up at him, her eyes wide with uncertainty. "I know, and I trust you, it's just…different. Scary, a little."

He kissed her, slowly, gently, wanting to show her with his kiss just how slow and patient he would be when it came time to claim her bottom.

Kara willed doubt and tension from her mind and body, gradually melting against him as his mouth settled over hers. His lips caressed hers, slowly, patiently. She let out a sigh which was captured and held prisoner by his mouth. She was safe and warm, cocooned within the warmth of his arms.

She opened her mouth to his kiss, eagerly inviting his tongue inside. She abandoned herself to the warm soft feeling expanding deep in her center. She felt like melted caramel, soft, warm, and gooey as she surrendered to him.

The sensation of melting beneath Slade's power was like a beacon guiding her. She wanted more of the sensation of being ever so gently conquered. She wanted to open herself to his dominance, to abandon herself. She wanted to feel his power slowly, patiently overwhelming her, swallowing her, taking her.

In her mind there wasn't a battle for her power. There was instead a slow opening up and a giving of her power to Slade. There was a feeling of rightness, of being welcomed, as Slade took the power she ceded. She gloried in the sensation and savored his control, his care, and the all encompassing trust she had that he would take care of her.

His tongue probed slowly, stroking deeply into her mouth. She whimpered in the onslaught. It wasn't enough. She still wanted more.

She felt his fingers tangle in her hair, holding her head as his tongue probed slowly, in and out of her mouth. In her mind she pictured his cock entering her bottom just as slowly, just as smoothly. She imagined her bottom relaxing, opening, and allowing his possession just as her mouth had.

The heavy tight feeling within her center expanded and grew greedy. She wanted Slade. She wanted him to possess her, to own her, to master every part of her.

She wanted more than the rhythmic probing of his tongue. She whimpered beneath his mouth, a feeble pleading for more.

Finally he drew back. She moaned at the sudden absence of his lips and tongue as her gaze lifted to meet his. Her body resonated with the need for more.

The kiss had been nice but it had not been nearly enough. It had made her yearn deeply for his possession. But now she was separated from him, alone in the maelstrom of passion he had ignited.

He stroked her hair, his own breathing ragged. She looked up at him consumed with the desire to give herself to him, wanting him to own every part of her.

His hand slipped from her hair to palm her cheek. His thumb teased her jaw line. His gaze met and held hers. The desire to have him claim her, the desire to belong to him completely, was like a wild thing trapped inside her. She couldn't get enough. "Please Sir," she whimpered turning her face into his palm, to press a kiss there. "Please make me yours…all of me…every part…nothing held back this time."

Slade looked down at her, loving her, wanting her, his body aching to take the gift she offered. His cock throbbed and pressed hard against his pants, his hunger suddenly threatening his control, urging him to take her, to claim her, to make her his as she had asked.

He clenched his jaw, fighting back the raw, ragged, untamed need that tore through him. He wanted her beyond all thought, yet what he felt was much more than simple lust.

He wanted to possess her, to exercise his power over her, but slowly, gently, with the kind of care that expressed the depth of love he felt for her. He wanted to join power with control so that when he claimed her it was an expression not only of his dominance over her but also his need to protect and care for her. He wanted the very act to express his love for her.

The physical need to have his body enclosed in hers was overwhelming, and yet it was more than need and desire that drove him. There was the knowledge that with her simple, straightforward words, she'd finally asked him to master her.

In some deep part of him he'd needed to hear the words, uttered of her own volition. He'd wanted her to offer him dominion over her body, her heart, her soul, with nothing held in reserve. He sighed at last feeling complete in his dominant role. She'd given him everything, not because he coerced or goaded, but because she wanted to.

The heaviness of his responsibility to her ricocheted through him filling him with reverence and wonder and absolute determination to live up to the trust she had placed in him.

He fought the rough jagged edge of desire, not because he had to, but because he wanted to, because he wanted to give Kara more than a brief moment of frenzied passion.

This time when he made love to her there would be nothing he couldn't ask of her. She had surrendered everything. She was his to command, and yet he knew that every command, every request would be voiced to care for her, to express his love, to give her pleasure.

He clenched his jaw, fighting the desperate desire to be inside her. His cock strained against his pants, throbbing almost painfully as he stroked her cheek, his light touch at odds with the raw, naked desire coursing through his body.

He waited till her gaze rested fully on him before he spoke. "I want to introduce you to a little sensory deprivation. I know it's new and it might be a little scary at first, but I want you to relax and trust me, focus on the sensations. Everything I'm going to do is intended to make you feel good."

Their gazes locked, his burrowing into hers in an effort to decipher her feelings. He found her calm, almost serene in her submission.

"I would use a blindfold, but this is new for you. I don't want you to be without the ability to look around if you need to, so I will just have you close your eyes instead." He stroked her arm lightly. "Okay so far?"

She nodded, looking up at him with eyes that had once looked at him with fear and dread but which now held only trust and passion. His heart swelled with pride as he looked down upon her.

"I want you to close your eyes now and keep them closed until I say otherwise. If you begin to feel uneasy and you need to look around to get your bearings all you have to do is ask. I will allow you to open your eyes but you are not to open them without permission, is that clear?"

She nodded, obediently closing her eyes.

"Good girl," he whispered stroking her hair.

She trembled, absorbing his praise.

He stood back admiring the quiet way she stood, eyes closed, head slightly bowed. God she's beautiful, he thought reaching out to trail his hand lightly over the slope of one lace covered breast.

He enjoyed the soft moan as he stroked her through her bra. He loved the way she whimpered in protest when his hand drifted away, arching toward him when his touch returned.

He continued to touch her. He purposely did not stroke the same place any two times in a row. He wanted her to realize that he controlled her experience. He would touch her where and when he wished. He could give her pleasure or he could withhold pleasure from her. The power was his.

He wanted her to relax within his power, to trust him, to accept his power over her. He wanted her to abandon herself to the sensations so that she was suspended within them.

Kara moaned. It was like heaven and hell rolled into one. It was heaven when he touched her. It was hell when his hand drifted away and she was alone with nothing but the memory of his touch and the desperate desire for him to touch her again.

She hovered on the precipice, wanting. She thought of asking for the touch she craved, yet she held her tongue, trusting Slade to give her the pleasure she sought.

Please, please, please! She thought as she waited, silently praying for the next touch of his hand, for the next shower of pleasure that would cascade through her when at last he touched her again.

She began to feel uneasy after several moments had passed and he had not touched her. She stood still, trying to sense him in the room around her. The room was silent, there was no sound from him, nothing to hint at where he was or where he had gone. Had he left the room? Surely she would have felt him leave, wouldn't she have heard his footsteps, even with the thickly padded carpet?

She licked her lips nervously, wondering where he was. Why he had stopped touching her. She wanted to open her eyes, she wanted to look around, to see where he was. Suddenly he was there, his hands cupping her breasts from behind, his fingers massaging her tight nipples between his fingers drawing a sharp gasp of mingled pleasure and pain. She arched thrusting her breasts more deeply into his hands, wanting more of the intriguing mix of pleasure and pain.

"You were a very good girl, keeping your eyes closed all that time," he said his voice loosening a scattering of tingles along the back of her neck.

She moaned deeply as his fingers tightened on her nipples, pinching, tugging, and rolling the tender nubs through her bra. The pleasure that spread through her began to coalesce into a hard ball of tension deep in her center. She could only manage a throaty moan as his fingers continued to pinch and pull. Her breath came in short gasps as the pain and pleasure merged and surged through her, carrying her higher. She felt her body tightening, in the way it always did just before she came.

"I know you're close honey, but I don't want you to cum yet. I want you to wait." His hands on her nipples gentled. His touch grew light. His fingers were tender as he stroked a circle around and then over each pouting nipple.

She wanted to cum. Her body was still tight with need, in spite of the fact that the sensation in her breasts had gone from the sharp bite of mingled pain and pleasure which had driven her to the edge of orgasm to a softer scattering of pleasure that radiated from her nipples making her want the sensation to go on forever.

"I want to move to the bedroom," Slade said softly near her ear. "I want to tie you to our bed, like in the fantasy."

Her mind was already fuzzy with pleasure and the need for more coiled within her. The tight neediness within her deepened, contracting as he stroked her nipple through the lace of her bra. "Yes Sir, please," she said her breath catching. She wanted nothing more than to abandon herself to Slade, accepting both the intense pleasure and the pain he would give her.

"I'm going to carry you there," he said as he lifted her into his arms. "You have permission to open your eyes if you feel dizzy or disoriented."

She leaned her head against his chest as he carried her, basking in the knowledge that he loved her, that she was safe with him. She didn't open her eyes to reorient herself. She didn't need to see where she was going. She trusted Slade to take her wherever he wanted her to be.

He stopped in the bedroom, settling her on her feet and holding her until he was sure she was steady before he released her. "Sweetheart, I love the outfit, but it needs to go," He said as his hands slid down her back until they rested on the clasp of her bra.

She didn't protest as he deftly unhooked her bra and slid it off her shoulders. His breath caught in his throat as the bra slid away revealing the smooth swell of pale breasts. He watched as the cool air of the room made the pink tips of her nipples tighten into hard nubs that begged his touch.

Instead of taking her with his fingers he bent forward, capturing first one nipple and then the other between his lips tonguing and sucking each one in turn. The sharpness of her moan as he clasped her hard nub between his lips laving it softly with his tongue echoed through his body making his cock ache.

With regret he withdrew from her breasts, his focus shifting to her panties and the desire to have her completely naked before him. He grasped the waistband of her panties and slowly slid them down over her hips, and past her thighs. His eyes followed their slow hypnotizing descent as she was slowly bared.

His body shook with need as he gazed at her. She was beautiful the way she stood there, her body so open, her trust in him complete.

He dropped to his knees before her, his fingers reverent as they stroked the soft silkiness of her mound before he spread the soft outer lips of her sex, opening her soft interior to his fingers. He inhaled deeply, enjoying the musky scent of her desire that mingled with the soft womanly scent of flowers.

She arched toward him, moaning. He steadied her, placing his hands one on each thigh as he pressed his mouth to her sex. His tongue followed the path his fingers had taken, gently probing between the soft outer lips of her sex in search of the softer, moister interior.

He used his thumbs to part her feminine folds, opening her as his tongue stroked deeper. Her hands knotted in his hair, and he heard the soft silky moans that issued from her as he pleasured her. He licked and sucked, focused only on stoking her pleasure, intensifying her need, making her feel good.

He feasted, savoring the sensation of her smooth moist center closing around his tongue as he probed her feminine center. His cock pulsed with need, jealous of the path his tongue had taken. His tongue sank more deeply into her warmth. In his mind it was not his tongue sinking into her cunt, but his cock sinking into her tight ass.

He felt her body tighten, heard her breaths grow choppy as he continued to stroke her with his tongue. She whimpered. He could feel her need coalescing as she arched toward him, her muscles taut. She was close, so close. He knew one more stroke of his tongue; two at the most would have her careening over the precipice as the climax overwhelmed her.

It was too soon to allow her to cum. He wanted her to wait. He wanted her on the brink and needy when he claimed her sweet little bottom for the first time.

He was breathing hard, his own need pulsing within him as he slowed the ministrations of his mouth, easing slowly away. He would give her pleasure but it would be a slow climb. He would take his time building her pleasure and maintaining it until he finally allowed her to cum as he claimed her.

He got to his feet, but stayed close enough to watch the nuances of her expression. He knew he was stretching her, pushing her, taking her into territory that they hadn't ventured into before. He wanted to be sure he wasn't taking her too far too fast. He wanted her to be happy.

"Are you doing okay?" he asked.

She didn't answer immediately. He watched the expressions that chased one another across her face. With her eyes closed her expressions were more difficult to read but they were there none the less. Raw unbridled need, disappointment, frustration. "I need," her voice caught. "I don't understand—"

His heart sank as he sensed her confusion. The knowledge that it was his fault she was confused settled over him. He should have known she wasn't experienced enough to know the reason behind his denial of her climax. She had no way of knowing that waiting would make it better.

He pulled her against him and wrapped his arms around her. He held her silently stroking her hair as he struggled to find the words to clear up her confusion and ease the hurt he could see on her face. "I know you were close honey. I know you wanted to cum. God, I wanted to cum too. Still do," he sighed.

He rubbed her shoulders, his hands making small circular motions that finally resulted in a small moan of pleasure.

"In all the times we've made love I have purposely only given you pleasure. I've always encouraged you to cum when you were ready. I've never asked you to wait before. I understand that you're confused." He stroked her cheek, wanting her to feel connected, close, supported even though he was going to continue to deny her what she most wanted for a little while longer.

She pressed her face against his palm

"You submitted to me honey. You gave me the power to control your orgasms. I want you to wait until I am in your bottom for the first time." He stroked her back. "I am not doing this to punish you or to tease you. I want the experience to be a good one for you. It will be if you trust me." He stroked her cheek softly, then lifted her chin so he could kiss her. He kissed her gently, willing her to understand, to trust him for a little while longer. "Okay?" he asked.

She nodded.

"Good girl," he said stroking her cheek and kissing her once again before he eased her onto the edge of the bed, urging her toward the center.

Her emotions were scattered as she lay in the bed, eyes

still closed as she listened to Slade moving around the room. She heard the zip of a zipper, and the clatter of his change being dropped into the jar on his dresser. She could imagine him undressing. She heard him opening drawers and heard things being shuffled around. It was the first time since he had asked her to close her eyes that she was really tempted to open them. She couldn't fathom what he was doing, why he'd need to open so many drawers.

After several minutes she heard his soft even tread moving across the floor toward the bed. She felt the bed give beneath his weight as he sat down upon it. "How are you doing sweetheart?" he asked softly, his mouth next to her ear.

"I am fine Sir," she answered determined to do everything she could to please him.

"Good girl." His voice was soft, it stroked her senses but made her feel somehow distant. "Everything I am going to do is to increase your pleasure and mine. None of it is supposed to cause you pain or discomfort. If you want to stop for any reason, at any time, just tell me and I'll stop."

She nodded her head silently praying she wouldn't need to stop. She wanted to give herself to him, wanted to please him.

She laid perfectly still on the king sized bed, her mind spinning as Slade lifted first one arm and then the other, positioning both above her head on the bed. She felt confused and overwhelmed as he began to bind her wrists. It felt odd and a bit discomforting to have her hands contained so that she couldn't touch him when she wanted to.

When she felt him ease away from her she tugged at her wrists, testing the bonds, testing her ability to move. Her wrists were bound tightly together and then anchored snugly. She could not move them more than a few inches in any direction.

She had not really understood the reason for bondage before. But now, with her hands bound above her head a sense of helpless began to invade her. The sensation was at once exciting and frightening.

She felt Slade's hands on her ankle lifting her leg and moving it out toward the corner of the bed. There was the sensation of something being looped around her ankle then a tightening of the rope as he anchored her leg, effectively parting her thighs. It made her feel vulnerable and open.

She shifted on the bed, suddenly struck by how confined she was, how open, how completely helpless she was in this position with her arms over her head and her legs tied to opposite corners of the king sized bed. She was stretched out before him, open, vulnerable, his to do with as he pleased.

Nervousness began to invade her. A sense of uneasiness pooled in her stomach. The knowledge that he could do anything he wanted and she would be powerless to stop him slid over her. Her heart began to pound, her breath catching and making her chest feel tight. She found it hard to draw a breath deep enough to satisfy her need for oxygen. She was breathing rapidly but the breaths failed to fill her need for air. She struggled to relax, her mind struggling to locate Slade in the room. She needed to touch him, hear him, she needed his presence to steady her, to reassure her. Though she wanted to reach out for the solace of his touch her hands were bound above her head and she could not reach out.

She wanted to open her eyes, needed to open them. She needed to see him to know that he was there, that she was safe.

"Easy honey, I'm right here," he said. She felt the bed give beneath his weight as he eased onto the bed next to her.

His voice was like a soothing balm that slid over her like the comforting softness of a down quilt. She sighed and relaxed a little. She felt his broad strong palm as it pushed her hair away from her face and stroked her cheek. She pressed her face against his palm enjoying the strong solidness of his touch, needing it to calm her scattered nerves.

He was still, cradling her face in his palm. "Do you need to open your eyes, get your bearings?" he asked near her ear.

She relaxed a little more. She loved him, trusted him. She had wanted this, had asked for it.

She shook her head and released a deep sigh relinquishing herself to his control fascinated by his ability to calm her with just a touch and a few words.

"You're sure you're okay? We don't have to do this now, or at all if you're feeling uneasy."

"I'm okay now. I felt shaky for a minute when you moved away. I just needed to know you were here. I'm okay now."

"Just relax," he said softly, drawing out the word. "I'm here and I'll be here. I'm not going anywhere."

She replayed the drawn out pronunciation of the instruction to relax in her mind and willed herself to obey the simple command. She closed her mind to everything except the soothing sound of his voice, and his instructions.

"Everything we're going to do is to make us both feel good," he said.

She nodded, her mind focused on the path of his hands, and on the sensations they created. His palm slid slowly down her neck and across her chest. He circled one breast, his palm caressing as it drifted lower, following the soft swell of her tummy before dipping lower to rest possessively at the juncture of her thighs.

His palm was warm against her splayed pussy making her feel open and vulnerable, owned and mastered. She longed to have his fingers enter her. But when they didn't, she mentally followed as his hands drifted back up, over the soft swell of her tummy and over her rib cage toward the softness of her breasts. He slid his palms in circles over her breasts, his touch circling her nipples which had already grown sensitive in response to his touch.

She arched toward him, suddenly consumed by the need to have her breasts in his hands, her nipples trapped between his thumb and forefinger as he squeezed and pulled inciting a shower of pleasure and pain.

He didn't take her nipples, he didn't even touch them as he

continued to massage her breasts, her tummy, her thighs and legs. His touches were pleasant. She enjoyed them, but they left her wanting.

She whimpered softly as she arched her body toward his hands. She wanted his hard, warm hands to stroke the throbbing tips of her breasts, or to move lower to the hungry space between her legs.

Need consumed her. "Please Sir," she begged as his hand circled her breast, barely brushing the puckered nub that strained toward him. "Please," she said again, the word seeming as if it was ripped from her.

Her hopes rose as he brought his hand to rest possessively upon her open and weepy pussy. She arched against his palm, wanting more, desperately wanting to cum. His fingers tapped lightly upon her splayed lips. The light taps sent showers of sensation rocketing through her. She moaned and arched toward his hand, wanting more. She wanted him to go on patting her forever. The need to cum began to intensify within her, her feminine core clenching and relaxing as he continued the soft percussive tap.

The need began to claw at her, becoming more insistent as his other hand teased her breasts his fingers stroking her nipples lightly, tenderly.

Desire was a hollow ache deep within her. It gaped and yawned making her want more. Frustration began to shaft through her as he continued to stroke her nipples as he lightly tapped her cunt. She strained against the ropes that held her to the bed, arching her body, offering herself. If only he would give her release. She was desperate, knowing if he continued just a little longer she would be there.

She arched and bucked on the bed, helpless to do more than moan in frustration as he slid his palm over her breasts yet again.

"What do you want sweetheart? Tell me, so I can make it so," Slade said. His voice dripped over her like warm honey, promising salvation from the torment of his hands that never quite touched where she wanted them to touch.

She wanted his touch too much to remain silent. "Please Sir, I want to cum," she begged uncertain exactly what she wanted him to do to make that happen.

She gasped as his fingers grasped her nipple hard. He pinched and pulled. Pleasure and pain mingled, each one fighting for dominance as he continued to tap her cunt. Though she was beyond caring whether the sensation was pain or pleasure, in the end it was both that carried her to the edge.

She moaned loudly, her body arching, held tight on the precipice of joyous orgasm. She was so close she could feel her body tightening, the pleasure a crescendo that drowned out every other thought.

"I don't want you to cum yet. Soon, but not yet," Slade whispered in her ear as his tapping slowed and his fingers released her nipple from his vice like hold. He continued to tease the sensitized tip by dragging his fingernail over it. The sensation was exquisite, like a thousand shards of glass shattering outward from her nipple, but with the slower, lighter tapping, it was not enough to carry her to orgasm.

She felt tight, on edge, unable to relax, the tightness that had gripped her body remained. She whimpered at the loss of the pleasure that had been so close.

Suddenly there was a light snapping sound and a sharp sensation of pleasure and pain that radiated outward from her left nipple. She sucked in a breath against the sharp sting trying to gather her thoughts, to figure out what was happening. Then there was another similar sting on her other nipple. It took her a moment to realize that Slade was slapping her nipples with some kind of an implement that stung as it struck.

She moaned as he continued to tap her breasts lightly, the small stingy nip of the implement caused her to gasp with the initial sting and then moan as the mingled pleasure and pain worked through her.

The knowledge that she was helpless to do anything but lay there accepting the strokes as he chose to apply them settled into her. Her mind grew fuzzy as she gave up trying to control where the spanks fell. Instead she focused on the sensation, longing for the sting and the radiating pain that turned to pleasure long before the next stroke fell.

She felt as if she was floating on the sensations of each stroke, all the while she knew she was held firmly and safely in Slade's power.

After a short time he laid something on her tummy, his hand making a slow measured descent toward the apex of her thighs. She wanted his hand there, between her legs, stroking her throbbing center so much she considered begging him to touch her there. Instead she bit her lip, waiting while his hand dipped ever lower. She trembled with need and pleasure when at last he stroked her open pussy. "Oh please, more," she begged wanting to feel again the same deep shaft of pleasure that had shot through her when he'd tapped her.

Slade stroked her again, just barely brushing her clit. She moaned deep in her throat, thrusting her hips off the bed, she wanted him to touch her again, harder this time.

"Please Master," she begged.

His response to her plea was immediate. He stroked her again. Pleasure jolted her. She arched upward, feeling as if she would explode if only he would touch her like that one more time.

She waited and waited for the touch that would send her to heaven, but it didn't come. "Please Master," she panted, knotting her fingers in the ropes that bound her hands.

"I don't want you to cum yet sweetheart," he said softly.

Frustration coiled in her. She wanted to cry, to beg him to let her have the release that she needed so badly.

"You know I'm going to fuck your bottom." Slade whispered in her ear. His voice was soft and sexy, his breath gentle against her neck. Tension sizzled in her. "Yes Sir," she whispered softly. She wanted him to take her ass. She wanted him to dominate her, she wanted to give him everything he needed, everything he wanted.

"I want you to cum good and hard for me when I fuck you. Are you ready?"

The question ricocheted through her. There was a momentary thought of the pain that she was certain would come when he entered her. It was followed immediately by the promise that she could cum when he fucked her. The tension coiled deep inside her, the desperate need for release was like a wild beast that clamored to get out. Even the pain wasn't a deterrent now. She wanted him to take her, to possess her, to claim her. She wanted to yield to him, to have the pleasure and joy he had promised. More than anything else she wanted to cum.

"Please, I'm ready, I need to cum," she said softly.

Slade pressed a kiss to her forehead, and whispered, "Good girl," before he went to work on the ties that held her feet in place. Kara was quiet, her mind focused on what was to come. When he had her feet untied he helped her roll onto her tummy.

"I need you to move onto your hands and knees," he instructed once she was lying on her tummy. She obediently moved so that she was on her hands and knees, her weight supported equally by each. "Good girl. Breasts down on the bed," he urged, a light touch on her shoulders compelling her downward until her breasts were pressed hard against the mattress. "Legs spread," he said softly. His hand ran down the inside of her leg, gently spreading her thighs apart.

Excitement and nervousness fought for dominance as she waited quietly for his next instruction. The bed gave and she sensed that he had moved onto the bed behind her.

Fear surged, sharp and hard as the moment of truth loomed. Suddenly the threat of pain was immediate, while pleasure was a distant promise.

"Relax honey," he said softly. He kissed the center of her back just above the curve of her bottom. The warm whisper of his breath and the smooth pressure of his lips sent shafts of pleasure through her.

He slid his hand slowly down her back and rubbed his palm slowly over each globe of her ass, before he slid his hand between the cheeks of her bottom. She wiggled at the unfamiliar sensation, but moaned when his hand dipped lower, his fingers slowly stroking her clit.

"We're going to do this very, very slowly," Slade said as he continued to stroke her. "Relax and trust me."

He nuzzled her neck as his hand stroked between her wet pussy lips brushing lightly against her clit. The touch wasn't enough to give her release, but it was immensely pleasurable and it tightened the noose of desire that made her want to cum.

"The first thing I'm going to do is open your bottom," Slade said against the back of her neck. "I'm going to use my finger and a lot of lubricant, which you can easily accommodate."

She moaned burying her face against the bed and squeezing her eyes more tightly closed. Embarrassment and an overwhelming sense of powerlessness flooded her. Her bottom was the one private space that hadn't been violated.

A sense of vulnerability and helplessness shafted through her as she felt his hands part the cheeks of her bottom. She felt cool wetness and his finger at the opening of her bottom. He stroked her there, his finger deftly spreading lubricant. She bit down on her lip, expecting pain. "Relax sweetheart," he soothed drawing out the command. "I'm going to be slow and easy. I'll take as much time as you need."

She did her best to relax, although nervousness still unfurled in the pit of her stomach making her wonder if she wanted this after all.

He was very slow. She felt the finger of one hand stroking her anus and the other stroking her pussy for what seemed like hours without him going any further. Gradually, she relaxed.

Once she was at ease with the finger that stroked against

her opening without ever breeching it he slowly pushed his finger against her opening. She gasped and then held her breath, everything focused on that one finger as it entered her. There was a feeling of pressure and stretching which created a sweet ache as her body yielded admitting his finger, allowing it to edge deeper. Once his finger was inside her he paused, giving her time to adjust to his presence.

She felt a deep sense of welcoming and a soft stirring of pleasure as her body stretched to accommodate him, accepting his presence inside her tight chamber. The intrusion wasn't painful. In fact she had enjoyed the sensation of her muscles relaxing and expanding to accommodate him.

She sighed, giving herself up to the pleasurable sensation of being opened, stretched, filled, as he began to move slowly inside her. A collage of emotion and sensation swept through her. There was a delicious ache, a longing, a feeling of completeness that combined with vulnerability and surrender. She relaxed further, her body automatically meeting him thrust for thrust. She welcomed the long slow shaft of pleasure that cascaded through her filling her with a deep need to cum.

The sensation wasn't sharp or hard. It was more like an unfolding within her, a blossoming. The more she yielded to Slade, the more she welcomed the deep probing thrusts and the more intense the pleasure. She bit her lip, the tension coiled deep in her, spiraling upward as the need to cum grew.

She moaned softly, as his other hand snaked beneath her to stroke the wet folds of her sex. The pleasure crescendoed lapping at her like waves that crashed on a silent shore. The sensation was unlike anything she had experienced before. There was a sense of docile surrender, a sense of abandoning herself to Slade's power, and a sense of welcoming his power over her which mingled with deep contentment. She moaned deeply, relishing the pleasure.

She willfully gave up all control to Slade enjoying the wonderful sensation of his finger moving deep within her, stretching her, preparing her. She rocked back against his probing finger eager for more.

"Feel good baby?" Slade asked, his voice soft against her neck.

"It's so good," she said on a soft sigh thinking that she had never imagined it would be like this, feel like this.

The pleasure that filled her voice stroked his ego making him feel strong, powerful, more determined than ever to give her everything she needed and more. He gloried in the knowledge that he could give her this pleasure, make her feel this good.

He slowly drew his finger from her bottom, putting a second finger with the first and adding more lubricant before pressing his fingers to her small puckered opening. He pressed slowly, smoothly, his focus on Kara and her response. He watched her facial expression and her body language, alert for signs that she was uncomfortable, that he was moving too quickly. He didn't want to hurt her with the addition of another finger, yet he knew he needed to open her a good deal more if she were to accommodate his penis.

He felt the tension as he pressed against the small ring of tissue and heard her moan. He wasn't sure whether the moan was one of pleasure or pain. She was still for a moment and he relaxed too, giving her a moment to get accustomed to his presence. Then he could feel her body adjusting stretching, slowly opening as he eased his fingers deeper.

Pride swelled within him as she sighed deeply and eased herself back against his fingers, slowly sinking against him until his fingers were buried to the hilt.

He was still for a moment, allowing her to become comfortable with his presence then he slowly drew his fingers all the way out and slowly pressed them in again, loving the way her body accepted him, clamping tight around him as she welcomed him into her.

He continued to thrust slowly in and out, in and out, gradually preparing her to take his cock. He listened to the soft sounds of her pleasure, feeling himself held captive by the sweet sounds of her surrender.

She was so tight, so tense, he could feel her need for release almost as if it was his own. His cock throbbed in anticipation of the moment when it would replace his fingers. He bit his lip, eager to bury himself within her, yet knowing it wasn't yet time.

He continued to use his fingers to open her. He knew that the time spent preparing her for his eventual possession would make the experience all the better for both of them and he wanted it to be a glorious event, a memory for her to treasure.

He clenched his jaw in concentration and determination as Kara rocked against his thrusting fingers her gasps and moans of pleasure inciting his need to claim her completely, totally.

He knew from the pants and gasps and the tension coiled in her body that she was as ready to cum as he was. One more time he withdrew his fingers buoyed by her moan of disappointment when they slipped free of her tight channel. Once again he added an additional digit lubricating all three. He put his three fingers together and pressed them to her. He clenched his jaw, and pushed very slowly, willing her body to open up, to admit him once again. He knew he was stretching her, he could feel her body stretching to accommodate him and he didn't want to cause her pain.

She was tight, her body protesting the additional girth. The tight ring of muscle failed to admit him as he pressed. She moaned softly, a sound that could have been either pain or pleasure. Her tension and her stillness coupled with the way she bit her lip, squeezing her eyes shut made him think that at least some of the moan stemmed from discomfort.

He paused his fingers exerting a soft steady pressure against the barrier. "Easy honey, I know it hurts, but it'll feel good again once I'm inside." He slowly kissed her neck and then her shoulders. "We're almost there. Relax baby. Let me in."

She moaned softly, her body still too tight to admit him. "I know you can do it. We're almost there."

"It hurts," she whispered softly.

"I know, and I'm sorry, do you want me to stop?"

She shook her head.

He remained still, exerting a gentle pressure till he felt her muscles beginning to relax. She whimpered softly as her body slowly began to open. He pressed harder, his fingers slowly breeching her defenses. "That's it," he sighed, as he pressed his fingers deeper. "Almost there." He pressed again, willing her body to open.

She whimpered as he felt her body give, her defenses gradually crumbling as his fingers pushed through.

He gloried, knowing that he was home free as she uttered a soft "Ahhhh," and raised her hips to meet him. He sank his fingers deep, intent on possessing her fully.

The soft moans crescendoed, growing louder as he took control, slowly fucking her ass with long slow deliberate strokes as he used his other hand to fondle her pussy, enjoying the silky wetness that coated his fingers.

It was clear from the frenzied thrust of her hips and the way her body spasmed against his fingers that she was close. "I don't want you to cum yet. Very soon, but not yet," he whispered against her neck as he felt her body grasping greedily at his fingers.

He continued to stroke her pussy, although more slowly than he had before. He didn't want her to cum yet, but he wanted her balanced on the precarious edge. Close, ready.

"Please... I need to cum," she whimpered.

"When my cock is buried in your ass, you can cum. It's a little bigger than my fingers. Are you ready for it?"

She nodded, her breath raspy. "Yes, Sir. Please." He could feel her need, her desire, her passion. It was all there expressed in the way her bottom spasmed around his fingers. He knew she was poised and ready. He could feel her tension, the ultimate pleasure hovering just out of reach.

His cock throbbed at the sound of her sweet, innocent voice

asking to have his cock buried in her ass. He was eager to be there too, his cock desperate to fill the space his fingers had just plowed. It was time. He wanted to give her the pleasure she craved.

Wasting no time, he moved behind her slathering his cock with lubricant. He throbbed, his own need sharp as he positioned himself at her opening. The need to have his cock enclosed in the tight sheath his fingers had just vacated drove him, made him want to drive himself into her, hot and hard, forcing her to take him, making her accept his presence inside her. But another, stronger part wanted the experience to be softer, more tender, more loving, something beautiful that she would look back on with pleasure.

Clenching his jaw against the urge to drive himself into her he edged his cock forward, slowly easing himself into her tight opening one small thrust at a time. "Oh god, it's so good," she whimpered as she shifted back against him, willingly accepting him inside her, welcoming him into her until the head of his cock pressed against her sphincter.

He could feel her resistance then. He pressed. Need ripped through him. He needed her to open, to admit him and yet he didn't want to cause pain. "Relax sweetheart, take my cock, I know you can," he said as he exerted slow steady pressure against her resistance.

She whimpered softly but didn't move away from the pressure he exerted. "Good girl, you're almost there," he whispered as he pressed a little harder his cock slowly breeching her opening.

"Owwwwwaaaahhh," she whimpered as she lifted her ass and pressed back against him.

"That's it. Almost there. Just a little more." She was so tight that he could feel every ripple and tremor as her body slowly opened admitting him. She moaned, the moan ending on a sigh of pleasure as he eased forward, gradually deepening his penetration.

He knew how close her climax was, he could feel her

muscles throbbing and rippling around his cock as he edged deeper.

He reached around her and stroked her clit as he buried himself in her warmth. She moaned, as he held himself still, giving her time to adjust to his presence inside her.

He felt the rhythmic contractions of her body intensify, as he began to thrust slowly.

She whimpered as his hand stroked her pussy. He knew she was close. Ready.

"Cum for me baby," he said softly as he thrust deep, his own need to cum taking over.

He felt her control break, felt her body contracting around his, even as his own climax hovered just out of reach. It was so good, the tension that encompassed him, driving him toward release. He could feel her straining for release. He could feel the contractions of her ass as she neared the precipice. Each contraction was harder and longer than the one before it.

His fingers lightly strummed her clit pushing her closer and closer to the edge. He felt her orgasm as it crashed over her, the contractions that squeezed his cock pushing him ever closer to his own release.

He felt her climax crash and rise again, as his fingers continued to stroke her clit. The sensation as her body clasped his finally pushed him over the edge as she reached the summit of her second orgasm. He could feel the tension in her body, even more intense now as she climbed the last few steps to the precipice where she trembled, holding her orgasm at bay. He could feel the contractions as her ass's grip on his cock tightened, its grip intensifying with each spasm. He knew she was ready, he could sense the impending release in the throaty moans and the tension that gripped her.

"Cum with me Baby. Cum now," he said as he felt her impending release. He thrust deeply, burying his cock deep inside her, claiming her completely as he felt her control shatter.

His body absorbed her contractions, even as his own

orgasmic contractions merged with hers. Pleasure ricocheted through him in waves of color and light. It was beauty and joy, pleasure and light, love and dominance, power and control, giving and taking. It was everything he wanted. Everything he needed. It was more.

The deep wails of pleasure as she ceded all control and existed for a time in the pleasure he had built for her served as a backdrop, that echoed through him making him feel at once possessive, powerful, and protective.

He existed for a time not caring where he was. As he began the slow descent to earth he realized he was curled over Kara's back, his cock still buried inside her, but softening now that the storm of passion had passed. He stroked her back, her hair, her neck, loving her, caring only that she was okay, that she was as happy and as sated as he was.

"Are you okay sweetheart? I didn't hurt you?" he asked softly as he stroked her back and her shoulders wanting to be sure not only that he hadn't hurt her physically but that the experience had been good for her emotionally as well.

"I am way better than okay. I am Perfect," she purred. He smiled at the reverence and awe coating her voice. He loved her and she was happy. Not much else mattered right then.

Suddenly he wanted her free of the ropes that held her arms in place above her head. He no longer wanted her bondage between them, separating them. He wanted her in his arms her head cradled against his chest. He wanted to feel the soft touch of her hands upon him. He wanted to be able to look into her eyes, to read her pleasure there.

As soon as he had loosed her from the ropes that had held her he told her she could open her eyes. He leaned over her looking down into her face loving the soft sensual bliss that he glimpsed there.

Satisfied she was happy he rolled onto his back carrying her with him, positioning her so that she was against him, her head upon his chest.

"That was magnificent," he said as he stroked her hair,

loving the way it felt against his hand and the way it tickled his chest when she moved her head slightly.

She snuggled closer. "I didn't know it would be like that," she said softly. "I expected it to hurt more."

He stroked her shoulders, feeling a little guilty for his rush to possess her at the end. "I did seem to hurt you a little there at the end. I should have taken more time."

She shook her head. "No, it was perfect. It did hurt a little but in an oddly good kind of way." She licked her lips and looked down at his chest before she continued. "I liked the sensation of my body stretching to make room for you. It hurt a little, but it was a nice kind of pain."

He settled his mouth over hers, kissing her slowly, leisurely, enjoying the sensation of his lips moving over hers, loving the tenderness as their tongues slowly twined. He was content to snuggle and kiss enjoying their closeness and the satiated after glow of their lovemaking.

After a long time he slowly withdrew from her mouth, holding her close, cherishing her and the gift of herself that she had given him. He smiled down at her, his mind taking him back to the day he had proposed as he thought about how far they'd come. "Remember how afraid you were when I first proposed?" he asked, remembering the fear that had clung to her as she'd considered his proposal.

"It seems a lifetime ago," she sighed as her palm slid across his chest.

"You were afraid of not knowing what to do with my fires," he said softly as he stroked the hair back away from her face so that he could look into the depth of her eyes.

She laughed, a soft musical sound that made him smile deep in his soul. "You promised you'd teach me everything I needed to know." She looked up at him a mischievous light filling her eyes. "I'm not sure I've learned it all, but I think I'm doing okay."

He hugged her close stroking her cheek and her jaw, her chin and neck. "You know everything you need to know honey.

You hold all the keys to my heart. Anything you learn from here will be icing on the cake."

He palmed her cheek. He loved the feeling of protecting her, nurturing her, watching her sexual confidence blossom under his tutelage. He wanted to give her everything she needed to be happy and confident in his bed and out of it.

He sighed, gazing up at the ceiling as Kara relaxed against him, her small hand slowly caressing his chest. They had been together only a short time, but already she was the most important part of his life. He was happy with her, happy with the relationship they were building.

His dominance and her submission felt right between them. It was part of the way they related to each other. His dominance flowed from the protectiveness he felt toward her. It made him feel strong, powerful, to use the control she had given him to give her pleasure and to encourage her self confidence.

He was utterly happy, utterly content.

As he held her, enjoying the soft sated sounds of her breath returning to normal after their passion there was only one thing that still caused him concern, and that was her past. He held her, gently stroking her hair, consumed with the love he felt for her, as he wished for the thousandth time that there was a way to take the brutality and the ugliness of her past and replace it with the pure, unadulterated love he felt toward her.

He supposed somehow being able to nullify the past was the hope he clung to. He figured it was probably the reason he'd spent so much time researching psychologists and psychiatrists that specialized in childhood trauma. He knew it was the reason he'd left work early to meet with the doctor whose credentials had topped every list he'd searched.

It wasn't that he saw Kara as damaged with a need to be fixed. It was that he knew the past still had a significant hold over her. She still had a significant number of bad dreams.

He shifted slightly and brought his mouth to Kara's, kissing her slowly, gently, his mouth making slow tender love to hers as he pushed the concern about her past to the back of his mind. She was happy now, and for now he wanted to share her bliss.

Chapter 21

Kara curled into Slade's body as he kissed her. Her hand splayed over the flatness of his belly as she enjoyed the tenderness of his kiss. Her body still hummed with remembered pleasure and she'd never felt more mellow, more content, or more sure about her decision to submit to him than she did now in the aftermath of their lovemaking.

As she thought back over the slow, patient, way he had made love to her she smiled to herself, remembering the way he had stoked her passion, making her want him so badly that the pain she might have felt was overwhelmed by need.

She remembered the frustration she'd felt as he had denied her one orgasm after another. She'd been so needy, so frustrated, but as his lips caressed her gently, reverently, she realized that in the end her need to cum, along with the tender way he had prepared her, had made her first experience with anal sex beautiful.

She snuggled closer, wanting to be as close to Slade as she could get as she reveled in the memory of his hard cock sinking into her tender bottom, his hard penis stretching her, forcing her to adjust to his girth as he claimed her bottom as his. She remembered the intimacy and the feeling of surrender, of giving herself totally to him. She'd felt totally mastered, completely subservient as he'd taken charge.

She basked in the memory of the way he'd, carefully, tenderly prepared her for his possession. She sighed wanting to belong to him this way forever.

Her mind drifted to his dominance of her as they fell quiet, both seeming momentarily lost in their own thoughts. He had dominated her right from the beginning. Even the first time she'd seen him at his office when she'd begged on her brother's behalf, he'd made it clear he made the decisions. But his dominance then or now wasn't mean or one-sided.

It was the exact opposite. From the very beginning he had used his power to protect her, to care for her, to make things better for her. She snuggled against him, appreciating all the ways he took care of her.

She loved him for the man he was. One who was strong enough to take charge, and yet one who was gentle and sensitive enough that his dominance was never brutish or bullying.

She cuddled against him, looking up at him from under her lashes, enjoying the rough five o'clock shadow that covered his chin and jaw. Her body felt warm and sated, her bottom alive with a soft ache that reminded her of his possession. She relaxed against him finally giving into the languorous sensation that filled her body.

Slowly she drifted, the soft edges of sleep lifting to encompass her even as Slade's arms cradled her. She allowed herself to drift peacefully, going deeper into the murky darkness of sleep.

Slade continued to stroke her, loving the way she nestled against him, seeking closeness even in her sleep. She seemed relaxed, content, her sleep undisturbed by memories and nightmares.

He relaxed, content to hold her as she slept, content with the soft sounds of her breathing, and the warmth of her breath that stirred the hairs on his chest at regular intervals.

She was safe within his arms, sheltered, protected, and loved. Life was good.

Chapter 22

Slade was aware of the nightmare's grasp almost immediately. Kara twitched in her sleep, her mouth moving, though no words came out. His gut tightened with familiar pain. He hated the nightmares, hated that even in her sleep the man who had kidnapped her and raped her still stalked her. He hated that he was powerless to stop this nightly rampage.

He tightened his arm about her, familiar dread rising as she began to whimper in her sleep, begging the unseen predator to leave her alone. Helplessness swept over Slade as he stroked her arm, hoping the gentle touch would still her torment and ease her back into restful sleep as it sometimes did.

His chest constricted as her whimpers and begging grew more intense, more laced with panic. He let out a deep sigh. It didn't matter how much he loved her or how well he took care of her, the past with all its brutality was still always there, haunting her.

"It's okay honey, you're safe. You're just having a bad dream," he whispered, stroking her shoulder as he did most nights when her nightmares woke him.

She jerked and startled awake. He watched as her fear and dread filled eyes focused on him before reality began to filter into her consciousness. She sighed, burying her face against his chest and scooting closer as his arms tightened around her.

He held her, doing his best to offer what little comfort he could. He could sense the pent up tension coiled within her and wondered what hideous memories had just played out across her mind's eye, what terror had pushed aside the beauty of their coupling to insert itself into her dreams.

Gradually she relaxed against him, her ragged choppy breaths growing more even. He felt the tension slowly ebb. He tightened his arms around her, wanting to protect her from ugly memories and bad dreams.

"The dreams seem pretty intense," he said softly as he held her.

He could feel the motion of her face against his chest as she nodded. "The dreams are pretty ugly," she sighed. "But I wake up in your arms and I am okay. It isn't like it was after the panic attack. It's not as sharp, it doesn't hurt as much." She pressed her face into his chest scattering kisses there.

He rolled in the bed so that he was facing her, his eyes studying the facial expressions that darted across her face as she looked up at him. She looked surprisingly serene in spite of the nightmare that had just gripped her. Her warm brown eyes met his with warmth and openness.

He thought back on their wedding night and the panic attack she'd had then and marveled at how much less the past controlled her now. There had been progress, and yet it wasn't near enough. He drew a deep breath and let it out. He wished that the bad dreams would stop.

He hated that she had to remember at all, hated that he couldn't replace the ugly memories of childhood with new memories of pleasure, joy, and intimacy. If there was a way to erase the past, to weaken its hold, to replace the ugliness with joy he would do whatever he could to make it happen.

He didn't suppose there was a way to erase the remnants of what had happened to her from her mind, though he wished there was. He knew it had been his desire to find a way to help her deal with the memories that had driven him to put aside his work and bail out of the office early that afternoon.

He'd had an appointment with Meredith Bellston PhD. He'd liked her credentials even before he'd met her but he had to admit, he liked the petite, redheaded psychiatrist even better after meeting her. She had an easy smile and an engaging manner that he'd liked right away.

He supposed the easy smile and the non-threatening manner were assets to a psychiatrist who specialized in adult survivors of childhood trauma. Surely, she had to build a foundation of trust with her clients, and the easy smile would be an asset.

He thought back over his conversation with her. She had been cautious, not promising any specific outcomes to the potential treatments they'd discussed. She'd told him that memories of childhood trauma rarely just went away. Rather, with treatment the memories intruded less frequently and became generally less powerful. Though the memories would likely always remain painful they had less impact on day to day life as treatment progressed.

He sighed. It wasn't perfect. Hell, it wasn't even close to perfect, yet it seemed that therapy did offer some hope. If it helped weaken the memories or helped ease the nightmares surely it would be worth it. He wanted Kara to be truly free, truly happy.

"Honey, I know you're better, but you're not really free of it even now," he said softly. He held her, loving her, wanting what was best for her. He stroked her cheek with the pad of his thumb wishing he could forget the haunted expression in her eyes as she'd looked up at him in the first moments after she'd woken.

A dull sadness filled him as he gazed at her. He wanted to take away the past with its ugly memories and see her happy and carefree.

"I'm not completely free of the memories and probably never will be, but I'm okay," Kara said softly. "I am happy for the first time in a long time."

"You're having bad dreams three or four nights a week, honey. That's not exactly my idea of everything being okay." He stroked the hair away from her face, hating the shadows and sadness that had crept in to replace the joy and serenity that had been there just after their lovemaking.

Kara dipped her chin, her gaze studiously avoiding his as she chewed her lower lip. He could feel her sadness. It emanated from her like an invisible cloud that surrounded her. Helplessness unfurled within him. He didn't know what to do to dismantle the memories or to erase the sadness though everything in him wanted to do both.

He sighed. He needed some help, even if Kara didn't believe she did. "I've done some checking and have found a very highly respected psychiatrist that specializes in adult survivors of childhood trauma. I think it might be a good idea for you to see her honey."

The words struck her, stinging like an unexpected slap to the face. Shock, hurt, anger and fear crashed over her leaving a sharp pain where just moments before bliss had dwelled. She turned her face from him, dark emotions tripping over each other as they ripped through her soul leaving a gaping emptiness where her heart had been.

Her lungs seemed to constrict. Her chest ached. She wanted space. She needed space. She needed to be away from Slade.

"Are you hungry?" She pushed the question past the tightness in her chest, desperate to put space between them.

"Yeah, I am actually," he said smiling down at her, seemingly oblivious to the emotions that churned within her. He kissed her slowly, gently, his mouth caressing hers. She kissed him back but inside she felt desperately alone. Her belief that he was strong enough to deal with the ramifications of her past was shattered.

They got up and she fixed supper, though what she really wanted to do was curl into a tight ball until the ugly, dark, feelings that filled her faded.

She sliced onions and mushrooms and cut sirloin into pieces, feeling disconnected from the task and lost within the emotions that surrounded her.

She felt as if she'd been plunged into an icy cold darkness, where no light could reach her and where only fear and anger resided. The ugly, bleak, desolate feeling surrounded her, closing out everything else. She wanted to believe in the love Slade had shown her, but it was as if his suggestion that she see a psychiatrist had poisoned everything that had come before, making her feel disconnected from the feelings of love and security that had once been so strong.

She wanted to forget his words, ignore the fact that he saw her as damaged, but she couldn't push the words out of her mind. The more his words tumbled through her mind the more tangled her feelings became until all that was left was a wall of distrust and hurt that closed in on her, trapping her in a desolate space where she was alone with the memories of abandonment that filled her soul, taunting her with the knowledge that no one had ever been able to stick it out in the face of the terror she had faced. Slade had been her champion, her beacon. She had believed in him in an almost worshipful way, seeing him as her knight in shining armor. She'd seen him as the one person whose love was strong enough to stand against the memories of the past. She'd believed that he had the power to restore her, to show her how to be whole again.

Darkness filled her soul as she realized he was no knight, no superhero with the superhuman capability to stand by her, protecting her from the ugliness of the past. No matter how much she wished she didn't, she knew the pattern of abandonment. She'd experienced it too many times not to recognize the signs, not to see it coming way before it arrived. The suggestion that she see a therapist always came before the abandonment. It had happened over and over again in her life with her family, her teachers, her mentors. No one she knew had ever been able to accept her the way she was, accept that the things that had been done to her were hellacious, that though she went on with life there wasn't a way to wipe them from her memory.

Everyone wanted to fix her. When she remained unfixed, because she remained impacted by the things that had happened during her eight days of hell they abandoned her.

Even more than she ached because Slade's words themselves hurt, she ached because she recognized the pattern. She saw the beginning of the end as she'd seen it so many times before. She didn't want it to end. She couldn't imagine life without his love, his power, his direction.

No matter what else happened around her his abandonment loomed on the horizon turning her world a deep, inescapable gray that remained, day after day, enclosing her in ever deepening layers of grief as the days passed one into the next in slow, sad cadence.

She cleaned the house, cooked the meals, made love with Slade, but there was no pleasure in any of it. There was always the knowledge that anything they shared was temporary and that when it ended she would be without him.

Her sadness deepened so far that when one of Slade's projects got off track and required him to work late into the evenings she felt nothing but relief. His absence in the evenings relieved her of the task of pretending that everything was okay while despair closed in on her like a giant tidal wave that she couldn't escape.

She released a deep breath, the hollowness within her threatening to swallow her. Even the reprieve his late nights had provided was destined to end. Slade had called early in the afternoon to let her know he would be home from work at the normal time.

Tears hovered but she pushed them down refusing to shed them. She couldn't allow them now. If she did she'd be all blotchy by the time Slade got home. He'd demand to know what was wrong and she'd have no answer, at least not one she wanted to share.

Chapter 23

Slade parked the SUV in the garage and cut the engine. He lifted his hand and massaged the tension and the ache at the base of his neck.

Things at work had been jammed up for the past week and a half and he'd worked late every night. He was tired and looking forward to a good night's sleep and a relaxing weekend, though both were out of the question till he sorted things out with Kara.

Things with her were in as big a mess as things at work had been. She had been listless and distant for the better part of two weeks. He didn't know whether she was angry about the fact that he'd had to work a lot of late nights or whether there was something else that was eating at her. He had asked her several times what was wrong but had only received a glum, "Nothing's the matter," in response to his questions.

He would have set matters right sooner except that he'd worked late and had come home most nights to find her already asleep.

On the nights she was awake when he got home he hadn't wanted to push her about her moodiness. He'd been bushed himself and in no frame of mind to deal rationally with issues she didn't want to talk about. He'd hoped that given a little time and space she would process whatever was upsetting her and bring it up herself.

Nearly two weeks had passed and she hadn't brought

anything up and her mood hadn't improved with time. Instead she had grown more and more melancholy, her moods seeming darker and bleaker with each passing day.

He sighed. At least the project at work was finally back on track. It was Friday, and he was home on time. He had the whole night, and the weekend if necessary, to put things back on the right track with Kara.

He thought back, trying to remember exactly when things had begun to go wrong. It had seemed like everything had been perfect between them. He smiled to himself as he remembered the night she had met him at the door in nothing but pink lace. He remembered the sweet way she'd told him she wanted him to master her and the tender way he had claimed her. They had been so close, so intimate that night.

He frowned, wondering how things had turned so quickly from the warmth and intimacy they'd shared that night to the cold and distance that dominated their relationship now. He thought back over the things that had been going on at around the time things had begun to go south, trying to pinpoint something that might have caused Kara's bleak mood. He wondered briefly if he had started it by mentioning the psychiatrist.

That was the only thing he could remember that might have caused trouble between them. He thought back. She hadn't said much about it at the time he'd brought it up, and he'd let it drop. He did remember that she'd been a little distant when they'd eaten dinner. She'd claimed at the time that she was just tired and he'd had no reason to doubt her.

In thinking about it, it didn't seem likely his suggestion that she see the psychiatrist was the cause of her moodiness. Her reaction to the suggestion had been almost non-existent.

His mind turned the events of the past week and a half over in his mind. Kara wasn't any less obedient or any less submissive. She always did the things he asked her to do and always tended to his wants and needs. The problem was that there was an edge to her actions, a sense that she was just going through the motions, doing what she needed to do to get by. There was none of the pleasure she had once taken in pleasing him.

She seemed to respond physically to his lovemaking, but the closeness, the intimacy, the joy she had once taken in it was missing.

He tunneled his fingers through his hair. He knew she was deeply unhappy and as long as she was miserable he could not be happy.

He turned the key in the lock and turned the knob pushing the door open and stepping into the kitchen. His gut tightened when he noticed Kara at the counter, her back to him as she sliced carrots into small round discs. He missed the excitement that used to race through him when she would meet him at the door, wrapping her arms around him and lifting her mouth for his kiss. Her greetings had always made him feel like he was important, like she couldn't wait for him to get home from work. Now it felt like she didn't care whether he came home at all.

He wanted the old Kara back, wanted their old relationship back. He stepped up behind her, wrapping his arms around her and hugging her against him, his hands lightly skimming her tummy and her breasts as he nuzzled her neck. She stood placidly within his embrace, neither encouraging nor overtly discouraging his touch.

He felt for a moment like he was trying to make out with a cold, impersonal, statue and he didn't like the feeling. Frustration swelled. His temper was controlled but it flared inside him. He'd had enough of the bleak mood and he wasn't in any frame of mind to hear again that nothing was the matter when clearly something was wrong.

"Alright. Enough Already," he said softly as he reached past her to take the knife she was using to massacre the carrots and slamming it onto the counter. He turned her towards him, and stood looking down at her, his jaw tight.

"Alright, what gives? You've groused around here like you'd

like to take my leg off for the better part of two weeks." She looked up at him and he noticed the dark circles beneath her eyes and the way her brown eyes darted away from his. "What is the matter Kara?" he asked softly.

She dipped her head, her eyes drifting to the floor in a way that reminded him of a puppy that had just been swatted with a rolled up newspaper.

"N-nothing." She answered backing away until her bottom bumped into the counter.

His frustration swelled. "I'm not buying that." His voice was soft, but he advanced on her, closing the space between them. He lifted her chin so that she had no alternative but to meet his gaze. "Whatever it is, you know I love you. You know we'll work it out. It's clear you're unhappy, now what gives?"

She jerked her face from his grasp and turned away from him, her back held ramrod straight.

"Nothing. Nothing is the matter." Her voice was tense, sharp.

Frustration surged through him.

He grasped her shoulders and spun her back around to face him, his patience spent. "I'm neither blind nor stupid. A blind man could see that you are unhappy, honey," he sighed trying to rein in his frustration. "I'm out of patience with beating around the block. Either you stop avoiding me and tell me what is the matter or I'm going to assume that you just need an attitude adjustment and paddle your ass like I should have done two weeks ago, when this sullen, moody, shit first started."

Kara's gaze flew up to meet his, her features cloaked in a combination of wariness and fear. He felt a wave of guilt work through him as he remembered how fearful she'd been of being spanked when they'd talked about it on their honeymoon.

She looked to each side, clearly looking for an escape route. His heart stuttered as he realized that this was the first time he'd ever spoken roughly to her. It was the first time he'd ever been even marginally angry with her.

He sucked in a deep breath. He was frustrated as almighty hell with the sullen, moodiness and her refusal to tell him what was the matter but his frustration didn't stop him from loving her or from caring that she was unhappy. It made him want to understand what was wrong so he could make it better.

He shoved his hand roughly through his hair, feeling ashamed of himself for using the threat of something he knew she was afraid of to make her talk. He didn't want to be short or harsh with her. He didn't want to hurt her. When it came right down to it, he didn't want to do anything but hold her and make everything alright again. The problem was he saw no way of getting to the point where he could do that without knowing what was bothering her.

Kara looked up at him, a shiver coursing through her. He was intimidating as he loomed above her, his jaw tight. There was a tired, edgy, frustrated look around his eyes that made her feel nervous and unsettled. If she could have, she would have backed away.

He had never looked at her with frustration or anger before and it caused a deep stab of pain that he was frustrated and angry with her now. The thought that he might actually carry through on his threat to spank her unfurled within her as her gaze ran up his length, pausing to take in the black wool coat that hung open at the front allowing her a glimpse of his crisp white shirt and the navy and black striped tie that was still knotted at his neck.

His threat, his expression, and the formal work attire all intimidated her. She longed to back away, to put space between them, but there was nowhere she could go. She was trapped between him and the counter.

"Which is it going to be?" His voice was soft, coaxing, but it felt menacing to Kara as the blood hammered in her ears. She pressed against the counter in a vain attempt to move further away from him.

"Slade, I don't want to do this."

"Tough. I don't remember giving you a choice."

She wanted to shrink out of sight. She didn't want to give voice to the terrible empty feeling that gnawed at her insides. She dipped her head and bit her lip, willing him to go away, willing the whole ugly situation to go away.

She wanted to avoid both him and the anguish that filled her. She wanted to avoid the pent up tears that made her chest and throat ache.

She sucked a deep breath. All she knew for sure was that she hurt, that the pain was a deep gaping hole she didn't know how to fill.

She felt betrayed, and angry. The trust she'd once felt was shattered. She no longer believed he wanted her or her submission. She didn't believe he wanted to care for her. She couldn't even think of any reason why he'd want to. She was damaged, broken. He deserved better.

She was consumed with grief, certain it was only a matter of time before he walked away and left her with her scarred and battered soul the same way everyone else had.

She swallowed hard, fighting back the unshed tears that had shadowed her for the better part of two weeks. She couldn't talk about it, but she knew it was time she accept the reality. There had never been anyone she could truly count on, and there never would be.

Slade's deep sigh drew her attention. Her gaze climbed slowly up his chest to his face. "Which is it going to be Kara?"

She bit her lip, trembling, the tears she'd vowed she wouldn't shed battering against her control. She'd once thought that him spanking her was the worst thing he could do to her, she now knew that that wasn't even close to the pain of him leaving her.

Her heart pounded in her chest as he stood looking down at her, his eyes dark, his jaw tight and inflexible. She didn't want him to spank her. The violence of the act frightened her and brought up bad memories. She closed her eyes, fighting back the tears.

"You promised you wouldn't spank me unless it was right

for me." She squeezed the words past the lump in her throat as she shrank against the counter.

He moved closer, his body almost touching hers, the closeness intimidating in spite of the softness of his voice when he spoke. "In part of that same conversation, when I took the spanking off the table, I said I wouldn't spank you unless you deliberately ignored an order, which is exactly what you're doing. But even so, the promise was before you gave yourself to me, before you asked me to be your master." He tipped her chin up and peered into her eyes. "Are you telling me you no longer want to submit to me?"

She shook her head slowly and blinked back tears as she met his steely gaze. She swallowed hard. She couldn't tell him she didn't want him to be her master, when she wanted his power, his stability so much. If only she could believe that he would be her master, that he'd stay her master, that he wouldn't tire of the impact of the nightmares and panic attacks and leave her when seeing a psychiatrist didn't cure her.

"You promised submission and obedience when we got married and you repeated that promise when you gave yourself to me. You knew what the consequences of disobedience would be then." He stroked her cheek, his slate colored eyes studying her intently.

She bit her lip feeling shaken and unsteady.

"All I've asked you to do, Kara, is tell me why you are unhappy. If you can do that then spanking can stay off the table. If not—"

Kara dipped her head and squeezed her eyes closed. She felt small and empty. Trapped.

He sighed and lifted his hand to stroke her cheek. She tipped her cheek into his palm, longing for the trust that she used to feel when he palmed her cheek. There was no sudden shaft of warmth, no sudden shaft of trust, only grief and loss that swept through her filling every part of her.

She wished to hell she could feel the trust, the warmth, the love and stability she used to feel when he touched her so gently, but she couldn't feel any of it. Now there was fear; fear that he'd make her see the shrink; fear that in the end he wouldn't be able to deal with her past, whether she saw the shrink or not; fear that he was grasping at straws with the shrink more because he couldn't deal with her past than because she couldn't.

She shuddered. More than anything else she feared that he'd walk away and leave her alone. She didn't want to be alone.

"Just tell me what's wrong, honey. I know you're not happy. Tell me why and let me make it better."

She felt his gaze upon her, felt his palm against her cheek, heard the soft baritone notes of his voice. She wanted to remain strong. She wanted the anger, the fear, and the pain she felt to stand strong as an insurmountable wall of protection against her fragile emotional center, but the walls began to crumble. As much as she wanted them to protect her delicate emotional middle from additional pain she couldn't keep them in place.

She hurt. He knew that she hurt and at least on some level he cared. The knowledge that he cared made the pain that filled her all the more stark, all the more sharp.

She dipped her head, biting her lip in an effort to keep her tears at bay. She swallowed hard against the tide of emotion as he tipped her chin, forcing her to meet his steady gaze.

"Please Slade, I don't want to do this. I want to finish cooking supper and go to bed. I don't feel good."

He lifted his palm, pressing it against her forehead as his eyes studied her with concern. "That'd ordinarily be fine Kara. But you don't seem to have a fever and you've been forlorn and sullen for the better part of two weeks. I don't think it is something that going to bed will fix."

She swallowed against the tightness in her throat and lowered her gaze to the floor.

"I have asked you to tell me what's wrong, not once but half a dozen times in the past two weeks. Each time I've asked you've told me nothing is wrong or you've tried to avoid me.

I'm out of patience honey. I am not prepared to let things fester any longer." He stroked her cheek with the pad of his thumb.

She felt a tingle of awareness, a longing for the gentleness and the strength that had always been such a part of him.

"I don't believe whatever it is that's bothering you will magically get better on its own. You've become more and more withdrawn, more and more sad."

He looked at her as if he was waiting for an answer, but she didn't have one.

"I don't want to punish you for being in a bad mood or for being upset over something. I want to understand why you are upset so that we can sort it out."

"Please Slade," she begged. "Just leave it alone. I don't want to talk about it."

"No Kara." He said, his voice firm. "Just ignoring it is not an option."

"Please Slade." She dipped her head, wanting to avoid his gaze, wanting to hide within herself as she had when she was seven, but all she felt was the same overwhelming loss she'd felt when she was seven and her daddy had died.

"No honey, I'm sorry, but this is not spilling into another day."

Her chest felt tight, constricted. She knew he was right, she knew she should talk to him but she couldn't. She didn't know where to start, what to say. The feelings were so dark, so bleak, so tangled up inside her that she no longer knew where one feeling began and another ended. The feelings were so strong and so dark that there was a sense that if she didn't push them down deep and keep them there they would overwhelm her and tear her to shreds. She couldn't bear to be any weaker, any more damaged than she already was.

"I know whatever is bothering you must seem overwhelming." He sighed. "I will do anything I can to help, but I can't help if I don't know what's wrong."

She stared at the floor, despair filling her. If only she could believe that he would be there, but she didn't.

He'd been with her less than two months and already he was casting her to psychiatrists, wanting them to fix her. She knew already what would happen when a couple months of talk therapy didn't cure her. He'd be frustrated and abandon her, the same as everyone else had.

She was numb, mentally, physically numb. She expected if he spanked her it would add another level to the misery she already felt, but she couldn't really imagine how it would be much worse. She didn't really care anyway.

She studied the pattern of the floor tile. She was just too emotionally tired, too emotionally devastated to care what he did to her.

She figured if he spanked her, when he was done he'd let her finish dinner and go to bed. She wondered if the spanking was a small price to pay.

"Which is it going to be Kara?" His voice was firm and yet held a thread of gentleness that stirred up a flurry of butterflies that filled her stomach. She wanted to reach out, to trust the gentleness inherent in his voice, but she couldn't. She felt only despair where the trust should be. "Just spank me and get it over with, if that's what you want," she said softly, her eyes still glued to the floor.

"It's not what I want Kara," he said softly. "What I want is for you to tell me what's wrong. Are you going to do that?"

She shook her head slowly. "I can't, I don't know where to start," she whispered brokenly.

She thought back to when he'd told her that a spanking was something he'd do for her because it would be good for her, because it would help clear the emotional air, help make her feel better after she'd felt bad. She hoped there was something about the act that would break her out of the dark emotional space she was in. She hated the bleakness, the grief, the anguish that surrounded her but she had no real hope of anything breaking her out.

His heart clenched at her words, so soft, so bereft. He wished to hell he could take the emotional load from her, but he couldn't if he didn't even know what was bothering her. The words and the way she'd said them touched something deep within him. He didn't want to spank her, at least not like this, not when she looked and sounded so completely and utterly sad that looking at her made his heart ache.

She hadn't left him much choice though. They were at an impasse. She wouldn't talk about what was bothering her and he couldn't help without knowing what was hurting her.

He thought back to what he'd told her about spanking on their honeymoon. He'd told her it was something he would to help her, to take care of her. That was especially true in this case.

He didn't want to spank her, yet it was his duty as her master to take care of her, to provide guidance and strength, to keep her safe in his care. He could either accept her decision to remain silent and let the distance between them fester and her depression deepen, which would do nothing to help her, or he could use the purposeful infliction of physical pain to systematically break down the walls until there were no walls between them, until he knew exactly what was bothering her and could do what was necessary to set things right.

He looked at her, noting the dark circles beneath her eyes and the listless emptiness within them. The utter desolation that clung to her like a heavy coat cemented his decision. She'd had 2 weeks to do things her way and it she'd only become more and more despondent. He had already let it carry on longer than he should. There was no way he was going to let it carry into another day.

"Kara, honey, I don't care where you start, or what is wrong," he said pulling her against him and nuzzling the top of her head. "I'm not looking for pretty words. Start at the beginning or at the end, or hell, start in the middle. I don't care. Just tell me what's wrong. Tell me why you are so unhappy."

She shook her head, burying her face against his chest.

"Please, just spank me and get it over with. I don't want to talk about it."

Her words hung in his mind. He hated the misery that coated her voice. He remembered how fearful she'd been of being spanked when they'd talked about it on their honeymoon and he wondered if spanking her was the right thing to do.

He knew that in the right circumstances, done the right way, it could be cathartic. He knew it could help release pent up emotions. But with her, with her history, her fears, he worried that it had the potential to bring on another panic attack. He hoped to hell it didn't, but wondered if even a panic attack would be better than the despair and despondence. At least the panic attacks had a focus. There was something specific that triggered it.   "This isn't the way I wanted it," he said softly as he took her hand and led her into the living room.

Chapter 24

"Clothes off," he ordered as he removed his long wool coat and laid it on the back of a chair. He watched as Kara fidgeted with the hem of her sweater. He slipped off his suit jacket and laid it atop his coat. Then he removed his tie and added it to the pile. Next he removed his cuff links and laid them on the end table. He stood watching her, his fingers deftly rolling up his shirt sleeves as he watched her.

When he was finished Kara still stood before him, her teeth worrying her lower lip, her fingers crimping the lower edge of her sweater as she shifted nervously from foot to foot. He wondered if she was reconsidering, if she was trying to put the words together, trying to figure out how to explain what was wrong. He hoped she was. He'd give anything to be spared the task of spanking her.

The task he'd once thought of as sexual intoxication was not sexual, or pleasant at all in this instance. It would not be a playful spanking given as sexual foreplay. He didn't expect it to be fun. He was not looking forward to it at all.

It would be hard, painful, intended to compel her to talk when he knew she didn't want to. He wasn't looking forward to purposefully inflicting pain, even though he believed that the situation made it necessary.

He opened a drawer in the lamp table and pulled out a thick wooden paddle with holes in it and tossed it onto the middle cushion of the couch before he turned back to Kara.

She still stood in the middle of the room, fiddling with her sweater.

He moved to her, feeling sympathy rise in his chest. "I said clothes off," he reminded her. "Are you having second thoughts? Do you want to talk instead?"

She shook her head, her gaze still pinned to the floor as she pulled her sweater off over her head. She bit her lip, tears squeezing through her lashes as her fingers went to the fastening of her jeans.

His heart felt heavy, constricted in his chest as he watched her step out of the jeans. She looked so small and defenseless, so miserable, as she stood before him in her pink cotton bra and panties.

"Come here," he said softly wanting to hold her and make everything right.

He watched as she moved slowly toward him, hating the hesitancy with which she moved and the knowledge that she felt no pleasure in this.

When she stood nervously in front of him he pulled her close to him and wrapped his arms around her, anchoring her to him. She buried her face in his chest as he stroked her hair. "I love you honey. I want you to understand that I'm going to spank you because I love you, and because it is part of the role I accepted when you asked me to be your Master. This is your last chance."

She shook her head sharply against his chest and pressed her face more tightly against him. He stroked her hair, everything in him recoiling against the idea of spanking her.

He swallowed hard and gathered his determination, determined to give her what she needed to break down the emotional walls she'd erected between them. He stepped back away from her, stroking her hair back away from her face, wiping at the tears that wetted her cheeks with his thumbs. His heart felt like lead in his chest as he accepted her decision.

Leading her by the hand he moved to the couch and sat down in the middle. Looking up to meet her sorrow filled gaze he tugged her down, moving her into position across his lap.

"I'm sorry your choices are making this necessary," he said softly. He rubbed his hand lightly over the globes of her panty covered bottom.

She didn't move, she didn't put up a fuss, she didn't resist. Quite simply, she submitted, and yet he knew it was only a physical submission.

"Submission is more than just physical, Kara," he said softly. "Sometimes it means opening yourself up, being emotionally vulnerable when you don't want to be. You asked me to be your master, you said you wanted me to care for all the parts of you, and yet you are keeping me at arms length, making it impossible for me to care for you emotionally."

He rubbed her bottom.

"I don't think that you mean to do it, but it isn't acceptable. I want it all honey, your body, your mind, your feelings I'm going to spank you to help you get back in touch with the submissive part of yourself." He continued to stroke her bottom through her panties.

"I know you are upset and unhappy. I've given you lots of chances to tell me why and every time I ask you refuse to say." He lifted the paddle, holding it against her ass where his hands had stroked, giving her time to become accustomed to its size and shape and the weight of it.

"I'm not happy about having to spank you, but I will do it because it is part of the role you gave me when you asked me to be your Master." He stroked her hair. "All I've asked you to do is tell me why you're unhappy so we can fix whatever is wrong."

She closed her eyes, her heart aching.

He massaged her shoulders, his hands sliding down her back toward the curve of her bottom. She wanted to lift her bottom, to welcome his touch. She wanted warmth to swell within her. She wanted the warm tender intimacy that they had shared before but it was not there. There was only a bleak feeling of impending loss and grief.

He lifted the paddle and brought it down hard against her left cheek. The sting was sharp and radiated outward from where the paddle had connected. It hurt, but the pain was not unbearable. She kept the small gasp locked tight inside.

"We've shared a lot in the short time we've been together. My love has never wavered. There is nothing you could tell me that would make me love you any less."

Her mind grasped onto his words, her subconscious mind arguing that he was already trying to foist her off onto a therapist.

He spanked her again, harder this time. The pain that seared into her flesh made her jerk and gasp. She longed to beg him to stop as the fresh pain blazed across her bottom.

"This isn't because I'm angry with you honey. It's because the course you've chosen isn't good for you or for us."

Kara bit her lip tasting the metallic taste of blood as she tried to hold her tears at bay. The gentle, matter of fact tenor of his words only made her feel worse, more alone.

She felt him shift, placing his leg atop hers and exerting steady pressure on her back he pinned her across his lap. Once he had her captive he struck her hard on the left cheek of her bottom. The sound of the paddle reverberated in the room intensifying the streak of pain that ripped across her ass cheek.

She hadn't been prepared for the bolt of pain. Tears filled her eyes. She was shocked that the pain was so much more intense than the first two swats had been. Pain radiated through her bottom making her want to cry out in shock in pain. She didn't want to believe Slade would hurt her like this.

Four spanks and already her ass blazed. She bit her lip harder as another stroke fell in the same spot.

"Ow," she screamed feeling helpless as Slade's legs trapped hers and his hand pressed down against her back, keeping her in position.

"This is a punishment spanking. I intend for it to hurt. It's the price of childish, disobedient behavior, and it will continue to be the price of that kind of behavior for as long as we are married," Slade said as another hard swat fell.

She winced, jerking as pain exploded high on her left ass cheek.

Tears squeezed past her eyelashes and fell on her cheek. The spanking intensified the bleak despair that filled her. That he was purposely inflicting pain, purposely hurting her rather than loving her, unleashed a torrent of deep emotional sadness.

The spanking had a surreal quality, like it couldn't be happening, and yet the pain of the spanks were sharp, so intense she screamed as the paddle connected with her thigh.

"You can decide whether you want to continue to be obstinate and stubborn or whether you want to straighten up and address things like a grown up," he said, adding another stroke atop the one that still sizzled through her thigh.

She shrieked, at the intensity of the pain that singed her. A bleak barren feeling, like standing at the abyss completely alone, forced to face everything alone swamped her, loosening the tight control she'd kept on her emotions.

Panic erupted. I can't do it all alone. I don't want to do it all alone.

Another stroke, this one harder than all the others connected with her ass. She gasped, and cried out, desperation to avoid the stinging blows filling her. She struggled in his grasp, trying to roll away from him, trying to get to her feet, but Slade kept her pinned across his lap.

"I'm sorry. I know it hurts."

Tears ran in rivulets down her face. She wanted it to end.

"It hurts," she sobbed lost not only in the intense pain of the spanking but also in the soul deep pain of being alone with only herself to rely on. She had depended on him to protect her, to love her, yet he was the one inflicting the pain that ravaged her ass. She thought of the gentle way he had made love to her and struggled to equate the gentleness he'd shown then with the purposeful infliction of pain now.

"You know how to make it stop," Slade said as another

stroke fell across her other thigh.

She gasped and expelled the breath on a wail as another stroke connected with her bottom.

She knew how to make the spanking stop, but she didn't know how to make the pain in her heart stop. That deeper emotional pain swelled, as the pain of the spanking intensified. Her soft sobs grew louder as the feelings she'd pushed down began to rise up within her closing out everything except the intense fear of being abandoned again.

Slade continued to land stroke after stroke on her bottom. She cried and fought to escape him as each one fell, but there was no escape from the physical pain or from the emotional pain that coalesced within her becoming less and less controlled with each agonizing stroke of the paddle. The pain sliced through her inciting her screams, but the soft sobs that shook her came from the overriding fear that he would leave her and there was nothing she could say or do that would prevent it.

He landed a searing lick across the center of her ass. Kara screeched, her hands grabbing his calves as she struggled to push herself up and out of his grip. She was desperate to avoid the searing pain of another stroke.

She gasped around the sobs that shook her as another half dozen strokes fell in quick succession. There was no time to think or to recover between his strokes. Helplessness engulfed her. She wanted him to stop. She wanted him to hold her, to cuddle her, to make everything better. She wanted him to make her feel safe. She wanted to believe in his power to make everything alright and yet she knew he was only a temporary part of her life. She knew she couldn't really count on him.

"Ow, ow, ow, please stop," she howled as he continued to spank.

"Oh no honey, I'm just getting started. This is a punishment spanking. It's supposed to teach a lesson and I'm going to make damn sure the lesson is learned. I don't want to have to spank you again," he said without pause in the cadence of spanks landing on her panty covered bottom.

Desperation clawed through her.

"You won't Sir," she whimpered.

"You're ready to tell me what has made you so unhappy the past couple weeks then?" he asked, the spanks finally stopping.

Relief at the reprieve coursed through her. Her chest constricted. She sobbed helplessly, not knowing how to put the deep, dark, ache that had swelled till it enclosed her into words that he would understand.

"Please Sir," she begged. "I'm sorry."

"Sorry is not enough Kara, you have to correct the transgression." His voice was smooth and matter of fact. There was no edge of anger or malice in his voice just a calm matter of factness. "Can you talk about it now?"

Anguish filled her as she shook her head. She felt broken. Shattered.

He sighed deeply. Kara could feel his displeasure radiating into her and felt shame and self pity creep through her. "It's your choice. There are only two choices, honey," he said softly near her ear as he spanked again, hard.

The pain that had streaked across her ass hadn't even dissipated before he tugged at her panties, pulling them down until her bottom and upper thighs were bare.

Panic chased through her. As much as it hurt with her panties on, it would be ten times worse with them off. She kicked her legs, and tried to roll out of his grip, her distressed sobs loud in the room. She dreaded the next spank and yet she knew she was helpless to avoid it.

All efforts at keeping her emotions under control evaporated as a series of slow, measured spanks landed on her unprotected ass. The emotions that she had fought so hard to keep under control surged to the surface overwhelming her with bleak anguish and despair. Even the pain of the spanking receded into the background as the anguish that she had pushed deep into her being was loosened and soared upward threatening to overwhelm her.

She shuddered feeling as if she were seven again, alone and facing everything by herself after the death of her daddy. She felt small in the face of overwhelming emotions that she couldn't bring herself to voice.

"You know how to make it stop honey," Slade whispered softly.

She heard his voice as if from across a great divide, like a beacon guiding her back to safety, back to warmth. The fear of being left, of being abandoned filled her soul with deep anguish and yet she wanted to make it all stop.

"Please Sir, it hurts," she cried brokenly. "It hurts so much."

Empathy filled Slade. He set the paddle aside, his palm caressing the red welts that marred her bottom. He knew her ass had to be causing her near agony. It was bright red and nearly singed his palm as he caressed it.

"Please, no more. Please," she begged.

He ran his hand over her ass again, feeling the heat that radiated off another cache of red welts. He was torn. He needed to know what was eating her, and if he stopped before she was ready to tell him he would just have to start again.

He was determined to get to the bottom of what was bothering her. He wouldn't have it following her into another day. He also knew she was about spent, emotionally, physically.

He couldn't push her much further. The broken way she cried as if she were trapped in agony so deep and bleak she couldn't see beyond it tore at him, making his soul ache. He wanted to make her pain go away.

The pain of watching her misery overcame him. "Come here baby," he said. He needed to hold her, needed to communicate that in spite of the pain he was inflicting, he loved her. He helped her up and lifted her so that when he settled her she was straddling his lap, her legs folded beneath her on each side of his legs. "Your spanking isn't over, but you look like you need a reprieve," he said softly as he pulled her against his chest.

She collapsed against him, her body limp, her sobs still a ragged reminder of the way he'd pushed her. Her posture, her weakness, reminded him of a rag doll that had lost its stuffing. The rough sobs and the tears that ran down her face and onto his shirt tore at him making him ache to make it all better.

He stroked her back and her hair, needing to touch her, needing to assure himself that she was okay, that the brokenness that seemed to emanate from her was the result of the physical pain he'd inflicted and not the result of some deeper emotional turmoil that he couldn't see.

He didn't want to spank her any more. He wanted to hold her, love her, take care of her the way he always had. He wanted to make things right between them again.

He palmed the back of her head, his hand pressing her face against his chest, thinking how he'd missed having her head there, how he wanted to feel it there again.

"How're you doing honey?" His voice was soft. The need to ease her pain and protect her filled him.

"It hurts." The tears still cascaded down her cheeks, her breath still came in short choppy gasps that ripped at his heart. He didn't feel like the caring, loving master he wanted to be and yet he knew he'd done what he'd done in an effort to care for her.

He held her close, loving her, wanting her to know how much he loved her.

"Let's try this again," he said softly as he stroked his hands down her back and over the roundness of her bottom where the welts marred the perfect smoothness of her bottom. "How is it that it is easier to take a spanking like this one than to talk to me?" he asked.

The question made the emotions that had bubbled up as she'd endured the spanking resurge filling her anew with all the despair, grief, and loneliness that had held her in its grasp.

The despair, the impending loss, the anguish that she would feel when he left her was too much. She was too tired, too emotionally drained to keep the feelings confined. The walls that surrounded her began to crumble. She couldn't hold the tide of raw naked emotion back anymore. Tears and emotions poured out of her in a torrent that she didn't have the energy to decipher. Instead she existed in the space Slade created for her.

She existed within his arms, within the soft sounds of his voice offering words of love and commitment, drawing comfort from his hands which stroked her tenderly.

Inside the circle of his arms, with the soft loving words cascading over her and his hands gently stroking her she was safe from the storm of emotion that filled and surrounded her.

"Please don't leave me." Her words were soft, almost shrouded by the soft gaspy breaths that still shook her, but Slade heard them.

His heart squeezed painfully. "I'm not going anywhere, sweetheart. I'm right here, for as long as you want me to be here." He stroked her hair and her back and what he could reach of her bottom loving the soft sounds of pleasure she made when he rubbed her back. He'd sit with her all night, holding her, loving her, if only she'd tell him what was bothering her.

His soft words of love and commitment caressed her as he held her slowly, tenderly stroking her. She cried until the emotions dissipated, until she was emotionally drained, until she was empty, until there was nothing left.

"I'm sorry Sir," she said softly as she rested against his chest feeling as if every bit of strength she possessed had been sucked from her.

"I know you're sorry honey." He stroked her back. "I never doubted you were sorry. I know that whatever is bothering you must seem pretty big, pretty insurmountable."

Emotion she thought was spent resurfaced. She sniffled helplessly as tears leaked from her eyes wetting his shirt front. The impossibility of their situation tore at her. The knowledge that he would eventually abandon her when he couldn't deal with the nightmares and the panic attacks rose again filling her with bleak despair. She didn't want to lose him. She loved him.

"Sh-sh honey, everything will be alright," he soothed as he stroked her back.

She sniffed feeling lost and overwhelmed, doubtful that everything would ever be alright.

"Please don't leave me, Slade," she asked, her voice stronger, more pleading than the last time she'd asked.

"I'm not going to leave you honey. You're safe. I've got you." He played her words over in his mind. There was something about them, something about the beseeching quality of her voice that stirred his attention.

He'd thought the first time she'd begged him not to leave her that she didn't want him to leave her in the aftermath of the spanking, that she wanted him to continue to hold her. But he wasn't so sure that's what she'd meant.

There had been something more in her voice this time, a beseeching quality, a desperation like she was begging for something she didn't expect him to give her. "What is it honey? Why are you so afraid of me leaving you?"

He felt a soft sigh that issued from her, felt her head burrow deeper into his chest. "I just don't want to be totally alone again, like—" She drew a deep, labored breath that sounded tight with pent up emotion.

"Kara," he shifted her, tipping her chin up so he could look down into her eyes. Guilt and shame filled him as he studied her face. Her eyes were red and swollen, her face blotchy, her lip swollen where she had bit it.

He stroked her back, hating the tears and the splotchy redness that were all part of the pain he had purposely inflicted to bring them to this point. He studied her face seeing only intense fear and sadness. "Honey, I have no intention of leaving you now or any time in the future. Where did you get the idea that I would?"

"You wanted me to see the psychiatrist," she said on a soft sob, as if that explained everything.

He drew a deep breath, his mind grappling as he tried to figure out what one thing had to do with the other. He came up a blank.

"Honey, I wanted you to see the psychiatrist about your nightmares. What has that got to do with me leaving you? I'm not going to leave you because you have nightmares."

"Just the nightmares?"

"Yes, pretty much. I just wanted you to be free of the past, free of the nightmares. I wanted you to have a chance to be happy and I thought she might be able to help." He was quiet for a moment. "You must have thought I brought it up for some other reason?"

He watched as she shifted on his lap. She seemed so small, so alone, so needy. "I thought you wanted me to see her because you couldn't deal with my past," she whispered.

"No honey, that was never it. There is absolutely no part of you or your past that I can't cope with. I'd like for you to not have the nightmares and the panic attacks because it would be better for you but—" He stroked her shoulder. "What happened to you when you were younger was a terrible thing, a tragedy, but it's in the past. All I want is for you to be happy. Your past and the nightmares and panic attacks has no bearing on my love for you or my commitment to you."

He stared down into her red tear strained eyes and her face that was still red and damp from crying. "If there was something about your past that I couldn't deal with, then it would be upon me to see the shrink, don't you think?"

Warmth flooded her. She smiled up at him, loving him.

"I don't understand—why—"

She looked up at him, her face soft, her expression bemused, happiness, and joy finally returning to fill the places where fear and dread had dwelled.

"Why did you let me spank you? Why didn't you just ask me what I meant or tell me why you were upset?"

He felt the shudder that worked through her and noticed her retreat behind sad eyes and lowered lashes.

She looked up at him, swallowing around the hard lump that still filled her throat. "It was just," she sighed. "When you said— When you suggested that I see her—" She stopped and drew a deep breath, then swallowed hard gathering her determination. There had been too many half truths and too many secrets between them. She no longer wanted to keep him at arm's length. She no longer wanted secrets between them. She wanted a clean break with the past and a future with him.

She swallowed hard. "When you suggested I see her, I felt dirty, used, not good enough." She drew a deep breath and let it out. "I thought it was only a matter of time before you left me." She swiped at her eyes.

"I don't understand honey, why would you think that?"

"Because—the past—the nightmares and panic attacks, they've been too much for everyone else," she said quietly.

He was quiet, waiting for her to continue.

"My parents were happy before… They were close. They laughed." She swallowed hard. Slade felt like he was three steps behind, trying to understand how it all fit together in her mind but he was determined to hang in, determined to understand what had hurt her so much she'd closed down and closed him out.

He stroked her back giving her time and space.

"After—" She shook her head. "They fought and yelled at each other, mostly about whether or not to take me to a psychiatrist, and which one." She was silent for a long time, so long that Slade began to wonder if she'd drifted into the sad memories of her parent's fights and the responsibility she thought she bore for them.

"My dad," she swallowed hard, her gaze rising slowly to meet his. "He shot himself in the same park where I was abducted." She squeezed her eyes shut and bowed her head. He watched as the tears squeezed past her eyelashes and slid down her cheeks.

He drew a deep breath and tightened his arms around her. He stroked her back, his voice soft and low as he told her that none of it had been her fault, that her parents were the grown ups and that they should have been there for her.

As he held her, her belief that he would leave her began to make sense, in an odd way. That her father had abandoned her in the worst possible way explained why she had thought he couldn't cope when he'd suggested she see the psychiatrist. The rapist had done a number on her, but her own family hadn't been much better.

"My—um-mom—checked out for awhile after that. Prescriptions. Alcohol. Ted and I pretty much fended for ourselves. He was just a toddler. We survived on what cookies and crackers I could scrounge from the cabinets.

"It's like every time someone suggests I see a psychiatrist more people check out of my life."

"I'm sorry honey."

"So am I. I just—" She squeezed her eyes closed and rested her forehead against his shoulder.

His arms drew tighter around her, holding her close. "You just—what honey?" he asked softly, wanting to hear it all once and for all so that they could put it behind them.

"I just—um-don't have the best history with psychiatrists. When you asked me to see one, all the history came back. Everything closed in on me at once." She nestled deeper into his arms.

He stroked her tenderly, loving her. He was sure there would be other issues that would raise their heads during their marriage, but at least she was talking.

They were quiet for awhile, each seeming lost in their own thoughts. Kara was content to sit on his lap, absorbing the warm safe feeling of being enveloped in his strong arms. She'd been unable to feel anything but the impending sense of loss since he'd suggested the therapist. It filled her with a deep pleasure to sit on his lap, enclosed in the warmth and security of his arms secure in the knowledge that he didn't intend to leave her.

"Tell me about the bad blood with psychiatrists," he asked after awhile.

Kara would have preferred to bask in softer thoughts, but a part of her wanted everything out. She didn't want any more secrets, any more half truths.

"The police wanted to nail the man – um – the man who raped me and who murdered my twin sister. Kayla."

She was quiet a moment, remembering Kayla, remembering how close they had been, how they'd done everything together.

"Jesus honey, you didn't tell me you had a sister or that she was part of this."

"I know." She drew a deep breath. "I never talked about her because—it hurts to remember the way she died." He nodded, pulling her closer and tucking her head under his chin as he stroked her back. The memory of the rapist killing Kayla exploded in her mind's eye. She remembered how she'd kicked and punched him, screaming at him to stop. She hadn't been able to kick him hard enough or to punch him hard enough to make him stop. The memory still hurt, but the pain was softer now than it had been.

"He—um—smothered her in front of me, then left her body in the basement as a reminder of what would happen to me if I didn't do what he said."

Slade held her tight. His lungs ached as he thought of Kara trapped in the basement with the body of her sister. "I'm so sorry baby," he whispered, wishing there was something more he could say, something more he could do that would ease the anguish that must still be very real to her, even this much later. "I can't even imagine how horrible that must have been for you."

She nodded and drew a deep breath. "It was. The whole ordeal was terrible, but I don't want to wallow in it anymore. I don't have an explanation for why I lived and Kayla died, but it happened that way. I don't want to spend any more time looking backward at the past. I want to build a life with you. I want to look forward."

Slade noticed she hadn't finished telling him why there was bad blood between her and psychiatrists, but he let it go. There would be another time for her to share that part of her past. He was more interested in building a future with her than looking back at a past which neither of them could change.

He felt his admiration for her swell. She'd been through a hell of a lot. She still bore emotional scars, but she was tough. They'd get through it together.

"I'd like that too honey. I'd like us to have kids someday, and take vacations, and do all the normal things people do."

Slade felt the tension that rippled through her, and knew that something he'd said had struck a nerve, even before she sat up, pinning him with soulful brown eyes that were still damp with tears. "There is something else." She bit her lip. "I didn't tell you when we got married because I didn't expect us to stay married and I didn't think it would matter."

She gnawed her lip, her eyes drifting down, away from him.

"What is it honey?" he asked. "I can tell it's bothering you."

"There is an—um—likelihood that I can't have children," she said, her beautiful eyes shuttered as she looked down, avoiding his gaze.

He gently lifted her face and looked deep into her eyes, wanting her to see that what he was going to say was honest and not just a bunch of platitudes. "Kara, I love kids, and nothing would make me happier than to make them with you, but if you can't have them then we'll adopt. There are hundreds of thousands of kids in the world that need families."

He stroked her hair, loving the soft light that filled her eyes as she tipped her head so that she rested her cheek in his palm as she looked up at him.

"Right now, all I care about is you and us. Are we okay? I know I was hard on you, probably harder than I should have been given the circumstances."

Kara nestled against Slade's chest and wrapped her arms around him, loving him. That he had spanked her rather than leaving her to suffer alone in the pit of emotional despair that had closed in on her had intensified her trust in him.

She curled into him, wrapping her arms around him. "We are perfect. All last week I wanted to feel safe, secure, loved and I couldn't feel it because there was too much fear and too much sadness in the way. The spanking hurt, but it took away the worst of the bad feelings. You holding me and talking to me took away the rest." She smiled up at him. "It was just like you said it would be."

"Ummmm," he sighed. "And how did I say it would be?" he asked lifting her chin and kissing her mouth.

"You said it was something you would do to take care of me. I feel very taken care of," she sighed.

"I always take care of what's mine," Slade said, his eyes meeting hers. "Make no mistake about it honey, you are mine."

Epilogue

Slade turned the key in the lock and pushed the door open to find Kara kneeling, naked near the door. He smiled as his eyes swept over her, following the pronounced curve of her tummy. He loved her more now than he ever had.

He smiled down upon her, the thought that he was going to have to find a new way for her to demonstrate her submission rising in his mind. Now that she was in her sixth month of pregnancy it was getting too difficult for her to get down and back up again.

His feelings for her were as they had always been. He loved her. He derived pleasure from caring for her, from protecting her, cherishing her. He didn't need her to kneel naked at his feet to demonstrate her submission. She demonstrated her love and submission in a hundred other ways every day.

Still he knew that the ritual made her feel mastered and it made him feel masterful that she wanted to submit to him in such a pronounced way. He knew he would come up with another ritual to meet their needs for expressing his mastery and her submission. It would just be one that didn't require her kneeling.

"How was your day?" he asked helping her to her feet and kissing her before she had a chance to respond.

"It was good. I stopped by to see my mom and at the vet clinic to have lunch with some of my friends from there. We had lunch in the restaurant where you proposed." She smiled up at him, her eyes sparkling. "It was nice to go back there...to where it all started."

He smiled down at her loving her.

"Your mom called. She wants us to come over for dinner." She smiled up at him, her eyes bright with mischief. "Dinner comes with strings though," she paused. "She has a problem with the drain, she wants you to fix for her."

Slade rolled his eyes. "Going to my mom's would entail you getting dressed," he sighed.

"I know, and I'd rather stay home, naked with you, but it will give us a chance to tell your mom about the babies."

Slade stopped dumfounded. He wasn't sure he'd heard her right. "What'd you say honey?"

She smiled broadly. "The doctor called today. You were right when you thought they were pointing out a lot of feet when they did the ultrasound." She laughed. "He said we're having two babies. Both girls."

Joy shot through him. He picked her up and spun her around as he kissed her. "Everything is okay with my babies and their mama then?" he asked still holding her.

She nodded grinning up at him. "Everything is good all the way around. I couldn't be any better or any happier if I tried."

About Alyssa Aaron

Alyssa Aaron read her first romance novel (*A Stranger's Kiss* by Sondra Sanford) when she was in eighth grade. She was hooked by the romance genre and became an avid consumer of Harlequin novels. It wasn't until she was in 9th grade that the praise of one of her teachers made her think about writing a book. The romance genre was a natural choice for her efforts.

Once the idea was born Alyssa was off like a shot. She completed her first novel a very tame marriage of convenience story and submitted it to Harlequin in the summer following 9th grade. It was rejected the following year but Alyssa continued to write dabbling in many other genres for many years.

His Perfect Submissive is her first, but she hopes not her last romance novel.

When she is not writing Alyssa enjoys gardening, quilting, collecting recipes, and volunteering for various causes.

Her volunteer positions have included working as an advocate for abused and neglected children, grooming police horses, and caring for cats at a no kill animal shelter.

Alyssa loves to hear from her readers. Email can be sent to her through her publisher at:

AlyssaAaron@blackvelvetseductions.com

or by snail mail through her publisher.

Alyssa Aaron
c/o Black Velvet Seductions
1350-C West Southport Road, Box 249
Indianapolis, IN 46217

Printed in the United States
111939LV00002B/28/P

ordered the youth before walking briskly toward the men sent to arrest him. He allowed them to close around him as he passed out of the door. They clattered down the stairs and out into the street, leaving John and Lady Eschiva standing on the upstairs landing in horrified paralysis.

"Treason?" Lady Eschiva asked the squire. "Did I hear correctly? Champagne has arrested my lord husband for treason? But that's not possible!" she protested.

"I've got to get word to my father at once!" John answered, his voice breaking with tension as the situation threatened to overwhelm him: he would not turn fourteen for another month.

"Mommy! Mommy! What are they going to do with Daddy?" It was the high-pitched voice of eight-year-old Burgundia. Ten-year-old Guy pushed past her, protesting, "They can't arrest, Daddy! He's the Constable!"

Eschiva turned toward her children, but then stopped to look over her shoulder to her husband's squire. "Yes, John, go to your father at once! If Isabella let this happen, he's the only one who might be able to help us now!"

The stables behind the house were cramped and dark. The four horses stirred uneasily, and one of them nickered at the unexpected intrusion. John was in such a hurry to get the terrible news of what had happened to his father that he hadn't thought to bring a light. He fumbled around in the dark, knocking things over, and nearly took the wrong saddle pad. He didn't bother with brushing his aging gray stallion, nor even picking out his hooves. In his mind, dark images of Lord Aimery chained to a dungeon wall spurred him to greater haste.

He tacked up the big gray in his stall, and then led him out into the narrow street. It was marginally lighter here because a three-quarter moon reflected off the pale limestone of the buildings. The big horse was fussing and nervous as he started to wake up and sensed John's agitation. John made for the eastern gate of the city. The hoof-falls of the shod stallion echoed through the silent streets. Everywhere the windows were firmly shuttered against the night; there was no sign of life until John reached the city gate itself.

The watchmen in the guardhouse were startled by a demand to open the gate in the middle of the night. One of the men came out and stood silhouetted against the warm orange light of the lamps inside. "Who goes? And what do you want at this time of night?"

Gambling that news of the Constable's abrupt arrest had not yet reached the watch, John answered as firmly as his nearly-fourteen years allowed, "I'm

John d'Ibelin, the Lord Constable's squire. He has entrusted me with an urgent message for my father, the Lord of Caymont. Let me out at once!"

The sergeant stepped closer to get a better look at John, and quickly verified he was who he said he was. The Constable's squire was not a nobody. He was a baron's son, an Ibelin—and half-brother to the ruling Queen. So the sergeant called to one of his men to open the gate, and saluted John. "Give your father my blessings, young man! I wouldn't have lived to make old bones but for him."

John nodded absently. Men said things like that to him all the time. His father was Balian d'Ibelin, the man who had led a breakout at Hattin, enabling some three thousand infantry to escape the Saracen encirclement. They were the *only* infantry to escape that day. His father had also negotiated the surrender of Jerusalem, enabling as many as sixty thousand more people to escape slaughter or slavery. Last but not least, he'd negotiated the Treaty of Ramla, which enabled tens of thousands of Christians who had been enslaved after Hattin to return to what was left of the Kingdom. In short, there were *a lot* of people who owed his father their freedom, if not their life.

As John emerged on the far side of the heavy barbican, he gently nudged the big horse with his un-spurred heels, and the stallion willingly took up a canter. He was on the main road south, and it was paved from Acre all the way to Haifa. Centurion, as the horse was called, was not particularly swift, but he was tough and trustworthy. He had served John's father as his warhorse for nearly fifteen years. He had carried the Lord of Ibelin at the Battle on the Litani, at Le Forbelet, to the relief of Kerak twice, and as recently as the Battle of Arsuf—but most important, he had carried the elder Ibelin off the murderous field of Hattin.

John was immensely proud that his father had given him Centurion along with a new hauberk, his first helmet, and a proper sword three months ago. The gifts marked his elevation in status from child to youth as he assumed the duties of squire to Lord Aimery. Lord Aimery was his cousin Eschiva's husband, the man she had married at the age of eight, when he was already nearing thirty. As a result, John had known him all his life, but John still respected Lord Aimery as a squire should. In his eyes, Lord Aimery was a paragon of chivalry: valorous on the battlefield, courteous to ladies, generous to the poor, pious and sober in word and deed. It was unthinkable that he had committed high treason. John was sure he was innocent, and the need to rescue him from injustice drove him to keep up the fastest pace possible in the dark.

After almost two hours, John reached a fork in the road. Here the right fork bent west to skirt Mount Carmel on the shore, leading to Haifa, while the left fork bent less sharply southeast to follow the valley on the backside of Mount Carmel. John was very fortunate to still have the light of the moon, because he had to take the left fork.

This road had once been the high road to Jerusalem, one of the most heavily traveled routes in the Kingdom. But when the armies of Saladin overran the Kingdom after Hattin, all peaceful travel had come to an abrupt halt. For the following five years, the only people to use the road had been the Saracens, and they had done nothing to maintain it. The Truce of Ramla signed this past August left both the Holy City and Nablus in Saracen hands, so the former highway ended abruptly at the new frontier just beyond Caymont.

The remnants of this once important highway were now nothing but a sad reminder of what had once been. The road was in poor repair, uneven and pocked with potholes. The farther John rode, the worse the surface became. The winter rains washing off the steep slopes of Mount Carmel to his right had deposited stones, rubble, and mud in some places and had broken down the road itself in others. There were whole stretches where the road had sunk and stood awash in muddy water. Centurion had to test his way forward cautiously. John gave him a long rein, trusting the old warhorse to find the best possible footing, but it was impossible to go faster than a slow walk.

While letting the horse find their way forward, John had more time to reflect on what had happened and what an absurd situation he was in. While Lord Aimery was John's cousin by marriage, the man who had ordered his arrest, the King of Jerusalem, was his brother-in-law, the husband of his half-sister Isabella, his mother's daughter by her first husband King Amalric of Jerusalem. Although Isabella was seven years older than John and an early marriage had taken her out of her mother's household, she had always been part of the family circle. John was close to her—at least he'd thought he'd been until now!

The problem, John suspected, was that Lord Aimery was the younger brother of the *former* King of Jerusalem, Guy de Lusignan. Guy had been married to Isabella's older half-sister Sibylla. Guy continued to claim the crown for himself, even though he'd usurped the crown in the first place and his royal wife was dead. Things had seemed settled when the English King conquered the island of Cyprus and then sold it to Guy de Lusignan. Guy had sailed away to claim his new possession last fall, but John was sure Lord Aimery's arrest had something to do with him nevertheless.

Dawn was coming. It turned the sky a murky gray, and the contours of the landscape began to emerge more distinctly. The valley had widened substantially, and along the banks of the river there were plowed fields marking where settlers had returned after the truce was concluded. On the far side of the river the hills rose up again, dark against the lightening sky, and there somewhere in the distance lay Nazareth. John could remember the town and the impressive Church of the Annunciation, but it remained in Saracen hands.

The sleepless night was catching up with him. John stopped beside a roadside well that had once belonged to a caravansary. The caravansary itself was abandoned and collecting old leaves and cobwebs, but the well was still functional. John dismounted, and threw a bucket down to draw water. The drum squeaked as it unwound, irritating Centurion, but the bucket splashed into water before it had gone too far. The rains had been good this winter.

John hauled the bucket up, removed it from the hook, and set it down for Centurion to drink. Since he was a small boy, John's father had taught him the importance of watering the horses first, but the lesson had become anchored in his brain by the knowledge that Hattin had been lost in part because many of the horses had been too dehydrated to withstand the rigors of battle. His father's younger stallion had refused to drink the night before the battle, and had collapsed under him; his father would have died if Centurion hadn't been in reserve. The older warhorse had drunk his fill the night before . . .

Now, too, Centurion sucked up the water greedily, so John hauled up a second bucket of water, but this time Centurion sniffed at it, drank a little, and then wandered off, more interested in grass. At last John dunked his tin cup into the water and drank himself.

His thirst quenched, John found he could hardly keep his eyes open. He convinced himself that there was no point arriving too early and waking everyone up. He was, he calculated, only five or six miles from Caymont. He could be there in less than an hour once Centurion was rested. So he unsaddled the big horse, lay down on the saddle blanket, and fell almost instantly into a deep sleep.

A bee woke him, and with a rush of guilt John jumped to his feet. The sun was halfway up the sky. He must have slept for three hours or more, he guessed. Meanwhile, Centurion had wandered a long way off. He grabbed the saddle and blanket and went after him, calling his name. When he was remounted, he set off at a fast pace to make up for his nap.

He had not ridden very far when, coming around a curve in the road, he abruptly came upon a large party of men and an oxcart that completely blocked the road. John drew up, annoyed, as he tried to figure out who they were and what they were doing. They were a mixture of Franks and Syrians, judging from their different head coverings: Syrians in turbans and Franks in fitted linen caps or bareheaded. The Syrians had hitched their kaftans up, while the Franks were wearing nothing but shirts and braies, with the sleeves rolled up over their elbows. They were all barefoot with their feet covered in mud, and they were armed with picks and shovels.

As John took in the little scene, he realized they were trying to clear the debris of a small landslide out of a relatively wide stone-lined irrigation ditch that ran beside the road. The ditch led from a spring farther up the hill to the fields on the upper slope to the right of the road. As they cleared the stones out of the ditch, they lugged them over to the ox-cart to dump them in the back, apparently for use in building or repairing walls elsewhere.

John was about to ride around the party when one of the men who had been wielding a pick to loosen a stone stood to wipe the sweat from his brow, and John recognized his father. "Papa!" John called out in shock and astonishment, before correcting himself to say, "My lord!" It was not at all right for a Baron of Jerusalem to be working with a pick in the mud, John thought.

Just last fall John had personally seen his father treated almost like an equal by King Richard of England. Only a month later al-Adil, the brother of Saladin, had visited the Ibelin stud at Tyre, and again John had seen the elaborate courtesies the Sultan's brother had shown his father. And now his father was clearing irrigation ditches with his tenant farmers?

Ibelin handed the pick to one of his companions and stepped across the ditch to approach his son, grinning. "John! What an unexpected surprise! What are you doing here?"

"I rode all night to bring you the news! They arrested Uncle Aimery for high treason—in the middle of the night—and the last thing he said to me was to get word to you straightway. But it can't be true. I'm sure of it. After all, I've been with him every minute for the last three months, and he's done nothing but his duties! He's completely innocent! You've got to do something! You've got to—"

"Calm down," Ibelin interrupted his excited son. "Give me a lift back to the manor, and we'll talk to your mother." As he spoke, he went around to Centurion's left side, put his foot on John's, and swung himself up into the saddle behind his son. Then he clicked to the faithful warhorse.

John didn't mind his father riding pillion with him; his best memories of early childhood were riding like this at the front of his father's saddle. He was distressed, however, by his father's calm. "You don't understand! They hauled Lord Aimery out of bed in the middle of the night and have taken him to the royal dungeon! He's probably chained up, and—"

"John, Aimery is Constable of Jerusalem, and he can only be tried for treason—or any other crime, for that matter—before the High Court of Jerusalem. I'm not the least bit worried that he will be able to defend himself there to the satisfaction of the majority. So don't worry. For the moment, you need some breakfast, and I certainly need a bath and a change of clothes."

The "manor" was the seat of his father's new barony of Caymont. The Truce of Ramla, signed the previous summer, entailed recognition of a new border between Frankish and Saracen territory based on the gains of the campaign led by King Richard of England. In the truce the Saracens recognized Frankish control of the coastal plain from Tyre to Jaffa. But the castle and town of Ibelin, the barony from which John's family drew its name, had not been included in the truce: it remained in Saracen hands. Likewise, the cities of Ramla and Mirabel, which had been held by John's uncle, and Nablus, his mother's dower lands, remained lost to the Saracens. Instead of his rich inheritance, John's father had been given the small but vacant barony of Caymont, a comparatively small wedge of fertile land southeast of Haifa and a good twelve miles from the sea. Caymont had never owed more than six knights to the feudal levee, and it had never been the seat of a castle, because it lay in a lush but indefensible valley.

Instead of a proper castle with strong exterior walls strengthened by towers, gatehouses, and barbicans like Ibelin, the manor at Caymont was a collection of farm buildings clustered around two courtyards. On one side of the road single-storied, barrel-vaulted storerooms of stone enclosed a square courtyard, with stables backed up against one long side of the square. On the other side of the road a stone arch led to a cobbled courtyard flanked by a mixture of two-storied and one-storied buildings. A second-floor chapel with a crypt under it took up one of the narrow sides of the courtyard. Opposite was the single-storied court-house. Between these were on one side a well, cisterns, kitchen, brewery, bakery, and wine press, and on the other side a two-storied tract of accommodations. Over the arched entrances to the rooms on the ground floor stretched an open terrace reached by a flight of exterior stairs.

They turned Centurion over to a groom at the stable, crossed the road, and passed through the arch to enter the domestic courtyard. Together father and son climbed the exterior steps to the terrace, where large amphorae sprouted small palms. "Mother's already started her garden," John remarked in surprise.

Ibelin laughed. "She's got her work cut out for her! There was once a walled garden on the back side of this building, but we've found over a dozen human skeletons there—along with the bones of pigs and dogs that the Saracens evidently slaughtered and then threw down on top of the Christian dead. We've tried to give the human remains a proper burial, but I can't spare the men to clean out the rest of the bones, repair the walls, and clean out the fountain just yet. We need to get the irrigation ditch cleared first, so we'll have a harvest next year. We also need to fix the vandalized oil presses and repair the damaged stable roof."

John nodded earnestly. He didn't like it here at Caymont. It wasn't home, and it was, he felt certain, haunted. The old Lord of Caymont and his son had both died during the Hattin campaign, and his wife, daughter, and daughter-in-law had failed to recognize the threat until it was too late. They had put up a futile defense against marauding Saracen cavalry and had been slaughtered (or had flung themselves out of the windows rather than submit to slavery) along with their household servants. Because they did not know exactly who had been at Caymont when it was overrun, they did not know if anyone had survived to be enslaved; they only knew they had found dozens of skeletons on their arrival here in early January. They thought they'd buried them all, but this latest story reminded John that there might be more in other unexpected places . . .

"We're making progress," Ibelin told his son, reading his distress from his open face, and clapping him on the shoulder.

John glanced up at his father and tried to smile, but as they passed from the bright sunshine of the terrace into the darkness of the hall, his spirits fell again. His mother, a daughter of the Greek imperial family, had been raised in the palaces of Constantinople. As a child she had never walked on floors of anything but marble or mosaic, but here there were nothing but rough flagstones and packed mud on the lower levels. It was more like a barn than a palace, John thought resentfully, glancing at the naked walls and the unglazed windows. How could his mother stand it here?

"Zoë!" Ibelin called, using his wife's middle name, which only he used with her. "John's here!"

A moment later Maria Zoë Comnena emerged in the doorway from the solar. She was dressed simply in accordance with her surroundings, in a rust-colored linen gown and a white surcoat of Gaza cotton. She had wrapped her head in saffron silk veils, however, and the dazzling smile she cast John reminded him that she had been a celebrated beauty in her youth. She advanced toward him with outstretched hands, but—still every inch a queen—she did not rush or shriek with delight. John hastened to meet her, bowing over her hand as he had been taught to do from earliest childhood.

"What brings you here? Are you alone?" she asked, delighted, but already looking beyond John, expecting Aimery and/or Eschiva.

"He's got bad news," his father answered for him. "It seems Champagne ordered Aimery's arrest for high treason."

"Ah, the Pisans," the Dowager Queen replied, nodding knowingly, while John gaped and his father nodded agreement.

"What do you mean?" John asked, looking back and forth between his parents.

"You tell him," Ibelin suggested to his wife, "while I go clean up and change."

Maria Zoë nodded, and slipped her arm through her son's elbow to lead him back into the solar as she explained. "The Pisans have been attacking ships bound to and from Acre. Acting little better than pirates, actually. Champagne is understandably furious, but he doesn't have sufficient naval forces to engage the Pisan corsairs, so he threatened to take action against the Pisan commune in Acre. The problem with that is that there's no evidence—and indeed, no reason why—the Pisans of Acre should be allied with those preying on shipping bound for Acre. Your sister Isabella wrote me that Aimery tried to stand up for the Pisan commune, which infuriated Champagne. I'm sure that's what's behind this arrest. Your father will soon get things cleared up." She paused to look at her son, smiling unconsciously to see him looking so mature and masculine. He might be only thirteen but, like his father, he was tall, and already handsome—at least in his mother's eyes. "Did you ride all through the night to bring the news?"

"Yes, I left immediately after Lord Aimery's arrest. I didn't even think to take food or money with me!"

His mother laughed. "Am I being too maternal if I suggest you're famished and need some breakfast?"

"I *am* famished!" John agreed readily.

"Then let's not stand on ceremony, and go straight down to the kitchens," Marie Zoë suggested, reversing direction.

Hungry as John was, he didn't like the thought of his Imperial Greek mother, the Dowager Queen of Jerusalem, going to the kitchens. He shook his head and stopped her. "Stay here, Mama. I'll go down and get myself something. But do you really think Papa can clear this up?"

"I'm certain he can. We'll return with you to Acre as soon as you've had a chance to eat something, your father has changed, and we can pack for a few days. Centurion can probably manage the distance again, or you can take one of the other horses. We want to get to Acre before nightfall so poor Eschiva doesn't have to spend another night in fear for her husband."

Chapter Two
The Great Negotiator

Acre, Kingdom of Jerusalem
April 1193

QUEEN ISABELLA I OF JERUSALEM WAS twenty years old. She had been married at eleven, divorced at eighteen, widowed at nineteen, and married a third time within days of her second husband's assassination. She had withstood Saracen sieges at Kerak and Tyre. She had taken part in the crusader siege of Acre. She had endured the uncertainty of a husband in Saracen captivity for two years, and the trauma of a husband dying in her arms after assassins struck. For all that, she was still a lovely young woman, who had inherited her mother's classical features and curly auburn hair. Furthermore, she bloomed with the inner beauty that came from being in love with her husband and a proud new mother, the posthumous daughter of her second husband.

After Mass and breaking their fast together, Isabella and her husband Henri de Champagne kissed before separating. He went to meet with the chamberlain, chancellor, seneschal, and viscount of the port of Acre, while she went to the nursery to check on her daughter Marie. It wasn't that Isabella had abdicated ruling her Kingdom to her husband. On the contrary, she took a keen interest in legal disputes, inheritances, wardships, and marriages, as well as correspondence with foreign powers. She was less interested, however, in the commercial and monetary issues discussed with the chamberlain and viscount. Besides, she was a young mother and felt an acute need to spend time with her baby.

The nursery had served this purpose for generations and was located on the ground floor facing one of the interior courtyards, so that growing royal children had a place to run about and make noise without disturbing the business of government or attracting the attention of their subjects. It was austerely furnished (as this was an age that believed children could do with less) but spacious, and Isabella already had dreams of filling it with half a dozen children. For the present, however, the nursery was occupied by her precious little Marie, the Syrian wet nurse, and Anne, the daughter of one of her ladies, who had been in Saracen slavery and had returned in a traumatized state.

As Isabella entered, Anne was beside the cradle, rocking it and singing a lullaby softly. Isabella smiled at her, pleased by the peaceful image, but Anne gasped at the arrival of the Queen and backed away as if she had been doing something wrong. "There's nothing to fear, Anne," Isabella tried to encourage the girl, but Anne dropped her chin to her chest and would not meet the Queen's eyes as she fell into a deep curtsy. Time, Isabella told herself, time and kindness would surely heal Anne's wounds. Then she bent over the cradle to look at her sleeping daughter.

Marie was perfect in Isabella's eyes. Isabella was sure she would grow up to be a great beauty, since her father had been one of the handsomest men of his age: the charmer Conrad de Montferrat. Isabella was glad that she had this last gift from the man who had taught her the joys of the bedchamber—and also glad that his child had been a girl, so her present husband Henri could sire the son who would one day rule her kingdom after her.

She did not want to wake her daughter, who was sleeping so blissfully, but she could not resist reaching out a finger to stroke the side of her cheek. Her skin was so amazingly soft that Isabella felt compelled to bend over the cradle to kiss her little girl on the nose. This, however, woke Marie, who squirmed, frowned, and let out a whining whimper of protest. Now Isabella had an excuse to take her in her arms to "comfort" her. She reached into the cradle and picked up her daughter. Placing her in the crook of her arm, she started very gently bouncing her up and down while she cooed to her. She was so absorbed in her joy with the child that she did not notice her mother stood in the doorway.

The Dowager Queen of Jerusalem watched her daughter in silence. It was good to see her eldest daughter so happy. It was good to see her enjoying motherhood, and even better to know she was at last happy with her husband after two marriages that had each been difficult in different ways. Humphrey de Toron had probably been a sodomite and certainly impotent, never consummating the marriage to Isabella; Conrad de Montferrat had been a good lover but overbearing and self-important, unwilling to recognize Isabella as an intelligent being. Henri de Champagne, in contrast, both adored his bride and respected her as his queen. Seeing Isabella like this was some compensation for the memories of the wreck Isabella had been during her wrenching divorce from Toron, much less the horror of watching Montferrat die in agony in her arms. Maria Zoë found it hard to break in on her daughter's private joy, knowing that she was going to shatter it the moment she raised the topic of Aimery de Lusignan's arrest.

"Mama!" Isabella noticed her mother at last. "How long have you been standing there?"

"I just arrived," Maria Zoë lied with a smile as she swept into the nursery. "And how is my granddaughter doing today?"

"She's as lovely as ever!" Isabella responded, willingly handing her daughter over to her mother as she offered both cheeks in greeting.

Maria Zoë smiled down at her namesake and bounced her in her arms gently, but when little Marie decided she'd had enough and let out a loud wail, she happily handed her off to the Syrian wet nurse.

Distracted by her mother, Isabella made no attempt to interfere with the nurse, asking instead, "What brings you to Acre? When you left after Christmas Uncle Balian" (as a child Isabella had picked up the habit of referring to her stepfather as "Uncle Balian") "said he didn't expect to be back until after the sowing was finished."

"True. We didn't expect an emergency."

"Emergency? What's happened? Have the rains caused flooding—"

Maria Zoë was shaking her head, "No, no. Shall we sit outside in the fresh air?" She indicated the courtyard bathed in morning sunshine.

Isabella slipped her arm through her mother's, and together they went out into the little courtyard. The sun was pouring in and the surrounding buildings protected it from the wind. They sat down on a plaster bench built against the wall, and Isabella looked expectantly at her mother. "Tell me! What is it?"

"Actually, you must already know," Maria Zoë started cautiously. Her relationship with Isabella was close, but it had also been stormy at times. There had been tense periods when Isabella had been rebellious and aggressive. "Your brother John rode all night to reach us."

"Oh!" Isabella gasped and drew back slightly, her face flushing. "You mean Aimery's arrest. Henri had to!" She defended her husband at once. "He can't risk him plotting against us for another hour! He promised me he would not put him in chains or anything like that, but he had to ensure Aimery could not communicate with his brother or the Pisans!"

Maria Zoë was relieved to hear that Isabella had at least extracted a promise of good treatment; that alone would mean a great deal to Eschiva. More important, it suggested that her daughter was not entirely indifferent to her best friend's husband. To her daughter she asked simply, "What is this all about, Isabella? You've known Aimery all your life. You know he's sacrificed the better part of *his* life for Jerusalem. How can you think he might have turned traitor now?"

"He's a Lusignan, Mama! And you know his brother has never stopped claiming the crown of Jerusalem. Guy did everything he could to prevent me obtaining what was rightfully mine. He even talked Humphrey into telling me I had no claim as long as he lived. And don't you remember how he tried to ingratiate himself with the Dowager Queen of Sicily, hoping to marry her? He's still looking for a new wife. If he marries again and has children, he will claim Jerusalem for them!" Isabella hardly stopped for breath as she fervently delivered this monologue.

Maria Zoë knew her daughter's passionate nature, and nodded before countering in a reasonable tone, "I don't doubt a word you're saying, Bella. Guy has been an intriguer, a seducer, and arrogantly blind to his own faults for as long as I've known him—which is more than a decade. But Aimery is not Guy—any more than you are Sibylla."

Isabella had always hated her older half-sister Sibylla, so the argument made her catch her breath and start biting her lower lip. Maria Zoë pressed her point. "I know Aimery backed Guy's usurpation six years ago, but he has lived to regret that a thousand times over. He's told me that himself, he's told your stepfather, and he's told your brother the same thing. I honestly do not think that he could be involved in any kind of plot against you or Henri, even *if*—as has not yet been proved—his brother is behind the Pisan pirates preying on our shipping."

Isabella was frowning and biting her lip in distress. "You're probably right, Mama. I *want* to believe you, for Eschiva's sake if nothing more, but arresting him was a precaution Henri *had* to take. If he's innocent, then I'm sure Henri will release him."

Maria Zoë took a deep breath and concluded this was probably the most she could hope to gain at the moment. Pressing Isabella too hard could easily trigger an angry rejection of "interference." It would have been easier to back off, however, if she hadn't spent the night with Eschiva and her children. Eschiva, usually so calm and self-possessed, had broken down and cried in Maria Zoë's arms. Eschiva had lived with Maria Zoë and Balian as a child, and the ties had never weakened. Maria Zoë loved Eschiva like one of her own daughters, and she knew how much Eschiva had suffered over the years—from Aimery's infidelities in his youth, from his captivity after Hattin and his absence at the siege of Acre, and more recently from the uncertainties of this last military campaign under the King of England. She and Aimery had only just started to rebuild their lives—and now this.

"That's really the best I can promise," Isabella spoke into Maria Zoë's thoughts, sounding faintly defiant already.

"I know, Bella," Maria Zoë chose tactical retreat. "That's all I ask." She smiled and kissed her firstborn on the forehead and then stood. "I must get back to Eschiva. She's understandably very distraught and frightened."

"You must assure her that no matter what comes to light about Aimery, she will always be a sister to me. I promise she'll never be made to suffer, even if Aimery is found to be a traitor."

"Ah, but sweetheart, if anything happens to Aimery she *will* suffer, because she loves him—not as you love Henri, nor indeed as I love your stepfather, but as a woman who has known no other husband since she was eight years old. Aimery is her life, Bella. If you take Aimery away, Eschiva will simply die." Maria Zoë patted her daughter's shoulder as if comforting her—but judging by Isabella's stricken face, her message had gone home.

Henri de Champagne, consort of Queen Isabella of Jerusalem, sometimes still felt as if he were a schoolboy who hadn't done his homework. He was not yet twenty-five, and he had not been raised to be a king. Furthermore, the laws of the Kingdom of Jerusalem were unique; he could not just apply his experience from home. He was completely dependent on the (not always patient) explanation of the customs and usages of his wife's kingdom provided by his bishops, barons, and counselors. Sometimes he wondered if everything they told him was absolutely true.

Take the custom of "restor," for example. Who had ever heard of such a thing? But the seneschal and chamberlain both insisted that it was the custom of the Kingdom of Jerusalem that the *king* was responsible for compensating knights and sergeants for horses lamed or killed in battle. This seemed a huge and unreasonable expense to Henri, who pointed out that in France a knight was responsible for supplying his own horses at his own expense.

"You are not in France," the Archbishop of Nazareth, his chancellor, reminded him in an unsympathetic voice.

"Obviously," Henri retorted, annoyed, "but this is quite unreasonable. A knight enjoys his fief and the profits thereof in exchange for owing service *with horse and squire*. If the king assumes the costs of the horse—"

"Only if it has been killed or lamed in his service," the chancellor corrected him.

"Yes, but that's when most horses are killed!" Henri protested. "You're talking about over fifty horses—Ah! Just the man I need!" Henri had caught sight of the Baron of Caymont in the doorway. "My lord of Ibelin" (everyone still called him Ibelin, even though the land that went with the title was in Saracen hands), "no one knows the laws of the Kingdom better than you, and as you're also an expert on horses, I'm sure you know this one doubly well. Tell me, is it true that the *King* of Jerusalem is responsible for compensating knights and sergeants for horses lost or irreparably injured in battle?"

Ibelin smiled faintly as he came deeper into the room. He bowed his head to the Count of Champagne before answering, "It is called 'restor,' my lord, and it is the law of the land—"

"But I've never heard anything like it," Champagne interrupted in protest.

"The spoils of war go to the King," Ibelin tried to explain, "including the countless Saracen horses we usually capture. I think you'll find that the drain on your treasury is bearable."

"Ah, but don't the Saracens ride mares?" Champagne asked, puzzled.

"They do, but not *only* mares, and sergeants can be compensated with mares or geldings."

"Hmm." Henri did not sound entirely convinced, but he was somewhat mollified, and stood scratching his head as he tried to come to terms with yet another curious custom. Then he started, realizing that Ibelin was supposed to be in Caymont. "What brings you to Acre, my lord? I thought you had planned to stay in Caymont until Easter?"

"I had planned to, yes. My son John, however, rode through the night to bring me word of the Constable's arrest."

"Oh!" Henri's face clouded, and a frown of annoyance crept over his features. Ibelin could almost see him regretting that he had not ordered John's arrest. Since it was too late for that, however, he went on the offensive instead, declaring indignantly, "The Constable's brother Guy has been inciting the Pisans to prey upon shipping bound for Acre. They've seized at least three ships that we know of, and this isn't just piracy! The Lusignan is trying to undermine my authority by proving I cannot protect my subjects, as well as denying me valuable revenue that I would otherwise have from the customs duties on the cargoes of the seized ships."

"That could well be," Ibelin agreed steadily with a glance at the other men in the room, one after another. The chancellor, seneschal, chamberlain, and viscount of Acre each looked away as if ashamed. He wondered which of them had advised Champagne to arrest the Constable. The Chancellor Archbishop of Nazareth should certainly have known better, he thought, looking again to the senior churchman, but Nazareth had barely escaped Saracen capture after

Hattin. The months he had endured in reputedly wild, dangerous, and terrifying circumstances until he finally reached Tripoli had left their mark on him. He was said to bear a bitter, almost ulcerous, grudge against Guy de Lusignan—which was one reason Champagne had selected him as his chancellor. The seneschal Ralph of Tiberius was the younger brother of the Prince of Galilee, and he was likewise an outspoken and bitter opponent of Lusignan. He was also very young, roughly Champagne's own age—which, Ibelin supposed, might have been a factor in his appointment: Champagne probably did not want to be surrounded by old men. That left the chamberlain and viscount. The former was one of Champagne's knights, a man who'd come out to Outremer with him—and was, Ibelin presumed, blindly loyal to his lord while equally ignorant of the laws of Jerusalem. The Viscount of Acre, on the other hand, was the elderly and highly respected Peter de Gibelet, a man with a long history as a juror and counselor of the law. He was well qualified to preside over the Court of the Bourgeoisie—but not the kind of man to challenge a king, even a young and inexperienced one.

"Then you approve of the arrest?" Champagne broke in on his thoughts.

"Of course not," Ibelin answered firmly, turning his attention back to Champagne. "Everything you said pertained to *Guy* de Lusignan; the man you arrested was *Aimery* de Lusignan. He is also the Constable of the Kingdom of Jerusalem."

"Blood is thicker than water, Ibelin. You know that. I cannot trust the brother of a man who is set upon my destruction!" Champagne balled his fist as he spoke, adding passionately, "You saw how Burgundy constantly undermined the authority of my uncle King Richard. I don't want to have to deal with the same situation—where the man who ought to be my deputy is actively working against me, trying to destroy me and humiliate me at every turn!"

Ibelin nodded, thankful for Champagne's candidness. He was beginning to comprehend, and said out loud in a reasonable tone, "I can understand that, my lord. May I sit?"

"Oh, I'm sorry!" Champagne was instantly contrite, ashamed of his bad manners. He gestured for Ibelin to take a seat at the table while sending a page to fetch water, wine, and nuts.

Once Ibelin had taken a place at the table, he looked again at the other men gathered around it. The Archbishop of Nazareth looked wary, the Chamberlain confused, the Viscount and Seneschal worried. Ibelin's eyes circled back to settle on Champagne. "My lord, I doubt any of us here would suggest that you be forced to depend upon a man you do not feel you can trust." This statement elicited vigorous nods from the Chamberlain, but the Chancellor still looked wary and the other two men puzzled. "However," Ibelin continued, "regardless of your personal trust—or lack thereof—in Aimery de Lusignan, he remains the Constable of the Kingdom. I would therefore like to know by what authority he was arrested." As he spoke, Ibelin looked directly at the most experienced jurist in the room. By the way Gibelet sucked in his breath, he was sure he'd hit a nerve.

"I arrested him on my own authority as King, of course," Champagne answered innocently and confidently.

Ibelin met his eyes and took his time answering, but when he did it was to declare bluntly: "You did not have that right."

"What do you mean?" Champagne bristled. "I may not have been anointed King, but—"

"This has nothing to do with being anointed. Even if you were, you would not have the right to arrest any member of the High Court on your own authority. Only the High Court can order the arrest of any member, and I know the High Court did no such thing, because I was not summoned."

The Viscount was nodding vigorously. "My lord of Ibelin is correct, my lord," Gibelet hastened to say. "I tried—"

"A King has executive authority! I can order the arrest of any of my subjects!" Champagne countered hotly.

"Not in Jerusalem," Ibelin answered without raising his voice. "Since the Kingdom was established under Baldwin I, the Kings of Jerusalem rule only with the consent of the High Court, and no member of the High Court can be arrested, sentenced, or deprived of his rights without a judgment of their peers."

Champagne looked to the Archbishop of Nazareth, frowning. "Is that true?"

Nazareth did not look pleased, but he admitted in a clipped voice, "It is."

"What that means," Ibelin continued, "is that if you doubt the Constable's loyalty to the Crown, then you must accuse him of treason before the High Court and let it—the High Court—rule on his guilt or innocence. The Constable has the right to defend himself before, and be judged by, his peers in the High Court."

Champagne looked again to the Archbishop, who shrugged and declared, "Ibelin is correct."

The Viscount jumped in more vigorously to explain. "All justice in the realm is based on judgment by one's peers, my lord. That's why we allow Syrian courts and even Muslim courts to operate, and why the Italian communes have their own courts, and why we have separate courts for commercial and maritime disputes."

Champagne felt slightly dizzy confronted by so many curious customs.

They all seemed alien to him, yet he was supposed to enforce them. He wanted to rebel, to say 'No, I am the King,' but he knew he could not. He was the interloper, the newcomer, tolerated more than loved. Worse, he owed his position in large part to his close ties to King Richard of England, but the mighty Lionheart had been treacherously seized by the duplicitous Duke of Austria on his way home from the Holy Land and was being held in a German jail, charged with a list of bogus "crimes." The news of this outrageous affront against a crusader and a fellow king had only arrived this past week with the first ships from the West. Henri was still reeling from it, and it made him less confident than he might otherwise have been. Last but not least, Henri was acutely aware that he owed both his wife and his crown to the man sitting opposite him: it had been Ibelin who had put his name forward as a suitable husband for the abruptly widowed Isabella. He'd been totally unprepared for the suggestion when it was first mooted and had halfway hoped his uncle King Richard would reject the proposal. When he hadn't, Henri had felt trapped—until Isabella had come to him.

Henri had been in love with Isabella since the first time he saw her during the siege of Acre, and when she stood before him as a widow eighteen months later, he'd been hopelessly enchanted. He wanted *Isabella* far more than he wanted the crown of Jerusalem! But one did not come without the other. And now he was in this absurd situation of being King but not being allowed to act like one!

"What do you expect me to do?" he demanded of Ibelin hotly. "Release a man who is plotting against me and let him continue to undermine my reign and to impoverish my subjects?"

"No—since we do not *know* Aimery de Lusignan is plotting against you. But, yes, I am asking you to release a man you *suspect* of treason long enough for the High Court to be summoned and for you to put your case against him before it."

"He might flee the country in the meantime!" Champagne protested.

"Then you will be rid of him, and he will be a threat to you no longer."

"Are you saying the King of Jerusalem does not have the right to punish a man who has committed treason?"

"Not at all. A man *found guilty* of treason *by the High Court* will be condemned and sentenced. If found guilty, the Constable will be deprived of his office, and banished from the Kingdom."

"If he is found guilty by the High Court?"

"Exactly, by his peers—or, should he so choose, in trial by combat."

Champagne looked again to the Archbishop of Nazareth as if hoping for a different answer, but the prelate, looking sour, admitted, "Ibelin is right, my lord. The Constable can only be condemned and sentenced by the High Court."

"Why didn't you tell me that when I ordered his arrest?" Champagne countered, feeling trapped.

"We tried," the Viscount spoke up; "you were not in the mood to listen."

Champagne glanced at the Seneschal and Chamberlain, but they were young men like himself and while loyal, they were in no position to oppose the three older men. Champagne threw up his hands. "Then I'll summon the High Court!" he decided.

"Before you do," Ibelin warned, "you would be wise to consider the fact that the Constable has many friends in the High Court. He has fought for the Kingdom four times as long as you have, my lord. Taking this allegation of treason before the High Court could divide the lords of the Kingdom. Are you sure you want to do that?"

"No!" Champagne lost his temper. "No, I don't want to do that, but I will not tolerate a traitor at the heart of government, either! The Constable is a senior official of the realm! He commands the army in the absence of the King. I cannot—will not—allow the brother of my worst enemy to hold that position a day longer than necessary!"

"He's right about that," Ralph of Tiberius spoke up for the first time, rushing his words slightly from nervousness. He was intimidated by Ibelin, who had confronted his stepfather the Count of Tripoli over his separate peace with Saladin, led the successful charge at Hattin, conducted an amazing defense of Jerusalem, and negotiated the Peace of Ramla. It took all his courage to speak up against him. "No one should be Constable who *might* have split loyalties. I mean, it's not a matter of whether we can *prove* Lord Aimery has committed treason. It is, as my lord of Champagne said at the start, a matter of *trust*."

Ibelin considered the young seneschal with sympathy and nodded. Then he turned back to Champagne. "If I could speak with the Constable and convince him to resign his office, would you let him go free?"

"Why should he resign? It is his only source of income, and his brother undoubtedly wants him in it so he can aid and abet him in his efforts to usurp my throne."

Ibelin waited until Champagne was finished and then repeated his question. "*If* he agrees to resign, will you let him go free?"

Champagne looked to the others for support, but they were all nodding. The Archbishop of Nazareth remarked sharply, "Ibelin is right. The Constable has more than one friend on the High Court. It will not be easy to get the Court to condemn him, no matter what evidence you bring. It would not be wise to risk your—" he cut himself off to seek the right word and finally settled upon "—credibility with the Court so early in your reign. It would be better to avoid a confrontation with your vassals. If my lord of Ibelin can convince the Constable to resign, it would be the best thing for the Kingdom—and for you."

Champagne's lips were clamped together, his cheeks flushed, but he had his emotions under firm control. He turned back to his wife's stepfather and nodded. "All right, my lord. See if you can talk reason to him, but make sure he knows I will summon the High Court if he doesn't go voluntarily. I will not have a man I *cannot* trust as Constable of the Kingdom."

Ibelin nodded and got to his feet. "Thank you, my lord. You will not regret this decision."

Aimery had seen worse dungeons. The first time he was taken captive by the Saracens he had been nothing but a young landless knight. The Saracens had rapidly assessed his ability to raise a ransom as marginal, and had tossed him into the pit with the other men just barely above the threshold for sale into immediate slavery. He was told he'd be given one year to raise his ransom, and was pointedly reminded that his father had died in Saracen captivity.

That pit had been windowless, foul, and overcrowded. They had shared it with rats, fleas, and lice. Food and water had been lowered to them once a day, and they had sometimes fought over it.

The second time he had been held in Saracen captivity, he had been placed in the large, cavernous cellars of the fortress at Aleppo with a dozen other lords captured at Hattin. Although this dungeon was equally windowless, the roominess had reduced the stench of the place, and the company of his fellow barons had been a comfort. Still, the knowledge that the Kingdom had been overrun and uncertainty about the future had gnawed at his sanity. It was the hope of returning to Eschiva and his children that had helped keep him sane.

But both times in the past he had been a prisoner of war, a man with some value in terms of ransom, and in no way guilty of any crime. This time he was accused of treason, and if the dungeon was not as filthy or fetid as the first dungeon, it was more ominous nevertheless. The chamber was windowless, no more than ten feet in diameter, and furnished with a straw pallet, a bucket as a privy, and chains. That he had not actually been put *into* the chains was a relief, yet their very presence was a reminder of what might yet come.

It did not help that he was utterly alone. There was no one to offer him comfort, much less hear his confession. As the time stretched out before him, unmeasured by the chiming of the hours or the waxing and waning of daylight, he started to imagine that he might never again see the light of day or hear the sound of a human voice. It had happened before. Men were simply locked away and left to starve to death. Or fed only enough food to keep them lingering for years, as their hair and nails grew and their strength, sight, and soul drained away.

Aimery knew himself well enough to know that he would lose his soul to bitterness without the aid of a priest. It had been a source of great comfort to have the Bishop of Lydda with them in the dungeon at Aleppo. Denied the means to read Mass, the churchman had nevertheless regularly heard their confessions and provided spiritual advice and comfort.

Nor did it help to picture the fate of a traitor's wife and children. No one would hurt them outright, of course, but Eschiva might well be pressured into a new marriage. With four young children, she could not afford the luxury of retiring to a convent. She would have to remarry in order to provide for them, but the children would bear the stigma of "traitor's spawn." The thought made Aimery cringe. Guy was just going on eleven, bright and fun-loving. He'd been a page to King Richard and loved being at the center of things. To find himself the unloved stepson of Eschiva's new husband would shatter him.

And all because of his brother Guy! Aimery had come to hate his brother—for losing the Battle of Hattin, for starting the siege of Acre, for bringing his wife and daughters to that siege where they had soon died, and most of all for—undeserving as he was—being given Cyprus by the King of England.

Aimery's love of Cyprus had started in 1191, when he'd gone to the island with his brothers Guy and Geoffrey. King Richard had been in the midst of conquering the island from the Greek tyrant Isaac Comnenus, after the latter had threatened his wife and bride and broken his word. The Lusignan brothers had been desperate for the King of England's support, because the King of France had declared his support for Conrad de Montferrat's claim to the throne of Jerusalem. As the liege lord of their eldest brother Hugh, the Lusignans believed Richard Plantagenet *owed* them his support. They could not understand why he was "tarrying."

Of course he wasn't. Richard had simply recognized that Cyprus was vital to the security of the Holy Land, because Cyprus sat astride the sea routes of the Eastern Mediterranean. As long as it was controlled by Franks, it could prevent Saracen fleets from attacking the remaining Christian ports of Tripoli and Tyre. Strategically, it was also an ideal staging ground for launching new attacks on the Saracens, including a campaign against Cairo as a means of forcing the surrender of Jerusalem. Richard the Lionheart had taken control of Cyprus in just one month. He'd chased away the Greek usurper, had taken oaths of fealty from the local nobles, and then had sold the island to the Templars, thinking they would ensure the island remained a bulwark against the Saracens. Richard of England had never seen in Cyprus what Aimery had seen: an island of almost idyllic beauty from its snow-capped mountains to its palm-lined shores, a source of security not in the strategic sense, but economically and emotionally.

After fighting almost two decades in Outremer, Aimery was ready to "settle down." He wanted land he could call his own, land he could cultivate, land he could bequeath. He wanted to sink down roots and leave a legacy. He wanted to plant olive orchards that would still be here at the next millennium. He wanted to build a house for his growing family that would shelter his descendants for generations. It didn't seem such an ambitious dream to him, but it was elusive. Or rather, unrealistic. With the Kingdom of Jerusalem reduced to a quarter of what it had once been, there simply wasn't enough land to go around. Great lords like Tiberius had nothing, let alone men like himself, who had never had claim to a barony.

Cyprus, however, was fertile and sparsely populated. It offered him opportunity—if only it weren't ruled by the brother he had come to hate. And worst of all, Guy didn't even want it. He still coveted the crown he'd lost: Jerusalem. It was madness.

Now this. He was imprisoned for allegedly supporting the brother he detested in his brother's stupid quest for Jerusalem, which he opposed! Guy knew better than to ask Aimery for anything—much less support for his moribund claim to Jerusalem. Guy would make the best witness for the defense, but no one was likely to let Guy testify—even if there was a trial. It would be so much easier to just let him rot here . . .

And then the key turned in the lock and Aimery sprang to his feet. He was a bundle of nerves, and he found himself facing the door, every muscle so taut he was almost trembling with anticipation. Had they come to slit his throat or simply bring him a meal?

The door was massive, braced, and studded with iron. It swung open only slowly and with a creak. The man who entered had to duck under the door frame, but even before he straightened to his full height, Aimery recognized him and cried out in relief. "Balian!"

"John brought us word immediately," Balian answered, pulling a loaf of bread and a jug of wine out from under his cloak. "I brought these along as well, in case you needed something fortifying."

"Is the news that bad?" Aimery asked at once, tensing again.

"Not at all. I just finished giving Henri de Champagne a lesson in the laws of the land, pointing out that he had no right to arrest you. I have received his assurance—in the presence of the chancellor, chamberlain, seneschal, and viscount of Acre—that he will release you, on one condition."

"What condition?" Aimery asked, wary at once.

"That you resign the office of Constable. The crux of the matter is that Champagne doesn't trust you and doesn't want a man he doesn't trust as his deputy. He's traumatized by the image of what Burgundy did to King Richard. I can't say I blame him. In the circumstances, it doesn't make any difference if you're guilty or not: if he doesn't trust you, he doesn't trust you. Shall we sit while we discuss this?" Ibelin gestured toward the straw pallet.

Aimery nodded absently and sank down onto the crude bed. Ibelin handed him a pottery mug that he'd stashed in an inside pocket of his cloak, and then removed the cork closing the jug to pour wine for Aimery. It was strong red wine, and Aimery swallowed it gratefully. Only after he'd had a few sips did he look hard at Ibelin and ask, "What are you suggesting? That I resign as if I were guilty? And then what? Go beg in the streets?"

"Hardly. You know perfectly well my lady and I will make you and your family welcome at Caymont—such as it is. I can certainly use another pair of hands to dig irrigation ditches!" Ibelin laughed dryly at his own joke. Aimery did not.

They looked at one another.

"We're not the brave young knights we once were, are we?" Ibelin remarked, remembering their youth, when both had been landless knights seeking their fortune at the vibrant court of King Amalric of Jerusalem. Then the Kingdom had stretched far beyond the Jordan . . .

"Is that my only choice? Resign and live on charity or rot here?"

"No. You can defend yourself before the High Court of Jerusalem. You have many friends there—and, unlike Champagne, they've known you for decades. You stand a good chance in the High Court." He paused before adding, "Then again, many on the High Court hate your brother. If you lose, you'll be banned from the Kingdom, such as *it* is. Or, you could choose trial by combat and put your future and that of your family in the hands of God."

Aimery tipped the mug up and drank in deep gulps, then held the mug out to Ibelin for more. He was beginning to understand how this man had managed to extract concessions from the victorious Saladin in impossible situations. He certainly had a way of making you see the risks of any decision! "What does Eschiva want me to do?"

"I haven't asked her. I came straight here."

"And your lady?"

"The same. I haven't had a chance to talk to her, but she did go to her daughter to plead your case. I daresay she will have succeeded in making Isabella feel guilty."

Aimery's lips turned up in acknowledgment of the debt he owed the Dowager Queen. Out loud he confined himself to remarking, "Indeed, she can be very persuasive." He paused and then remarked with a deep sigh, "I gather you think I should take this offer to resign?"

"I do. I don't want your case to come before the High Court, because it will tear the Kingdom apart, and we've just barely patched it back together again. Champagne's rule is far too fragile as it is. And it *certainly* doesn't help that the King of England is rotting in a German jail. No one is going to come to our aid if al-Afdal, hothead that he is, decides to break his father's truce. We're entirely on our own, and our resources are tiny. The only thing that keeps me from despair is Cyprus."

"Cyprus," Aimery echoed wistfully.

"Yes. It's rich enough to feed us, close enough to receive us, and it could be a source of men and materiel, too—if it were in the hands of a good lord."

"Meaning my brother is not?"

"Is he?"

"God help us all!" Aimery threw up his hands.

"Amen. But assuming the Lord helps those who help themselves, then the first step might be for *you* to go to Cyprus."

"Are you crazy? Guy told me flat-out he didn't need my help and he didn't want it!"

"That was before Geoffrey gave up on him and sailed back for France," Ibelin pointed out.

Aimery thought about that. There was something to it. Their older brother Geoffrey had been pulling Guy's strings ever since he came out to Outremer in 1188. While he didn't share Aimery's resentment of Guy, he had shared his assessment of him. Geoffrey had counted on Guy being fully restored to his kingdom and so receiving from him the rich county of Jaffa and Ascalon for himself. When King Richard recognized first Montferrat and then Champagne as the rightful King of Jerusalem, and—worse still—bartered away Ascalon in the Treaty of Ramla, Geoffrey had lost interest in the Holy Land altogether. He'd gone with Guy to Cyprus the previous fall, only to sail for France this spring. Guy was now alone on Cyprus with only a handful of followers.

"It's worth a try," Ibelin prodded.

If only you knew how you are tempting me, Aimery thought, his memories of Cyprus starting to banish the walls of his prison. And why shouldn't he give in to this temptation? What did he have to lose? His position as Constable was precarious at best and deadly at worst. Champagne would almost certainly find a new excuse to imprison him—assuming he could even talk himself out of the charges he'd already leveled.

"Eschiva and the children can stay with us, of course," Ibelin sweetened the lure even more.

Aimery knew that the happiest years of Eschiva's life had been when she lived with Balian and Maria. Caymont wasn't Ibelin, of course, but she'd be with people she loved and trusted. The children would be in the countryside where they could grow up in the fresh air, riding, swimming, and climbing trees with their cousins. And maybe, just maybe, he could talk his brother into giving him that slice of Cyprus that he so desperately coveted. Outwardly he shrugged to disguise his inner excitement. "You're right. It's worth a try."

Ibelin's face broke into a smile, and then he flung his arms around the prisoner. They hugged each other in mutual relief before Ibelin got to his feet and pulled a still somewhat benumbed Aimery up after him.

Aimery was feeling slightly manipulated, yet comforted himself with the thought that he was in good company. Ibelin was the man who had reconciled Tripoli with Lusignan, obtained terms for a city already conquered, and secured a kingdom already lost. What chance had he against the Great Negotiator?

Meanwhile Ibelin pounded on the door with his fist and demanded, "Open the door! The Constable has resigned!"

"Please, my lord," John pleaded earnestly with his father. He was dressed in his chain-mail hauberk and straining to look as mature as possible. "I want to go with Lord Aimery. It's my place. As his squire."

Balian frowned. Watching his eldest son grow into a resourceful, responsible, and yet optimistic young man was one of his greatest joys. He did not like being separated from John at all, but up to now he'd been in Acre, only a few hours away. Balian had been able to visit him, or call him home, on short notice. Cyprus was different. Cyprus was across the water, a strange and unfamiliar place. He knew Aimery would do his best to look out for John, but ultimately they were both at the mercy of Guy de Lusignan—the last man on earth Balian trusted.

"Has Lord Aimery asked you to go with him?" Balian growled, preparing to give the former Constable a piece of his mind.

"No, he didn't. He told me I was released from his service, but I—I told him I wanted to go with him." John stumbled a little over his words.

Balian knew his son well, and by his reaction quickly guessed he had already pledged himself to Aimery. "Did you give him your word?"

John swallowed guiltily, but stood his ground. "Yes, my lord."

"You had no right to do that without my permission," Balian reminded his son sharply.

"My lord—Papa—Lord Aimery's completely alone! You know how much Guy hates him. He's as likely to throw Lord Aimery out of his court as Champagne did—"

"Yes, exactly, so what good will *you* being there do?" Balian retorted dismissively.

To his father's astonishment, John had a ready answer. Meeting his father's eye, John declared firmly, "I can make sure his armor glistens and his spurs gleam and ensure that no one can sneer at him for a beggar. I can show him the respect he deserves, and in so doing shame them. Most of all, I can remind them of where you stand, my lord. I can remind them that the Lord of Ibelin holds Aimery de Lusignan in greater honor than either claimant to the crown of Jerusalem."

Balian caught his breath and held it. When he let it out it was with a sense of rueful respect. "If you don't master the sword and lance, John, you can make your living in the courts."

"Does that mean I can go with Lord Aimery?" John jumped at the unspoken shift in his father's stance.

"Yes, damn it. It means you may go with him, but don't think I can't come after you! If I have any reason to think you're not safe, not keeping good company, or not remembering your duty to God, I will haul you back to Caymont and make you dig irrigation ditches with me!"

John broke into a smile of relief and excitement. He flung his arms around his father with a heartfelt, "Thank you, father! You won't regret this! Wait and see—Lord Aimery plans to demand land from his brother, and when he does, he'll reward me, too. We'll have something for Philip and a dowry for Margaret. I promise you, Father, I'll make our family richer and stronger!"

Balian shook his head at so much youthful optimism and enthusiasm, but held his son tight for a moment before stepping back with sigh of resignation and capitulation to warn, "You're very young, John. You have a lot to learn, and not all of what you need to learn will be pleasant. Whatever happens, remember who you are: that the blood of the Eastern Roman Emperors runs in your veins."

John sobered immediately and looked at his father squarely and earnestly.

"I won't forget that; but even more, I won't forget that I am the son of Balian d'Ibelin, the man who saved the *people* of Jerusalem."

The unexpected blow almost felled his father. He could only defend himself by embracing his son a second time in gratitude and pride.

Chapter Three
Encounters in Seaside Taverns

Caesarea, Kingdom of Jerusalem
April 1193

THE WIND WAS HOWLING AROUND THE corners of the stone buildings crowding the little harbor. It chased anything not tied down along the streets and rattled the shutters of the warehouses and taverns. Waves crashed against the sea wall, sending spumes twenty feet into the air before the water cascaded down in tatters on the glistening surface of the massive stones. The ships huddling in the shelter of the harbor were tossed about on the swells, their masts rolling from side to side and their rigging banging incessantly. The galley captain had been right when he'd refused to sail yesterday, John registered to himself. At the time, Lord Aimery and he had been extremely annoyed (and the former a little insulting) about the captain's refusal to put to sea. Now that Lord Aimery had taken leave of his family, he was anxious to quit the Kingdom. By the look of the weather, however, it might be two or three days before the wind let up and the seas settled.

Unfortunately, the Lord of Caesarea, a friend and supporter whose hospitality they had counted on, was unexpectedly absent. They'd been forced to rent a room at a tavern near the Cathedral of St. Paul. This had seemed a final insult to Lord Aimery, and he had retreated into the room in a bad mood. John could understand how he felt, but he couldn't stand being cooped up in the small, stuffy room with a brooding Lord Aimery, either. With the excuse of "checking on the horses," he had extricated himself. The horses, however, had been fine, contentedly nibbling at their hay nets, so he had decided to take a walk along the harbor front. He was enjoying the spectacle of the waves shattering on the outer wall built by the Romans. Each wave flung up fountains of glistening water that caught the sunlight. It wasn't cold, although a bank of clouds hung over the Western horizon, threatening rain by nightfall.

The waterfront was all but deserted. The ships were battened down to withstand the storm, and both loading and offloading were too difficult with the swells bashing vessels against the sides of the quay. Only at one of the many taverns had a couple of tables been set up in the lee of a large warehouse. John decided to pause for a glass of ale and a bite to eat. (John was always hungry, but Lord Aimery had largely lost his appetite since leaving his family behind.) Only one other customer, an old salt staring morosely into his pottery mug, was braving the wind. John chose a table with a good view of the harbor and settled himself.

His father had given him a purse of coins so he would not be entirely dependent on Lord Aimery. His father had stressed that he should always have the cost of the passage home tucked safely away "just in case." John had conscientiously sewn this sum and a little more (to cover meals and such) inside one of his boots. Even so, there still seemed to be a lot of copper and silver coins weighing down his purse. He felt an "obligation" to lighten the load a little.

The fact was, this was the first time in his life that he'd ever had his own purse and the right to spend money as he pleased. Not that John had any intention of wasting his money "foolishly," but it made him feel "grown up" to sit down at a table, signal the proprietor over, and ask what he had to offer.

"Fish soup, pig's feet, and cabbage stuffed with rice and cheese," the Syrian proprietor answered, eyeing John suspiciously. He might be tall for his age, but he had no need to shave, his limbs were thin, and his chest hadn't filled out. He looked like the teenager he was.

"I'll take the pig's feet and your best ale," John answered with a shrug, to imitate nonchalance and familiarity with something that was actually novel.

"If you can't pay, boy, I'll haul you inside by your big ears and make you work off the price of the meal in the kitchen," the proprietor warned gruffly.

"I can pay," John answered indignantly.

The proprietor huffed off, and John returned to watching the entertainment offered by the waves and the boats in the harbor until a big dog with a thick coat of shaggy brown hair came around the corner from the nearest alleyway and stopped to stare at him. John had always wanted a dog, but after they were driven out of Ibelin and had to live in cramped quarters, his mother firmly prohibited dogs from the house. He'd tried to befriend some strays, but they all disappeared somehow. This dog immediately captured John's sympathy, because the wind was blowing hard enough to reveal his scrawny skeleton underneath his fur. Furthermore, he looked at John with large, intelligent eyes. After a glance over his shoulder, he padded forward to sit three feet away from John. From here he watched John solemnly—until the proprietor arrived with a dripping bowl, a wooden spoon, and the mug of ale. Immediately the dog ran a dozen feet away before stopping to look over his shoulder. No sooner was the proprietor gone than the dog returned. Reading John's mood correctly, he now risked coming closer, his ears half cocked, his nose lifted, and his tail swaying slowly from side to side, hopeful but wary.

John reached into his bowl of stewed pig's feet, removed one, and tossed it to the dog. With practiced ease the dog snatched the morsel in his teeth, but rather than gulping it down and waiting for more, he darted with his prize around the corner to the alley. John was sorry to think people had made him so afraid. But he soon returned, and since the pig's feet weren't very good, John shared another one and then two. Each time, the dog disappeared around the corner to eat.

Having given most of his meal away to the dog, John was still hungry when he'd finished, so he ordered a loaf of bread and sausage. The proprietor put his hands on his hips and looked down at him. "You'll have to clean pots for two days to work that off!" he warned.

John indignantly showed the proprietor his purse to prove he could pay, and the man shrugged and retreated. Too late, John noticed that the man at the next table had also seen him show his purse, and he started to feel a little nervous. He'd been so absorbed in the dog that he'd failed to notice that the establishments around him were starting to come to life as the sun went down. The tables were filling up.

To distract himself from his own foolishness, John looked for the dog again. He was waiting as before, watching with big solemn eyes what John would do next. John patted the side of his thigh. "Come here, boy!"

The dog took a step closer, and then another, but then lost his courage. A moment later the landlord returned with John's second order and the dog retreated in guilty haste. As soon as the latter was gone, John tore off the end of the loaf of bread and tossed it to the dog. The dog at once disappeared around the corner, only to return shortly. John cut off a piece of sausage and held it out to the dog, trying to get him to come closer. He stepped nearer, his ears lifted and his tail thrashing the air, but he could not actually eat from John's hand. John gave up and threw it to him, and again he disappeared with it.

By now all the tables were full, and the men at them were starting to make John feel uncomfortable. John didn't like the looks the women were giving him, either; they were both patronizing and predatory. But the men were worse. John saw or imagined that some of them were eyeing him like "easy pickings." When he noticed the man who had watched him show his purse to the proprietor elbow the man beside him, he put his hand to his hilt. This only made a man with an ugly scar on his neck and a mouth full of broken teeth smirk at him condescendingly; his expression implied contempt for both John's sword and his ability to wield it.

It was time to get out of here, John concluded, shivering as the first drops of rain sprinkled from the now overcast sky. He called for his bill, paid off the proprietor with an (unintentionally excessive) tip, and rose to return to his lodgings. To avoid the clientele on the dockside, he decided to return through the town, and so turned into the same alley where the dog had always disappeared. Almost at once he tripped and nearly fell headlong over a man wrapped in a blanket.

The dog was beside him and jumped up with a defensive bark, followed by a hopeful wagging of his tail as he recognized John. John found himself looking down into the face of a skeletal man. Although his hand was completely covered by the blanket he was clutching around himself, it still held the half loaf of bread John had given the dog. The dog had been feeding *him*, John registered in amazement. Embarrassed by the whole situation, John turned and hastened back the way he'd come.

Lord Aimery had already gone to bed when John returned, and only grunted something about it taking "rather long to look after the horses." John apologized, admitted he'd stopped for something to eat, and offered to fetch something for his lord. Lord Aimery said he wasn't hungry and turned his back on John.

John undressed himself and got into the other side of bed, but he couldn't sleep. As the rain grew heavy and splattered against the shutters of the rented room, he pictured the man in the alley clutching at his wet dog for warmth. Why had he run away? The man was obviously harmless. Indeed, the very loyalty of the dog suggested he was kind to it. John shuddered at the thought of sleeping in the alley on a night like this. But why did the old man do it? Why didn't he seek out the hospice of St. John?

John's guilt was increasing. His father had sacrificed his entire inheritance, including the lovely and rich barony of Ibelin, to secure the release of twenty thousand Christians from Saracen slavery. His father said they had no right to a barony when so many Christians did not own even their bodies. Yet there were so many of them, and none of them had money, land, or jobs. John was certain that the man in the alley was a returned captive. Unable to sleep, he resolved to return the following morning to bring the man a loaf of bread and a round of cheese—unless the winds died down and they could sail, of course.

The next morning, the wind was stronger than ever and laced with showers. John bought a loaf of bread and cheese and returned to the alley beside the harbor-side tavern. When he came around the corner (half hoping there would be no one there), he found the man rolled against the wall, completely covered by his filthy and ragged blanket.

At the sight of John, the dog sprang to his feet and started howling piteously. It wasn't the defensive barking of the day before, but a mournful wailing that made the hair stand up on the back of John's neck. The man beside him didn't move.

"Hello!" John called out, instinctively keeping his distance. "Hello! I've brought you bread and cheese, but you really ought to go to the brothers of St. John."

The man under the blanket didn't stir.

"Christ!" John muttered to himself. His instincts were screaming, "Run away," but that would be cowardly, and Ibelins were not cowards. "Hello! Wake up!" he called louder still, with the same response: none at all.

Swallowing down his revulsion, John took a step nearer, and with the toe of his boot he nudged the man in the back. The slight jostling made him roll away from the wall and sprawl out at John's feet. The hand that had been clutching the blanket flopped down, opening the blanket to reveal the man more clearly. John gasped in horror. The man was a leper! And he was very clearly dead.

Crossing himself fervently, John said a prayer for the dead man's soul, and turned to flee. He should have told the brothers of St. John about the man yesterday, he admonished himself. They would have taken him to the brothers of St. Lazarus. Maybe if he'd spent the night in the leprosarium he could have survived. "Forgive me, Father," he muttered to himself in guilt. "Forgive me, Father, I didn't know. . . ." But he could have looked harder, or asked, or just gone to the good brothers, his conscience said.

John fled from his crime of negligence—only to be stopped in his tracks by the howling of the dog. Poor thing. He'd just lost his master, John registered, and he stopped and looked back. The dog stopped howling and looked at him with big, mournful eyes. "Do you want to come with me, boy?" he asked the dog.

The dog looked back sadly.

"Here." John held out the loaf of bread. "It's all for you, now," he told the dog.

The dog looked at the bread, up at his face, back at the bread, up at his face. But he didn't move.

"You'll have to come and get it. I won't bring it to you," John told him.

The dog took a step forward, then stopped to look back at the corpse. His chest was heaving as if the parting hurt him physically. John broke down. He crossed the distance to the dog, went down on one knee beside him and, stroking his head, gave him the loaf of bread. The dog took it in his teeth, only to drop it on the ground. Again he looked over his shoulder at his dead master, and then up at John again.

"If you come with me, boy, I'll take care of you." *If Lord Aimery lets me,* John added under his breath. "But first we'll go to the brothers of St. Lazarus, and pay them to bury your master and say a Mass for him." The thought made John feel better, and getting back to his feet he set off in the direction of the leprosarium—with frequent checks to be sure the dog was trailing him.

At the leprosarium John rang the bell, and informed the lay brother who answered that he had seen the corpse of a leper lying in an alley by the quay. The man, himself a leper, nodded, "That'll be old Oliver! We warned him he'd end like this—but, no, he was too good to live with the likes of us! Old ornery bastard! Don't worry about him, boy. We'll collect his rotten bones and see they get underground." Then he held out the palm of his fingerless hand for alms.

John dutifully pulled out his purse and dropped a dinar into the leper's palm with a sense of relief for having done his Christian duty. But as he went to put the purse away again he also noticed how much lighter it felt than the day before. Had he really gone through most of his coins already?

The chiming of the church bells ringing terce made him realize he was long overdue at his lodgings. He'd told Lord Aimery he was just nipping out for breakfast. As he hastened across town with the dog still trailing him, he started to prepare his arguments for keeping the dog. When he reached their lodgings, rather than plunging inside, he stopped and patted the side of his leg. "Come here, boy."

The dog hesitantly came nearer, then stopped with wary looks at his surroundings.

John returned the half-dozen steps to the dog and went down on one knee to scratch him behind his ears. The dog closed his eyes in contentment. John explained, "I'm going to ask Lord Aimery if I can keep you, but you'll have to wait for me here."

The dog gazed at him solemnly.

John got back to his feet, but before turning to go inside he bent to pet the dog one more time. "One way or the other, I'll be back and see that you get a decent meal. I promise."

The dog finally wagged his tail a couple of times, as if hope of some kind was returning.

"John!" The voice of Lord Aimery from the window overhead made John jump. Aimery had opened the shutter and was looking down into the street. "Just bring the cur in with you!"

"My lord?"

"Bring the shaggy mutt inside so we can wash the fleas out of his hair before we go aboard ship."

"You mean I can keep him?" John asked hopefully.

"Why not? He reminds me of the flea-bitten mongrel I had at your age."

The smile that broke out on John's face brightened the day for Aimery. It was going to be just the two of them for an indefinite period to come, and Aimery was determined to ensure John had no reason to regret his decision to come to Cyprus. Besides, John was his best means of ensuring Ibelin's support in the future.

Lord Aimery insisted on calling the dog "Barry" in honor of his father-in-law and John's uncle, the Baron of Ramla and Mirabel. John wasn't entirely sure that was a compliment to either of them—but then, Lord Aimery's relationship with his wife's father had often been strained. John's own memories of his uncle were few, and were overshadowed by his uncle's dramatic decision to go into self-imposed exile rather than take an oath of fealty to Guy de Lusignan. The entire Kingdom had been amazed by such a dramatic gesture of contempt for the usurper, and John's father stressed the nobility of putting one's principles ahead of one's interests. John's mother, on the other hand, noted that compromise was the essence of politics, and suggested that the good of the Kingdom sometimes had to come ahead of one's personal feelings. Either way, John could not remember his uncle ever smiling, so the name in some ways fit the melancholy dog. Still, John couldn't help but wonder if it wasn't the idea of giving commands to "Barry" that made Lord Aimery name the dog after his father-in-law.

Of course, it didn't matter to John as long as Barry was accepted into their little traveling party of two humans, four horses (two for Lord Aimery, Centurion, and their packhorse) and, now, a dog. The galley captain made no objection to Barry, simply confining him below deck with the horses, and they set sail shortly after sunrise on Palm Sunday.

John and Lord Aimery stood on the stern watching the land recede until there was nothing to see, not even the spires of the churches. John was acutely conscious that he had left his homeland for the first time in his life, and it frightened him a little. Some evil voice was whispering, "You might never see it again, or your father or mother or brother and sisters. . . ."

For Lord Aimery, on the other hand, the severing of ties seemed to have a liberating effect. He took a deep breath of sea air, then looked down at John with a slight smile on his face and declared: "Well, lad, we're committed now. Let's go up to the bow and look forward rather than back."

Together they made their way across the waist of the ship, which was increasingly pitching and rolling as they headed into more open waters, and pulled themselves up by the ladders onto the forepeak. Here spume from the waves breaking on the bow made the planking wet, and now and again a wave broke in greater force, splattering water, but Lord Aimery just laughed and took a firm hold on the railing.

"Cyprus," he told John, "is the closest thing to Paradise on earth. It's fertile, gets plenty of rain, and has massive forests full of game. You can grow anything on Cyprus—olives, wine, wheat and barley, citrus trees and sugar cane." That sounded no different than home to John, but he just nodded, happy to see Lord Aimery's spirits picking up.

As the wind got colder, however, they retreated to the shelter of the main deck and accepted an invitation from the captain to join him for the midday meal. The captain of this vessel was Venetian. He was a wiry, darkly tanned man with a neatly trimmed beard already flecked with grey. His eyes sat deep in their sockets and seemed almost permanently focused on the horizon, shunning eye contact with humans. He was taciturn, which had suited Aimery well enough up to now, because he was traveling incognito and had not wanted any questions asked. Now he was in the mood for talking, and he sought to draw the man out more.

"Tell us of affairs on Cyprus," he urged.

The Captain raised his eyebrows. "I thought you knew."

"I have not been there for about a year."

The Venetian remarked rather grimly, "Much has happened since."

"Are you from Cyprus?" Lord Aimery asked next.

"Me? I was born in Constantinople. My brothers and I were one of the few crews that managed to escape impoundment by the Emperor Manuel when he treacherously imprisoned the entire Venetian commune and confiscated our property! My father was not so lucky. He was arrested on his way down to the harbor, and is still in a dungeon in Constantinople—for nothing! For simply being a Latin!" the Venetian spat out furiously, and Aimery thought he was beginning to understand his dour temperament. The man was being eaten from the inside by hate and guilt.

"But the Emperor Manuel was friendly to the Kingdom of Jerusalem," John burst out, forgetting his place in his eagerness to defend his mother's great-uncle.

"Friendly? When he wanted to be!" the Venetian snarled back.

"He sent his nieces to marry our kings, and he married his only son to the Princess of Antioch," John reminded him, with a glance at Lord Aimery requesting both forgiveness and permission for speaking up. The latter gave both with a shrug.

"A lot of good that did!" the Venetian retorted. "She only made the mob hate us Latins more. When they turned on the Genoans and Pisans, they didn't just arrest them as Manuel did us: they tortured and slaughtered them." There was, Aimery thought, almost satisfaction in the Venetian's voice as he reported the fate of the men from rival city-states who had sought to profit from Venetian misfortune.

"You can't trust the Greeks," the Venetian added. "They lie and cheat and stab you in the back at the first opportunity. They do that even with their own— look how Andronicus killed his nephew Alexius, and then the mob tore him to pieces, and put Isaac Angelus in his place—a nobody and a coward."

John had heard this from his mother, too, and nodded.

"But they'll do it first and foremost to any Latin. Take my word for it, they hate us all, and they will cheat us any way they can. Richard of England did Christendom a favor when he seized Cyprus from the Greeks." The captain continued, "But then the Templars took over," the captain complained, adding viperously: "A covetous and bigoted Order!"

John had been raised to respect the Knights Templar. His father had frequently praised their discipline on the battlefield and their piety. "What do you mean?" he challenged the captain, with a quick look at his lord to be sure he was still going to be allowed to speak up.

"The Templars are bankers first and knights second, believe me! They are more interested in amassing wealth than in fighting for the Holy Land!"

Worlds were clashing—the mercantile world of the Venetians with the chivalric world of Aimery and John—and both the latter looked shocked. This time John did not need to speak, because Aimery himself hastened to defend the Templars. "You speak out of place, Captain. I have seen how selflessly the Templars fight—at Hattin and Arsuf. More: I saw the survivors of Hattin cruelly and brutally executed by Muslim Sufis after the Battle. They were brave and pious men!"

"Oh, the sheep for the slaughter may be brave and selfless enough, but their leaders are more grasping than the Pope himself!" His passengers only looked more offended at this remark, so the Captain dismissed them as naive and stupid, remarking disdainfully, "Well, don't take my word for it; but if you plan to spend any time on Cyprus, you'll have the pleasure of reaping the consequences of Templar greed. They tried to tax too many and too much, and the people rose up in rebellion. You'll see. Taxation and the persecution of the Orthodox Church have turned all Cypriots into our enemies. Never meddle with a man's faith, if you want to live at peace with him," the captain advised; he downed the rest of his wine standing before pounding up the ladder and back on deck.

Their ship put in at the small fishing port of Famagusta.** Lord Aimery would have preferred to land at Limassol. As the main port on the south coast of the island, Limassol had a cathedral and a royal castle, where they could have requested hospitality. Their captain, however, flatly refused to sail on, pointing out, "You paid for passage to Cyprus and didn't quibble about which port when we struck the price." Aimery now was beginning to suspect the captain of smuggling, and that he wanted to avoid ports at which customs officials could be expected—but Aimery was in no position to challenge the Venetian, so they disembarked at Famagusta.

The town appeared poor and rundown. There were no more than a half-dozen churches, all Greek Orthodox, a small marketplace surrounded by shops under an arcade, and a collection of narrow whitewashed houses with flat roofs. There were only two inns offering rooms, neither of which looked free of fleas—but it was rapidly getting dark by the time Aimery and John offloaded their goods and horses, and they could not ride in the dark on unfamiliar roads to a place they had never been.

They agreed on the least disreputable-looking of the two inns, put the horses in the pathetic shed that was identified as the "stables," and then settled

---

** The place names used throughout the book are the currently familiar names instead of the historical names used in the period. The point is to tell the reader the location of action, not demonstrate the quality of my research by using contemporary designations that mean nothing to anyone but scholars.

into the tavern for wine and a meal, with Barry clinging unhappily to their heels. There were only four tables in the entire tavern, and none were taken when they first sat down.

Before their meal was dumped in front of them by a slovenly and resentful landlord, all the other tables had been occupied—and served. That they were kept waiting so long while the others were served first was obviously intentional and insulting, but the alternative was not to eat, so Aimery kept his temper in check. He did, however, feel bad that John's first impression of Cyprus was so poor.

John, on the other hand, was far less disappointed than Aimery suspected. The very rundown, seedy character of the town suggested "adventure" to John, who shared his lord's suspicions about their captain. John had convinced himself the Venetian was really a former pirate now engaged in smuggling. Which meant he was now in a smugglers' den, John reasoned. Furthermore, being surrounded by people speaking Greek underlined the fact that they had left the familiar behind.

John had learned Greek in the schoolroom from a Greek priest who had accompanied his mother as a bride to the Court of Jerusalem. Father Angelus had been one of John's two tutors and responsible for both the language and the history of the Greeks, as well as mathematics and geometry. John had practiced Greek with his mother now and again because it pleased her, but he had never been terribly enthusiastic about the language. Now, as his ears began to separate words from the flood of sounds, he found himself straining to understand more.

"Please" and "thank you," "another," "more," "wine," "good," and the like were easily understood, but while Lord Aimery slipped again into his thoughts, John started to pick up whole phrases. "Who do you think they are?"

"Franks; that's enough for me."

John caught his breath and tried to look over at the men talking about them without being obvious about it. Pretending to look for the proprietor, he let his eyes slide over the men at the table to the right. They looked like farmers to him, except for a young Orthodox monk with a thick black beard under a wide nose. John didn't dare let his eyes linger. Finding the proprietor, he signaled and called for more wine—in French. Instinctively he shied away from using Greek, both because he didn't trust his knowledge of the language entirely and because some part of his brain suggested it might be better if the others didn't know he understood them.

"The one's a knight," the conversation continued.

"Another [something John didn't understand] looking to [incomprehensible] us dry."

The proprietor brought the wine jug and then turned his back to serve the table on the right.

"Yes, yes," John heard the proprietor say. "They're staying here. I put them in the back room over the latrines."

Laughter answered him.

John felt something creep up his spine. "I don't think they like us here," he remarked to Lord Aimery, reaching down to pet Barry as he spoke. The dog's presence at his feet was somehow reassuring.

"What?" Aimery had been deep in an imaginary conversation with his brother Guy.

"I don't think they like us here."

Aimery looked around and shrugged. "What makes you think that? They'll like our money well enough. I'm tired. Let's go to our room. You can bring the wine with you if you like."

John would have preferred to stay and see what more he could understand, but he was in service and his lord wanted to go to bed. He took the wine and both their pottery mugs and followed Lord Aimery to the chamber they had been given. Barry, John noted, slunk behind them with his belly so close to the floor he collected dirt on his belly hairs, and his tail hung limply. John smiled reassurance at him, but Barry answered by looking up with questioning eyes. Barry didn't like it here either, John concluded.

The room they had been given had a low ceiling dark with grime, a box bed with straw covered by a blanket, and a window closed by partially broken shutters. The window overlooked the shed that housed the latrines, and the broken shutters let in the stench.

Aimery swore and kicked out at the bed. "Shit house!"

"I'll go ask for another room," John volunteered, and without waiting for an answer, turned and scampered back down to the tavern. At the foot of the stairs he stood still in the shadows and surveyed the scene. He didn't know what he was looking for, but he could smell the hostility, and something frightened him. He just couldn't pinpoint what it was.

He caught sight of the proprietor as he left the stairwell and approached him. "The room stinks," he announced. "My lord wants another."

"I don't have another," the proprietor answered sullenly, with a glance in the direction of the men sitting with the young monk. Then he shoved John out of his way.

Rather than retreating back up the stairs, John slipped out into the courtyard to check on the horses. It was a good thing he did. They greeted him with indignant snorts and whinnies. Centurion kicked at the stall door so hard it leapt on its hinges, and John was sure it would break if he kept it up. Checking their feed boxes, John realized they had been given nothing at all; worse, there were no water buckets in their stalls.

John started to get angry. Whatever these people had against Lord Aimery and himself, they had no right to take it out on the innocent horses. Simmering with resentment, John led each horse to the open trough and let them drink their fill. He then helped himself to the barley in a sack near the tack room, giving a scoop to each horse. While they devoured this, he looked around for hay and spotted it in the loft. He scrambled agilely up the ladder and was just about to throw a bale down when voices below him made him freeze.

"… came on the Venetian galley."

"From Caesarea, then?"

"I say we [incomprehensible] tonight."

"They are armed."

"You can't count the boy."

"Wait until they are both asleep. Costas will give you the key."

"With your blessing, Brother Zotikos?"

"Go with God and do His work!" The monk made the sign of the cross over the other man's head. John could see the monk's face clearly. He was burly but handsome in a solid, powerful way with a full, dark beard. His most powerful feature, however, were eyes that burned with passion as they caught the light of the torches inside the tavern.

"The boy, too?" the second man asked. He was standing with his back to John, and all John could make out was that he was broad-shouldered and had long hair.

"It is as wise to kill a small viper as a large one," the monk answered, and then, taking his donkey by the halter, he led it out of the stables followed by the others.

John was left paralyzed behind them. He was certain that these men meant to kill Lord Aimery and himself in the night—but how could he convince Lord Aimery of that?

After giving hay to the horses, John returned to the stinking room. Lord Aimery was sitting on the bed with the wine jug at his feet. He looked expectantly at John. "Did you get us another room?"

"No, of course not. The proprietor put us here intentionally. My lord, I overheard two men talking about killing us."

"Don't be silly."

"I swear, my lord." and without stopping for breath he spilled out the whole story of what he had overheard.

Aimery gazed at him in apparent disbelief, but his brain was working, too. He was beginning to wonder if the Venetian captain were in cahoots with these men, or if they were simply facing anti-Latin hatred. But there had been no hostility to Latins two years ago, Aimery argued with himself. The Greeks, high and low, had welcomed Richard of England. The nobles had flooded into Limassol to offer homage, and the common people had lined the roads to offer him bread and salt. Isaac had been defeated as much by the hatred of his subjects as by the prowess of the Lionheart.

The captain had blamed the Templars, Aimery recalled, but what had his brother been doing since? He looked up at John. "We're not going to get much sleep in this shit-hole anyway. Let's take the horses and find ourselves a place to camp."

John let out a sigh of relief and agreed with alacrity, "Yes, my lord!"

"No need to pay the landlord for his hospitality," Aimery decided next, getting to his feet. "Let's slip out as silently as possible. You go down first, like you're going to the latrines, and saddle up. I'll follow in a few minutes with our gear."

"Yes, my lord! Come on, Barry!" John patted his thigh and the dog, who had been lying with his head on his paws, jumped up with wagging tail to follow him.

In the stables, John first got Lord Aimery's palfrey tacked up and then Centurion, while Barry kept watch at the door warily. It seemed a long time before Lord Aimery loomed in the stable door, but he had their gear, and together they tied it on the packhorse. From the tavern came the sound of men grumbling and calling for their bills. "Closing time!" John whispered to Lord Aimery.

"They'll all be coming out, then," Lord Aimery drew the correct conclusion. "Hurry."

John grabbed the lead of the packhorse and took Centurion by the bridle, while Lord Aimery took charge of his two horses. They made it out into the courtyard, but before they had a chance to mount, men spilled from the tavern into the yard.

"Mount!" Lord Aimery hissed at John, but before he could even get his foot in the stirrup one of the Greeks lunged at John, drawing a knife as he did so.

John saw the steel blade in the darkness and tried to jump aside, only to collide with the packhorse. He felt the blade hit his side and then slide over the rings of his hauberk. The man drew his arm back for a second strike as, with the clatter of hooves, Lord Aimery spurred forward, his sword raised. Most of the crowd fled to the safety of the building, but the attacker grabbed John by the throat of his hauberk with his left hand and swung about, using John as his shield against Lord Aimery's sword. John felt him draw back his right hand for a second stab. In his mind he registered that at this range his chain mail wouldn't save him.

Suddenly his assailant was screaming in pain and terror as Barry sank his fangs deep into the man's buttocks and dragged him away from John. Immediately Lord Aimery spurred past a dazed John and, leaning down from his saddle, swung his sword in a blow strong enough to nearly decapitate the would-be murderer.

As the man collapsed in a spume of his own blood, Lord Aimery turned his horse again, shouting to his still-dazed squire: "Mount!"

John turned, grabbed the near stirrup, and pulled himself up into the saddle. Lord Aimery spurred toward the exit to the stable yard with his destrier on the lead. Centurion leapt forward without awaiting any human instructions, and the packhorse followed out of habit. Barry brought up the rear at a lope, his tail in the air and his ears up, as if he were enjoying himself for the first time since he'd acquired a new master.

Lord Aimery didn't stop until they were at least two miles beyond the limits of the town. This far they'd followed a paved road by the light of the waning moon, but the sound of water tumbling over itself and rushing under a low bridge reminded them of how thirsty they were. Aimery pulled up and, after checking one last time that they weren't being followed, he gave his palfrey a long rein. At once the horse plunged off the road and found his way to the soggy banks to drop his head into the water, the destrier beside him.

While the horses and Barry drank gratefully, Aimery turned to John, his face white in the night, to ask anxiously, "Are you all right?"

John nodded, but at once started to relive in his mind how close he had come to being stabbed. "My hauberk saved me," John said out loud.

Aimery snorted, and with a nod toward Barry loudly lapping up water beside the horses, retorted, "I'd say Barry saved you! He's earned *his* keep, if ever a dog did." Aimery was as badly shaken as John. They had come within a whisker of being cut down by common thieves in a seedy tavern. Aimery no longer had any doubt that John had overheard a genuine plot to murder them—and had he not, they might have had their throats slit while they slept. As it was, for those few seconds when the murderer held John between them, Aimery had believed John was a dead man. How would he ever have explained his death to Ibelin?

Aimery had given his word that he would look after the boy—and here, on their very first night on Cyprus, he had nearly lost him. Ibelin would never have forgiven him, never.

John decided to dismount so he could give Barry some well-deserved thanks—only to discover his legs were shaking. When he landed on the uneven surface of the riverbank, they just gave way, and he fell and slipped in the mud.

Aimery at once jumped down to help him back onto his feet.

"I'm fine, I'm fine!" John insisted, ashamed to have his lord discover he was trembling.

Aimery, however, already had him under the arm, and after he pulled John to his feet, he put an arm around his squire's shoulder to steady them both. "We both had a bad fright back there," he assured his squire. "It's a good thing you can understand Greek, or we'd both be dead. Let's see if we can find a dry place to catch some sleep."

John nodded his head vigorously.

Aimery let go of him and started searching under the bridge for a dry spot to roll out their blankets. Meanwhile, John went in search of Barry. The dog had stopped drinking and was looking over at him with lifted ears. As soon as John patted his thigh, he bounded over to have his ears scratched as John praised him profusely. "Good boy!" he told him. "Well done! You get the next sausage I can find."

"Offload the packhorse and bring our kit over here!" Aimery ordered, and John turned to his duties.

After they untacked and hobbled the horses, they settled down under the bridge. The ground was damp and uneven, and John tossed and turned before he could find a halfway comfortable position.

"At least it doesn't stink," Aimery commented as John adjusted himself yet again.

"No," John admitted. "And look? Isn't that Gemini?" He was looking out from under the bridge to the crystal-clear sky beyond. The moon was down and the stars were more brilliant than ever. The Milky Way was a smear of white, while the outlying stars were so vivid they seemed to prick like needles.

"What?" Aimery asked, confused.

John flung out his arm. "That pair of bright stars there! They're the constellation Gemini—they represent the twins Castor and Pollux, Helen of Troy's brothers."

Aimery snorted. His education in Poitou hadn't included the constellations of the Greeks, much less their mythology. The evidence of his squire's education reminded him again of the boy's parents. "John," he started hesitantly.

"My lord?" John was young and resilient. The trembling had ceased and his breathing was steady. He was enjoying his adventure again.

"There's no need to tell your father about what happened tonight."

John cracked a smile at his lord. "There's no way I can; he's a hundred miles away."

"Yes, true—but frankly, we didn't exactly cover ourselves with glory tonight, and sometimes it's better fathers don't know all the scrapes their sons get into."

"If you don't want me to say anything to my father, then I won't," John agreed.

Aimery sighed with relief, remarking as casually as possible, "Good. Then let's get some sleep and hope we can find better lodgings tomorrow night."

Chapter Four
The Ineffective Despot

Nicosia, Cyprus
April 1193

BLOOD. GUY DE LUSIGNAN STARED IN horror at the stream of urine the color of Cypriot rosé wine, and his stomach cramped in fear. He didn't need to pay a physician a pretty price to know that blood in his urine was not a good sign. This, combined with the pains in his groin and intestines, warned him that he was ill. Seriously ill. If only Sibylla were alive. She would have comforted him, but there was no one to turn to anymore. No one he trusted. They all wanted him dead. Because of Hattin, which wasn't his fault.

The stream of urine had tapered off to a drip, and Guy closed his braies and tucked the tails of his shirt back inside before tightening the drawstring and letting his surcoat fall back in place. He stopped at the basin just outside the garderobe and poured water over his hands. He used a bar of balsam-scented soap to wash them more vigorously than usual, as if by washing his hands he could cleanse away the undefined illness that was eating away at his innards.

His squire, the awkward and bumbling Dick de Camville, was hovering uncertainly at the door to the outer chamber, moving nervously from foot to foot. It still galled Guy that none of his former barons had been willing to put their sons in his service. That they had elected Conrad de Montferrat and then Henri de Champagne King of Jerusalem in his place *might* have been rationalized on legal and political grounds, but refusing to let their sons serve him was a personal insult. Guy therefore found himself dependent on this semi-moron, the younger son by a second marriage of one of the men Richard of England had left on Cyprus more than two years ago. While the boy was willing enough, he was not the brightest youth Guy had encountered, and he stuttered half the time.

"What is it now?" Guy snapped at him, feeling exposed just because the boy had been so nearby while he urinated blood.

"Th-th-there's a man here, w-w-who says he is your b-b-brother," the squire stammered out, getting bright red from agitation in the process.

"My brother? Is Geoffrey back?" Guy asked hopefully. After Sibylla's death, Geoffrey had been the only soul to wholeheartedly support Guy. He had badgered the English King into recognizing Guy as the rightful King of Jerusalem, and had been furious when Richard abruptly abandoned the Lusignans and accepted Conrad de Montferrat instead. After Montferrat was murdered and Henri de Champagne married Isabella, even Geoffrey conceded defeat. Champagne was the Plantagenet's nephew, and blood is thicker than water. Still, Geoffrey had seemed willing to accept Cyprus as an alternative to Jerusalem— until he got here. From the start, he hadn't liked Cyprus. No sooner had the spring sailing season opened than he abandoned Guy. That left Guy utterly alone in this hostile world of treacherous Greeks and greedy Italians.

"N-n-no. Another b-b-brother," the squire squeaked into Guy's thoughts.

It could hardly be his eldest brother, Hugh "le Brun," Guy calculated; he'd returned to his lordship in Poitou even before King Richard departed. That left only the third of the four Lusignan brothers. "Aimery?" he asked in disbelief.

"Yes, it can hardly come as *that* much of a surprise," Aimery answered from behind him. Guy spun about as his brother stepped into the room from the balcony.

Guy gaped at his elder brother, completely confused by his own emotions. It *was* good to see a familiar face, a face that had shadowed him for so much of his thirteen years here in Outremer. But the voice still had that condescending ring to it, and Aimery's eyes betrayed his continued disdain for his "little brother." Aimery had never accepted that his "little brother" had been more successful than he, had risen higher, was a king . . .

"What brings you here?" Guy asked warily.

"Well, it seems that—because of you— Henri de Champagne does not trust *me* anymore, and since he does not trust me, he wanted me removed as Constable. Since I can't draw on the Constable's income anymore, I'm penniless—all because of you. Under the circumstances, the good Baron d'Ibelin thought I might find more lucrative alternatives here on Cyprus."

"The *good* Baron d'Ibelin," Guy sneered sarcastically, "who *never* supported me, who undermined me at every turn, who worked *against* me—" Before he got more insulting, his elder brother gestured with his head to the youth in the doorway to the balcony, and Guy belatedly recognized Ibelin's eldest son. Instantly, his resentment boiled. The barons refused to let their sons serve him, but Ibelin—the ringleader of the lot!—allowed his *eldest* son and *heir* to serve Aimery! It was ridiculous.

His anger spilled over into his voice as he snapped back, "Well, if 'lucrative alternatives' is what you're looking for, you've come to the wrong place! The Greeks and Italians between them have stolen everything of value. Nobody pays me a penny in taxes, customs, or fees, and if I ride so much as five miles outside of Nicosia I have to fear for my life. Indeed, I'm hardly safe in Nicosia, either. I never know when or where an assassin might be lurking with a poisoned knife, ready to send me the same way as that bastard Conrad de Montferrat!"

The tirade was out before Guy had a chance to consider what he was saying—but that was typical Guy, Aimery reflected. He had always been one to speak before he thought. What surprised him was rather how haggard Guy looked. Guy was very vain. He had always loved the way he looked, and consequently had given his appearance the utmost attention. He was, to be sure, still dressed like the king he no longer was, but his hair was thinning and receding from his forehead. The skin on his face was sagging noticeably, too, and his eyes were sunk in wrinkled sockets darkened by shadows. He looked considerably older than his forty-three years, older and less well (or so Aimery thought) than Aimery himself.

"And you are doing nothing about the situation?" Aimery asked calmly, sinking down on the arm of a heavy wooden chair and swinging his free leg.

"Of course I'm doing something about it!" Guy shouted at his brother, all his anger and fear erupting into this outburst. It was actually a relief to be able to shout at someone; Guy had been ashamed to shout like this at his servants, his soldiers, or the few men who had followed him here. Yet trying to disguise his fear had exhausted him. To his brother he explained, "I've sent Sirs Galganus de Cheneché and Henri de Brie to ravage all of Karpas as punishment for their effrontery! If the people refuse to pay their lawful taxes, Galganus and Henri take their valuables and burn their miserable houses so they learn a lesson. They've especially made an example of the monasteries. I hate the way these pompous Greek monks pretend to be poor! Ha! If the example of Karpas doesn't work on its own, I'll send Barlais to Kyrenia and Bethsan to Paphos next! I'm not going to tolerate people lying and cheating to me!"

Only gradually did Guy realize that he was ranting and raving while his brother and the two squires just stared at him as if he were mad. He fell silent.

"What is it?" he asked nervously, looking from his brother to his brother's astonished squire and then over at Camville, who hastily looked down. Before anyone could answer, Guy felt the urgent need to urinate and dashed back toward the garderobe.

Aimery looked over at John with an expression pregnant with discussion for later on. Then he glanced at his brother's squire and asked, "What's your name, boy?"

"Dick, my lord, Dick de Camville, after my father—and the King." He obviously meant the English King, since there was no King Richard in Outremer and never had been.

Aimery nodded, then asked in a low voice with a jerk of his head in the direction of the garderobe, "Is he like this often?"

"I-I-I don't know what you mean, my lord. Isn't this the way he always is?"

Aimery drew a deep breath and rubbed his forehead in uncertainty. Then he drew himself to his feet and declared, "We're going to take lodgings in the khan across the street. When my brother is more disposed, he can send for us." Beckoning John, he briskly left his brother's chamber before the latter re-emerged from the garderobe.

As they descended the stairs to the street, he remarked in a low voice to John: "Well, at least he didn't order us to leave the island."

The stone caravansary (known locally as a khan) that sat opposite the royal palace in Nicosia was one of the largest and nicest Aimery had ever seen. It had evidently been built in the reign of Isaac Comnenus to cater to clients attending the court. It had a large courtyard with a central cistern surrounded by washbasins, and two large plane trees for shade. While the rooms on the ground floor behind the arcade encircling the courtyard were small and functional storerooms, the second floor offered spacious suites with access to the interior gallery and small balconies over the street. The floors were plaster and were obviously washed regularly by the cleaning staff, so that the entire complex made a pleasantly clean impression. The stables behind were equally spacious and well kept, and John had no qualms turning their horses over to the grooms, all of whom spoke passable Latin and went by Italian names. John rapidly surmised that the proprietor was Italian, and this was soon verified.

The man introduced himself as Carlo di Rossi of Pisa. He explained in Latin that he had settled on Cyprus after the expulsion of the Pisans from Constantinople in 1182. He had enjoyed the patronage of Isaac Comnenus' guests, but proudly claimed to be one of the first citizens of Nicosia to do homage to Richard of England. He gave them a corner room, told them that his brother Mario ran "the best tavern on Cyprus" (just around the corner), and assured them that the Greek baths behind the khan were "first class and completely safe."

Although Aimery and John had stopped on the outskirts of the city to clean themselves up after their night in the rough, they welcomed both a proper bath and a good meal. After a good hour in the baths steaming out the dirt and stiffness, they changed into clean clothes, leaving their dirty things with the khan's efficient-looking laundry mistress, and headed for the tavern, which was tucked in a side alley.

This establishment was small and quiet, with a notably high-class clientele composed of Italian-speaking merchants, guild masters, and marine officers. The proud prices, apparently, made it unattractive to the locals or sailors, and this in turn justified a greater investment in the furnishings. There were flagstone floors, tile paneling on the walls, glazed windows facing the street, and cushions on the wooden benches. The smells coming from the kitchen were nothing less than mouthwatering.

Mentioning Carlo's name as instructed, they were immediately shown to a small corner table, and Mario told them to leave everything to him. A moment later a very pretty young woman in a crisply clean apron and scarves covering her hair came out to lay down trenchers and cutlery and ask their wine preference.

Before she had finished, Mario came back to see that all was in order, and Aimery asked him to join them for some wine. "We have only just arrived and would be interested in hearing the latest news," he explained.

"I will join you shortly," Mario promised and disappeared back into the kitchens.

Their wine was brought and exceeded all expectations. John swore he hadn't had anything so good since leaving Ibelin, and Aimery agreed that the wine matched even the best from Poitou. "I told you Cyprus is rich in resources," Aimery insisted, feeling that so far John's introduction to the island had been less than felicitous.

"Yes, true," Mario intoned, coming up behind Aimery and asking with a gesture if he could sit. Aimery welcomed him. He had his own goblet and a glass carafe of wine with him, which he set on the table but did not immediately pour or drink. "So, you are newly come from Acre?" he asked, identifying them as natives of Outremer by their dress and shaved faces.

"Yes," Aimery agreed. "We arrived two days ago."

"And what brings you here, if I may ask?"

"I have a brother here," Aimery replied evasively, preferring not to reveal his identity.

"I see," Mario answered, but he glanced at the table next to them, at which four distinguished-looking gentlemen were engaged in an animated conversation in Italian. Catching his look, one of the gentlemen immediately got to his feet and came over to bow to Aimery. "My lord Constable," he started, shattering Aimery's illusions of anonymity, "you may not remember me, but I am Francesco Pasquali, bailli of Pisa here on Cyprus. May I join you?"

"I'm honored," Aimery countered diplomatically, although inwardly annoyed at being recognized so readily and even more for being called "Constable;" it meant he would be forced to explain that he no longer held the title.

Mario surrendered his seat to the Pisan bailli and withdrew. The bailli poured the wine left behind by Mario and raised his glass to Aimery.

Aimery answered the gesture and they both drank without a formal toast. "My lord, let me assure you that your reputation precedes you," the Pisan bailli opened as he set his glass down. "My brothers in Acre sent word of your courageous defense of their innocence."

"Thank you," Aimery answered stiffly; he had long since regretted his actions. Had he just kept his mouth shut, maybe he would still be Constable of Jerusalem, living with his wife and children. . . .

"My colleagues and I assure you that we have nothing to do with the attacks. They are completely unauthorized—but, I fear, a sign of the times. We live in very troubled times." He shook his head.

"We do have a truce," Aimery pointed out.

"A desert truce, my lord. The seas are still at war, and now this unnecessary violence on Cyprus." He shook his head. "I know you are not a man of trade, but surely you understand just how devastating your brother's policies are? Men of trade need peace and security above all else. Much as we hated the despot Isaac Comnenus, at least he maintained law and order on the island. The roads from one end of the island to the other were safe. We had no need to fear for the safety and honor of our wives and daughters when they ventured onto the streets. All that is gone!" He gestured dramatically with his hands.

"Why?" Aimery asked, leaning back against the wall and watching the Pisan carefully.

"Why? Because your brother's ham-fisted attempts to assert his control have sparked widespread rebellion. Angry young men don't ask if the people they attack are the same people who caused the problem. We've had four warehouses torched in the last three months! Several inland convoys have been shot at by archers hiding in the hills. Camels and horses have been killed or stolen. So far the ports are safe, but for how much longer, my lord? If things continue this way, we will have to cut our losses and relocate."

Aimery considered that an empty threat. Where would the Pisan mercantile community relocate to? Like the other Italian merchants, the Pisans were in the Eastern Mediterranean because of the riches that could be made trading with Constantinople, the crusader states, and Alexandria. Nevertheless, Aimery recognized that the crusader states needed the Italian merchant communities for their own economy—and for their fleets, which kept the Saracen ships bottled up in their harbors. He also recognized that trade was greatly inhibited and disrupted by unrest and violence. "And what do you expect me to do about it, good sir?"

"Convince your brother to call off his dogs! Brie and Cheneché are worse than rabid wolves!" Aimery glanced at his squire, and John squirmed uncomfortably. The Pisan continued, ignorant of the squire's identity and the fact that Brie was his cousin. "They have set the entire Karpas peninsula aflame, and as people flee before their mercenary soldiers, they spread fear and hatred to the rest of the island. They must be stopped!"

"My brother claims he has not received the taxes owed him."

"Well, there are better ways of collecting taxes than destroying the means to pay them!" the man of commerce informed the nobleman sharply. "How are people supposed to pay taxes without income? Without mills or workshops? He's destroying his own tax base with his scorched-earth policy!"

The Pisan had worked himself up into a rage of righteous indignation, and one of his colleagues rose from the next table to pat him on the shoulder. "Calm yourself, Francesco. Take a sip of the wine." Then turning to Aimery he added, "Forgive my dear friend Francesco for his little outburst, but believe me it is justified. The situation here is very dire, very dire indeed. We all hope you will be able to talk sense to your brother Lord Guy."

Aimery smiled cynically. He might talk "sense" to Guy until he was blue in the face, but his brother rarely listened. . . .

Just as Aimery had anticipated, Guy was not receptive to advice—at least not from his older brother. Gathered in the council chamber on the far side of the heavy wooden door were nearly all the men who had thrown in their lot with Guy de Lusignan and come with him to Cyprus. They were only a handful of knights—no barons among them—and most had been made paupers by Saladin's invasion of the Kingdom of Jerusalem. The exceptions were the two Englishmen left on Cyprus by King Richard—Robert of Thornton and Richard of Camville—along with Reynald Barlais, a Poitevin sergeant-at-arms who had been in the service of the Lusignan family for decades. He'd come out to the Holy Land with Geoffrey, but had elected to remain on Cyprus with Guy.

From what John could hear through the door, the Englishmen, both older men left on the island by King Richard for their administrative and financial talents rather than the strength of their arms, were the only two men in the other room backing Aimery's calls for de-escalation and peace overtures to the rebels. Barlais—strongly backed by John's cousin Henri de Brie, Walter de Bethsan, and Galganus de Cheneché—was furiously and loudly insisting that the rebels had to be "crushed," "obliterated," or "exterminated."

"At what cost?" Thornton asked in an exasperated tone. "You're destroying the economic base of the entire island!"

"Better that than let these snakes get away with biting us! If we don't crush them now, they'll attack us again and again!" John's cousin Henri snarled.

Henri de Brie was the son of Balian's half-sister Ermengard. As a very young knight, he had taken service with Reynald de Châtillon, the Baron of Oultre-jourdain. It was with was Châtillon that he had won infamy by command-ing one of the galleys Reynald de Châtillon launched in the Red Sea in 1182. Châtillon's fleet had wreaked havoc with the Muslim pilgrimages and spread panic across the Arabian Peninsula. Brie was practically the only survivor of the raids, and he'd been rewarded by Oultrejourdain with an heiress. After Oultre-jourdain's death, he'd attached himself to Guy de Lusignan.

"These 'snakes,' as you call them, are Christian men and women," Camville reminded Brie. "Men and women who for the most part assisted King Richard to capture this island in the first place!"

"Well, Christian or not, they are defying us!" Henri de Brie replied force-fully, adding in a more conciliatory tone, "I've got a suggestion: Give each of us defined territory and let us deal with the situation therein as we see fit. We'll soon see whose methods work best!" He flung out the words as a challenge.

"You're just angling for a barony!" Guy objected petulantly, leaving John nodding in agreement. It had always galled his cousin that despite his close ties to the Ibelin family, the Bries were rear-tenants rather than barons.

A loud bang from the opposite side of the room made John start and turn sharply. A man had just entered the anteroom, and it had been the door banging against a chest as it was flung open that had startled John. He was even more stunned when he recognized the man standing in the doorway: it was his former brother-in-law, Isabella's first husband, Humphrey de Toron.

Toron drew up sharply and stared. "John?" he asked uncertainly. Humphrey hadn't seen John d'Ibelin in nearly four years—not since the day he'd left Tyre with his then-wife Isabella to take part in the siege of Acre. Toron blamed John's parents for the annulment of his marriage some fifteen months later, and had refused to set foot in the same city, let alone the same building, they occupied ever since. In the intervening years, however, John had grown from boy to youth. Indeed, it was more his increasing resemblance to his father than to his former boyhood self that allowed Humphrey to recognize him.

"Yes, my lord," John answered, feeling acutely uncomfortable.

"What are you doing here? Your father isn't—" Humphrey immediately looked toward the closed door, registering the raised and angry voices on the other side.

"No, no," John hastened to reassure him. "I'm squire to Lord Aimery, and he came to join his brother."

Humphrey relaxed visibly, and he glanced back at John. John had been his brother-in-law for seven years, and lacking brothers of his own, he'd looked on John as a younger brother. He'd enjoyed reading from the *Iliad* and the *Odyssey* to a wide-eyed John, and John had been one of the first to hear Ernoul's songs. The thought of Ernoul wrenched at Humphrey's heart.

Ibelin's squire Ernoul had been the only other living soul, besides Isabella, who admired Humphrey's learning and gift for languages. For years Humphrey and Ernoul had exchanged manuscripts and recited poetry to one another. When the Dowager Queen and Ibelin tore Isabella away from him so they could use her as a pawn in their dynastic game to make Conrad de Montferrat king, they had taken from him not only the woman he loved, but his best friend as well. "How is Ernoul?" Humphrey heard himself asking. His own emotions—hatred and grief mixed together—made his voice sound faint and far away.

"Ernoul's just become a father," John answered quickly, relieved that Humphrey had asked about his father's squire rather than Isabella herself. He knew he would not be able to lie convincingly about how happy Isabella was with Champagne, and he knew just as certainly that that was *not* what Humphrey wanted to hear.

Humphrey's face twitched. He'd forgotten Ernoul was now wed. Humphrey had been held in Saracen captivity longer than the other Christian barons and not released until May of 1189. By the time he reached Tyre to be reunited with Isabella at last, he had been bewildered to discover that his friend Ernoul was married. Not just married, but in love with his wife as well. Although welcoming, Ernoul had been more interested in practicing his next duet with Alys than in spending time with his old friend. In retrospect, Humphrey had fled Tyre to avoid the disappointment of Ernoul's coolness as much as to escape Ibelin's contempt. "Send Ernoul my congratulations," Humphrey replied stiffly. "Was it a son or a daughter?"

"A daughter; they've named her Helen—for Helen of Troy," John offered, apparently remembering those nights reading the works of Homer just as Humphrey did.

Humphrey nodded sadly, as the door from the inner chamber opened abruptly and young Gauvain de Cheneché burst out with a frown on his face. "John! You've got no business jawboning with Toron! We need refreshments! Wine and water and something to eat, too! Hurry!"

"I don't take orders from you, Gauvain!" John bristled. "I'll—"

"*Sir* Gauvain, to you!" the younger Cheneché snarled, cuffing John for good measure. "Now get moving before I teach you your manners!"

"Manners you obviously never learned yourself!" Toron admonished, grabbing the younger Cheneché by the arm and pulling him back. "Do you think raping little girls gives you the right to treat other men the same way the infamous Châtillon did?"

"Well, at least I'm known for raping girls, not bending my ass for other men!" Cheneché shot back.

Toron blanched and John gasped.

"What? Didn't you know?" Cheneché sneered in John's direction. "Why do you think your sister dumped Toron at the first opportunity? She wanted a real man in her bed, not a sodomite!"

"We sent you for refreshments, Gauvain—not to stand about insulting the only baron on the island!" The growl came from the older Cheneché, and at once both Sir Gauvain and John fled in the direction of the kitchens, leaving Humphrey to face the other men alone.

Stiffly, Humphrey walked into the council chamber overheated by the tempers simmering in the men around him. He wished he could convince himself that they hadn't all heard what young Sir Gauvain had just said, but in his heart he knew that, whether they'd heard the remark or not, they agreed with it.

And then his eyes met those of Guy de Lusignan, and he saw profound and unexpected sympathy in the former king's eyes. Guy, too, had lost the woman he'd loved, and he'd lost the respect of his vassals and his men. Guy de Lusignan knew what it was like to be scorned and despised by one's peers.

"It's good to see you," Guy greeted Toron verbally, indicating a vacant chair. Guy would never forget that it was Toron's defection from the High Court to do homage to Sibylla after she'd been crowned without their consent that had prevented the Count of Tripoli and Ibelin from crowning Isabella as a rival queen. It would have come to civil war in 1186 if it hadn't been for young Toron. Without Toron's "betrayal" of his wife and father-in-law, Guy knew he might never have been king at all. Guy remembered that, and it was more important to him than whether Humphrey preferred boys to girls. "I need your loyal counsel," he told Toron with a tired, but sincere, smile.

Toron smiled back, weary but thankful, and took his place at the table. Ibelin had never forgiven him for betraying the barons in 1186. He even blamed Humphrey for the catastrophe of Hattin, arguing that if Humphrey hadn't "gone crawling on his belly" to Sibylla and Guy, the barons could have prevented Guy from becoming king. And, so Ibelin's reasoning went, if Guy had not been king, he would not have led the feudal army to defeat. Another king, Ibelin contended, would have listened to his advisers; another king would not have fallen into Saladin's trap; another king would not have lost the battle and so would not have lost the Kingdom. . . .

Humphrey and Guy were both burdened with the guilt for that catastrophe, Humphrey reflected, like two oxen yoked to a plow. They strained together to move forward, but the plow caught in the earth, held back by the bloody mud of a defeat no one could—or should—ever forgive.

Chapter Five
Of Beggars and Kings

Nicosia, Cyprus
October 1193

SIX MONTHS ON THE ISLAND HAD dramatically improved John's command of Greek. A lifetime of classroom lessons, so long stored away in his brain like dusty volumes in a forgotten trunk, had been unlocked by the sounds around him. Growing understanding had slowly been transformed from hesitant into more fluent speech. With the confidence that he could understand what was happening around him (and ask his way if necessary) had also come increasing curiosity about his new world.

When John realized that just by changing into a different set of clothes he could also blend in with the native population, he had started exploring Nicosia from the ground up—enjoying the utter freedom of anonymity. When John slipped out of the khan in his Greek clothes, he left John d'Ibelin behind, and with him the burden of being the son of the savior of Jerusalem and a paragon of chivalry.

Not that John transformed himself into something despicable or dishonorable. John had not grown into a taste for loose women and had no natural proclivity to alcoholism. Because he was alone on his adventures, he was also not in a position to be led astray. His only companion was Barry, who clung to him as loyally as a shadow, ever ready to share a meal—or an adventure.

Today John was looking for firewood. The nights were chilly, and as the frequency of the rain showers increased, the air turned damp as well. The khan provided each resident with an allotment of wood, but it was far too little, in Lord Aimery's opinion. John wanted to surprise him with a big stack of wood to get them through the next few days. Having no illusions about how much wood he could personally carry, he borrowed a donkey and panniers from the khan and headed toward the outskirts of town where the potters had their kilns. Kilns consume an enormous amount of firewood, and John reckoned he would either encounter one of the suppliers or be able to purchase directly from the kiln enough wood for their modest needs.

Unfortunately, the potters occupied land northeast of Nicosia, so it was a bit of a hike, and John opted to cut through the cattle market and past the slaughterhouse beyond. It was a good place to find a bone or two for Barry, although he disliked the number of beggars that prowled around on the lookout for edible refuse. As always, the beggars clustered near the stinking bins behind the abattoir, and stray dogs licked the blood seeping out of them. Barry lifted his ears and wagged his tail in anticipation, but John braced himself for the smell and tried to hold his breath as he scanned the fresh heaps of bones for the best pieces. He rapidly chose one, handed it off to Barry, and then took a second for later, stashing it into a sack he had over his shoulder. Then he turned away and put a dozen steps' distance between himself and the bins before letting out his breath.

He found his path was blocked by a young beggar with a bad bruise on the side of his face. John had seen him here several times over the last couple of months, but without the bruise. Evidently he'd run into some kind of trouble. Although he was smaller than John, John guessed they were about the same age. Unlike the younger children, who worked as a pack and had to surrender all their earnings to the adults, this youth usually worked alone.

"I've made a collar for the dog," the beggar announced, holding out a collar made of woven straw with a crude buckle carved from bone. "You can have it for just five obols," he told John.

John looked down at Barry. The faithful dog did not need a collar; he followed John everywhere without it. On the other hand, John's mother had taught him that it was better to reward industry than sloth. She always made a point of offering alms to the working poor, or institutions that cared for those not yet or no longer able to work, rather than beggars. She had warned him never to give to children who begged because, she claimed, they only grew up thinking everyone else owed them their livelihood and became thieves and pickpockets. This boy, however, was clearly trying to earn his keep.

Seeing his hesitation, the boy pulled another object out of his pocket. "Or what about a comb?" he asked, offering a comb likewise carved from cattle bone. "It will cost you ten obols."

"That's too much," John protested. The money his father had given him was long since used up (except for the cost of the passage home, still sewn in his boot), and he had to make do with the allowance that Lord Aimery gave him. "Besides," he added, "I have to get firewood, and I don't know how much it will cost. Maybe another day."

"I'll help you with the firewood," the boy offered. "I know a place you can get it cheap."

"I was going to the potters," John explained.

"They'll charge you double," the beggar dismissed the idea. "I know a man who resells wood from damaged structures. There is always some waste he doesn't care about."

John weighed whether or not to trust the youth, and decided to go ahead. After all, he had Barry with him and his dagger. "OK."

The beggar smiled, stuffed the collar and comb back in his pockets, and indicated the way. John fell in beside him with the donkey and Barry trailing. "What's your name?" he asked the beggar.

"Lakis. And yours?"

"Janis. How did you get that bruise?"

"That bastard Niki tried to take my earnings from me," Lakis told him bitterly.

"Did he succeed?"

"Sort of. I had some coins hidden."

"Why do you hang around the slaughterhouse? I'll bet you could get work somewhere in the city," John suggested, trying to implement his mother's policy of encouraging work.

"Where?" Lakis asked back hopefully.

John was embarrassed to have to shrug and admit he didn't know. "Didn't you learn a trade?" he asked instead.

"My Dad was a miller," Lakis declared, his lip a grim line, and he refused to meet John's eye.

John understood the use of the past tense, and concluded that something terrible had happened to Lakis' father. After a few minutes of trudging along in silence, John decided to reopen the conversation by asking, "May I see the collar again?"

Lakis brightened up at once, and pulled it out of his pocket. John examined it carefully. The straw collar was only crudely woven, uneven, and not very strong, but the buckle was cleverly made. "You're good with carving," John told Lakis. "Where did you learn?"

"After I went to live with my uncle (he's a butcher in Karpasia), I met this man, a refugee from Jerusalem, who used to collect the bones from behind the butchery so he could carve them into things for sale. He taught me how to make things, but my aunt hated him. She always chased him away whenever she saw him and forbade me from visiting him. She said he was evil, a Musselman."

"Had he been a slave?" John asked, suspecting this was one of the released captives trying to start his life over again but tainted by six years in Saracen slavery.

"Yes," Lakis admitted. "He'd learned to carve from the Saracens, only they had ivory rather than bone, he said. He spoke Arabic, but he assured me he was a good Christian." Lakis sounded uncertain.

"Of course he was," John defended the unknown man. "Many of our—" John had just been about to say "vassals," only to realize that would betray that he wasn't the Greek servant boy he pretended to be.

"What?" Lakis asked.

"Nothing. What happened? I mean, did you disobey your aunt and see the man anyway?"

"Yes, until she caught me and had my uncle beat me. It was terrible, and I hated it there, anyway. I don't want to be a butcher, and my cousins will inherit anyway, so what's the point?"

"You should apprentice to a carver—someone who makes book covers or the like," John decided enthusiastically, thinking of the magnificent carved ivory cover of one of his mother's books.

"Book covers?" Lakis asked in a skeptical tone.

John suspected he'd given himself away again. "Or combs or whatever," he added with a dismissive gesture.

"What's your trade?" Lakis countered.

"Me?" John shrugged. "I'm just a servant. How far is it to this place with the firewood?"

Lakis returned his attention to their goal and led them to a noisy workshop in a back alley, squeezed in behind an iron-worker's forge and a candlestick maker. In the courtyard, wood had been heaped up in a messy pile. Most of it was charred in places. Much of it was broken and splintered. Large, twisted nails reached out of the beams in awkward places, ready to tear open a man's hand. Behind the pile of wood were some workbenches and vises where a couple of young men sawed away damaged portions of the wood to rescue the still-sound portions. The good wood was stacked along the far wall by length, while the rubbish landed in a second, smaller heap. Lakis pointed to the latter, and John nodded. Partially charred wood made excellent kindling. "Do you know the proprietor?" John asked Lakis. "Can you ask him what he wants for the wood?"

Lakis nodded, adding, "Go around the corner. If he sees you with the donkey, he'll charge you more."

John dutifully removed himself and waited until Lakis returned with an armload of wood. He dumped it on the street and went to get more while John loaded the wood into the panniers on the donkey. After Lakis had made five trips, they had all they could load on the donkey, and John asked how much he owed. "Ten obols," Lakis declared, holding out his hand.

John suspected the wood was free and that Lakis was simply taking what he'd refused to pay for the comb, but he didn't mind. He wanted the firewood, not the comb. Having paid Lakis, he turned the donkey around to start back across town to the khan.

"Where do you live?" Lakis asked.

"Other side of town," John answered vaguely.

"The nice side of town," Lakis observed.

John shrugged, and they continued in silence for a few more minutes.

"Are you sure you don't want the collar?" Lakis asked a little plaintively. "It's only five obols."

"Maybe another day," John demurred, and they parted.

After that, John saw Lakis at various places. He diligently tried to peddle his bone objects—combs, hairpins, buttons, and the like—at the daily markets. He also made a couple of crosses that he tried to sell on the steps of St. Sophia. John always greeted him and they would exchange a nod and a smile, but it wasn't until the lion tamer came to town that they spoke again.

The lion tamer had taught two aging lions tricks, and he gave a performance every night on the field where the monthly horse market was held. It cost two obols to get in and was immensely popular; even King Guy went with his brother and household knights. John, however, had been stuck looking after the horses and Barry, who had made a frightful fuss, barking incessantly. So the next day he asked Lord Aimery's permission to go back on his own. While Lord Aimery agreed in principle, they first had to make a trip to Paphos for King Guy, and by the time they returned to Nicosia, the show had been in town almost a week and the crowds were thinning. John spotted Lakis and waved to him.

Lakis made his way around to John, and they stood at the railing side by side as if they were old friends.

"Have you ever seen lions before, Janis?" Lakis asked as they waited.

John shook his head. "My father said that when he was young there used to be wild lions around, and the old king hunted them sometimes."

"The old king?" Lakis asked puzzled. "You mean Isaac Comnenus?"

John bit his lip; he'd slipped up again. "Yes," he said to cover his blunder.

To his surprise, Lakis seemed to believe him. He looked back at the improvised arena and nodded. "The brothers of Antiphonitis say there are still lions up in Trodos. The Romans used to capture them from here for their games in Rome."

"Really?" John asked, astonished.

Lakis looked over his shoulder at his companion with a frown of concentration, "Where are you from, Janis?"

"Here," John insisted. "Nicosia."

The look that Lakis gave him was full of doubt, but he was rescued by the arrival of the aging and less-than-impressive lions.

After the show was over, John, being famished as usual, suggested they get a pocket of flatbread stuffed with fatty lamb sold by a street vendor. Lakis shook his head vigorously, and John surmised he wasn't making much money with his street sales, so he said (somewhat grandiosely), "Oh, this one's on me," and pulled out his purse.

Lakis' eyes widened a little at the sight of the comfortably bulky purse, but he didn't say no. By the way he devoured the meal, John concluded that Lakis was a lot hungrier than he was himself. As Lakis finished his meal with a sigh of satisfaction, John took advantage of their now stronger friendship to ask, "What happened to your father, Lakis?"

"He's dead," Lakis answered, his face closing.

Lakis nodded grimly. "And your mother too? Was it an accident?" John asked, sensing that there was some terrible story behind Lakis' condition. The son of a miller and nephew of a butcher wasn't a street urchin by birth.

"No, they killed them," Lakis croaked out, that grim expression returning to his face.

"Who?" John asked innocently.

"The Franks, of course! Who else? Lusignan's Wolves! Brie!" Lakis lashed out, and John felt as if he'd been punched in the stomach. "Don't you realize what is happening here?" Lakis asked in disbelief. "Where do you think all those charred beams came from? They're the broken bits of burned-down houses and mills!"

"They burned your father's mill?" John asked in horror.

"With my parents and sisters still inside!" Lakis screamed it out because it had been pent up inside him for too long. Then he turned and ran away into the afternoon crowd. John tried to follow, but Lakis was lost to him.

John went over in his mind all the things they'd heard from the Pisans and men-at-arms and, indeed, from King Guy himself. John didn't doubt that what

Lakis said was true. His problem was not understanding how his own cousin could be responsible—and not knowing what he could or should do to make it up to Lakis. How do you compensate a youth for his parents? His sisters? His inheritance? His future? Lakis wasn't like Barry. He couldn't just be adopted, could he? John looked down at Barry, and hugged him firmly in a gesture really meant for Lakis.

As he helped Lord Aimery out of his clothes that night and prepared to brush them out and fold them for the next day, John kept stopping, completely distracted by his thoughts.

"Just spit it out, John! What's troubling you?"

John looked up at his lord with a sigh of relief to have been given an invitation. "My lord, I met a boy my own age at the lion show today, and—and," it spilled out in a rush, "he said his parents had both been burned alive in their own mill by my cousin Henri."

Aimery started, then shook his head. "He was just trying to get alms from you."

"No, he wasn't. He doesn't know who I am. He thinks I'm a Greek servant named Janis."

"Ah, is that what you do in your spare time? Lurk around taverns in disguise?"

"I don't lurk!" John protested. "And I told you, I was at the lion show, not in a tavern. Besides, all that matters is whether it's true or not. Did my cousin burn down mills with innocent people—women and girls—still inside?"

Aimery took a deep breath. "That's what people are saying. I don't know for sure—but if you must know, I think it's probable. Your cousin was one of the leaders of the Red Sea raids, remember?"

"Then they have every reason to hate us, don't they?" John countered angrily. "It's not just about taxes and revenues, is it? It's about making boys orphans—and beggars."

"I'm sorry if I'm the first to tell you this, but life isn't pretty and it isn't fair!" Aimery snapped back. It was bad enough that his brother was an idiot, without his squire rubbing his nose in it!

"You think I don't know that, my lord?" John shot back, his jaw set stubbornly, and the boy's stance reminded Aimery so sharply of his father-in-law, he almost laughed. Meanwhile, John was continuing, "I've lost my inheritance, too, remember?" But even as he protested, he was reminded that while he'd lost his wealth, he hadn't lost his parents or siblings, and at once his stance of defiance crumbled.

He felt a heavy hand fall on his shoulder, and Lord Aimery spoke more gently now. "Don't blame yourself, John. There is nothing you can do."

John didn't like that answer. He *wanted* to do something. He frowned and looked down in frustration and shame.

"John, I know it's hard being separated from your brother and cousins. You need to spend more time with boys your own age. Why don't you try to befriend the Camville boy? He was asking about you only this morning. I'm sure he needs a friend, too, and you're both from the same class, the same church."

"Can you hold Barry's front paws while I remove the burrs from his belly?" John asked Dick de Camville. It was worded as a request, but it was really an offer of friendship, and Dick jumped at it. He loved John's big, furry dog and wished he was allowed to have a dog of his own.

"W-w-where did you get B-b-barry?" he asked the other squire, as he took Barry's paws in his hands and held him upright while John took a comb to his belly to vigorously remove a collection of burrs.

"He was a stray," John answered without looking up or stopping in his task. "Or, well, he belonged to a leper, who died. I adopted him."

"And your f-f-father let you?" Dick asked in wonder.

"I'd already left home and was with Lord Aimery. My father wouldn't have minded, though. The problem was always my mother. She said our house in Tyre was too small for dogs—but then she let my little sister Meg have one!" John added in disgust.

"Is it true your mother is a Greek princess?" Dick's stutter was subsiding as he became more comfortable with John.

"Yes," John confirmed without looking up from his task.

"And you speak Greek?"

"Yes, pretty well now."

"Do—do you think you could help me?"

"How?" John asked without looking up; Barry had started to fuss and squirm, and he had to concentrate on his task.

"My lord wants to consult an apothecary—a Greek apothecary. He says the Italian apothecaries are all quacks."

That got John's attention and he looked up at Dick, fully conscious of how significant this was.

Misinterpreting his stare, Dick shrugged. Barry yapped in protest, so Dick let go of his paws and patted him on the back of his head to calm him. As if talking to the dog, he added, "I think he's afraid the communes will find out he's sick if he goes to an Italian apothecary."

"Yes, I imagine he does," John admitted. "What's the problem?"

Dick shrugged and stammered out, "I d-d-don't know." His stammer betrayed that he was lying, but John decided not to push for an answer. They were only just becoming friends, after all.

"You want me to find a Greek apothecary and bring him to Lord Guy?" John asked instead.

"Yes, but only after d-d-dark and in secret! No one must f-f-find out. Not even L-l-lord Aimery."

"You can't ask me to keep secrets from Lord Aimery," John protested.

"Then f-f-forget I said anything!" Dick retorted hotly, his face flushed. He stopped petting Barry and turned to leave.

"Wait! Stop!" John understood their budding friendship was on the line.

Dick stopped and looked back over his shoulder, waiting.

"I promise to keep it a secret."

"You'll do it, then?" Dick asked.

John nodded again.

Andreas Katzouroubis was a cautious man. He had survived the many vicissitudes of recent years largely by minding his own business, which was healing the sick. So long as the island had been part of the Eastern Roman Empire, he had done his duty in the large municipal hospital in Nicosia. In accordance with the custom throughout the Empire, he had tended patients there every other month for nominal payment, and had earned his living in the other six months by tending private patients. That system broke down, however, when the despot Isaac Comnenus took it into his head that the Head Doctor was poisoning him and had the man tortured to death. After that, no one wanted the job of "Head Doctor," and soon no one was being paid. So they stopped going to work in the hospital and withdrew to private practice, treating penniless patients on a charitable basis at their own discretion.

Financially this had not proven such a bad development, but Andreas Katzouroubis had not joined the medical profession for the sake of income alone. For one thing, he was genuinely interested in healing the sick, or at least easing their suffering—but the driving passion behind his choice of profession had really been fascination with the human body and how it worked. He loved the study of medicine more than the practice of it, and to this end he had studied both in Constantinople and in Alexandria. He had also spent one year as a "guest physician" in the famous Al-'Adudi Hospital in Baghdad, and another at the renowned Hospitaller establishment in Jerusalem. Andreas Katzouroubis was a man of the world as well as a highly respected pharmacist.

The request from a Greek-speaking squire to come attend on the hated Latin despot Guy de Lusignan did not fill him with particular enthusiasm. He saw no particular reason why he should either heal or help this man who had unleashed so much misery on his beloved homeland. Nor did he believe the man could be suffering from an ailment that would interest him intellectually. The pay might, admittedly, be good—or it might be death, as in the case of the Head Doctor. Dealing with despots was always a dubious proposition.

On the other hand, it was usually not wise to refuse a summons from a despot, either. It was, in short, a situation of "damned if you do, and damned if you don't." Not being by nature a man with fragile nerves, however, Katzouroubis simply raised his eyebrows, told the squire to wait, and then took his time collecting his bag of utensils—the urine jar, lancets, string for the tourniquet, clean gauze bandages, ointments, and small bottles filled with various liquids and powders used in common remedies. His bag packed, Katzouroubis took a cloak from the wall and flung it over his robes, leaving his distinguishing cap visible. At last he nodded to the squire that he was ready.

Outside it was misting more than raining. Although there was no noticeable precipitation, the air was thick with moisture and the cobbles had a wet sheen. The apothecary's cloak soon glistened with tiny droplets. They moved silently through the darkened streets like two shadows until they came to the royal palace. Here the squire led past a sentry, who evidently recognized him and his authority to bring a stranger inside. They ascended by a back stairway and followed a service corridor until the squire stopped before a closed door and gave a distinctive knock. He was answered almost at once by the opening of the door from the inside. The squire nodded for the apothecary to enter, murmuring, "This is where I leave you, sir apothecary. Lord Guy's squire will look after you from here."

A youth on the other side of the door took over, gesturing for him to follow. Katzouroubis soon found himself deposited in an elegantly appointed chamber with mosaic floors and marble facings on the wall. There were soft Egyptian carpets on the floor, an abundance of silk cushions on the benches and chairs, and dozens of glass oil lamps flickering around the room. It took him a moment to even find the patient.

Up to now, Katzouroubis had seen the Latin Lord of Cyprus only from a distance when he rode through the city. He had always been in armor and mounted. He had looked impressive. Now Guy de Lusignan was wearing a long, loose kaftan, belted with a richly embroidered cord. He wore sandals on his naked feet. He looked smaller, frailer, and older than he had looked mounted and in armor.

"You are the apothecary?" the Lusignan asked in a sharp voice.

Katzouroubis bowed deeply. "I am a physician and, yes, an apothecary as well. At your service, my lord."

"Ah, you speak French." The Lusignan sounded relieved.

"I spent sixteen months with the Brothers of St. John at Jerusalem, my lord."

"Good, good. I need your help," Guy confessed.

"Shall we sit?" Katzouroubis countered, gesturing toward a bench softened with cushions whose gold threads caught the light of the lamps.

Guy nodded absently, pulling his kaftan straight at the back as he sat down and folding the extra material over his knees like an old matron.

"So, what symptoms do you have?" Katzouroubis asked in his calm, professional voice.

"Blood in my urine," Guy admitted in a tight, frightened voice. "And pain in my lower guts."

"Hmm. I will need a urine sample," the doctor told him, turning to open his bag and remove his urine flask. "As for the pain, does it hurt to urinate?"

"Yes, very much."

"A burning? Or stinging?"

"Yes, as if my urine were liquid fire."

"And you need to urinate frequently?"

"It feels like it, but there's nothing there half the time. Just the pain."

"How long have you been impotent, my lord?"

"What makes you think I am?" Guy shot back defensively.

Katzouroubis' eyebrows shot up and he looked at the Frank skeptically.

Guy flung up his hands, grabbed the urine flask from the doctor's hand, and stormed in the direction of the garderobe.

Katzouroubis looked around the room while he waited. The second squire had discreetly disappeared. The only other occupant of the room was a tiger cat who lay on a cushion looking at him with large, half-closed amber eyes.

Guy returned and thrust the flask at him. Even in the poor light, the apothecary could see that the fluid inside (not much, but enough) was murky and brownish. Not healthy at all.

Katzouroubis jammed a cork stopper firmly down the throat of the flask to seal it, and placed it upright in a leather loop sewn inside his bag that would keep it upright. "I will need to examine it in my laboratory," he told the patient. "Meanwhile, do you wish to share any other symptoms with me?"

"The pain keeps me awake at nights," Guy told him, asking himself if it was really the pain or the loneliness and hopelessness of his situation.

"You need to drink more water and less wine," Katzouroubis advised at once.

"I urinate all the time as it is!" Guy protested.

"You feel the *need* to urinate, you told me, often with meager results. The discomfort would be less if you had water—plenty of water—to pass."

Guy grunted ambiguously.

"You should also drink the juice of crushed pomegranates morning and night. Five or more pomegranates, to be precise. The harvest is just starting, so you should have no trouble with that."

"Will it ease the pain?" Guy asked, and Katzouroubis heard an echo of desperation in his voice.

"No," the doctor admitted honestly before adding, "but I can give you something else for the pain, if you like."

"Can you give it to me now? Tonight?"

Katzouroubis hesitated, but then nodded, and looked through his bag for the opium.

Chapter Six
Interlude in a Precarious
Peace

Caymont, Kingdom of Jerusalem
December 1193

FROM THE "LISTS" ERECTED JUST OUTSIDE the manor came the sound of excited young men shouting and cheering. It was a familiar and comforting sound to Maria Zoë. At thirty-nine, she still thoroughly enjoyed watching skilled knights face off against one another in a joust or melee. Far more important, however, was the fact that so many young men training in the skills of knighthood gave her hope for the future. The Kingdom of Jerusalem had very nearly been lost by Guy de Lusignan on the Horns of Hattin. It had, with the help of large armies of Westerners, clawed back important territories along the coast under the able leadership of Richard of England. However, the heartland of the Kingdom—Jerusalem, Bethlehem, Nazareth, and her own dower lands of Nablus—were still occupied by the Saracens. If they were ever to win those holy (and economically vital) places back, they needed a new generation of knights eager and ready to fight for the Holy Land.

Here on the plain of Caymont, a dozen youths were engaged in the rough-and-tumble training so essential to later battlefield competence. They were being schooled by her husband and his knights, who maintained their own skills not only in mock combat against one another and out hunting, but by playing target to the squires—and more often than not, defeating them left-handed.

Drawn by an explosion of excited shouting, Maria Zoë knelt in the window seat and opened the small casement set in the thick, milky glass so she could get a look at what was causing all the shouting. In the middle of the lists her husband sat on his youngest destrier, a black stallion called Ras Dawit, and he was blindfolded. In the four corners, younger men sat their horses, and as she watched, one put spurs to his horse and launched himself at his lord, blunted lance lowered. Based on the sound alone, Balian nudged his horse around on his fore hand and lifted his shield in time to parry the blow from the blunted lance. As the lance slid off the shield and the rider galloped past, the bystanders cheered the blindfolded baron.

At once another youth launched himself from a different corner, and again Balian deftly swung his attentive horse to face the threat. Maria Zoë, an excellent horsewoman, could see Ras Dawit's ears twitching and swiveling. He was responding as much to the threat as to his rider's legs, and she smiled as she realized that this was part of the trick: a horse trained to face any man attacking his rider.

It was likewise obvious to the horsewoman Maria Zoë that the youth attacking now wasn't riding very well. He was bouncing too far out of the saddle, and when he collided with her immobile husband, he tumbled backwards into the sand—to the hoots and laughter of the youths collected around the lists.

Maria Zoë sucked in her breath in sympathy and glanced over her shoulder at her waiting woman, Beatrice, who had come to join her at the window. It was Beatrice's eldest son who had just been so publicly disgraced.

Beatrice grimaced and shook her head. "He'll never make up the lost years," she commented realistically. Beatrice's father, Sir Bartholomew, had held a knight's fief from Ibelin for half a century. Despite his sixty-some years, he had been with his lord at Hattin, but in the aftermath of that defeat, Beatrice and all three of her sons had been taken captive by the Saracens. They had been slaves for five years before the Treaty of Ramla freed them. As a result, from the age of eleven to sixteen, her eldest son Bart had sat cross-legged on the dirt floor of a hovel knotting cotton to a frame, the slave of a carpet maker, instead of learning the skills of knighthood.

Before Maria Zoë could comment, she and Beatrice were distracted by the next attack. This came from Beatrice's second son, Amalric. He had been sold to a smith rather than a carpet maker and had returned from captivity not only big and strong, but burning with hatred. He launched himself at his blindfolded lord with the fury of a man who pictured himself in combat with his worst enemy—or maybe just with the determination of a youth who wished to wipe away his brother's humiliation. His attack was strong enough to make

Ras Dawit whinny as the horses collided. When Balian leaned forward to knock him back, Amalric grabbed the edge of his shield and tried to twist his opponent off his horse. Balian responded by spurring his horse forward, and Ras Dawit flung himself into the other horse with enough force to stagger him. Meanwhile, Balian wrenched his shield loose and used it to bludgeon the unfortunate Amalric, who (as the hooting and shouting indicated) was soundly outmatched.

"It must be reassuring to see how well your lord husband fights," Beatrice noted behind Maria Zoë as her second son also hit the dust.

Maria Zoë nodded. "It is—and I don't doubt your father taught him much of it. He was the drillmaster for the squires when Balian was a youth."

Beatrice nodded and looked away quickly, because she still had not come to terms with her father's death. He had lived to see her and the boys return from captivity, but he had died this past autumn. He had found peace at last, she told herself, and he had certainly earned the rest of heaven, but she missed him desperately. He was the only one who fully understood the pain she felt over her youngest son, Joscelyn. Jos had been only six when he was captured, and he had returned a Mamluke and a Muslim. To this day he insisted he would not worship "idols," called the rest of them "polytheists," and swore he would return to "his master" (al-Adil) as soon as he reached maturity at fifteen.

She felt a hand on her arm and looked over at the Dowager Queen. The expression in Maria Zoë's eyes suggested that she did understand. "It is hard to bury a child," she said softly, "but far harder to watch a child willfully destroy himself."

Beatrice nodded, blinking back her tears, and drew a deep breath, oblivious to the fact that Maria Zoë was referring to the temper tantrum her eldest son was throwing in the lists below the window. Maria Zoë had not given up hope for Joscelyn—who was, after all, only twelve. He showed an increasing interest in riding and jousting with the other boys his own age, who were all eager squires-in-waiting. Bart, on the other hand, was handicapped not only by the time lost in captivity, but also by a sullen and whiny temperament that alienated his comrades.

"I suppose it's time we got back to work," Maria Zoë announced to change the subject, and left the window seat to return to the pile of linens the two women had been sorting through. The linens had been discovered in some trunks under a semi-collapsed roof in one of the partially burned out-buildings. While badly mildewed on discovery, after a thorough washing they were looking quite serviceable. Given the state of their finances, Maria Zoë was determined to let nothing go to waste, and these linens could, she felt, be turned into surcoats, tunics, or, if quilted, gambesons for the squires and aketons for the men-at-arms.

For now, however, she was hoping to use them on the tables for the upcoming Christmas feast. Last year they'd had only bare tables; this year she wanted the feast to be more festive. A little more pomp, she felt, would signal hope.

Wild shouting from the lists, however, again distracted her. This had a different ring to it. It wasn't the usual shouted advice and insults, nor the cheers and boos of judgment. She rushed back to the window and stuck her head out just in time to see two men ride into the lists. Before she had fully recognized who and what they were, her husband (who was no longer blindfolded) flung himself from his horse to embrace one of the riders, who had vaulted down to meet him.

"It's John!" Maria Zoë exclaimed in amazement. "And Aimery! They must have come for Christmas!"

She leaned as far as she could out of the window into the brisk wintry air and called as she waved, "John! Aimery! Welcome home!"

John heard her and waved back, a broad grin on his face.

Maria Zoë had learned dignity at the court in Constantinople. For the first twenty years of her life, she had been trained not to show her emotions, not to "betray" herself to those around her—who were (by definition in Constantinople) her inferiors. But over the last nineteen years she had, piece by piece, broken out of that prison. She grabbed a shawl in passing and hurried out of the solar, calling up the spiral stairs to the floor above, "Eschiva! Come quick! Your lord husband is back!"

Eschiva had been in the nursery with her daughters Burgundia (nine) and Helvis (seven) and her youngest child, four-year-old Aimery. She appeared almost at once at the top of the stairs to ask, "What did you say? Aimery is here? At Caymont?"

"Down in the lists, but he'll be inside shortly."

Eschiva put her hands to her hair, her gown, her face. "I'm not ready for him! I have to change! I need—"

"You have rarely looked as lovely as you do right now," Maria Zoë told her with a smile. She was not lying. Eschiva had bloomed in the more simple rural life of Caymont. At court, in her former capacity as lady to Queen Isabella, Eschiva had been constantly exposed to the problems of the realm—from finances and disputes over land to threats and rumors—without, of course, being able to do anything about any of them. Here at Caymont, she had nothing to worry about but whether her eldest child, eleven-year-old Guy, was taking care of his pony and whether the girls were learning to stitch.

"Oh, no, I must change," Eschiva insisted, disappearing from the top of the stairs. It was not vanity that motivated her; Eschiva had no illusions about being particularly attractive. Rather the opposite—a nagging insecurity that Aimery, who had so often cheated on her in the past, would be disappointed.

Maria Zoë let her be, and turned instead to cross the great hall and descend the stairs to the inner courtyard, reaching it just as her son and Aimery came through the archway from the road with Balian and a gaggle of young men around them. Aimery had his arm draped over the shoulders of his eldest son, Guy, while John's younger brother Philip, who was the same age as Guy, bounded beside John like an excited puppy.

The past year had been good for Philip, Maria Zoë noted mentally. He had always stood in John's shadow, and to escape it he had often been disobedient, foolish, or wayward. The more John strove to please his father and be ready to step into his shoes, the more Philip rebelled. Maria Zoë could hardly blame her husband for the attention he had showered on John, but she knew Philip had been jealous—until John went away with Aimery and his father turned his attention to his remaining son. Without John to compete against, Philip had become more stable and more congenial. Caught red-handed in a misdemeanor, he had always had the most outrageous excuses, but this last year he had shown he could use his glib tongue to entertain them all. His sharp wit seemed capable of finding the humor in almost any situation, and Maria Zoë could not count the times he had saved them from feeling sorry for themselves with some remark that made them laugh. She was glad to see her husband reach out to Philip and pull him into the circle of his arm as he said something to John that made Philip blush, struggle, and then punch his father—laughing all the while.

Behind the principals trailed Henri de Brie's two sons, Anseau and Conan. They too had been left at Caymont with their mother, Heloise, while their father served Guy de Lusignan on Cyprus. They were clearly trying to attract John's attention, while bringing up the rear was a big, furry dog. The latter was evidently confused by the large crowd and was trying frantically to push his way through them all to John. Maria Zoë laughed: John had his dog at last.

It was nearly midnight before Aimery could be alone with Eschiva. First there had been the boisterous reception by Ibelin's men, then greetings from the household, followed by a meal in the hall with nearly a hundred people, including servants and tenants. Even after the public portion of the day was over, his family had demanded attention. They had eventually seen the younger children off to bed, which meant Aimery had to carry his already sleeping namesake up to his little pallet and tuck Helvis into the big bed she shared with Burgundia and

Balian's Meg. But Aimery's oldest son Guy wanted his attention, too. Aimery could have said no—but this last nine months, watching his brother brooding in his loneliness, had made Aimery see his family in a new light. His brother Guy had worn a crown, but he was now nothing but a lonely, prematurely aged man. So Aimery took the time to talk at length to his brother's namesake until the boy's eyes were falling shut. Only after young Guy had also been sent to bed could Aimery and Eschiva retreat to their own cramped quarters under the eaves.

Closing the door to their little chamber and throwing the bolt, Aimery looked at his wife. Eschiva had always been eclipsed by the women around her: the Greek princess selected for her beauty to be bride to the King of Jerusalem, and that woman's daughter by the notoriously good-looking King Amalric. Eschiva had also served the infamous Eleanor of Aquitaine's daughter for a bit, when the latter accompanied her brother King Richard to the Holy Land. Yet even in the absence of more celebrated beauties, Eschiva would never turn men's heads when she walked into a room. She was too slim, too flat, too small. Her hair was a medium brown rather than blond or dark chestnut. Yet her features were harmonious, her lips soft, and her eyes a rich, amber gold—and most of all, she was his. She had been his since she was eight years old, and he so much older that he thought of her not at all.

He would never forget that day he rode back to Ibelin after her father, the Baron of Ramla and Mirabel, was taken captive on the Litani. The Sultan's ransom demands were so ridiculous that he'd pictured Eschiva's entire inheritance—*his* future lands— mortgaged to the hilt to pay them. He'd come to Ibelin to secure those lands by consummating his marriage to Ramla's heiress. He hadn't much cared what she looked like, and he couldn't remember how old she actually was. He'd been waiting impatiently in the hall for what seemed like hours, fuming at the entire situation, when the Dowager Queen had walked in with a lovely little dove beside her, and he'd been stunned to realize that that dove was his wife!

He had consummated their marriage, not with the cold efficiency of greed that had brought him to Ibelin that day, but rather with genuine delight and passion that had fostered a sense of protectiveness and affection. Those feelings had grown into love as time passed. Not that he hadn't dallied with other women in the early years, but his year in Saracen captivity had cured him of his wayward eye. He had returned determined never to stray again, for the sake of his marriage and his soul.

These last nine months had reinforced those feelings. What other woman would ever love him as unquestioningly as Eschiva? Who else would look at him with admiring eyes despite his graying hair and thickening waist? Where else could he be assured of complete acceptance, regardless of what he did? Even now, after a long absence in a strange land, Eschiva did not question him or ask what he had been up to. Instead she gazed at him, watching his every move, listening to whatever he had to say, smiling whenever he looked at her. She returned even the most casual touch with hungry eagerness.

Now all he had to do was stretch out his arms, and she came into them wordlessly. He folded them around her and swiveled back and forth as if to calm a child, when in fact it was his own racing emotions that he needed to calm. There was so much to say, he could not find any words. So they made love instead, frantically like young lovers and then languidly like old ones, and then they cuddled together like children, and Aimery thanked God for his wife.

While Eschiva fell into a deep, contented sleep, breathing evenly in his arms, Aimery lay awake thinking. For nine months he had argued with his brother Guy about the latter's counterproductive policies. He had been frustrated to the point of madness by Guy's stubborn refusal to consider alternatives. He'd been driven to silent rage by his brother's sullen adherence to the poisonous advice of men like Barlais, Cheneché, and Henri de Brie. He'd begged Guy to at least leave Nicosia and take a look at things for himself—all in vain. For nine months he had racked his brain for an explanation. And tonight he had discovered it.

Guy didn't care what his policies did to Cyprus, and he didn't care if the Cypriots hated him. Guy clung to Cyprus because he had nowhere else to go, but he did not love it or cherish it. Because he had no one to leave it to.

For as long as John could remember, his father had taken him along on rounds of his barony. As a very little boy, he had ridden in his father's lap; later he'd ridden his own pony. His earliest memories were of his father showing him the fields, orchards, mills, and villages of Ibelin. Always, his father had been at pains to explain to him about the different crops and different peoples that made Ibelin rich. Ibelin lay on the fertile coastal plain south of Jaffa, and the sound of seagulls crying and the smell of the salt air, like the yellow dunes, had been part of the landscape.

Caymont, in contrast, lay in an inland valley along a lazy river that almost disappeared in the dry season but after the rains flowed slowly, a muddy brown. The principal crop of the manor domain of Caymont was sugar cane rather than pomegranates and citrus fruits. Irrigation was essential to the production of sugar cane, Balian explained to his son, as they rode down toward the river from the manor that stood higher up the slope of the rugged hills. Aqueducts brought the water from springs in the mountains to large, stone-lined reservoirs, and ditches funneled it to the upper edges of the fields, where gravity led it down the rows of cane. The fields were divided into plots large enough to be harvested in a single day. They cut off the water to each plot one month before it was due to be harvested, and harvested the sugar one month later. The stalks were brought to the large limestone sugar mill, located in the middle of the fields, to be crushed and processed. Only during the rainy season did the sugar production halt.

They left the manor shortly after the sun lifted itself over the mountain range to the east. Balian urged John to try one of the younger stallions at the stud, with the irresistible argument that "You'll need a second horse once you're knighted." John's spirits soared at the mere thought of knighthood, and he selected a bay stallion with a billowing mane that his father assured him was one of their best. "He's cheeky if you don't pay attention, but intelligent." Philip joined them, riding his own stocky gelding and in irrepressible high spirits.

There were several hawks floating on the morning air, and twice they stopped to let shepherds herd their charges down to the river for watering along the designated paths between the fields of sugar. After crossing the river by ford, they picked up an easy canter through the cane fields on the far side until they reached the vineyards that rose up gently behind the sugar. The vines stretched parallel to the river, and Ibelin slowed to a walk so they could pick their way carefully. Many of the stalks were very tiny and barely visible above the surface of the soil, replacements for the vines trampled down by the Saracen cavalry as they swept through. Fortunately, Balian told his sons, the Sultan's cavalry had not taken the time to systematically destroy the vineyards, and some of the vines had survived. These survivors stood upright and proudly spread their leaves along the strings stretched between the stalks. The leaves were a mustard yellow at this time of year.

Beyond the vineyards the slope became steep and was dotted with olive trees. Here at last Ibelin gave his horse his head. With his eldest son close behind and his younger son trailing, he galloped up a steep, rugged path, both exciting and exhausting the horses.

When at last they crested the hill, the horses slowed of their own free will, breathing heavily, but snorting and shaking their heads in pleasure. Ibelin drew up and, gesturing toward the next valley, remarked, "This is the border."

"It looks like the Sultan hasn't awarded the land to anyone yet," John noted observantly, taking in the fact that the valley lay fallow, sprouting weeds rather than useful crops.

"That, or the recipient is too busy intriguing against al-Afdal to spend time here," his father countered.

John looked over, unsure what this meant; Philip was less inhibited. "Why don't we take it back?" he asked cheerfully.

"There's a treaty—" John started to remind his brother in exasperation, but his father cut him off, explaining in a far more patient voice, "Because I swore to uphold the Treaty of Ramla, Philip, a treaty I personally negotiated."

Philip sighed and looked duly chastised for half a second. Then he cheered up and announced, "I'll bet there's lots of game in those woods over there. There's not anything in the treaty against hunting in unoccupied land, is there?"

His father laughed. "No, I didn't think about that at the time. Maybe another day." He turned his horse around and they started to descend at a more decorous pace, letting the horses find their footing carefully among the loose stones.

"How are things, Papa?" John asked earnestly.

"Good," his father answered. Then, recognizing that this answer was not enough for his heir, he elaborated. "We've been very lucky. Edwin Shoreham agreed to leave his flourishing business in Tyre to come help us rebuild." Edwin Shoreham was the carpenter son of Ibelin's former master sergeant. Ibelin had knighted the elder Shoreham during the defense of Jerusalem, and two of his younger sons had died there. John understood that Edwin (and his shrewd but shrewish wife) had come to Caymont to support the aging Sir Roger and comfort him in his lingering grief over his lost sons.

Balian was continuing, "The rains were good, which helped; but more important, we found good tenants for the outlying farms, the ones producing millet and barley, and—what's more astonishing—we were able to recruit two score families willing to work in the vineyards and cane fields. They're almost all Syrians, refugees from southern Galilee and Bethsan."

"So they're Orthodox Christians?" John asked, pricking up his ears.

"Yes, Jacobites," his father confirmed.

"Do they come to church?" John asked next.

"What do you mean? They don't attend *our* Mass. Most of them don't speak more than a smattering of French, much less Latin. Their own priest conducts Mass in Arabic according to their rites after our Latin Mass in the chapel is finished. Of course, that's only because they don't have a church of their own yet. I've allotted them land near the sugar factory, and most of the rocks we cleared from the irrigation ditches have been piled there for reuse. They hope to start construction soon, now that the rainy season has started and we can't cut the cane anyway."

John nodded thoughtfully, explaining to his father, "Carlo—that's the man who runs the khan where Lord Aimery and I live—says that King Richard promised to let the Greeks on Cyprus retain their churches and monasteries and to live under the laws that had been valid under the Emperor Manuel I. But the Templars tried to make the people follow the Latin rites, and now King Guy is trying to make the churches and monasteries pay taxes to him, although they were exempt in the time of Manuel I. Carlo says that's the main reason the people of Cyprus are up in arms against King Guy."

"Is this rebellion serious, then?" Ibelin asked frowning slightly.

"It's terrible!" John exclaimed. "King Guy claims he doesn't have any income and is afraid to leave Nicosia, while Brie, Barlais, and Cheneché spend all their time burning things down to make people pay up. The Pisans say King Guy and his men are destroying the tax base and impoverishing everyone, not to mention sowing hatred of all Latins and Franks!" John told his father hotly.

That didn't sound good to Balian, and he shook his head. "What does Lord Aimery say?"

"That his brother's crazy, but King Guy won't listen to him any more than to the English knights King Richard left on the island. He doesn't listen to anyone, really. Not even Cheneché and Brie, because *they* keep urging him to assign them territory and let them pacify it, each in their own way."

Balian laughed shortly. "Your cousin wants a barony, John."

"Is that so bad?" John asked back cautiously. After all, that's what Aimery— and in his own heart John, too—wanted. Not one like this, though, cut off from the sea, dependent on unreliable rains, vulnerable to Saracen attack, and haunted by the ghosts of past tenants. . . .

"No, it's perfectly natural," his father answered his question reasonably. "It's what men fight for—land, wealth, fame, and faith—probably in that order. Why does Guy de Lusignan" (John noticed his father did not dignify him with the title "king") "resist carving the island up? It's big and rich enough to support more than a score of baronies, much less reward the handful of men with him."

John weighed his head from side to side. "I'm not sure, but once when Bethsan was pressing for 'clear authority' in one place or another, King Guy snarled that he wasn't about to set up another High Court that could turn against him."

"Ah," Balian nodded knowingly. "So that's the problem." When John and Philip stared at him questioningly, he elaborated, "Guy's never forgotten or forgiven the High Court for opposing him. He's afraid of independent barons, men who have independent opinions, and—more dangerous—sufficient resources to stand on their own feet."

That made sense to John and he nodded, but then he had another thought. "Did you know Humphrey de Toron was with King Guy?"

"I guess I had heard that, but I'd forgotten. You've seen him?" Balian asked with a sideways glance. He too could remember when Humphrey had been like an older brother to John.

"He agrees with Lord Aimery about using less force, but he won't speak up. He says if he spoke up it would do more harm than good."

Balian snorted and conceded, "He's probably right."

"Why do people look down on him so much?" John asked cautiously.

"I don't know about 'people,'" Balian's tone turned tart, "but *I* will never forgive him for betraying us at Nablus, sneaking out in the dark of night to go pay homage to Sibylla, thereby undermining the authority of the High Court and denying Isabella her rightful crown. It was because of him that Guy was crowned king, that your uncle Baldwin fled the Kingdom, that the Count of Tripoli sought a separate peace with Saladin, and ultimately that we found ourselves on the Horns of Hattin."

John knew all that, but it wasn't what he was actually asking about. He tried again. "But that's not everything, is it? I mean, Gauvain de Cheneché accused him of being a sodomite. . . ." John concentrated on guiding his horse as he said this, too embarrassed to risk a glance at his father.

Balian gave his son another sidelong glance and asked back, "You know what that means?"

"I think so. I can't really picture it."

"Oh, I'll show you!" Philip offered, making John snarl at him to "shut up" and Balian laugh before warning sternly, "You'd better not, or I'll have your hide in *this* life—before the Lord sends you to hell for all eternity in the next."

"I just meant I can show John two sodomites painted on the mural of the Last Judgment in the Cathedral of the Holy Cross in Acre. Ernoul pointed it out to me at Easter."

"I'll have *his* hide for that!" Balian responded, but in a tone that made his sons laugh, and they dropped the topic. John, however, registered that his father had not denied the charge against Toron.

Later that day, a weather front swept in from the West. Stiff winds lashed rain mixed with snow across the valley, and howled around the walls and towers of the manor. By nightfall the peaks of the hills around them were dusted white with snow, but Balian was pleased to have the reservoirs and cisterns refilled.

Meanwhile the household, forced inside by the weather, set to work decorating the hall and chapel for the Feast of the Nativity. In the kitchens, preparations were under way for a banquet, and the tenants had brought their solstice payments with the intention of staying through Christmas in order to enjoy Mass at the manor chapel and then partake in the traditional baronial Christmas festivities.

John found himself helping out in a variety of ways, from hanging holly on the walls to helping Father Angelus note and provide receipts for tithe payments. During the latter, John surprised (and amused) Father Angelus with his fluent but eclectic mix of imperial and colloquial (Cypriot!) Greek. They chatted away in this tongue as they worked. "You must show your mother how your Greek has improved!" Father Angelus urged. "She'll be delighted!"

John was not reluctant to follow that advice, but he had a hard time finding an opportunity because his mother was so busy organizing the Christmas festivities. It was not until after compline, when his mother sank down into her favorite chair before the fire in the solar and announced she was exhausted but would like a cup of mulled wine before retiring, that John got his chance.

"*Thelis krasi levko ee kokino?*" John asked his mother, springing to his feet to serve her.

She smiled and answered, "*Levko, parakalo.*"

All that was quite simple, but now John surprised her with a flood of Greek—assuring her he would bring her mulled white wine, but only on the condition she stayed up to talk to him a little more. He had a thousand questions for her, he warned.

The smile she gave him would have melted the hearts of monks and mercenaries, much less her teenage son. "Janis," she assured him in Greek, "to hear you speak my mother tongue like that, I would stay up *all* night. Send someone else for the wine!" Switching to French, she twisted around in her chair to call, "Ernoul? Ernoul? Where did he get to?" Although her husband had two squires, there was a division of labor between them. Ernoul, who had been too badly wounded at Hattin to carry arms ever again, no longer kept his lord's armor, arms, or horses; those tasks fell to Georgios. Instead, he was expected to serve them at table and afterwards.

"Practicing his Christmas concert, of course," her husband answered, coming up behind her. He laid his hands on her shoulders and his thumbs started rubbing the back of her neck, making her close her eyes with a sigh of contentment. "He is more troubadour than squire, and it's time we acknowledged it. He's a father, too. Far too old for squiring. I think I need a new squire, don't you?" he spoke into her serenity.

"Who were you thinking of?" she asked without opening her eyes, while John ducked out to get her the mulled wine she wanted.

"Amalric, Beatrice's middle boy."

Maria Zoë's eyes flew open, and she craned her neck to look up at her husband. "Passing over his older brother? Won't Bart be jealous? Insulted?"

Balian sighed and moved around to seat himself in the chair waiting for him beside her. "Yes and no. He thinks he's already his father's successor and should be knighted."

"He's nowhere near ready!" Maria Zoë protested.

"And he never will be—as he well knows. He wants to avoid the unpleasantness of training and failing for all to see. The bigger problem is, I cannot afford to give him a fief. I need tenants who can work the land, not youths too taken with their alleged status and 'birth rights' to bend their backs to labor. I don't think he'll ever willingly accept that fact. He's already threatened to haul me before the High Court for not giving him a fief."

"The impudent little brat!" Maria Zoë declared indignantly, adding, "He should be grateful you waste time with him at all!" Yet at another level she understood Bart's problem. Precisely because he had been a slave five long years, he was overly sensitive about his status. The Baron of Ibelin might clear irrigation ditches with his tenants, but never Bart d'Auber. She noted cautiously, "On the other hand, you *do* still owe six knights to the feudal army."

"True, and Bart d'Auber will never be one of them," Balian answered firmly, then checked over his shoulders to be sure Beatrice was not within hearing. He'd only broached the topic because he had not seen her here.

"Beatrice asked to go to bed early," Maria Zoë answered his look. "She seemed very tired. I hope she's not ill."

Balian nodded agreement. "I hope she's not, too. Not now, just before Christmas, when you need all the help you can get. But as I was saying, I don't believe Bart will ever make a knight. Amalric, on the other hand, has the right instincts for a fighting man. He's aggressive and daring without being foolhardy. He's had the nonsense knocked out of him the hard way, and he's surprisingly cagey for a youth of just sixteen. Nor does he shy away from hard work. He's always the first down at the lists, and often the last to leave as well. He knows he's not yet good enough with a sword to survive real combat, which makes him try harder, not less. If I give him a chance, I believe he'll grow into a very solid and trustworthy knight—like his grandfather."

"But if you knight the younger brother and give him a fief, Bart will hate you."

"I didn't say I'd give Amalric a fief. I see him as a household knight. No more. Unless our fortunes change." Changing the subject, he asked after Eschiva and Aimery.

"Off to bed early," Maria Zoë answered with a knowing smile.

"I hope Eschiva *wants* another child," Balian remarked with a slight frown, remembering how frightened his niece had always been of pregnancy.

"She does," Maria Zoë assured him simply.

Balian chose not to pursue this discussion, because at this point John returned with a tray laden with goblets and a wine carafe. He presented both to his mother with a new flood of Greek.

Balian got to his feet. "If the two of you are going to chatter in that incomprehensible tongue, I'll leave you to it." Although he pretended irritation, he was very pleased to see that John had finally mastered a language he had long resisted, and he understood that his wife wanted time alone with her son. He kissed her hand in parting, and left John with his mother.

First John told his mother about his many adventures: how he'd found and adopted Barry, the attack in the tavern (he'd only promised not to tell his *father* about that), King Guy's reception of them, the complaints of the Italian communes, and his adventures in disguise. His cheerful, almost bragging narrative elicited frequent laughter from his mother, sometimes as much for the idiomatic slang picked up on the streets of Nicosia as for the content. When he started talking of the encounter with Lakis, however, his tone turned thoughtful and worried. He ended by asking his mother plaintively, "How could I have helped him?"

He was seated on a cushion at his mother's feet, with Barry's head in his lap. Maria Zoë bent down and kissed the top of his head. "The important thing is that you *wanted* to help him, John."

"From *his* point of view, I don't think that's good enough!" he answered testily.

"No, perhaps not," his mother conceded. Her pride in a son who worried about how to help others rather than about his dignity (like Bart d'Auber) or his skills at horse and arms (like Amalric) was almost overwhelming. She knew better than to patronize him, however, and so answered practically. "Finding him an apprenticeship would help him most—a bookbinder would be perfect, if there is such a thing in Nicosia. I could ask in Acre if they know of an appropriate shop on Cyprus."

The school of manuscript illustrators, previously attached to the Church of the Holy Sepulcher, had re-established itself in Acre. They had been some of the primary beneficiaries of Ibelin's surrender, as there was little doubt that, had Jerusalem fallen to Saladin by assault, the precious Christian texts decorated with images abhorred by Islam would have been destroyed. Because Ibelin's surrender terms allowed the inhabitants of Jerusalem to ransom themselves and remove their portable property, the canons of the Holy Sepulcher had been able to rescue their most precious manuscripts and much of their vellum, parchment, paints, and brushes as well. Furthermore, the monks themselves had looked death in the face as the northern wall of Jerusalem collapsed, and they said daily prayers of thanks for their salvation—and for the Baron of Ibelin. Maria Zoë had no doubt that she could ask a favor of them. "I don't suppose this orphan speaks any French or Latin?" she asked her son, thinking that a place with the scriptorium itself would offer the greatest chance of betterment.

"Lakis? No, he only speaks Greek. Mother?"

"Yes?"

"Just what are the differences between the Greek and the Latin Church?"

Maria Zoë drew a deep breath, and then shook her head. "It's far too late, I'm too tired, and I've had too much wine. We'll have to take up theology another day, if you don't mind."

"But you were raised in the Greek Church," John insisted. "It can't be that different from the Latin Church."

"It's not. The churches differ more on matters of form than content. We—I mean the Greek Orthodox Church—does not recognize the authority of the Pope to determine doctrine, for example, believing that only an ecumenical council of the heads of all the churches can do that. All Eastern Orthodox Churches, as far as I know, also believe that the Holy Spirit springs from the Father but not the Son."

"Is that important?" John asked, frowning.

His mother laughed shortly. "I'm far too tired to know, John, and I can't say it ever mattered to me, but you really ought to put these questions to Father Angelus and Father Michael. They have been your tutors since before you could read or write, and they have spent the better part of twenty years arguing—amicably, I might point out—about these very matters. If, however, you insist on asking a daughter of the Imperial family of the Eastern Roman Empire, then I will give you a political, rather than a theological, answer."

John grinned. "That's what I want, Mama!"

Maria Zoë laughed, recognizing her husband in her son. "The principal issue is who controls doctrine, and so what people think and believe. In the West, the Pope has established a position of unassailable dominance that allows him to excommunicate kings and call crusades, for example. My ancestors, on the other hand, resisted the idea of allowing any prelate to become that powerful. They preferred to let Church matters be determined by collective discussion—which inherently fostered competition and diversity of opinion and so opportunities to, shall we say, *influence* matters. At times, the divisions could be quite bitter and destructive, as during the iconoclastic strife, but on the whole the tactic allowed the Emperors to retain a powerful voice in Church matters."

"Yes, but that doesn't explain why millers and butchers on Cyprus should prefer to impale themselves on Templar lances than go to a Latin Mass," John protested.

"True," Maria Zoë conceded. "That has little to do with either theology or politics. One might even argue it has to do with the very *absence* of theological understanding. Illiterate people, who inherently understand little of the concepts behind the rituals they follow, often mistake form for content. And then there's the issue of celibacy," she added in a playful tone. "Greek Orthodox priests can marry. They are not prepared to sacrifice that privilege lightly, so they generally rile up their flocks to protect their pleasures."

John's scowl made her realize she had offended him. With a deep breath she forced herself to get serious again and continued, "Mostly, I think, it has to do with preferring to hear services in a language we understand."

"So, why don't we let people worship in whatever language they like?" John asked back earnestly.

"But we do! The Jacobites here hold their services in Arabic," she pointed out. "And have you forgotten there were synagogues and mosques in Nablus? They were only banned from Jerusalem itself—and that more for military rather than theological reasons."

John started slightly. He had forgotten. His mother's lands of Nablus seemed as far away as ancient Rome to John. "Didn't the King of Jerusalem object?" John asked, puzzled.

"Object to what?"

"Letting mosques and synagogues flourish?"

"Not at all. He simply taxed them more heavily," Maria Zoë replied a bit flippantly, and again regretted it. John was still very earnest. To make up for her tone, she leaned down, put her hands on both his shoulders and spoke very seriously. "There are good and bad men of every faith, John. The beauty of Christianity is it shows us the road to salvation through forgiveness and understanding. But if you really want to know my personal opinion"—Maria Zoë was a little drunk by now and about to confess something she would not have voiced to her more Catholic husband—"I don't honestly think God cares what rite or formula we use for prayer. I think the only thing that matters to *Him* is *what* we pray for and the sincerity with which we do it."

John twisted around and looked up at her. "Thank you."

She kissed his forehead, and then pushed herself to her feet. "And that is the last you will get from me tonight, John. I am going to bed, no matter what you say."

Chapter Seven
Rebels Against the Hospital

Island of Cyprus
April 1194

Kolossi

IT WAS THE STINK OF BURNED sugar that John would remember the rest of his life.

Word that rebels had attacked the hospital and sugar factory at Kolossi, run by the Knights Hospitaller, had reached Nicosia late on Sunday, but it had taken Lord Aimery two days to convince his brother Guy to let him go to investigate. Aimery and John had left the following morning and ridden hard to reach Limassol by nightfall. Here they had requested and received the hospitality of the Templars, staying overnight in the fortress-like commandery in the heart of the town. Aside from the obvious advantages of a clean bed, hearty food, and security, the Templars had also given refuge to the victims of the brutal attack, and Aimery had been able to interview the Turcopole commander as well as some of the Brother Sergeants from the hospital.

These men reported that a mob two to three hundred strong had attacked the Hospitaller commandery as darkness fell on Friday night. The attackers were not heavily armed, but the Hospitallers swore they must have been tipped off that the Hospitaller commander and all ten knights had left Kolossi to answer a call for assistance from a Venetian vessel in distress off the coast. At the time of the attack, therefore, only the Turcopoles, hospital staff, and lay brothers were on the premises. Furthermore, the factory had already closed for the day. Except for the night watchman, who tended the vats, the workers had dispersed to their homes in the surrounding villages.

Because the Hospitallers had taken over the factory and manor only eight months previously, they had not yet built any kind of defenses. Low stone walls marked the perimeter, while the manor itself consisted of a rectangular stone building over a vaulted chamber that was partially underground. The hall was accessed by a broad exterior stairway, but there was neither a gap nor a drawbridge separating the top of the stairs from the building. The hospital was nothing but a low vaulted chamber of fieldstone held together with mortar. The church was an old Greek structure, another low vaulted building with a single apse and narrow windows.

The Hospitallers had not been expecting any kind of aggression against them. They had established a hospital that served the poor of the surrounding countryside, and had been treating no fewer than thirty-two patients when the attack occurred. In addition, they had restarted production in the sugar factory, which had lain idle since the fall of Isaac Comnenus, thereby providing jobs to half a hundred workers from local communities. The Brothers of the Hospital were unanimous in expressing their bewilderment at the attack.

"Had there been complaints about wages or the like?" Lord Aimery asked the senior Turcopole.

"No, not at all! We pay better than the local landlords, let alone the mines! Besides, it wasn't our workers who did the damage. The mob consisted of outsiders, for the most part. We recognized only a handful of local youths, troublemakers we had dismissed." The Turcopole was lying in the Templar infirmary, his head bandaged over one eye and his arm in a splint, evidence of his efforts to stop the mob.

"This sounds well organized," Lord Aimery observed dryly.

"Very well organized! They came armed with clubs and axes and they had torches, too. But they looted first. They took not just the plate and furnishings from our hall, they took the wine from our cellars, the grain stacked there, and the olives, too. They even stole the personal belongings of the patients—their own people!—before setting the building on fire!"

"With the patients still inside?" Lord Aimery asked in horror.

"No, no, they dragged them out into the yard, and then went in and searched for valuables, stuffing anything they found into sacks they'd brought with them. *Then* they set the place on fire."

"Who was leading them?" Lord Aimery wanted to know.

"A monk, a Greek monk!" the Turcopole reported, spitting on the floor to show his contempt.

"Young? Old? Fat? Thin? What can you tell me about him?"

"He was young, no more than twenty-five. Not tall, but strongly built with a barrel chest. If it hadn't been for his robes, I would have taken him for a black-smith or a carpenter. He had a thick black beard, like they all do, and a broad, strong nose. His most striking feature, however, was his eyes: they burned with hatred."

"Anyone else you noticed?"

"Not really. It was getting darker by the second and the torches and fires were blinding, casting everything else into shadow."

Lord Aimery nodded understanding, and asked if there had been serious casualties. The Turcopole reported that no one had been killed and that he and the other Turcopoles had suffered no injuries more serious than broken bones and bruises, but that the patients and lay brothers serving them were trauma-tized. There had been four women patients, all more or less elderly women, and they were saying they would never return to Kolossi. One was even demand-ing admission to a nunnery, although she had not been violated, just roughly handled and insulted.

"They demanded our names—almost as if they were looking for someone, or at least Franks."

Lord Aimery nodded. He had heard similar stories. The rebels might steal from their fellow Greeks if they were, like the workers and patients of the Hospital, benefiting in any way from the new regime, but they didn't want to kill their fellow countrymen. Even the Turcopoles were probably spared greater violence because they were natives of Syria, Orthodox rather than Latin. The worst violence was reserved for Latin Christians—Franks and Italians, but espe-cially Franks.

"What happened to your priest?" Lord Aimery thought to ask.

"They stripped him naked and bound him backwards on a mule. Then they hit the mule on the rump to make him run away. We found him the next morning in a field several miles away, still tied to the mule, scratched, cut, and bruised from collisions with trees and God knows what else. He was in a terrible state of mind. He had seen the fires and assumed we were all dead."

Despite these stories, it was still the smell and sight of the gutted sugar factory that shocked John the most. It was just four months since he had visited his father's sugar mill. His father had led him around, pointing out the equipment and explaining the process of cutting, crushing, and boiling the raw sugar multiple times until thick molasses formed and dripped into pottery molds. At the time, he had been bored and only pretended interest to please his father. Yet he understood instinctively that his father had spent so much time explaining things to him because he was proud of reopening the sugar mill. From his father's description of all the problems encountered and costs incurred, John understood it had been very difficult. It would have been no different at Kolossi. The Hospitallers had invested time, money, and heart's blood to get this factory working again. Now it was a charred hulk oozing foul-smelling smoke, and the floors were glazed with sticky black pools of burnt sugar.

"Why burn down the sugar mill?" John asked. "It benefited the people in the local communities."

"And because of that, the locals are not so hostile to Frankish rule. The rebels want everyone to hate us," Lord Aimery answered. "What I don't understand is why the workers didn't defend their livelihoods, their employer, their hospital. And who tipped the rebels off that the knights were away? They clearly didn't want to risk a fight with armed knights. Or should I rather ask, who sent word to the commander that a Venetian ship was in distress just down the coast? A phantom ship, it seems, as the Hospitallers rode up and down the coast all night looking for it and never saw any sign of it."

They had not been able to talk to the commander of the Hospitallers at Kolossi, because he and his knights had already left Limassol by ship to report to headquarters in Acre. All in all, Aimery did not think the Hospitaller commander had covered himself in glory, but it wasn't his business. The Order would have to deal with him.

"Do you think you could find anything out from the villagers?" Lord Aimery asked his squire.

John shrugged. "I doubt it. I'm dressed like a Frank."

"Try. I'll be in the church."

While the interior of the manor house and hospital had been torched after the looting, the church had not. The rebels had, of course, helped themselves to the cross, candlesticks, and even the icons, but they had not burned the building itself. Tethering his horse outside, Lord Aimery slipped into the empty church to await his squire's reconnaissance.

John, with Barry loping behind him, rode the half-mile to the nearest village, which sat astride the Limassol-Paphos road at the place where the road to Kolossi branched off it. The village consisted of a well, a threshing floor, and a church similar to that at Kolossi, surrounded by some two dozen low cottages covered with rough, dirty plaster and topped by flat roofs.

As John approached, the barefoot children ran away to their respective houses, and the chickens in the yards scattered. A woman at the well, hearing the high-pitched screams of the children, paused, looked over her shoulder, and at once let go of the rope to flee down the street. The released bucket splashed at the base of the well and the spool continued to unwind several turns, unraveling a yard of rope.

John stopped and looked around for someone to talk to. The village appeared abandoned, but he was certain that many eyes were watching him from inside the narrow windows.

With a sigh he dismounted, tethered Centurion, and approached the first house, with Barry at his heels. He knocked on the closed door. Something scraped and bumped on the far side, but no one answered his knock. He went on to the next house. This time he could hear voices, but still no one answered. Moving to the third house, John felt foolish and frustrated, but he stubbornly decided to knock at every single cottage.

At the fourth, the door cracked and he looked into the face of a young woman. She was anything but pretty. She had a mouth full of crooked teeth and her nose was set at an angle in her face. She looked up at him with the blank eyes of the mentally deranged. "I'm trying to find out what happened to the hospital," John explained.

The girl shook her head vigorously and tried to shut the door in his face.

John got his foot in the door and shouldered it open. Although the girl tried to stop him, she was much weaker than he, and when she realized it was pointless, she ran to the back of the room and squatted down on the far side of a central hearth with her arms crossed over her head. It made John feel like a marauder.

His eyes swept the room, and he felt his mouth go dry as he registered just how poor these people were. There was literally nothing in this cottage but straw pallets on the floor and a pottery cauldron sitting somewhat precariously on some fieldstones that surrounded a fire. The cauldron was steaming lightly and smelled of garlic, while smoke clouded the whole room; there were neither chimney nor windows for the smoke to escape. An old crone squatted beside the cauldron and squinted at him silently, not daring to challenge his intrusion.

John knew it would be pointless to ask her anything about the attack. He shook his head, mumbled an apology, and withdrew, abandoning his plan to go to every house. Instead, he collected Centurion and rode on to the next village.

This was far enough away so that people did not immediately make a connection between a young Frank and the attack on Kolossi—until he started asking questions. Then they clammed up, shook their heads, and denied all knowledge of events.

Frustrated and hungry, John wanted to return to Kolossi so he and Lord Aimery could get back to Limassol for the night. He did not want to spend a night surrounded by the charred remnants of Kolossi. It emanated not only a foul smell but an ominous threat from the still-smoking ruins. On the other hand, he was reluctant to return to Lord Aimery empty-handed, and so with a sigh he stubbornly retraced his way through the nearest village to continue on to the village farthest west.

Two priests stood talking in front of the small church, but they slipped inside at the sight of John approaching. John had spotted them, so he rode straight to the church, tethered Centurion to a ring on the surrounding low wall, and ordered Barry to stay with the horse. Barry dutifully sat down at Centurion's feet as the horse voraciously tore up tufts of grass and weeds from the base of the low wall with his teeth.

The door was so low that John had to duck to enter the little church. It was so dark inside that the only thing he could make out was burning candles lighting up a silver icon of the Virgin with the Christ Child on her arm. Immediately John went down on one knee, shoving his coif off his head at the same time. He crossed himself and silently prayed to the Mother of God for help. "Holy Virgin, Lord Aimery wants these people no harm," he argued with her in his mind. "We want to end the violence. Please help me. "

When he stood, his eyes had adjusted enough to see the two Orthodox priests—or rather, a priest and a monk—staring at him warily from the railing before the dark, dilapidated screens. He approached them and addressed them respectfully in his best Greek: "Good sirs, forgive me for interrupting, but I was hoping you could help me." The looks of astonishment on their faces to have a young Frank address them in fluent Greek pleased John.

Their surprise also gave him a moment to study them. The priest had wavy gray hair and a soft, fluffy beard of the same color, but his face was not really old—no older, John guessed, than his father. It was marked by lines made more by smiling than frowning. The monk, on the other hand, was younger, with dark hair and beard, and his face was lined by anger. It also reminded John of someone, but he couldn't quite remember who.

It was the monk who replied hotly, "What do you Franks need help with? Killing, burning, and raping?"

The priest immediately put his hand on the younger man's arm and shook his head. "Curb your tongue, Brother," he told his companion before addressing John to ask, "What might we be able to help you with?"

"The hospital at Kolossi was attacked last Friday by a large mob. They plundered the entire complex, even the church," John stressed, "and they stole from the patients as well. The priest was stripped naked and tied backwards on a mule and then chased away." As he related this incident John watched the faces of the two men opposite him. The monk frowned, while the priest raised his eyebrows and looked over at the younger man as if asking for verification.

"He was not harmed—unlike many of *our* priests, monks, and nuns!" the monk defended the outrage. "Indeed, no one was raped or killed."

"You seem to know a great deal about what happened," John observed. "Can you tell me more about who was involved in the attack and why? Why attack a hospital caring for the poor? Why destroy a factory that brought work and income to these poor communities?"

"The land was stolen from us! It is our land! Our country! You are not welcome here!"

"Would it be better for people to have neither medical care nor jobs?" John asked with the simplicity of youth.

"You understand nothing! Just like the rest of your stupid, brutal, barbarian people," the monk dismissed him angrily.

"You say he understands nothing, yet he asks good questions," the priest spoke up in a calm, firm voice. "It is what my parishioners have been asking me all week," he added. "They had little enough as it was. Now they have nothing. They do not know how they are going to feed themselves, and they are terrified of retribution. Up to now, all the trouble has been in the north and east; now they fear the Franks will come and take revenge on us here for this."

"The Franks need to be shown they are neither wanted nor invincible! They need to learn they have no place here, and that we can fight them! You," the monk turned on John, "you are not wanted here! Go back where you came from!"

"I can't," John answered, his beardless chin raised in proud defiance. "Salah ad-Din took it away." He pronounced Saladin's name as he had learned it, in Arabic.

"Well, go fight *him* for it, then! Just because you were beaten by the Saracen doesn't give you the right to steal from us!" the monk snarled back, raising his voice in anger.

His elder colleague laid a hand on his arm again and spoke to John in a reasonable tone. "Tell us, young man, do you know what will happen to the innocent people who had nothing to do with this attack? Will Lusignan send men to scourge the villages that have already suffered?"

"Not all the villagers were innocent, my lord," John countered. "Some were young men dismissed from work for being troublemakers—"

"Patriots!" the monk corrected.

"That's enough!" the priest admonished his colleague. Turning again to John, he asked, "If we were to deliver to you the ringleaders, would you spare the others?"

The monk gasped in shock and looked at his colleague in outrage. The priest looked him straight in the eye as he spoke in a slow, deliberate, and admonishing tone. "Don't you think that is *fair*, Brother Zotikos? Young men who plunder, burn, and terrorize a hospital are not productive members of society." Turning back to John, he noted sternly, "But we must have a guarantee that the innocent people will be left in peace. Many of my parishioners have come to me in tears saying they will help rebuild everything, if only the Hospitallers will return and re-establish the hospital and the mill. They deeply regret what has happened. They should not be punished."

"I will tell my lord what you have said. I'm sure he will want to discuss this with you. Who should he ask to speak with?"

"I am Father Andronikos. He can find me here any time. And who is your lord?"

"Lord Aimery de Lusignan," John announced proudly, harvesting a hiss of hostility from the monk and a startled look from Father Andronikos.

"And you?" the monk snarled. "Who the hell are you, and where did you learn Greek?" He inferred that John's command of Greek was tantamount to deception.

John smiled at him and announced with relish, "My name is John d'Ibelin, and my Greek I learned from my mother, Maria Comnena."

The name had the effect intended. The clerics dropped their jaws and gaped at him in astonishment.

John took advantage of their amazement to bow deeply to the priest and nod curtly to the monk, then he turned and exited the church, trying hard not to reveal his excitement. Outside, he untied Centurion and pulled himself up into the saddle, so full of pent-up hope that the old horse picked up his ears and started prancing in anticipation. John was so elated, in fact, that he felt almost as if he were flying as they cantered along the road back to Kolossi, with Barry pressed hard to keep up. This little incident convinced John he had inherited some of his father's diplomatic skills, and that made him immensely proud.

Nicosia, Cyprus

Lord Aimery was considerably less ecstatic about John's "negotiations." He pointed out that they had no way of knowing if the priest would deliver the real culprits—or someone else. He also grumbled about the fact that it would be hard to convince his brother to agree to talks—but he eventually agreed to try. They spent the night with the Templars at Limassol again and headed for Nicosia the following day. They arrived well after dark in a rain shower, and Lord Aimery opted to get out of their wet clothes, have a warm meal, and confront his brother in the morning.

John had a hard time sleeping. He kept going over in his head all the arguments for at least meeting with Father Andronikos again. If the priest failed to deliver men that the Hospitallers could identify as part of the mob, they could still opt for retribution, John thought. He was acutely conscious that the lives—or at least the welfare—of many souls depended on what he did or said. He wished he could have turned this over to his father and let his father do the talking from now on. He was certain that his father could have talked Guy into negotiating; John was not so certain about his own or Lord Aimery's ability to do the same.

Since he wasn't sleeping anyway, John rose early, washed and dressed, and then took a brush to Lord Aimery's suede boots and even scrubbed his chain mail. By the time Lord Aimery finally woke up, everything was waiting for him. After helping him dress, John went out for fresh bread, while Lord Aimery got a shave from the khan barber. Fortified with breakfast, they at last crossed the street to the royal palace. They were admitted immediately by the guards and proceeded to Guy's apartments, only to find Dick de Camville guarding the door to the inner chamber against a room full of audience-seekers. Humphrey de Toron was here, as were both the elder and younger Cheneché, Bethsan, Barlais, and the Venetian bailli.

"Well, if it isn't Lord Aimery!" Cheneché called out as they stopped just inside the door, both surprised and irritated by the sight of the others. "Let's see if he'll see *you*. He hasn't been willing to see any of *us* for days."

"Why is that?"

Cheneché shrugged eloquently, and Bethsan grumbled, "If we knew the answer to that, we probably wouldn't be here."

Lord Aimery turned to his brother's squire. "Tell my brother I'm here," he ordered.

"Yes, my lord." Dick bobbed his head respectfully and disappeared through the door between the outer and inner chambers.

Toron left the window seat and came across the room to speak to John in a low voice. "Did you find out anything about the attack on Kolossi?"

"Yes, we were able to talk to the victims, and I found a priest who said he'd deliver the perpetrators if we promised not to take action against the innocent." John spoke in an excited rush, but with his voice pitched so only Toron could hear him.

Toron looked startled at his news, but pleased, too. He smiled faintly and seemed on the brink of asking something when Dick returned and announced, "He'll see you, my lord."

"What?" Cheneché sat up sharply and exchanged a startled look with his son, while the Venetian looked outright offended.

Lord Aimery strode between them with John clinging to his heels, much as Barry clung to his most of the time, but Dick shook his head at John. "He said his brother. Just his brother."

Deflated, John stopped in his tracks and watched as Lord Aimery disappeared into the room beyond. Dick closed the door firmly behind him and resumed his guard-dog stance.

Beyond the door, Aimery found himself facing his brother Guy. His first thought was that Guy was looking worse than ever. He'd lost weight, and the skin of his face and neck sagged like an old man's. His eyes were sunken in sockets lined with blue. "Well?" Guy asked anxiously. "What did you find out?"

Aimery was taken aback by his brother's intense interest in this case. After all, it wasn't the first time the rebels had attacked. Then again, it was the first instance of violence on the south coast, and also the first time the insurgents had struck at one of the militant orders rather than just merchants and isolated knights. Glad of his brother's interest, Aimery responded readily, "We were able to talk with the Hospitallers, and John spoke to some of the locals as well. The men behind the attack first lured the Hospitaller knights away with a decoy, a request for assistance from a Venetian ship, and attacked at dusk after the workers had left the factories. They looted and—"

"But who *were* they?" Guy interrupted him anxiously. "And where are they now? They all got away, didn't they? They could be anywhere! Anywhere! Even here in Nicosia! Indeed, right here in this palace!" Guy's eyes were burning with fear—no, Aimery revised his assessment, with sheer panic.

He tried to counter the panic with a dismissive, "Of course they're not here in the palace!"

"YOU ALWAYS THINK YOU KNOW BEST!" Guy shouted, springing to his feet. His voice was so loud and furious that Aimery drew back slightly.

"Guy, calm down," Aimery urged in a soft voice to get his brother to lower his. Guy glared at him, breathing hard, the panic still in his unsettled eyes. "Listen to me," Aimery continued as calmly as possible, although his pulse was racing at the obvious irrationality of his brother's reaction. His mind was racing, too, trying to figure out what had so unnerved Guy that he would be in a state of panic about this comparatively minor incident. "Listen to me," Aimery repeated, as Guy's eyes darted around the room as if expecting assassins to spring out from behind the furnishings. "The leader of the mob was a young Greek monk."

"A monk? You mean we can't even trust their monks? Where are we? Are we both dead and in hell? Does the devil have monks in his service?" Guy asked the question as if he seriously meant it.

"You're not dead, Guy, and I seriously doubt the devil has monks, but evil men have been known to wear clerical robes often enough. The point is: there are no Greek monks here. You're perfectly safe. You're well guarded. As I was saying, these men first lured the knights away from Kolossi. They are afraid to fight us face to face."

"All the more reason that they will send an assassin!" Guy answered, spinning around as if he had heard something behind him. "Or poison! They could use poison!"

"Guy, listen to me," Aimery tried again. "There's nothing to fear. These are cowardly rabble-rousers, not assassins. They tied a helpless priest to a mule. They aren't going to attack *you*. They wouldn't dare."

"How can you be so sure?" Guy countered sharply, his eyes narrowing. "You always think you know best, but you told me to come here. You told me Cyprus was beautiful—and bountiful. You *lied* to me, Aimery."

Aimery gazed at his brother, speechless: it was true, he had urged Guy to come. He had indeed called Cyprus beautiful and bountiful. He still thought it was, but what did his brother know of it, since he hardly ever left these rooms? And slowly, day by day, it was going up in smoke, slipping from their fingers.

"Leave me," Guy ordered abruptly, sinking down into a chair, his shoulders sagging.

"Don't you want—"

"No, it doesn't matter," Guy declared as if he were talking about a spilt glass of wine. He wiggled his fingers in a belittling gesture for Aimery to go. "I know you lied, but I suppose you meant well. It doesn't matter anymore. Leave me. I'm tired."

"Do you wish to speak to any of the others?" Aimery asked as he withdrew toward the door.

"What others?" Guy asked listlessly.

Aimery looked sideways at the door and then back at his brother. "There's an anteroom full of men waiting to see you, Guy. The Chenechés, Barlais, Toron, Bethsan, the bailli—"

"Oh, them. Yes. I'd forgotten. No. I don't want to see them. Just leave me alone. No! Send Dick in. I need to see the boy!"

"All right, Guy. I'll send Dick in to you," Aimery answered evenly. Then he turned and exited the chamber with a rising sense of panic—not because his brother's panic was contagious, but because his brother appeared to be going mad.

"My lord?" Dick asked as the door clunked shut behind him, dampening the sound of the others as they pounced on Aimery to ask what had happened. Guy beckoned his squire closer, and Dick approached warily. In the last few months Guy had struck him more than once, always without warning—much less cause. As a result, he treated his lord with the same caution he would use with a bull or a mean-tempered horse.

Only when Dick was directly beside him did Guy speak in a whisper. "I'm out of medicine. I need more. Go at once."

"But the doctor said—"

Guy lashed out. Despite his deteriorating health, he had been a fighting man for thirty years, and his balled fist could still deliver a substantial blow. He also knew where to aim, and his punch landed firmly in Dick's gut. The squire doubled over in pain, and Guy hissed at him. "Don't talk back to me, you miserable milksop! I said I need more medicine! Get it now or I'll have you flogged for your rudeness!"

Biting down on his lip and trying to hold back tears of pain and indignation, Dick turned away. He did not right himself until he reached the door. There he took a moment to collect himself, pulled the door open, and slipped out.

Chapter Eight
Disinherited

Acre, Kingdom of Jerusalem
June 1194

"Is my mother here yet?" the Queen asked breathlessly as the contraction eased.

At once one of her women ordered another to go and see if there was any sign of the Dowager Queen, while another patted the Queen's arm and told her to relax.

"How can I relax?" Isabella shot back irritably, and then gave a cry of pain as the next contraction overwhelmed her.

"Everything's fine," the midwife assured her with professional calm from her position squatting in front of the birthing stool and looking up the Queen's skirts.

"Why doesn't the baby come?" Isabella wailed back at her. She'd been in labor for what seemed like eternity. She was exhausted, drenched in sweat, stinking, and miserable, and the spasms of excruciating pain would not end until it was over. She was sure it had not hurt this much or lasted this long when she gave birth to little Maria. For a son, of course, it would be worth it. She so wanted to give Henri a son, an heir, the start of the Champagne dynasty on the throne of Jerusalem, but first she had to survive this ordeal and the baby had to be born alive, and—the pain obliterated all thoughts as she screamed.

In the courtyard, Maria Zoë and Balian looked up toward the window from which the scream escaped, a long, distant wail that seemed frail and weak by the time it drifted down to them. Eschiva put their thoughts into words. "Poor Bella!" she exclaimed, and at once began to clamber down from the horse litter without waiting for assistance from anyone. Eschiva was herself seven months pregnant, and Maria Zoë had tried to dissuade her from making the trip from Caymont at all. Eschiva, however, insisted, because she remembered how emotionally fragile Isabella had been at her last lying-in.

"I'll see if I can find Champagne," Balian told his wife. "I expect he's suffering nearly as much as Bella is, and he'll either want distraction or be ready to kill anyone who comes near him. If he's in the latter mood, I'll retreat to the hall."

"What were you like in these circumstances?" Maria Zoë asked curiously.

"I generally wanted to kill someone."

"Charming."

"Just concern for you, my love." He bent and brushed his lips to her forehead.

Maria Zoë, trailed by Eschiva and Beatrice, made her way up the stairs and through the familiar corridors of the palace of Acre to the royal apartments. She had occupied these herself as Queen of Jerusalem twenty years ago. Isabella had herself been born in the very chamber where she now labored.

As they approached the Queen's apartments, Beatrice's sister came out, and catching sight of her sister, ran forward to embrace her. "I was hoping you'd come!" Constance exclaimed. "I'm having such a terrible time with Anne. You have to talk to her. Maybe she'll listen to you." Constance, like Beatrice, had been in Saracen captivity for five years, and her daughter Anne had been circumcised and sold to a man she abhorred at the age of eleven. The scars left on her body and psyche had been evident the moment she was freed.

"Of course I'll talk to her," Beatrice assured her sister. While Eschiva and Maria Zoë continued to the birthing chamber, the Auber sisters slipped down the corridor to have a private chat and reunion.

Isabella lifted her head at the sound of the door opening. Seeing her mother, she exclaimed in a voice that expressed both relief and exasperation. "Mama! What took you so long?"

Maria Zoë went to her daughter and took her hand from one of her waiting women, who at once withdrew. She smiled down at her eldest daughter. "So, you held back just so I could be here, did you?"

Isabella started to protest, and then realized her mother was teasing her and didn't know how to react. Her mother took advantage of her confusion to continue, "We took longer to get here because Eschiva wanted to come, too, and couldn't ride in her condition. I hope you *appreciate* Eschiva coming all this way in her condition to be with you. Your stepfather and I tried to dissuade her—"

Isabella's eyes shifted to Eschiva as she exclaimed, "Oh, I *am* grateful, Eschiva! I can't *say* how grateful I am. I swear I'll be with you when your time comes, no matter what."

"I'll hold you to that promise, Bella," Eschiva told her with a smile, moving around the midwife to take her other hand, which she squeezed as she looked sympathetically down at her childhood friend. Although her tone was light, Eschiva knew she was going to need all the support she could get when her time came. Much as she wanted more children, she still had a deathly fear of childbirth.

"Now that that's settled," Maria Zoë continued matter-of-factly, "tell me what names you've selected," she ordered her daughter. "Henri, I presume, if it's a boy, but what does your lord husband want to name a daughter?"

"Oh, I told him not to worry about that. I assured him it was going to be a boy," Isabella declared.

"Hmm. I'm not sure that was wise, sweetheart, but what's done is done. I guess we'll just have to think up something for ourselves—just in case. What names do you recommend, Eschiva?"

The midwife glanced up at the Dowager Queen with a faint smile and shook her head in bemusement. She had been dismissive of the Queen's demands for her mother, thinking she had enough assistance with four ladies and an experienced midwife such as herself. Now that the Dowager was here, however, she understood: the Dowager distracted Isabella with a sovereignty that could not be dismissed. Queen Maria simply commanded attention, even from another Queen.

The Count of Champagne was actively seeking distraction, with little success. His household knights, bachelors who had come with him from Champagne, tried to interest him in a game of dice, but after only a short interval Champagne threw the dice down and, with uncharacteristic harshness, told them that it was "heartless" to dice while his wife struggled for her life. They took the hint and withdrew.

Next the Chancellor attempted to interest Champagne in the business of his realm, only to realize that Champagne wasn't listening to a word he said. Rapidly recognizing that any decision Champagne made under the circumstances was likely to be a poor one, the Chancellor Archbishop somberly suggested that Champagne retire to the chapel and pray for the well-being of his wife and child. "Prayers are needed regardless of whether they live or die, after all," the celibate churchman pointed out with great sincerity.

"Get out of my sight!" the usually soft-spoken count shouted. "Out! Out!" Champagne seemed on the verge of throwing something at him.

The shocked chancellor beat a hasty retreat, leaving all the documents lying on the desk, and feeling most unjustly mistreated. As he scuttled down the hall, he nearly collided with a man coming the other way, and was taken aback to find himself confronted by a tall man in chain mail. The figure looming out of the darkness made him catch his breath, and then a voice assured him, "No need for alarm, my lord archbishop. It's just me. Ibelin."

"Praise to the Father and Son! Then your lady wife is also here to be with her daughter?"

"She is. How is my lord of Champagne taking things?"

"Badly," the archbishop summarized sourly.

Ibelin just laughed. "I'll brave it." He continued past the archbishop and knocked while opening the door.

Champagne spun around with an expression on his face that suggested he was preparing to throw whoever it was out. At the sight of Ibelin, his expression changed to relief. "Thank God! They tell me Isabella has been asking for her mother every few minutes, although for the life of me I can't think what difference it could make. Your lady could hardly have had *her* mother with her during the birth of her children, did she? I know my mother didn't, seeing as my grandmother was very much persona non grata in the house!" Ibelin recognized Champagne's need to let out his thoughts, so he simply helped himself to a chair, then removed his leather riding gloves and ran a hand through his tangled hair.

"You look very hot and dusty," Champagne noticed at last. "Shall I send for something?"

"Sherbet would be very welcome. How long has Isabella been in labor?"

"Almost a whole day now. Did your wife take this long?"

"Longer with Helvis, less with John and Meg. Philip was the hardest birth, as I remember. Or maybe it was just the weather. He came in a dreadful storm, and I had nowhere to escape to."

"So you didn't stay near?" Champagne asked.

"Near enough, but I admit I was cowardly enough to prefer the stables or the tiltyard to sitting where I could hear every scream."

Champagne took a breath and then shook his head. "I can't. I just can't. I'm terrified that if I'm not within hearing, she might call for me and I wouldn't be there. At least when she was brought to childbed with little Marie, I could spend the time cursing Montferrat! Now I have no one to blame but myself!"

Ibelin laughed. At moments like this he both liked the young man who was his king and understood why Isabella was head over heels in love with him. With sympathy, he gently kept Champagne talking about things he cared about, first asking after little Marie, and then turning the conversation to the County of Champagne, asking what Henri had heard from his brother. Eventually, as the sun sank down to pour through the windows, they talked about the full-scale war that had broken out between Henri's two uncles, the Kings of England and France.

"I can't blame my uncle of England!" Henri declared decisively. "Philip betrayed him in every way! He intrigued against him while he was still here with us, and would have put the crown of England on that spider John! You'd know just how ridiculous *that* idea is if you'd ever met my cousin John!" Henri assured Ibelin. "And while Philip was not to blame for Richard's capture *per se*, he offered to pay *more* than any ransom my grandmother raised to free Richard, for the Holy Roman Emperor to turn Richard over to *him*! I shudder to think what he would have done to Richard once he had him in his power. Chains would have been the least of it! There are times," Champagne admitted, "when I am ashamed to be related to Philip Capet. He is a weasel. A man without a shred of honor."

"I so wanted to like him," Ibelin reflected. "He was the first of the Western monarchs to come to our aid, and I wanted him to be, well, like Richard of England was."

Henri snorted. "They couldn't be more different, could they? I think, sometimes—" Henri cut himself short and his head came up sharply. "What was that? Didn't you hear it? I think it was the cry of an infant!" Champagne jumped to his feet and rushed to the door to stick his head out. Ibelin waited patiently.

"There it is again!" Champagne exclaimed. "No! Christ! It's sobbing, wailing!"

Ibelin calmly got to his feet and joined Champagne at the door to the hall, his ears cocked. From here it sounded as if the shouts and screams of pain that had punctuated the entire afternoon had been replaced by the wailing of a woman in grief.

"The child's dead! Or Isabella herself!" Champagne concluded, his face blanched in horror.

But then another wail pierced the air, clearly an infant crying loudly and indignantly. "Isabella!" Champagne concluded. "She's died giving birth—"

"I think not," Ibelin countered, taking Champagne by the arm and guiding him back into the room.

"But if the child's healthy—and he sounded healthy—why else would they be weeping and lamenting?"

"Did you ever consider the possibility that this child might be a girl?" Ibelin asked.

Champagne looked at him blankly.

"The Dowager Queen gave King Amalric a daughter, and then our first child was also a daughter. Isabella might well take after her."

"A daughter?" Champagne asked back, still looking rather dazed. "Why would they lament the birth of a daughter? It can't be that. Something must have gone wrong!"

Ibelin was relieved by Champagne's response, and suggested, "Let's go to your wife's apartments and see what we can find out."

Champagne nodded, grateful to have company, as the sound of hysterical weeping grew louder the closer they got to the Queen's chamber. Then suddenly the Dowager Queen was standing in their way, smiling broadly. "I was just coming to see you, my lord," she addressed Champagne. "Your wife has been safely delivered of a lovely little girl."

"Is she all right? Is Bella all right? Why is she or someone else crying so piteously? What's wrong?" Champagne demanded.

Maria Zoë rested her hand reassuringly on Champagne's arm. "I promise you, my lord, there is no cause for alarm. Bella is only disappointed she did not give you a son. Give us a few moments to clean things up, and then come see her and your daughter. Meanwhile, I will tell Bella that you are very pleased with your little girl. Did you have a name in mind? Bella insisted there was no need, but I'm *sure* you had more foresight." There was a hint in those words that Champagne instantly understood. If he showed himself ready with a name, Isabella would believe he was not so disappointed.

"Marguerite," he told her instantly. "I had a sister Marguerite."

"It is a lovely name, my lord. We favored it ourselves. I'm sure Isabella will be delighted with it." She bowed her head slightly and then withdrew, leaving Champagne with her husband.

Maria Zoë and Eschiva left Isabella sleeping contentedly in a fresh, clean bed, with the cradle of little Marguerite in easy reach, and Champagne sitting on her other side holding her hand. Together they found Balian in the hall, and Maria Zoë suggested, "I could use some fresh sea air. What do you say we go down to the harbor? Do you feel up to a little walk, Eschiva?"

Eschiva nodded vigorously. Like Maria Zoë herself, she had had more than enough of the stale, sweat- and blood-drenched air of the birthing chamber. She wanted to clear her head of the sounds and sights as well as the smells. It would all start again too soon, but for now some fresh air and chilled wine would do her good. "We should celebrate little Marguerite's birth," she told her aunt and uncle as they left the palace. "At the very least, we ought to light a candle for her and for Isabella. St. Sebastian is not far away," Eschiva suggested; she had fond memories of this little monastery nestled near the port, because she and Aimery had once enjoyed an unexpected and blissful night together there.

Balian remembered it as the house where Beatrice and Constance's father had sought refuge and faith, when they were in captivity and he had lost all hope of them ever coming home. He noted, "They serve very good wine and simple but good food."

"We might as well stay there rather than at the palace," Maria Zoë concluded; "neither Henri nor Isabella will be entertaining for a bit."

"I'm agreeable," Balian assured the women, and turned to give instructions for his squire Georgios to return to the palace for the horses and their luggage, and to tell Beatrice (who was staying with her sister) where to find them in the morning. "Tell her we'll want to leave no later than terce," Maria Zoë added. Georgios nodded and departed.

They agreed to walk along the harbor front first, enjoying the cooling breeze off the water and a spectacular sunset that turned the horizon a vivid orange. The port, as always, was bustling with ships loading and offloading, street vendors catering to the newly arrived sailors desperate for fresh fruits and women, and customs officials and shipping agents intent on getting their due. With the truce now eighteen months old, trade had built up steadily. Furthermore, with fewer ports in Frankish hands, more trade passed through Acre than ever before. Although ships from the Italian communes—Pisa, Venice, and Genoa—dominated the harbor, there were a pair of Egyptian coastal dhows offloading on the backside of the mole, and a large buss hailing from Marseilles hogging much of the main quay, while a Sicilian round ship was demanding access through the chain. All these larger ships almost obscured a low-lying galley, but Ibelin spotted and recognized the Norse snecka. "Look, isn't that the *Storm Bird*?" He pointed.

The ship was painted black with red trim. She sat low to the water and boasted twenty banks of oars. She stood out from the other galleys because she carried a large square sail rather than the more popular lateen rigs of the Mediterranean. Furthermore, the bird on her raised prow—with spread wings, open beak, and blood-red eyes—was familiar.

"It does look like her," Maria Zoë agreed, following her husband's finger. "I thought Master Magnussen had left the Holy Land for good."

"That's what he said, but unless he's dead or has sold the *Storm Bird*, he must have changed his mind."

The trio changed direction and headed over to the snecka, which seven years earlier had been the first ship to successfully run the Saracen blockade of Tyre, bringing a shipload of Norsemen eager to regain the Holy Land. The captain and Ibelin had worked closely together thereafter. Ibelin regularly used the ship when the land route was impassable or too slow.

The Norse ship lay neatly tied up at the quay, but there was no sign of her captain, or indeed any of the crew except an unfamiliar boy. Ibelin asked the latter when the ship had arrived and from where.

"We left Limassol last night," the boy readily told them.

"Do you know where Master Magnussen is?" Ibelin asked next, but the boy only shook his head.

"Let's go back to St. Sebastian," Eschiva suggested; "you can send Georgios to ask after Magnussen later."

Her companions agreed, and they retraced their steps to the little monastery, knocking at the door with the brass ring hanging from a lion's head.

The brother that opened for them looked astonished. "My lord d'Ibelin!" he recognized Balian at once. "How did you get word so soon? We hadn't even—"

Beyond him in the courtyard there was a bustle of activity punctuated by the barking of a dog. "That's John's dog!" Maria Zoë exclaimed, recognizing Barry. "John must be back again!"

Eschiva pushed through the door that the monk was holding open for them, asking even as she searched the courtyard with her own eyes, "And my lord husband, Lord Aimery de Lusignan? Is he—Aimery!" She started running forward as fast as her heavy, unbalanced body allowed.

Aimery had been bending over going through one of his saddlebags when he heard the sound of his wife's voice. He straightened and spun about to face her.

Eschiva was halfway to him when she registered his face, and her steps faltered. There was no answering smile, no open arms. Her husband looked like he had turned to stone, a middle-aged man with deep lines in his face and gray in his hair. "Aimery?" Eschiva asked, frightened. "Aimery? What is it?"

Aimery turned his back on her and plunged into the shadow of the church porch. Eschiva gave a cry of pain, and her knees started to give way under her. Aimery had rejected her. He was discarding her, just as her father had discarded her mother. He was—Eschiva felt dizzy with confusion and hurt, and Maria Zoë only barely caught her elbow in time to stop her from crumpling up onto the stones.

But on her other side and coming from the other direction, John bounded forward to embrace his father, flushed and breathless. Then he stood back to announce, "Guy's dead! He's been sick for over a year, but he tried to hide it. His insides rotted. He was in terrible pain toward the end, and then even the opium didn't help anymore."

"But what are you doing here?" Balian asked frowning. "If Guy's dead, Aimery—"

"That's just it! On his deathbed, Guy named his brother Geoffrey his heir!"

"Holy Mother of God!" Maria Zoë gasped, tightening her hold on Eschiva, who was swaying in her distress.

Her husband was more explicit. "Idiot. Absolute idiot! Right to his dying breath: an idiot! Not to mention a thankless bastard."

"Lord Aimery couldn't bear to stay a moment longer," John explained breathlessly. "I hardly had time to pack our things, and we headed for the coast. And you wouldn't believe it! Just as we reached Larnaka, we spotted the *Storm Bird* lying alongside. I jumped on board and told Master Magnussen what had happened. He didn't even bat an eye. He just ordered his men to lay down a plank for our horses and then put out to sea again. He hasn't changed at all," John added in obvious enthusiasm. For John, the excitement of all that had happened in the last forty-eight hours still obscured the implications.

Balian clapped a hand on John's shoulder, both in pride and to calm him down a bit. His eyes had already shifted to the darkness of the church porch where Aimery had disappeared, but his expression was impenetrable.

"I must go to him," Eschiva said at last, pulling herself together.

Maria Zoë nodded, but also tightened her hold around Eschiva's waist and started forward with her.

"We were on our way to Caymont," John continued explaining to his father behind them. "We had no idea you were in Acre. Is the High Court in session?"

"No, Isabella just gave birth. She sent for your mother," Balian answered his son.

"Is Bella all right?" John asked anxiously.

"Yes, she's fine. She had a second little girl."

"Oh!" John sounded more disappointed than the father had been. "But we need an heir for Jerusalem."

"There's plenty of time for that," Balian answered.

Ahead of him, the two women disappeared into the church. As their eyes adjusted, Eschiva registered that Aimery was not in the church, but that the door opening to the cloisters was open. She nodded in that direction, and they crossed the church to step down a couple of steps into the arcade of the cloister. Here Eschiva's eyes found Aimery. He was on a stone bench with his head in his hands. She nodded to Maria Zoë. "I'll be fine. Let me go on alone."

Maria Zoë reluctantly let her go, and stood watching as Eschiva bravely made her way around the cloisters to the bench, sat down beside her broken husband, and put an arm over his shoulders.

Aimery gasped out without even lifting his head: "I've failed you, Eschiva. You and the children. I've failed completely. I have absolutely nothing. Our child," he glanced at her distended belly, "conceived in so much hope, will be born in poverty."

Eschiva didn't have an answer. All she could do was hold him closer to her. Just as long as he wasn't divorcing her, she kept thinking, just as long as he wasn't setting her aside, turning her out like her father had discarded her mother. "We are still together, Aimery," she squeaked out, so shaken by the way he'd turned his back on her that it came out more like a question.

Aimery sat up straighter and looked into her frightened face. "Eschiva? I'm sorry!" He opened his arms and pulled her into them, clinging to her as much for his own comfort as for hers.

At the far side of the cloisters, John and Balian joined Maria Zoë. Balian waited respectfully for Aimery and Eschiva to finish kissing, but then he started to make his way toward them.

"Balian." Maria Zoë reached out a hand to stop him, thinking that Aimery and Eschiva needed a little more time.

Already the sound of Balian's boots on the flagstones had caught Aimery's attention, and he drew back and sat up straighter. His entire body and face were taut with wary anticipation.

John and Maria Zoë fell in behind Balian, sensing that he must have something important to say.

Balian came to a stop in front of Aimery and Eschiva, and the older man looked up at him grimly, unsure what he should say. Part of him wanted to blame Ibelin for sending him to Cyprus in the first place. He should have stayed and defended his innocence before the High Court. He should never have resigned as Constable. He should—

"Look, Aimery, your idiot brother may have *named* Geoffrey his heir, but I wouldn't bet on his chances of ever claiming that inheritance."

"Why not?" Aimery snapped back, frowning. "What do you mean?"

"Do you honestly think that the men who have spent the better part of two years fighting to gain control of Cyprus are about to relinquish their gains—or claims—to someone who hasn't been risking his hide with them? My nephew Henri, you can be damned sure, wouldn't dream of such a thing, not even in a nightmare."

Aimery's eyes narrowed, and he slowly withdrew his arm from Eschiva to sit tensely focused on Ibelin. "What are you saying?"

"How many times in the history of this Kingdom have men from the West been the 'rightful' heir, only to lose out to men already here? The precedent was set from the very start with the election of Baldwin I. Now is no different. My nephew, Toron, Cheneché, Bethsan, even Barlais—they know you, they trust you, and they respect you. If you want them to recognize you as Guy's heir, do what Guy, in his stubborn idiocy, wouldn't do: give them each enough land so they can feel richly rewarded, and keep enough for yourself to win new vassals. This city and Tyre are *flooded* with men who have lost everything. If you promise them something, *anything*, just a *foothold*, they will flood to your banner. They will practically swim across to Cyprus for the chance of a new beginning." Maria Zoë found herself wondering if her husband was speaking of himself.

Balian continued, "You've been a loyal brother, Aimery. Again and again. You backed Guy against your better judgment. You stayed by him on the Horns of Hattin, when you could have broken out with Tripoli or me. You went into captivity with him. You joined him at the siege of Acre. You supported him against Montferrat. And what did he ever give you in return? Nothing. Not one miserable thing. Why, in the name of our ever-loving Christ, should you respect his last wishes?"

"You sincerely think your nephew would back me?"

"For a barony? Henri would back John's dog!"

Suddenly they were all laughing, and although Aimery growled, "I'm not sure that's much of a compliment," his shoulders had squared, and Eschiva could feel the energy surging through his muscles again.

"Let's discuss this over dinner and wine," Maria Zoë suggested practically, with an eye on Eschiva.

The little monastery of St. Sebastian only had two guest chambers and most guests took their meals with the brothers in the refectory, but Ibelin asked for wine and food to be brought to his chamber, and John lugged the small table and both chairs from Aimery and Eschiva's chamber to his father's, then pulled up a chest for himself. The decision, however, had been made in the cloisters; all that remained was to discuss was details. Georgios quickly sent back to the *Storm Bird* to bring Magnussen as soon as he appeared, and Ibelin had the monks bring them papyrus, so Aimery and John could give him a better picture of the island, the situation, and what was at stake.

"There's a very long, narrow peninsula that extends to the east at the end of the Pentadaktylos range. Then along the south coast are three large bays, each with a small port: Famagusta furthest east, then Larnaka, and finally Limassol— the only port that can be called anything more than a fishing village. The west of the island curves around to the north, with a small but ancient town facing due west, Paphos. Then there's a fairly sharp peninsula and two bays that face northwest, but are practically uninhabited because of the Troodos mountain range that sits here." Aimery thumped his hand over the western third of his self-drawn map.

"But Troodos has copper and, they say, silver. And there are salt fields near Larnaka and Limassol," John added eagerly. In his tone of voice Aimery heard confirmation that John had, despite everything, fallen in love with the island as much as he had.

"The forests are so dense, tall, and broad, you could build a thousand ships and hardly notice a tree had been felled," Aimery added.

"And the wine is as good as at Ibelin, Papa. Truly it is!" John's enthusiasm made his parents laugh.

Aimery continued with the geography lesson. "Beyond Morphou Bay here in the north there is a sharp peninsula pointing due north; after that the north coast is a long, straight line right to the tip of the Karpas peninsula. The Pentadaktylos comes down almost to the edge of the sea, so there is only a narrow, but incredibly fertile, coastal plain from here to about here, and there are two ports on the north coast, Kyrenia and Karpasia, of which Kyrenia has the smaller but better protected harbor."

"So, if you divided up the island based on the ports, much as we did here, you'd have baronies at Karpasia, Kyrenia, Paphos, Limassol, Larnaka, and Famagusta."

"And Salamis. I forgot that. It's here on the southern shore of the Karpas peninsula. Little more than ruins, really, but a lovely location. It could be revived."

"That would still leave you this enormous inland area as the royal domain—to be bestowed on worthy vassals at a later date."

"There's a problem, Balian," Aimery pointed out, sitting upright and glancing at Maria Zoë. "Only a king can make barons. Guy was King of Jerusalem, but he was only Lord of Cyprus."

"But Isaac Comnenus called himself 'Emperor,'" Maria Zoë pointed out.

"And everyone called him a usurper. Before that, Cyprus was only a province of the Eastern Roman Empire."

"So was Palestine," Balian reminded them. "All the states we have established out here were mere provinces of the Eastern Empire before. All you need do is—"

A knock on the door interrupted them, and on their invitation Georgios entered, followed by a tall, sinewy man with a beak-like nose and blond hair streaked with grey that fell down to his shoulders. Ibelin jumped to his feet, and a moment later found himself in the short but powerful embrace of the Norse captain.

"Master Magnussen, I thought you said you were gone for good!" Ibelin exclaimed as he stepped back to get a better look at the Norseman.

"Stinking boring back in Western Ocean and the North Sea. Nothing doing but a little piracy—which, of course, I abjured long ago."

"I would have thought King Richard could have used your services in his war with King Philip."

"I tried, but for some reason he prefers English and Scottish crews. Besides, I thought I remembered the climate being better here. I'd forgotten it was an oven worse than hell in summer."

"Come, join us. Wine, or should I send for ale?"

"The ale here is lousy—I'd forgotten that, too—but still better than grape juice."

"Georgios?" Ibelin looked to his squire.

"Yes, my lord." The young man disappeared again.

"So, aside from missing my beautiful face, why did you want to see me, Ibelin?" The Norseman took a seat on the chest John vacated for him.

"You heard that Guy de Lusignan is dead and has named his brother Geoffrey his heir."

"That's what *this* Lusignan said," the Norseman replied, nodding his head to Aimery almost insultingly, but then softening the gesture by flinging a smile his way. Magnussen had always retained his independence, taking an oath to no man. He had worked closely with Ibelin—not the Lusignans. The latter had been "the enemy" during most of his stay in Outremer, and had it been Aimery rather than John who had asked for passage, he would probably have turned him down.

"Well, for a variety of reasons, we don't like that solution," Ibelin noted.

Magnussen grunted and waited, his eyes fixed on Ibelin.

"Geoffrey only campaigned briefly here; he's not as familiar with the situation, and despite his unquestioned courage, he did not make many friends."

"He'd sell his own mother to the devil if it suited him. Last I heard he was thinking of betraying King Richard to Philip."

"What?" John asked, scandalized. After his father and Magnussen, King Richard was the man he admired most in the world.

Balian wasn't letting himself get distracted, however. He remarked firmly, "We think Aimery would make a better Lord of Cyprus."

Magnussen looked over at Aimery and then back at Ibelin with slightly raised eyebrows.

Ibelin didn't explain himself. He simply declared, "Aimery needs to return as soon as possible to establish his claim. It is important that he is well established and recognized before Geoffrey finds out he has been bequeathed a fabulous lordship," Ibelin explained, only to be taken aback by his wife contradicting him.

"I'm not so sure," she noted, earning a look of confusion from her husband and son, a scowl from Aimery, and a look of outrage from Eschiva. They all gaped at her, while Magnussen looked amused by her apparent rebellion. Maria Zoë answered their looks by pointing out, "Geoffrey returned to France because he didn't like Cyprus, remember?"

"Or he didn't like playing lieutenant to Guy!" Aimery countered, adding bitterly, "It's an unpleasant and thankless job, I can assure you. Geoffrey didn't have the temperament for it. Being lord in his own right is something else."

"Certainly, but Geoffrey will want to weigh his options," Maria Zoë insisted. "If he thinks he will be welcomed on Cyprus with rapturous relief by devoted followers that is one thing. If he knows he has been rejected by the men in control of the island and that he will have to fight his own brother for it that is something else again."

"Ah," Balian caught the drift of his wife's thoughts. "You're saying we *want* Geoffrey to find out that Aimery is staking his claim."

"Yes; it might help him make, shall we say, the *right* decision. In fact, I think the *sooner* he finds out, the better."

"I can see to that," Magnussen volunteered. "If you give me a day or two to purchase a cargo of spices, silk, or ivory, I can sail for Cyprus the day after, drop *this* Lusignan off, and continue back to Marseilles. There we'll spread the news in every tavern of the city that Aimery has been acclaimed Lord of Cyprus."

"At what price?" Balian asked evenly. He'd long since learned that Magnussen did most things merely for the sheer fun of it, or the challenge, but he always pretended to be mercenary. It was essential to negotiate a price up front.

"Well," Magnussen leaned forward to prop his elbows on the table. "Cyprus, as we see here, is an island, and its security, therefore, will depend upon a fleet. I always fancied commanding a whole fleet—not of merchantmen, but of fighting ships. I want to be Admiral of Cyprus." He looked up and smiled straight at Aimery.

Aimery spluttered with indignation. "For one single voyage?"

Magnussen looked at Ibelin. "Was it only one?"

"It's a good deal, Aimery," Balian advised. "You were still in captivity when Magnussen almost single-handedly broke the Saracen blockade of Tyre. If he hadn't, Tyre would have been lost, but Montferrat never properly thanked him."

"That man got what he deserved. Almost made me like the Assassins," Magnussen observed. "Besides, if you don't take me, you'll end up being dependent on the Pisans or the Venetians or the Genoese, and *they* will cut your throat to sell you your own blood or sell you your own p—sorry, my ladies." He stopped himself with a bow of his upper body in the direction of Maria Zoë and Eschiva.

Aimery recognized that he was in no position to haggle. Of course, he could take passage with another ship, but the Norse snecka was one of the fleetest ships he'd ever seen, much less set foot upon, and the captain was an independent man beholden to no one. Furthermore, the Dowager Queen had a point: if the news reached Geoffrey that Cyprus wasn't really his before he'd had a chance to get accustomed to the idea of being Guy's heir, Geoffrey might prefer to stay in Poitou. He might opt to stake his fortune on playing off Capet against Plantagenet. It was a game Geoffrey understood well, and was likely to seem more certain of success than another adventure in Outremer.

Aimery signaled his consent by adding, "Be sure you also spread the word about how precarious the situation is. Stress that even the militant orders have been attacked and that no one is safe."

"Horrible place! Worse than Sicily!" Magnussen answered with a straight face. "Ship was nearly swamped by people desperate to escape the carnage. I wouldn't be surprised if all the Franks on the island are already dead—slaughtered in their beds."

The men laughed, leaving the monk delivering Magnussen's ale completely discomfited. How could good Christian men laugh about such a state of affairs?

Eschiva had hardly spoken over the meal. She was particularly intimidated by Magnussen, who seemed to her more a heathen Viking than a Christian captain. Mostly, however, she was still shaken by that moment in the courtyard when Aimery had turned his back on her. It didn't matter that his reason had been shame. In that single gesture, she had been confronted by her worst nightmare: divorce. Her father had divorced her mother after twenty years of marriage. Eschiva had been married to Aimery for the same number of years.

Suddenly she realized why she had never made a fuss over Aimery's frequent affairs. In the deepest core of her being, she knew she could survive anything except being set aside, dismissed, discarded. Let him have his mistresses, as long as he didn't take from her the status of wife. For twenty years—nearly her entire conscious life—she had been Aimery de Lusignan's wife. It was who she was. Yes, she had been born an Ibelin and inwardly often sided with her uncle against her in-laws, but she was still Aimery de Lusignan's wife.

That moment in the courtyard had been all the worse for being so unexpected. Since Aimery's return from captivity five years ago, they had found new affection for one another. They had been like young lovers, as the child in her womb testified. Her hand fell automatically to her belly, feeling for the sign of life within. This past Christmas at Caymont had been the most beautiful interlude of her entire life. She had felt loved, respected, cherished, and content. Aimery had spent all his waking hours with her or the children. Indeed, he had lavished attention on the children as never before. Furthermore, although he had complained about his brother's policies, his love for Cyprus and hope of building a future there had shone through.

The door fell shut with a loud clunk, and Aimery shot the bolt. "You know," he started at once, not noticing his wife's fragile mood (as was so often the case), "it's risky, but Ibelin is right. We have nothing more to lose. The only thing I regret is, it means we'll be separated again for God knows how long."

"No."

"No?" Aimery looked around, baffled. He had unbuckled his sword and hung it over the bedpost, and was about to sit to remove his boots. "But, Eschiva! You heard the arguments. On Cyprus I have a chance, a real chance, of becoming a king in all but name—maybe in name, too, if we appeal to the Pope—"

"I didn't mean you shouldn't go, Aimery," Eschiva declared steadily. "I only meant I wouldn't let you go *alone*. I'm coming with you."

"Eschiva! You can't come now! Not in your condition!"

"What do you mean, 'in my condition'? I'm carrying your child, Aimery—a child whose future is at stake. A child who might one day be the ruler of Cyprus."

Aimery crossed the distance between them with two giant steps and put his hands on her shoulders. "Eschiva, Cyprus is—not safe."

"This has nothing to do with being *safe*. I don't *want* to be safe, if it means being separated. And, more important, if you are laying claim to a kingdom, then you need to show your future barons that in choosing you they aren't choosing a single man, but a dynasty—a man with a wife, two sons already, and more on the way."

Aimery registered that Eschiva was making sense—as she almost always did when she ventured to voice an opinion. Before he had decided what to answer, Eschiva continued, "Nor does it hurt that I'm an Ibelin."

Aimery had thought of that already. Eschiva's father had been a respected nobleman; her uncle was nothing short of legendary. "I know," he admitted, "but you're in the seventh month. Do you think I've forgotten how frightened you are of childbirth? Do you think I don't understand what a chance you are taking already? I want you safe, and I want you to be among people you trust when the time comes."

Eschiva thought briefly of how earlier today she had made Isabella promise to be with her when the time came, and instantly recognized how unimportant that was compared to being with Aimery. She lifted her chin, looked Aimery straight in the eye, and declared: "And I'm telling you, Aimery, *you* are the only one I need to have near me. Any midwife can deliver the child, but I want you beside me when I hold *our* child in my arms for the first time. I want you beside me when we christen him in Nicosia, your future capital. I would rather give birth in a manager like the Virgin Mary than in a palace, if the former means you are with me."

Aimery pulled her into his arms and held her closely but gently, conscious of her big belly between them. "Eschiva, you are more precious to me than anything else on earth. How can I put you at risk?"

Eschiva rested her head on his chest with a sense of deep gratitude for his words, his presence, and his warmth, but she spoke firmly. "I'm at risk in childbed—no matter where I am. I could die just as easily at Caymont or in the royal palace at Acre. It's not as if you're going to the wilderness where there are no midwives, no physicians, no houses, baths, or churches." Eschiva had listened very well to his enthusiastic descriptions of Cyprus over Christmas. "Indeed, the way you described the royal palace in Nicosia, it was hardly less splendid than the Imperial palace in Constantinople where Maria Zoë grew up."

Aimery winced inwardly as he realized he was now trapped in a web of his own making. He was being repaid for his earlier eagerness to make her want to come, anticipating reluctance rather than this untimely zeal.

"And you said the physicians were highly trained, the sewage systems very modern, and the wine excellent," she recited further.

"God help me, Eschiva." Aimery bent to seal her lips with a kiss to stop her saying any more. Then, pulling away, he admitted, "It is all true, but . . . " He searched for an argument that would hold water. "I would feel happier knowing you are with Maria Zoë or Isabella. I'm going to have my hands full. I'm not going to be able to devote the time and attention to you I did at Christmas."

"I understand that," Eschiva told him bluntly. "I don't expect you pay *me* attention. I'm coming to support you, not the other way around." Taking a deep breath, Eschiva drew away from Aimery's embrace and faced him. "Aimery, it doesn't matter what you say. I'm going with you to Cyprus."

For a moment more, Aimery tried to resist. He wanted to do what was right for her and their unborn child, but deep down inside, selfishly, he wanted her with him. He knew she would be a comfort to him, and a source of strength. Aimery pulled her back into his arms and laid his head on hers. "So be it then, sweetheart."

Chapter Nine
Staking a Claim

Cyprus
June 1194

THE WIND GOT UP AFTER THEY had lost sight of the mainland. Eschiva at once started to feel queasy, and decided she should lie down. Although her hastily recruited handmaiden Anne was here to look after her, Aimery insisted on going below with her. This left John on deck alone and free to approach the crew.

John would never forget the first time he laid eyes on Haakon Magnussen. He and his father had gone to an armorer about repairs to a hauberk, and Magnussen had burst in with half his crew still bleeding and bruised from a brawl with the Marquis de Montferrat's men. In their old-fashioned leather armor, with axes as large as ox heads and long, flowing hair, the Norsemen had seemed like characters right out of a Viking saga. John had been entranced from the start, but his father had not been keen on him making a more intimate acquaintance with the Norsemen. John wasn't entirely sure why, since they were all good Christians. Even now, he noted, all the crew wore heavy wooden or bone crosses around their necks, most of which were elaborately carved.

"Either out of the way or give a hand!" Magnussen's voice bellowed from the afterdeck. "We're coming about!"

John looked back over his shoulder, saw men dividing up to unleash both corners of the sail, and went to join the men on the leeward side. He'd watched this maneuver on the outward voyage and thought he understood what was going on.

At a shout from Magnussen, the helmsman flung the tiller over with all his might. The sharp prow of the vessel swung into the wind. The great striped sail started to shiver, sag, then fill from the wrong side. The ship lost momentum, and the pitching of the deck became so pronounced that John found it hard to stand (although his companions seemed to have no problem). John glanced nervously over his shoulder toward the captain, awaiting the order to release the sail and adjust it, but one of the men around him told him to relax. "We need to back around more," he explained to John.

After what seemed like an eternity of wallowing, the order came. The man at the head of the rope released it, and they walked the end forward to make it fast as close to the bow as possible. John was conscious more of tagging along than of doing any good, but that earned him at least a grunt of thanks from one crewman and a smile from another. The latter was a youth who seemed about his own age and startled John by asking in Latin, "Want to learn seamanship, do you?"

"Well, I want to *understand* it better," John corrected, asking back, "Where did you learn Latin?"

"My father sent me to a monastery to atone for his sins three years ago, but I ran away. It didn't seem fair, *me* suffering for *his* sins. I couldn't stand being cooped up all the time. I need the wind and sea." He gestured vaguely toward the prow, which was again plowing the sea in a steady, purposeful manner. He had long blond hair, tied at the back of his neck by a leather thong, but the wind had freed many strands that now whipped around his face. John thought he looked magnificent.

"You'll find most of Haakon's crew are running away from something," the youth flung at John with a smile, and then a wary glance toward his captain. "I'm Christian Arendsen, by the way," he announced, holding out his hand. "Come. I'll show you the ropes." John followed eagerly.

By dusk John was utterly exhausted, and they hadn't once had to man the oars. With the sunset, however, the wind died down, and they found themselves becalmed in the middle of nowhere. Aimery, Eschiva, and Anne came back on deck. Here they shared a meal of fresh-caught fish over an open grill in the fresh, cool air under the stars.

"It's like being in the desert," Eschiva remarked, looking around uneasily at the emptiness. "Not another living soul, no landmarks, nothing." She wasn't comfortable entrusting her life to the fragile structure that they called a ship, and she felt very lost and far from everything she knew. The magnitude of the risks they were taking crowded in on her.

"But there are fish to feed us," Magnussen remarked, gesturing to the remnants of the grilled fish they had just finished off, "unlike in the desert. And we don't have to drag ourselves through the heat, but can let the *Storm Bird* carry us forward even in our sleep."

Eventually they settled themselves on some sheepskins with light cotton coverings. Aimery and John were soon asleep and snoring softly, but Eschiva lay awake in Aimery's arms, reminding herself that she had asked for this and trying to ignore Anne's sniffling.

Anne was Constance d'Auber's daughter, the girl who had returned traumatized from Saracen captivity. Everyone had assumed that being home with family would enable her to bury the past, but she seemed unable to fully adjust. Queen Isabella, served by so many high-born ladies, had lost patience with her. Anne was so timid that she never looked anyone in the eye, mumbled when she spoke, frequently dropped things, and ran away from every responsibility. Her mother, sensing that Anne had become a liability, had asked Eschiva to take the girl with her as her handmaiden. Since Eschiva had no one else, she had readily agreed. Only now, listening to her sobs, did Eschiva realize no one had even thought to ask Anne if she *wanted* to come. Her tears gave a depressing answer. They also added to Eschiva's guilt at leaving her children behind without a goodbye.

Of course, the children would be fine at Caymont. It was the nearest thing they had ever had to a real home. Even before Hattin, the Constable's quarters in the Tower of David had been cramped. They'd been ejected from them by the Saracens only to go to the even more crowded accommodations in besieged Tyre. That had always been "temporary," just a place to stay until the Franks recaptured the Kingdom. After the Truce of Ramla they'd rented the little house in Acre, another residence with little space, and again they'd been expelled. Caymont was the first manor house her children had ever lived in, Eschiva reflected, and they all loved it there.

In the dark and silence of a ship at sea, however, Eschiva asked herself what would happen if things went wrong. What if the Frankish lords on Cyprus refused to support Aimery? What if they insisted on supporting Geoffrey? How would Aimery react? What if he blamed Uncle Balian for sending him to face such a humiliation—and by association blamed her? Surely he wouldn't, but . . . Her thoughts kept going in circles, until the wind came up again and the gentle hiss of the waves along the hull lulled her into a deep sleep.

They made landfall at Famagusta—but Aimery, remembering his reception there the previous year, insisted on sailing back to Gastria, where the Templars retained an austere castle. Although the distance from Gastria to Nicosia was greater, Aimery was acutely aware that the roads on Cyprus were not safe. He and John had relied on being fast and armed, but with Eschiva in his party he could not travel fast, and he wanted a stronger escort than he and John could offer.

John's friend from the crew grumbled about the decision. When John questioned why, he laughed and answered, "No taverns or wenches in Gastria. A bunch of stone-cold sober monks!" John felt a little foolish for not being interested in "wenches," while what he remembered of the taverns of Famagusta had not whetted his appetite for more.

Aimery was relieved to find that the Templar commander of Gastria was away. He was not at all sure the Templars would throw in their lot with him in his bid to become Lord of Cyprus. Everything would depend on the new Master of the Temple, Gilbert Erail. Aimery knew too little about the man to venture a guess at how he would react to rivalry between the Lusignan brothers.

With the commander away, however, a sergeant was in charge at Gastria. This semi-illiterate local man didn't dream of challenging the former Constable of Jerusalem (or was it the brother of the late King Guy?). He at once agreed to provide an escort of eight sergeants, as well as a horse litter for Eschiva and Anne. So they took leave of Haakon Magnussen and his crew—who, after taking on water, put out to sea again.

After only one night in the austere guest quarters at Gastria (with the men strictly separated from the women), the little party set out. While Anne sat motionless with her shoulders hunched up and her head down, Eschiva kept the curtains pulled back to see as much of her new home as possible. The land here was flat and treeless, cultivated by peasants dressed in unbleached homespun kaftans and wearing head coverings of the same material. They were for the most part hoeing the fields of evidently rich but sun-baked earth, hacking at the caked soil in preparation for fall planting. There was no evidence of oxen or plow horses, just humans doing this back-breaking labor in the oppressive heat. Occasionally light breezes swept dust into tiny cyclones that shattered the shimmering heat, only to dissipate again in the already hazy air. The peasants spared the travelers only scant and wary glances.

The road itself was comparatively empty, although they passed several shepherds with sheep, goats, or a mixture of both moving their small flocks along the side of the road. More often they encountered women driving little donkeys laden with amphorae to and from the wells. The women were barefoot and kept their skirts hitched into their belts to avoid the dust, thereby exposing their ankles. They kept their heads covered by large white shawls wrapped around their shoulders, despite the heat. They kept their eyes down and averted for the most part, only rarely risking a glance at the strange women. At first Eschiva smiled and waved, but she was met with such consistent blank or hostile stares that she soon gave up.

The bank of purple mountains that had blocked the horizon to the north-west gradually came closer. The mountain range was dramatic. It had tall, sharp peaks and was clothed in dense forests—something Eschiva had never seen before. The range ended dramatically in precipitous cliffs down to the fertile plain on which they were traveling. Aimery pointed out some white rocks and claimed there was a castle there. Eschiva could not make out what he was talking about. The top of the hill was sharp and ragged, not flattened to support a castle, and there were no rings of masonry anywhere.

"We'll spend the night there," Aimery assured her. "It's where your cousin Henri has his base of operations."

"He built a castle already?" Eschiva asked, astonished.

"Good heavens, no! It was built by the Greeks. Allegedly by the Dowager Queen's ancestor, Emperor Alexis I—or, shall we say, at his behest by the governor at the time."

Eschiva leaned out of the litter to try to see the castle again, but she could not for the life of her find it. All she could see were vertical limestone bluffs interrupted by crevices in which pines grew. She said nothing, however, for fear of Aimery's scorn. He would doubtless be disgusted that she couldn't see something as substantial as a castle.

In the afternoon they started to wind their way up the face of the mountain range, and soon the horses were toiling hard on the incline. Eschiva felt vaguely guilty, conscious that without her in a litter, her husband would have made much better time. He might even have been in Nicosia by now, she supposed. It was also decidedly uncomfortable in a horse litter on a steep hill. Had she not been so heavily pregnant, she would have preferred to walk. As it was, she and Anne sat facing backward so that they did not have to lean forward the whole time.

As the sun slid down the sky, Aimery sent one of the Templars ahead to Kantara to warn Henri de Brie that they were on their way. This proved a wise precaution, as the forest was getting denser and they were having increasing difficulty finding their way on narrow trails that sometimes twisted back on themselves or just petered out.

Suddenly a half-dozen knights burst out of the forest to their right and surrounded them. After a moment of alarm, Eschiva was relieved to see her cousin
Henri at the head of the party. He greeted Aimery curtly, and then rode straight
over to the litter and bent down from his horse. "Dearest cousin! This is no place
for a lady! Much less a pregnant one," he told her bluntly. "I've ordered the most
habitable tower made ready for you, but in this thing"—he looked contemptuously at the litter—"you're at least an hour away from Kantara. Do you have
anything warm with you? When the sun goes down, it gets chilly up here."

"Yes, I have a shawl, thank you, Henri. I *do* so appreciate your hospitality,
cousin."

She had succeeded in making him feel rude, and he caught his breath,
paused, and looked at her again. Their eyes met. Eschiva was reminded of all
the horror stories that had circulated about him. He had taken part in Reynald
de Châtillon's Red Sea Raids, plundering, burning, slaughtering, and whoring
all the way to Aden and back. Rumors had circulated that he'd kept a half-
dozen women as his sex slaves and had tortured prisoners to make them reveal
their treasure to him. But Uncle Balian told her not to believe everything she
heard. . . .

"We'll talk in Kantara," he answered, sat up straighter, and started giving
orders.

They were being led by men carrying torches by the time they finally made
it to the outer works of the castle, which abruptly reared up out of nowhere.
These consisted of two very tall towers of white limestone blocks flanking a
narrow wall, rather than a perimeter wall as at every other castle Eschiva had
ever seen. The castle itself loomed above them atop a slope so steep she had to
tip her head all the way back to see the walls. She might not have seen them
at all if men with torches had not been moving back and forth along them in
apparent agitation.

Aimery came to help her out of the litter and announce that she would have
to walk the rest of the way. The stables were here and the path was too steep for
horses. Eschiva said nothing, only helped Anne, who was now trembling from
fear or cold or both, out of the litter. She put an arm around the girl's shoulders
to comfort her, and to give herself something to lean on. Then Aimery seemed
to remember himself. He came back, took her arm, and started leading her up
the narrow path that zigzagged up the face of the mountain. Anne was left to
trail behind them like a lost puppy.

Eschiva didn't understand a great deal about military architecture, but even
she felt as if she were trapped in a killing field. Behind them was the barbican, and

on both flanks there were towers, even more massive than those of the barbican. These protruded forward from the cliff ahead of them on bedrock ledges. Straight ahead, but a good hundred feet higher than where they dismounted, was a tall, crenelated wall. In short, from all sides the dark, windowless walls loomed up, crowding in on her. If those walls had been manned by hostile men, they could have been slaughtered from four directions. Any unfriendly force trying to storm the arched gate into the still-invisible castle would be subjected to murderous fire—all the while struggling up a steep and uneven slope.

The surprise beyond the gate was almost as great. There *was* no castle inside the wall: just buildings scattered among the rugged outcroppings of limestone and the pine trees. The wall itself, however, was four yards deep, with batteries of vaulted chambers honeycombing the backside and spilling light into the interior space, which was far too rugged and overgrown to be called a courtyard.

"This is a military camp, my lady," one of her cousin's knights remarked, seeing her expression, "not a residence."

"We're on our way to Nicosia," Aimery answered for her. "We only ask your lord's hospitality for the night."

"And you have received it," Henri answered, looming up behind them. "Come."

He led them along a rough stone path that wound its way through the scrub brush. By the way it caught at Eschiva's skirts, tearing them when she tried to free them, she realized they were thorns. A singularly inhospitable garden, she thought.

At last they reached a rectangular tower topped with crenelation. Entering through the arched door, they found themselves in a spacious chamber paved with mosaics under a soaring cross-vaulted ceiling. The tower was actually divided into two rooms, both with fireplaces, although a small and smoking fire had been lit in only one. An interior stone stairway led up to the floor above. By the light of the struggling fire and the torches held by their escort, Eschiva could make out sparse, crude furnishings that appeared to have been taken from peasant huts. Yet in addition to the mosaic flooring, she could faintly see the hint of wall murals. Once upon a time, she surmised, this had been an elegant and magnificently appointed chamber fit for the chatelaine of the castle—or at least the Emperor of the Eastern Empire's deputy on the island.

"This is a command center, Eschiva," her cousin intoned, echoing his knight's comment, "not a lady's chamber. There's a bed on the floor above that we'll make up for you and Aimery. John and your woman can bed down here. I'll also have some lamps, a meal, and a chamber pot brought for you, so you don't have to use the garrison latrines."

"Thank you, Henri, I appreciate that. I hope you will join us for the meal?"

"I can't *wait* to hear what you are doing here in your condition," Henri answered, and then with a brief bow withdrew.

There was an awkward silence in the tower chamber as the footsteps, voices, and torchlight from Sir Henri and his men retreated. Then Aimery started to defend himself: "I warned you! I told you—"

"Aimery," Eschiva interrupted him. "I don't mind. But I would like that chamber pot, and I expect poor Anne needs one, too. I would also like to sit down." She looked around at the three-legged wooden stools, and chose a chest with a broken foot instead. She eased herself carefully onto its slightly sloping top, a hand on her belly.

"Are you all right?" Aimery asked in alarm, his anger already dissipated by her calm.

"Yes, Aimery, I'm just tired."

"I'll go see about the chamber pots and some lamps," John volunteered, uneasy about the situation and not sure if Eschiva was really as calm as she appeared. Although he'd been to Kantara before, it was only tonight, with a lady present, that he registered just *how* Spartan the accommodations were. He was sure Aimery had promised her the palace at Nicosia, not this barren fortress, when he'd induced her to return to Cyprus with him.

John first made his way to the latrines and then worked his way back through the dark to the large tower beside the main gate, which his cousin and his knights occupied. Here the sergeant cook loaded him down with a chamber pot, a pair of crude pottery oil lamps, a loaf of unleavened bread along with a bread knife, and a crock full of lard.

Returning to the tower, John found Anne crouching beside the fire holding her shoulders, while Aimery and Eschiva spoke in low tones in the dark of the adjoining room. "Dinner!" he announced as cheerfully as he could, hoping to dispel any lingering tension.

Aimery and Eschiva at once broke off their conversation and returned to the lighted room. John set the bread and lard on the chest, handed the chamber pot to Eschiva, and went over to the fire to light the wicks of the lamps. Anne at once drew back into the shadows as if afraid of him. John tossed her a reassuring smile, but she only looked down, ashamed to meet his eyes. John felt sorry for her, but there was no time to try to win her over.

With a loud knock, his cousin Henri was back. He'd removed his helmet and was carrying a pottery pitcher in both hands. He clunked these down on the chest beside the bread, declaring, "Well water, and local wine. Oh, we need some goblets, spoons, and bowls. Stew's on its way." He was gone again, but returned shortly with the missing items. He then looked around the room critically and decided they needed a chair or two.

Two men-at-arms manhandled two chairs into the chamber a few moments later, and a third brought a deep cauldron filled with a surprisingly savory-smelling stew. "Local hare," Henri announced as he personally scraped the bottom with the ladle and emptied a large portion into a bowl, which he handed to Eschiva. There were carrots and leeks as well, all flavored with rosemary, bay leaf, and black pepper. John dutifully served Eschiva and Aimery wine and bread as they sat before the fire, and even took a bowl over to Anne before he sat on the chest and shoveled the stew down between bites of bread. He was absolutely famished.

Not until the leftovers had been carted away by John and Henri's own squire and a second pitcher of wine brought did Henri sit down on one of the stools facing his guests and open the conversation that had been hanging over them all. "So what is this all about, Aimery?" Henri asked bluntly. "First you just disappear, leaving the rest of us to bury your brother, and now you're back with a pregnant wife?"

"Did you bury Guy?" Aimery deflected the question. "I thought he asked to be buried in Acre."

"He did. Which would have entailed embalming his corpse and then, of course, petitioning the Archbishop of Acre for permission to bury him in Holy Cross Cathedral. We opted to bury him in the Templar church at Limassol instead."

Aimery nodded. That was good news. If they were willing to ignore Guy's last wishes in something as personal as his place of burial, they were likely to ignore his choice of successor as well.

"Of course, if you'd been here, we would have respected your wishes, Aimery. He was your brother, after all. We couldn't imagine where you were off to all of a sudden—unless it was flying off to France to offer your sword and services to your beloved brother Geoffrey." Henri sounded very cynical as his eyes bored into Aimery.

"I have no intention of serving my brother Geoffrey," Aimery answered bluntly.

"Meaning?"

"I don't think Geoffrey has earned an inch of Cyprus—much less all of it. Do you?" He sounded more defiant and self-assured than he really was.

"No, not particularly," Henri answered so reasonably that Aimery wondered if he had already guessed what they were about.

"And the others?" Aimery asked next.

"Barlais backs Geoffrey, of course. Bethsan and Toron think we should respect Guy's wishes. The English think Cyprus has reverted to the English Crown and want to consult with King Richard."

Aimery snorted in disgust, and Henri agreed: "My sentiments exactly."

"And Cheneché? Yourself?"

"Let's just put it this way: We didn't come here to enrich someone else."

"I'll make you a baron, Henri. I'll make you all barons. If you back me." Aimery hadn't intended to blurt it out like that, and the look of alarm on Eschiva's face made him think he'd blundered. He wished, in that moment, that he had Ibelin's skills of persuasion—or better yet, that Ibelin were with him now. But he wasn't, and now that he'd said it out loud there was no taking it back. He waited.

Henri was staring at him with narrowed eyes. After a tense moment he remarked in a cautious tone, "You and I haven't always seen eye to eye."

"Is there anyone you see eye to eye with *all* the time?" Aimery asked back.

"The devil, maybe—or that's likely what the semi-sainted Balian d'Ibelin would probably say." Henri turned to throw this remark pointedly at John.

John bit his tongue to stop himself from blurting out what his father *had* said: that Henri would follow even a dog for the sake of a barony. Fortunately, his cousin had turned back to Aimery to complain: "You have spent almost every day you've been out here trying to rein me in, to stop me from doing what I do best—spreading terror."

"Has it gotten you what you wanted?" Aimery countered.

Henri didn't answer. The tension grew. Aimery kept trying to think of something to say, but his thoughts were racing in circles. Balian had been so certain Henri would back him over Geoffrey—and yet here he was, just staring at him. Aimery opened his mouth, and then thought better of it. He needed some fresh air to clear his brain out. "I need to go to the latrines," he announced abruptly. "Wait for me." He stood and exited.

Eschiva had been racking her brain trying to figure out how she could contrive a moment alone with her cousin. Now it was abruptly here, and she pounced. "Now that we are among ourselves, let me speak plainly," she burst out.

Henri looked over at her, surprised. He was not used to this cousin speaking her mind, at least not on matters of policy, nor did he entirely know what she meant by "among ourselves." Except for the girl, they were only family, anyway. And then it hit him: with Aimery temporarily out of the room, they were all *Ibelins*.

Eschiva knew she had only a few short minutes and could not afford an indirect approach. "Back my husband now, Henri, and no one will benefit more than you. Not because I or even my husband will reward you, but simply because if you do you will be the kin of the *next* Lord of Cyprus. If you back Geoffrey, on the other hand, you'll see the island flooded with his Poitevin friends and *his* wife's relatives. Support Aimery—and my son, who is even now growing up with yours, will one day rule."

The sound of Aimery returning put an end to her short speech. Eschiva ended with a faint smile under eyes that were deadly serious. Then she looked down at her hands as Aimery entered and pretended she had said nothing at all.

Aimery hardly noticed as he launched into his own new argument. "Henri, you've known me for decades. You know I'm a reasonable man. We may disagree on tactics from time to time, but on the whole we have agreed on more than we have fought over—including our assessment of my recently deceased brother. May God have mercy on his soul."

"Indeed," Henri answered, getting to his feet with a significant glance at Eschiva as he announced, "I'll think about it. Now your lady needs some rest." He bowed to Eschiva gallantly, then nodded curtly to Aimery and John before striding out.

They sat in silence, listening to his retreating footsteps. It had not been an auspicious start. Aimery was seized with a sense of helpless rage that he dared not voice, while Eschiva didn't know if she should offer comfort or pretend she didn't recognize the gravity of the situation. If they couldn't win over even her cousin . . . But he had said he would think about it, she told herself. It would be wrong to despair already. With a sigh she stood, took an oil lamp, and beckoned to Anne. Together they passed into the darkened room and slowly mounted the stairs to the room on the floor above.

There was not a single stick of furniture here except the bed and the chamber pot. The windows were neither glazed nor shuttered and let in the brilliant darkness of the star-studded sky. It was as beautiful here as it had been at sea, Eschiva thought, but a chill seemed to cling to the walls, and she hurried to remove her surcoat, shoes, and stockings so she could slip into bed in her shift. The rough woolen blankets smelled vaguely rank, and she wondered who had used them last and where she might find a bath. Then, exhausted beyond even worrying, she fell asleep.

She awoke disoriented in the same chamber, utterly alone. She remembered Aimery being with her in the night, but he was not here now. Sitting up and looking around, she noted that here, too, the walls had traces of murals on what plaster remained. The plaster was cracked and chipped and much had fallen away, revealing the naked stones underneath. The sun pouring in the end window was brilliant, however, and warmth came in with it, chasing away the chill of the night before.

Eschiva threw back the blankets and pushed her stiff and heavy body upright. She needed that chamber pot, and she needed to wash: if not a proper bath, at least some warm water to sponge off the worst dirt. Furthermore, her hair hadn't felt a comb since leaving the Templar commandery. Where on earth was Anne?

"Anne?" she called out in the direction of the stairs, and was answered by the sound of scurrying feet. Apparently the girl had only been waiting to be summoned. She appeared at the top of the stairs, head down, hair a ragged, unkempt mess, skirts and hands dirty with soot from the fire downstairs. She bobbed a curtsy but said nothing.

"Anne, where's my lord husband?"

"Dunno, m'lady," Anne answered, face down.

"Can you find us some wash water? There must be a well somewhere."

Anne turned and fled down the stairs again. With a sigh, Eschiva used the chamber pot, and then noticed there was another stairway in the corner of this chamber.

She went to it and peered upwards. It climbed inside the thickness of the walls to the roof above, and sunlight was pouring down it. She couldn't resist. Taking a fistful of skirts in her left hand and putting her other hand on the outer wall, she started up the stairs to the top. As she stepped out onto the roof, the splendor spread out before her took her breath away. She had a view down a steep, forested cliff to a stripe of brilliant green coastline outlined by the white of breaking waves. Beyond, a brilliant and glittering blue sea spread out to infinity. To her left, layers of purple mountains tumbled in echelon down to the sea. To her right, a patchwork of green, yellow, and brownish fields stretched outwards like a broad finger flanked on both sides by water. It was, she thought, the most beautiful sight she had ever seen in her life. No wonder Aimery was in love with the place!

Eschiva walked slowly around the roof of the tower, feasting on the changing panorama as her point of view shifted and the imperfect overcast blowing across the sun changed the patterns of sunlight on the sea. To the north the sea was so close she could make out the lines of breakers as they approached the shore and the whitecaps farther out. To the south, on the other hand, the sea only shimmered silver in the distance. The fertile peninsula to the east was pinched by the water until it became smaller and smaller, but it was richly cultivated. Along the near shore to the north, Eschiva could discern villages dotted along the coast, often with orchards around them. There were small, gentle bays, dotted with bobbing fishing boats and a larger roundship off the coast, heeling over in the wind.

"Beautiful, isn't it?" a male voice said behind her, and it wasn't Aimery. It was her cousin Henri.

Eschiva started and spun around, flushing violently. She was wearing nothing but her shift, and the wind up here was blowing it about her wildly. Her hair, too, was uncovered and fluttering in the wind. She felt practically naked, and the look in Henri's eye and his crooked smile suggested he was seeing more than he should.

Strangely, he looked as if he liked what he saw. This was confirmed by his next remark. "Not more beautiful than you, perhaps, but you already belong to someone else. Karpas, on the other hand, might be mine." He strode to the edge of the parapet and stood looking due east with hungry eyes. "That," he continued, pointing to the peninsula that gradually narrowed as it disappeared into the distance, "is Karpas."

He turned, his eyes narrowed on either side of a nose that hung down from his forehead like the nose guard of a helmet. "Karpas is my price, Eschiva. Tell your husband he can have my backing—up to the hilt—if he gives me Karpas. And Kantara." As he said the latter word, his gaze shifted from the distance to the immediate surroundings, the buildings scattered apparently haphazardly between the rocks and gullies that formed the crest of the sharp, narrow mountain.

Eschiva followed his gaze and then looked back at him. Their eyes met. She sensed that this was a very steep price—rather like Haakon Magnussen expected to be named Admiral. She was certain that Aimery would resist. He would protest. Just as he had about Magnussen. Aimery had never had enough money (or titles) to throw around. He had learned frugality the hard way, and he would find it hard to be generous. But Eschiva also knew that her Uncle Balian was right: they had to give the island away if they were ever going to hold it. She nodded, adding cautiously, "I will tell my lord husband."

Her cousin nodded without breaking eye contact. "Tell him. And tell him it is non-negotiable. Karpas and Kantara, or I will throw my lot in with Geoffrey." Then Brie ducked down into the stairwell again and left her alone with the splendor that had enchanted not only Aimery de Lusignan, but the hardhearted Red Sea Raider as well.

Nicosia, Cyprus, July 1194

Aimery had not exaggerated in describing the "imperial" palace. It was as beautiful and well-appointed as he had claimed. It had taken days for Eschiva to explore it all, and a week or more before she no longer got lost in its maze of courtyards and corridors. The gold mosaics, the blue, turquoise, and aqua-colored tiles, the marble fountains, and the potted hibiscus all reminded Eschiva of the stories Maria Zoë told of her childhood in Constantinople. Yet, despite—or was it because of?—its unquestioned luxury and beauty, the "imperial" palace of Nicosia was a frightening place to Eschiva. For one thing, her brother-in-law Guy had died in the very bed she shared with Aimery, and for another, she felt trapped in a strange dream. Around her was magnificent luxury, yet when she reached out for it, it seemed to recede.

It was just the language barrier, she told herself. All the servants in this beautiful palace were Greek-speaking, and they did not understand even simple requests. Or was it that they *did* understand but *pretended* not to?

Eschiva's attempts to get a meal ordered, a bed made up, or furniture moved, much less a message to her traveling husband, ended in blank stares and shaking heads. She hadn't been so conscious of the lack of understanding around her as long as Aimery had been with her, because John was their constant interpreter. But Aimery had been gone for ten days now, trying to win over others for his cause. The longer he was away, the more the palace around her seemed hostile. The servants seemed to grow scarcer, their looks more antagonistic, their whispering more conspiratorial.

Or was it all in her imagination? Eschiva put her hand to her belly. The child was very heavy now, but like the palace, he seemed unnaturally still. Her instincts said that wasn't good, but when she'd tried to ask for a midwife, the women gave her blank, uncomprehending stares and shook their heads. She'd tried to get Anne to go out into the city to locate a woman from one of the Italian merchant communes, hoping to ask about a midwife, but Anne had looked at her in sheer terror and then run away for half a day.

If she'd been feeling better herself, Eschiva would have ventured out into the streets on her own, but she wasn't feeling well. She was having repeated dizzy spells that left her queasy at best. Once or twice she almost blacked out. This wasn't normal. She knew it wasn't normal.

Guy had sickened and died in this palace. His insides had rotted. Or had he been poisoned?

John was starving (nothing unusual for him), and in his eagerness for some "real food" he turned Centurion over to the palace grooms. He took the steps to the second floor two at a time, thinking he was surely in time for dinner, and confident that his cousin would have organized the kitchens by now. Women were good at that.

"Eschiva?" he called out as he reached the royal tract, bewildered by the stillness around him. Things had never been this quiet before. When Guy lived here, the corridors had always been filled with petitioners and servants, hangers-on, and salesmen. "Eschiva?"

Something crashed loudly in the room to his right and he started, drew up, and looked toward the sound. "Eschiva?"

Anne darted out of the room from which the noise had come, saw him, and turned around to run back in. Alarmed, John followed her. Eschiva was standing upright behind a chair, pale as a ghost. A toppled table spilling broken crockery lay between her and the door. Her giant eyes met his. "John? Is Aimery back?"

"No, not yet. He—he sent me ahead. He should be here by evening," John stammered as his heart beat in his chest. His cousin didn't look at all well.

"John," she started. "You must help me."

"Of course. How?" He skirted the broken things while Barry happily started lapping up something, confident that anything on the floor was his.

As John reached Eschiva, she was swaying on her feet. "I need a midwife—or a doctor," Eschiva told him, grasping his arm to hold herself upright.

"I know a doctor!" John announced, relieved that this was a task he could fulfill.

"Thank God for that, John," she smiled at him wanly. "You must fetch him before Aimery gets back. Go for him now!"

Andreas Katzouroubis did not consider pregnancy his specialty. Indeed, he had had very little to do with it, preferring to leave it to those better trained and inherently more knowledgeable: the midwives. On the other hand, he could not refuse a summons from the palace, and he could not suppress his curiosity about the new despot's wife, either. He was also considerably less worried about unpleasant consequences, having survived this long already. So he dutifully donned his robes and followed the Greek-speaking squire to the familiar apartments of the despot.

Here he was surprised to find himself confronted by a middle-aged woman with pleasant features who was not in the least haughty or proud, but for all her dignity and restrained demeanor, desperately frightened. Andreas did his best to dispel her fears, assuring her that dizzy spells could be caused simply by the child in the womb sucking up more blood. "Perfectly normal," he repeated blithely, without having a clue of whether it was true or not. He next advised her to rest as much as possible. "There's no harm in spending the last couple of weeks in a sedentary state," he told her in his best doctor's voice before asking, "Do you have no relatives with you?" As he spoke he looked around, surprised at the empty room. Women nearing childbed were usually surrounded by a bevy of clucking female relatives.

Eschiva shook her head solemnly.

"And no handmaidens?"

"Only Anne." Eschiva looked around for the girl, but she was nowhere to be seen.

"Hmm," Katzouroubis remarked, displeased. "I will send a midwife to you," he concluded. "Are you having any pain?"

Eschiva shook her head, adding anxiously, "But the baby's so still."

"Nothing to worry about," Katzouroubis assured her again with a dismissive gesture. "Just take it easy, and get plenty of sleep. Do you want a sleeping potion?"

Eschiva shook her head.

"Good; then there's nothing more I can do for you. You can send for me if you feel the need, but it would be better to send for the midwife," he admitted professionally. Then he packed his bag and departed without even requesting a urine sample.

When he was gone, John knocked hesitantly on the door, and poked his head around. "Is everything all right?" he asked.

"The doctor thinks so," Eschiva answered hesitantly. She was, however, biting her lower lip, something John had seen his sister Isabella do when she was uncertain.

"Don't you believe him?" John asked, coming into the room.

"I don't know what to think, John," Eschiva admitted, and she looked at him with huge eyes in her pale face. "I think something's wrong. I've never been this dizzy before, almost blacking out. And the baby isn't kicking anymore. But I can't admit that to Aimery! He *told* me not to come. He *said* it was too dangerous. *I* was the one who insisted on coming—and now, if something goes wrong, it will be my fault. Aimery will never forgive me if I miscarry this child, or if it's born deformed. It would be such a terrible omen, a curse upon the entire dynasty he is determined to establish." It was all spilling out of her, because for over a week she'd had no one to speak to at all. Normally it would not have occurred to her to confide in a fifteen-year-old boy.

John sensed that this was a much worse problem than he could handle. Eschiva sounded so *afraid* of Lord Aimery—and he didn't understand that, because in his experience Lord Aimery could be caustic, sarcastic, and short-tempered, but never unkind, cruel, or unjust. It didn't help that Lord Aimery was due by nightfall and the sun was already very low in the sky.

As if reading his thoughts, Eschiva drew a deep breath and sat up straighter. "Find Anne, will you, John? I need to fix myself up for Aimery. And then see if you can explain to someone in the kitchens that we need to make a proper meal. They don't understand me." Her frustration was reflected in her voice.

John nodded. "Yes, of course, I can take care of that, but—" John couldn't just carry on as if Eschiva were fine. She obviously wasn't; whether it was physical or just in her head didn't matter.

"Aimery mustn't know I'm so worried, John," Eschiva insisted, sensing his hesitation. "Promise you won't tell him."

John frowned. He thought Lord Aimery ought to know.

"Please!" Eschiva begged. "I couldn't bear it if he sent me away!"

John was rescued by the sound of horses, men, and Barry's barking as he ran joyfully down the corridor to greet his second master; Lord Aimery had just arrived in the street out front. John immediately announced, "I'll go down to the kitchens and send Anne to you—she's just out here!" Then he ducked out of the room without making any promises.

John intercepted Aimery on the stairs as he came pounding up them eagerly. Aimery had been more successful than expected, and he looked forward to telling Eschiva all about it.

"My lord!" John put himself in Aimery's way.

"John, go down and check on the horses; I don't trust the grooms here. And find out what's for dinner; I'm starved. Bring some wine back with you."

"Yes, my lord, but first—"

Aimery had started up the stairs again, and he turned his head to scowl back at his squire.

John stood his ground. "My lord, Lady Eschiva is not well. She asked me to fetch a physician, but she doesn't want you to know—because, you see, she's afraid something is wrong with her baby."

Aimery froze. His breath froze in his chest. All thought froze in his head. He stared at John.

"My lord, I think I should go for my mother. I think it would be better if she were here."

"Your mother? The Dowager Queen?" Aimery asked, still dazed by John's blunt announcement. Part of him was thinking: *I knew this would happen. I warned her not to come.* And part of him was feeling overwhelmed by guilt for not having insisted that she remain in Caymont. Another part was just denying everything, saying she'd been fine when he left ten days ago.

John was still talking, trying to explain his thinking, but it was difficult because it had less to do with thought than instinct. He understood the fear he'd seen in Eschiva's eyes, and he also knew he couldn't put what he'd seen into words on a piece of parchment. "I was thinking, my lord," he stammered out, "that if I went to my mother and told her personally—"

"Look, John, if you want to go home, just tell me! You don't have to make up excuses!" Aimery snapped, trying to convince himself that John had made up everything about his wife feeling ill as an excuse to go home.

"I don't *want* to go home," John countered, with a stubborn expression Aimery had come to know well in the last eighteen months. "Well, not to stay," John modified his statement, adding, "I mean it, my lord. I think my mother should come. She speaks Greek. She's a Comnena. And Eschiva trusts her."

Aimery looked into his squire's eyes and saw nothing but sincerity in them. John genuinely cared about Eschiva, and he wasn't making this up.

"We were going to seek out Richard of Camville next," John spoke up, trying to anticipate Aimery's next objection. "You could ask Dick to serve as your squire while I go to Caymont. You could use two squires, anyway, and there's nothing wrong with Dick." John defended his friend, knowing that only Guy's treatment had made him seem so timid.

Aimery nodded absently. He wasn't worried about himself. He was worried about Eschiva. "Do you really think your mother would come?"

"Yes," John insisted, knowing he was overstating his own confidence. But his mother loved Eschiva almost as much as she loved her own children. Surely if she knew Eschiva was so afraid . . .

Aimery turned away from John to look up the stairs, and at that moment Eschiva emerged from the shadows of the gallery. She had put on one of her best gowns and a silk scarf the color of coral. It was usually one of her most flattering scarves, but (warned by John) Aimery saw the pallor of her cheeks and the dark circles under her eyes. His heart twisted in his chest. Eschiva had a terror of childbirth. She should not have to face it here among strangers, no matter what she had said to him in Acre a month ago.

Aimery smiled and continued up the steps to take his wife gently in his arms, very conscious of the belly between them. He bent and brushed his lips on her forehead, and then stood back to smile at her. "Thornton's with us, sweetheart. He agrees the King of England has no more interest in Cyprus. Tomorrow John and I will go to Camville—"

"So soon?" Eschiva seemed to stagger, almost fall.

Aimery caught her firmly. "We must go as soon as possible so Dick can serve me while John goes to Caymont."

Eschiva looked over at John, bewildered, hurt, and reproachful. "You're leaving us? But—"

"Only to get my mother," John assured her. "I'll bring her back in time to be with you."

"Tante Marie?" Eschiva's face brightened at once, "Do you think she'd come, John?"

The hope that lit up Eschiva's eyes was enough to shatter the last doubts Aimery had about this scheme. If the mere mention of Maria Zoë was enough to bring some color back to Eschiva's cheeks, then her presence would surely be enough to help her through the coming ordeal. He glanced back at John with a wink and a smile, and John grinned with relief.

Chapter Ten
Call of Kin

Caymont
Early August 1194

MARIA ZOË'S DREAM TURNED ABRUPTLY ALARMING. The banal, wandering plot, having something to do with planting carob trees that were yielding figs, suddenly became threatening. An ill-defined "evil" was trying to climb over the wall of her garden, causing the dogs to crawl away on their bellies rather than bark. A bloody hand took hold of the top of the wall—

Maria Zoë shook herself awake so sharply that she almost woke Balian. Then she lay in the dark, listening to the beating of her heart and trying to calm herself. It was just another nightmare. She'd had many since coming to Caymont. The dead were not at rest. Somewhere, she was certain, the remains of Christians still lay in unconsecrated ground. Until they were properly buried and Masses could be said for their souls—

She sat bolt upright in bed, realizing that she was wide awake and that the barking and shouting were real. "Balian! There's something going on!"

Balian groaned, stirred, and then tensed, hearing what she had heard. "There's someone at the gate," he concluded.

"It's the middle of the night," Maria Zoë protested.

Balian, who had been sleeping on his belly, pushed himself up and swung his legs over the edge of the bed in an easy, fluid motion. Naked, he stepped down from the bed platform and crossed to the window. He opened the shutter and peered out into the night, but could see nothing. This window did not give a clear view of the courtyard gate anyway, but the night was dark. "No torches," he announced. "I'll go see what it's about." He turned back into the room and started pulling on his shirt and braies.

Maria Zoë slipped out of bed. Unlike her husband, she did not sleep naked. In her nightgown she went to the door and, opening it, called into the anteroom to her husband's squire. "Georgios! Come help my lord dress."

Georgios dutifully roused himself from his straw pallet and stumbled into the chamber to help Balian into his hose and gambeson. He hadn't quite finished before a loud pounding at the outer door interrupted them. An excited voice shouted through the wood: "My lord! Lord John is here!"

"John?" Maria Zoë asked, and crossed the anteroom with hurried steps to open the outer door herself.

A young sergeant stood on the landing. He hadn't expected to be confronted by the Dowager Queen of Jerusalem wearing nothing but her nightgown, and he flushed in embarrassment as he stammered, "Uh, yes, my lady, Lord John is here."

Balian came up behind his wife, buckling on his sword. "Alone?"

The sergeant gratefully directed his gaze at his lord. "Except for his dog and his lame horse. He said something about being thrown. . . ."

"I wasn't *thrown*," John's voice protested out of the darkness of the stairwell. "Centurion shied and landed on uneven ground. He lost his footing, and we both went down." With a nod to his lord and lady, the sergeant made way for the heir of the house. John emerged, limping. His parents backed up into the chamber, taking in the caked mud on his shoulder, hip, and down the side of his leg. The side of his face was bruised, too, and his hose badly torn and bloody at the knee. "I would have made it before sundown if that hadn't happened, but Centurion came up so lame I couldn't ride. I think he's torn a tendon, or maybe it's a twisted pastern. He won't put any weight on his right foreleg—"

"We'll look after Centurion in due time," his father interrupted. "First, sit down and tell us what you're doing here." He took hold of his son's arm and pulled him into the anteroom, guiding him toward one of the chests.

Maria Zoë sent Georgios for water and vinegar to wash John up, while John continued talking about the accident. "Everything had gone so well until then," he explained, as if someone were accusing him of being irresponsible. "I didn't even get cheated by the Genoese, because Haakon told me what to watch for, and what the going rates for passage are. The Genoese galley couldn't sail anywhere near as close to the wind as the *Storm Bird*," he added, showing off his newly learned seamanship, "but we still would have made Acre in two days if we hadn't been forced to run from a Pisan corsair that hove into sight just ten nautical miles off Bodrum. We ran before the wind to get away from her, and had to beat back to windward after we'd shaken her off. It was quite rough, too. I think Centurion didn't have his land legs yet. I mean, it's not like him—"

"John." His father's voice was soft, but firm and commanding. "Why are you here?"

Rather than answering his father, John turned to look at his mother. "It's because of Eschiva," he said earnestly. "She's—she's frightened. The doctor said everything was all right, but she—she just doesn't trust him. Or, I don't mean she doesn't trust *him*, it's just that she's alone, among strangers." The words were tumbling out in an excited rush. "Lord Aimery and I have been away a lot. We had to go to all the Frankish lords to put our case to them" (his mother noted that he called it "our" case, identifying with Aimery de Lusignan), "and they are scattered across the island. Eschiva was alone—you can't count Anne. She's more frightened than a sparrow and hardly ever says a word. Sometimes I get the feeling she's not right in the head." Maria Zoë sometimes had that feeling, too, but who could blame her after what she'd been through? She nodded.

John continued. "But no matter what the doctor says, Eschiva's convinced there's something wrong with the child, and—"

"Did she say what exactly?" his mother interrupted him.

John shrugged uncomfortably. "No, not really. Something about the baby not kicking enough, I think. But that's not the point"—his mother raised her eyebrows, but he didn't notice and forged ahead breathlessly—"it's just that she's frightened. I don't think it's anything specific. She's just, you know, frightened. It's all so strange. The doctor recommended a midwife, but the woman's French is terrible. I tried to get one of the Italian women to come, but most of the Italians leave their wives in their home cities. Or, I guess, they *used* to have them with them, at least some of the time, but because of the growing unrest they've sent them home. They don't feel safe anymore, they say, and—"

"We can talk about that later," his father interceded again, with a glance at his wife. "Right now we need to hear more about Eschiva."

John took a deep breath. "There's really nothing more to tell, except that she's having these dizzy spells and doesn't feel well, and nobody speaks French, you see, so she can't talk to anyone. I'm not sure there's anything really wrong, but she's lonely and frightened, and . . . " John hesitated, but then continued with the utter sincerity of youth, "She couldn't bring herself to say it, Mama, but she desperately wants you to come and be with her when her time comes. She's ashamed to ask, because she insisted on going to Cyprus in the first place. Lord Aimery wanted her to stay until she was safely delivered, but she wanted to be with him, and now she's ashamed to admit she made a mistake. She didn't ask me to come get you, but when I said I would—you should have seen her face! She was *so* relieved, Mama. She *needs* you to be with her—more than Isabella ever did." John put all his heart into his case, the images of Eschiva still vivid in his mind's eye.

Before his mother could answer, Georgios returned with a large pitcher of water, a bottle of vinegar, and gauze. Maria Zoë thanked him and told her son to take off his hose so she could get a look at his knee.

"I'll go check on Centurion," Balian announced, hauling himself to his feet and leaving his wife to look to his son's injuries.

John's knee was scraped, cut, and badly swollen. After washing as much of the dirt and sand out of it as possible, Maria Zoë started to apply the vinegar to clean it more deeply, but John's yelps and squirms induced her to send Georgios for wine, which she could lace with a pinch of ground henbane.

By the time John had been sedated, his wounds cleaned and bandaged, and he had been put to bed, the dawn was breaking. There was no point in going back to her own bed; Maria Zoë knew she would not be able to sleep. Not wanting to wake Beatrice so early, she sponged herself down with some of the water brought for John, changed into a day gown, re-braided her hair, and covered it with a pale-blue silk scarf. Then she took a shawl against the morning chill, and made her way down to the rooftop terrace to await the sunrise.

It was here Balian found her, facing east as the sun rose over the distant mountains and flooded the valley with a pale, hazy light. He came up behind her, and before he could speak she turned to tell him she must go to Eschiva.

She didn't get a word out. He put his finger to her lips, and asked her instead, "Do you remember when I came to you in Jerusalem? The Patriarch, the burgesses, the sisters of St. Anne, the brothers of the Hospital, the common people in the streets, Syrian, Armenian, and Frank alike—they all expected me to stay. But defense was futile, so staying meant condemning us all to death. Or so I thought at the time. I went to the Holy Sepulcher, down into the tomb itself, and I lay there beside where our Savior's corpse had been stretched out after his crucifixion. I tried not to think at all. I emptied my mind of all thought and will. And after a time, I don't know how long, I knew I had to stay even if it was futile.

"We now know that it wasn't futile—that God had a plan—but at the time I could not know that. I dreaded telling you that I had chosen to sacrifice you and our four little children to something I could not even define. Was it duty? Was it symbolism? Was it the will of God? I just knew I had to stay—but didn't have the words to explain myself.

"But I didn't have to, because you understood. You didn't even ask for an explanation. All you said was: 'I know.'" He paused, remembering that moment seven years earlier, savoring the memory. Then he continued, "Well, I know now, too. You have to go to Eschiva. Sooner rather than later; the fall storms could start any day. The only thing I'm unsure about is whether I should let you go alone or come with you."

"Would you?" Maria Zoë looked up at him so hopefully that it made him laugh.

"You want me to come?"

"Yes, I do! Don't tell John, but I don't *entirely* feel he's a match for pirates, assassins, or thieves just yet. But mostly, I just hate being separated. I've become accustomed to having you around me these last two years. I like it. But can you leave things here?" she asked anxiously.

"I will need to make arrangements, and they will delay your departure."

"How much?"

"Two to three days."

"That's nothing," she exclaimed with relief, adding happily, "John's in no state to ride today or tomorrow as it is. Besides, I don't think Eschiva is due for another three to four weeks. We should still be able to make it in good time. Didn't John say he made the crossing with Magnussen in under twenty-four hours?" She was excited, pleased to think she could go to Eschiva without being separated from Balian. After a moment, however, she paused her racing thoughts, cocked her head, and asked, "Why do *you* want to come? It's not just to be with me, is it?"

He laughed, bent and kissed her, and then admitted, "No, not entirely. I'm curious. First Aimery and now John have fallen in love with the place. And . . . " his voice faded out.

"What?"

He took a deep breath and looked out from the terrace across the walled garden to the paddocks beyond. They were brown and barren at this time of year, places where the horses could move freely and get fresh air but not graze. Beyond them the domain fields started, plowed but not planted, waiting for the first rains. His eyes swept north toward the river, the sugar-cane fields, and the mill amid its cluster of low, plaster-covered houses, and he sighed. Rather than putting his feelings into words, he asked, "Are you happy here? Does it feel like home?"

Maria Zoë nodded in understanding rather than agreement. "Those are two different questions. Yes, I am happy here, because we have peace and I have my family around me. As for it being home . . . it's different for me. Girls are raised from the cradle knowing that the home of their childhood will not be the home of their adulthood. They know that when they marry they will go to a new place, which will become their home. In my case, I was sent to a completely different land filled with strange people and strange customs, which made it hard for me to feel at home for a long time. It didn't help that Amalric and I lived not only in Jerusalem, but in Acre, Tyre, and Jaffa. I'm not sure I felt at home anywhere before he died. When I was widowed and moved to Nablus, I started to feel at home, but then you entered the picture, and I had to divide my time between Nablus, Ibelin, and Jerusalem. We'd only been married ten years when King Guy lost the kingdom at Hattin. After Hattin we were in Tyre for five years, living in someone else's house on borrowed time. We've been here two years. So does this feel like home? No, not particularly. Home is where *you* are, or should I say, where you are happy. If you want to go to Cyprus, I have no objection." She paused, smiled a little impishly, and added, "Of course, if you want a piece of it, you'll have to recognize Aimery de Lusignan as your overlord."

Balian burst out laughing. "Didn't I say Henri would recognize John's dog Barry for the sake of a barony? Well, I'm not much better. I'm willing to bend my knee to Aimery. I did it to his idiot brother, remember?" The bitterness was still there.

"And regretted it ever after."

"Aimery's not Guy."

"No," Maria Zoë conceded, thinking it through, "and he will never be able to treat you like his vassal, either. You've been equals for far too long—not to mention you're his wife's uncle—and, if nothing else, you'll still hold Caymont from the Crown of Jerusalem."

"Or the Sultan, depending on how you look at it," Balian quipped before becoming more serious and noting, "Perhaps more important on Cyprus: you're a Comnena."

"Hmm. We'll soon see if that holds any water anymore. Isaac was, by all accounts, not very popular."

"Perhaps, but he was feared and respected." Balian paused and then announced, "Then it is settled. We will go to Cyprus, both of us. I'll take six of my household knights, so with them, their squires, myself, and my squires, you'll have fifteen armed men as your escort. And John. Is that enough for you, my lady queen?"

Maria Zoë replied, "Indeed, my lord. It should be enough." Then she leaned forward and kissed him.

Over the next two days, Balian set about appointing officials to run his barony in his absence. He named the Syrian Christian who had been most active in reorganizing the community after it resettled in Caymont "ra'is," the official responsible for serving as an intermediary between his estate officials and the native tenants. To enforce the law and keep order, he named Sir Roger Shoreham "dragoman." Shoreham had been one of the sergeants Balian knighted during the defense of Jerusalem, and he had proved his solid reliability and incorruptibility many times over his fifteen years of service to Ibelin, but he was aging and in no mood for new adventures. He was happy to remain in Caymont with his grandchildren. The last appointment, that of scribe, had been most difficult. Far more than their title implied, scribes were the financial administrators of a lordship, the tax and rent collectors, the bookkeepers and accountants. Balian would have liked to appoint his confessor of many years, Father Michael, but after much mental agony he decided to name the perpetually dissatisfied Bart d'Auber. While he hated rewarding someone for nothing, Balian had to face the fact that Bart might become even more disruptive of the community if he wasn't given some authority. Since the position of scribe was usually filled by a man of knightly rank and it came with a fief and house, it assuaged Bart's damaged pride. The fact that Bart's command of Arabic was (due to his years in Arab slavery) exceptional helped justify the appointment—and Father Michael was given the task of reporting to Balian any abuses or complaints against him from the tenants.

With these officials appointed and sworn in before tenants, Balian was ready to plan his own departure. Meanwhile Maria Zoë had decided to take Beatrice with her, leaving the nursery of children in the hands of Henri de Brie's wife, Heloise. What Balian and Maria Zoë had not reckoned with was a revolt by the older boys.

Their youngest son, Philip, and Aimery de Lusignan's firstborn, Guy, were both twelve, and Joscelyn d'Auber was thirteen. Just after vespers, when Balian and Maria Zoë left the chapel preparing to retire to the solar for a few hours of peace before bed, the three boys blocked their way.

"We have to talk, Papa!" Philip opened belligerently. "I'm not a baby anymore. I shouldn't have to stay in the nursery with the girls and the *children*." He was referring to Aimery's youngest son and namesake, who was only four, and Henri de Brie's young sons.

Guy immediately backed him up, declaring, "It's *my* mother who wants help! She would want me to come. I can cheer her up!"

Joscelyn kept his mouth shut, but his presence expressed his position. He, too, wanted to go to Cyprus.

Maria Zoë put a restraining hand on her husband's arm, half expecting him to explode with indignation at such a disrespectful confrontation. The boys arguably needed a good hiding for confronting the Baron of Ibelin in this rude manner, but Balian seemed less offended than Maria Zoë expected. Instead of reproaching them for their tone and attitude, he dismissed them with a wave of his hand. "I can't afford to take deadweight along. That's an end of it."

"But we're not *deadweight*!" Philip protested indignantly. "I can take care of Ras—"

"We're not taking any destriers, just palfreys," his father interrupted him.

"But I'm even better with Hermes!" Philip spluttered, referring to his father's favorite riding horse. "And Guy and Joscelyn can help with the horses, too!" he added, harvesting vigorous nods from his companions.

"We have our squires; what do we need the likes of you for?" Balian countered dismissively.

"But the squires can look after the weapons, and—and—we can serve you at table and look after your clothes and run errands and—and—anything you want us to do," Guy piped up. "Just like I did for King Richard."

"Really?" Balian asked, looking from one boy to the other in mock disbelief, while Maria Zoë bit her tongue to keep from laughing; she now knew he was teasing the boys.

"John got to ride out with you in Tyre!" Philip reminded his father indignantly.

"He *couldn't* have been as young as you are," Balian answered as if irritated.

"Yes, he was!" Philip insisted. "He was *younger*! He was only *ten*!"

"Really? You're sure about that?"

Philip was beginning to suspect his father was teasing him. "Yes, you *know* he was. My lord."

"Ah, that's better," Balian noted with a quick twitch of his lips. "Because I'm certainly not taking any impudent little boys who have not yet learned their manners."

"No, my lord," Philip adjusted his tactics instantly, echoed by Guy and Joscelyn.

With them now standing contritely in front of him, Balian asked, "So, you want to come with me to Cyprus. Why? It's just to get away from your lessons, isn't it?"

"No, no! Not at all, my lord!" Philip's eyes widened in a look of such perfect innocence that Maria Zoë couldn't hold her giggles in any longer and had to cover her mouth with her hand.

"Well, I'm glad to hear that," his father answered seriously, ignoring his wife's unhelpful behavior. "Because Father Angelus is coming with us, and *if* I were to let you come, then you would be expected to spend at least two hours every day perfecting your Greek."

Philip's eyes darted between his mother and father. He wasn't sure about his father yet, but he sensed his mother was not at all opposed to this suggestion. That meant she would be his ally behind closed doors. He smiled an angelic smile at her and then assured his father, "But I *love* learning Greek, my lord—"

That was too much for Balian. He burst out laughing—and then cuffed his son lightly with the admonishment, "Don't lie to me, boy. You hate it. You always have. Just like John. But that doesn't interest me. If you come with us, you'll spend five hours in the classroom every day, not just four, until your Greek is at least as good as John's. Then we'll see whether Father Angelus thinks we can reduce class time or not. Last I heard, your Latin was nearly as bad as your Greek, your French spelling was nothing short of comic, and you thought Edinburgh was in the Holy Roman Empire."

"Well, Hamburg and Rothenberg and Regensburg are," Philip defended himself, adding hastily before his father could get out a disgusted word, "and I'm good with geometry, my lord. Ask Father Angelus!"

"I will," his father promised. "Now go to bed. All of you!"

Joscelyn and Guy said a hasty, "Yes, my lord. Good night, my lord," happy to have escaped without actually provoking any rage, but Philip started to leave and then turned back. "Was that a 'yes' or a 'no,' Papa?" he wanted to know.

"I haven't decided yet," his father told him truthfully. "So scat before I decide you're a nuisance."

Philip took the hint and ran after his friends.

Maria Zoë took Balian's arm but said nothing, leaving him to sort through his thoughts on his own. In the solar, she seated herself in her favorite chair by the fire. Georgios was waiting with wine, which he poured into two of the beautiful enameled goblets they had saved from the house in Jerusalem. Only after Balian had also seated himself did she speak. "I think it *would* do Eschiva good to have Guy with her, and he did serve in the *household* of Richard of England, admittedly more a page to Queen Berengaria than Richard. Still, he knows the duties. We've been giving them both a little too much freedom here."

Balian nodded and looked over to her. "That's what I was thinking, too. But I'm also serious about them not interrupting their schooling. The older a man gets, the less time he has for education. If I hadn't found myself serving a prince under the tutelage of a great scholar like William of Tyre, I would be a half-ignorant man. It was also a perverse benefit of being cooped up in Tyre that John had more time to study than otherwise. I don't want Philip to be less educated."

"We'll have access to more learned men on Cyprus than we do here in Caymont."

"Greek scholars, I presume you mean."

"Yes, but one learns a language by hearing it all the time. Cyprus will be good for Philip's Greek."

"It certainly did wonders for John's. And Joscelyn? What do you make of his request?"

"That he no longer wants to run away to al-Adil. That's a first and important step to returning to the True Faith. I think it is a very good thing."

Balian nodded thoughtfully. "So, we'll take them along?"

"Yes, I think we should."

Balian smiled. "Good. I rather like the thought of seeing what sort of trouble Philip will get himself into next."

Chapter Eleven
Faltering Dynasty

Nicosia
Late August 1194

ESCHIVA WANTED TO DIE. IT WAS that simple. She wanted to die, and she couldn't understand why God had taken her infant son and left her alive to face the shattered wreck of her marriage. She couldn't bear to face Aimery ever again.

They had torn the little baby out of her womb and told her he was dead. They hadn't even shown him to her, or let her hold him in her arms. They had just whisked him away, scolding her in their incomprehensible tongue.

She had screamed and screamed in protest, but it had done no good. They had taken him away wrapped in a shawl, and she wasn't even allowed to see that he was really dead. Maybe they had just stolen her baby so the hated "despot" would not have a child here? Or maybe one of the women just wanted him for herself? How would she ever know? She couldn't understand a word they said.

But without the baby, she could not face Aimery. She had stopped them from fetching him. They didn't understand much of what she said, but they had understood that much. Shaking their heads and clucking, they had gone out and just left her here alone. In the filthy sheets. With the stench of death and failure all around her.

She did not know how long she had been alone, but long enough for her sweat and tears to turn cold where they had soaked the linens. Cold enough to make her shiver, though God knew the room was stiflingly hot, or had been when she struggled to deliver a dead child . . .

Oh, God, why? Why don't you just take me away so I don't ever have to go through this again? Or see the disappointment and anger on Aimery's face? Or worse, hear him renounce me, turn me out. . . .

The door crashed open and women rushed into the room, chattering and tripping over themselves as they tried both to move and to fall on their knees at the same time. Their voices were anxious, urgent, defensive, and then silenced by a single command. Eschiva gasped and struggled to lift her head enough to see to the door. A woman was sweeping past the kneeling servants with shimmering golden veils pinned to her head by a crown. Pearls gleamed on the bodice of her gown. The image was so reminiscent of an icon that for an instant Eschiva thought God had heard her prayers: she was dead, and the Virgin Mary was striding toward her.

But then the Virgin Mary let out a stream of words in Greek that didn't sound mild or sweet-tempered, as Eschiva expected of the Virgin. Furthermore, the words scattered the women in all directions as if in panic, and Eschiva had come to herself enough to recognize Maria Zoë.

A moment later Maria Zoë had reached the bed and, seating herself on it, pulled Eschiva into her arms. "I'm so sorry, Eschiva! I'm so, *so* sorry! I thought your time was still weeks away!"

"It was," Eschiva gasped out, breaking down into miserable, choking sobs. "It was, but—but—he came early. He was dead. Or they *say* he was dead. They took him away from me!" She wailed this out, reliving it all over again.

"Hush, hush, hush," Maria Zoë whispered, stroking Eschiva's face and head, while tightening her hold so Eschiva could gain strength from the warmth and comfort of her arms and bosom.

Feeling the pearls of Maria Zoë's bodice, however, Eschiva tried to pull back. "I'll ruin your beautiful dress, Tante Marie. I'm so dirty!"

"Then the lazy hussies will have something else to do—after they've cleaned up the mess here, made a proper meal, and washed down the corridors as well! This palace looks as if no one has taken a mop to it since Isaac Comnenus died!" Maria Zoë retorted indignantly. "But first and foremost, we need to get you cleaned up so you can see Aimery."

"No! I can't face him! I've failed him! He'll renounce me, Tante Marie—just like my father—"

Maria Zoë put her fingers to Eschiva's lips. "Shhh!" she ordered.

Eschiva swallowed down the words, but they burped back up as hiccups and gasps for breath.

Maria Zoë pulled her back into a close embrace. "Listen to me, Eschiva."

Eschiva tried, but she couldn't stop the sobs, so Maria Zoë just sat and held her until they ebbed on their own. Then she asked gently, "Can you listen now?"

Eschiva nodded in resignation.

"Aimery is outside banging his head against the wall and blaming himself. He thinks the reason they won't let him in is that you're dead or bleeding to death. He has called for a priest, and he just told me that he would—"

Women burst in on them, carrying a tub and several amphorae of steaming rose water. Maria Zoë turned to give orders for setting up the bath, and then turned back to Eschiva and pulled her soaked and bloodied gown up over her head. She tossed the gown across the room in disgust and then helped Eschiva onto her feet and helped her hobble to the bathtub, all the while giving further orders to the women. These rushed to strip the dirty sheets from the bed, remove the basin full of blood beside the birthing stool, manhandle the stool to the side of the room, and start wiping up the marble floor.

"They told me he was dead, but they wouldn't even show him to me," Eschiva told Maria Zoë in a notably calmer voice as she sank into the warm water of the tub.

Maria Zoë stroked her forehead, turned, and demanded a sponge. Then, pushing back her outer sleeves and heedless of the inner sleeves, she dipped the sponge in the water to start gently washing Eschiva's face with the clean water. "Sweetheart, John told us the babe had not been kicking in the womb. If that's true, he had probably been dead for some time before the birth. Which means, of course, that development had stopped and he was not—whole. That's why the midwife didn't want you to see him."

Eschiva bit her lower lip as she began sobbing again, but this was a different sobbing, the sobbing of grief rather than protest. She knew it was true. She had known it before she first sent for the doctor, before she'd told John. . . .

The warm water was calming her, as were the gentle strokes of the sponge on her face. Maria Zoë spoke to her again gently: "We brought Guy with us, and Philip and Joscelyn."

Eschiva opened her eyes and lifted her head from the padded rim of the tub. "*My* Guy? My son? He's here? On Cyprus?"

"Yes, but we can't let him see you like this. Come. We need to wash out your hair." As she spoke Maria Zoë put the sponge aside to unbraid Eschiva's hair, and then ordered her to dunk her head under the water.

Eschiva did as she was told. (People rarely disobeyed Maria Zoë.) The water made her long hair swim and swirl around her. When she came up again for air, Maria Zoë started combing it away from her face with her long fingernails. Eschiva had always admired her for those long, beautifully filed nails. She couldn't seem to grow her own. They broke or got chewed off. . . .

"I'm going to have a long talk to the midwife," Maria Zoë was saying now, "but if I understood her apologetic babbling as I came in, she said you will be fine. She insists there is nothing fundamentally wrong with you at all. The bleeding stopped very promptly, she said, and the afterbirth came out cleanly. Are you in any pain?"

"Not more than normal," Eschiva admitted.

"Good." Maria Zoë turned and issued orders again, and promptly a woman was beside the tub with a large linen towel, which she held open between outstretched arms. But Maria Zoë shook her head and sent her scurrying away.

"They're so obedient to you," Eschiva observed, with a wan smile. "They always pretend not to understand a word I say."

"For which I've promised to have them stripped naked and flogged through the streets of Nicosia," Maria Zoë told her briskly.

Eschiva put her hand to her mouth. "You didn't!" She was at once both horrified and delighted.

"I did, but I'll probably be persuaded by much contriteness into commuting that sentence to throwing them all out and hiring new staff. I won't have this—what's that wonderful German word Mistress Shoreham always used? *Schlampenwirtschaft*—slut household. But first—Beatrice?" Maria Zoë looked around the room and found her own lady helping to make up the bed with clean linen sheets. "Beatrice, come help Eschiva finish her bath, while I go tell Aimery his wife is *not* on her deathbed."

"No!" Eschiva caught her aunt's arm. "No, I can't. He—"

"Listen to me!" Maria Zoë hushed her firmly. "You've miscarried a child. It happens to all of us. I miscarried one of Amalric's children, too. Your mother miscarried several times. It is God's will, though we cannot understand it. It was His will to call this child to him early. That's all there is to it. You're fine. You're not yet thirty. There's every reason to think you can conceive again—and if not, you have two wonderful sons already. You were right to come here, Eschiva. This island needs a government, not an army of occupation. Now, I'm going to tell Aimery the good news before he suffers any longer. I'll be back."

Outside the birthing chamber John waited anxiously, but he relaxed at the sight of his mother's calm face. "She's going to be all right?"

"She's fine. She lost the baby, that's all. It happens. Take me back to Lord Aimery." The birthing chamber was traditionally a room far from the royal apartments—so the screaming would not be too disruptive of government—

and Maria Zoë did not yet know her way around this palace. As John led her through the apparent maze of corridors, Maria Zoë had time to note in greater detail the little signs of neglect. King Guy had obviously not been concerned with the maintenance of his principal residence, and Aimery hadn't had time. Eschiva had her work cut out for her, Maria Zoë concluded—but that was a good thing, as it would distract her from this latest loss. They would start by replacing the entire staff, including poor Anne, who was clearly too traumatized to be of any use. Hopefully she would find peace in a convent. In her place they would hire a local girl, and they would replace the entire pack of servants. People who owed their positions to the new regime were more likely to be loyal to the House of Lusignan. Maria Zoë found the thought of turning the palace on its head invigorating.

Men's voices, low and strained, greeted them as they entered Aimery's private apartment. Dick de Camville was waiting anxiously by the door and, not knowing Maria Zoë, he could not read her face instantly. "Is my lady dead? Is the Lady Eschiva dead?"

"No. She's going to be fine."

Dick crossed himself, and his lips moved in a prayer of thanks. In the short fortnight he'd been in the service of Aimery and Eschiva, he had developed a deep affection for Eschiva. Lord Aimery was certainly no Guy, just as John had promised, but it was Lady Eschiva who had won his heart by her kindness. She had made him feel like part of the family.

Maria Zoë continued deeper into the room, where Aimery sat crumpled in a chair with his face in his hands. Balian stood opposite him, and he interrupted himself at the sight of Maria Zoë. As Balian's voice fell silent, Aimery sat bolt upright and twisted around to look at Maria Zoë, an anguished look on his ravished face.

"She's fine, Aimery," Maria Zoë assured him, coming closer and laying her hand on his shoulder. "She's miscarried a child, but she's fine. The bleeding has stopped; the afterbirth discharged cleanly; she has no fever. The midwife seemed quite competent, from what Eschiva said, but the household servants are a pack of slovenly hussies who should all be flogged publicly. This entire palace is filthy—as you apparently haven't noticed—and where there's filth, there's corruption. They're probably robbing you blind by selling off bits of stores, supplies, pieces of valuable furnishings, even the very substance of the palace decorations. I will demand to see an inventory shortly, but for now the important thing is that Eschiva is physically fine." She paused and waited as Aimery caught his breath and stared at her expectantly. She had used the flood of words to give him time to get a grip on his emotions; she used the pause to make sure she had his full attention. "Eschiva's problem is not physical, Aimery. It's emotional. She seems to think you will not forgive her for losing this child."

Aimery scowled. "Where does she come up with nonsense like—"

"That doesn't matter. The point is, she thinks you will blame her for this dead child, so much so that you will set her aside—"

"That's ridiculous! I—"

Maria Zoë held up her hands. "I'm only telling you so you know what to say to her when you go to her. Reassure her, Aimery. Tell her how much you love her. I'm going back to her now, but I'll let you know when she's ready to receive you." She was gone as soon as she finished speaking.

Aimery turned his baffled eyes to Balian to ask, "How can she possibly think I would reject her after this? I've never *once* threatened to set her aside. Christ in Heaven! I have no grounds for it, and the Church wouldn't allow it even if I wanted to."

"It's my brother's fault," Balian concluded simply. "It's not just that he set her mother aside after twenty-odd years of marriage; Eschiva feels he abandoned *her* when he renounced his titles and went to Antioch, never to be heard from again. If my little girl, Helvis or Meg, had been married, say, to a prince of Armenia, who was then taken captive by the Seljuks, while the whole country was overrun and my daughter was trapped in a besieged city—"

"I know," Aimery interrupted. "You would have ridden through hell itself to bring her home."

"How do you know that?" Balian asked, astonished.

"Because you did, didn't you? You went to Jerusalem to free your wife and children—something none of the rest of us would have done. Tripoli even advised *against* going to his wife's rescue, remember?" He paused just long enough to suggest his respect for this action before continuing, "Fortunately, I don't have to go to such extremes. All I have to do is cross the palace and go down on my knees before her. I've been thinking, Balian, ever since I came back. It's not enough to give men "control" of one area or another. That's not a legal or heritable status—even if dear brother Geoffrey doesn't come back and reverse everything I've done!" His frustration and uncertainty over his brother's reaction was evident in his raw tone. He added tensely, "I need to be able to make barons, and for that I need a crown."

Balian nodded.

"Who created the Crown of Jerusalem?" Aimery asked.

"The leaders of the First Crusade."

"Not the Pope?" Aimery sounded surprised by the answer.

"The Pope would have preferred an ecclesiastical state headed by the Patriarch, but the men who'd fought their way to Jerusalem and then extended the boundaries one bloody square mile at a time weren't about to accept that solution. Besides, the Patriarch was helpless without armed protection. An ecclesiastical state would not have survived a decade, even against the weak and fragmented Muslim lords who controlled the surrounding territories at the start of this century. The barons made the king, Aimery, which is why the High Court still has the right to select the next monarch."

"But how can barons create a king, if only a king can create barons?"

"A paradox, I admit. The law of conquest helped with the creation of the early baronies. John tells me that you had success in winning the leading men already on the island to your cause; am I right?"

"Yes, both Englishmen admitted that Richard of England is too entangled in a desperate struggle for his hereditary lands to taken an interest in ruling Cyprus. If only he'd chosen the crown of Jerusalem over that of England!" Aimery exclaimed, shaking his head. Then, drawing a breath, he returned to the subject at hand. "Your nephew Brie demanded a ridiculous price, by the way! I had to cede him one of the six royal castles on the island, Kantara, *and* promise to give him a free hand throughout the Karpas peninsula. That's little short of highway robbery!" Aimery told Balian indignantly.

"Speaking of which," Balian interposed, "Famagusta is a pirate's nest. The corsairs are literally anchored three deep, and they dart out to prey on merchant shipping traveling between the Levant and Europe. It's no wonder Champagne thought your brother was behind them and believed their purpose was to destabilize his reign. They are a severe menace to the Kingdom of Jerusalem, because they threaten the Kingdom's lines of communication and supply. You need to clean them out."

"I know, but I've got more important things to do first," Aimery answered, irritated. "Haakon Magnussen, as my *admiral*," he noted sarcastically, "will have to deal with them—if he ever comes back. First I've got to get control of Cyprus itself, whether dear brother Geoffrey decides to turn up or not. Walter de Bethsan has taken control, in my name, of the most impregnable castle ever built—much better than Kerak or Krak des Chevaliers. I'll have to show it to you. The Greeks call it St. Hilarion, but for some reason the Italians call it Dio d'Amore—Dieu d'Amour. Galganus de Cheneché is holding the other mountain fortress of Buffavento, and Barlais is holding the castle and port of Kyrenia—though I'm not sure whether he's holding it for me, himself, or dear brother Geoffrey," Aimery admitted. "The same holds for Rivet at Larnaka. The Templars still maintain a presence in Gastria and Limassol, which is the only reason the latter port is still halfway functioning, but God only knows whose side the Templars are on or for how long. If Geoffrey shows up, they're just as likely to recognize him as me. The Hospitallers, on the other hand, have pulled out altogether—cutting their losses, they say, after their sugar mill at Kolossi was burned down. And now, for the first time, trouble has also broken out in the west part of the island. A large roundship bound for Marseilles with returning pilgrims was wrecked just north of Paphos, and apparently the locals slaughtered every single poor soul who survived the wreck—in violation of the laws of God. They *certainly* seized all the salvage, in violation of the laws of Comnenus! You may say that's not so important," Aimery hastened to counter the argument he presumed was on Balian's tongue, "but it's indicative of the spirit of contempt in which the people here hold me—and all Franks."

"You need to win over the Church." It was the voice of Maria Zoë, who had returned unnoticed by the men.

Aimery started and looked over at her. "May I go to Eschiva now?"

"Shortly. But I am serious. If you want to win the people of Cyprus, you must first convince the Greek clergy on the island that you will not try to impose Latin rites on them or their flocks, that you will not confiscate their properties or tax them, and then that you will treat their people fairly. How we define 'fair' may be a matter of interpretation and negotiation, but you will not have peace on this island until you have the Greek Church on your side."

Aimery stared at her, still absorbing her message, but Balian shrugged and announced, amused, "*ee vasilissa exee lalisee*: the Queen has spoken."

Aimery looked at him askance, and Maria Zoë smiled. "Come. Eschiva needs some rest, but she won't be able to sleep until she's been reassured you still love her and do not blame her."

Aimery nodded and then remembered to ask, "How do I look?"

"Terrible," Balian answered, "which is just the way you *should* look. She should see how distressed you have been."

Aimery nodded absently; in his mind he was already preparing his words. Maria Zoë led him through the corridors, and as he approached the chamber containing his wife, he was pleased by the way the women all went down on their knees and bowed their heads nearly to the floor—until he realized it was for Maria Comnena, not himself. Damn it, he thought, but then he was inside a room gleaming with wet marble and smelling of roses. The sheets were so white they seemed almost to glow. There were even fresh hibiscus in a glass vase beside the bed. Eschiva was all but lost in the puffy pillows, and her huge eyes followed him as he approached the side of the bed. She reached out a hand to him tentatively: it appeared to plead more than to welcome.

Aimery fell on his knees beside the bed, took her hand and kissed it, and then held it to his cheek. "Forgive me, Eschiva," he croaked out. "I should never have allowed you to risk your own life or that of our child by coming with me."

"Aimery, my love," Eschiva assured him, struggling to sit up more, and Beatrice at once came to help her. "Aimery, it's all right as long as you aren't angry," she told him.

"Why, my love, should I be angry with you? You have done nothing wrong. You risked your life and that of our child to support me, and any setbacks we have are my fault—but, believe me, Eschiva." Aimery's voice was getting stronger as he spoke, reassured by how serene, self-possessed, and loving Eschiva looked. "I swear to you, Eschiva," Aimery declared, "I will make you a queen. They will recognize *you* as their queen. And, so help me God, our children and our children's children will rule this island kingdom for the next three hundred years!"

St. Hilarion, Late October 1194

The boys had never seen anything like it. From a distance the castle blended in so well with the crags and rugged contours of the landscape that they thought the towers were outcroppings. As they came closer, they realized that cascading down the steep slope of the mountain face was a wall that enclosed a partially overgrown area with a slope of 45 degrees or more. At the top of this a series of towers nestled against the back of a sheer limestone cliff. But they soon discovered that even these towers were only the outer line of defense. On the very top of the cliffs that reared up in jagged peaks and teeth of stone, there were more towers still. One crowned the top of a spike of rock with a skirt of pine trees all around it. The boys could only gape in wonder.

At the lower barbican, the party of Franks led by Lusignan and Ibelin dismounted, and the squires stayed there to see to the stabling and feeding of the horses, while Lusignan and Ibelin continued. They proceeded on foot up a steep, winding path punctuated with shallow steps to the wall against the cliff. The knights of their escort trailed them, with the three boys forming the tail of the formation. The towers built against the side of the cliff were solid, crenelated, and well-fortified with gates, portcullis, murder holes, and more. Furthermore, they were dog-legged, sometimes twice, so that after entering, one faced a blank wall of stone and had to turn to continue. Only after emerging from the far side did it become evident that the second chamber was carved out of bedrock. Beyond that they exited onto a narrow spine of land that faced north rather than south.

This was like no castle the boys from Palestine had ever seen. The buildings were strung along the corniche of the mountain and connected by narrow footpaths that wound amid the outcroppings and the undergrowth, and—following the rugged contours of the mountain crags—dipped down steeply or scaled to new heights in a series of steps.

Almost as amazing as the structures themselves were the large gnarled trees that grew wherever the surface was too steep for either a path or a building. If the south slope by which they had gained the castle had seemed steep, the drop-off to the north was dizzying. The mountain dropped straight down for hundreds of feet before the forest resumed, clinging to the side of the mountain as it fell to the coastal plain. The latter was cultivated with patches of orchards, vineyards, pastures, and fields. A little port with a double harbor inside a breakwater and a powerful castle could be seen to the northeast—but mostly it was the lushness of the countryside that amazed the boys raised in the Holy Land.

Until they started exploring, that is. The "middle" castle, as they came to think of it, lay just behind the cliff they had passed through, and it had what seemed like endless storerooms, pantries, wine cellars (chock-full of wine!), a curing room for meat with a fireplace, a bakery, a brewery, an oil press and a winepress, even a stall for goats and a henhouse and pigeon cote. There were barracks here as well, only sparsely furnished and partially occupied, and an impressive basilica constructed of limestone interrupted by thin layers of brick to create a horizontally striped wall. The three apses of the church faced due east from the tip of the mountain crest. Unless one went to the window to look down, they offered views only of the sky—as if the building were suspended in the air.

Heading west through the maze of buildings, some connected underground, the boys eventually came to a narrow path that led beside the rocky face of the mountain upwards by means of narrow, steep steps toward a cluster of buildings crowning the top of the highest point on this ridge. The elder Lusignan and Ibelin and their knights had taken this route immediately, while the boys had been distracted by exploring the middle castle.

Now the boys followed, discovering that the "upper castle" was more cohesive, with a paved courtyard, and a number of impressive buildings with batteries of arched doors and double-light windows offering spectacular views in all directions. The ground floors of these buildings were often at least partially carved out of bedrock and usually windowless, but well stocked with grain, oil, wine, and weapons. The second floors of the buildings, in contrast, were paved with either tiles or marble. There were window seats in the windows, hooded fireplaces, and other signs of the luxury accommodations conspicuously lacking in the barracks of the middle castle.

When they had completed their round of the buildings facing the court-yard, they passed out by way of a gate facing west and discovered there was yet *another* lone tower, standing upright and defiant on a little peak of white rock roughly a thousand feet away. This tower was very narrow and tall with no windows, but topped by crenelation.

"How do we get *there*?" Philip asked in awe. There was no visible path. In fact, right in front of them the rocks fell sharply away, and they were looking at the tops of the pine trees. In short, they were separated from the tower by a shallow gorge.

"I think there's a trail over here," Joscelyn decided. He had wandered a little to one side.

Guy and Philip followed him and looked at the narrow, naked path that struck out into the trees from the foot of the rocky platform they were standing on. "I'm not so sure," Guy prevaricated. "It looks like nothing but a goat track to me."

"But look!" Philip pointed. "You can see it emerging from the trees there!" He pointed toward the tower. Sure enough, at the foot of the tower the trees parted a little, and a narrow white path wound up out of them to go along the base of the tower and disappear around the corner. "The door must be at the back of the tower," Philip concluded.

"But how do we get down to the start of the trail?" Guy asked. The begin-ning of the trail was a good six or seven feet below where they were standing.

"Oh, that's easy!" Philip announced. Dropping down onto his buttocks, he rolled over and, face to the rock, slowly lowered himself. The rock face being rugged, he had handholds and footholds. Once his feet hit the trail, he backed up (oblivious to the white dust smeared across his front) and waved at the other boys. "See! Easy!"

Joscelyn was already on his belly and following, leaving Guy little choice.

They followed the trail through the woods, the pine needles under their feet and birds crying indignantly as they were disturbed from their perches. It was chilly here in the deep shadow, although the trees broke the wind somewhat. None of the boys gave a thought to the fact that some of the chill came from the fact that the sun was very low in the sky. They were too busy concentrating on the trail, which was more rugged than expected. The last hundred feet was a climb up the escarpment on which the tower was perched. They had to use their hands to haul themselves up as much as their feet to push them off. They were filthy, scratched, and breathless—but triumphant—by the time they reached the foot of the tower.

As they came around the first corner, however, they gasped in terror. The trail broke off abruptly and plunged down a thousand feet to a heap of broken masonry already half overgrown with gorse and thorn bushes. The outer half of the tower, concealed from view up to now, had collapsed.

Still shaken by how close they had come to stepping off the cliff, they turned around to return the way they'd come. Only now did they notice that the sun had already set, and night was closing in on them rapidly. "We'd better get back fast," Guy summed up the situation.

He got no contradiction from his companions. Rather, they all started to hurry, afraid to admit to one another how frightened they were becoming. The first challenge, of course, was getting down the face of the rock they had climbed up earlier with so much élan. Again they resorted to going down the face of the rock backwards, but in the fading light it was harder to find footholds. Now and again one or the other missed and slid more than stepped, scraping knees, elbows, and hands. But they made it.

The trail, however, was harder to find now that the shadows had enveloped it. Footing was harder to find, too. Partway, Joscelyn tripped over a root, staggered forward out of balance, and in trying to catch himself put his foot sideways on another root. With an audible "knick," his foot fell sideways off the root. He crashed down face first with a cry of alarm and pain. Philip was leading, and he stopped at once to look back. Guy turned and went back to Joscelyn to help him up.

"My ankle," Joscelyn gasped out. "It's broken."

"You probably just twisted it," Guy countered. "Here. I'll help you up."

Joscelyn shook his head. "I can't! I can't!" There was a whine and sob in his voice that was utterly unlike him. Joscelyn was no crybaby. He could usually take more and worse than the others, always anxious to prove that a Mamluke was better than any Frank. The pain and panic in his voice now made Philip turn around and return to find out what had happened.

With Guy's help, Joscelyn had pulled himself into a sitting position with his back against the trunk of a tree, but his face was ghostly white, and he was holding up his right leg at the knee. The foot hung uselessly from it.

"Christ!" Philip whispered in shock.

"*He* can't help, you stupid polytheist!" Joscelyn snarled, and he started praying in Arabic.

"What are we going to do?" Guy asked Philip.

"One of us has to stay here with Jos, and the other better go get help."

Guy nodded.

"You'd better go," Philip decided; "it's your father's castle and his men. My father's here for the first time and doesn't know his way around."

Guy nodded again, but he didn't move.

"What's the matter?" Philip asked.

"I'm not sure I can find my way back or climb up the rock at the other end," Guy admitted.

"You have to!" Philip told him in a tone that was sharp with rising panic. "We can't stay here all night!"

It was starting to get decidedly cold now that the sun had set, and the wind seemed to have picked up as well.

"I know; it's just—"

"All right, then *you* stay here. I'll go for help!" Philip declared. He was inwardly just as afraid he might lose his way or fail to scale the rock, but now he was determined to show off his courage. He forged ahead with blind determination for a few hundred paces, only to stop abruptly. He was surrounded by darkness, and overhead the trees whispered to one another alarmingly. He hadn't a clue where the trail was. His breathing was getting louder and he could feel the pounding of his heart. He turned on his heel to return the way he'd come, but now he couldn't find the trail back, either.

Philip felt an intense need to pee, but he knew it was just fear. He *had* to find the trail. After looking this way and that, he gave up, and just struck out through the trees in the direction he thought the castle *should* be. The first time he tripped over a root, he froze with a new terror. If he broke his ankle like Jos had done, no one would ever find any of them. And there were lions up here in the mountains, John had said.

Philip held his breath to listen. Everything was still except for the rustling of the treetops. Maybe that was because a lion was already stalking him! Philip started praying frantically and plunged forward through the forest, telling himself that as long as the ground was sloping upwards, he had to be going in the right direction.

It seemed like an eternity, but eventually he began to make out a rocky cliff, lighter than the forest, behind the trees. He'd made it back to the base of the castle. Only this wasn't the same place where they'd descended. The cliff was much taller—at least ten feet. Worse, to his left the ground dropped hundreds of feet into the darkness. Philip broke out into a cold sweat and started back along the base of the rock on which the castle perched.

He hadn't gotten very far when he saw light overhead. It was an unsteady light, yellowish and swaying. A torch!

"Hello!" he called out at the top of his voice. "Hello! Can anyone hear me?"

The torch swayed. "Hello?" came an answering call.

"Help!" Philip cried out with the strength of hope. "It's Philip d'Ibelin! I'm down below you!"

The torch moved, and a head silhouetted against the light of the torch looked over the edge of the cliff.

"How did you get down there? What are you doing?" With relief Philip recognized the voice of his father's squire Georgios.

"We just wanted to see the outer tower, but then Jos broke his ankle and it got dark, and I couldn't find my way back, and—"

"Stay there!" Georgios ordered. His head disappeared again and Philip could hear voices muttering. Then Georgios' head reappeared and he called down, "Follow the trail, keeping your right hand on the rock all the way until you come to some stairs. We'll be waiting for you there."

Philip had never been so relieved in his life. He turned, and keeping his hand on the surface of the cliff he slowly made his way back. After a few minutes he saw two torches descending in front of him. Georgios was accompanied by a sergeant from the garrison and his father's other squire, Amalric d'Auber, Jos's older brother.

As Philip came into the circle of light cast by the torch, Georgios could see his torn and dirty clothes. The squire frowned. "Are you all right?"

"I'm fine! It's Jos who broke his ankle."

"Are you sure?"

"It looks like jelly on the end of his leg," Philip answered graphically.

"Where is he?" Amalric asked tightly. Jos was, after all, his little brother, even if the boy's conversion to Islam was almost as much a shame to him as his elder brother's incompetence at arms.

"There's a trail that leads to that tower over there!" Philip explained, pointing. The tower, pointing upward from the highest hillock to the west, stood out in sharp silhouette against the luminous western sky.

The sergeant grunted and added, "I know it."

"Can you lead us there?" Georgios asked

The sergeant nodded.

"Do we need a stretcher for Jos?" Georgios thought to ask.

"Surely we can carry him between us," Amalric answered irritably, already annoyed by how much trouble his stupid brother was causing.

Georgios nodded, and they followed the sergeant first along the base of the castle and then into the woods. With the torches it was a lot easier. As they approached, Guy called to them in a voice that was high with fear: "Over here! Over here! Help!"

When they reached the two other boys, Georgios went down on one knee to examine Jos's ankle and gasped. It was badly swollen and discolored already, but just as Philip had said, it was completely wobbly—which could only mean that every tendon and ligament had also snapped.

"You idiot!" Amalric burst out at his younger brother. "This is what comes of abjuring Christ! If you never walk again, it will be what you deserve! You brought it on yourself, you—"

"Amalric! Enough!" Georgios cut him short. Although Georgios was the son of a native tradesman, he was twenty-five years old, and he'd been in Ibelin's service since before Hattin. Amalric might be the son of a knight, but he was just seventeen, and he'd been a slave for five years. When Georgios stared him down, Amalric looked at his feet resentfully.

"Take your brother under his arms from behind," Georgios ordered Amalric next, and then addressed himself to Jos. "We can't walk backwards on that trail. You'll have to straddle me with your legs so I can hold them at the knees. I don't want to touch that ankle. Understand?"

Jos nodded, swallowing hard, but tears were streaming down his face and his teeth were chattering.

"Doesn't anyone have a cloak?" Georgios asked, recognizing shock.

The others shook their heads helplessly, so Georgios unhooked his aketon, pulled it off, and put it around Jos's much smaller shoulders. Then he turned around, stepped between Jos's legs, and hooked his hands under the boy's knees. "Ready?" he called to Amalric, and on the affirmative answer ordered, "Lift him up!"

Jos screamed at the jostling, but cut off his own cry. Then they set off, with the sergeant leading with the first torch and Philip bringing up the rear with the second.

It wasn't until Jos had been delivered to the castle barber (who doubled as surgeon) that Philip had time to start worrying. By now he knew that their absence had set off a massive manhunt. Well, maybe not *massive*, but the Lord of Lusignan's concern for his heir had resulted in search parties being sent in multiple directions. Because they'd been in such a hurry to get Jos and Guy out of the woods, their rescuers had not sent word that they were found. Their arrival at the castle barber set off such an explosion of shouts and activity that Philip and Guy knew they were in deep trouble. "Shit!" Guy kept saying. "Shit! My Dad's going to have my hide!"

"He'll have to fight my father for the honor!" Philip answered grimly, before adding, "We've got to tell them Jos broke his ankle on the way—no, that won't work, either. Maybe we could say—"

"The truth!" Balian's voice came out of the darkness behind them, making them both jump.

"Ah! Yes, my lord. You see—"

"No! I don't see." The next minute Balian had them each by the scruff of their neck and was pushing them in front of him to the steps leading up to the great hall.

The hall was full of people and oppressively hot after the cold of the night. Torches were lit all along the wall. A fire was roaring in the main fireplace on the inside wall. A sideboard had been set up with cold leftovers from the midday meal, and large pottery jugs of water and wine for the knights and squires to help themselves.

As Ibelin entered with the two boys, a ragged cheer went up, and Lusignan signaled for Ibelin to bring the boys up onto the dais. As they passed through the crowd, everyone turned to look at them, and Philip became conscious of how dirty, scruffy, and ragged he looked.

"You don't think he'll put us in the stocks, do you?" Guy whispered beside him, his eyes fixed on his father, who glowered at them from the high table. Guy sounded genuinely afraid, and Philip realized that Guy didn't know his father very well. Lord Aimery had been away most of the last two years, the very years when Philip had been getting to know his own father. Philip wasn't afraid. He knew he was in trouble, but he trusted that the punishment would be fair.

"So! What do you have to say for yourself?" Lusignan snarled at his heir as the latter came to a halt in front of him, Ibelin holding him firmly in place. "What were you doing? I had a hundred men out looking for you!"

Philip, with a glance over his shoulder at the roomful of men, thought the number was greatly exaggerated.

"We were just exploring," Guy squeaked out uncomfortably. "We wanted to get to the outermost tower. We didn't know it was a ruin."

"Why didn't you return before dark?" Lusignan demanded. "Don't you know how dangerous it is to wander around in a forest after dark? Are you idiots, or what?"

"Jos tripped over a root and broke his ankle, and then I got lost trying to find the way back in the dusk. It was my fault," Philip announced, and was gratified by the squeeze his father gave his shoulder. His father approved of him taking the blame.

Lusignan shifted his gaze to Philip, then back to his son. "Whose idea was this?"

"Mine!" the boys declared in unison, then looked at one another and smiled.

"Well said." Ibelin patted them both on the back, and Lusignan nodded.

Ibelin added, "I hope you've both learned a lesson. A good soldier never loses sight of the sun, and always makes sure he has a secure place for the night. Never forget that!" The boys nodded vigorously.

Lusignan waved his hand in dismissal. "Go get yourself something to eat and then clean yourselves up."

Balian released his grip on the boys so they could run back to the sideboard; then he mounted the dais, pulled out the chair next to Aimery, and sat down, remarking, "As long as they're both safe and sound . . . "

Aimery pushed a pitcher and goblet in his direction as he answered: "Yes, but if something had happened to Guy so shortly after losing this last baby, I don't know what Eschiva would have done."

"We can't coddle them," Balian reminded him.

"I know," Aimery answered with a sigh, running his hand through his graying blond hair. "Nor do I want to, but—"

"My lord?" A knight with wind-blown hair was standing before the dais.

"Yes?" Aimery sat upright and asked expectantly.

"I was out looking for your son on the upper ramparts, and from there I spotted a sail far out to the west. The light was fading fast, so I can't be sure, but I think it was a snecka. At any rate, it was very low in the water and running before the wind with shortened sail."

"Magnussen!" Aimery exclaimed at once, instantly filled with tension. Would the Norseman hurry back with good or bad news?

"We can't be sure," Balian warned.

"But the sailing season's over. We haven't seen a merchant ship in over a fortnight, not sailing west to east."

"Send someone to Kyrenia to find out what ship it is," Balian advised, adding, "presuming she puts in to Kyrenia."

"I'll send John. He knows and likes Magnussen."

Balian bit his tongue. Hadn't he said just two minutes earlier that they should not coddle their sons? Still, he didn't like the thought of John alone on the roads here, or in a port town—not after what he'd seen of Famagusta. "I'll have Amalric go with him," he decided, and Aimery made no objection.

Kyrenia, Late October 1194

The imperial road, built in the reign of the Emperor Manuel I, led from Larnaka via Nicosia to Kyrenia. It had been paved with massive square stones and had been wide enough for four men to ride abreast or for an ox-cart to move comfortably. From Larnaka to Nicosia it was still in good repair, but as it started up the backside of the Pentadaktylos range, although still intact, it became more rugged. The edges had often broken or been washed away. By the time it reached the pass itself, large portions of the road had been completely washed away by landslides. Instead of a road, there was just a dangerous trail of broken masonry, gullies, and rubble.

John, still distressed by the injury Centurion had taken on his trip home, at once jumped down and led the young bay palfrey his father had helped him choose in Caymont. Troubadour was a pretty, intelligent bay with a smooth gait and an easygoing temperament—an ideal palfrey. He was also very curious, and he found this unfamiliar landscape very provocative. He had to stop every few feet to look around and sniff at things, making Amalric impatient. "Just yank on the reins!" Amalric suggested irritably.

"Why?" John replied. "He's just looking around, and once he's figured things out he'll be calmer and more settled."

Amalric muttered something under his breath and then said out loud, "At this rate we won't make Kyrenia before dark!"

"We'll make it," John insisted, patting Troubadour on the neck as they continued.

John was right, and they reached Kyrenia well before nightfall, although it was late afternoon. The gates were open, and no one stopped them for papers or tolls. Once in the small city, they passed quickly down a sloping paved street between low stone buildings with flat roofs and plastered walls, heading straight for the harbor. This consisted of a nearly perfectly round inner harbor enclosed by a chain in the north. The chain stretched from a sea wall extending out from the foot of the castle in the east to a large customs house on the western shore. Beyond the chain was a man-made outer harbor created by two breakwaters that reached out like enfolding arms from east and west, almost meeting in the middle but leaving a gap just wide enough for ships to sail through. A lighthouse sat on the tip of the western breakwater, showing sailors the small harbor entrance.

The harbor was nearly empty. Local merchantmen had been laid up for the winter, leaving the harbor to a handful of fishing craft and a single oceangoing vessel that looked decidedly the worse for wear. The mast was broken about two-thirds of the way from the top and the prow was missing its figurehead. John gasped at the sight of her. He thought it was the *Storm Bird*, but without the figurehead he couldn't be 100 per cent sure.

There was a lot of activity on deck, however. It looked as if all the rigging had been uncoiled and laid out on the deck, apparently to dry or to find weaknesses. The crew was also busy hanging out their clothes to dry and tossing rotten supplies overboard into the harbor—despite the outraged protests of a local fisherman who was shaking his fist at them.

John rode straight to the quay, looking for a familiar face. When he spotted Christian Arendsen, he started waving and shouting. "Christian! Christian! Welcome back! Is the *Storm Bird* badly damaged?" John jumped down from Troubadour and had to drag the horse closer to the ship. (Troubadour had not enjoyed the journey to Cyprus and was not the least inclined to repeat the experience. Barry, on the other hand, had been spoiled by the entire crew and now raced past his master, yapping in delight.)

Christian smiled broadly at the sight of John and Barry as he waved back. Grabbing a halyard made fast to the outer rail, he hauled himself onto the gunnel and jumped down onto the quay. "The mast broke a day out of Rhodes, taking the Bird with her, but she's fine! We could jury-rig it pretty easily and the rest of the mast apparently didn't split, but we'll have to replace it here. Great forests, I'm told." He looked left toward a bank of mountains covered with tall trees, a rarity in most of the Mediterranean.

Haakon himself appeared at the side of his ship, hands on his hips, as he glowered down at John. For all that Christian had made light of their ordeal, John had only seen Haakon look this bedraggled once before: when he'd been part of a relief fleet for the besiegers of Acre in the winter of 1189. On that infamous trip they had been forced to break off the relief attempt and run back to Tyre after losing two ships. Certainly Haakon's leather aketon was encrusted with salt, his hair stringy, and his beard untrimmed. "Where did you come from?" Haakon demanded. "We only tied up two hours ago!"

"We saw a sail from up there," John pointed in the direction of St. Hilarion, "and Lord Aimery thought it might be you, so he sent me to find out. With Amalric here," he added with a gesture toward his companion before asking anxiously, "What news from Lord Geoffrey?"

Haakon's rugged face formed a twisted smile. "You'd better start calling me 'sir,' young man, because you're looking at an admiral."

"Lord Geoffrey's not coming? He turned Cyprus down?" John couldn't believe it. Not only did it seem too good to be true, it was simply impossible for him to imagine anyone *not* wanting Cyprus.

"He thinks the Plantagenet is a wounded lion that he can now take down with impunity."

"But why would he want to? King Richard is a great king!" John protested naively.

"Yeah, well, a great king who dumped the Lusignans in favor of Montferrat, remember? Lord Geoffrey hasn't forgiven him for that. His official answer was entrusted to a Genoese captain, but we left *him* wallowing under swamped decks in the Straits of Messenia. God knows when he'll make it—might not be till next spring."

"Do you want to bring the word to Lord Aimery yourself?" John asked. "Or should I ride back with the news?"

"We only docked two hours ago, for Christ's sake!" Haakon answered irritably. "I haven't been out of these clothes in a month, below deck it stinks enough to make even me want to puke, the rigging needs a complete overhaul, and we are all going to celebrate our successful passage tonight. Then, *after* I've recovered from the hangover, I'll think about getting on something as terrifying as a horse and taking the message to Nicosia."

"Lord Aimery isn't at Nicosia. He's at St. Hilarion." John pointed again in the direction of the castle, although it was quite impossible to see it from here.

"Well, wherever. You're not going to make it back tonight, either. Why don't you join us for a little well-earned celebration?"

John looked hastily back at Amalric. If it had been the steady and responsible Georgios, he would have received a shake of the head and dutifully said no. But Amalric was all for this idea. Norsemen had a reputation for wild parties. He nodded enthusiastically, and John agreed.

"Go find some lodgings, then," Haakon waved him off. "We need to get this ship tidied up a bit, but we'll be ready for some entertainment come sundown."

John nodded again, waved to Christian, and then turned to lead the way to the castle, where he and Amalric could ask for hospitality from the castellan, Reynald Barlais. With the horses put away, they left their bedrolls against the screens in the great hall and then returned to the harbor, Barry at their heels.

It wasn't sundown yet, however, so they decided it wouldn't hurt to get something to eat before joining the Norsemen. They found a small street stand selling freshly grilled octopus soaked in olive oil, and bought themselves a portion each. Then they returned to the *Storm Bird* and found the crew collecting on deck in their "best."

It was, John thought, an excitingly frightening collection of muscular men in an eclectic collection of armor and weapons, all jabbering in their peculiar language. John was both fascinated and uncomfortable. He found Christian and attached himself to the former cleric. Amalric, in contrast, despite having no common language, seemed surprisingly at ease with these men. He was very muscular, too, of course, and three years older than John.

At last Haakon emerged from somewhere aft and they set off. As they moved along the quay, John noticed that some of the establishments quickly closed their doors and bolted them. But as they got closer to where the fishermen were tied up, a couple of taverns remained open.

With the sun down, the air was chilly, and they moved as a horde into the vaulted ground floor of the tavern. Here they occupied the bulk of the tables, and Haakon ordered ale for everyone. The proprietor answered in Greek that he couldn't understand a word they were saying. Haakon turned and stared at John. John ordered ale for everyone.

"Let's hope it tastes better than horse piss," Haakon muttered generally, "or my crew might get out of hand. Better find out about the food," he added to John (who now understood why Haakon had wanted him to join them for the evening).

The ale, fortunately, met the approval of the Norsemen, as did the food— and the mood, rather than turning ugly, was becoming decidedly jolly. One of the Norsemen stood up on a bench and started singing-speaking, to the apparent approval of his shipmates, who occasionally cheered or pounded the tables with their mugs in a kind of chorus. Now and then they even joined in, apparently as familiar with the saga he was reciting as the performer himself. When the latter sat down, they all started singing, beating the time with their mugs or their feet.

At first John loved the singing because it was melodic and forceful, but not understanding the words, he gradually became bored. It was now nearly compline anyway, and he was used to going to bed at this time. He always started the day at prime. He was trying to think of a way to excuse himself when Christian leaned over and said in his ear, "It's time for the wenches. Ask the landlord."

"Wenches?" John asked back, feeling completely out of his depth.

"Yeah. Just ask. He'll know what we want."

John took a deep breath and called the landlord over. "Ah. My friends here were wondering—ah—about—um—women." Wenches was just not a word he used. . . .

The landlord didn't seem surprised. He nodded and went away. Within a quarter of an hour, a score of women sauntered into the tavern and spread out among the tables. They were all shapes and sizes, some older, some younger, and yet they were also all the same in the way they smiled at the men, helped themselves to their ale, winked and gestured with their heads. One after another, the men started disappearing out the back with the women. John knew perfectly well what was going on, of course, but he'd never been a witness to it before. He felt acutely uncomfortable—aroused despite himself, yet also embarrassed.

Amalric didn't suffer from the same inhibitions. He had his arm around one of the girls and was kissing her hotly. When his hand started kneading her breast, however, John stopped watching them out of sheer shame.

A moment later, Amalric was beside him. "John, can you lend me ten dinars?"

"What?"

"I'll pay you back next month," Amalric promised, his breath laden with ale, and his hose poking through the slit in his surcoat. Seeing John's glance to his crotch, he flashed a smile. "Yeah, you can see the state I'm in! But if I can't pay she'll go with one of the others. Please! You must have it!" Amalric insisted, starting to get genuinely antsy.

John reached for his purse to pull out the coins, and Haakon's hand closed over his wrist in an iron fist. "Don't pull out your purse in a place like this!"

John looked at him blankly. "But Amalric—"

"I heard him. Where's the madam?" He looked around and signaled to a woman who was standing with the landlord watching. She was not fat or old, as John had always assumed madams would be. Rather, she was tall and lithe with black hair and black eyes, and she moved toward them with a fluid grace that was almost like the sea itself.

She reached their table and greeted them with a smile on her lips and narrowed eyes. "Monsieur le Capitaine, I presume?" She, at least, spoke French, albeit with a strange accent.

"I'm good for every man in the room. Understood? Ten denier a turn, right?"

She nodded with that mirthless smile, her eyes shifting to John and Amalric.

Amalric muttered, "Thank you!" to Haakon and darted back to the girl, who was flirting with someone else. He grabbed her under her arm and dragged her up off the bench. She laughed, waved to the others, and put her arm around Amalric as he led her away.

The woman seated herself opposite them, her eyes fixed on Haakon. "What about you, Captain? It was a long, difficult crossing, or so I heard. So late in the year, and the ship nearly dismasted." Her voice was like olive oil, soft, fluid, slippery.

"Join me for a drink," Haakon answered instead.

"I don't drink that horse piss," she answered with a gesture of contempt toward the ale, making Haakon laugh. Then he asked, "Wine?"

"Red."

"Of course." Haakon looked to John, who with a sigh signaled the landlord. "The—" he'd been about to say lady, but that was clearly not the correct term in this case— "ah—we'd like a carafe of red wine, please."

The landlord nodded and withdrew warily, leaving the three of them at the table. John felt very much like a fifth wheel. He looked frantically for Christian, but the younger Norseman had already disappeared. He turned to pet Barry instead, as he reckoned in his head: ten deniers a turn, times sixty men plus Amalric, and some of the men seemed to be taking two turns, or had they just passed out drunk? Any way you looked at it, it was a lot of money. How much money had Haakon made with his cargo of opium seed, root of camphor, and arsenic?

"Your girls. Are they clean?" Haakon asked.

"A lot cleaner than your men," the madam answered back, with that same smile that never reached her eyes.

"You don't know my men."

"And you don't know my girls."

Haakon raised his eyebrows, looked pointedly at the room around them, and then back at the madam with an amused expression. "Pardon me, Madame, I didn't realize we were talking about blushing virgins. Somehow that escaped my notice."

"You, captain, think we are the scum of the earth because we give you what you want. But you're wrong." She paused, then shook her head slowly and deliberately. "The scum of the earth is *you!*"

John caught his breath, expecting an explosion from Magnussen—and he was right, but it was an explosion of laughter, not rage. "Almost," Haakon declared as his laughter died. A smile still on his face, he declared, "We're the scum of the *sea*, not the earth. Here's your wine. Let me pour."

The landlord set the wine jug down and added three glazed pottery mugs, then withdrew again.

Haakon reached for the pitcher, poured wine into all three cups, and they each took one. "What's your name?" Haakon asked the madam.

"You don't care," she answered. "You don't *want* us to have names and stories. They just get in the way of business."

Haakon shrugged. "We haven't gotten to business yet—unless you want to consider a flat-rate price for the whole night. It would save us both the trouble of keeping tallies."

"A thousand dinars," she answered.

Haakon laughed. "You may have the only goods on offer, Madame, but they aren't *that* good."

"If you think we're less than perfect, then take a look in a mirror!" the madam shot back. "We are what you have made us. All my girls were abused and discarded by the likes of you, or worse," the madam spoke into the stillness. "Now they work for themselves."

"Not you?" Haakon asked skeptically.

"I provide a home for them, protection, and medical treatment, if necessary. They pay me a percentage of their earnings in return."

"Not a small percentage, I presume," Haakon ventured with a cynical smile.

"Less than half."

"So if I choose you, I get it for less than ten dinars?" Haakon asked, making John squirm in discomfort. He wished he weren't here.

"No. I don't take customers," she answered with her cold smile. "And one of the rules of my house is that any of my girls can say no to *any* customer without explanation—just as long as they earn enough each month to pay their keep. We're not anybody's *property* anymore."

Haakon's eyebrows shot up, but he said nothing and took a deep drink of ale. John was confused. He blurted out, "What do you mean?"

Her eyes shifted to John, and something in them softened. She cocked her head. "You look a little displaced among these hardened seamen, young man. Like a fish out of water, or should I say, a puppy at sea? That's a silk shirt, isn't it? With—" she stopped herself, frowning, "—aren't those the arms of Ibelin?"

Damn it! John thought. Why hadn't he thought to change into something less obvious?

Haakon laughed.

The madam glanced at him and then back at John. "You serve the Lord of Ibelin? I'd heard he came to Cyprus not long ago."

"He doesn't *serve* the Lord of Ibelin," Haakon announced, clapping his arm over John's shoulders as he bragged, "he *is* an Ibelin. His eldest son and heir, to be precise."

The madam gave Haakon a look as if she didn't believe him, and John felt he had to say something. "Right now I'm just a squire to Lord Aimery de Lusignan."

The madam looked back at him and her eyebrows twitched. "I see," she said, but John wasn't sure if she believed them. He rather hoped she *didn't* believe them, because he didn't want his father hearing about this evening!

"John has never been in an establishment like this before," Haakon admitted. "I brought him along as an interpreter, but I shouldn't have . . . " He looked over, considered John, and repeated, "I shouldn't have."

She nodded. "And yourself? Aspasia's available." As she spoke she gestured a girl over to their table.

Haakon looked at the girl, but shook his head. "She's too young for me. I prefer older women. Women as cynical as me."

"Too bad," the madam retorted, standing and drawing Aspasia away with her. The girl glanced over her shoulder and flashed a smile at John.

"I like him!" she whispered to the madam with a giggle.

"Well, forget about him. He's the heir to the Lord of Ibelin. The captain was wrong to bring him here, and he's not likely to come back."

Chapter Twelve
Unhealed Wounds

Nicosia
October 1194

Two women were on their knees with scrub brushes and a bucket of soapy water, while another two followed with mops to wipe up the dirt the first two scrubbed from the corners and cracks. Although she had been sent by Maria Zoë to see that they were doing a proper job, Beatrice was not without sympathy for the cleaning women. She knew exactly how hard it was to kneel on marble floors, and how your hands became cracked and raw from the soapy water. She knew, too, how the skirts of your dress became soaked and worn. It was only a little over two years since she had been doing the very same task. Just over two years ago, she had been a slave.

Most of the time she avoided thinking about the years in slavery, but that was not the same as escaping the consequences. Slavery had changed her as profoundly as it had changed her sons. It wasn't just a matter of learning hardship and humiliation—it had altered her entire value system. She simply did not value or covet the things she had thought were important "before." Instead, she appreciated the "luxury" of occasional idleness, of occasional privacy, of choosing her own food, of a pair of shoes. . . .

The experience, furthermore, set her apart from most of her peers, and it had made it impossible for her to completely reintegrate into Frankish society. That was the reason she preferred the reclusive life at Caymont over life at the court in Acre. In Caymont, Ibelin and his lady had welcomed her into their household for her father's sake, and respected her need to bury the past. Lady Eschiva of Lusignan had followed their example. In Acre, on the other hand, Isabella's ladies and Champagne's knights followed her with surreptitious glances and whispering. Everyone at court knew she had been repeatedly raped by Saracen soldiers before ending as a household scullery maid.

Cyprus, however, was proving an unsought surprise. To the Greek women she was a Frankish *lady*, a widow, and—more important—one who enjoyed the confidence of the Lady of Lusignan, not to mention "the Comnena." Three years ago she had not dared dream she would ever again wear silk, be shown respect, or be obeyed by even a child.

Nor had she dared to dream she might ever be reunited with her sons. Thus the sight of Amalric in chain mail, with a surcoat bearing the arms of Ibelin, still warmed her heart, no matter how often she saw him dressed like the squire he now was. She smiled unconsciously as he approached up the length of the long hall.

"Mother! I've been looking all over for you. We just got back from St. Hilarion," her son exclaimed even before he reached her. His blond hair was wind-blown, and she noted with motherly pride that he had some almost invisible hairs on his chin.

"Was the castle all Lord Aimery promised it would be?" she asked, breathing in the masculine perfume of horse sweat, leather, and greased iron. These were the smells of knighthood, a status she had thought lost to her sons forever.

"The castle? Oh, yes, it was quite amazing," Amalric admitted, before continuing—with a teenager's carelessness of the impact of his words—"but Joscelyn, the idiot, went and broke his ankle doing some crazy thing outside the castle walls. We had to bring him back in a litter. The castle barber said he didn't have the skills to reattach the ligaments. All he could do was stabilize the ankle, but he said if we don't get the ligaments fixed, he'll be a cripple the rest of his life."

"Joscelyn?" Beatrice gasped. He was still her baby, although no one had ever hurt her more—not even the men who gleefully raped her and spat and kicked her when they finished. All her sons had seen it happen. It had broken Bart as much as her, and made him ashamed of them both. It had filled Amalric with rage, hatred, and a determination to avenge her. But Joscelyn had just been bewildered—until the Mamlukes convinced him his mother was "nothing but a whore" who deserved what she got. When Beatrice was reunited with Jos in Tyre, he had called her a whore to her face. Because his grandfather had taken a belt to his backside until it was too sore to sit on for a week, he'd never said the word aloud again. Yet she saw the word "whore" in his eyes every time he looked at her.

Amalric was still speaking. "It's what he deserves for abjuring Christ—not to mention how he treats you! But I thought—"

"Don't say that, Amalric. He's still your brother, my son. Where is he?"

"I'll take you to him. Ibelin has sent for the apothecary who tended King Guy."

Joscelyn had been laid on a straw pallet on a rope bed. There was a pitcher of water on a small table beside him, and sunlight poured through the open door from the courtyard. It made his tangle of blond hair seem like spun gold. He had dropped off to sleep from the exhaustion of the painful journey, but his face was pinched with pain nevertheless, and traces of tears streaked his face. He was still dressed in the dirty clothes he'd been wearing when the accident occurred. All the barber had done was to cut away the hose around the broken ankle, then bandage and splint the injury.

"Will you be all right for a moment, Mama?" Amalric asked, in a hurry to be gone. "I need to see to my lord's armor."

"Yes, I'll be fine," Beatrice answered as she sank down on the floor beside the bed and hesitantly reached out a hand to stroke her son's arm. Ever since they had been reunited, Joscelyn had angrily resisted her attempts to caress him. He said it was because he "wasn't a baby" anymore, but Beatrice suspected the real reason was that he didn't want to be touched by a "whore." Now he was too tired to feel her touch at all.

Beatrice sighed. She wanted to pray, but why should Christ help a boy who stubbornly refused to recognize Him? Every priest she had consulted agreed that Christ would forgive a seven-year-old for converting to Islam while in slavery. The problem was that he had not returned to the Church now that he was free. It was his stubborn insistence that they were all "polytheists" and that he alone had found truth through the prophet Mohammed that endangered his soul.

She found herself pleading with Christ to inspire her son to repent, but even as she prayed she believed it was hopeless. An open heart was the prerequisite of grace, and Joscelyn didn't have an open heart.

She did not know how long she sat there, lost in a vicious circle of doubt and confusion, before the light streaming through the door was cut off by a figure. Recognizing the doctor, Beatrice struggled to her feet as Andreas Katzouroubis swept into the little chamber in his red robes. "So, what have we here?" he asked as he came to stand beside the bed.

Beatrice stammered out that it was her son and that he had broken his ankle. The physician carefully drew back the blanket covering Jos' legs and examined the bandaged foot and ankle. He dropped on his heels and professionally removed the splint. Then, taking hold of the toe, he moved the foot from side to side, eliciting a gasp from Jos as he woke up.

"Who are you?" Jos demanded in outrage.

"A doctor," Katzouroubis answered simply. "How long ago did this happen?"

"It was dusk the day before yesterday," Jos told him.

"I have to remove the bandages to see the swelling and bruises," the doctor announced.

Beatrice caught her breath, certain that this would be very painful, while Jos protested in a voice sharp with fear, "But the barber surgeon said the leg had to stay still or it would never heal! You're *trying* to cripple me! You *hate* me because I'm Muslim!" Jos flung at the astonished doctor.

It was his fear speaking, Beatrice realized, and she reached out to put a hand on his shoulder to reassure him. Jos shook her hand off as if it burned him, casting her a look of sheer hatred. Wounded, Beatrice drew back in helpless despair.

Katzouroubis watched the little exchange with narrowed, intelligent eyes, and when he next spoke to his patient it was in Arabic, a tongue Beatrice had mastered during her years of slavery just as her son had. "You should be ashamed of yourself for treating your mother like that! Did not the Prophet, may Allah's blessings be upon him always, teach us to respect our mothers?"

Jos' eyes widened in astonishment, while Katzouroubis continued indignantly, "And why should I want to cripple you because of your faith? I had the honor to learn my trade in Baghdad with some of the greatest physicians of the Dar al-Islam. Now, to the matter at hand: the barber surgeon did the best he could to ensure there was no *more* damage, but he told the Lord of Ibelin that he believes all your ligaments have snapped, and unless we can sew them back together, you will never walk again. So you have a choice: either you let me examine that foot so, if the barber surgeon was right, I can fetch a skilled surgeon to sew the ligaments back together again, or you become a cripple."

Jos' face was flushed with fear of pain and confusion, but he swallowed and nodded.

"You want me to try to save your ankle?" Katzouroubis demanded confirmation.

Jos nodded.

"Then *first* you will apologize to your mother and beg her forgiveness."

"But my mother is nothing but a Frankish whore—"

Katzouroubis slapped Jos so fast that neither Beatrice nor Jos saw it coming. Beatrice started to protest—to say that the insult was nothing new—but the doctor gestured her silent as he told Jos harshly, "You have no right to call your mother that! She is your mother. You owe her your life. Without her you would not exist. I will not help a boy who is so foolish as to insult and reject his mother—especially when she is only trying to comfort him. The Koran teaches respect for mothers above all other women! If you do not respect your mother, you have no right to expect the benevolence of Allah, because you will have broken *His* law. We men of medicine can do our best, but it is always the will of Allah that prevails. You believe that, don't you?"

Jos nodded vigorously.

"Then you must do that which is pleasing to Him. A boy who does not respect his mother has a crippled and misshapen spirit, and it would be only justice if Allah allowed his body to reflect that inner imperfection. If you want His help, therefore, you must honor your mother by begging her forgiveness for your insults." When Jos hesitated, he added, "Now!"

Jos swallowed and snuck a glance at his mother.

Beatrice held her breath in fear of Jos' response. The boy looked back at the doctor, his expression more confused than defiant.

"Apologize to your mother and promise you will never insult her again, or I will let you become a cripple in body to match your crippled spirit," Katzouroubis insisted firmly.

Jos looked at his mother again, and said in a soft and contrite Arabic, "I'm sorry, mother."

Beatrice wanted to fling her arms around him and shower him with kisses, but she did not trust this truce and feared an exuberant response would reawaken his resistance. Instead, she just nodded as tears started to trickle down her face.

"Good," Katzouroubis nodded his approval to Jos, "and now promise you will never insult her again," he insisted.

Jos took a deep breath, swallowed, and said in a soft voice, "I promise I will never insult you again."

Beatrice started sobbing, while Katzouroubis simply said "good" and got to work removing the splint and efficiently unraveling the bandages.

Jos tensed and gritted his teeth as the first jarring pain stabbed him. Beatrice risked reaching out a hand to steady him, expecting him to shake it off, but Jos did not. With a flood of gratitude toward the doctor and God, Beatrice sat on the head of the bed and put her arms around her son. She held him against her as he gasped and stiffened in response to the increasing pain.

By the time the doctor finished, Jos' face was wet with tears, and he clung to his mother's arm as if were a lifeline. As Katzouroubis moved the foot clinically by the toe from side to side and forward and back, Jos' fingers dug deep into his mother's arm as he writhed in pain. He was grinding his teeth together to stop any sound from coming out.

Katzouroubis finished his examination, stood upright, and announced to Beatrice rather than Jos, "He must be operated on as soon as possible. I know a very good surgeon. I will fetch him. We'll need to sedate your son, however. This will be very painful."

Beatrice nodded.

Katzouroubis redirected his focus to Jos and said, "This is the only way we can save you from being a cripple, young man. Be thankful there is a surgeon here in Nicosia that has done this kind of operation before, and be thankful your mother is with you."

Jos didn't answer—he just closed his eyes, still oozing tears, and laid his head on his mother's breast. Beatrice didn't dare move, although she was sitting awkwardly on one folded leg and the circulation to it was cut off. With one hand she gently stroked the tears from Jos' face, while she gave thanks to Christ for the privilege of holding him like this. She had not held him in her arms since he had been torn from them in the slave market in Damascus. Now it was almost as if he were that little six-year-old again. Except he was so heavy. . . .

Within the hour Katzouroubis was back, accompanied by a stocky man with a square face and stubby fingers. The surgeon spoke no French at all, and only nodded briefly to Beatrice before he rolled up his sleeves and started laying out his instruments on the little table.

Beatrice felt Jos tense in her arms, and the terror on his face was so eloquent that she almost asked the surgeon to go away. Katzouroubis, however, came over and patted her shoulder. "It's time for you to leave him with us, Madame," he told her in French. "I have a very potent sedative."

Beatrice nodded, but countered, "I'll stay at least until he's asleep."

"Very well, but we'll need some wine—"

"I don't drink wine," Jos protested, rubbing away the tears pouring from his nose with the back of his hand.

Katzouroubis snorted. "We'll see about that. Bring me both water and wine, Madame."

Beatrice reluctantly withdrew, hobbling on the leg that had gone to sleep. A part of her was terrified that by leaving she would break the spell, and Jos would reject her again when she returned. She hurried to the kitchen and was received there by a flutter of agitation. The new kitchen staff was eager to prove they were efficient. They shooed her out with assurances that the wine and water would be brought to her shortly.

She hurried back, relieved by their diligence, as it shortened the time she was separated from Jos. As she re-entered, the boy cast her a look of relief and almost desperate welcome. The enchantment hadn't broken! She sat again on the head of the bed and took him back into her arms. He was trembling with fear.

The water and wine arrived, and the doctor poured water into a pottery goblet, added a powdered mixture into the water, and brought it over to Jos. "Here."

Jos brought it to his lips but then he drew back, making a face and holding his breath. "That smells vile!" he told the doctor in outrage.

"It does, doesn't it?" Katzouroubis answered. "Now, you should know as well as I do that the Koran explicitly allows wine if it is necessary for one's health. This is one of those times."

Jos took a deep breath and nodded assent. The doctor returned to the table and mixed the powder into red wine. He brought this to Jos, and the boy reluctantly but dutifully took one sip at a time until he had drained the goblet to the last dregs. By then he had already stopped trembling and his breathing was becoming deeper, his pulse slower. "Everything's going to be fine, Jos," Beatrice assured him, bending to kiss his forehead under the tousled hair. (How often had she longed to do that in the last seven years?)

"Help me, Mama. Please. Help me." The words were just a whisper, and Jos's arms were too weak to hold her, but he had chained her to him: these were the words he had screamed in terror as the slave trader tore him out of her arms. She had tried to cling to him, but the men in the market had closed in around her, kicking her legs out from under her and then kicking her in the gut, the back, the head, and the breast until the slave trader himself called them off. When he yanked her back onto her feet, bleeding from her nose, half crippled from the pain in her ribs and her kidneys, the man who had pulled six-year-old Jos after him by ropes around the child's wrists was nowhere to be seen. She had not seen Jos again until she arrived in Tyre after the Truce of Ramla.

"I really don't think you should stay, Madame," Katzouroubis told her soberly. "This is going to be a very delicate operation, and there is going to be a lot of blood."

"I don't care," Beatrice told him softly, smiling down at the sleeping boy in her arms. "You can blindfold me if you like, but I want to stay here holding him."

"Hmm." Katzouroubis took a deep breath and then nodded. "Then at least close your eyes, Madame."

"No, I'll just focus on Jos," she told him.

With another sigh and a shake of his head the doctor turned his attention to supporting the surgeon, who was ready to proceed.

The operation took a long time. The sunlight stopped flooding the little room as the sun moved westward, and the temperature grew chilly. The doctor and surgeon spoke only Greek to one another, which was just as well, since that way Beatrice could not tell exactly what they were doing. She was conscious only that the surgeon gave the orders, and that the learned doctor responded by bringing tweezers and clamps, string, or gauze as required. The physician also daubed away the blood again and again, throwing the bloody rags away to apply more until there was a heap of bloody gauze near the door. Finally he laid cobwebs into the wound, and then bandaged it up again and replaced the splints.

"We have done the best we can," he assured Beatrice, washing his hands clean in a bowl of water as the surgeon packed away his instruments. "Only time will tell if it was adequate."

"How long before he wakes?" Beatrice asked, gently extricating herself and stretching her cramped muscles.

"I expect it will be three or four hours, maybe even six. He needs the sleep, and when he comes to he will be in acute pain. I have left two doses of painkiller on the table. Mix them with a large glass of wine and give him something light to eat. No fat, no meat or fish, just bread and something fresh: figs are very good, grapes, or plums."

Beatrice nodded; she thanked the physician profusely and the surgeon, too. The latter nodded matter-of-factly and seemed in a hurry to go, but Beatrice clung to Katzouroubis' hand. "What you said to him, sir, about respecting his mother—how can I ever thank you? I mean, it wasn't the first time it was said to him—my father and the Lord of Ibelin both punished him for insulting me— but it never had any effect before."

Katzouroubis squeezed her hand and smiled at her. "Sometimes, Madame, it is only when we are facing a new crisis that we go back into our inner souls and discover ourselves. Your son, perhaps, blamed you for something?" He raised his eyebrows a fraction, and Beatrice caught her breath. "I'm not saying you *were* to blame, Madame," the doctor continued—"in fact, I'm almost certain you weren't—but is it possible that something you did made him *so* angry that he hated you? It was surely hate that made him call you the worst name he could think of. All I did was remind him of the essentials: whatever you did, you are still his mother, and every religion in the world calls on children to honor their parents. That is not a monopoly of Christianity. His conversion to Islam in slavery—I presume that's what it was?" Beatrice nodded. "Could it have been his way of punishing you for not protecting him from that very fate? But you see Islam, too, teaches sons to respect and honor their mothers above all other women. By reminding him of that, I yanked away his crutch—and his weapon. I simply showed him that he cannot use Islam to punish you, because Islam demands that he honor you. Now, try to get some rest, Madame. I'll come again tomorrow to check up on him."

But Beatrice couldn't possibly rest. What the doctor said made sense, and it filled her with hope. It wasn't the Mamlukes who had turned Jos against her—or rather, they had succeeded only because he was already filled with fury because she had "let" him be taken from her. She had not wanted to. She had been as helpless as he—but to a six-year-old, who had seen her as all-powerful until then, it must have *felt* like betrayal or abandonment. And now? She had to rebuild his trust by explaining the reality of her own weakness. For the first time since she had been confronted by Jos's conversion and hostility, she began to hope that she could win him back.

Chapter Thirteen
An Eye for an Eye...

Nicosia
Late January 1195

A CROWD HAD GATHERED IN THE street before the palace. Angry voices were raised and fists were being shaken. "What are they shouting?" Dick asked John anxiously. The two squires waited by the gate to admit the knights who pushed their way through the crowd outside.

"Just crude insults, for the most part," John answered, more unsettled than he wanted to admit. Although there had been sporadic and localized violence and unrest ever since he'd come to Cyprus, most had occurred in the outlying regions, such as Karpas or the region between Famagusta and Larnaka. The capital had generally remained calm. Certainly, angry crowds had never assembled in front of the palace like this before.

"What sort of insults?" Dick pressed him.

"Bastards, cutthroats, godless whoresons, blasphemers—I think." John fell silent as he peered through the crack in the door to judge the progress of the party of roughly twenty horsemen making their way through the outraged mob.

The approaching men were all armored, and wore helmets on their heads to cover their faces in shadow if not behind visors; they were and acted immune to the violence around them. The horses, on the other hand, were visibly unnerved. They fretted, shaking their heads, dancing sideways to avoid this or the other loud noise or sudden gesture. Now and again one swung his haunches around and kicked out. That frightened the crowd back for a few moments.

At last they were close enough for John and Dick to act. With a nod of agreement, they sprang forward to pull open the wings of the gate. At the sight of the yawning opening, the lead riders spurred their mounts forward. The unnerved horses leapt forward, as eager as their riders to escape the mob. In less than a minute, the entire column of knights had clattered into the cobbled courtyard. Dick and John slammed the gate shut and barricaded it against the mob. The latter rushed the gate too late and found themselves pounding on the iron-studded oak, screaming more loudly than ever before.

The gate secure, the two squires turned their attention to the men who had just arrived. They were jumping down from their sweated and dusty mounts, shoving their helmets up off their red and perspiring faces. They talked among themselves in angry, agitated tones, cursing the crowds and grumbling about orders not to draw their weapons. John and Dick ignored the bulk of them and made for the two leaders: John's cousin Henri de Brie and Reynald Barlais.

The men were almost a comedy of contrasts: Barlais short, stocky, and round-faced, Sir Henri tall but with a gaunt face and a nose that fell straight from his forehead like the nose guard of a helmet.

"We heard Lusignan was back," Sir Henri tossed in John's direction as the latter came up beside him to take his horse. Aimery and the Ibelins had spent the Christmas season in Caymont and had only returned to Cyprus two days earlier.

"Yes, my lord," John answered respectfully, while his cousin lifted the saddle flap to loosen his horse's girth.

"We need to see him right away. Someone else can see to my horse. Take us to him immediately," Sir Henri ordered, flipping the reins over the horse's head and handing them off to one of his knights.

John nodded to Dick, who had hold of Barlais' horse, and led his cousin and Barlais under the arcade surrounding the courtyard, through a passageway to a walled garden, and from here up an exterior stairway that brought them to a gallery. John's feet were light on the checkerboard of brown and white tiles, but behind him the boots of his companions pounded heavily and in accidental unison. To John it sounded like an ominous drumbeat.

At the tall arched door to the anteroom of Aimery's suite of rooms, John knocked and then entered to announce: "My lords of Karpas and Kyrenia, my lord." Both titles were self-appropriated by Henri de Brie and Barlais, respectively. No one had formally invested them with the titles—certainly not Aimery—but he had given them the task of establishing "authority" over the respective regions.

Aimery had been dictating a letter to the Pope, his secretary hunched over a writing pulpit and scratching away furiously with a quill pen to try to keep up with the flood of words—frequently interrupted, corrected, and started over. "*Who* did you say?" Aimery asked his squire, frowning at the interruption.

The door was pushed open, and Sir Henri and Barlais surged past and around John to stand before Aimery with their arms akimbo. "Don't act so surprised!" Barlais growled.

"You're right," Aimery retorted, with a wave in the direction of the windows from which the dull roar of the agitated crowd still seeped into the room. "I should have known you two would be the cause of any riot! What have you done now?"

"We've got the ringleaders," Sir Henri answered with evident satisfaction.

Aimery looked surprised. "Are you sure?"

"Yes," Sir Henri insisted. "I'd been suspicious for months, but a week ago I finally found a treacherous weasel willing to puke out the whole story for a laughable reward of a herd of sheep—and the grazing rights, of course."

Not willing to let Henri de Brie take all the credit, Barlais growled, "I'd had men watching them for weeks. A nest of vipers, that's what they are. It would have been better to smash their heads with our heels immediately, but Karpas here" (he too used the title that Henri had expropriated for himself, in a tone that seemed to say, "I'll call you this because you want me to, but don't think I don't know you made it up") "insisted that we arrest them instead. He thought they might be persuaded to identify their friends and allies."

Sir Henri smiled. "I did suggest that. You'd be surprised how easy it is to make men squeal—particularly when they aren't hardened fighting men, but monks—"

"Monks? You didn't arrest monks?" Aimery asked, aghast.

"Of course we did!" Barlais barked back. "We have evidence they are the men behind all the unrest. Everything points to them! Like the spider spins a web, they sat up on their mountaintop at Antiphonitis and cast their web of protest and revolt across the whole island."

"Just how many monks did you arrest?" Aimery demanded.

"Not many," Henri assured him in a calming tone.

"Seven and the abbot—he's the real ringleader, of course," Barlais added more precisely. "And a slimier snake you could not imagine! All pious pose and poison!" he spat out the last.

"Arresting monks is not going to make us popular!" Lord Aimery retorted angrily. "No wonder there's a riot out there!" He gestured again to the window.

"Who gives a damn about being popular?" Barlais snarled back. "It's better to be feared than loved! Love is as fickle as a woman. Fear, on the other hand, is what these people understand. It's how Isaac Comnenus ruled."

"And how he lost the island to Richard of England, too! No one was willing to raise a finger in his defense. They all came running to offer the English King their fealty."

"We don't need them to lift a finger to defend us! We can damn well defend ourselves," Brie retorted. "But with this viperous abbot and his sanctimonious apostles in a dungeon, the attacks against us will soon stop!"

"It doesn't sound that way to me." Aimery nodded again toward the undiminished sounds of men shouting insults and threats.

"Oh, just give them time. Without their leaders to rile them up, they'll soon calm down," Henri assured him confidently.

"Where have you put them?" Aimery wanted to know.

"The dungeon at Kyrenia—where it's dank, dark, and smelly," Barlais declared smugly. "Lots of rats down there, too, and no windows. It's under water, actually. If they try to dig their way out, they'll drown."

Aimery knew more than he wanted to about dungeons; he'd spent far too much time in them himself. He asked instead with raised eyebrows, "And now?"

"We let them rot for a bit and then see how willing they are to talk to us about their accomplices and how they are going to publicly submit to us. Sir Henri's—sorry, *my lord of Karpas'*—'sharper' methods may not be necessary. I say a week with only foul water and no food in the damp cold will make them grovel at our feet like we were the second coming of Christ."

Aimery stared at the two men before him with narrowed eyes. He didn't like what they had done. To be sure, he'd long had his own suspicions against the Orthodox clergy on the island. The Templars had heaped angry abuse on them for their "stubbornness" and "wiles." Likewise, the Dowager Queen had been saying ever since she arrived that the clergy was the key. While she urged approaching them to effect reconciliation, her stand nevertheless gave credence to these accusations. And if Aimery had no reason to think this particular abbot was at the heart of things, there was also no reason to assume he was innocent, either.

But arresting men of the cloth was always dangerous. The murderers of the Archbishop of Canterbury had intended only to arrest him, and had been provoked into the horrifying murder of an archbishop in his own cathedral by Becket's stubborn refusal to comply. If these Greek monks died—even if it was from cold and hunger rather than from torture or execution—they would *still* be declared martyrs. And everyone involved in their arrest would find themselves cursed, if not by God then by the people of the island.

The problem was that Aimery was not certain Barlais would obey him if he ordered the immediate release of the monks and their abbot. Furthermore, the damage had already been done. Would anyone in the crowd outside seriously believe he was not behind it? That it had been done without his knowledge and consent? No. They called Barlais and Brie "Lusignan's wolves." They all thought these men did his bidding.

"Still no word from your brother Geoffrey?" Barlais broke into his thoughts, evidently getting impatient with the silence.

Aimery answered defensively, "We've had word he's *not* coming. He has rejected—renounced—the inheritance."

"So your tame *Norseman* says," Barlais scoffed, adding, "I want more proof than that."

"Then you'll have to wait. The Genoese ship he entrusted with his written response won't be here until the next sailing season."

"Well, don't get too comfortable in your pretty palace!" Barlais sneered, with a contemptuous glance at the luxury around him. "Your brother may be here *before* his messenger!" Then he turned on his heel and stormed out.

Brie waited until Barlais was out of hearing before remarking in a bemused tone, "I don't share Barlais' conviction about your brother, but I support this arrest, Aimery. I tell you, the Greek Church is behind all this opposition. They feed the people lies about us: say we'll increase the taxes, reduce them all to slavery, force them to drink blood instead of wine, and God knows what more."

Aimery sighed, and when he spoke his voice was both tired and irritable. "Maybe, but by arresting their monks we only give credence to their lies. It makes us appear opposed to their Church, and we're *not*. Holy Cross! Muslims, Jews, and Samaritans—let alone Armenian, Jacobite, Maronite, and Coptic Christians—were all good subjects of the Crown of Jerusalem. A more or less homogenous population of Greek Orthodox subjects ought to be far less troublesome."

"Ought to be, perhaps, but they aren't proving to be. The situation isn't getting any better, Aimery. If you don't come up with a strategy to get control of this island soon, you're going to lose it—just as the Templars did—whether Geoffrey comes back or not." With a sarcastic bow to Aimery and a nod and a wink for John, Sir Henri also withdrew.

Early February 1195

Master Afanas was the best ivory carver in Nicosia. Although he worked predominantly in wood, his workshop also produced magnificent ivory inlays. He had a large workshop near the Kyrenia gate, and he frequently received commissions for altar screens, choir stalls, and other furniture for churches and monasteries. The work with inlaid ivory, on the other hand, was rare, small scale, and usually for the Italians.

It was, Lakis reminded himself, a privilege to learn your trade under such a master. But as an orphan, Lakis had no contract. He'd obtained his position by showing the master the combs and buckles he'd made from bone, and Master Afanas had been interested enough to agree to take him on under conditions that Lakis increasingly saw as slavery.

To be sure, he was allowed to sleep in the workshop, which wasn't bad since the wood shavings made a sweet-smelling, soft bed, and he was given the same hearty midday meal provided all the apprentices. But that was where "remuneration" ended. Lakis received no pocket money for baths, clothes, or wine. Since he had no home at which to obtain breakfast or dinner, he was almost always hungry. Worst of all, he could not sell what he produced, because "the Master" had the right to everything made in the workshop.

Work started early, ended late, and was accompanied by what seemed like constant criticism from Master Afanas combined with sneering and heckling from the other apprentices, all of whom felt themselves better than "the beggar." Sometimes their insults and jokes inspired Lakis to work harder and be better— but sometimes, like tonight, they just made him miserable and tired. One of them had "accidentally" knocked over the little chest of drawers he'd been working on for two weeks and it lay on the floor, a heap of broken pieces.

Master Afanas had hit the boy responsible with his stick and vowed to deduct the cost of the materials from his allowance as he chased him and the others home for the night. But the chest was still ruined, and two weeks of work had been for nothing.

"Don't look so broken-hearted," Master Afanas advised in a businesslike tone. "Your work wasn't *that* good. Hopefully your next try will be better. You certainly aren't going to be entrusted with any ivory if you can't do better than that." He indicated the broken box with a dismissive gesture. "I told you when I took you on that you had just one year to start producing things I can sell to real customers. You've only got until Christmas to meet my standards. After that you're back out with your friends behind the abattoir!"

"I don't have any friends!" Lakis shot back at him, hardening his feelings.

"No wonder, either! Sullen little brat that you are. I don't doubt your last master ran you out for being impudent and rude! I didn't ask any questions when I took you on—but believe me, if I hear something that makes you a liability, you're out on your ear! Now clean up that mess and bar the door after me. I'm late for dinner as it is."

The Master was out the door, leaving Lakis behind feeling sorry for himself as he squatted down beside the wreck of his masterpiece and started picking up the pieces. He had been so proud of it. He had thought it was up to Master Afanas' standards. He'd pictured it in an apothecary, filled with precious drugs, or maybe adorning a lady's table, holding beautiful jewels.

Tears started to well in his eyes, and to defeat them he deflected his emotions into rage. He threw the pieces across the room and screamed "Damn you! Damn you!" Only he didn't know who he was damning: Master Afanas, his fellow apprentices, or the Franks who had killed his parents and left him an orphan.

The thought of the Franks, however, reminded him of Janis. He had almost been a friend. At least he'd been *friendly*, but Lakis had sensed something was fishy right from the start. Lakis had suspected he was the son or servant of an Italian merchant. But then, months after their last meeting, he'd caught sight of someone who looked like Janis all dressed up in fine Frankish clothes and riding a beautiful horse beside one of the Frankish lords. He hadn't wanted to believe it, so he had started lurking around the palace. Sure enough, "Janis" came and went with easy familiarity, although he lived in the khan opposite. By asking around a little, Lakis soon discovered that the man Janis was usually beside was none other than Aimery de Lusignan, the brother of the tyrant himself. Then the tyrant died (terribly, it was said), and now this Aimery de Lusignan had taken over as tyrant.

It made Lakis sick and angry that Janis was one of them, but it was also Janis who had suggested he apprentice to a real carver. Angry as Lakis was, he still recognized that he'd learned a huge amount in the last ten months. Even if Master Afanas threw him out, he'd be better able to fend for himself.

With a deep sigh of resignation, he went and barred the door, then collected the broken remnants of his box and carried them over to the fireplace. A low fire burned there day and night, fed just enough discarded, unsuitable, and remnant wood to keep it from going out and so keep the chill off the air. With great solemnity Lakis fed the shattered pieces of his masterpiece into the fire and watched them burn, one piece at a time. In the flames he imagined his father's mill burning.

He hadn't actually seen it burn, because he'd been sent up to the brothers of

Antiphonitis to ask for help before the Franks set fire to it. The brothers had not allowed him to go down the hill for weeks afterwards. Nor had they allowed him to see the remains of his parents and sisters. They had put the bodies in a coffin and nailed it shut before they let him near it. It had smelled so terrible he had gagged and backed away. The brothers had comforted him, and now they *too* were in the hands of the Franks. Some said they had been put into a dark hole to starve, and others said they were already martyrs, crucified just like Christ. Lakis didn't know what to think.

A loud pounding at the door made him jump clear out of his skin. He sprang to his feet and called in a voice high with alarm: "Who's there? What do you want? We're closed!"

"Lakis!" The voice was low, unfamiliar but urgent.

"Yes, I'm called Lakis," the orphan answered sullenly, going closer to the door to stand in front of it, arms crossed stubbornly. "Who are you and what do you want?"

"It's me, Brother Zotikos! From Antiphonitis. Let me in!" The man had dropped his voice to nearly a whisper.

Lakis was terrified. Had he conjured up the dead? Summoning all his courage, he declared to the closed door as forcefully as possible: "Brother Zotikos is in a Frankish dungeon! Whoever you are, go away!"

"Lakis, listen! I can't shout or it will attract attention. Father Eustathios and seven of my brothers were arrested, but I wasn't at Antiphonitis when the Franks came. I'm still free. Let me in. I need your help!"

Lakis couldn't deny help to Brother Zotikos. He lifted the bar holding the door shut, and cracked the door open. In the darkness he saw only a monk in black robes looking anxiously over his shoulder. Then the monk turned toward the door and his dark eyes fixed on Lakis. He gasped. It was Brother Zotikos— but rather than the mild and kindly man that he had been at the monastery, he looked fierce and sinister.

Lakis backed up, opening the door only a little wider. The monk squeezed himself inside. Lakis shut the door and replaced the bar. Brother Zotikos waited for him. When they were facing one another again, the monk explained, "Your uncle told me you had run away; he wanted us to track you down and return you to him."

"Is that why you're here?" Lakis asked, disappointed and betrayed.

"No, I found you months ago; but since you seemed to have landed on your feet and not to be in need of your uncle's care, I decided to leave you here."

Lakis let out a slow sigh of relief. He did not want to return to his uncle, no matter what.

"Lakis, listen to me. I dare not stay in Nicosia very long, but I need someone—you—to deliver a package to that dog Lusignan."

"Me? Why me? I don't have anything to do with the despot!"

"I know. You're a good boy. But this message is, well, a warning—to stop the Franks from doing any harm to Father Eustathios. I'm very worried that the Franks could torture or kill him. We have to stop that if we can."

"Of course, but how? People say he may already be dead."

"No, he's not. I've checked on that. He and my brothers were taken to the Castle of Kyrenia, but the—ah—" he interrupted himself, cleared his throat, and continued "*women* who have, um, dealings with the garrison have been able to discover that they are being kept in the underwater dungeon. They are being given water and bread, and that is all, but so far none of them have died. We have to ensure they get better conditions soon. You know how old and ill most of my brothers are."

"But how can I help?" Lakis wanted to know.

"It is better if you don't know the details, but in this box is a message for the tyrant Lusignan." From a satchel he had been carrying over his shoulder, Brother Zotikos removed a beautiful carved wooden box inlaid with mother-of-pearl.

"Oh, that's beautiful!" Lakis exclaimed, for an instant the craftsman in him overcoming everything else as he reached out to it in wonder.

"Don't open it!" Brother Zotikos warned just as Lakis went to flip open the tiny brass latch holding the box shut.

Lakis looked up at him, alarmed.

"What's inside is for the Frankish dogs only! You must deliver it to *them*—as a gift." The way Brother Zotikos smiled as he spoke sent a shiver down Lakis' spine. "Will you do it?"

"But—I mean—how am I going to get past their guards?"

"You sell carved objects, don't you? You make and sell them? Everyone in Nicosia knows that. The Franks will have seen you hawking your wares all over the city."

Lakis looked down at the box in the palms of his hand and shook his head. "I've never even *seen* anything as beautiful as this. No one will think I made it. Where is it from?"

"It comes from a land beyond Arabia. You don't have to pretend *you* made it. Say your master made it and has sent you to deliver it. We *must* get it to the Lusignan." There was desperation in Brother Zotikos' voice, while his eyes burned almost feverishly. Or maybe he *was* feverish, thought Lakis, as the monk continued in a low, breathy voice: "I am certain God whispered your name to me, Lakis. I came to Nicosia with this mission, but without knowing how I was going to perform it. Then God whispered your name to me, and I remembered you were here, apprenticed to a master carver. I knew you were the one chosen by Him to deliver this box, this message. If you refuse, Lakis, you are not only being ungrateful for all Father Eustathios and my brothers did for you when you were orphaned, you will also be defying the will of God."

Lakis stared at Brother Zotikos, hypnotized by his words, and a chill ran down his spine, making him shudder. Truly, he thought, only God could know that he *did* have a "friend" in the tyrant's own household: his "friend" Janis. He nodded solemnly. "I'll deliver the box, Brother Zotikos—if I can convince Master Afanas to give me some time off, that is," he added uncertainly as he tried to rehearse what he would say.

Brother Zotikos reached out his hand in blessing. "God will reward you, Lakis!" He made the sign of the cross, then bent and kissed Lakis on both cheeks. "Tell your master it is the anniversary of your parents' death and that you wish to attend Mass and pray for their souls. No Master would deny you time to do that."

Lakis nodded solemnly. He had to find a way to do what Brother Zotikos said. It was not often that an orphan-turned-beggar-turned-apprentice was tasked directly by God.

"There's a disreputable Greek youth outside asking to see you, sir," the sergeant of the guard told John, catching him as he returned from putting his and his father's horses up in the stables.

"Me?"

"Well, he said 'Janis, the despot's servant,' and I don't know who else he would have meant."

John's heart missed a beat. It had to be Lakis! "Where is he?"

"I told him to wait on the other side of the street by the khan you used to live in. I didn't want him accosting people or trying to slip inside. You can't trust these Greeks, sir. They're all slippery as eels—liars and cheats at best and outright rebels at worst. If you want me to come with you—"

"No, I'll be fine!" John insisted, and hastened back out onto the street. He didn't spot Lakis right away because he was sitting on the ground with his back against the side of the khan. As John approached, Lakis got cautiously to his feet. He had grown inches, and although he was still thin, he was somehow less feral-looking than the last time they'd met.

"Lakis! It *is* you!" John exclaimed, grinning broadly.

Lakis did not return his smile. He gazed at John with piercing eyes and an earnest expression. "You lied to me," Lakis opened the conversation.

"I—"John's smile faded. "I had to. I was in disguise. I wanted to get to know Nicosia without anyone knowing who I was. I wanted, for a little while, *not* to be a Frank."

"Why?" Lakis demanded.

John took a deep breath and tried to think through his answer very carefully. "Because I knew that if everyone saw me as a Frank, I wouldn't get to know the real Nicosia or have an honest conversation with anyone. That's true, isn't it?"

"But why did you care?"

"My mother's Greek," John answered with a shrug. "I don't hate Greeks."

That took Lakis by surprise. He started, frowned, and looked at John harder than before. He'd heard that one of the Franks was married to a Comnena, but John had been there before the Comnena arrived with her Frankish husband. Surely he couldn't be related. "You're not—I mean, you can't . . . "

"What?" John asked back, baffled. "What's so strange about having a Greek mother? Many of us born here in Outremer are of mixed blood. Queen Melisende was half Armenian—"

"But not the Comnena? Your mother isn't the Comnena?" Lakis broke in, sounding desperate for reassurance that this wasn't the case.

"What's wrong with that?" John asked back irritably. He was proud of his mother's blood.

Lakis crossed himself and started to back away.

John reached out and grabbed him to stop him from escaping again. "Lakis, what is it? Why are you looking at me like that?"

Lakis froze. He had been raised to think of the Emperors as semi-divine. His father had taught him that: no matter how unjust Isaac Comnenus had seemed, he was still a member of the Imperial family and, and, and . . . now a member of that family was touching him. Lakis stared at John's hand on his arm.

John instantly let him go, but he pleaded with him. "Lakis, I'm sorry for what some of the Franks have done. I told my mother about you and how your parents and sisters had been killed. I think that's one of the reasons she's here. She wants to stop this violence—"

"By arresting monks and abbots?" Lakis flung at him.

John took a breath to answer and then just shook his head. "No. That's wrong. My mother has told Lord Aimery that it was a terrible mistake. Even Lord Aimery recognizes that it is wrong, but . . . " John cut himself off, realizing he had been on the brink of revealing the internal divisions in the Frankish leadership. Instinctively he knew it would not be good to talk openly about them. "Listen to me, Lakis. Despite what has happened, we aren't monsters and blasphemers and all the other things you call us. Let's go someplace where we can talk. I'll buy—"

"No! I have to get back to my master. I'm an apprentice now," Lakis told him proudly. "With a wood and ivory carver. I only came to tell you that—and to give you this." He thrust out the box from Brother Zotikos, at the same time taking a step back in preparation for flight.

John stared at the beautiful box, and he knew instinctively that whatever it contained was evil. "What is it, Lakis?" he asked in a low, serious voice.

"A gift."

"But from whom? And why?"

"My master wants commissions from Lord Aimery or his lady. He sent me to bring you this box to show you what good work he does. Give it to Lord Aimery—and if he wants more, come find me in the workshop beside the Paphos gate." He gave a completely wrong address, in the certainty that the Franks would soon want to kill whoever had delivered the box.

John saw through the lie, but he also had no compelling reason to reject the box. To buy time and to think things through, he cautiously flipped open the little latch to look inside the box. As he did so, Lakis darted away as fast as his feet could carry him. Distracted and dismayed, John started after him—then, realizing it was pointless, he stopped and looked down into the box.

A crumpled cloth or rag covered with dark brown stains was all there was inside. Frowning, John started to extract the rag. It was stiff, and the brown stains started to flake off as he touched the cloth. John froze and pulled his hand away. He couldn't be sure, but he strongly suspected the stains were dried blood. But whose?

John snapped the box closed and ran to the palace. He didn't stop until he had reached his parents' apartment. He knocked once on the door, but didn't wait to be invited in. "Mama! Papa!"

They were seated opposite each other in the window seat, his father with a goblet of water in his hand, having just returned with John from a morning ride around the city to assess the situation. He looked up sharply and met John's eyes. One look at his son was enough to make him get to his feet and step down from the window seat. He was already tense and wary.

John crossed the distance with the box in his hands. "Papa, this was just delivered—a "gift" to Lord Aimery. But—look inside!"

Balian took the box from John cautiously, his eyes looking at his son's ashen face more than the box. He flipped the latch and slowly opened the lid. John watched him closely, but his father's face was guarded. He studied the contents and then put a finger inside to shove the cloth aside, and with his fingernail extracted a note lying on the bottom of the box. He removed the note, but it was in Greek, so he handed it to his wife, who was hovering beside him. Then he reached inside the box again and pulled out a heavy gold ring.

"All it says is: 'An eye for an eye, and a tooth for a tooth. . . .'" Maria Zoë informed him.

Balian was turning the ring over in his hand, frowning. It was a man's ring, large enough for him to wear on his thumb. It had an exceptionally large, irregular stone set in heavy gold. The style was quite exotic—neither Frankish nor Greek, more oriental, although nothing on it was overtly Islamic such as an Arabic inscription. He felt as if he'd seen this ring somewhere before, but he couldn't place it. Holding it up, he asked his wife, "Do you recognize this or know to whom it might have belonged?"

Maria Zoë gasped. "That's Humphrey de Toron's ring! The one he inherited from his grandfather the Constable. It was too big for his fingers, so he used to wear it on a chain around his neck."

"Of course!" Now Balian recognized it, too. "It was a gift from the Caliph of Cairo! Given to the Constable when he negotiated with him in the 60s."

Balian and Maria Zoë's eyes met.

"Humphrey de Toron?" John asked anxiously. "You think he's dead?"

Maria Zoë shook her head sharply. "Not unless the abbot of Antiphonitis is. I think we can assume, however, that the rebels have poor Humphrey in their power, and his fate depends on how we treat the abbot and monks of Antiphonitis."

"Who gave you this?" Balian asked his son intently.

John drew a deep breath to lie, but he couldn't. "Do you remember the orphaned beggar I told you about? The one whose parents were killed by Henri de Brie—burned alive in their own mill? He—he—please don't go after him!"

"No, there's no need. What you said is enough. He has reason to hate us, and he's probably active in the rebellion, which confirms what this is: a clear threat to Toron. Where was Toron last we heard?"

"Paphos," Maria Zoë answered. "In the West," she answered her husband's question before it formed; "Aimery sent him to demand salvage from that pilgrim ship and see if he could find out what had happened to the survivors. It seemed an easy enough job, as there has been no open rebellion or unrest in the region."

"And Toron, of course, doesn't inspire fear," Balian noted cynically. Then, taking a deep breath, he announced: "Come with me, John. We need to take this to Aimery."

Aimery turned the ring around in his hand and considered it with narrowed eyes for what seemed like an inordinately long time, before setting it down on the beautiful mosaic table in front of him and declaring with a nod, "This is a very good turn of events."

"Aimery! How can you say that?" Eschiva exclaimed in outrage. "Have you forgotten that poor Humphrey backed the Lusignans when the rest of the High Court would not? You can't still begrudge him the better treatment he received from Saladin! He's suffered. . . ." The flood of words died on Eschiva's lips as she realized that Aimery was nodding calmly to everything she said. Falling silent, she looked nervously to her uncle and aunt. The two were waiting alertly for her husband to continue, rather than joining in her protests. She didn't understand.

"It's very simple, my dear," Aimery explained once she fell silent. "*This,*" he took the ring in his fingers and held it up again, "gives me the excuse I need to order Barlais to improve the conditions in which the abbot and his monks are held. Obviously, we can't and won't release them until we can be sure Toron's kidnappers will release him in exchange, but it gives me an excuse to enter into negotiations with the rebels. Not even your nephew could object to us talking with the rebels now, could he?" The question was directed at Balian.

Balian shook his head. "No, Henri wouldn't insist on putting Toron's life at risk."

"Good. I don't think Barlais will, either." Aimery turned to his wife and assured her, "I'll order the abbot and his monks confined in more humane conditions until we can find out where Toron is and who is holding him." Then he focused again on Balian and Maria, his eyes shifting between them as he asked, "Do you think you could find out who sent this and where Toron is?"

Balian nodded slowly. "I think so." He studiously avoided looking at his son.

"And do you think you could negotiate with them?"

Balian glanced at his wife before answering. "I think so."

"Good. Then I would ask you to set out for Paphos tomorrow. These people appear to have slaughtered innocent pilgrims. I am not happy thinking about what they might do to Toron."

Balian nodded, then turned and ordered John out of the room.

John drew a breath to protest, but thought better of it. "Yes, my lord."

Maria Zoë raised her eyebrows, but waited to see what her husband had in mind.

Balian waited until he heard the door shut with a clunk. Then he announced: "John is fifteen and a half. If I were dead, he would have come of age. He's been in your service for two years, and you have done well by him. He has matured fast and excellently. He is ready for knighthood. I would like to confer it on him at his sixteenth birthday in April. Meanwhile I would like to take him with us, for my lady and I will travel together, and I would commend to you my younger son to take his place."

"Philip? He's not exactly a comparable replacement," Aimery noted wryly, but with a twitch of a smile. "I could offer to let you take Guy—" Eschiva's gasp was audible to all of them, and Aimery smiled at her—"but as I was about to say, I can't bear to be separated from him just yet. So take John and leave Philip with me."

"Thank you. Now, what terms do you authorize me to negotiate?"

"What was your mandate from King Richard?"

"The best deal possible."

Aimery nodded. "I want peace, Balian. I don't just want Toron returned, I want an end to the insurrection. I want people to be safe traveling on my roads, regardless of what faith they are. I want people to be safe to go about their daily business, no matter what that is. I want crops sowed and harvested, not burned in the fields. I want—peace."

Balian nodded, and then crossed himself. "In the Name of the Father and the Son and the Holy Ghost. Amen."

Chapter Fourteen
A Lawless Land

Cyprus
February 1195

AFTER THE SLEEPLESS NIGHT AND THE encounter with "Janis," Lakis was having difficulty concentrating. Luckily for him, Master Afanas appeared to be feeling guilty about his callous reaction to the willful destruction of Lakis' box the day before, or maybe he was just preoccupied with something else. In any case, he had allowed Lakis to take the morning off, and he'd largely left him alone since his return.

Lakis selected new wood carefully, then traced the outlines of the pattern he intended to carve on the first panel. As he worked he kept going over his conversation with "Janis." He wanted to be angry and full of hatred, but he wasn't. Instead he kept seeing the smile with which "Janis" had approached him. He'd been so *glad* to see him—like nobody else in the world since his parents had died. His aunt and uncle certainly never greeted him with a smile like that!

A customer came into the shop in front of the workshop, and Master Afanas rushed to greet her. Lakis looked up out of mild curiosity, but from where he sat he couldn't see much except that it was a woman in a richly embroidered surcoat. Women like that didn't come to the shop very often; they usually sent their servants. Janis was curious, but the other apprentices were so shamelessly peering out the door, jabbing each other, and giggling that Lakis became uninterested. He hated them!

He turned his eyes back to his work, polished the surface of the wood with the back of his sleeve, and picked up a fine chisel. Fragments of conversation filtered through the door, and he noted the cultivated but low-pitched voice of the woman: "... your reputation," "source your ivory," "book covers." Janis had once talked about carving book covers, Lakis remembered, and realized now that he was probably literate. The lady in the showroom said something about "... such a beautiful box . . . very rare . . . your workshop," and the other apprentices scatted back to their workbenches.

When Master Afanas appeared in the door, gesturing for a lady to precede him into the workshop, they were all back at their places and studiously pretending disinterest. Lakis, in contrast, glanced up and caught his breath: not only was the woman dressed in embroidered silk, she was strikingly beautiful despite being no longer young, and unlike most rich women, she was trim and still shapely rather than fat. Her eyes swept the room alertly, looking at each of the apprentices in turn, but then turned her head slightly to listen to someone behind her. Before Lakis could sort out what was happening, she was coming straight towards him, asking: "Are you Lakis?"

Lakis' jaw dropped, and then as he gaped at the lady, he registered that "Janis" was following in her wake. It could only be his mother! Lakis scrambled off his workbench as fast as he could and dropped onto his knees. "It's the Comnena!" he hissed at his fellow apprentices, shocked that they were so rude as to stay sitting.

Master Afanas' head snapped around. "My lady?" he asked, but then dropped to one knee to be safe rather than awaiting an answer.

"That's not necessary," the Comnena assured them, gesturing for them all to get up again—but while Master Afanas and the other apprentices obeyed, Lakis remained firmly on his knees with his eyes down.

"I'm interested in this boy," she said, standing directly before him, but addressing Master Afanas. "What are the terms of his contract?"

Master Afanas cleared his throat. "He, um, being without a sponsor, I've taken him on for just a year as a charity case. He gets free bed and meals—"

"One!" Lakis couldn't resist throwing out in a flare of defiance.

"—and a half-day off every month," Master Afanas ended complacently.

"Hmm, but evidently no shoes, no work clothes, and no bath money," the imperial lady noted, making Lakis cringe to think she could smell how dirty he was. He curled the toes of his filthy bare feet.

"If he completes his first year satisfactorily, I will pay for a set of work clothes," Master Afanas declared, "but before I took him in, he was a beggar. He ran away from his last master, and I was not going to spend money on him until he had proven himself."

The Comnena gave Master Afanas a look so contemptuous that Lakis almost laughed. Then she remarked, "This boy's parents and sisters were burned alive by the Franks, Master Afanas. Don't you think you could have found it in your heart to be a little more charitable?"

Master Afanas' expression of astonishment was enough to make Lakis look down and bite his lips to keep from laughing. "I had no idea, my lady," the master craftsman assured her. "Not a clue. Lakis never said anything about it." To be fair, that was true, Lakis thought, but he still suspected that the Master's astonishment pertained more to the fact that the Comnena referred to "the Franks" in a tone that suggested disapproval.

"I wish my confessor, Father Angelus, to have a word with the boy in private, while you and I discuss more reasonable terms of service. I am prepared to sponsor the boy." With a rustle of silk she turned away and returned to the shop, leaving Lakis to gape after her.

Then a Greek priest was smiling down at him and offering his hand. "Will you come with me, Lakis?"

"Yes, father, but . . . " Lakis looked around, confused. Had he heard right? The Comnena was going to sponsor him? Get him better conditions of work? All because of "Janis." Lakis risked a glance at the other youth, who was standing in the doorway between the showroom and the workshop. He was smiling tentatively at Lakis, and Lakis felt intensely ashamed of his behavior this morning. But what had been in the box? He'd been so certain it was something terrible, something that would make Janis and the despot angry. He looked at the Greek priest in bewilderment.

The man looked like he was in his early fifties, with a lined, tanned face and salt-and-pepper beard. His eyes were gentle and his smile genuine. "Where does that door lead?" he asked as Lakis looked at him.

"That's just the woodshed," Lakis explained.

"Can we step inside?"

Lakis nodded vigorously and led the way, in a hurry to get away from the stares of the other apprentices. He closed the door behind him and they stood in the dusty little room, where the wood was stacked neatly by variety, age, and length. Sawdust softened the floor underneath and drifted in the air. The room had no window, so the only light came from under the crack of the door they had just closed. It took a while for their eyes to adjust, and neither spoke.

Finally the priest started softly, "Lakis, this morning you brought Lord John—Janis—a beautiful box inlaid with mother-of-pearl."

Christ help me! Lakis thought, swallowing hard.

"Where did you get it?"

"Please don't ask me that! Please!" Lakis begged.

Father Angelus nodded. "I understand. You think we want to hurt the man who brought it."

"Don't you?"

"No. Not at all. My lord of Ibelin has been entrusted with an embassy to the man. Lord Aimery wishes to negotiate with him about the release of the abbot of Antiphonitis and his brothers. You want to see the abbot and brothers released safely, don't you?"

Lakis nodded vigorously.

"That will only happen if the Franks can meet and talk with men who sent that box."

"Why? They can just let them go, can't they?" Lakis countered.

"Unfortunately, it's not that simple. You see, the men who sent that box have taken a Frankish lord hostage and are holding him in an unknown place. The Franks won't release the good abbot and his brothers unless they are certain that the Frankish lord will be released in exchange. The lives of nine men depend on you enabling us to establish contact with the men who hold the Frankish nobleman hostage."

Lakis shook his head. "I can't help you."

"Can't or won't?" Father Angelus pressed him, but not unkindly.

"*Can't!*" Lakis insisted.

"Why not?"

Lakis shrugged his shoulders. "Because I don't know. The man who brought the box to me was Brother Zotikos. He's a brother of Antiphonitis, too, but he wasn't there when the others were arrested, so he's still free. He found me here—"

"Why would he want to find you, Lakis? Who are you to him?"

"My father's mill was located below Antiphonitis. When Lusignan's wolves came and started burning everything, my father sent me to the brothers for help. Only they couldn't help. Not against Frankish knights and sergeants! My parents and sisters were burned alive, and the brothers of Antiphonitis let me live with them until they could get word to my uncle about what happened. Then I had to go live with my uncle in Karpasia. That's how Brother Zotikos knows me."

"Why did he seek you out?"

"He needed someone to deliver the box. He said I shouldn't open it. He said—What was in it?"

"A message. Just a message. Or rather, a threat to kill the Lord of Toron if anything happened to the abbot and his brothers. Why did he think you could deliver the box?"

Lakis shrugged, ashamed to say anything about God's will to a priest. "Just because I make boxes. I could take it as a gift from my master, he said."

Father Angelus nodded. "And you don't know where he might be now?"

Lakis shook his head vigorously. "He left as soon as he'd turned over the box. He didn't stay more than a quarter-hour."

Father Angelus nodded again, although Lakis wasn't sure he believed him. "Thank you for telling me all you know, Lakis," the priest continued in an even voice. "If God blesses us, we will save many lives—not just the nine now at stake, but many more to come—because Lord Aimery truly wants peace on this island, and so do the Lord of Ibelin and his lady. Now, if you have nothing more to share with me . . . " The priest gave Janis another chance to confide more information, but Janis pressed his lips together stubbornly.

Father Angelus concluded he would get no more out of Lakis at this time, and with a smile suggested, "Let's return to the others," as he opened the door and held it for Lakis. In the workshop the other boys stared at them, but Father Angelus ignored them. They crossed the room to where "Janis" was still waiting for them. At a nod from Father Angelus, Janis broke into a broad smile and gestured for Lakis to come with him into the shop.

In the shop, the Comnena turned to smile at the youths, and then asked Lakis seriously, "So, young man, what do you think of these terms: three meals a day, a half-day off each *week* and a full day at the end of each month, a work apron and work shoes once a year, and an allowance of a two deniers per week?"

Lakis' eyes widened in amazement at these terms; they would make him equal to the other apprentices. He wouldn't be the "beggar" anymore.

"Good." She turned back to Master Afanas. "Then we are agreed on the terms for the next two years."

Lakis caught his breath and looked at his master. Two more years would enable him to finish his apprenticeship properly. He'd be a genuine journeyman if he could stay two more full years. Master Afanas nodded without noticeable hesitation or reluctance.

The Comnena turned back to Lakis and gestured to Father Angelus. He understood her gesture and produced a purse that he handed over to her. She removed two silver bezants and offered them to Lakis. He just stared at them. He'd never seen so much money all at once in his life.

"This is your allowance from the last year that Master Afanas failed to pay you. I am donating it now so you can get yourself some proper clothes, some shoes, and a haircut, and you should still have money left over for the baths."

Lakis looked up at her. It wasn't that he had a problem accepting alms; he'd been a beggar, after all. He just couldn't grasp his sudden change in fortune.

"It's not charity, Lakis. You've earned this," she told him, mistaking his hesitation for pride.

"Thank you, my lady! Thank you!" Lakis held up his hands and she dropped the coins into them as Lakis glanced over his shoulder at Janis, who was smiling more broadly than ever.

"I will send John over to check on you now and again, Lakis. I am hopeful that you will work diligently and develop skills that will make you self-sufficient in due time."

Lakis nodded. "Yes, my lady."

"Then take your day off and go buy yourself your clothes and have a bath—or two!" The smile she gave him as she said this was dazzling, and left Lakis so dazed he just stood rooted to the spot as she departed with Janis and Father Angelus in tow.

When they were out of hearing, Maria Zoë asked her confessor, "Well?"

"He could only tell us that the man who gave him the box was a brother from Antiphonitis. Apparently he was traveling and so escaped arrest when Barlais' men came for the abbot. Very likely he wasn't there because he was engaged in stirring up trouble," Father Angelus added with a sour expression.

"Did he give a name?" John asked anxiously.

"Brother Zotikos."

"That's it!" John exclaimed, excited. "I couldn't remember, but I'm sure that's it. It's the monk who was so angry and bitter at Kolossi! I'm sure he was behind the fire there! And he was an outsider. The priest, Father Andronikos, clearly objected to the fires, saying the destruction of the factory had only put people out of work and furthermore would bring retribution on the innocent villagers. Father Andronikos cared about his flock, but Brother Zotikos was an outsider and didn't give a damn what happened to them. In fact, he might even have been the same man who told the men in the tavern at Famagusta to kill Aimery and me. . . ."

His mother and Father Angelus were staring at him, astonished. After a moment his mother asked, "Where do we find him?"

"I don't know," John admitted, a little deflated, but then he brightened. "But we can start by going to Kolossi and finding Father Andronikos. He agreed to see us again, and I'm sure he will support our efforts to bring peace. He understands that the violence is hurting the people of Cyprus as much as it hurts us."

Kolossi, February 1195

It started to snow sometime during the night, and by the time they were ready to depart Limassol, it was already collecting in cracks and shadows. The Templars questioned if it was wise to proceed to Kolossi, and Maria Zoë at once agreed to let her new serving woman, Dimitra, remain behind in the warmth and security of the commandery. Balian was considerably more reluctant to reduce their escort, but the Templars assured them there had been no further signs of trouble since the attack on the sugar factory. "We think the troublemakers moved on—west. All the recent trouble has been around Paphos."

So Ibelin agreed to let the bulk of his knights with their squires remain in the comfort of Limassol, and proceeded with just John as their guide, Amalric and Georgios to look after their horses and be on hand for errands, and Sir Galvin, an aging Scotsman with the strength of a bull, as extra protection.

They made good progress at first, and when they reached the ruins of Kolossi, the sun broke through the cloud cover and began to melt the snow that had already fallen. This seduced them into spending longer than initially intended looking over the gutted factory. As John had anticipated, his father identified strongly with the Hospitallers and kept shaking his head in mute distress at the scale of the destruction.

It was thus noon before they were ready to proceed to the village in which John had encountered Father Andronikos. By then the sun was lost again behind thick, low clouds that threatened new snow. Ibelin wondered out loud whether they ought to return to Limassol, with a significant look at his wife.

"We didn't come all this way in the cold to see ruins, but to talk to the priest," she answered, turning on her son. "How much farther is it, John?"

"Not more than a half-hour ride, if we hurry."

"All right," his father agreed. They remounted, trotted back to the main road, and there took up a gentle canter, but they still didn't make it before the storm broke. It came down out of the Troodos Mountains with a vengeance, and suddenly they were being lashed by freezing rain and gale-force winds. There was, however, nothing to do but keep going. Balian rode around to be to windward of Maria Zoë, and he ordered Sir Galvin to ride ahead and be sure they weren't surprised by anything.

By the time the village with its low church came into sight, they were all soaked through. They made immediately for the church to get out of the sleet, tethering the horses in the imperfect lee of the little structure. While the church offered some shelter from the sleet and wind, it had no fireplace and was bitterly cold. John at once volunteered to go in search of the priest.

He stepped back out into the storm, but had not gone more than a score of paces before a figure in the black robes of a priest emerged out of the freezing rain. With relief John recognized the man coming towards him by his white beard whipping in the wind. "Father Andronikos! Thank God! My mother and father have come to see you, but we got caught in the storm. They're in the church."

"Janis, wasn't it? Lord Aimery's squire?"

"Yes, it's me. I'm sorry I didn't come back sooner, but—it's a long story. My parents are with me now."

"Didn't you say your mother was Maria Comnena?" the priest asked.

"Yes, that's right."

"Merciful heavens! And riding about in this weather? Hurry!" The priest stretched his stride and John had to scurry to keep up. They burst back into the church, and the priest focused quickly on the only woman among them. He strode straight to her, and bowing his head he went down on one knee. "My lady! It is an honor to welcome you to my humble church, but in this weather I fear that I must offer you the hospitality of my even *more* humble home. Please! Come! Come!" He was back on his feet and gesturing for them all to follow him.

There was no resistance. Not only did the travelers welcome any place with a hearth, Father Andronikos himself exuded goodwill. Despite the circumstances, John felt that they had been right to press on with the journey.

Father Andronikos' house was directly beside the church and only a little better than the peasant cottages. It did, however, have a large fire already blazing around large logs. Indeed, it was warm and dry and smelled of fresh-baked bread. A middle-aged woman with an ample bosom and an even more generous lower half looked up astonished as the visitors crowded in, but taking her cue from Father Andronikos, she gestured everyone in to the fire in a motherly fashion. John, remembering the horses, told his host they had to get them to shelter.

"My stable's too small for six of your big horses. We'll have to distribute them. I'll show you!" Father Andronikos went back out into the storm with John, Amalric, and Georgios. Each youth collected two horses. They left Ibelin and his lady's horse in Andronikos' own small goat and donkey shed, then took the others to the animal sheds of neighbors. By the time they returned to Andronikos' home, Maria Zoë had already been supplied with a complete change of clothes and sat by the fire in the overly abundant linen robes of her hostess, while her own gown, surcoat, and cloak were spread out on the bed in the adjacent room to dry. Ibelin and Sir Galvin, meanwhile, had stripped down to their braies and draped their hose, shirts, gambesons, and surcoats over other pieces of furniture, while their chain-mail hauberks were spread out on the flagstone apron of the hearth.

"Better get out of your wet things," Ibelin advised his son and squires. "I don't want you catching a cold."

John was not reluctant to comply, as his clothes now clung to him like icy plaster. He found a stool near the door into the kitchen, and sat to remove his wet things one layer at a time. Just as he got down to his shirt and hauled it up over his head to stand naked from the waist up, he found himself face to face with the most beautiful female he had ever seen in his life. She was gazing at him with a tray loaded with pottery mugs and a steaming pitcher. By the smell, she was bringing hot cider to the chilled guests. As their eyes met, she blushed such a bright red that John felt instantly ashamed of his nakedness. He held his wet shirt helplessly over his naked chest, but the girl had already turned away to offer the objects on her tray to Maria Zoë. Father Andronikos smiled broadly at the sight of her and announced proudly, "Here is my daughter Eirini."

"Ah," Maria Zoë smiled at the girl, "let us hope that is an omen, for we have come on a mission of peace, Father."

"I know, my lady," Father Andronikos smiled back at her, his arm encircling his daughter's slender waist as he spoke.

Maria Zoë was duly astonished and asked, "How can you know that, Father?"

"Would a queen ride through this weather with only two armed men to bring war? I have hoped ever since I heard you had landed on the island that you would be a peacemaker, for you have been both Greek and Frank and can see both sides."

Ibelin cleared his throat to indicate he wanted a translation. With a nod to his mother, John hastened over to his father's side, went down on his haunches, and whispered a translation in a low voice. From this position his own scrawny nakedness was hidden from Andronikos' beautiful daughter by his father's broader figure, but he had a clear view of Eirini as she poured the cider for his mother.

Meanwhile Father Andronikos was continuing, "Of course, I couldn't be sure what role you *would* play. Some royal women are more concerned with their wealth, dignity, and pleasure than the people they rule. Such was the wife of Isaac Comnenus. But when Janis said you were in my church, then I knew you had come in peace."

"Point out," Ibelin urged his son after this was translated, "that in the state we're in, anyone who wishes us harm will have child's play cutting us to pieces."

John demurred. "He knows that, Papa."

Meanwhile, Maria Zoë was remarking cautiously, "I am glad to do what I can, Father, but you must not think I come on my own. Lord Aimery de Lusignan bade my lord husband see what he could do." She gestured to her husband while John translated, shifting a little more to his father's rear to secure more cover as Eirini also looked in their direction.

Father Andronikos nodded earnestly. "That is even better news, my lady. I welcome you both," he continued, bowing deeply to Ibelin, and Eirini hurried to bring the tray to her father's guest. As the elder Ibelin reached out and poured himself a portion of cider from the pitcher, the girl peered around him toward John and smiled. "You too, sir?" she asked in a whisper.

John's throat constricted so sharply it was impossible to get out more than a croaked "*parakalo!*" (Please.)

Eirini smiled and brought the tray closer. John had no choice but to surrender some of his cover to reach out, take a mug, and help himself to the cider. He thanked Eirini as she, with another smile, continued to Georgios and Amalric.

Father Andronikos, meanwhile, looked about, found a vacant stool, and brought it closer to the fire, so he could sit down at his visitors' feet. "Please tell me, my lord, how you think a humble priest such as I can help."

When the priest's words had been translated, Ibelin nodded to his wife and authorized her to explain rather than insisting on continuous translation. Maria Zoë started carefully, "We have reason to believe, Father, that certain members of the Greek Church on this island are hostile to Frankish rule here. Even before the Templars came, a priest tried to foment rebellion, posing as a Comnenus Emperor," she reminded him.

"He had no support, or very little," Father Andronikos countered.

"Not among the population, perhaps, but what about in the Church? Wasn't he a priest?"

Father Andronikos shook his head. "There was no hostility here until the Templars came. They behaved very badly."

"Just what did they do, Father?"

"They imposed new taxes, and when the senior tax collectors came to them collectively—all worthy men with many years of loyal service—to explain that the new taxes violated King Richard's promise to rule by the laws of Manuel I, the Templars had them flogged and put in the stocks as if they were criminals. Men with long beards and university degrees!"

Maria Zoë asked John to translate this for his father, and only when he was finished and Balian nodded understanding did she urge Father Andronikos to continue. "What happened next?"

"At first, nothing. Tax collectors are not popular, even if in this case they were representing the interests of taxpayers rather than the Crown. But soon the Templars noticed that they were getting no revenues at all—much less new ones."

Maria Zoë nodded and gestured for John to translate again.

"And then?" she asked when her son finished.

"Then the Templars sent some of their men out to key sources of revenue—to the harbor masters at Limassol and Kyrenia, to the millers and bakers in Nicosia, and to important oil and wine presses round about. Everywhere, they broke into the homes and seized all the valuables the owners had. They rough-handled the men and their servants and mocked the women."

Maria Zoë nodded and paused again for translation, which John provided his father.

"But again," Father Andronikos continued, "these were rich men, and there were many who may have felt they got only what they deserved. At the start of Lent, however, there was an incident in which the Templars, returning late one evening, found their way blocked by crowds gathered in front of St. Michael's. The people had come together innocently to hear Mass and had simply collected in such numbers that they overflowed into the street, blocking the road. The Templars rode into the crowd, ordering people out of the way, and lashing out at them with their sheathed swords. When a priest protested the rough treatment of peaceful Christians gathered to honor Our Lord, one of the Templars grabbed him by the beard so firmly that he pulled him clear off the ground. Several young men came to his assistance, and the Templars beat them back with so much force that one had to be admitted to hospital with a concussion, and another lost several teeth. The—"

"Stop." Maria Zoë held up her hand. "I need to tell this to my husband." This time she handled the translation herself, while Father Andronikos watched the baron's face closely. At first his face was impassive and well controlled, but at one point in the flood of French narrative, he flinched and then frowned until his wife finished speaking. She turned back to Father Andronikos and told him to continue.

"The word of this incident spread like wildfire through the city, and people started getting agitated. After that the Templars could not ride anywhere without people shouting insults at them—from a distance. Sometimes stones or refuse were thrown as well, but always from behind or from overhead. When the Templars turned around or looked up, no one was visible anymore."

Maria Zoë translated this, and her husband nodded grimly. At her signal, Father Andronikos continued. "As Easter approached, the mood was getting uglier and uglier. A group of young men got very drunk one night and came out to 'serenade' the Templars with a silly drinking song in which they compared the Templars to—don't ask me why!—she-goats in one stanza and accused them of sodomy in the next. Apparently they assumed there was no one among the Templars who understood Greek. Unfortunately, they were wrong. The Templars understood and were enraged. They sent their sergeants out to arrest the youths, chasing them through the streets of Nicosia until they had caught a half-dozen of them, although allegedly two escaped. The youths they captured were mishandled, and then made to stand naked in stocks in front of the commandery for two days and a night. Several of them, it turns out, were from very good families, and their parents were treated with contempt when they tried to intercede." He stopped and nodded for Maria Zoë to translate.

The Baron of Ibelin sat back in his chair, the warmth from the fire now sufficient to make him comfortable in his half-naked state. His expression was resigned, and he nodded now and again at his wife's words.

"Then on Good Friday, the devil must have possessed them. Four Templar Knights, including their commander, burst into the cathedral during Mass and, shoving the Archbishop roughly aside, started shouting at the people that they were "schismatics" and "heretics" who would soon learn to "pray properly." It was like tossing a torch into a haystack. All at once everyone was shouting at the Templars that *they* were the schismatics and heretics. Then something snapped, and they fell on the Templars with the force of numbers and ripped their weapons off them before they could be used. They tore off their tunics and their armor, and—kicking and beating them—drove them out of the cathedral."

John hastily provided the translation this time, nodding when he had finished. Father Andronikos continued, "Humiliated, the four Templars staggered and dragged themselves back to the commandery, hounded the entire way by men still spitting and insulting them. They made it inside, but by morning the Templars found themselves completely surrounded by a mob that was larger by far than the one that had hounded them the night before. The mob started to smash windows and batter the gate with an improvised battering ram. Furthermore, they were calling for blood. The Archbishop had retired to his home, still shaken by the rough-handling he had endured during Mass the night before. Other voices of reason were intimidated by a mob that was clearly set on violence. The majority were being egged on and riled up by the more volatile elements in the population—journeymen and sailors, teamsters, even some of Isaac Comnenus' Armenian mercenaries, the ones who had married locally and remained. They brought out their crossbows and began firing at the Templars whenever one of them showed himself." At a signal from Maria Zoë, Father Andronikos halted so John could provide the translation.

As John finished, he drank his mug empty, and Eirini hastened over to refill it with a shy smile.

John thanked her in kind, while her father resumed his narrative. "The Templars raised a white flag and requested a safe-conduct to the coast, but there was no real leader of the mob. Besides, many of the young men suspected a trick; at least, that's what I was later told. Maybe they were simply full of hubris and believed they could truly eliminate the Templars. There were, after all, only fourteen knights and twenty sergeants altogether, supported by fifty or sixty lay brothers." As John translated this he watched his father's expression carefully, and saw him nod at the numbers.

Father Andronikos took up the narrative again. "Thinking they had nothing to lose, the Templars, I am told, confessed their sins and heard Mass. Then, at the hour of dawn on Easter Sunday, they armed themselves, mounted their war horses, and sortied out of their commandery. By then most of the crowd had dispersed and gone home to welcome the Resurrection. The sortie was actually quite unnecessary."

Maria Zoë nodded agreement while John translated.

"Tragically, the Templars confused the crowds of people on their way to Easter morning Mass with the rioters of the day and night before. They rode them down with leveled lances. Enraged witnesses rallied to fight them, storming out of all the surrounding streets with whatever weapons they could grab. The Templars were better armed, however, and by now they were fighting with fury or desperation or both. In the end they all escaped, leaving behind sixty-eight dead and more than a hundred injured. Among the dead were six women and eleven children trampled by God knows whom in the confusion." Father Andronikos ended with a deep sigh, and sat looking very sad as John provided the translation.

"The Templars seem to attract some singularly stupid men," Ibelin noted when John finished the translation. "In addition to Gerard de Ridefort, of justifiably infamous reputation," Ibelin noted, "I met this Arnaud de Bouchart, the Templar commander here. Without self-reflection or self-doubt, he blamed all the trouble here on the Cypriots, calling them 'mad dogs' and saying they were totally 'ungovernable.' He predicted Guy would fail, by the way."

Maria Zoë translated her husband's remarks for Father Andronikos, who nodded understanding before explaining additionally: "After this incident the population turned vehemently anti-Latin. When King Guy landed with his few men, no one was willing to see them as anything other than a continuation of Templar rule. Many believed they had only come to make way for a return of the Templars, a view reinforced by the re-establishment of a Templar presence at Gastria and in Limassol. Certainly no one was prepared to pay taxes, tolls, or customs duties to him." He paused for the translation and then continued.

"And what can I say? Tragically, Lusignan proved even *worse* than the Templars. While the Templars had broken in to men's houses to take the monies they wanted, Lusignan sent out troops not only to collect money, but also to *punish* the recalcitrant. He burned down the houses of those who refused to pay taxes. When his men were ambushed by outraged inhabitants—or more commonly, when Cypriots took out their anger on the Italian merchants— Lusignan responded by sending out more men, who took hostages or burned and slaughtered whole villages in retribution. The spiral of violence has continued ever since." Father Andronikos shook his head in distress and sadness.

John, however, stood up, his thighs and calves aching from squatting so long, and announced proudly, "There has been no retribution for the fire at Kolossi, and there won't be! King Guy is dead, and Lord Aimery is different."

John's father looked up at him suspiciously and asked his wife, "Is John speaking out of turn?"

"Not really—if a little rashly," she assured her husband with a smile. Then, turning to Father Andronikos, she noted, "We are very grateful to you for your candid explanation of what happened here. It will, I hope, help us find a solution. What my son says is right: Lord Aimery de Lusignan is a very different man from his brother."

"We have seen no evidence of that," Father Andronikos answered soberly. "Has he not just ordered the arrest and incarceration of a worthy abbot and seven brothers?"

"Actually," Maria Zoë answered, slowly sipping her cider, "he didn't. Certain lords who are impatient carried out the arrest without Lord Aimery's knowledge, much less consent."

Father Andronikos didn't answer, but his eyes were fixed on Maria Zoë, watching for some indication that she was dissembling.

She continued, "And now someone has seized a Frankish lord, Humphrey de Toron, and we have received an anonymous threat to his life."

Father Andronikos raised his eyebrows, sat up straighter, and smiled to his daughter. "Go help your mother with the bread," he suggested, and she scurried away, hastily loading empty mugs on her tray as she went. Andronikos said nothing even after she was gone, however, and Maria Zoë was compelled to ask, "Have you heard of this?"

Father Andronikos nodded.

"Do you know who is responsible?"

He shook his head, but a little too sharply to be convincing.

"We *must* establish contact with them," Maria Zoë explained.

"Couldn't you just let the abbot and his brothers go?"

"Not without the release of Toron. If we release the abbot and his brothers and they retain Toron, then they will threaten his life to gain other concessions."

"Very possibly," Father Andronikos conceded, while John whispered a quick translation of the dialogue to his father.

Ibelin got abruptly to his feet and stood towering over the priest, who hastened to stand as well, wary of what was coming. "People may not like paying taxes, but without taxes no government can function. Since driving the Templars out, government on this island has broken down. Lawlessness is increasing by the day—whether it is pirates on the waterways or robbers on the highways. I understand that you might prefer to be ruled by your own, but I wouldn't be so sure the current Greek Emperor is so benign."

Maria Zoë translated his speech quickly.

Father Andronikos answered, "We are not asking for rule from Constantinople. Better a despot of our own, here on the island, readily accessible to our complaints and pleas. King Richard promised a restoration of the laws of Manuel I. That is all we ask and expect." Andronikos' tone was reasonable and his expression mild, yet there was pride and determination underneath his words, too.

Ibelin nodded at the end of John's translation, but made no promises. Instead he insisted, "We must speak to the men who hold Lord Toron. It takes two to have a dialogue."

"I suggest, then, that you do not live with the Templars," Father Andronikos advised a touch tartly.

"No? Where else are we safe?"

"Go to Paphos. The castellan of the royal fortress on the shore is an old and honorable man, appointed by Manuel himself. Tell him your mission and request his hospitality. You'll find the accommodations far more comfortable than with the Templars, my lady," Father Andronikos added, turning to Maria Zoë. Then, focusing again on Ibelin, he promised, "I will see what I can find out and send word to you there."

Paphos, Cyprus

Father Andronikos had not lied about either the accommodations or the castellan at Paphos. The old man had welcomed them graciously, opening up the royal apartments that had been unused since the last visit of Isaac Comnenus in 1189. As with so many structures built in the previous century by the Greeks, the masonry consisted of layers of different-colored stone to create stripes. Although the ground and second floor were windowless, the upper story, on which the royal apartments were located, had batteries of arched windows between delicate marble pillars. From the inside, the rooms initially seemed dingy and stuffy because the windows had been sealed with hides against the storms of winter, but the day after their arrival a strong southwest wind chased away the snow with unseasonably warm, sunny weather. Removing the heavy hide coverings from the windows, they had let in the fresh air and sunlight. At once the suite of rooms was transformed: the gold and silver mosaics glistened, and the polychrome marble in elaborate geometric designs on the floor and the frescoes on the walls came to life in full color. The castle also boasted a very welcome bath.

Ibelin was even more pleased by the defensibility of the compact fortress. It sat astride the start of a hook of land that extended out southwards from the shoreline and curled to the east to form a small harbor. The castle was thus protected by water on three sides: by the sea to the west, the harbor to the east, and a salt-water moat on the north. Furthermore, it provided generous accommodations for both man and horse. With the men he had with him, Ibelin felt confident he could withstand a short spasm of violence, although the stores were inadequate to endure a long siege.

After settling in and setting a watch, Ibelin and his lady set out to explore Paphos. The city was still enclosed in a massive but largely ruinous wall, from which (evidently) the residents regularly obtained masonry for new buildings, creating a sense of decay. Within the wall, the sense of ancient majesty brought low continued. Between monumental buildings with marble columns and expressive statues, rough stone and plaster houses huddled like beggars. In the once-grand agora the columns lay toppled, the individual disks of marble lying like sliced salami on top of one another—evidently the work of an earthquake. In the Greek theater, people were living in the three-story structure behind the stage, their laundry fluttering on lines dangling from the windows.

Everywhere they went they were accompanied by a flock of noisy boys, more pickpockets than beggars. Although Georgios and Amalric kept the boys well out of range by flanking the Ibelins warily and chasing the most impertinent boys away with well-aimed kicks and sheathed swords, the pack of boys still clung to the Franks like flies. Older beggars, many with crutches or missing limbs and eyes, tried to block their way. They took expert advantage of the fact that the sewers appeared to be blocked or broken, so that in many places foul-smelling water spilled onto the once well-paved streets. Ibelin also noted that the fountains were dry and filled with rubbish, much of it stinking.

"The earthquake that destroyed the agora may well have broken the aqueducts and underground drainage," Ibelin concluded.

"Obviously," Maria Zoë observed as they stepped over yet another leaking sewer.

"The point is: the fountains and drains prove that the city *had* a functional water and drainage system. This isn't like Ibelin, where we had to build everything ourselves. All that's needed here is to find out where the damage is and repair it."

"Easier said than done."

"Not cheap, but the stink and rubbish creates a false image of poverty."

"False?" Maria Zoë asked skeptically, wishing it was not beneath her dignity to hold her nose.

"Didn't you notice the ships in the harbor as we set out?" her husband answered.

"Yes," Maria Zoë answered cautiously, not sure what he was driving at.

"Didn't you notice the cargoes?"

"One was loading timber," John spoke up eagerly, earning a smile from his father.

"Exactly, and not just ordinary timber: huge logs such as I've never seen before in my life. You can see a wagon with them there. They must come from the Troodos Mountains, and they are worth nearly their weight in gold. The Italian cities need timber like that for the masts and keels of their ships, but it is almost impossible to find in any land on the Mediterranean. Logs like that usually have to be imported from the Baltic Sea, and that takes forever and costs a fortune. From here, those ships can sail directly to Genoa, Pisa, or Venice at much lower cost. Did you notice anything else, John?"

"There were sugar cones on the quay," John readily answered, "and vats of honey, too."

"You *would* notice that!" his mother observed, knowing John's addiction to sweets.

They laughed together, but Balian quickly turned the conversation back to the exports at the port. "Anything else?"

"Wine, I think," John ventured, less sure of himself. There had been a lot of activity at the port as the winter was drawing to a close and ships were making ready for the first sailing of the season. The first ships out would reap the greatest profit in Western markets starved throughout the winter of whatever produce they could bring.

"Wine, olive oil, and ore of some sort—which is a waste to export when they could be smelting and refining it here. And did you see any evidence of someone recording and taxing these exports?"

Maria Zoë and John stared at him in astonishment. Neither had even thought to look for evidence of that.

"No, you didn't," Ibelin answered his own question, "because the customs house was an empty ruin, gutted by what I think was a recent fire."

"Ah." Maria Zoë was beginning to sense the drift of her husband's thoughts.

"With the revenues from the exports in the harbor, it would almost certainly be possible to repair these sewers and the aqueduct, but people are too short-sighted to understand that. They prefer not to pay customs and export duties—and live in filth." He gestured to the heaps of rotting vegetables collected in a clogged ditch beside the road.

"John!" he continued, coming to an abrupt halt. "Do me a favor and go across to that bathhouse and ask the price of a bath."

John looked at him, puzzled. "But there's a bath in the castle."

"I don't intend to use that dump," Ibelin countered, "but we know for a fact that Aimery hasn't seen a denier in revenue from Paphos in the last six months, right?"

Maria Zoë and John nodded.

"Well, I'll wager if you ask them what they're charging, they will name a price higher than in the best bathhouses in Acre—without giving an obol to the Crown. Which means that the owners are enriching themselves shamelessly."

Now John was interested, too. With a smile he darted across the cobbled plaza to duck into the bathhouse, which was covered with a low dome that appeared to date from the Turkish occupation. His parents waited for him in the square, while Georgios yet again chased off the beggars and pickpockets with a flood of inventive curses.

"Why do I get the impression," Maria Zoë started, "that you like it here?"

Balian threw back his head and laughed. "Am I that easy to read?"

"Sometimes. You do like it, don't you?"

"Maybe it's being near the sea again," Balian tried to explain himself. "Listen to the gulls. They remind me of home."

"Ibelin smelled considerably better!" Maria Zoë countered, but inwardly she was pleased by Balian's reaction to Paphos. Up to now he had been curious and intellectually challenged by the problems facing Aimery, but he had remained detached as well, as if waiting for something. Here, at last, the enthusiasm Aimery, John, and even Philip felt for the island appeared to have ignited in her husband, too.

John was back. "Eight obols!" he declared triumphantly. His father was right. This was two obols *more* than the baths of Acre asked—after tax.

"No wonder no one protested when the Templars seized the treasure of the millers, bakers, and bathhouses," Maria Zoë noted with a snort.

"Exactly. If we ask, we'll probably find that prices for grain, bread, wine, oil—everything that is usually taxed—have exploded in the last four years since the fall of Isaac, but *not* because of excessive taxation—as the people have been led to believe. What's happening is that the people who control the resources are keeping what they used to pay to the Crown for themselves, and more. As a result, the rich get richer, the poor get poorer, and no money goes for the public good anymore—whether it's fixing the aqueduct or the sewers or simply driving out the robbers and pirates. This island is sinking into greater and greater lawlessness, not just because of the rebellion against us, but out of the sheer greed of the inhabitants themselves."

"Isn't that what Mother said practically the day we arrived?" John reminded his father. "She said, 'This island needs a government, not an army of occupation.'"

"Did she?" Balian looked at his wife in admiration.

"Yes, I think I did say something like that," Maria Zoë agreed, inwardly preening that John had taken note.

"Well, she's right," Balian agreed with a smile for Maria Zoë. "But how do we re-establish royal authority without a king—and, more important, without recognition of our legitimacy?"

"Aimery thinks the Pope and the Holy Roman Emperor will give him a crown."

"And he's probably right," Balian agreed, "but the people here aren't going to recognize that as legitimate, are they?" he asked his Greek wife.

"No," she admitted. "Both authorities are seen with suspicion, if not outright hostility."

"So whose authority would they accept and respect?" John asked.

"I think," Maria Zoë started cautiously, "that you—we—need to appeal to their pride and love of independence. Didn't Father Andronikos say they would prefer a local despot to a distant one?"

"I'm not so sure about that. It's easier to cheat a distant despot than a near one," Balian countered.

They had reached the wall on the far side of the city. It was in an even more crumbling and ruinous state. Balian turned around, and they started back toward the harbor and castle.

"As I've said before, I believe the Greek clergy is key," Maria Zoë returned to her favorite thesis. "If we could get the local Church hierarchy to advocate Frankish rule—not necessarily as legitimate, but as the lesser evil to lawlessness and spiraling violence—that would go a long way towards buying acceptance."

"Undoubtedly—but we haven't been very successful so far."

"Father Andronikos was friendly," John pointed out.

"And we've heard nothing from him since," Balian pointed out.

"It's only been four days," John protested.

"True, but each day in a dungeon is a day in hell," Balian reminded him, and John was at once contrite for having forgotten about Humphrey of Toron—and the abbot and monks of Antiphonitis.

Chapter Fifteen
The Saint in the Cave

A Cave on Cyprus in an
Unknown Location

HUMPHREY'S TEETH WERE CHATTERING AGAIN. THE chills came irregularly and were interspersed with fever. The fever was better because it made him lethargic, while the chills made him conscious of his misery. He had not had a change of clothes since his capture, and he had been given only a single ragged blanket to supplement his garments. This was inadequate to hold off the cold. Clothes and blanket, furthermore, were equally soiled and caked with mud from the floor of the cave. His hair and beard were encrusted with it as well, because he had nothing on which to rest his head except the rocks or the damp, naked floor.

Humphrey hated the filth even more than he hated the shackles on his wrists and ankles or the near-permanent hunger. When he was in Saracen captivity after Hattin, it had been the offer of a bath from Imad ad-Din that had shattered his desire to resist. He had been so grateful for that bath and the clean clothes. The others had detested him for having "special privileges"; they had even accused him of converting. In fact, Imad ad-Din, despite hinting that someone as intelligent as Humphrey "must see" the error of "polytheism," had never pressed Humphrey to renounce his faith. For his part, Humphrey had never been seriously tempted, but he had learned much from the Islamic scholar. He had endured the jealousy and seething anger of his fellow Frankish captives for the sake of intelligent conversation with a truly educated man—and for the baths. The hostility of the others had simply made him long to be alone.

Now he knew better.

He had been alone since his capture on Cyprus, except when they deigned to feed and water him. Sometimes it seemed as if they had forgotten him entirely, and the thirst and hunger nearly overpowered him. Or rather, it *did* overpower him, and he sobbed in self-pity or pleaded frantically for help or screamed wild threats at the solid stone of his cave prison. It didn't matter what he did. No one saw or heard him.

Now and then, however—irregularly—someone *would* come to throw moldy bread at him and taunt him as he begged for water. There was no question that they hated him, as the Saracens had not. The Saracens had treated all the noble Frankish prisoners with the respect due a worthy enemy. The Saracens felt themselves superior, and they felt the Christians had been punished by God for their foolish "polytheist" beliefs, so they pitied more than hated their prisoners. Indeed, Imad ad-Din had genuinely liked him, Humphrey told himself.

Not so his current jailers. They wanted him dead. The only question was why they hadn't already killed him. It couldn't be because they were holding him for ransom; he was penniless. The only person who *might* have paid an obol for his release was Aimery de Lusignan, but Aimery hardly had sufficient revenues to pay his household, let alone the ransoms for his dead brother's friends. Besides, Humphrey had no illusions about Aimery *liking* him. Aimery had never forgiven him for the better treatment he had received from Imad ad-Din. . . .

If his captors knew he had no monetary value, why didn't they kill him? Humphrey asked himself. Or *were* they killing him? Just slowly, so it would be as terrible as possible?

This slow death left Humphrey time to reflect upon his life, and that was the greatest torture of all. He would turn thirty this year, if he lived until the Feast of St. John the Baptist. And what had he accomplished? He had surrendered his proud inheritance to his stepfather Reynald de Châtillon before he was sixteen. He had rejected a kingdom at twenty-one. He had lost his mother's heritage at twenty-two, and lost his wife at twenty-five.

Since then, his life hadn't been worth living.

So why didn't he just die? Why didn't God let him die?

It wasn't just his anonymous captors who hated him, he reflected: it must be God Himself. But he didn't understand *why* God hated him, any more than he understood why his captors hated him. As far as he knew, he had never met any of his captors anywhere or anytime. Nor had he engaged in any violence against the inhabitants of Cyprus. But maybe they didn't know that?

As for God, however, *He* knew that Humphrey was guilty of no violence against the Cypriots or anyone else. Why did *He* want Humphrey to suffer? It wasn't as if he had ever denied Christ. He couldn't. Much as he recognized the humanity and intellectual sophistication of men like Imad ad-Din, Salah ad-Din, and his brother al-Adil, he had never been tempted by Islam, simply because it offered him nothing. He could pray five times a day as a Christian. And he could give alms, fast, and go on pilgrimage, too. To the Muslims, both Mohammed and Christ were prophets, and so Humphrey could not see why a pilgrimage to the tomb of one prophet was more valuable than to another. No, Islam offered him nothing at all. At least in Christianity he had the Virgin Mary and the saints.

So many saints had suffered for their faith. They had been tortured and humiliated. So had Christ. Hadn't Christ himself despaired in the hour of his death, calling out to his Father to ask why He had deserted him?

"Father, why hast Thou forsaken me?" Humphrey formed the words. First silently, and then as the chattering receded, he said it out loud: "Father, why hast Thou forsaken me?" The words were lost in the vastness of the cave. "Father!" Humphrey raised his voice, "Why hast Thou forsaken me?" Now his words came back at him, reverberating with deathly tension.

Humphrey pulled his disintegrating sanity together and forced himself to form the words in Greek, a language he had mastered as a youth but spoke far less fluently than Arabic. Still, he had learned his Greek by reading the Gospels, because his grandfather claimed they had originally been written in Greek. Greek was the most "authentic" form of the Holy Word. When he thought he had the phrase right, he lifted his voice and asked loudly of the darkness: Patera mou, yiati exeis me evkatelepsyes?" The last word, *forsaken*, reverberated in the cave, getting softer and more conspiratorial with each repetition.

As the echoes died down to a whisper, Humphrey lifted his voice and shouted even louder: "*Patera mou, yiati—*"

"He has not," a voice interrupted him in Greek, and Humphrey leapt out of his skin in terror. He broke instantly into a cold sweat, certain that God had answered his cry and terrified of a confrontation with the Almighty in his present state. Then he realized a light was approaching through the tunnel by which they always brought his water and food.

Humphrey went stock-still and stared toward the unsteady, yet steadily approaching, light. Within seconds a man emerged out of the tunnel, which was only about four feet high and allowed no grown man to walk upright. As the man righted himself, Humphrey realized that he was dressed in the robes of an Orthodox priest, complete with hat and a flowing white beard. Behind him scrambled some of the shabby men who had been keeping him prisoner. The latter looked strangely subdued. There was no taunting, sneering, or threatening now; they just waited uneasily by the tunnel entrance as the priest advanced.

"He has not forsaken you, my son," the priest repeated in Greek as he approached with the torch. He advanced until he was beside Humphrey and then laid a hand on his shoulder as he repeated, "He has not forsaken you, and nor have your friends. They are trying to negotiate your release. It has not yet been secured, but I am here to take you to a more comfortable place." Then, turning on the shabby men with him, he signaled for Humphrey's jailers to unlock his shackles. When they finished, he helped Humphrey to his feet and led him back to the tunnel.

Humphrey was so weak he could hardly shuffle along. The priest had to hold him upright and half-drag him along. He was a strong man despite his long white beard.

As they neared the entrance of the tunnel, the light started to blind Humphrey. He put his hand over his eyes and resisted moving forward. The priest snapped at the young men, and one returned with a strip of cloth that they used to bind Humphrey's eyes. Even when he was blindfolded, the light was almost painful, and then suddenly Humphrey felt the warmth of the sun. It was like paradise.

A cacophony of Greek erupted around him. Men were exclaiming, cursing, mocking, and chattering. The priest silenced them. Humphrey clung to his arm, and he led Humphrey across some uneven ground to something wooden. It moved. "Here, I'll help you up," the priest said and then turned Humphrey around. With the help of a second man, he lifted Humphrey up onto the wooden thing. It moved again and Humphrey gasped. The men around him laughed. The priest silenced them again. He put his hand on Humphrey's knee to comfort and steady him. Then he clicked with his tongue, and Humphrey's seat moved sideways. After a couple more strides, Humphrey realized he was sitting on the pannier of a donkey. No wonder the men around him laughed! Despite his filth and hunger, Humphrey was ashamed of this ultimate humiliation: to be transported on the back of a donkey like a peasant woman.

The trail, however, was steep, and the donkey had to brace and find her footing carefully. Humphrey had no choice but to cling to the sides of the pannier. The priest never left his side, however, and as time passed he was glad not only of that warm hand, but of the donkey itself. He could not have walked this far.

At times the air became very cold and the light went away, suggesting they were traveling through shade. Sometimes Humphrey could hear the wind rustling the trees around him, but not always. He couldn't figure out what made the shade if it wasn't trees. Eventually they came to a stream. Humphrey heard the water even before they stopped and the donkey dropped her head to drink.

"We've made it," the priest announced at last, and Humphrey felt hands untying his blindfold. Although he had to blink and squint, his eyes had adjusted enough to enable him to see his surroundings. They were in a mountain clearing by a stream. Set back a little from the bank stood a small stone church with a single apse. Beside the church were several hovels slowly leaking thin columns of smoke.

Monks emerged from one of these huts and came toward Humphrey. They shook their heads at the sight of him, in pity or perhaps disapproval at his treatment rather than hostility. Without speaking they gestured for him to follow them, as if they had taken a vow of silence. The priest who had brought him smiled at him and gestured for him to go with them. "You'll be safe here," he assured Humphrey, "until your friends can arrange your release."

The monks led Humphrey to a goat shed and gestured for him to strip out of his filthy clothes. When he was naked, they made him get into the trough and brought him scrub brushes to clean himself. Although the water was cold, Humphrey still welcomed the bath. By the time he was finished they returned with one of their own robes, and Humphrey gratefully put it on.

Next they led him inside one of the huts and had him sit at a table. They gave him a pottery cup of water straight from the spring and unleavened bread. The water was cool and clean; the bread was fresh and still a little warm. He ate it ravenously. Indeed, he could not remember another meal ever tasting better.

After the meal, the monk led him to another hut filled with wooden beds laid with straw and gestured for him to lie down. Gratefully he did. It was soft and wonderfully dry after the floor of the cave. With a deep sigh, he started to drift off to sleep. As sleep swept over him, he was wondering who his "friends" could possibly be. He felt that he had none left in the whole world—ever since Isabella had abandoned him.

Paphos, Cyprus

John dropped his visor over his eyes, lowered his lance, and spurred down the sandy stretch of beach that his father's knights had turned into an improvised tiltyard. His father, his knights, and their squires came here daily to practice their skill at arms. A knight could not afford to let his skills become rusty any more than he could let his chain mail rust. Usually John fought Amalric, Georgios, or one of the other squires, but today Sir Galvin had challenged him.

"Come on, John!" he'd called out. "You've got the best horse here! What have you got to fear? I'm without a lance! I'll take you on with shield and ax alone!"

It was a taunt no youth could ignore, although John inwardly thought that Troubadour's obedience and agility hardly made up for Sir Galvin's greater strength, weight, and experience. Hoping that speed might compensate for his much lighter weight, John urged Troubadour to a full gallop. His lance tip hit Sir Galvin's shield, but it had no apparent effect on the knight himself. The tip snapped off and the butt slid off the curvature of the shield. Then, just as John started to ride past, the Scotsman's blunted ax came smashing down on his shoulder. It hit John with such force that he swayed in the saddle. Grabbing Troubadour's abundant mane with his left hand, he just managed to keep from falling off as the horse continued down the tiltyard at full gallop.

As he reached the far end of the lists, Troubadour automatically fell into a trot and then halted. John dropped his reins and the broken lance to feel his left shoulder with his right hand; he was convinced something was broken. Instinctively he stretched out his arm, but the fact that he could move it belied the theory that the shoulder was broken. But it was killing him all the same.

Sir Galvin trotted over, grinning from his old-fashioned, open-faced helmet. "Well done, lad! You're very good!" he announced in a loud voice.

"Oh, is that why I'm covered with bruises?" John snapped back, frowning inside his own helmet.

It was only when his remark was met with general laughter that John registered how many men had gathered to watch the little joust, his father included. His father's face was guarded, but the set of his lips suggested he was not pleased. What John couldn't tell was whether his father was displeased with his performance or with Sir Galvin's challenge.

"Again?" Sir Galvin asked.

John tipped open his visor to glare at the older man, but with his father listening, he couldn't answer any other way than, "Sure. Why not?"

"Good, lad! Now remember, if you hit me squarely enough to fling me back against the cantle of the saddle, it'll make it much harder for me to hit you with my ax."

John nodded, took a deep breath, and turned Troubadour around, while Sir Galvin trotted back toward the far end of the lists. As he waited for Sir Galvin to take up his position, his father brought him a fresh lance and paused to pat

Troubadour on the neck. He didn't look at John, but spoke as if to the horse. "Fool the old man. When you're three strides away, cut across in front of him and shift your lance over your horse's head to ride past him on the right. No need to hit his shield; just avoid his ax."

John only had time to nod once as his father stepped back. He started down the tiltyard, his teeth clamped together in determination and concentration. When he asked Troubadour to pivot sharply left, the stallion executed a perfect flying change, as they had often practiced. At the same instant, John ducked down and hunched over the pommel as he rode past Sir Galvin without even attempting to place his lance.

The Scotsman let out a bellow of protest. "Cheater! Who taught—My lord, you're a bad influence!" He shook his fist at Ibelin, adding indignantly, "How is the lad ever going to learn to fight properly with tricks like that?"

Ibelin was grinning with satisfaction, and he called back without remorse: "Every knight has to cultivate his own advantages. Yours is your great strength. John and I don't have that muscle power, so we have to use tricks. Well done, John!"

Sir Galvin was still grumbling, but Ibelin paid no attention. He'd been distracted by someone who tapped him on the shoulder from behind. As he turned in response, the man threw something at him, then ducked down and disappeared in the crowd. Ibelin felt his blood run cold as he realized how easily it could have been a dagger flung into his belly. As he recovered from the shock, however, he looked to his feet where the object thrown at him had fallen. He reached down and picked up a rolled piece of parchment. It had Greek writing on it. Now his heart was pounding. He turned back toward the lists and gestured John over.

John trotted over, grinning with pride, but his face fell when he saw his father's expression. "What did I do wrong?" he asked, bewildered.

"Nothing. Here. Read this. Someone just threw it at me."

Relieved, John dropped the reins to take the parchment from his father. "Coral Bay. Saturday. Nones," he read out loud. Then he looked up with excitement igniting his eyes. "Father Andronikos has done it! We have a rendezvous!"

His father nodded much less enthusiastically. All he acknowledged was, "It would seem so. I want you to ride back to Kolossi and ask Father Andronikos to join us. I want a witness whom everyone can trust."

John nodded eagerly. He'd be able to see Eirini again, and this time he wouldn't be half naked or looking like a drowned rat!

Coral Bay

Ibelin took all of his knights, their squires, and both his own. With John and himself that made sixteen armed men, and he made sure all of them were in gleaming armor, polished helmets, and clean surcoats; their horses were brushed and curried until their coats were like satin. Georgios was entrusted with the swallow-tailed Ibelin banner: red on the lower half, marigold on the top, with a red cross pattée on the golden half near the staff. Amidst all that chivalric pageantry, Father Andronikos on his donkey was almost a comic figure, but he gave no indication of feeling either ridiculous or intimidated.

They followed the coastal road, which roughly paralleled the shoreline, although it continued straight when the coast jutted into the sea in a series of peninsulas. To the right the Troodos Mountains loomed up purple and majestic, and to the left the sea, almost always visible, glistened. The coast of Cyprus was far more rugged than that of the Levant. Great slabs of limestone tumbled down into the water, forming promontories that extended underwater as treacherous ledges. A ship unfortunate enough to be wrecked on this coast had almost no chance, Ibelin reflected, and began to wonder if there had been any survivors from the pilgrim ship wrecked here the previous fall. Aimery had always accused the locals of killing the survivors, convinced that not *every* soul on board could have drowned. Balian was no longer so sure.

It was well past noon, and Ibelin was beginning to get anxious about making the rendezvous on time, when they crested a shallow hill and suddenly found themselves looking down on a magnificent bay. Limestone arms enclosed it, but in the concave interior the shore was lined by pristine white sand. Furthermore, unlike the water of the Levant, which was muddied by the constant churning of waves and currents on the sandy bottom, the water here was crystal clear. It was possible to see rocks scattered across the bottom, a turtle paddling in a leisurely fashion, and schools of silver fish darting about. The water itself was aqua in the shallows, but gradually turned turquoise before it became a bright cobalt blue in the distance.

Ibelin drew up to gaze in silent amazement at the beauty and serenity of the scenery, while beside him John put his feelings into words with an enthusiastic, "That's beautiful!"

"Coral Bay," Father Andronikos told them simply.

Ibelin glanced toward the sun, judging they were not more than a half-hour ahead of the rendezvous time. He searched the road ahead and the rocky escarpment that fell from the road down toward the beach. There was not another living soul in sight. He frowned. He did not want to think they had come this distance with so much show only to be ignored.

Father Andronikos read his expression and said, "Be patient, my lord. If I am not mistaken, that is a boat." He pointed out to sea.

Since the sun was already sinking down the sky, Ibelin had to shade his eyes and squint to see what the priest had seen—but, indeed, there was a black spot far out upon the cobalt water. That made sense, of course, Ibelin noted; what better way to keep one's whereabouts secret than to use the sea as your highway? No one could track a boat.

He nodded and ordered his men to dismount. When he started to lead them off the road to descend to the beach, however, Father Andronikos stopped him. "I think," he said softly, "you will have to meet Brother Zotikos alone. He will not land if he sees so many armed knights waiting for him. He will think it is a trap. Your men can stay up here where they can see what is happening and come to your aid if there is any foul play, but we must go alone, on foot, and unarmed."

Ibelin stared at him while Georgios translated, then grimaced, not at all happy with this suggestion. After a moment, however, he nodded once, unbuckled his sword, and handed it to Sir Galvin. Then he turned to Father Andronikos and announced, "I need a translator, and it will be my son John." He could have chosen Georgios, of course, but he recognized that this was an opportunity for his firstborn to learn about negotiations with an enemy.

Father Andronikos nodded when the words were translated, adding, "As long as he is unarmed."

John at once removed his sword and handed it to Georgios, his heart pounding with excitement. Ibelin turned the reins of his stallion over to Amalric, and John handed Troubadour's reins to another of the squires before following his father off the road, Barry at his heels as always.

"Leave the dog here," his father advised.

"But he's a concealed weapon!" John protested a low voice.

Ibelin looked down at the dog, gazing up at him with his tongue hanging out of the side of his mouth and his tail lashing from side to side, and found it hard to believe. His skepticism was easy to read from his face, and John added earnestly, "He saved my life once already. I promise, he'll kill anyone who tries to lay a hand on either of us."

Ibelin glanced at Father Andronikos, but the priest appeared uninterested in the dog, so he shrugged and they started down the steep, rocky, winding trail to the beach. Meanwhile, the black dot on the water became larger and larger until it resolved itself into a boat with four oarsmen, a coxswain, and a passenger. By the time Ibelin's party reached the start of the wide beach, the boat was well into the little bay. The passenger was indeed an Orthodox monk with a thick black beard.

Father Andronikos laid a hand on Ibelin's arm. "Wait here. Make him cross the sand to meet you, leaving his men behind as you have left yours."

Ibelin nodded at the translation and waited, watching as the bow of the boat collided with the shore at the far end of the beach. One of the oarsmen jumped over the side to land in thigh-deep water. This lightened the boat enough to float the bow again, and the sailor took hold of the gunnel to guide the boat back onto the beach as a second oarsman jumped over the other side. Together they pulled the boat far enough onto the sand for the monk to clamber over the side onto dry land.

"They look like a bunch of pirates," Ibelin observed as the remaining sailors disembarked. Below the waist they wore long, baggy braies that ended just below the knee, leaving their calves and feet bare. On their upper bodies they wore shirts with short sleeves, open at the neck but bound at the waist by thick leather belts. Prominently displayed in the belts were long, curved knives, shorter straight knives, and in one case a sling. Their skin was darkly tanned, their hair long and unkempt, and they were all bearded, though only the monk wore a beard long enough to reach his chest.

John had not translated his father's remark, and Father Andronikos did not request one. He announced instead: "The monk is Brother Zotikos of Antipho-nitis."

John, having passed the message, added in a whisper, "I recognize him! He's the same monk who told the men in Famagusta it was as wise to kill a little viper as a big one—meaning me."

His father turned and stared at him in shock; John had forgotten that he'd told his *mother* of the incident in Famagusta, but not his father. "I'll tell you later!" he promised, as there was no time for an explanation now. Brother Zotikos was striding toward them, his eyes burning with hatred.

From the top of the escarpment, Sir Galvin and Ibelin's other men watched anxiously. They shared Ibelin's assessment of the sailors, and while they could not see Brother Zotikos' eyes, they hardly needed to. His every gesture exuded hostility and aggression, so much so that Barry lowered his head and curled his lips in a threatening stance. Sir Galvin glanced over his shoulder to Sir Sergios. The Maronite Syrian had served the Count of Tripoli at Hattin, but had been fighting under Ibelin's banner ever since the great armed pilgrimage from the West that had wrested control of the coast back from Saladin. He was a superb archer, and he already had his bow out of its case. His quiver hung from the pommel of his saddle.

Sir Galvin nodded to him, and he fitted an arrow onto the string, lifted the bow, pulled the string back to his ear, and looked down the arrow with narrowed eyes at his target: the Greek monk's broad chest. He nodded, then gently eased the string back to the uncocked position, yet kept the arrow notched. At this range, he was confident he could kill the Greek monk before he could do any harm to their lord.

None of Ibelin's men could hear what was being said, but they could see the monk gesturing wildly with his arms. He threw them out wide, then rotated his right arm like a windmill. Then his hands formed fists that he held under Ibelin's nose. A moment later he thrust out an index finger and jabbed the air in front of Ibelin's face—eliciting an angry warning bark from Barry, whom John was visibly restraining from attacking.

Throughout it all, Ibelin appeared impassive. His stance was relaxed, his arms akimbo, his weight on his right leg with his left bent and slightly forward. His men recognized he was actually poised to swing his weight forward with his right fist if he needed to. Compared to the apparent flood of words that accompanied the dramatic gestures of the monk, Ibelin appeared to say very little. Once or twice he lifted his head as if to make a short remark. Each time his words provoked a new round of angry gestures from the monk, followed by increasingly violent gestures from Barry.

Once Father Andronikos tried to intervene, only to harvest a series of stabs with an index finger in his direction from the younger cleric. John, meanwhile, was having trouble holding his dog, and was clearly distressed, confused, and a little frightened. He looked at his father for guidance, but the elder Ibelin remained calm, signaling for him to restrain the dog.

"I don't think things are going well," Sir Galvin observed generally, and Georgios shook his head sadly.

Abruptly, Ibelin turned his back on the monk and started back up the escarpment. The monk shouted furiously after him, making Georgios wince at the crude threat. Sir Galvin looked over, on the brink of asking for a translation, but then thought better of it. On the beach Father Andronikos was evidently trying to reason with the angry young monk, his hand on the latter's arm. The younger man shook him off, and with a violent, dismissive gesture started striding toward his boat. The sailors were already shoving it back into the water; the stern floated while the bow remained on the sand, ready for Zotikos to re-board.

Ibelin reached the top of the escarpment slightly breathless from the climb, and held out his hand for his sword belt. "Hopeless!" he announced to his men, snatching the belt and wrapping it around his waist to buckle it snugly. "He insists that they will keep fighting until we are either driven from the island like the Templars, or all dead." He grabbed the reins of his stallion, threw them back over the horse's head, and gathered them up as he pointed his toe in the stirrup to haul himself into the saddle.

He was so agitated that he swung his horse around and started to ride off before John had had a chance to mount. Then he caught himself and waited, his expression grim.

"So they wouldn't consider exchanging the abbot for Toron?" Sir Galvin asked, puzzled and disbelieving.

"No. That monk is a fanatic. He is incapable of compromise or negotiation. Saladin was pure reason compared to him!"

John's seat hit the saddle, and his father set his horse into a canter from a standstill. He had rarely been so angry. Most of all, he hated to think that his nephew Henri de Brie was right: that the only answer to this rebellion was to crush it with unrelenting and merciless force.

Paphos

It was a long time since Maria Zoë had seen her husband this upset. He could not sit still, but instead paced around the hall, the heels of his boots clacking on the marble floor. It had been dusk by the time he and his knights had returned, and the bells ringing across the town to the north now marked vespers. Georgios entered with a burning reed with which to light the lamps, and as he went from one brass lamp to the next, the mosaics on the walls began to glint in the firelight. In the groined arches overhead, the gold stars painted on the blue field caught the light of the lamps and began to twinkle. It was for this reason that Maria Zoë loved this room after dark.

In his present mood, however, her husband had no eye for the beauty around him. "The man's a fanatic," he kept repeating. "A blind fanatic who cares nothing about the cost of his intransigence. He literally said he would rather see the entire island go up in flames than give us a single a province, a single city, a single inch of his 'sacred' Cyprus! He was no more rational than John's damned dog!"

"And does he answer to no one?" Maria Zoë asked cautiously. "Surely a man so young is not the leader of the entire rebellion?"

"He *said* he answered only to God!" Balian scoffed.

"But he is a monk. He must have vowed obedience to his superiors."

"Yes! The abbot whom Barlais so *stupidly* threw in his dungeon," Ibelin snapped back. "I think we did this damned madman a favor by freeing him of any restraining voice of reason!"

"Do you think that if you released the abbot, he might be able to bring his subordinate to reason?"

"After a month in Barlais' tender care? The abbot is more likely to have been radicalized himself! Prison rarely breaks strong men. Think of Reynald de Châtillon. He endured fifteen *years* in horrible conditions to emerge more violent and hate-filled than ever before. My fear—"

A knock on the door silenced Balian; he cut himself off to call out, "Yes?"

The door opened and Georgios bowed. "My lord, Father Andronikos is here and begs an audience."

Balian shrugged and gestured for the squire to bring him in. As they waited, he remarked to his wife, "Father Andronikos is not to blame for this outcome. I believe he is sincere in wanting peace."

Maria Zoë nodded agreement, and then rose to her feet as the Greek priest was ushered in. Father Andronikos bowed his head first to her and then to her husband. Balian indicated he should take a seat, and sent Georgios for wine and nuts.

"I won't stay long," Father Andronikos countered. "I simply came to beg a favor of you, my lord."

Balian raised his eyebrows as his wife translated, and indicated with open palms that the priest should continue.

"There is a very wise man on this island, a highly educated hermit, who lives in a cave less than a day from here. He—he is greatly venerated among the people of this island. Many believe he is a living saint." Father Andronikos paused so Maria Zoë could translate.

As she finished, Balian pressed him to continue with an audibly skeptical, "Yes?"

"I want you to come with me to meet him," Father Andronikos confessed.

"Alone, I presume," Balian noted cynically as his wife translated.

"With your son, or your Greek squire—but no other men, and unarmed."

Balian nodded, his expression grim, when she explained the terms. "I thought as much," he remarked sharply.

"This is not a trap, my lord, I swear it upon my soul," Father Andronikos assured him, clasping the silver cross he wore on his breast. "I have taken the captive Frankish lord there for safekeeping as well. You will be able to see him if you come with me."

Maria Zoë could not restrain her own excitement as she passed this information to Balian. The news made Balian catch his breath, and they held each other's eyes for a moment as Father Andronikos continued. "Father Neophytos is very strict about excluding women from his monastery," Father Andronikos explained apologetically to Maria Zoë in Greek, "or I would welcome your presence on our journey, my lady."

"No," Balian said sharply, mistaking the meaning of the monk's remarks so evidently directed at his wife rather than himself. Answering what he thought the monk had said rather than his actual words, he announced, "My lady and my son stay here. I will travel with Georgios alone. When do we leave?"

"If we can leave just before dawn, my lord, that would be best. From the northern gate."

Balian nodded agreement, and through his wife answered, "I will meet you there at dawn."

By midmorning, the trail into the wooded flank of Troodos had become so steep and rocky that Ibelin had to dismount and lead his palfrey Hermes. The stallion was not happy, and kept stopping to look around as if he expected lions to jump out at him from the surrounding woods. To a horse born and raised in Palestine, forests were strange and dangerous places.

Ibelin wished he didn't share his stallion's apprehension. There was, he thought, something primordial about a forest as thick, dense, and tall as the one that surrounded them. The trees reached forty or fifty feet into the sky, higher than any mast he had ever seen; their trunks were broader than a man could embrace with his arms, and their roots twisted between the rocks with the power to crumble them.

As they climbed higher and deeper into the forest, a silence encased them. The sound of the sea was long since silenced; they were nowhere near habitation, and even the wind seemed to have been absorbed by the trees. There was just the chink of hooves on the rocky trail and their own heavy breathing—and the birds, of course. They called sharply overhead or twittered near at hand. Large birds of prey occasionally flew up, startling Hermes into abrupt sideward leaps or making him stand quivering as he looked about expecting the next attack.

Just about noon, when Ibelin was hot, sweaty, and hungry, Father Andronikos turned sharply to the left, leading them down an even narrower path that wound its way in zigzags down a fold in the mountain to emerge in a clearing beside a stream. On the far side of the clearing, a sheer rock outcropping reared up, pierced by several caves that opened some fifteen feet above the valley floor.

To the right, beside the stream, was a small chapel, and beyond it several flat-roofed huts.

Several monks emerged out of one of the houses, and one came to meet the three men. He crossed the stream on stepping stones while holding the skirts of his black robes out of the water. Father Andronikos went forward to meet him and they spoke together in low voices, the monk frowning darkly at Ibelin and Georgios. "He's protesting our presence, my lord," Georgios whispered. "He says Father Andronikos had no right to bring Latins here."

Father Andronikos did not appear intimidated, and answered calmly. Georgios narrated: "He is vouching for us, my lord. He insists that we be allowed to see Father Neophytos."

The local monk answered sharply, gesturing angrily, but then he turned and splashed back to the far shore, ignoring the stepping stones and getting his bare feet wet, but still holding the skirts of his cassock out of the water. Father Andronikos followed him, but Ibelin and Georgios opted to remount for the crossing and arrived on the far shore dry-footed.

Here they were required to dismount again, and Father Andronikos asked them to wait while he went to the face of the rock and called up in the direction of the caves. After he had done this twice, a rope ladder was flung out of the cave, and Father Andronikos hauled himself up the face of the cliff one difficult step at a time until he reached the ledge outside the entrance. He left the ladder and disappeared inside the cave.

After that, nothing happened for a long time. Ibelin considered his surroundings. The stillness of the forest was broken by the gurgling of the stream, which rendered it less ominous. Furthermore, to build the church and dwellings, the forest had been felled, expanding the clearing. As a result, the sun poured down, bright and warming. Because they were surrounded on all sides by higher peaks and slopes, there was no wind. Protected from wind and warmed by the sun, the little valley was already ablaze with wildflowers, and the grass was long and rich. The two horses were grazing contentedly, occasionally expressing their satisfaction with short, conversational snorts.

"*Kirios* Ibelin!" The voice came from the ledge before the cave. Father Andronikos was standing there waving. "Ela!" (Come).

Ibelin and Georgios got to their feet, and Ibelin led the way up the ladder. As he reached the ledge before the entrance, Father Andronikos backed up into the cave, as there was room for only one man on the ledge at a time. Ibelin ducked through the entrance and immediately caught his breath in amazement and wonder. He was standing in the nave of a church carved completely out of bedrock. Even more astonishing, the walls were adorned with paintings in vivid colors. Lifelike and life-sized figures on the narrow wall to his left depicted a tall golden-haired angel with spread golden wings hovering over a kneeling maiden: the Annunciation. Along the wall ahead of him, in painted arches, were the Nativity, Christ teaching in the Temple, Christ sharing the loaves, Christ turning water to wine, Christ walking on the Sea of Galilee. . . .

Behind him Georgios gasped as he too stepped inside the stone church. Ibelin glanced over his shoulder at his awestruck squire with a smile of shared emotion. These were some of the most beautiful paintings either of them had ever seen—not excluding the paintings in the Holy Sepulcher, Nazareth, and Bethlehem.

Father Andronikos was standing at the wooden screens dividing the far bay of the little church from the nave they had entered. He was smiling faintly, evidently enjoying their reaction. "Father Neophytos brought a famous artist from Constantinople to do the painting. Your wife may have heard of him," Father Andronikos remarked: "Theodoros Apseudes."

Ibelin nodded absently as Georgios translated in an awed whisper. It wasn't that Georgios had ever heard of the artist, but *anyone* brought from Constantinople sounded impressive, and the graceful vitality of the paintings spoke for themselves.

"Come." Father Andronikos gestured again for them to come with him through the screens, and somewhat hesitantly Ibelin and Georgios followed. They found themselves in a small semicircular chamber from which another door led out the far side. On their right, however, an altar carved out of rock was lit by several candles that burned on either side of a silver icon showing the Virgin with Christ in her arms.

Ibelin and Georgios both went down on one knee facing the altar and crossed themselves. Ibelin said a Pater Noster, adding at the end a formless prayer for assistance from the Prince of Peace. When he finished, he found the door from the room beyond filled with a tall, thin monk with a gray beard that was longer, though not as full, as Father Andronikos'. Ibelin got to his feet, but respectfully bowed his head to the old man.

"You are a Frankish lord," the old man said in a firm, dry voice.

Georgios whispered the translation into his ear from behind, and Balian answered, "Yes. I am Balian, Baron of—"

"Ibelin. I know. You defended Jerusalem against the infidel Saracen."

It surprised Ibelin that Father Andronikos had provided such a comprehensive biography, but he bowed his head in acknowledgment.

"Do not mistake a conscious decision to withdraw from the world for ignorance, Frank. I do not like living among the temptations of the world, but I keep myself very well informed of world affairs." The hermit paused for Georgios to perform the translation. Then he continued, "When I was younger, I sought advice and guidance from several hermits in the Holy Land, but my bishop insisted that I had no right to keep my inspired insights to myself. He made me take disciples. By recording my thoughts, I can reach many men—even women—without having to see but a very few, or none at all of the latter." Again he paused for the translation.

Ibelin nodded, and Father Neophytos continued, "I do not write simply about theology. I have been recording the events of the world, particularly as they affect this island, because they may well indicate that the end of the world is coming. Since the death of Manuel I, Constantinople has fallen into the hands of unholy men, while holy Cyprus has been visited by the tyranny of the cruel and rapacious Isaac Comnenus. Worst of all: Jerusalem has fallen to the infidels. A dire omen."

Ibelin was discomfited as Georgios translated this last sentence. He wondered just how much guilt for the loss of Jerusalem the Cypriot monk placed on his individual shoulders.

"Not all the armies of the West could drive the infidels out of the Holy Land," the monk continued. "Rather, they brought new horrors, for although the English King ended the rule of terror by Isaac Comnenus, the traitorous scoundrel turned around and sold this sacred island—as if it were nothing more than a pasture or a piece of livestock—to that horde of money-grubbing abominations that call themselves by the heathen name of the Knights of the Temple! How do men dare to call themselves Christian monks when they bear arms? How dare they take their name from the Jewish Temple? Surely they must know they are an offense to God!"

As Georgios translated this lengthy diatribe, Ibelin began to wonder if he'd been dragged all the way here just to hear a lecture against the Templars.

The Cypriot monk continued, his voice getting louder and angrier. "And as if that weren't enough, after the God-fearing people of Cyprus had driven the offensive Jew-loving Templars away, the English scoundrel sold the island yet *again*, only this time to that notorious instrument of the devil: Guy de Lusignan!" The monk was clearly working himself into a rage, and Ibelin needed no translation to know he was now talking about "Guy de Lusignan"— though he had not thought of Guy as an "instrument of the devil" before Georgios provided the translation.

"Since his arrival on this island, we have had no peace. Rather, we are smitten with one calamity after another. Anyone who can afford to leave has fled, leaving behind the poor, the helpless, and the uneducated. This island, the birthplace of love and beloved of the apostles, is daily becoming poorer and more benighted."

"It is, isn't it?" Ibelin snapped back, when the last was translated for him.

The interruption and his tone took the hermit-monk by surprise. He started visibly and fell silent with a puzzled, angry look at Father Andronikos.

Ibelin took advantage of this break in the monk's monologue to launch into a speech of his own. It had not been prepared, but the intensity of his feelings gave him words. "This island is suffering from a lack of government. Pirates control the sea lanes, and smugglers clog the ports. Everyone who can, enriches himself at the expense of his neighbors, and no one looks after the common good of the people. The aqueducts spill their water in the wilderness rather than feeding the fountains of the cities. The sewers pour their infectious odors into the homes of rich and poor alike." Georgios translated all this in a rush of words, his heart pounding in fear at the audaciousness of his lord toward such a holy man.

Father Neophytos was too astonished to respond at once, and Ibelin continued, asking provocatively, "And why? Because people—monks—have set themselves up in the place of emperors and governors. People no longer respect the proper authorities, nor obey the laws, nor pay taxes. Lawlessness is spreading, and with it comes the tyranny of anarchy."

Ibelin waited for his words to be translated, and saw the holy hermit lift his chin and look at him with piercing, intelligent eyes while Georgios delivered his words in Greek. He watched as the anger was replaced by something closer to surprise, if not respect. As Georgios' translation ended, the hermit remarked simply, "You speak the truth."

Ibelin understood the word "*alithea*"—truth—and breathed out a little.

The monk continued with a question: "So we agree on the diagnosis. What do you propose as the cure?"

"Aimery de Lusignan is not Guy. He is a wise and prudent man. He would bring peace and prosperity to this island, if given a chance. He has asked me to help bring peace."

The hermit turned to Father Andronikos with a question, but Father Andronikos shook his head and looked at Georgios. The squire put the question to his lord. "He asked, why you? Why did Aimery not come himself?"

"Tell him kings do not negotiate; they send envoys and ambassadors."

"Aimery isn't a king," Georgios pointed out anxiously.

"He means to be. Tell Father Neophytos what I have said."

Georgios did what he was told and received the next question. "Is it true your master negotiated the peace between the English King and the infidel Sultan Saladin?"

"It is," Georgios answered for his lord.

"Then I am honored." The hermit let a smile flit over his lined face. "Let us sit." He backed out of the little church, and Father Andronikos gestured for Ibelin and Georgios to follow him into the final room. This was more spacious than the altar room, although much smaller than the nave. It was as beautifully painted as the rooms before, and in addition offered modest creature comforts such as a ledge carved out of rock on which a straw mattress lay, and another bench carved along the far side behind a stone table. The monk sat on his bed and indicated that Ibelin should sit on the bench behind the table. Ibelin did so warily, not sure what to expect now.

"What terms does Aimery de Lusignan offer in exchange for peace?" the hermit asked via Georgios.

"First, the release of Humphrey de Toron in exchange for the release of the abbot and monks of Antiphonitis."

The hermit nodded but made no comment in response, so Georgios looked back at his lord and nodded for him to continue.

"Second, the restoration of the laws of Manuel I Comnenus for the native inhabitants of the island, and their own courts and churches."

The monk cut Georgios' translation short to ask sharply, "*Ecclisies?*" Churches?

Again, Ibelin understood the word; having a wife who was a native speaker and two sons who were learning rapidly had started to improve his own understanding. He answered in Greek, "*Ne, ecclisies.*" Yes, churches.

The monk still didn't seem to believe him, and turned to Georgios. "He said we will be allowed to retain our own churches?"

"Yes, courts and churches."

Surmising that the hermit was questioning his promise, Ibelin told his squire: "Remind him that we never suppressed the Greek, Maronite, Jacobite, or Armenian churches in the Kingdom of Jerusalem."

The hermit nodded thoughtfully once this was conveyed to him by Georgios, and then muttered, "This too is true. I traveled across the Holy Land, and Greek and Latin clergy shared many churches and monasteries. Indeed, new Greek churches and monasteries were built under Frankish rule." He was speaking more to himself than to Ibelin, but Georgios translated nevertheless. Neophytos nodded again, and then announced, "I must pray. Leave me." He made a gesture of dismissal, and Ibelin got to his feet, bowed his head respectfully, and returned the way he'd come. Father Andronikos, however, lingered longer in the little cell, the recipient of a flood of instructions from the hermit.

Georgios tensed and grabbed his lord's arm. "My lord! I think, if I heard correctly, he just ordered Toron's release. As a goodwill gesture. He said that will test the truth of your words, and it is the Christian thing to do."

"Are you sure?"

"No, but we'll soon find out."

Father Andronikos took his leave of Father Neophytos, and as he emerged from the altar room, the smile on his face said it all.

Humphrey was not unhappy. Indeed, in some ways he had never been happier. The monks hardly spoke, so he was not plagued with questions, critique, or even inanities. In the isolated little monastery there were no problems, no crises, no threats, no risks, nothing but peace. One heard Mass five times a day, and in between one ate, slept, and did household chores like cleaning, tending the kitchen garden, preparing meals, and darning clothes. The monks here spun and wove their own cloth. They also grew vegetables and raised ducks and chickens. Humphrey was not confronted by his failure here—until he looked up from scattering feed to the cackling and fluttering chickens and saw his former father-in-law coming toward him.

In his astonishment he exclaimed, "Uncle Balian!" It was a form of address that he'd picked up from Isabella when they were still children imprisoned at Kerak under the iron fist of his stepfather, Reynald de Châtillon. He had not used it since that horrible day in Acre when Ibelin had turned his back on him. All because he'd supported Lusignan's usurpation in 1186.

It made no sense that he was here in this isolated Greek monastery.

Ibelin started visibly at being called "Uncle Balian," but then his face softened and he came forward more quickly. "Humphrey, I hardly recognized you in those robes."

It was true Humphrey was dressed as a monk, but that was not the reason Balian had failed to recognize him. Balian had not immediately realized he was facing Humphrey because Toron looked twice his age. He was thin, haggard, frail, and losing his hair.

"Are you here—because of me?" Humphrey asked in disbelief. When Father Andronikos said his "friends" had not forgotten him, he had not once thought of his former father-in-law. Aimery de Lusignan, even Henri de Brie, but never Balian.

"Yes. Father Neophytos has released you to me. You can come back to Paphos with me. If we leave now, we should be back before nightfall."

"Paphos?" Humphrey asked.

"Yes; my lady is there. She will be very relieved to see you safe and sound."

"Isabella's mother?" Humphrey asked, dazed.

"Yes," Ibelin assured him, beginning to think Humphrey was not right in the head.

Humphrey shook his head. He couldn't bear the thought of facing the Dowager Queen. She had been the one who talked Isabella into turning on him. She had been the one who told Isabella that she must choose between her crown and her husband. And even worse. Humphrey instinctively took a step backwards, away from Ibelin. Isabella, he was thinking, probably told her mother that he had never consummated their marriage. The Dowager Queen knew he had failed to fulfill his marital duties. The others might suspect—they might call him a sodomist in their ignorance—but she *knew* the truth.

"You cannot think that my lady holds anything against you." Ibelin tried to reason with Humphrey, dismayed by his reaction.

Humphrey shook his head ambiguously, and then announced, "I don't want to leave. I am happy here."

Ibelin frowned slightly and glanced over his shoulder at Georgios. His squire could only shake his head to indicate he was as perplexed as his lord.

"I should have been a monk!" Humphrey burst out in an unintended confession. He had not really thought about it before this moment—but suddenly, confronted with the choice between staying with the monks at this isolated monastery and returning to the pressures and humiliations of his former life, he realized that it was *before* he came here that he'd worn the wrong clothes. He had played the wrong role his whole life.

"I was never good at fighting," he reminded Ibelin. And chastity, he added silently, suited him better than marriage. His failings in the bedchamber had always disappointed Isabella. They had turned her against him. If he had not been expected to consummate their marriage, they could have remained best friends, just as when they were still children. To Ibelin he said defiantly, "You never valued my strengths—that I could read and write in three languages, that I had read the works of the ancients, that I could write poetry and play instruments. . . ."

"You are wrong, Humphrey," Balian answered solemnly. "I did—and do—value your intelligence and your studiousness. I always defended you, even to others, as a good soul. What I could not condone was that you should become king—not after you betrayed us at Nablus. You bear the blame for Hattin, for the loss of Jerusalem, for the slaughter of thousands and the enslavement of many more—"

"DO YOU THINK I DON'T KNOW THAT?" Humphrey shouted at him. "Do you think there is a night that I sleep in peace? You have no idea of my nightmares! I had to watch them slaughtering the Templars and Hospitallers!

They haunt me constantly! I spend half my waking hours begging their forgive-ness. And the forgiveness of God."

They stared at one another for a moment, and then Ibelin took a deep breath and nodded. "If that is so, then it is indeed best that you stay here where you can pray in peace—assuming you truly feel safe here?"

"I have rarely felt so safe, or so at peace, in all my life," Humphrey answered, so sincerely he sounded almost angry.

Ibelin nodded. "Then, if that is what you want, I will leave you here. I must return to Nicosia to bring word to Aimery of what we must do to bring peace to this island."

Humphrey nodded. "Yes. That is what I want." He sounded defiant, even a little petulant, as he declared this, and in his eyes was a challenge, as if he dared Ibelin to contradict him.

Balian, however, with an inward wince of contrition, recognized that it was guilt, not captivity, that had ravaged Humphrey's young face and body. As he recognized that, he felt the anger he had carried with him for far too long seep away like melting snow. As his anger dissipated, his heart softened as well. It was past time to forgive Humphrey for his betrayal.

Balian crossed the distance between them. Before Humphrey knew what was happening, he embraced him. "I am sorry that you were your father's only son," he told Humphrey earnestly. "Sorry you were forced to bear a cross too heavy for you. I have judged you too harshly, and I ask you to forgive me for that. I should have been more understanding." He paused to let the words sink in before adding, "I will tell Isabella that you are at last where you belong, and at peace. It will be a comfort to her, because she loves you still."

"Truly?" Humphrey asked, brightening at the mere thought.

"Truly," Balian told him, drawing back to look him in the eye. It was, he thought, the least he could do for a young man who had suffered far too much only for being what he was, rather than what he should have been.

Chapter Sixteen
The Light at Dawn

Nicosia,
April 1195

ESCHIVA LOVED THE WALLED GARDEN. IT had a fountain in the center, cypress trees in the corners, and potted palms, hibiscus, and oleander in the arches of the surrounding arcade. Protected from the wind, it was never really cold, and the arcade offered shade, ensuring it was never too hot, either. Here she could sit and spin or sew while Joscelyn read or sang to her.

Although the youth could walk again, the injury had been too severe for him to fully recover the strength and agility needed to resume an active life. A future as a Mamluke was as closed to him as a future as a knight or even a squire. He would remain a quasi-invalid with a severe limp the rest of his life. Surprisingly, he had accepted this fate with far more equanimity than his mother or anyone else had expected. It seemed as if the injury had resolved his conflict of loyalty. Now that he could serve neither his "master" al-Adil nor his "lord" the Baron of Ibelin, Joscelyn was free to choose a profession that did not involve taking sides at all. He was determined to become a surgeon or apothecary, although it was not yet settled where and how such an undertaking could be arranged and financed. Meanwhile he served as a willing companion to Eschiva, while Beatrice handled the day-to-day running of the household.

Eschiva sometimes felt guilty for not being more active in the household, but she still felt very weak—almost perpetually exhausted—and occasionally still had dizzy spells. She presumed this was because she was pregnant again, and her fear of losing this latest child made her all the more cautious. She was determined to carry this child to term even if it meant she hardly set foot outside her chamber, let alone the palace. After this next child was born, she promised herself, she would take up her duties as Lady of Cyprus. Just another five months, and she would be become more active. . . .

Voices echoed in the passageway to her right, and she looked up to see Aimery burst in. He was dressed for riding in leather boots and hose. His hair was wind-blown, his face reddened by the sun and exertion. "My love!" He strode across the garden toward her, and pushed her down as she tried to rise to greet him. "Sit! Sit! I'll join you." He dropped down on the bench at her side, and took her hand in both of his. "Geoffrey's ship put into Kyrenia at last! He delivered a formal written renunciation of his rights to Cyprus or anywhere else in Outremer!"

Eschiva was surprised by how elated her husband sounded. "Did you ever doubt Magnussen's word?" she asked.

"*I* didn't, but Barlais and Cheneché certainly did!" Aimery reminded her. "Now they have both caved in and are vying with one another to assure me they supported me all along! Hypocritical bastards!" Aimery was grinning as he spoke, betraying how much his relief outweighed his resentment.

"I saw Renier de Jubail off as well," Aimery continued, dropping his voice slightly and glancing at Joscelyn.

"Leave us, Joscelyn," Eschiva suggested with a smile, and the youth dutifully set the book on the bench and slipped out. Aimery watched him go, and then got up and followed to make sure he wasn't lurking in the passageway. Apparently he was, because Eschiva heard her husband say, "Go on! Fetch me lime sherbet and pistachios!"

Returning, Aimery sat down beside Eschiva, took her hand again, and continued, "The Archdeacon of Latakia sailed two days ago with my message to the Pope, and Jubail put to sea yesterday with my letter to Emperor Henry VI."

Eschiva was very supportive of her husband's appeal to the Pope to elevate Cyprus to a kingdom. She recognized the advantages to her husband and her son, when the time came, of being crowned and anointed. She also saw that it was important to establish Cyprus' independence from Jerusalem—as long as Henri de Champagne was king there. Although Aimery's arrest by Champagne had been brief—thanks to the intercession of her uncle and other members of the High Court—she could not forgive Champagne for what he had done. The mere thought of that night when he sent men to drag her husband from his bed for a crime he had not committed made her blood boil. She was as determined as her husband, if not more, that he never again bend his knee to Champagne. If they ever met again, she vowed to herself, it would be as equals.

She was less comfortable, however, with the idea of Aimery ceding Cyprus to the Holy Roman Empire and doing homage to the Holy Roman Emperor for it. Aimery had explained the logic: he needed protection from Constantinople, which had never accepted Isaac Comnenus' secession from the Greek Empire or Richard of England's conquest, much less Templar or Lusignan rule. Twice the Greek Emperors had equipped and sent fleets to regain control of the island. Aimery was convinced that the rebels, too, had ties to Constantinople. He needed an ally against Constantinople, an ally strong enough to deter attack. Jerusalem, Tripoli, and Antioch were too weak to help them—and Aimery would *never* ask a favor of Champagne anyway. The Armenians were gaining strength, but they were not a seafaring people, and so not much help if faced with a fleet from Constantinople. The Holy Roman Emperor Henry VI, on the other hand, had a tradition of hostility toward Constantinople, and he now controlled Sicily, which had a powerful fleet.

Eschiva understood all that, but she still detested the man for the way he'd treated the English King. She considered Henry VI a treacherous, unscrupulous rat, and she didn't like the thought of her husband taking an oath of fealty to him. But she had voiced her reservations as forcefully as she dared earlier, and held her tongue now.

"With luck, we could have an answer before the sailing season closes. Maybe in time for your next confinement," Aimery announced, laying a hand on her belly with a smile. Eschiva smiled back and put her hand on top of her husband's for a moment. It pleased her that he was taking such a strong interest in this child. It was their seventh, after all. Many men lost interest after they had secured an heir, and Guy was growing like a beanstalk at the moment, thriving visibly.

"I've decided to christen him Hugh, after the founder of the Lusignan dynasty," Aimery declared, patting her belly before removing his hand.

"And if it's a girl?" Eschiva asked.

"Then we'll name her after you," he answered with a shrug. "But this one is a boy. I'm sure of it."

Eschiva nodded, knowing that he couldn't possibly know.

"The other thing I wanted to tell you is that Ibelin thinks he has a solid agreement."

Eschiva sat up straighter and held her breath. For three weeks her uncle had been negotiating with the abbot of Antiphonitis and Father Neophytos on Aimery's behalf. "The Greeks want us to celebrate 'reconciliation' in a joint Mass in their cathedral with the Archbishop officiating." Aimery's tone reflected his uncertainty.

"There's no harm in that," Eschiva encouraged him.

"It means kneeling down in front of their archbishop."

"It means kneeling down before *Our Lord*!" Eschiva corrected him firmly.

Aimery nodded his head, but his expression suggested he remained unconvinced. "They want a public display of us recognizing their church and clergy. They specifically demanded that not only all my knights participate, but that you and Guy do so as well."

"That's a good sign," Eschiva told him.

"How? What do you mean?"

"The participation of your son and heir is intended to bind him publicly and in the eyes of God to this agreement, but it is also a pledge by the Greek clergy to recognize *him* as your heir."

"I worry that such a public pageant—procession on foot from here to the cathedral and back, not to mention a three-hour church service—will exhaust you," Aimery admitted, his eyes full of worry. It had not escaped him that Eschiva had not recovered from her miscarriage, nor that she was paler than ever he remembered, her skin almost transparent.

Eschiva reached up and hooked her hand behind his neck to draw his face down for a kiss. "Thank you for worrying about me," she told him warmly, before releasing his head and declaring in a more practical tone, "Did you know Maria Zoë found her coronation robe in a chest here when she was doing the inventory? She sold it to Isaac Comnenus back in 1188, when she and Uncle Balian had lost everything after Hattin. Isaac, being a usurper, was keen to have anything that hinted at legitimacy, and Maria Zoë exploited his insecurity to sell him first her coronation crown and then her coronation robe. Richard of England apparently took and kept the crown, but didn't have an eye for women's clothes. He probably didn't even think to look for valuables in the clothing chests of Isaac's wife! Maria Zoë found it, but she has outgrown it, of course: it was made for a thirteen-year-old. I certainly can't wear it in my condition, but Burgundia would look lovely in it. It is in the style of the Eastern Empire, with broad bands of gold embroidery studded with pearls." She smiled up at her husband.

Aimery considered her with a bemused expression. "You're saying not only that you want me to go through with this, but also that you want me to bring our younger children to Cyprus, aren't you?"

"Yes, I am. It's time for them to start identifying with this island as their future.

"It's the best white wine on the whole island," John declared enthusiastically as he poured for his parents. They were celebrating the successful conclusion of a peace agreement between the Greek Patriarch and Aimery de Lusignan in private. The real spirit behind the agreement had been Father Neophytos, but he had no official position, and the Patriarch was recognized by the entire Greek population as an authority. Ibelin, however, was in some ways even more gratified by the fact that his nephew Henri, along with Barlais and Cheneché, had also embraced the peace. The latter expressed doubts about whether the peace would hold, but all agreed that it was worth trying.

Balian himself was astonished by how good he genuinely felt. His last two forays into diplomacy had ended "successfully"—but at incredible cost. The first, the surrender of Jerusalem in 1187, had saved the lives and freedom of three-quarters of the Christian population, but left the Holy City itself and its poorest inhabitants in Saracen hands. The second, the Treaty of Ramla in 1192, had secured the coast of the Levant for the Franks, but left his own heritage of Ibelin and Ramla and his wife's dower of Nablus in Saracen hands. The agreement they celebrated today (not a treaty, as it was not between sovereign powers) was far more modest. It might not even find a mention in the chronicles, but it was more satisfying because Balian could see no drawbacks to it.

The Greek churches were to retain not only their structures but their tithes, and Latin churches would be built on royal land and draw revenues from land allotted to them from the royal domain. Furthermore, the laws of Manuel I were to be reinstated, with all customs, taxes, and tolls at the same rates as in the last year of his reign. The penalties for criminal and civil offenses for the Greek population were likewise to be restored to those of the last Comnenus; only treason and other crimes against the "Crown" were to be tried in Latin courts on the basis of the laws of the Kingdom of Jerusalem, which were to apply generally to the Frankish and other immigrant populations.

Maria Zoë lifted a red glass goblet, with crosses of gold enameled into it, and toasted her husband. "My lord! To the finest diplomat in Christendom!"

"With the grace of God," he modified before sipping the wine. His eyes widened and as he set the goblet down and he turned to his firstborn son to exclaim, "That *is* good! Where is it from?"

"A village called Paradisi." John pronounced it in the Greek fashion, as "Paradhisi." "It's on the south coast just east of the ruins of Salamis."

"We need to secure *barrels* of it," Balian concluded.

"I can see about that," John agreed with a smile. "But shouldn't I first take word to Father Andronikos about this agreement?"

His father dismissed the suggestion with a wave of his hand. "Father

Andronikos isn't important anymore. His intervention saved us from further bloodshed, and God will bless him for that, but at this point he has no further role to play."

"I know," John conceded, "but we should at least have the courtesy to tell him about the agreement and thank him."

"I thanked him most emphatically the very day that Father Neophytos agreed to intercede. Being a man of peace, the agreement itself is his greatest gratification."

"I'm sure," John agreed again, "but surely he has a right to hear the terms?"

"He'll hear them from his bishop, as will all the other priests on the island."

"But shouldn't he hear it *first*," John insisted (his tone was becoming decidedly impertinent), "since he was partly responsible? Surely you see—"

"What I see is a young man talking back to his father!" Balian snapped. "I've given you a great deal of freedom, John. Don't think that gives you the right to talk back to me as you never would have done to Lord Aimery. Don't forget you're still only fifteen, and you aren't knighted yet."

"I don't see what this has to do with my age or whether I'm knighted or not," John rejoined stubbornly, his jaw hardening in a way so similar to Balian's that Maria Zoë thought she was seeing her husband at fifteen. "All I said was that Father Andronikos deserves to hear about this agreement before—"

"I'm not deaf, and I can't see why this means so much to you—unless the real reason you want to ride halfway across the island is to see Father Andronikos' *daughter*."

This accusation took Maria Zoë completely by surprise, but the way John flushed and then started denying it in a breathless rush of outrage made it all too obvious that Balian had hit a nerve.

"*Now* we're at the root of things," Balian declared, sitting back and crossing his arms. "I hereby forbid you from *ever* going back to Kolossi! I won't have you dishonoring me—or such an honorable man of God as Father Andronikos—by debauching his innocent daughter!"

"Balian!" Maria Zoë exclaimed in shock. His accusation seemed groundless and his tone unjustified. But before she could say anything in the defense of her son, John jumped to his feet and shouted at his father, "You're not being fair! What have I ever done to make you think I'd dishonor Eirini? I'm not Haakon Magnussen or Amalric! You have no right—"

"I have every right!" Balian barked back, raising his own voice in face of so much impudence. "And if you keep on like this, I'll have you flogged."

"I'm not a child!" John shouted. "I won't stand here and let you insult me and humiliate me!" With these words, John flung his chair over on its side and strode toward the door. Despite his father's shout to turn around and come back, John charged out of the room and slammed the door behind him.

"He's going to regret this!" Balian announced with controlled anger, his jaw clenched.

"Frankly," Maria Zoë countered pointedly, "I think John was perfectly justified! You *were* being unfair. You have no grounds for imputing such dishonorable behavior to John. He has never been anything but honest, upright, and chivalrous in his dealings—"

"You haven't a clue what goes on inside a fifteen-year-old boy!" Balian scoffed. "They're all ruled by their loins, and when it comes to an attractive girl, they think with what's between their legs. I can't, and won't, risk having John shatter everything I've worked for! Imagine it: a Frankish youth rapes a Greek priest's daughter! The island would explode—"

"John isn't going to rape *anyone*, much less Father Andronikos' daughter!" Maria Zoë protested, losing her temper.

"Rape, seduce. What difference does it make? It—"

"Let me tell *you* that the difference is like to the difference between heaven and hell!" Maria Zoë cut him off furiously. "If you don't recognize that, then you're no better than—"

"This isn't about what the *girl* feels!" Balian cut her off. "It's about the way it would be *perceived* and *exploited* by the likes of Brother Zotikos! I don't give a damn if the girl seduces and rapes John! If she's deflowered by a Frank, everything I've worked for these past weeks is ruined!" Balian jumped to his feet and paced to the far side of the room to stand with his back to his wife.

Maria Zoë took a deep breath to get a grip on her anger. While she remained convinced that Balian was completely in the wrong, she also recognized that this outburst had more to do with his inner fears that something could still go wrong. She wanted to reassure her husband, and she wanted to reconcile him with his firstborn. She just wasn't sure how. The silence extended from seconds to minutes.

At last Balian turned around and returned to the table. He didn't sit, just took his glass and sipped from it standing. At last he looked at his wife, and the reproach in her eyes irritated him. "I know John doesn't intend to do anyone any harm," he told her firmly. "I know he's exceptionally responsible and mature for his age, but he's playing with fire and doesn't even know it! He doesn't *know* how unutterably powerful sexual desire can be!"

"Come," Maria Zoë tried to reason. "Are you saying you wouldn't have been able to control yourself at his age?" Maria Zoë tried to make it a joke, but it fell flat.

"That's *exactly* what I'm saying! Damn it! Why did he choose this time and this girl to lust after?"

"I expect," Maria Zoë observed dryly, "that he didn't *choose* either. Love is notorious for taking us all by surprise when and where we least expect it. I hardly intended to fall in love with a landless knight, either, you know. But let's not assume the worst. Sit down and drink with me. You forbade John from going to Kolossi. He won't defy you. He's a good boy."

But that's exactly what John did. He stormed out of the confrontation with his father, went to his chamber and packed a bunch of things in a saddlebag. He took all the money he owned, and then went to the stables, with Barry anxiously at his heels. Just as on that night when Lord Aimery had been arrested two years ago, he saddled his stallion in the dark and set off into the night. Now, as then, no one thought to stop the son and heir of Balian d'Ibelin.

He had ridden far beyond Nicosia and was on the treacherous highway to Limassol before the anger had burned itself out enough for him to moderate his pace and take stock of his situation. A part of his brain suggested he should turn around and return to Nicosia rather than pursue open defiance. He could express his indignation in other ways. He could seek his mother's intervention. He could appeal to Lord Aimery and Eschiva. He could treat his father with icy-cold politeness, freezing any attempt at friendliness.

But after considering his options, he concluded he couldn't go back. The injustice of his father's accusation drove him forward. He had never, *ever* done anything that anyone in their right mind might interpret as dishonorable when it came to women.

Taking pity on Troubadour and a lagging Barry, however, he dismounted, removed the saddle and bridle, and hobbled the horse where there was plenty of grass. He lay down on the saddle and took Barry into his arms (something the dog loved) to help keep him warm. Eventually he put himself to sleep with imaginary conversations in which he defended himself to his father. At dawn he rose unrested, re-tacked Troubadour, and set off again, with Barry loping along, tongue hanging out, at their heels.

John was beginning to fear his father would send men after him to bring him home, so he avoided villages as much as possible. He skirted any habitation, riding through open countryside. He paid a shepherd to share some cheese and bread with him, paying far too much and giving half to Barry. He regretted setting off in his Frankish clothes, remembering nostalgically his adventures in Greek attire.

On the second night he begged the hospitality of a peasant family. They were far too terrified of a Frankish "knight" to say no. Again he paid handsomely, particularly for meat for Barry, because he knew they had little to share. In return the housewife served him a generous breakfast and gave him bread and cheese for the next stage of his journey.

John spent his third night in Limassol, but far from the Templar commandery where he might be recognized and arrested on his father's orders, seeking a humble hostel instead. The other guests were mostly old, decrepit, and poor, and they looked askance at him and his big dog, but his silver remained welcome. The snoring and smells of the other guests in the common room, however, sent John to sleep in the stable. He climbed up into the hayloft and made his bed there, with Barry as his pillow.

In the morning he gave Barry a washing in a fountain and then found a bathhouse for himself. He indulged in a thorough cleaning and a haircut. He sent his underwear and shirt to a laundry while he steamed away the grime of the road. Thus it was midmorning before he embarked on the last stage of his journey to the village beyond Kolossi where Father Andronikos lived.

By now a new kind of nervousness had overtaken him. What if Eirini wasn't glad to see him? What if her father shared his father's views of his intentions?

He had already resolved to pretend he was representing his father and had come to share the terms of the agreement, but that wouldn't give him any excuse to be alone with Eirini. . . .

John's changing thoughts and moods produced an erratic pace. Sometimes he pressed ahead eagerly. Sometimes he slowed to a walk as he rehearsed speeches and imagined encounters in his head. He had already passed the turnoff to Kolossi when abruptly, out of a grove of trees, an armed knight burst out to block the road in front of him. John reached for his hilt as his heart leapt into his throat. It didn't help that he recognized Sir Galvin almost at once. John was (naively) more afraid of his father's wrath than he was of robbers.

"Been taking our sweet time about this trip, haven't we?" Sir Galvin mocked with a grin as he blocked the road.

John drew up. Sir Galvin was bigger, stronger, and more experienced in combat. He also rode a larger and heavier horse. Nor did it help that Barry recognized Sir Galvin as the man who often gave him scraps of meat and started wagging his tail in delight. The dog would be no help to him now, and John did not stand much of a chance trying to force his way through anyway. He didn't try. Instead he called out defiantly, "I'm not going to just turn around and go docilely back with you! You'll have to tie and gag me."

"Now why would I want to do that, laddie?" Sir Galvin asked with a grin. "You father simply suggested you shouldn't be riding about on your own at your tender age." That was a provocative and calculated insult, John noted furiously as the old knight continued, "He sent me to *escort* you."

Damn him! John thought resentfully. Now he would have someone watching his every move and word when he was with Eirini! He glowered sullenly at Sir Galvin for half a minute, while trying to think what he could do or say to shake off this unwanted "nursemaid," but his brain was empty. After another half-minute he conceded defeat and nodded.

Sir Galvin turned his horse on his haunches and fell in beside John, Barry trotting happily beside them, and John rode the remaining mile to the village where Father Andronikos lived in resentful silence. They arrived as the priest was ringing the little bell in the rectangular frame over the church door. He smiled and waved at them. "Welcome, welcome! Join me in thanking the dear Lord for your lord father, young Janis. He has worked a miracle."

"Did you *tell* him already?" John hissed furiously at Sir Galvin.

"How else was I to explain my presence?" Sir Galvin defended himself. "I was sure you would get here ahead of me, given your head start, so I rushed in, only to discover no one had seen hide nor hair of you. It was very awkward— especially considering my nearly nonexistent Greek. All I could do was stammer '*ola kala, o baron exei epitichi*' or something like that." (Everything's good, the baron was successful.) While Sir Galvin's French remained heavily accented by his native Scottish burr, his Greek was so badly mispronounced that John wondered how anyone could understand it at all; had he been in a better mood he would have laughed.

Meanwhile they both dismounted, tied up their horses, and proceeded into the church to join the women, children, and elderly streaming from various houses to the church for Mass. The men were evidently in the fields.

Father Andronikos' wife was in the first row on the women's side of the church, and Eirini was beside her. Eirini turned to see who had entered, and her face lit up into a smile before she covered her mouth with her hand and then hastened to face the screens. After that she dutifully kept her eyes ahead, crossing herself, kneeling, and giving the responses like a good priest's daughter.

John, however, couldn't keep his attention on the Mass. He looked over at Eirini so often that Sir Galvin stomped on his foot and hissed at him to "stop making a scene." John concentrated on the Mass for at least thirty seconds after that, but then he looked over again and this time met Eirini's eyes. She blushed sharply as she turned back to the front, only to look over her shoulder at him again almost at once.

Now he was sure! She was as excited to see him as he to see her.

When the Mass concluded, John crossed the aisle to bow before Eirini and her mother. He tried to direct his words to the elder woman, but he simply couldn't keep his eyes off Eirini. She stood demurely with her eyes down—except when she snuck little glances at him, her cheeks so infused with blood that they were the color of roses.

Father Andronikos came up behind John and Sir Galvin. Clapping his hands together, he suggested, "Come! Let us celebrate together."

"Yes, please. I so wanted to be the one to bring you the news—but Sir Galvin, I understand, beat me here."

"No matter, Janis," Father Andronikos assured him. "He couldn't tell me any details. I heard from Father Neophytos, however, that you accompanied your father to most of the negotiations." Father Andronikos sounded impressed, and John's chest swelled with pride because Eirini's eyes grew wide with wonder.

"Just as his squire," John hastened to explain, anxious not to seem like a braggart.

"Of course; what else at your age?" Father Andronikos remarked genially. "But very few young men have such an opportunity to be a witness to history. It must have been very exciting. You must tell us all about it!" He herded his guests, wife, and daughter toward his modest house, the Franks leading their horses, and Barry wagging his tail in anticipation of food.

Once inside, however, the women disappeared into the kitchen, and John could hardly discontinue his narrative and insist on waiting for Eirini. Fortunately, he hadn't got all that far in the story before Eirini emerged with a tray of refreshments. As she came to offer them to him, she briefly stood between her father and John, her back to her father, and she risked smiling straight at him. John felt as if his bones were melting, but he didn't dare say a word. He took a cup with a murmured "Thank you," and Eirini continued to Sir Galvin. Unfortunately, she returned to the kitchen as soon as the men all had something to drink, but John had to continue his narrative.

Eirini next returned with nuts and raisins, and after a few more minutes, she emerged to set the table. John sat a little straighter and spoke as loudly as he could without (he thought) being too obvious. Eirini studiously focused on the table, but she was so slow about her duties that her mother called out from the kitchen, asking what was keeping her. She finished in a hurry and darted back to the kitchen, only to re-emerge a few minutes later with two steaming platters of food. Her mother came after her, and Father Andronikos invited his guests to the table. He asked them all to join hands while he blessed the food, then with a smile gestured for them to sit. As he served, he launched into a lengthy speech about how delighted he was about the outcome of the negotiations.

"There's only one thing that disturbs me," Father Andronikos concluded, his tone taking on a serious note, in contrast to the optimistic tone that had prevailed up until now.

"Yes?" John asked attentively.

"Brother Zotikos," Father Andronikos answered, "has refused to accept the agreement."

"But his abbot," John started, "he—I mean—Brother Zotikos can't disobey . . . "

Father Andronikos took a deep breath and shook his head. "He should not—but, if what I have heard is right, he got very angry and accused the abbot and, indeed, the Patriarch of taking Frankish bribes. He said that they might be "corruptible," but he was not. He stormed out and has not been seen since. There are rumors. . . ."

"Yes?" John pressed him.

"He was very close to some notorious smugglers—not to say pirates. Particularly a man who goes by the name of Kanakes. It was his boat that brought Brother Zotikos to that first rendezvous with your father in Coral Bay."

John remembered that day vividly, and the way his father had said they all looked like a "bunch of pirates."

"Zotikos has vowed to continue the fight," Father Andronikos admitted with a sigh.

"Then this isn't peace?" John asked, confused.

"No, no. It's not as bad as that. The Patriarch has sanctioned this agreement and ordered the people to respect it. The vast majority of people want peace and truly praise Our Lord and Savior for this agreement. Things will calm down. I just wanted to warn you that Brother Zotikos may yet try to cause trouble. Now, if you're done, why don't you let me take you to see the ruins I told you about during your last visit? That way we won't be underfoot while the women clean up."

John very much *wanted* to be with the women, but he had no choice but to assent. Dutifully he followed Father Andronikos to an overgrown site on the edge of the village where, among the weeds, capitals of marble pillars and fragments of mosaic were visible. "Cyprus was very important in the centuries before Christ," Father Andronikos explained as Barry sniffed about, excited by a thousand scents. "There were powerful kings who ruled from Salamis and Paphos." John listened politely as Father Andronikos gave him a history lesson, but he heard with only half an ear; his mind was focused on how he could find time alone with Eirini.

By the time they returned it was late afternoon, and Father Andronikos excused himself to prepare Mass, heading straight for his little church. John's hope of a moment with Eirini were dashed, however, by the sight of Sir Galvin blocking the doorway. "It's time to head back for Limassol," he announced with a meaningful look; "otherwise we won't make it before dark."

"But we can—"

"It would be most improper to impose on these poor people, John. They've shared more than they can afford already. It's time to go. *Now.*" He was very firm.

"But we can't go without taking leave of Father Andronikos, and he's in the church," John protested.

"If you explain things to his wife, she will understand and tell him we have left. Tell her we must get back to Nicosia, *or your father will have your hide.*" Sir Galvin enunciated very precisely with a fake smile. "Now I'll go tack up the horses, and you go tell Madame Priest we're leaving."

Fuming inwardly, John entered the little house, calling out as he entered, *"Kireea?"* (My lady).

He was answered by Eirini, who came toward him with her finger to her lips. "She's napping," Eirini told him in a whisper.

At last! They were alone together, and just a foot apart. John felt his throat close so tight he couldn't breathe. His pulse was racing. "Eirini!" he whispered.

She gazed up at him with wide, dark, expectant eyes.

John licked his lips. "Eirini. I love you!" He gasped out.

She went on tiptoe and pecked at his cheek with a little kiss in answer. Then, just as she was about to dart away, ashamed of her own audacity, John caught her, pulled her back into his arms, and held her for a moment of sheer ecstasy. "I have to go," he murmured into her ear, holding her tighter still, "but I'll be back. Trust me. I love you."

Now she lifted her face to his, and he bent his own to place a kiss on her lips. He had never known anything like this. He didn't want it to end. Not the embrace or the kiss or—

"John! I'm waiting for you!" Sir Galvin shouted from the yard.

"I have to go!" John whispered, pulling back. "I have to go, but I'll be back. I love you!"

"I love you, too!" Eirini answered, glowing with the same excitement that had overwhelmed John.

"John! Do you want me to come in and get you?" Sir Galvin threatened.

John dropped a last, fleeting kiss on Eirini's lips and fled out the door, almost tripping over a stool and wooden clogs just inside the entry.

Sir Galvin was already mounted, sitting with one hand on his hip and Troubadour's reins in the other. Barry was panting at Troubadour's heels. At the sight of John, Sir Galvin just shook his head. "It's going to be damned uncomfortable riding in the state you're in, but at least I can see you didn't have time to spill it in the wrong place. Come on. Mount up."

John obeyed, too dazed by all the sensations surging through him to resist. As Sir Galvin picked up a trot past the little church, John turned and looked back over his shoulder at the priest's house. Had Eirini been in the doorway, he would have ridden back to her at once, willing to face any fate *whatever* just to hold her in his arms again, but she was not. John turned forward and reluctantly urged Troubadour to a trot to catch up with Sir Galvin.

"I'm not sure your father would approve," Sir Galvin remarked as John fell in beside him, "but I've found that when I'm inflamed with passion for a woman I *can't* have, it helps to comfort my body with a woman that I *can*. If you want, we can stop at a place I know in Limassol where the girls are clean, pretty, and totally lacking in virtue."

John didn't answer, but he nodded wordlessly. He had to learn more about this whole business of physical attraction to the opposite sex.

Chapter Seventeen
The Old Kingdom

Sidon,
June 1195

THE BIRTH AND CHRISTENING OF A son and heir is always a good excuse for a celebration, but the Baron of Sidon had more reason than most for a feast. He was sixty-six years old, and despite two previous marriages, this was the first time a live child had been born to him. In the old man's eyes, to be blessed with a son so late in life was nothing short of a miracle. He knew the life of his infant son was fragile. He knew the infant might not live a month, a year, or a decade, much less more than a half-century as he had. But the baby had been born whole and healthy, and Reginald de Sidon was overwhelmed with joy and pride. He wanted to share his feelings with the whole world.

For his servants and the commoners of Sidon, he ordered the slaughter of two oxen and six sheep, all of which now roasted over open pits in the outer ward. Dozens of trestle tables lined with benches had been set up, and tents erected over them to shield the guests from the summer sun. In addition to the roasted meat, mounds of bread and casks of ale were dished out. A dancing bear, jugglers, fire-eaters, and acrobats were also on hand to entertain the crowd and ensure a festive mood.

In the great hall of the castle, Sidon's tenants and retainers gathered around sideboards laden with mounds of roast pork under crusted fat, heaps of goat soaked in red wine and bay-leaf gravy, and mutton smothered in mint-flavored yogurt. There were loaves of wheat and barley bread, casseroles of carrots and celery baked under a layer of cheese, puddings of umbles spiced with cumin and nutmeg, marzipan cakes, candied fruits, and much more. Each empty platter was replaced with a fresh one, offering either more of the same or something new.

Guests came and went as they pleased. They made their way to the high table to offer their congratulations to the host before partaking of the feast. They chatted with acquaintances and friends at the lower tables. They wandered out to the ward to see the entertainment. Later in the day a tournament was planned, so many of the younger men were already checking on their horses and equipment.

Tournaments were not common in Outremer, and were nowhere near as popular as in France. Real warfare had been too prevalent for too much of the history of the Latin Kingdom in the Holy Land for anyone to feel a need for mock combat. The truce with the Saracens, however, was almost three years old, and youth was restless. Or, one could argue, the truce was due to expire in less than a year, and it was time to hone one's combat skills again. Either way, the tournament had attracted the chivalry of the Kingdom of Jerusalem in large numbers.

Most of the barons of the High Court had assembled, and not a few of the bishops as well, although the King had sent regrets because Queen Isabella was still in her confinement after the birth of a third daughter, this one christened Alice. At the high table with Sidon were two of the Tiberius brothers, Ralph and Hugh. In addition, the Lord of Caesarea and his heir (both called Walter) had joined their host at the high table. The place of honor, however, had been given to Sidon's father-in-law, the Lord of Caymont, Balian d'Ibelin.

Ibelin was twenty years younger than his son-in-law, which in the circumstances provoked a great deal of good-natured teasing. "You must feel *ancient* being a grandfather!" Reginald ribbed him.

"Being a grandfather is actually quite satisfying," Ibelin countered; "it almost makes me feel like I'm founding a dynasty." The others made dismissive gestures and not very polite noises, and were about to change the subject when Balian added, "What disturbs me is the idea of sleeping with a grandmother."

The remark caught the others by surprise and harvested guffaws of laughter accordingly—until the Lord of Caesarea quipped, with a nod toward the door opening from the solar behind them, "Then again, when the grandmother looks like *that* . . . "

Balian spun about with a guilty conscience and got hastily to his feet, bringing the other men at the high table with him. From Maria Zoë's serene expression, however, he surmised she hadn't heard his joke. Reginald was calling for another chair to be brought, as Ralph of Tiberius chivalrously vacated his own seat for the Dowager Queen.

"Is everything all right?" Reginald asked anxiously.

"Helvis seems to think she's the *first* woman in the *world* to give birth to a son," Maria Zoë answered with a pseudo-disgusted shake of her head. "Honestly," she added, nodding to her husband as he silently offered to pour wine for her, "she practically floats when she walks around the room, and I'm worried the poor little thing will starve to death, because she can hardly let go of him long enough for the wet nurse to feed him. She wants him in her arms every second. I don't know where she gets it. I was *never* that maternal." She tossed Balian a smile that seemed to contain some private joke, because he laughed.

Then she turned back to the beaming father and declared, "You're going to have trouble with her, Sidon. She now thinks that she can walk on water, that the sun and moon rise at her command, and I don't know what else."

Sidon and Ibelin both laughed at this, as Maria Zoë intended, but she recognized in their laughter a large portion of nervous relief. Sidon quite obviously doted on his pretty young bride, and it did not help that his first wife had died in childbed. It was only natural that he be both very concerned and very relieved that this birth had been comparatively easy and successful.

For Balian, on the other hand, Helvis was his firstborn child, conceived in sin, and still barely seventeen years old. Balian, Maria Zoë knew, had a partially guilty conscience for marrying her to a man old enough to be her grandfather. At the time of the betrothal it had seemed like a blessing because they had lost all their lands to the Saracens, whereas Sidon had a promise of a fief from none other than Saladin himself. The situation had changed with the grant of Caymont, but by then it was too late to break the agreement with Sidon. Besides, Helvis herself had never expressed any dissatisfaction with the proposed marriage. On the contrary, she had very early realized she could get her own way in nearly everything from the besotted Sidon, and she visibly enjoyed her status of married woman and Lady of Sidon.

Inwardly Maria Zoë shook her head over a daughter who was so radically different from herself in almost every way. Helvis had always been a timid child, afraid of horses, and so pious there were times when Balian thought she might have a calling to the Church. Since her marriage she had become completely focused on her husband, her household, and now her baby. She took no interest in anything beyond her little circle. Maria Zoë found that incomprehensible, but she accepted that Helvis was happy in her narrow world.

The Bishop of Sidon, in full episcopal regalia, was making his way across the hall, trailed by a couple of fellow clerics. He mounted the steps to the high table and approached Sidon. "My lord, we are nearly ready for the christening. You can start assembling in the chapel, and have the godmother fetch the child."

Sidon nodded, raised his voice, and announced the message to the larger crowd, while Maria Zoë excused herself to return for the baby. "What have you decided to name him, by the way?" she asked curiously.

"Oh, didn't Helvis tell you?"

"No, she was being very coy about it. Saying it was to be a surprise."

"Balian, of course," Reginald answered with a grin to his father-in-law. "What else could we call him?"

Balian was surprised by how flattered he felt.

The christening over, the spectators started to drift in the direction of the large field that had been cordoned off for the tournament. This was to be a melee, with two teams competing across an area roughly a mile wide and half a mile deep. It had gullies, wadis, rocks, and scrub brush, just as a real battlefield would have. The objective was to capture or unhorse as many of the opposing knights as possible. Capture was effected by forcing the opponent to surrender or by physically dragging him, with or without his horse, to the area behind the starting line of each respective team. The tournament ended when all members of one or the other team were unhorsed or captured.

Maria Zoë had been mildly surprised that Balian chose not to participate. "This sort of thing isn't for *grandfathers*," he'd replied, adding, "it's for the next generation."

He was probably right, she reflected, but by not participating he also gave John a chance to shine. In ways Maria Zoë could not fully fathom, John and Balian's fight earlier in the year had resulted in a stronger bond between them. Balian, of course, had already recognized by the next day that his son's safety was more important than his obedience. He had sent Sir Galvin not to drag him home, but merely to ensure nothing happened to him. Ever since the incident, which neither of them spoke about, Balian treated John more like an adult. Even more surprising to Maria, John seemed more at ease with his father too. He was less deferential and more self-confident without being disrespectful. In May, in a public ceremony celebrated with as much pomp as they could afford, Balian had knighted John. It was therefore as Sir John d'Ibelin that he would compete in the tournament today.

Another advantage of Balian not taking part in the tournament was that it freed up Georgios to serve as John's squire. Georgios had once been squire to the famous tournament champion William Marshal, during the latter's sojourn in the Holy Land. Georgios still lionized the old tournament master, who had evidently regaled Georgios with many tales of his tournament successes. The squire had been giving John tips ever since they heard about the tournament, and Maria Zoë had the impression that Georgios was at least as (if not more) excited about the event as John himself.

John would be riding the destrier his father had given him on the occasion of his knighting. He was a young black stallion, a younger brother of Balian's own Ras Dawit, and he had been named Trojan. John, Maria Zoë knew, was more than a little nervous about riding the still-unfamiliar horse in an event like this. The risks of serious injury resulting in the need to put the horse down were very real. At a minimum there could be cuts, abrasions, bruises, strained muscles, wind and bog spavins, or bowed tendons as a result. To not participate, however, would have been to concede defeat before he even started, and John was dogged if nothing else.

With John participating, Philip on Cyprus, and Helvis confined with baby Balian, the Ibelin spectators consisted of only Balian himself, Maria Zoë, Margaret, and Barry. The latter had been entrusted to Meg, to keep him from getting underfoot in the melee. Meg, however, had gone to change, leaving the confused dog with her parents. She now came breathlessly down the spiral stairs from the chamber she was sharing with a half-dozen other noble maidens to join her impatient parents. As a maiden, she wore her hair long and uncovered. She had inherited her mother's curly dark-auburn hair, and had expertly braided two little strands leading back from her temples and from behind her ears to meet in a single braid at the back of her head. This had the effect of pulling her bushy hair away from her face, thereby highlighting its aquiline symmetry, while allowing her generous and luxurious tresses to explode around her shoulders. Added to the natural beauty of the hair itself were little gold wires that she had inserted into her thick hair so that it was highlighted by gold. Her gown was crimson, but the linings of her wide sleeves were the brightest of marigold silk: Ibelin colors.

Balian nearly gasped at the sight of her. What had become of his little girl? He did not remember her being on the brink of womanhood when they left Caymont ten months ago. Had she grown up overnight? Or had he been blind?

Maria Zoë's reaction was far more practical. "You are *not* wearing that gown to the tournament!"

"But it's made of Ibelin colors to support John!" Meg pointed out in astonishment.

"It's very fine silk, cost a fortune, and is *totally* unsuitable! You could have worn it to the christening, but not to a tournament!"

"But it's the prettiest thing I *have*!" Meg countered, revealing her true motives.

"All the more reason you don't want it getting covered in dust, much less risk getting the sleeves or hem torn and trampled on! Honestly, Meg! Use your head. Now go change, or we'll miss the start!"

Trumpet signals were already sounding, calling the teams to marshal.

"But, Mama—" Meg started to argue.

"Do as your mother says, or you aren't going to the tournament at all," Balian warned.

Meg knew she was defeated when her father weighed in against her, and with a furious expression she turned and ran back up the stairs in an angry huff, frantic to change rapidly. She *had* to be at the start! Sir Walter of Caesarea the younger had whispered to her in the great hall that he wanted to wear her colors!

Left at the foot of the stairs, her father asked her mother, "When did she grow up?"

"Don't deceive yourself, my love, she hasn't. She's still a child. She's only *flirting* with the idea of growing up—without a clue about what it means."

"How old is she?"

"Fourteen," Maria Zoë answered readily, only to pause, surprised, before admitting what she had only just remembered: "A year older than I was when I married King Amalric."

"Hmm." Balian thought about that, too. Maria Zoë had been a very poised, disciplined, and distant young queen. At times she had seemed more like a doll than a human: beautiful but so impassive that she seemed indifferent to everyone around her. It had taken their shared love of a young prince isolated by his leprosy to give Balian a glimpse beyond her façade. He had then discovered what a lively, passionate, and intelligent person she was. Not once, however, had he seen her as a *child*.

"I was forced to grow up fast, just like Helvis. We've let Meg remain a child longer than usual, but I don't regret it."

Already the sound of light footsteps, almost tripping over themselves as they hurried down the stairs, warned them that Meg was returning. She was now dressed more suitably, in a sky-blue linen gown with a sheer green surcoat of Egyptian cotton. "Much better," Maria Zoë praised her, but Meg was still seething with resentment and refused to acknowledge her mother's remark. Instead she took her father's elbow and looked up at him expectantly.

"Um hum," he remarked ambiguously, and then offered his other arm to his wife.

They were late getting to the improvised grandstand beside the tourney field, and it was already crowded, but people automatically made way for the

Dowager Queen of Jerusalem and the Lord of Caymont/Ibelin. They climbed easily to the middle of the bench on the highest rung to settle down next to the host, Reginald de Sidon, and the bishop. Barry had absorbed the excitement and was looking about curiously, his wagging tail slapping spectators in their faces, so that Balian realized he would have to be tied to the base of the grandstands and returned with him.

Meg, meanwhile, was anxiously searching the men lining up on either side of the grandstand on nervous destriers. They wore full armor, which meant nowadays that most of the helmets had visors, and she couldn't see faces anymore. The identity of the rider could only be discerned by the colors and insignia they wore on shields, surcoats, and the trappers of their horses. John had adopted his father's colors and shield: a gold field with a red cross pattée. His surcoat was marigold with red crosses on it, but Trojan's trapper was red with marigold crosses on it. The bright combination made John stand out amidst his fellows. Meg, however, was looking feverishly for Walter of Caesarea, but she wasn't sure of his device. Was it a black falcon or a black tower? She was sure it was black on blue. A knight separated himself from the others and came to the foot of the grandstand, saluting with his lance.

"Meg!" Her mother discreetly trod on Meg's foot to make her pay attention. "The knight requests a token from you."

"But—" Meg broke off, flushing furiously. It wasn't Walter, but Hugh of Tiberius.

"Give him something," her mother told her.

"But—"

"I don't care. A lady does not humiliate a young knight in front of everyone by refusing. *My* daughter certainly won't," she added ominously.

Meg swallowed, pulled from her sleeve the red-and-yellow ribbon she had been saving for Walter, and with a forced smile reached down and tied it to the tip of the offered lance. Sir Hugh bowed his head and saluted her with his hand before riding off.

"Now I don't have anything for Sir Walter," Meg hissed angrily to her mother.

"That's perfectly all right," Maria Zoë assured her with infuriating calm. "Ribbons mean absolutely nothing in the real world." Maria Zoë knew that Meg had been devouring romances this past year. "In the real world," she continued, "your father will choose your husband for you, and it need not be anyone you've ever given a ribbon to."

Meg opened her mouth to say something, but was interrupted by the return of her father. Just as he re-seated himself, a trumpet fanfare set the knights cantering in echelon to their starting positions. Compared to the elaborate pageantry of French and Flemish tournaments, this was a very crude affair. There were no heralds, for a start—but then again, in this close-knit society everyone knew everyone anyway, and heralds were hardly necessary. There was also no parade of knights. They cantered to the start positions, and at a renewed trumpet signal they charged from either end of the field to clash more or less in front of the grandstands.

Within a very short space of time, so much dust had been stirred up that it was increasingly difficult to see anything at all. They could hear shouts, occasional threats or insults, the clash of weapons, and the snorting and whinnying of horses—and Barry's frantic barking. Now and then a horse and rider appeared on the periphery, usually turning to return to the fray. A couple of men staggered out on foot, one limping badly, and the barber-surgeon immediately went to his aid. Riderless horses also escaped the cloud of dust, happy to get away from the madness, and were quickly captured by waiting grooms.

Soon the spectators closer to ground level were racked with coughing fits, and Maria Zoë pulled the upper flap of her scarf down from the top of her head to cover her face.

"I can't see a thing," Meg complained impatiently.

"John's still mounted and fighting," her father answered.

Meg didn't dare *say* she didn't care about John, but she was far more interested in what had happened to Sir Walter of Caesarea. She was also getting bored. Since she couldn't really see what was happening, it was not very pleasant sitting out here in the heat and dust. Fortunately, a canvas awning over the grandstands kept them in the shade, but even so, it was June in Palestine and very hot. Meg could feel herself sweating, and inwardly thanked her mother for making her change. She would have ruined her beautiful gold-and-scarlet dress out here.

"Ah!" Her father sprang to his feet, and his wife and daughter looked up at him.

"I think John's down!"

"No, there he is!" Sidon elbowed his son-in-law. Sure enough, John had just ridden out of the dust toward the sidelines, to be greeted by frantic barking from Barry. John was hunched over the saddle, but still in it. As they watched he righted himself, and Georgios trotted over to give him water and a new lance. He drank, thanked the squire, took up the new lance, and turned Trojan around to re-enter the mock conflict.

The dust was slowly beginning to thin and settle, however, as more and more riders were either unhorsed or forced off the field. Of the nearly one hundred knights who had initially clashed, only about a quarter of them were still engaged.

"Which side is winning?" Balian asked Reginald.

"Haven't a clue," Sidon answered honestly. "Next time we should have one side dress up as Saracens. It would make for a more realistic test anyway."

"Who would want to be the Saracens?" Balian countered.

"All right, we can make it English against the French, or Pisans against Genoese. *That* would be realistic!"

They laughed, and in so doing breathed in so much dust that they both started coughing. Maria Zoë signaled for water from one of the waiting pages.

A half-hour later it was over. The team under the Prince of Galilee had won. Still mounted and uncaptured were Ralph of Tiberius, the elder (but not the younger) Caesarea, and John d'Ibelin. It was a very strong showing for such a young knight.

The spectators gratefully climbed down from the bleachers and started drifting back to the castle for refreshments. Balian, however, wanted to congratulate John, and he urged Maria Zoë and Meg to go ahead of him. Maria Zoë agreed, but Meg said she'd wait for him. She released Barry's leash and sat down on the lowest bench with Barry at her feet, gratefully gazing up at her as she petted and scratched him indulgently.

Meanwhile, Balian ducked under the perimeter railing and waved to John, stopping him from returning to the stables. John trotted to meet his father, and flung open his visor as he drew up. He was grinning broadly. Balian stood beside him, patting Trojan on the neck. The horse, dripping sweat, tried to rub his nose on the Baron of Ibelin, shoving him this way and that as he talked to his son. Then, stepping back, Balian signaled for John to return to the castle just as Barry broke free of Meg and streaked across the field, barking wildly in greeting as he caught sight of John.

As he joined his daughter, Balian was smiling almost as broadly as his son, and he gladly gave Meg his arm. Now that her mother was not around, Meg leaned her head on her father's upper arm. "Daddy?"

"Yes, dove?"

"I know Helvis is very happy, but . . . "

"But what?" Balian was already frowning slightly, afraid of what was to come.

"Well, we're different."

"You think I haven't noticed?"

"No, I just mean . . . "

"What?"

"Well, when you start looking for a husband for me . . . "

"Ah. Yes?"

"I really do like Walter of Caesarea the younger."

"Hmm. Aiming high."

"What do you mean?"

"He's heir to Caesarea. The lordship includes the port of the same name, which used to be very prosperous before Hattin. Although it hasn't recovered fully by any means, there's no reason to think it won't. It once owed one hundred knights to the feudal levee—compared to ten for Ibelin or a mere six for Caymont. In short, you'd better lower your expectations, child." The use of the word 'child' said it all. He was not taking her seriously.

Meg tightened her jaw (much as her brother and father did) and considered her answer carefully. At last she settled for, "Well, will you promise me my husband won't be as *old* as Reggie?"

"No. I won't promise you anything, dove. Marriage is politics and very rarely takes affection or attraction into account; it's about land and alliances. So don't wish for it too soon. Enjoy your freedom instead."

Tyre, July 1195

Ayyub crawled out from under the nailed-together pieces of rubbish that he used as a roof and brushed the worst creases and dirt from his kaftan. He slid his feet into his dilapidated sandals, and then ran a wooden comb through his long hair before tying it with twine at the back of his neck. Rubbing his cheeks, he measured the stubble, and could only hope that today he would earn enough for a bath and a shave.

The thought drove him forward. Yesterday he'd heard rumors that work would at last begin on the expansion of the sea wall. The Archbishop had engaged a master builder, and people said he would be recruiting laborers at prime today. With a glance toward the east, Ayyub increased his pace. He didn't want to be late and risk not getting a job.

As he came around the corner, his heart sank. There were already at least two score men clustered inside the main gate, the "job market" for any construction work in the city. As he watched, a well-dressed man with a clerk in attendance rode up and was immediately besieged by the crowd of job seekers. The master builder waved the suppliants away irritably and gestured for them to line up with their backs to the wall. The scribe dismounted from his mule, withdrew his utensils from a leather pouch attached to his belt, and started down the line of job applicants.

Ayyub had no choice but to go to the end of the line, and he wasn't the last. By the time the clerk reached him, another score of jobless men had joined the lineup. Work for unskilled laborers was scarce in Tyre in 1195.

"Name?" the clerk barked at Ayyub.

"Ayyub ibn Adam," Ayyub answered readily.

"Age?"

"Twenty-two."

"Place of birth?"

"Nablus."

"Any skills?"

"I was an apprentice mason before Hattin."

The clerk looked up and their eyes met. Ayyub saw understanding. The priest nodded once. "Good enough. Join the men over there." He pointed and jotted a note on his scroll. Ayyub gratefully joined the cluster of men selected.

After the clerk had found fifty suitable workers, the hired men were divided up into teams of ten, each under a journeyman mason. Ayyub's troop was led outside the city gates and across the two drawbridges to the start of the causeway that led from the mainland toward the city. Here a long convoy of ox-carts, loaded with freshly cut quarry stone, waited patiently. These unwieldy and heavy carts exceeded the weight limits of the drawbridges; they could not be allowed in.

"That's today's first job!" the mason announced smugly. "Offload the quarry stones from those wagons and load them onto the barges down there." He pointed to four barges tied up in the moat. While it made sense to transport the heavy stones by barge to the seaward side of the city where the work was to begin, the task of carrying the massive stones down the steep slope of the moat to the barges was daunting. It didn't help that a stiff southerly breeze had whipped up the surface of the moat, making the barges bob and sway. The mason warned, "And watch what you're doing. Any cracked or chipped blocks will be deducted from your pay."

Ayyub thought that far worse than paying for cracked or chipped stone was the prospect of a broken foot or fingers. A man could be crippled for life if he mishandled stones like these. But a fellow laborer was more concerned about compensation and shouted out, "Just what *are* you paying?"

"Should have asked that earlier," the mason answered with a shrug.

"I'm asking now," the workman answered, crossing his arms over his chest in a defiant stance.

Ayyub frowned. He didn't want a troublemaker on his team. Employers didn't always distinguish between individuals and might just fire the whole team. To express his opinion of the other man's obstinacy, he started in the direction of the cart.

"There are plenty of men willing to work, if you fancy yourself too good for it," the mason articulated Ayyub's gesture.

"I didn't say that; I just asked what the wages are," the first man prevaricated, uncrossing his arms and taking a more cooperative stance.

"Two dinars a day," the mason answered.

"With or without lunch?" a third man asked. By the looks of him, he hadn't had a square meal in several weeks and probably would have worked for the meal alone.

"Lunch is included," the mason answered, and that clearly satisfied the man who had asked about lunch, but not the man who had asked about wages. Although he joined the others at the cart and started to lend a hand, he grumbled. "Slave wages, that's what they're paying, the fat bastards! Slave wages!"

"You don't know what the hell you're talking about!" Ayyub snapped at him bitterly.

"The hell I don't!" the troublemaker bristled. "I've worked construction sites from Paris to Marseilles, and the going rate is two and half! The Archbishop of Sens was paying *three* for the work on his cathedral."

"And I've worked construction sites from Aleppo to Cairo, and *slave* wages are f***ing zero—nothing—shit, spit, and kicks in the ass!" Ayyub snarled bitterly.

The others looked at him with varying degrees of sympathy. The troublemaker just looked baffled. "Huh?"

"Stop jawboning and get to work!" The mason put an end to the exchange, and they all put their backs into it.

It was hard work. They took turns standing on the bed of the cart and lowering a stone onto the back of a comrade, who then staggered down the steep slope to two men aboard the barge. There, one took the stone from the man carrying it and handed it off to the last man, who stacked it on the barge to keep the weight as evenly distributed as possible.

By terce they felt as if their backs were nearly broken, and all had stripped down to loincloths as they worked in the fierce summer heat. There was still a cart waiting to be unloaded when a wagon arrived laden with water, a cauldron of steaming stew, and loaves of bread. The construction team quit work, too hungry to obey the mason's orders to finish offloading the last cart first.

Ayyub grasped for water first and helped himself to two ladles full, pouring it down his parched throat so fast that some of it spilled down the side of his chin. It was lukewarm and tasted stale, but he hardly minded. He then grabbed a loaf of bread and tore several chunks off with his teeth. He'd had nothing to eat since yesterday noon, and had been having dizzy spells in the noonday heat by the time the food arrived. Only after he'd gobbled down half the loaf did he line up for the stew, which smelled strongly of onions and looked greasy. Ayyub wasn't fussy. He took the bowl offered and started soaking up the soup with what was left of his bread.

With two dinars, he calculated mentally, he'd be able to afford a bath, a shave, and a decent meal tonight. Furthermore, if he'd been hired for the whole job, not just the day, he had the prospect of earning two dinars per day, or sixty dinars a month, for the next six, eight, maybe even twelve months. Maybe he could start to look for real lodgings, rather than sleeping under an improvised shelter in an alley. It wasn't that bad now, in the height of summer, but he knew that when the rains and cold set in this fall, sleeping under a leaking roof would be miserable. He didn't want to have to do that again.

"Get up! Get up!" the mason started yelling at them. "The master's coming! Get back to work!" The journeyman sounded rather frightened, Ayyub thought, but he was no more willing than the others to drop his meal just to make their young overseer look good to his master.

Unable to motivate the workers, the journeyman mason ran forward to meet the master builder with a flood of excuses. The master builder, still flanked by his clerk, frowned, but did not voice any audible reproaches. Instead he ordered (in a sarcastic voice), "When you *do* get finished, bring your team back to the quay."

"Yes, sir!" the young mason promised. "We'll be there in an hour, sir! You can rely on me, sir!"

The master builder ignored his subordinate and turned his horse around to return into the city. He found the drawbridge blocked by a party of horsemen riding out of the city. These men wore armor and surcoats, and longswords hung at their hips, spurs glinting on heels: knights.

"Aren't those the crosses of Ibelin?" one of Ayyub's companions asked, pointing to the trapper of the nearest horse. "It must be Balian d'Ibelin! I heard he was passing through on his way back from Sidon to Acre."

"No, the rider's too young," one of the others retorted.

Ayyub eagerly turned his attention to the party of knights. He'd been born and raised in Nablus, a city held by the Dowager Queen of Jerusalem. He could still vividly remember the siege of Nablus in 1184, when all the citizens had to take refuge in the citadel while Saladin's troops sacked the town. The citadel had been awash in frightened humanity, and it was soon obvious that there weren't enough supplies to feed so many people for more than a day or two. But the Baron of Ibelin had ridden through the night to their relief, and Saladin's men had fled before him. Ayyub would never forget the moment when the frantic howling of horns announced the baron's approach and he'd scrambled to the top of a stairway to get a better look.

Now, a decade later, he could still recognize Ibelin from his memory of that day. Pointing excitedly, he declared, "Beyond the youth, on the chestnut! *That's* the Baron of Ibelin!"

The master builder, too, had recognized the leader of the party blocking his way, and bowed deeply from the waist. Ibelin's voice, speaking Arabic, carried on the breeze to the curious workers.

"… on Cyprus . . . aqueducts and drains . . . recommend . . . "

The master builder was shaking his head vigorously, but because he faced the opposite direction they could not catch his words.

Ibelin spoke again, but he leaned forward on his pommel to speak more personally with the builder and lowered his voice. None of the workers could hear what he said, but they saw the master builder respond by shaking his head and gesturing vaguely.

Ibelin nodded, sat upright again, and signaled his men to turn around. Ayyub got a look at his face: he looked discouraged, Ayyub thought.

The distraction over, the journeyman turned his attention back to his charges and complained, "What are you gawking at? We need to unload the last cart."

"What did my lord of Ibelin want?" Ayyub asked, as he brushed the last crumbs of bread from his hands and stood up to show his readiness to get back to work.

"Oh, he's looking for a master builder willing to go with him to Cyprus. He says there are major building projects that need to be undertaken, but no skilled labor on the island. He'd heard about the master from someone and came here to try to recruit him, but the master's got more than enough work here." The journeyman was proud of the fact. "Come on! We need to get this job done."

Ayyub dutifully left his chipped bowl back on the stack beside the cauldron, and climbed aboard the last wagon to get the process started again. All the while, his mind was racing. Major building projects. He'd heard the words "aqueducts" and "drains." Those were things that took *real* skills: mathematics, geometry, proper plans, and detailed, properly scaled sketches. Not that this project didn't, but he was as far away from the plans as the earth was from heaven. But once upon a time, when he'd been apprenticed almost a decade ago, he had dreamed of building aqueducts. That was why he'd asked his father to get him a contract with Moses ibn Sa'id. Master Moses was the man who'd built the third aqueduct at Caesarea. He'd come to Nablus to carry out construction of an even more ambitious aqueduct project. They'd only just started work on the aqueduct when Saladin invaded. The army had been called up, and Moses ibn Sa'id had followed the call, joining the feudal host armed with a spiked mace. As a man who'd learned his trade from the ground up and was adept with chisel and hammer, Master Moses was a formidable fighter. But the catastrophe of Hattin had swallowed both of them.

Ayyub found himself in Nablus when it was overrun by the Saracens just two weeks after Hattin. He'd made the mistake of not fleeing to Jerusalem when the Dowager Queen left with her household, foolishly thinking he'd be fine and still hoping that Master Moses would miraculously turn up. Instead, Ayyub had been picked up in a Saracen dragnet, and despite his fluent command of Arabic and his ambivalent name, was identified as Christian by his inability to produce the right answers about the Koran. Clamped into chains, he'd been sent back to the slave market in Damascus and a nightmare that lasted five years. Slavery had shattered not only the world he had known, but his future as well. When he was finally released by the Treaty of Ramla, he was nineteen years old and trained in nothing but how to endure humiliation, starvation rations, blows, flogging, and endless labor. In five years, Ayyub swore, he had never had a kind word, a gesture of sympathy, or a day of rest.

The cart was empty at last, and the journeyman released the barges to their respective crews and led his troop of laborers back through the city to the inside quay. Here they found that two cranes had been assembled and mortar was being mixed. As the barges came alongside the outside of the quay, the stones had to be offloaded again and lined up ready for use. Having worked all morning on the eastern edge of the city in the full heat of the rising sun, they now had the pleasure of working on the western edge of the city as the sun sank. The temperature had risen steadily throughout the day, but the breeze had died down. As they worked, the sun glinting off the water was almost blinding, and the heat stewed them in their own sweat.

The ringing of vespers marked the end of the twelve-hour day at last, and the men dropped whatever they were doing and lined up for their pay. The clerk, protected by two burly sergeants, placed himself behind a crude table, and each man made a mark beside his name on a scroll to confirm receipt.

Ayyub nodded his thanks to the clerk as he took the two dinars, and stashed them inside a purse tied to a cord *inside* his kaftan. He then hastened around the corner and up the street to a small square with a public fountain. Here he removed his kaftan again, knelt with one knee on the rim, and reached as deeply as he could into the basin to wash his arms. Then he cupped water so he could wash his face, and poured it with his hands over his head and splashed at the back of his neck. Finally, he splashed his upper body and armpits liberally with water to remove the worst of the sweat and grime. As clean as he could get himself in this manner, he pulled his kaftan back over his head, combed out his wet hair, and retied it behind his head.

Feeling somewhat restored, although sore all over, he started up the street to the Cathedral of the Holy Cross. He had a plan, but it all depended on Master Moses.

His former master had suffered even more than he had himself. Taken captive on the field of Hattin, his very prowess with the mace had attracted the attention of his enemy. He had killed one man too many, or maybe just the wrong man. In any case, his captors were so full of rage that, once they had disarmed him, they made him lie face down on the bloody field and hacked off his right hand halfway to the elbow. A cripple, he had gone into captivity, and there found himself the property of a bathhouse owner, who used the former master builder to clean out the latrines.

On his release after the Treaty of Ramla, Master Moses—like thousands of other former slaves—had washed up in Tyre. In a city overrun with released captives, he was nothing special, just another ex-slave—and a crippled one at that. No one cared what he'd been before Hattin, and a man of forty-something with just one hand could not compete with hordes of healthier, younger men like Ayyub himself. He had ended up a beggar, and it was in this capacity that Ayyub and Moses had met again roughly a year earlier.

Since then Ayyub had made a point of sharing some of his earnings whenever he was lucky. That was rare enough, and Master Moses was visibly failing. He was permanently bent, skeletally thin, and increasingly mentally absent as well. Ayyub was terrified the former master might be too far gone to help him now.

At least he was sitting in his usual spot, nestled into one of the niches formed by the receding arches of the main portal. He had a dirty rag spread out before him for people to drop coins into as they entered or departed. His unkempt mane of graying hair hung about his shoulders, but it had thinned so much that his scabby scalp showed through in many places. His wrinkled face was dirty and blank. He sat with his knees bent before him and his stump propped on them for all to see: a silent plea for alms.

"Master Moses!" Ayyub called as he reached the foot of the stairs up to the portal and started up them.

His former master's head swung slowly and stared at Ayyub as he approached. He did not smile in pleasure; he just stared.

"Master Moses." Ayyub went down on his heels in front of the beggar. "What would you say to working as a master builder again? To building aqueducts?"

"I'd say you've gone mad," came the bitter answer.

"But could you do it? Could you design and build an aqueduct? Like we were going to do together?"

"Have you been drinking or chewing khat?" the master builder asked, narrowing his eyes and eyeing Ayyub suspiciously.

"Neither! I can't afford such luxuries. The Baron of Ibelin is looking for a master builder to build aqueducts and sewage drains on Cyprus."

"I've seen more *sewage* drains than I ever want to see the rest of my life!" the ex-slave growled. "Go away!"

"This isn't about cleaning them out," Ayyub protested frantically, his dreams collapsing around his ears. "It's about designing them and watching other people build them."

The beggar snorted skeptically and snarled, "What's in it for you?"

"Just that you take me on as your apprentice, like before: that you take me with you."

"Where?"

"To Cyprus! Didn't I already say that? Ibelin wants a master builder willing to go with him to Cyprus."

"That's what *you* say!" Moses scoffed. "Sounds like a drunkard's dream to me."

"I'm not drunk. I'm stone-cold sober, and I heard the exchange myself. What's the harm in trying?"

"Trying what?"

"Going to find the Baron of Ibelin and presenting yourself."

Moses ibn Sa'id made a rude noise.

"Come with me!" Ayyub insisted, reaching out to pull Moses to his feet by his forearm.

Moses tried to shake him off, but Ayyub was stronger. "You're coming with me," Ayyub insisted.

Moses was too weak to effectively resist, and so he found himself being dragged through the streets to a small and rather disreputable bathhouse run by a fellow Syrian Christian. Ayyub handed the bathhouse owner twelve obols and pulled Moses inside with him. The bath boy made a face at the sight and stink of the beggar, but his employer cuffed him and told him to get to work. The two guests stripped out of their filthy rags, and each lay face down on a bench. At once they began to soak in a sense of luxury and relaxation as their bodies sweated away the accumulated filth of weeks (or months, in Moses' case). They were washed down by the attendant, lathered in soap, washed again, oiled, and washed a third time.

Ayyub's stomach was growling long before they were finished, and it cost him considerable discipline to pay for a barber, gutting his food money, but the transformation in Moses was significant. Except for their clothes, they both looked quite respectable by the time they showed up at the Archbishop's palace and requested an audience with the Baron of Ibelin.

"Beggars go to the back. You can get leftovers from the kitchen there," the Turcopole guard dismissed them.

"That's a good idea," Moses agreed, turning away at once. Ayyub stopped him. "First we talk to the baron," he told his companion.

"Didn't you hear the young man? He's not going to see us."

"Yes, he will," Ayyub insisted, turning back to the Turcopole. "Sir," he addressed the Turcopole, "listen to us. We're not here to beg. We're here to offer our services to the Baron of Ibelin."

"Don't make me laugh," the Turcopole answered. "Move along."

"Not until you've at least sent word to the Baron of Ibelin that the master builder who built the aqueduct at Caesarea, the man who was building the aqueduct at Nablus, is here requesting an audience."

The Turcopole narrowed his eyes and looked from Ayyub to Moses and back again. "If this is a hoax, I'll have you both in the stocks for a week," he threatened.

"And we'd deserve it," Ayyub answered steadily, meeting his eye, "but I'm not lying. The Baron of Ibelin is looking for my friend. He'll be angry if he finds out we were here and you turned us away."

"How would he find out?" the Turcopole countered, and for a moment Ayyub feared he was going to send them away after all. After a moment of letting them dangle in doubt, however, he pointed to a stone bench built beside the gate and told them to wait there. He turned around and shouted to a colleague to man the gate while he took a message to Ibelin.

It seemed to take forever, and Moses was grumbling about having wasted money on baths that they could have spent on food. "We can beg for food at the Archbishop's kitchen," Ayyub retorted.

"Sure, and all we'll get is *slops*. You think I don't know? I've filled my belly there more times than I can count. They feed *pigs* better than what he gives us."

"Hey!" It was the Turcopole guard. "Come with me!"

They jumped up and hurried to follow him. *Now* Ayyub was nervous. Up to this moment, he'd been so sure he'd fail to get an audience that he hadn't envisaged actually *facing* the Baron of Ibelin. As the Turcopole led them across the courtyard, up a flight of stairs, and down a corridor, Ayyub frantically tried to think what he should say, but everything sounded stupid in his own ears. They found themselves in a small chapel, apparently used for private prayer, and were told to wait. Ayyub took the opportunity to address the icon of the Virgin and Christ Child over the altar in a desperate plea for divine assistance.

Suddenly a lady swept into the little chapel with a smile on her face, only to come to an abrupt halt as her eyes lit upon the two men in front of her. Ayyub went down on one knee and bowed his head with a respectful, "My lady." He recognized the Dowager Queen of Jerusalem. Moses, however, seemed to have turned to stone, and he just stared at his former patroness.

The Dowager Queen glanced from Moses to Ayyub and back to Moses. "Master Moses?" she asked uncertainly in French.

Although Ayyub did not speak French, it was obvious to him that she did not recognize the former master builder, shrunken and broken as he was, so he hastened to explain in a flood of Arabic. "Yes, my lady! It's Master Moses ibn Sa'id, the master builder you commissioned to build the aqueduct at Nablus, and I'm Ayyub ibn Adam. I was his apprentice for two years before Hattin landed us both in slavery."

The Dowager Queen looked rather strangely at Ayyub and shook her head to convey that she could not understand him. Then she turned again to Moses and repeated "Master Moses?" followed by something else that made Moses look down at his stump and shrug. After a moment he answered with a single word: "Hattin."

"But there's nothing wrong with his brain!" Ayyub pointed out frantically in Arabic, certain that the Dowager Queen was dismissing Moses as a cripple. Mentally, he asked God why the Lady of Ibelin had come rather than her husband. At least the Lord of Ibelin spoke fluent Arabic. . . .

The Dowager Queen silenced him with a raised hand, but then gestured for him to wait. She withdrew. At least they hadn't been thrown out.

After another long stretch of time, the Baron of Ibelin ducked through the doorway. He had removed his armor and was dressed in a cotton surcoat over leather trousers and a silk shirt. Although he looked comfortable and prosperous, up close Ayyub registered that he, too, had aged significantly since that day a decade ago. He had a streak of gray in his silky, dark hair, and the network of lines around his eyes was deep, the shadows dark. The eyes themselves, however, were alert and took in the two men awaiting for him. He seemed to assess them both before he addressed Master Moses in French.

The latter nodded, and looked down hopelessly and glumly at his stump.

Again Ayyub protested in Arabic. "It doesn't matter about his arm! He doesn't need it to direct others. The Saracens didn't take away what he *knows*. He can still *design* aqueducts, and I can be his draftsman. All he has to do is tell me, and I'll make the drawings. I can . . . " His voice faded away under the baron's steady gaze.

"And who are you?" Ibelin asked into the silence.

To Ayyub's amazement, it was Master Moses who answered for him before he could take a breath. "He is my apprentice, or he was once. He's a good boy, my lord. Ayyub ibn Adam."

"And is he right?" the baron asked. "Can you still design buildings and teach Ayyub how to do the drawings? The surveying?"

"Yes—yes, I think I can." Moses sounded uncharacteristically uncertain and added apologetically, "It's been a long time."

"Of course he can," Ayyub insisted, pleading desperately with his eyes.

"And you are prepared to come to Cyprus?" Ibelin asked.

"Of course! Gladly!" Ayyub assured him emphatically. Anything to get away from the poverty here, to have a new start.

Ibelin looked pointedly at Master Moses, and the old man nodded hesitantly.

"The population on Cyprus is more homogeneous than here," Ibelin warned. "They all speak Greek and dress in the Byzantine fashion. You will want to adapt as fast as possible. I fear they will look on you as Muslims because of your names, speech, and dress."

"I'll wear anything you give me—or tell me to," Ayyub corrected himself hastily. Learning another language was more intimidating, but he dared not express any doubts.

Ibelin nodded again. "I'm willing to see what you can do. Do you have families you wish to bring with you?"

Ayyub and Moses shook their heads.

"It's probably better that way. If you marry on Cyprus, it will help you assimilate more rapidly." He smiled at that, and then told them matter-of-factly, "I'll send my squire to show you where to get a meal and where to sleep tonight. We leave for Acre first thing in the morning, so I'll have Georgios organize a couple of hired hacks for you as well." He nodded one last time and withdrew.

Ayyub and Moses stood staring at one another in stunned disbelief, and then Ayyub flung his arms around his still-bewildered former master in speechless relief. He didn't care what awaited him on Cyprus: it was a new beginning.

Royal Palace at Acre, August 1195

"I'm sorry to see you go," Champagne admitted to his father-in-law somewhat awkwardly. "And Isabella misses her mother very much. She was very upset that she wasn't here for Alice's birth."

Ibelin nodded but countered, "Isabella *likes* having her mother with her, but she doesn't *need* her; she's strong and attended by the best physicians in the Kingdom. My niece Eschiva, on the other hand, nearly died at the last birth," he exaggerated. From Balian's perspective, Isabella had been spoiled much of her life and, now that she was a ruling queen with a doting husband, she was on the brink of becoming insufferable. Isabella truly did not need her mother waiting on her. Eschiva, on the other hand, was emotionally fragile and intensely grateful for Maria Zoë's moral support.

"I suppose you're right," Champagne admitted reluctantly, "but I miss your sage voice in my council as well." He flashed Ibelin a smile that was intended to be winning.

It very nearly was. Ibelin was not immune to flattery. Part of him felt he *ought* to remain in the Kingdom of Jerusalem and play his hereditary role in the High Court. Furthermore, here he was recognized as the premier baron in the realm by virtue of being stepfather to the Queen. If Champagne recognized him as an asset, it increased his value to the Kingdom. Didn't he owe it to Jerusalem to give her everything he had? Did it matter if his greatest contribution was no longer the strength of his arms but rather the quality of his advice?

He hesitated, rethinking his decision to return to Cyprus. He had expected to feel more "at home" here, but Caymont still felt alien—while Acre and Tyre, and indeed the entire country, struck him as overpopulated and over-cultivated. The countryside seemed dry and dusty and the cities smelly and crowded, after the forested mountains and well-watered plains of Cyprus. The sun seemed hotter here, too, because Cyprus was cooled by strong winds, and the castles sat a thousand feet or more above sea level.

Shifting uncomfortably in his chair, he recognized that after nearly a year away, he'd also been discomfited by the large number of Arab caravans that used Acre and Tyre as their market for West-bound goods. They were a constant reminder of the defeat the Christians had suffered and the threat that remained. On Cyprus, on the other hand, it was so easy to forget about Hattin. . . .

And there was Paphos. Aimery had offered it to him. "Rebuild it, and it's yours," he'd said plainly. The offer was more than tempting: it was seductive. On the one hand, the city's Roman/Greek heritage was so dominant that it was almost like returning to the age of Christ. On the other hand, it was in such a state of decay and disrepair that it begged for help. The vision of a new city with a modern castle and a Latin cathedral was far more compelling that Champagne's offer of a seat on his council. Ibelin took a deep breath. "Thank you. I'm honored, but no. I promised Aimery I would return."

"Aimery." Champagne's face turned sour and his voice tart.

That surprised Ibelin. Champagne had been in the wrong with his accusations of treason against Aimery, and the Lusignan's gracious withdrawal to Cyprus had saved them all an unpleasant confrontation. Champagne, Ibelin thought, ought to be grateful to Aimery. "Surely you can have nothing against him now?" Ibelin asked with an edge of exasperation in his voice.

"Is it true he is trying to have himself made king?" Champagne returned sharply.

Ibelin registered Champagne's resentment and tried to reply in a mollifying tone. "He needs the authority of a crown to keep the likes of my nephew, Cheneché, and Barlais in check. By offering Cyprus to the Holy Roman Emperor in exchange for a crown, he also gains an ally against the Greek Emperor, who still claims Cyprus."

"In case you've forgotten, the snake calling himself Holy Roman Emperor is the man who held my uncle Richard in a dungeon!" Champagne retorted hotly. "He treated the King of England—a *crusader*—as if he were a *criminal*! The Hohenstaufen is a madman!"

"I wouldn't know. I haven't met him," Ibelin demurred, "but he *is* a very powerful monarch. Furthermore, he's taken the cross and is recruiting a substantial force to come to your aid. The truce with the Saracens, don't forget, runs out in nine months."

"No, I haven't forgotten," Champagne answered grimly. "It's one of the things that keeps me awake at night—and, indeed, *another* reason I wanted you to stay. I wanted to consult with you about our strategy. When the Holy Roman Emperor comes, I don't want all his men wasted on a futile assault on Jerusalem. Twice the French forced my uncle to waste men and horses on a goal that was never achievable. Even if we could capture it, Jerusalem cannot be held now any more than it could have been held three years ago. When reinforcements arrive from the West, we need to direct them toward a goal that is strategically sound and will strengthen this kingdom in the long run."

Ibelin nodded, relieved that Champagne had learned this lesson from the Lionheart. "I couldn't have said it better myself," he told his young king.

Champagne looked pleased by this reply, and Ibelin was both flattered and unsettled. It was flattering that Champagne valued his opinion, but not good for a king to be so obviously unsure about his own military instincts.

Champagne continued, "So, Ascalon? I know how reluctant my uncle was to withdraw from Ascalon—not to mention the effort he put into rebuilding it."

Ibelin's heart missed a beat. To retake Ascalon, they would have to recapture Ibelin first. For a second the image of Ibelin hovered in his consciousness, calling to him like the sirens of the Odyssey. Then Ibelin shook his head sharply to banish it to Hades. "No. Ascalon, like Jerusalem, is far too vulnerable. Your uncle, however, was planning an assault to retake Beirut when Saladin's attack on Jaffa diverted him. Re-establishing control of the coast from here to the County of Tripoli ought to be your priority. It will greatly strengthen all three remaining Christian states if we eliminate the Saracen enclaves separating us."

Champagne nodded and admitted, "Yes, that makes sense. I'll see what the others say."

Ibelin nodded and got to his feet. "Then with your leave, I'll go find my wife and say goodbye to Isabella."

Champagne stood and they embraced briefly.

"Go with God," Champagne ended the audience, and Ibelin bowed deeply. He liked Champagne, but as he exited the chamber he still felt a sense of relief and excitement to be returning to Cyprus.

Chapter Eighteen
Pirates of the
Mediterranean

Paradisi, Cyprus,
November 1195

THE PLACE WAS WELL NAMED, ESCHIVA thought. There was surely no place on
earth more like paradise than this manor, nestled between low hills encircling a
small cove on the south shore of Cyprus. There was a beach of fine white sand
between arms of white limestone, and water so clear it was like glass the color
of aquamarines. Even when the wind blew, it remained transparent, yet transported the gently wiggling beams of light to the minnow-rich floor of the cove.
The meadows behind the beach were a brilliant green after the first rains of
autumn. They sprouted tiny yellow and white wildflowers. The orange trees on
the slopes were heavy with ripening fruit and harbored hosts of songbirds. The
hills formed a natural protective wall around the small complex of whitewashed
stone buildings, giving Eschiva a sense of utter security and privacy.

Beyond the hills, people labored, traveled, traded, and tilled the soil.
Beyond these natural walls, they quarreled, competed, and complained. Out
there, Aimery was still struggling to establish his control over this unruly island,
and she was expected to be his consort. But here she had no duties and no one
expected anything of her. Instead, she lived in simple peace and harmony with
her little brood of children. Except for Guy, who was with Aimery, they were all
with her, including the latest addition to her growing brood: Hugh. He'd been

born in October, a perfect little Lusignan with hair so fair it was almost invisible and bright blue eyes. He was sure to seduce all the ladies of his brother's court when he grew up, Eschiva thought, just as his father had.

Hugh was not objectively more perfect than any of his older siblings, of course. Eschiva recognized that. Yet after the nightmare of last year's miscarriage, bringing Hugh into the world healthy and whole had seemed miraculous. As if by divine intent, he'd also made things easy for her, coming a little early but with little fuss, and from the start he'd been sweet-tempered. He slept well, fed well, and smiled more than any infant she could remember. With Hugh in her arms, Eschiva felt utterly content and complete.

He would be her last child, she had resolved privately, feeling that three sons and two daughters was enough. Maria Zoë had confided in her that there were safe ways of preventing a new conception without even telling Aimery about it, and Eschiva was resolved to take her advice as soon as she'd recovered enough strength to return to Nicosia and take up her duties.

The need for her to do both—get well *and* take up her duties—was evident to everyone. For all Aimery's concern for her health, he was also impatient for her to take a more active role in his realm now that a tentative peace had been established. A lady dispensing charity and showing an interest in the cultural and social life of the island would do much to bolster his fragile popularity. It was also more appropriate for a lady to be reconciliatory and forgiving than for the lord himself. A lord needed to be feared and respected; a lady to be loved and cherished. Aimery argued persuasively that the time had come when a gentler face would win them more support than his sword, and he wanted her to be that face.

But there was also no question that Eschiva was too weak to take up her duties just yet. She tired just from walking from one end of the palace in Nicosia to another. She had frequent dizzy spells, and her skin was so pale and bloodless it was like ivory. The apothecary Andreas Katzouroubis prescribed complete rest and a diet rich in seafood, particularly mussels and clams, and cheese. He also suggested she eat as many oranges as possible and cook with lemon juice.

Eschiva was determined to follow the doctor's orders, and Paradisi was surely the perfect place to do so. Not only was it surrounded by orange groves, while bountiful lemon trees filled a walled garden, but local fishermen brought their catch to the cove daily. The local women brought their fresh cheese as well, along with olives soaked in their own oil. Eschiva had convinced herself she was feeling better already, although she'd only been here a fortnight.

"Mama! Mama!" six-year-old Aimery called excitedly from the beach. "Come see! Come see!" His high-pitched voice was frail and distant, partially carried away by the light but freshening breeze.

Eschiva was sitting under a roof of vine leaves woven through a framework of bamboo with Hugh in a cradle beside her. She lifted her head to see what had excited her middle son.

"Baby turtles, Mama!" The high-pitched voice of nine-year-old Helvis joined her little brother.

Eschiva could see all three of the older children clustered around something on the beach. Her lethargic body wanted to remain where she was, but her heart said she should go to the children. When would she ever again have time for them like this? If Aimery succeeded and was given a crown, she would become a queen. She would have endless duties and obligations, not to mention the duty to protect her dignity. She would not be allowed to wade barefoot into the lusciously warm waters of the Mediterranean to look at baby turtles with her children.

She glanced around for the wet nurse, but the young Italian woman, Cecilia, had gone inside to fetch some needlework for them. So Eschiva scooped little Hugh into her arms and started down the sandy trail through the soft grass toward the beach. Before she reached little Aimery and Helvis, however, eleven-year-old Burgundia came running toward her. "Give Hugh to me, Mama!" she demanded, adding, "You know it exhausts you to carry him!"

Eschiva smiled at Burgundia's concern and handed off the easygoing Hugh, not because she felt exhausted, but because she liked to see her eldest daughter taking such an interest in her infant brother. Aimery was already talking about marriages for Burgundia. Thinking like a king, he was looking for alliances that would serve Cyprus best. He was currently most taken with the thought of forging ties of kinship with Leo of Armenia. Leo had been systematically expanding his territory and his power for several years now, and he had proved effective in holding his frontiers against the Turks as well. Furthermore, he favored independence over close ties to Constantinople. However, he had no sons, so any ties would be indirect, via one of his nephews. Eschiva had asked for more information about these young men, and Aimery had promised to find out what he could. Meanwhile, Aimery had suggested as an alternative that they ask the Holy Roman Emperor to suggest one of his nobles as a means of binding the ever-slippery Hohenstaufen more closely to them. Or there was the Venetian option. As an island kingdom, Cyprus needed maritime ties, and Venice, so Aimery claimed, was on the ascent.

Eschiva had reached the beach, and with a sense of self-indulgence she kicked off her sandals to enjoy the near-visceral pleasure of walking barefoot on the soft, still cool sand. She loved the way her heels sank down and her toes spread out as she rolled forward on first one foot and then the other. Meanwhile

Helvis and little Aimery ran toward her, and each took a hand to lead her to the turtles farther down the beach.

Peripherally something caught her attention and, still smiling from mindless contentment, Eschiva turned lazily to see what it was. She was expecting a seagull, a dolphin, or at most a fisherman with his catch to sell. To her astonishment, she saw the low, sinister prow of a galley oozing its way into the little cove.

In sheer amazement, she stopped dead in her tracks to stare at the ship. The oars were barely moving as it advanced cautiously. No sail was set. No banners flew from the masthead. It was painted black. Just black. Without a trace of trim or heraldry. Even the oars were black.

As if a cloud had crossed the face of the sun, Eschiva felt a shiver run down her spine. Something wasn't right about this galley.

Little Aimery and Helvis had stopped when she did, and their looks followed hers. "What ship is that, Mama?" Helvis asked, frowning.

"Is it a pirate ship?" Little Aimery asked eagerly.

"I don't know," Eschiva answered, adding as a second inexplicable shiver ran down her spine, "I think we should go back to the manor."

"No, no!" Little Aimery protested, tugging at her hand. "Come see baby turtles!"

Eschiva's eyes were still on the ship. Men were pointing at her and she heard shouts in Greek. Men started running about frantically, and the ship pivoted as the starboard oars backwatered. At the stern men appeared to be launching a tender.

"No, Aimery!" Eschiva told her son firmly. "We need to go back to the manor *now!*" She turned around, but little Aimery was still trying to pull her in the opposite direction. Although Helvis and Burgundia scolded him jointly, little Aimery did not take his elder sisters seriously and dug in more determinedly.

"Burgundia, hurry back with Hugh!" Eschiva ordered her eldest daughter, as the sense of danger grew greater with each heartbeat. The tender had plunged into the water with a splash, and half a dozen men jumped overboard from the galley to clamber up into it from the water. Yet the very threat that emanated from the strange ship made Burgundia cling to her side.

Eschiva reached her sandals and bent to pull them onto her feet. Behind her the sound of oars striking the water came nearer and nearer. She glanced in the direction of the approaching tender. There were four men pulling at the oars, their backs to her, and two other men in the boat. They had thick black beards over naked torsos. The hilts of multiple knives and swords lined their belts. Little Aimery in his innocence was right: they must surely be pirates.

Eschiva kicked her sandals aside and tried to run barefoot across the field to the manor, but little stones and crabgrass hobbled her. Despite the rising panic, her feet were too tender, and her strength was giving out. "Run, children! Run!" she screamed. Behind her the keel crunched on the sand of the beach. Soft thuds told her men had jumped onto the sand.

Only Helvis obeyed. Little Aimery turned around to see what was happening and froze at the sight of the men running toward him; Burgundia clutched Hugh in her arms and started whimpering.

The next thing Eschiva knew, she'd been grabbed from behind by a powerful arm around her waist. The stench of the man, as much as the brutality of his grip, made her feel faint. Her legs gave way under her, and she felt them flying through the air as the man spun about and started back to the boat with her. She tried to scream, but his grip was choking the wind from her. Her cries came out in short gasps in rhythm with his strides.

Burgundia managed to get out a bloodcurdling scream before they silenced her somehow, and little Hugh wailed at a pitch to wake the dead. Little Aimery joined in and then Helvis, but Eschiva could see nothing anymore. She was forcefully shoved over the gunnel into the tender. She fell headfirst into the boat, and hit the edge of the seat so hard she was winded. Then her head cracked against the side of the boat, and she felt herself spinning. Still, she struggled to drag herself upright, grasping the side of the boat. A foot kicked her arm, breaking her hold on the side of the boat, and someone clambered into the boat on top of her. She caught a glimpse of a pirate wrenching Hugh away from Burgundia before she was shoved back to the bottom of the boat and held down by the man's naked foot. Eschiva started screaming hysterically as Burgundia was hurled into the boat like a sack of grain, and tiny vibrations indicated the boat was being shoved down the beach. Just as it began to float, a pirate with Hugh in his arms stepped over Eschiva to go to the bow.

The oarsmen took their places and deftly turned the tender back towards the galley. Abruptly the boat tilted sharply to the side. Eschiva screamed, thinking they were about to capsize. Instead, a pirate with her howling son under one arm and dragging Helvis by her hair with the other appeared at the side of the boat. He flung Aimery at his fellows, then dumped a struggling Helvis into the bottom of the boat. One pirate boxed Aimery into silence, while a second stood straddling Helvis with a drawn sword lifted over his head. He shouted at them in Greek.

The side of Helvis' face was torn open with cuts and bruises. Blood oozed out of the side of her mouth and tears streamed down her face. Burgundia was sobbing hysterically as she stretched out her arms to the pirate holding Hugh. "Give him back! Give him back!" she kept pleading frantically.

On the wind behind them came the sound of shouting, and Eschiva strug-gled to right herself. The man holding her down with his foot glanced over his shoulder and laughed. Confident of their escape, he took his foot off her chest, and Eschiva dragged herself upright enough to see back to the shore.

Cecilia was standing at the edge of the shore, gesturing wildly, while a half-dozen men rushed onto the beach. Most were bareheaded and without arms or armor. Only one man had a crossbow. He raised it to take aim—but then, shaking his head, lowered it again. He could not risk killing the Lady of Lusignan or one of her children.

With a clunk that sent a shudder through the whole boat, they collided with the galley. The pirate who had captured her shook his naked cutlass in Eschiva's face and pointed for her to climb up netting that had been flung over the galley's side. Eschiva shook her head to indicate she didn't have the strength, but the man grabbed Helvis by the hair again and lifted her clear off the bench to hold her suspended, squirming and sobbing in both terror and pain. With his other hand he held a knife to her throat. "Help me! Help me!" Helvis pleaded.

Eschiva *had* to find the strength to go up the nets. She grabbed them with both hands, and sobbing like her nine-year-old, tried to pull herself up, but she *couldn't*. Then she felt a man's hand shoved between her buttocks, and with brute force he pushed her upwards, as her heart stopped in shame at his intimate grasp. Fortunately, two men leaned down over the railing of the galley and grabbed her under the arms from either side. She was dragged up over the railing and flung onto the deck like a fish. Other pirates were pushing, pulling, or carrying Helvis, Burgundia, little Aimery, and Hugh up the netting.

Eschiva crawled on her knees to pull the terrified Helvis into her arms as the galley started to pivot once again. The tender abandoned, the galley scuttled out of the cove. Clutching Helvis in her arms, the last thing Eschiva saw was the loyal Sir Simon splashing furiously into the water of the cove. He was swinging his sword over his head and shouting insults, curses, and threats. But it was pointless. He couldn't swim in armor, and the galley was surging forward under the power of forty oars.

The pirates locked them in the hold. They were below the water line, and the sound of water rushing past was a constant reminder of the growing distance from home, safety, and civilization. Hugh, usually such a sweet baby, could not be quieted, because he was hungry and his diapers soiled, but Eschiva's breasts were dry and they had neither food nor clean diapers with them. Little Aimery, after an initial temper tantrum pounding his little fists on the deck, collapsed into a ball of misery and fell asleep. Burgundia kept trying to soothe Hugh, and Eschiva left her to it; as long as Burgundia focused on Hugh, she had less opportunity to think about her own situation. Helvis, lying in her arms, cried herself to sleep.

Eschiva had no sense of where they might be heading, but it was certainly as far away from Cyprus as possible. Nor had she any sense of time, beyond the fact that it was long enough for them all to get very hungry and to be forced to relieve themselves as best they could in a bucket they had found amidst the other nautical supplies.

Eschiva was not naive. She had no illusions about what would soon happen to her, and Burgundia, at eleven, would most likely share her fate. Even Helvis wasn't safe. Not if these pirates were desperate for a female body. As soon as the pirates believed they were safe from pursuit, they would settle down to enjoy their "prizes."

Eschiva tried to remember everything Beatrice had said about the repeated rapes she had endured after her capture. The problem was that Beatrice had not *talked* about it. Not really. She had only, very occasionally, made oblique references with phrases like, "One can learn to endure anything." Or, when someone complained too thoughtlessly, she might remark tartly, "Things could be worse." Still, Beatrice *had* survived with her sanity intact. She had survived long enough to be freed, and because of that, she had been restored to dignity and even authority.

Anne, on the other hand, had not. She had returned from captivity a stunted human, a girl so terrified of the world around her that she literally could not function in it and had retreated to the cell of a convent. She had been transformed from a happy child into a girl who abhorred her very essence, all because she'd been circumcised and then raped by a man she detested at the age of eleven. Burgundia's age . . .

To make things worse for Eschiva, she recognized that while the Saracens viewed Christian women as despicable objects to use as they pleased, they were nevertheless marketable commodities that could be sold to the next man when they tired of them. The pirates might not have that option, which made it far more likely they would simply kill them when they were done with them. By the time the fifty to sixty men aboard were tired of the three females, Eschiva reflected, she and her girls would probably be glad to die. . . .

But what could the pirates possibly want with Hugh? They might raise Aimery to be one of their own. He could serve them like a slave until he either died from the treatment or grew strong enough to fight back and win their respect. A pirate version of the Mamluke fate. Hugh, however, was too small to be put to work for years to come. He was and would continue to be a perpetual irritation. If they didn't feed and clean him, he would die—so why hadn't they just left him behind? If only they had left Hugh behind . . . If only . . .

Eschiva only realized she had drifted off to sleep when she woke up again. Someone, presumably Burgundia, had dragged a coil of ropes closer and bedded her head upon it. Hugh was whimpering weakly from another coiled hawser, while the three older children had fallen asleep in each other's arms. Although the hold was still warm, the sun no longer burned down on the deck overhead, and the darkness was greater than before. It must be night, Eschiva registered.

She lifted her head and tried to look around the hold, conscious that something had woken her. She struggled to sit up, clamping her teeth against the pain from the bruises to her ribs. Her neck had a crick in it and her shoulder and hip were throbbing with pain. The bruises on her forehead were swollen and hot to touch. She burned with shame as she remembered the feel of the pirate's hand in her crotch, but that thought reminded her of the worse that was bound to come.

The shock had worn off enough, however, for her to try to think what she could do to save her daughters. She could offer to sleep with all of them—but with sixty men, even three women were too few to go around. She wasn't so beautiful that she would be viewed as a special prize. . . .

Of course, her household knights would have sent word to Aimery, but it would take them a day to reach Nicosia, and by then the sea would have swallowed their tracks, and no one would ever find them again. Not unless their corpses washed up in still-identifiable condition on a shore where people had heard about the kidnapping.

There seemed to be a lot of shouting and running about on the deck overhead, Eschiva registered. That probably meant they were approaching a port or an anchorage. She glanced around the hold, pointlessly looking for a place to hide her children. It was a futile thought, because while she could hide them from sight, the pirates knew their own ship better than anyone. They knew, too, that their prisoners could not escape. No matter how good their hiding place, they would be found eventually. . . .

Oddly for going into port, the sound of water hissing along the side of the ship appeared to be intensifying, and the oars were slapping into the water at a faster rate. They were increasing rather than slowing their speed. Perhaps there was a headland or strait they needed to pass around or through?

Abruptly, with a violent jolt and a loud bang, the galley was flung sideways. The children awoke with cries of fear, and overhead all hell broke loose. Shouts, screams, curses, thuds, and crashes could be heard—followed by the clang of weapons.

Eschiva sat bolt upright and then struggled to get to her feet, only to fall down again. The galley was unsteady, wallowing in the waves.

A crash almost directly overhead was followed by splinters raining down on her, and the children started screaming. Burgundia swept up Hugh and clutched him to her, while Helvis and little Aimery cowered down behind one of the coils of rope. Eschiva stepped out of the shower of splinters so she could look upwards. An ax tip pierced the deck, was withdrawn, and then appeared again more fully. It took another half-dozen blows before one of the planks gave way enough to be kicked in. Immediately the ax blows were directed at the adjacent planks until a hole large enough for a man was smashed open. A moment later, a man with an ax in one hand landed in the hold.

Eschiva had been hoping it would be Aimery or one of his knights, and was bewildered to find herself facing a man in leather armor and an open-faced helmet. Then she recognized Magnussen, and called to him in relief.

Magnussen had been searching the darkness. He spun around at the sound of his name, and crossed the distance to Eschiva with a single stride. "Hurry! We can't hold them for long." He had hold of her upper arm.

"The children!" Eschiva countered, pointing.

Magnussen turned, saw them, nodded, and then turned back to Eschiva. "You first! I'll lift you up to my men standing by the hole in the deck!"

Eschiva didn't have the strength to argue. She let Magnussen grab her around the hips and lift her up toward the break in the deck overhead. As her head emerged above the level of the planking, two men reached for her and helped drag her free. No sooner had she gained the deck enough to crawl aside than she gasped out, "My children! They're with me!"

Magnussen's men were already reaching back into the hole to help Helvis out. Eschiva didn't have the strength to stand, but her eyes turned to the battle raging across the deck of the galley. In the darkness, it was impossible to tell friend from foe. All she could make out were scores of men fighting furiously with sword, ax, and cutlass. She saw a man gutted, his innards spewing out of his mouth as he doubled over, and she turned her head away, screwing her eyes shut.

Magnussen was beside her again. He grabbed her upper arm and dragged her to her feet. "We can't hold them much longer!" he repeated. "Come!"

Eschiva stumbled and tripped as he dragged her to the railing. The *Storm Bird* lay alongside, but about ten feet lower in the water. Eschiva hadn't realized the freeboard of this galley was so much greater.

"Over the side!" Magnussen ordered.

"I can't," Eschiva gasped, clutching the side of the ship. The world was spinning around her as she was overwhelmed by one of her dizzy spells.

Even as she spoke, a dozen men closed around them, pursued by the pirates. Magnussen's men were fighting—and dying—to keep this small piece of deck in their control. If they hesitated another second, they would all die here—and Eschiva would still be a captive. She recognized that, but she did not have the *strength* to lift her legs over the railing. "The children! Take the children! Leave me!"

"Hugh!" Burgundia thrust her little brother into Magnussen's astonished arms. "Take Hugh to safety! I'm staying with my mother!"

"Haakon!" It was one of his men calling as he slid on his own blood and went down with a terrible crash. A cutlass slit his throat as he lay at the pirate's feet.

A bloody hand closed around Helvis' hair and dragged her backwards. Another pirate grabbed hold of a paralyzed little Aimery.

Magnussen vaulted over the railing to land on the deck of his own ship with Hugh still clutched in the crook of his arm. The next instant Eschiva was yanked away from the railing and flung backward. As her head hit the deck, she lost consciousness.

The news of the kidnapping of the Lady of Lusignan and her children spread like wildfire across Cyprus. It was the only topic of conversation in the markets and the taverns of city and town, and across the island Masses were sung for the safe return of the hostages in churches both humble and grand. No matter what people thought of the Franks in general or Lusignan in particular, there was widespread condemnation of the abduction of a young mother, her infant, and three young children. Expressions of distress, sympathy, condolences, and offers of help almost overwhelmed the palace staff.

Sir Simon had dramatically offered Aimery his sword hilt first and spread out his arms, inviting execution. Instead Aimery had cuffed him and ordered him out of his sight. Cecilia had been questioned mercilessly about what had happened until she collapsed in misery and had to be put to bed to recover. Beatrice, confronted with memories she preferred to forget, wore an expression both haggard and haunted as she tried to keep the household functioning. Maria Zoë found sleep impossible and felt lamed by her helplessness as she watched both Balian and Aimery rage futilely.

"Who could possibly want to harm Eschiva?" Aimery asked them collectively and rhetorically for the hundredth time. "Who? And why? If it had been pirates—as they all claim," he dismissed his wife's household contemptuously, "why haven't there been any ransom demands? I'd pay anything! Anything at all!" He dropped his grizzled head in his hands and cried out inarticulately to Christ.

Aimery hadn't shaved or combed since the news arrived, and with blood-shot eyes and tangled hair he looked quite wild. He was grayer, too, the news having aged him overnight. The sleepless nights made his voice raw when he roared his frustration at everyone in hearing. Nor he could stay still. Instead, when he wasn't chasing after someone for possible information, he paced about the solar, kicking at the furnishings and pounding his fist randomly on tables, walls, and window sills. His thoughts spun around him viciously. His instinct was to attack, to fight, to kill—but he didn't have a target.

Balian's anger had burned itself out sooner, and he now sat looking worse than at any time since his arrival in Tyre after the surrender of Jerusalem. His eyes were sunken in the sockets of his face, and the skin around his eyes and jowls sagged like an old man's, although he was not yet forty-seven. "Pirates will have wanted to put enough distance between you and them to prevent a rescue attempt. They will then have to send someone back across that distance, possibly by a circuitous route to disguise their whereabouts, with their demands," Balian responded to Aimery's most recent outburst.

"What are you saying?" Aimery demanded, staring at him belligerently, although they had never been as united in their feelings as they were now. Over the years they had disagreed over politics, strategy, and tactics. There had been times when Aimery resented Eschiva's affection for Balian, and times when Balian had blamed Aimery for his treatment of Eschiva. Certainly they had been on opposing sides during the succession crisis after Baldwin V's death and again after Queen Sibylla's death. But their love of Eschiva had always bound them together and forced them to find common ground again and again.

"All I'm saying is that the ransom demands may yet materialize," Balian noted wearily.

"We need to burn out the whole nest of pirates at Famagusta!" Aimery declared, pounding his fist on the nearest table.

Balian looked up at him with a sour expression, too tired to refrain from pointing out, "I *told* you to do that a year ago! Besides," he added in a more dis-couraged tone, "the pirates anticipated you and have cleared the harbor. It hasn't been this empty in two years, John tells me."

"Where the hell is Magnussen?" Aimery burst out next. "He's supposed to keep my waters safe!"

This time Balian bit his tongue rather than pointing out that Aimery had given Magnussen no resources with which to build up a fleet. It was obvious that Aimery was in no mood for a discussion of what he might have done wrong, and Balian conceded that there was little point in such debate anyway. There would be time enough for recriminations *after* they learned who was behind this kidnapping, and what they needed to do to set Eschiva and the children free.

Aimery growled, "When I find out who told these bastards where Eschiva was, I'll skin him—or her—alive."

"You've been in the East too long, Aimery," Maria Zoë remarked. "Torture is such an Eastern custom—and one Eschiva abhorred."

The clatter of horses, followed by shouting and pounding, erupted in the street below at the entrance to the palace. Maria Zoë, who was sitting in the window seat, leaned forward to try to see what the commotion was. "It looks like a rider has just arrived, but I can't see who it might be. He's completely hooded. It's raining," she added, as she noticed the way the torchlight glistened on the cobbles of the street.

Aimery immediately headed for the door, declaring more from hope than conviction, "It must be someone with news of Eschiva!"

At the door to the hall, he saw a crowd of people burst in and start moving toward the dais in an excited mob. Philip d'Ibelin, sitting with his brother John and cousin Guy at one of the tables, leapt up and started running toward the solar. He bounded onto the raised dais with a single leap, and seeing Aimery in the doorway, called to him, "My lord! Someone's coming—"

"I'm not blind and deaf!" Aimery answered irritably, his eyes riveted on the man in the rain-darkened cloak coming toward him. The hood still shielded his face, but it was clear from his posture that he carried something under his cloak, something precious by the way he moved. He reached the foot of the dais steps and climbed them with a weary doggedness that spoke of long hours in the saddle. Then he looked up and was close enough for Aimery to see his face.

It was a stranger.

The stranger reached up to push his hood off his head with one hand, revealing long, red-blond hair. His other hand remained hidden under his cloak, the elbow still crooked. "My lord," he croaked out, in a voice laden with grief and warning of bad news.

Aimery backed up into the solar, a sense of foreboding freezing his face and making his movements lame and clumsy.

The cloaked stranger followed him into the room. He was wearing old-fashioned leather boots bound to the leg with thongs, and something clicked in Aimery's memory. This was surely one of Magnussen's men.

"My lord," the man repeated, going down on one knee and then gently pulling back his cloak to reveal a baby sleeping in the crook of his arm.

"Hugh!" Aimery exclaimed instantly, as Maria Zoë and Balian both sprang to their feet in amazement.

"Yes, my lord. Your son Hugh," the man declared, holding the infant up to Aimery.

Aimery took the little bundle into his arms and looked down at him with wonder. But then his brows knotted in bewilderment. "But what of his brother? Where is Eschiva? The girls?—"

"My lord, Haakon managed to board the pirate ship with half the crew. He broke into the hold where your lady and the children were being held. The crew held the pirates off long enough for Haakon to get them all on deck, but your lady was too weak to climb over the side. As the pirates overwhelmed the crew, your lady thrust the baby into Haakon's arms and begged him to save at least the infant. That's what he did."

"Where is he?" Aimery demanded, and from his grim expression and tone it was clear that he was not satisfied with this story.

"He's dead."

Aimery, Balian, and Maria Zoë all gasped at once, and stared at the messenger.

"The pirates fired crossbows as we pulled away. One went straight through Haakon's back, killing him instantly. We barely managed to catch Hugh as he fell. Almost all the men who had boarded the galley with Haakon were killed, and we lost six more to the crossbows. The *Storm Bird* was so badly reamed from the collision she nearly sank on the return to port. She'll never be seaworthy again." Tears were running down the Norseman's face as he spoke of the fate of his ship, but they were for his captain and his shipmates, too.

Aimery stared in stunned horror, and Maria Zoë hastened to take the baby out of his arms before he dropped the little bundle in his state of shock.

"Eschiva and the girls? They're still in the hands of the pirates?" Aimery asked, not wanting to believe it.

"Yes, my lord."

"But . . . " But what?

"It was Kanakes," the Norseman added.

"What? Who?" Aimery shook himself out of his shock.

"Kanakes," the Norseman repeated. "He's quite a famous pirate."

"I know! I put a price on his head!" Aimery answered, irritated. "But why hasn't he sent me ransom demands? What does he intend to do with my wife and children?"

"I don't know, my lord, but he was headed for Antiochia Mikra on the southwest coast of Cilicia when we intercepted him."

"Isaac!" Maria Comnena recognized the ruler of this rebellious enclave of Cilicia immediately.

"Isaac who?" Aimery and Balian asked in unison.

"I forget what he calls himself. He's nothing but a petty warlord, a traitor to the Emperor. I believe he has been meddling in the dispute between Leo of Armenia and Bohemond of Antioch. He was *certainly* allied with Saladin as long as the latter lived. God knows who he's allied with now, but his only interests are his own power and wealth."

"Then he will sue for ransom?" Aimery asked.

Maria Zoë drew a breath and held it, hesitating with her answer. In the end she said, "It's hard to know what someone like that wants. I fear he will seek more than money. That would be too mercenary for him. He sees himself more as a power broker." She paused and then reminded them of the positive: "At least we now know to whom we can direct an embassy."

Aimery swung around and looked Balian in the eye. "Will you go?"

"Of course; I'll leave as soon as possible." As he spoke Balian reached out to raise the Norseman to his feet, remarking to the sailor, "You need rest and food. I'll see that you get both, and then I will ask that Masses be said for the soul of one of the bravest and truest men I have ever had the privilege to meet: Admiral Haakon Magnussen."

Cilicia

After the rescue attempt, the treatment of the Lusignan hostages deteriorated. They were bound hand and foot and watched continuously. Although given water on demand, they were given no food nor any chance to relieve themselves. This treatment robbed them of any strength and all pride. But what did it matter? The pirates had gloated over the fact that the rescue had been a disaster. As they tied them up, they'd told Eschiva that Magnussen had been killed, and that Hugh had fallen overboard to drown. The news had broken Eschiva's heart, leaving her numb to her own fate.

The sounds of oars being shipped, and feet running back and forth overhead, followed by the thud and shudder of the ship going alongside a quay, dragged Eschiva from her oblivion. She lifted her head to glance at her three terrified children. Although Burgundia was trying to be brave, Helvis and little Aimery were both whimpering again. The children were not too young to realize that their arrival at whatever the destination was would bring them new horrors. Helvis' face was swollen and covered with dried blood from the injuries she had received during the kidnapping. Burgundia's gown was soiled from holding Hugh in his dirty diapers. Eschiva glanced down at her own gown and realized it, too, was torn and filthy.

And Hugh was dead. Drowned.

Voices were shouting down to the hold, and the man guarding them stood with a grunt. A ladder was lowered, and their guard cut the cords binding their wrists and ankles before gesturing with his knife for them to climb the ladder. Aimery was closest, and at the sight of the threatening knife blade he scampered up the ladder with astonishing energy. Helvis followed quickly, but Burgundia looked back toward her mother. "Mama?"

The man with the knife shook it at Burgundia, and she grabbed the ladder and mounted it with evident reluctance, but steadily enough to avoid any more threats. Lastly, the man gestured for Eschiva to go. She tried to stand, but the world started spinning around her. She staggered forward, lost her balance, and crashed down onto the floor of the hold. A sharp pain stabbed up from her hip, and she tasted bile in her throat. Over her head the pirate stood shouting at her, his knife just inches from her face. But just trying to sit upright brought the dizziness back and she grayed out.

The pirate shouted furiously. Eschiva expected to feel cold steel on her throat. Instead, men thudded down beside her and roughly dragged her up the ladder to dump her on the deck of the ship.

The fresh air smelled amazingly good, and started to revive her. Burgundia was beside her, too, her little hand on her shoulder saying, "Mama! Mama! Are you all right?"

Eschiva put her hand over Burgundia's and nodded, but did not speak.

"My mother's sick!" Burgundia spiritedly told the pirates gathered around them. "She can't walk."

Eschiva noted mentally that they didn't need her upright to rape her. They could do that well enough with her lying right here.

Babbling voices and much commotion, however, ended in an improvised stretcher being brought. To her amazement, Eschiva was carried off the galley on this, with Burgundia close beside her. Eschiva had glimpses of a quay laden with barrels and crates being on- or off-loaded. There were some weathered warehouses crowding the quay, and a tavern filled with gaping people in shoddy clothes. The women wore their hair loose and uncovered (whores), and the men looked like sailors from all the seas on earth.

The stretcher was put on the back of a wagon, and the children were ordered to crawl onto the back beside their mother. From where she lay, Eschiva could see nothing but the side of the wagon, so she squeezed Burgundia's hand and whispered, "Tell me what you can see."

"It's a port," Burgundia started.

"Can you see minarets?" Eschiva asked, fearing they had been landed in Saracen territory and were headed for a slave market.

"No. There's a church up on the hill."

"A church?" Eschiva could hardly believe their good fortune. "What does it look like?"

"It's made of red brick with a dome, more like a Greek church than one of ours."

Eschiva nodded in relief and let her eyes roll back in her head as unconsciousness overcame her.

She was woken by Burgundia shaking her shoulder. "Mama! Mama! They want us to get out."

Sure enough, the wagon had halted and men were crowding around it, peering over the sides. These men were dressed differently from the pirates. They had long-sleeved shirts rather than naked torsos, and some had armor that was fashioned primarily from leather but with chain mail in places where flexibility was particularly important, like the neck and under the arms. The children were ordered off the cart with gestures, and then someone grabbed the handles at the end of Eschiva's stretcher and pulled them far enough for a second man to get hold of the other end. They carried her a few yards and then set her down again in the grass.

From here Eschiva could see what looked like a poor, rundown farm with a lofty barn, some smelly and muddy pens for pigs (further evidence they were in Christian-held territory), and a stucco house with a smoking chimney. Two women in brown homespun dresses and linen aprons stood staring at the commotion. After some shouting in their direction, the women came over and took charge of the three Lusignan children, gesturing for them to come into the house. Although the women did not look very bright and were clearly taking orders from the armed men, they were instinctively maternal, and one gently touched Helvis' bruised and scratched face, saying something that sounded comforting.

Eschiva was left lying outside for several more minutes. Eventually she saw a man in long black robes come out of the house. The robes looked like those of an Orthodox monk, but that didn't make sense to Eschiva. Surely no man of God would be involved in kidnapping, rape, and whatever else was going on here? This man handed a purse over to the leading pirate. The pirate chief opened the drawstring and poured the coins into his palm, counting carefully. Satisfied, he nodded, replaced the coins in the purse, and climbed back onto the seat of the wagon. The other pirates clambered onto the back, and the wagon slowly turned around in the little yard. Evidently the pirates had been contracted to conduct this abduction by the men here. That meant the objective was not merely rape and murder, Eschiva reasoned.

After the pirates had departed, the man in the black robes approached Eschiva with long, purposeful strides. He had a full black beard that extended a good four inches from his chin. His black hair was long and wild. His nose was broad, and his eyes were pools of black hatred. Eschiva recognized that, even if his expression was completely at odds with the large wooden cross that hung on his breast. This man was indeed an Orthodox monk, she registered.

He stopped, looked down at her for a long moment, and then spat on her. "Lusignan!" he hissed. "Lusignan's woman and brats!" he spat again, followed by a furious diatribe in Greek. All she could understand was the visceral hatred it expressed.

Another man had come up behind the monk and laid a hand on his shoulder. He said something in Greek and then turned to Eschiva and spoke in heavily accented and poorly constructed French. "My friend Brother Zotikos would rather I kill you and the children, but I have convinced him you're worth more to us alive than dead. We will send your husband your wedding ring to prove we hold you in our power, and we will give him a choice. Either he and his wild dogs depart Cyprus and leave it to us Greeks, or we will kill his children one by one and then kill you, too—but not until we've turned you over to our men to enjoy." He smiled at the thought, evidently anticipating that Lusignan would sacrifice his family for his throne.

Eschiva looked him in the eye and said with all the strength she could muster, "Your men will find little pleasure in raping a corpse."

The man frowned and snapped, "We'll kill you *afterwards*, stupid."

Eschiva shook her head. "It will be too late. I am already dying." She closed her eyes, crossed herself, and started reciting the Lord's Prayer with a sense of peace. She could not know what would happen, but she was certain that Aimery would not abandon their children. As for herself, she had said the truth. She could sense that she was dying. She would surely not live long enough for her fate to be of consequence in the power struggle between her husband and her captors.

Chapter Nineteen
Leo of Armenia

Sis, Cilician Armenia, December 1195

IBELIN SET SAIL FROM KYRENIA IN a Venetian galley and made landfall at Antiochia Mikra before sundown. Here, however, his vessel was denied entry. After being fired upon by crossbowmen in the breakwater tower, the ship put about and headed east. They followed the coastline to the Armenian port of Corycos.[†]

This much more significant port was guarded far more effectively. It had a magnificent fortress built on the island guarding the entrance, and a second, somewhat smaller, castle on the mainland. In addition, a pier or breakwater that would effectively close the waterway between them to a narrow passage was under construction. But this was a friendly port; they sailed in without obstacle.

No sooner had they docked than an Armenian customs official boarded. The Venetian captain explained that he was not trading, simply bringing passengers. Ibelin's party of six knights included a man with Edessan roots and an Armenian mother, Sir Constantine. Sir Constantine spoke Armenian well and rapidly explained their situation. The customs official immediately agreed to take them to Simon, Baron of Corycos.

Ibelin and his party were welcomed at the Armenian baron's town house, where news of the Lady of Lusignan's kidnapping ignited indignation and anger.

---

† Greek: Κώρυκος; Latin Chronicles: Gorhigos

Their host and his knights were quick to offer their support, and there was brief talk of an immediate assault on Antiochia Mikra. ("We should have taken that rats' nest long ago!" was the widespread feeling.) In the end, however, the calmer voice of the Lord of Corycos prevailed. Ibelin was promised horses and an escort commanded by the Baron's eldest son, Ravon, to take him to Leo, the ruler of Armenian Cilicia.

After a night's rest, Ibelin, his knights and escort set off for Sis, the Armenian capital, some two hundred miles to the northeast. They covered the distance in just over five days, entering Sis in late afternoon on the second Sunday in Advent, according to the Armenian calendar.

Sis, located at the foot of the Taurus Mountains, was a fine town with many stone houses behind a strong perimeter wall reinforced by tall, square towers at regular intervals. The domes of the churches dominated the skyline of the lower town, but the castle proudly stood above the town, banners fluttering boastfully from all its towers.

Ravon of Corycos was sufficiently important to gain them immediate and unquestioned access to the fortress. Their horses were taken by attentive grooms, and in a very short period of time a household official appeared. He bowed deeply to Ibelin, welcoming him in excellent French to Cilician Armenia and the residence of its ruler. He offered the hospitality of his lord to Ibelin and his party, indicating that the knights should share in the common meal in the great hall, while offering to take Ibelin to a guest chamber where he could bathe and change before an audience with Leo. Ibelin asked that one squire and Sir Constantine accompany him, a request readily granted.

Ibelin followed the household official up a series of stairs and down corridors to a tower chamber well-appointed with fur rugs, including an entire bear. The other furnishings consisted of elaborately carved chests, tables, and chairs, as well as a large box bed hung with fine curtains. The temperature here at the foot of the Taurus Mountains at this time of year was decidedly chilly, and the steward promised that a fire would be laid immediately. He also promised that a bath and hot water would be brought to the chamber along with refreshments. Adding that he could not know when his lord would grant an audience, he suggested that Ibelin make himself comfortable and partake of the refreshments. Then he withdrew.

Ibelin went to the window and opened the shutters to orient himself. He was confronted by a spectacular view of distant snow-capped mountains, and an extensive brick monastery complex with a large domed church on a nearer hill. The bells of the monastery clanged faintly on the cold air, and, as if they were a signal, the bells of the churches in the city started to ring in their different notes. Ibelin crossed himself and drew back into the room, shuddering from the cold air.

This was the farthest he had ever been from Ibelin in his entire life. The world here seemed stranger to him than Damascus. At least in Damascus he had spoken the language. . . .

He turned back into the room, and his eyes fell on Sir Constantine. The knight was slight and wiry, his strength not visible but, Ibelin knew from experience, dogged. Sir Constantine was somewhat taciturn by nature, not to say melancholy, a function perhaps of his history. His grandfather had been killed in the skirmish that led to the capture of Joscelyn II of Edessa, and with the fall of Edessa six years later his family had lost their lands. The family fortunes further deteriorated when his father was taken captive alongside Bohemond III of Antioch and Raymond III of Tripoli when Constantine was not yet a year old. He had not seen his father again until he was eight. Constantine himself had fought with Tripoli at Hattin, and had been one of the knights to fight his way off the field with the Count—but like Sir Sebastian, he had sought service with Ibelin following the surrender of Jerusalem. Sir Constantine had no land, no family, and no clear purpose in life.

"Tell me everything you know about Leo of Armenia," Ibelin ordered, stepping down from the window seat in search of warmer air. As the sun set, the chill was becoming greater, and Ibelin could see his breath in this tower chamber.

"He's about your age," Sir Constantine opened. "His father was treacherously murdered when he was only fifteen, and he and his brother had to seek refuge with his mother's kin. Ten years later, the man who had probably instigated the murder, Leo's paternal uncle, was in turn assassinated by his own bodyguard. Leo's older brother, Rupin, was recognized as prince. Rupin was a strong friend of the Franks; he was married to Humphrey de Toron's elder sister Isabella."

That piece of news took Ibelin by surprise. "Is she still alive?"

"I don't think so—or if so, she is in a convent, for she retired there at the same time as her husband went into a monastery."

"I thought he was the ruling prince?" Balian asked, confused.

"He was, but Rupin was lured to Antioch on the pretext of negotiations over the disputed border, and was immediately seized by Bohemond and imprisoned. The Armenians had to secure his ransom at huge cost, including recognizing Antioch's suzerainty over Armenia, and the agreement took years to negotiate. Meanwhile, Leo held the reins of government, and with very few men had to defend his brother's territory from both the Seljuks and the Greeks.

Eventually Rupin returned from captivity, but he was a broken man. He retired to a monastery rather than resuming his rule."

"Was that his choice or his brother's?" Ibelin asked sharply.

Sir Constantine shrugged. "I can't be sure. I was not here. But my Armenian relatives always spoke highly of Leo. They did not ever suggest foul play on his part."

Ibelin nodded. "Go on. What happened next?"

"Although Armenia had been humiliated, Antioch was in no position to exploit the advantage, because it was 1187. With the collapse of the Kingdom of Jerusalem following Hattin, Antioch had to prepare for an onslaught from Saladin. In fact, the situation was so desperate that Antioch and Leo buried their differences, and a marriage between Leo and Bohemond's niece cemented their new alliance. Meanwhile, with the Seljuks striking almost to Sis itself, Leo gathered what forces he could and went to meet them head-on. He won a dramatic and unexpected victory over the Seljuks, driving them back into their own territory. After that he supported the crusade of Friedrich Barbarossa, providing horses, supplies, and medical care for the many wounded. After Saladin abandoned the Templar castle of Baghras, Leo seized it, rebuilt it, and garrisoned it. That, however, provoked outrage from Bohemond of Antioch, who felt the castle belonged to him. Leo invited Bohemond to discuss the dispute at Baghras, and promptly took him, his wife, and his entourage hostage."

"What?" Ibelin gasped in sudden alarm.

Before Sir Constantine could answer, a troop of servants arrived with burning coals, tinder, and logs. Although they had been speaking French, which the servants presumably did not understand, Ibelin and Sir Constantine waited until the fire was devouring the kindling voraciously and the servants had withdrawn before continuing.

"Is Antioch still held?" Ibelin asked as the door clunked shut.

"Last I heard," Sir Constantine replied evenly, "but we have not always been well informed of events here."

"Last you heard, *where* was he being held?"

"Right here, in Sis."

Ibelin stared at Sir Constantine. "Why didn't you tell me this earlier? We may have just walked into a trap!"

"How so?" Sir Constantine answered levelly. "Leo seized Bohemond in revenge for what Bohemond had done to his brother. That is the Armenian way. But he has no quarrel with us. He will treat us with great hospitality. As you see." Sir Constantine indicated the servants now lugging buckets of steaming water and a tub into their chamber.

Ibelin watched warily as the tub was set on a mat before the fireplace and water was emptied into it. Then, with resignation, he beckoned Georgios over to help him undress. Lost in thought, he undressed and stepped into the tub. He supposed that Sir Constantine was correct about the lack of motive for any hostile act, and their reception so far had been exemplary. Still he felt uneasy. Maybe it was just being so far from familiar surroundings—or the increasing sense of chasing a mirage.

The only evidence they had that Eschiva was in Antiochia Mikra was the statement of a Norse sailor that the ship carrying her had been headed that way when it was intercepted. Who was to say the pirates hadn't changed course thereafter? Then again, the fact that he'd been denied entry to Antiochia Mikra seemed to confirm the hostility of its ruler. Nor had Corycos' men doubted for an instant that the tyrant there was capable of such an act of perfidy as the kidnapping of a young mother and her children.

With a sigh, Ibelin stood up and accepted the towel Georgios held out to him as he stepped out of the tub. While Balian dressed in clean clothes, from his braies to his best silk surcoat, Sir Constantine bathed, followed by Georgios. Meanwhile red wine, flatbread, cucumber yogurt, and bowls of beef, beet, and bulgur stew had arrived. The food was loaded onto the table along with wooden cutlery and local pottery. Ibelin, Sir Constantine, and Georgios gathered around to eat heartily.

They had not finished, however, before a knock interrupted them, and the household official bowed deeply before proclaiming, "My lord would see you now, if it is convenient to you, my lord."

Ibelin nodded and stood. Sir Constantine grabbed one of the flatbreads to eat as he followed behind his lord. They were escorted through a large and crowded hall in which they saw the other knights of their party and nodded greeting, but continued to an audience chamber. Here the walls were covered with bright frescoes of scenes from the Gospels, the saints' heads surrounded by solid gold halos. At the center of the far wall was a raised dais with a carved throne on it, and magnificent carpets covered the floor around it. But the throne was empty, and before Ibelin had fully oriented himself, a man in long silk robes and a heavy velvet cloak trimmed in gold strode toward him with an outstretched hand. "My lord of Ibelin," he opened in French (to Ibelin's relief).

Ibelin went down on one knee and bowed his head. Leo of Armenia, however, grabbed him firmly by the elbow and pulled him up to deliver a kiss on each cheek. "Any member of the House of Ibelin is welcome here. I will never forget how your brother was one of the few men to stand by me when the Sultan Saladin joined forces with that snake Isaac Angelus and tried to crush Armenia!"

Balian staggered physically at these words, but Leo of Armenia was too busy talking to notice. "He fought like a lion—not to say St. George himself! Alas, he was not immortal, and he died of the wounds he had suffered as we pursued the Turks all the way to Sarvandikar. It was a grave loss, and I bitterly regret that he did not live to enjoy the reward I would have given him. Did you not know this?" Leo asked, astonished, as he paused long enough to register his guest's expression of amazement.

"You are speaking of my brother Baldwin, Baron of Ramla and Mirabel?" Balian asked back, dazed and disbelieving.

"Yes. Didn't you know he had died?"

"I presumed it, because I have heard nothing from him in the last eight years. But I had no idea where, when, or how. He—he fought with you against Saladin?"

"And Isaac Angelus, that traitorous bastard!"

"When—when, again, did you say he died?" Balian asked, beginning at last to understand the silence that had so puzzled him after Hattin.

"1187. That was the reason I could not send help to Jerusalem. Surely you knew that? I was fighting for our freedom, our very existence, right here—with your brother at my side. He was a wonderful man, a great knight. I gladly called him friend and would have happily made him a baron, with a good Armenian wife."

"My lord, forgive me. I honestly did not know. When my brother left the Kingdom of Jerusalem, he said he was going to Antioch. We heard that he was received there with great honor. After that, however, we heard no more from him. He seemed to just disappear. We had no idea where he was or why he did not send us word of his doings. It is a great comfort to hear that he died as he would have wanted, fighting for Christ." But the greatest comfort was to think that he had not abandoned his only child out of indifference or because he had a new wife and a new family. Balian begged God to be allowed to tell Eschiva this news, while the prince of Armenia assured him that he spoke the truth.

When the Armenian finished, Ibelin told him, "If it is as you say and you were my brother's friend, then the news I bring will cause you distress. I am here on account of his only surviving child, his daughter Eschiva, the Lady of Lusignan."

It was Leo of Armenia's turn to look astonished. "Is the Lady of Lusignan not well?"

"The Lady of Lusignan was kidnapped by Kanakes from a coastal manor to which she had retired with her youngest children in order to recover from her last childbirth. A galley in the service of Lusignan intercepted Kanakes' ship off Antiochia Mikra and managed to rescue the youngest child, but the Lady of Lusignan herself was too weak to make the transfer from one ship to the other. She, her daughters, and the Lord of Lusignan's middle son were, we believe, landed by Kanakes at Antiochia Mikra. We presume that Kanakes was in the pay of Isaac of Antiochia Mikra."

"The whoreson!" Leo burst out emphatically. "If it is true, he will either release them to me or I'll crush him!" He grabbed Ibelin by the arm and assured him earnestly, "I swear to you, I will secure their release. Have no more fear for their safety. I will secure their release—not just for your brother, whom I loved well, nor indeed for the good Lord of Lusignan, whom I respect, but for Christ Himself. This was a *despicable* deed!"

Ibelin liked the sound of that, but what if they were wrong and Eschiva was held by someone else?

Mountains of Cilicia, January 1196

Dying was proving to be much harder than Eschiva had expected. It was now, Eschiva calculated somewhat uncertainly, over a month since their capture. Although she could not stand without feeling dizzy and so remained in bed most of the time, her condition appeared to have stabilized.

Since their arrival at the isolated farmhouse, they had been in the care of the two women. Although the Lusignans and their caretakers had no common language, humanity was a language in itself. The women had taken an instant liking to bright-haired, curious little Aimery, and he was already their darling. He followed them around as they went about their chores, and his laughter rang out like church bells, always lifting Eschiva's heart—until she thought of Hugh.

When she thought of Hugh, she felt the desire to join him wherever he was. But if she died, would they be reunited? *He* had been without sin, but she had many sins on her conscience and no confessor to give her absolution. Besides, whenever she found herself wishing she could hold Hugh in her arms again, she was called back to the present by little Aimery, Helvis, or Burgundia.

The women had been very solicitous of Helvis, cleaning her face gently and with sympathy. They seemed concerned that she might have scars, and had produced ointments that they smeared on the cuts with obvious good intent. Indeed, although they showed boundless indulgence for little Aimery, they were no less kindly and motherly to Helvis and Burgundia.

With Eschiva, admittedly, they were more reserved. It was hard to tell if they were following orders to keep their distance or simply intimidated by what they had been told about her. Whatever the reason, they avoided meeting her eye, and seemed embarrassed in her presence. Nevertheless, they had cleaned all their clothes and provided them water and sponges so they could clean themselves as well. They brought fresh bread and milk for little Aimery daily, but otherwise the diet consisted of salted or dried meat or fish, lentils, and occasionally dried fruits. At times Eschiva felt she couldn't face this mixture again and refused to eat altogether, but then Burgundia would come and coax her.

"Don't die, Mama!" Burgundia pleaded. "What would we do without you? We need you! Please eat at least a little," she begged. Whereupon Eschiva would dutifully take the flatbread and nibble on it until it was consumed. Then Burgundia would kiss her with a heartfelt "Thank you, Mama!"

Eschiva saw little of the guards keeping them here, and nothing of Brother Zotikos. She supposed everyone was awaiting Aimery's response. She tried to picture it, and depending on her energy level she pictured either him storming ashore to rescue her, or negotiations that dragged on for years. The absence of her wedding ring, however, led to terrible nightmares. She had been only eight when Aimery slipped it on her finger, and as she grew older, the knuckle had grown but not the first section of her left ring finger. They had been forced to cut through the gold and pry it open to remove it from the finger that had worn it for twenty-two years. In her sleep, her subconscious combined the missing ring with her most sinister fear: divorce. Instead of Brother Zotikos and his minions cutting off the ring, it was Aimery himself. More than once she had woken up thrashing in her bed, whimpering for Aimery not to leave her.

Her cries inevitably woke the children, and Burgundia would put her arms around her to calm her. Apparently she called out to Aimery in her sleep, because each time Burgundia assured her, "Papa is coming to free us. I know he is."

To which Eschiva could only reply that yes, she was sure, too—although her nightmares seemed to belie her faith.

Suddenly men were bursting into the room with drawn swords—but they weren't Aimery's men. They wore unfamiliar armor and were speaking Greek. They seemed initially confused, until someone saw her and pointed. His commander stormed over to the bed, his sword still raised. Eschiva stared up at that blade and started to pray.

As suddenly as he had entered, he sheathed his sword and asked in hesitant French, "Ma dame, *vous êtes Madame de Lusignan?*" ("Are you Madame de Lusignan?)

"*Oui, je suis,*" (yes, I am) she answered him.

The man looked immensely relieved. "I come to rescue you," he declared in his broken French. But no sooner were the words out of his mouth than he frowned and, looking around, started giving orders angrily. Moments later the two women were brought into the chamber and roughly flung on their knees. Eschiva protested. "Monsieur, don't punish them! They were only doing what they were told. They have taken care of us as best they could. They have been kind."

The commander nodded but continued to berate the women, who looked very frightened.

Eventually, after what seemed like several hours of chaos, Eschiva found herself again on a stretcher, but this time the front was tied to one horse and the back to another, and in this improvised horse litter she began a new journey. Little Aimery was held in front of the saddle of one of the men, and her daughters were both riding pillion behind other men. Eschiva still had no idea exactly what was happening, beyond the assurance of the commander that he had come to rescue her.

They spent one night in another farmhouse, where the inhabitants were clearly in a state of alarm over their unexpected guests, but on the following night they arrived in a small town. Here Eschiva and the children were handed over to the care of nuns, and by the next morning Eschiva found that she and her daughters were the recipients of silk underwear, silk gowns, velvet surcoats, fur-lined cloaks, dainty slippers, sheepskin boots, silk scarves, and fur-lined hoods, as well as combs, soaps, perfume, and rouge for lips and cheeks. Where this wealth had come from she did not know, but she suspected it had been arbitrarily confiscated from some innocent individuals who had the misfortune of being roughly the same size as the captives.

Furthermore, in place of the two peasant women who had kindly tended them in the farmhouse, two hussies of dubious virtue were sent to attend them. The nuns were disapproving, but the women were assertive. They appeared determined to make Eschiva and her daughters look like they had been visiting at the court in Constantinople, rather than imprisoned in the hold of a ship and then at a peasant farmhouse.

After these women were finished dressing up the captives in their new finery, Eschiva and her children were escorted to a real horse litter, painted brightly red and gold and hung with damask curtains. Sitting two to a seat facing each other, they set off yet again. There could be little doubt, however, that whatever their next destination was, their fortunes had taken a turn for the better.

It was a four-day journey by horse litter from wherever they had been to

Corycos. Nor would the Lusignans, who had never been there, have known where they were if their escort had not been intent on informing them.

"Corycos?" Burgundia asked. "Where's that, Mama? I've never heard of it."

"Cilicia," Eschiva answered. She was not feeling well. Sitting upright all day in the horse litter left her dizzy and lightheaded to the point of nausea. She tried to swallow it down and did not want her daughters to notice. Fortunately, there was so much commotion outside the horse litter that even Burgundia did not seem aware of her mother's state.

"All these people," the eleven-year-old exclaimed excitedly. "They're cheering and waving. You don't think it's because of us, do you?"

Eschiva forced herself to open her eyes and pull back the curtains to peek outside. Burgundia was right. The streets appeared to be lined with cheering crowds! Eschiva couldn't remember anything like it since King Baldwin's coronation—and to top it all off, trumpets were blowing.

Eschiva again risked a look out of the curtains. The people on the side of the road were throwing their hats in the air or waving them over their heads. The little cavalcade came to a halt, and Eschiva's view was blocked by a big chestnut horse. The horse fretted, and the rider, in splendid armor and velvet cloak, flung himself to the ground. "I think we are about to be greeted by someone important," Eschiva told her children, pulling back into the horse litter and letting the curtains drop into place so they could prepare themselves. "Aimery! Stop picking your nose and try to look like a young nobleman! Helvis, sit up straighter!"

From beyond the curtains a voice intoned, "Madame de Lusignan, welcome to Armenia. We assure you of the most gracious hospitality our humble land can provide until your husband arrives to escort you home."

Eschiva appreciated that the man had not simply flung back the curtains as he might have done: this was a civilized man.

Taking a deep breath to collect and steady herself, she pulled back the curtains to smile out at the speaker. "Thank you, my lord, from the bottom of my heart. Thank you!" What else was she supposed to say? The world seemed to be spinning around her again. Everything was happening so fast.

Something moved behind the splendidly dressed man in the velvet cloak, but Eschiva had to close her eyes against the dizziness. She heard Burgundia explaining apologetically in an earnest child's voice, "Forgive her, my lord. My Mama is not well."

"I'm fine," Eschiva protested weakly. "I'm just—"

"Hush." The voice was deep and close, and so familiar that Eschiva caught her breath in disbelief. It was a voice from her childhood, the voice of comfort in all her early nightmares. Even when the Saracens sacked Ibelin, he had ridden to the rescue. His hand was on her shoulder—dry and wiry but warm and reassuring. Eschiva's eyes flickered open to be absolutely certain this was no hallucination. "Uncle Balian?"

"Yes, 'chiva, I'm here. Don't worry. You're safe with my lord of Armenia, and now that we have seen you safely in our hands, we'll send word to Aimery. You're almost home." He squeezed her shoulder, and Eschiva sank back against the seat of the horse litter with tears of relief running down her face.

Kyrenia, March 1196

The harbor was packed with galleys, so many that not all could come alongside and several were moored beam to beam, clogging the harbor. The quay was hardly less busy, as scores of men were preparing to go aboard the waiting ships, and the last chests laden with gifts for Leo of Armenia were being carried precariously over the gangways.

John had been sent to stable his mother's and his own horse at the castle, but there had been no room left. Obviously, for the Dowager Queen they would have thrown some of the other horses out, but John preferred to take the horses to a good livery stable around the corner. He knew the proprietor and grooms at this establishment and trusted them more than the overworked castle grooms in the service of Barlais. Almost as important, he knew they'd look after Barry, too. (His beloved dog had been banned from this expedition.) But the diversion cost him a half-hour, and by the time he returned to the quay, King Aimery and his immediate entourage were preparing to embark.

John hurried around the edge of the curving harbor, dodging excited dogs, crates, and barrels of cargo awaiting ships displaced by the galleys. An attractive woman in a shawl smiled at him and he nodded to her, before he remembered where he'd seen her before: in the brothel. It was the madam who had mocked Haakon Magnussen, and John flushed to think he (a knight!) had acknowledged her in public. It was bad enough that he *recognized* her, but to dignify her with a greeting was terribly gauche.

Still flustered by his mistake, John joined the party clustered around Lord Aimery, which included his mother. Maria Zoë was dressed for the sea voyage in practical gray-green cotton under a surcoat of forest-colored damask and a woolen cloak trimmed with beaver against the expected chill of the ocean air. The cloak appeared quite superfluous at the moment, however, as the sun was blazing down on them from a cloudless sky. Beyond the breakwater, the ocean glistened like a flat blue disk just lightly textured by a steady but moderate breeze.

The fine warm weather also mocked the Bordelais shipmaster, who appeared to be trying to dissuade Aimery from boarding. The sight of the Frenchman commanding this impressive array of ships sent a stab through John's heart. He still could not grasp that Magnussen was dead. In some part of his imagination, John had believed the Norseman was immortal, a man of legend more than flesh and blood, the kind of eternal hero that cannot die.

John was certain that Magnussen would have put to sea in a raging storm—let alone on a day like this—but the Frenchman was whining, "… Something's brewing." He frowned at the beautiful sky. "This is very early in the season for crossing—"

"We're not sailing for Sicily or France, for God's sake," Aimery retorted irritably. "We're only crossing from here to Corycos. That's little more than a hundred nautical miles, I'm told."

"Yes, we should be able to make the crossing in a day, but I'm not so sure about the return. This sunny calm won't last for long this time of year."

"Then no more dithering!" Aimery commanded. "I have sent word ahead to the good Lord of Armenia that I am coming with many notables to bring my lady and children home! I am not going to break my word—much less leave my bride and children in a stranger's hands a day longer—most especially not for a storm that no one can even see!" He turned from the evidently insulted seaman, took Maria Zoë firmly by the elbow, and guided her across the gangplank to the deck of his flagship.

Behind them, Dick de Camville followed quickly—but Philip, either to prove a point or in answer to a dare, tried to jump from the quay onto the railing of the ship without using the gangplank. He almost made it, started to fall backwards, and grabbed one of the lines tied up to the nearest pin rail to keep from falling. The line, however, was only loosely made fast, and Philip found himself spinning just above the level of the dock, hanging on like a terrified monkey. The incident attracted the attention of the sailors, who started hooting—while young Guy de Lusignan, who was being left behind, was laughing himself silly at his friend's precarious position.

"Philip!" John shouted angrily as he strode over. He grabbed hold of the line above his brother's frantic clasp, and stopped the swing and spin of the rope. Philip let go of his hold to drop onto the quay, with a heartfelt, "Thanks, John."

"What the devil got into you?" John scolded. "This is no time for pranks and games!"

Philip, who had been genuinely grateful for his brother's intervention, now frowned and snapped, "Oh, leave me alone! I'm just getting my sea legs!"

"You don't know what you're talking about!" John snapped back. "Hurry! They're preparing to cast off!"

The brothers rushed together over the gangway, and the sailors standing by on either side hauled it in as their feet touched the deck. Forward, the lines were being cast off and the forward oars eased out to shove the bows gently away from the quay. Within a quarter-hour they had cleared the harbor and set sail, while the five remaining ships in their little flotilla straggled out of the harbor behind them.

Lusignan and his party were traveling on a big three-masted galley, an example of the finest and most modern of ships now coming off the skids of European shipyards from Tynemouth to Florence. The great seaborne expeditions to the Holy Land financed by the Kings of England and France in the last decade had given a dramatic boost to shipbuilding across Europe. Perhaps more important, they had given young naval architects an opportunity to demonstrate the advantages of their sometimes radical designs. This ship had no less than fifty-two oar-banks, twenty-six per side, which could each be manned by two men. She also carried three lateen sails on her three masts, the aftermost of which was stepped just ahead of a wheel rather than a tiller. The latter stood in front of a two-story deckhouse that provided luxury accommodations for a limited number of passengers, and more basic accommodations for the officers. The crew, both sailors and rowers, slept forward, in a lower and less solid deckhouse on the foredeck.

Lord Aimery had selected this ship to bring Eschiva and the children home because of the gracious accommodations, but Maria Zoë, no less than John, preferred to stay on the roof of those accommodations rather than go below. This was where the captain or his officers kept watch, as it provided a splendid overview of the entire length of the vessel, right to the low-lying bow with its long snout. The latter butted into the small waves, sending showers of spray upwards, but John found it stiff and awkward compared to the elegant, upward curving bow of the *Storm Bird*.

"It's a ram," his mother told him, when he grumbled about how ugly it looked. "It can be used to pierce the side of an enemy vessel and sink it. It is based on the ships of the ancient Greeks. The snecka, in contrast, is essentially a Viking ship, designed to allow men to navigate up rivers and for beaching. A snecka cannot fight at sea."

"Magnussen could certainly fight with it!" John reacted as if his mother had insulted the dead Norseman.

"Magnussen used his ship as a fighting platform to launch his men against other crews, but he did not fight with the ship itself," his mother corrected.

With a sigh, John drew aside to grieve for his lost friend by staring out at the sea Magnussen had loved. He stood sharing the dead man's love for the endlessly shifting surface of the water, the play of light and shadow, and the unique smell of salt water on wind. Later John stood at the break of the poop to watch the helmsman for a while, wishing he could try his hand at the wheel, but he didn't dare ask. Lord Aimery wanted the fastest possible crossing, and that meant leaving the helm to the professionals.

They had a light midday meal below deck, and Maria Zoë remained there for the afternoon to escape the intensity of the sun. Only after they sighted land off their larboard bows late in the afternoon did she return on deck. The sun was behind them now as they steadily swept along the shore of Cilicia, the wind freshening across their larboard quarter. It was, in fact, ideal conditions for sailing and they were making at least ten knots, John estimated, trying to remember everything Magnussen had told him about judging the speed of a ship by its wake and the bubbles rushing by the side.

On land, the bright banners streaming from the towers of irregular fortifications dipped in apparent greeting, and as they swung north into the harbor of Corycos itself, they were greeted by fanfares of trumpets from both the island castle and the shore-side towers. They handed sail to take speed off the vessel and manned the oars to ensure maximum maneuverability.

A bright red tender flying a red banner with a lion rampant on it started toward them. A man standing braced against one of the benches signaled the Frankish galley to follow and then led them into a quay at which, with great pomp, a large number of people waited. There were priests and monks with silver incense burners, knights in gleaming armor, and ladies in bright-colored dresses. All looked very magnificent, yet there was still no mistaking Leo himself. He was dressed in jewel-studded robes, a massive sword in a jewel-encrusted scabbard at his hip.

Maria Zoë grumbled in an aside to John that they had not been warned they would be met at the quay; she had expected to have time to change before meeting the Armenian lord. She disappeared briefly below deck to brush the snarls out of her hair, re-braid it, and change into shimmering silk veils, but none of the rest of them took the time to make any adjustments in their appearance.

Lord Aimery was standing very tensely at the poop rail, his eyes narrowed and his jaw set as he scanned the crowds for Eschiva and his children. "I can't see them!" he growled in exasperation to Maria Zoë.

"I don't think they're there," she assured him, scanning the crowd herself as the galley moved closer, half the oars already shipped to reduce speed. "No. They must have remained at the palace or wherever the feast will be. There's Balian, beside and behind the Lord of Armenia." She pointed, adding, "He would surely be with Eschiva if she were here."

Aimery made a grimace that reflected just how worried he remained. Balian's report had stressed that Eschiva had suffered no assault or abuse, but also that she was very weak and badly shaken by the experience. He had also related that the pirates had deliberately lied to her, saying Hugh had drowned, and she had grieved intensely for an infant she believed lost. She had almost not believed Balian's assurances that Erik Andersen had managed to rescue the boy and bring him to Nicosia. Aimery, however, also knew that Balian was unlikely to have told him everything. Indeed, Eschiva herself would not have admitted all that she went through. He was tormented by his own imagination of what she must have undergone.

John, on the other hand, was suffering from a sense of deep shame that his father and Lord Aimery and even, exceptionally, his mother looked so plain and dowdy in the presence of this Armenian lord and his nobles. They were all in silks, velvets, and gold embroidery, while the Lusignans and Ibelins were dressed in cotton and linen. In John's eyes his father was every bit as important as the Armenian prince, but although his father stood a head taller, he managed to hang back and give the impression of being a mere servant.

With a gentle clunk and a slight jolt, the galley went alongside the quay. A cheer went up; trumpets sounded. Aimery swung himself onto the ladder leading down to the main deck and descended face first like a sailor. John gallantly helped his mother descend more cautiously, facing backwards. By the time John had reached the deck, Philip and Dick de Camville had already jumped onto the gangway to proceed before their lord and bow before him as Lord Aimery went ashore. It was a brave (and John suspected improvised) attempt to give the Lusignan a touch of dignity, but quite pathetic compared to the Armenians' display.

Leo of Armenia strode toward Lord Aimery with outstretched arms. As Lord Aimery started to bend his knee, he caught him and embraced him instead. "My good and dear friend! Lord Aimery!" Leo's voice carried across the quay. "Welcome to Cilicia! My house is yours!"

"My lord, there are no words equal to the depth of my gratitude for what you have done—" Aimery had prepared the speech, but he found himself overwhelmed by the situation nevertheless, and his voice caught slightly.

Leo of Armenia jumped in easily, "What I have done is not worth a word! It is only what any man of honor would have done, and for a lady of such perfect grace and innocence! I'm sure you would have done the same for me if our roles had been reversed. Come, I know how anxious you are to see with your own eyes that no harm has come to your lady or your children—and, I assure you, your impatience is only exceeded by *her* desire to lay eyes on *you*." He took Lord Aimery's arm and started leading him through the cheering public.

Balian fell in beside his wife and son. "How is Eschiva really?" Maria Zoë asked, confident that Lord Aimery could not hear her over the cheering and commentary provided by his host.

"She's deathly ill," Balian answered candidly. "I think only the hope of seeing Aimery and Hugh again keeps her alive. She is fundamentally bedridden. She can stay sitting up for an hour or two, but she can hardly stand at all without getting dizzy. She would have fainted dead away had she tried to come down and meet Aimery on the quay, as was originally planned."

"What is it? Have you consulted physicians here?"

"Yes, but they only shake their heads and talk of humors and weak blood." Balian shook his head in frustration. "I feel as if she needs to move more and breathe fresh air. When a man is wounded and immobilized, he loses strength in his healthy limbs just from inactivity. I can't help feeling that part of Eschiva's problem is that *because* she doesn't move, she is getting weaker and weaker."

"But if standing makes her dizzy . . . " Maria Zoë pointed out, and her husband threw up his hands with a sigh. "What of the girls and little Aimery?" Maria Zoë asked next.

"Little Aimery is happy as a healthy puppy," Balian assured her, "and Helvis also seems to have recovered well. She plays with the other girls and is already learning some Armenian. I'm more worried about Burgundia. She seems to feel she should stay with her mother, reading to her or playing chess. She is far too sober for a girl her age. Even our Helvis was more carefree—bossing Sidon around, actually."

Maria Zoë laughed at the memory of their eldest daughter at Burgundia's age. She was by then already betrothed to Reginald de Sidon and, as Balian noted, had quite shamelessly taken advantage of her elderly bridegroom's kindness and chivalry. Returning to the present, she remarked, "Let's hope that once Burgundia gets safely back to Cyprus, she'll get over her current mood and become more cheerful again."

The sun was setting as they reached the Lord of Corycos' palace, which, as the largest and best-appointed residence in the port, was housing the freed captives and Leo himself. The Lord of Corycos had spared no expense to deck his residence with bunting and bright ribbons, and torches were lit all across the front of the building and on the roof as well. Lord Aimery was led up the interior stairway that wound around the courtyard toward a hall—but Eschiva, hearing the commotion in the courtyard, could not wait for him. She dragged herself to her feet, and leaning heavily on Burgundia's arm, made her way out into the corridor just as Aimery reached the top of the stairs. He saw her and ran to her, without a thought to his dignity. As he reached her she started to reel, the world spinning around her, and he grabbed her in a fierce grip. Eschiva closed her eyes and dropped her head on his chest.

"Sweetheart, can you ever forgive me?" Aimery whispered as her legs gave way. He held her upright only by the strength of his arms, conscious of how terribly light she was in them. She had lost a great deal of weight, and she had had none extra to lose three months ago, he registered.

"Hugh," was the first word out of Eschiva's mouth. "Is Hugh—"

"He's fine! I swear, he weighs more than you do!"

Eschiva smiled without opening her eyes. She just seemed to faint into a contented sleep. Aimery bent and slipped his arm under her knees to carry her into the room behind her. She came to again as he set her down on a large cushioned bench. She smiled up at him and whispered, "I love you, Aimery."

Leo of Armenia had arranged a magnificent banquet to honor the Lord of Lusignan and celebrate the reunion of husband and wife. In fact, he had arranged three days of feasting, hunting, and other entertainment. The day following the arrival of the Cypriots started with a Mass at the main cathedral to give thanks for the safe delivery of the captives. Eschiva declined to attend, but the three Lusignan children dutifully accompanied their father. Lord Aimery led his little namesake by the hand, and the two girls went before him. Their bright blond hair was brushed out and free for all to see under garlands of almond blossoms.

Maria Zoë, imperial princess that she was, had thought to bring something appropriate to wear, and looked suitably regal. She also provided gold-trimmed surcoats from her sea chest for her husband and son, but the Lusignan girls were dressed entirely in Armenian charity. The debt, John thought, just kept growing.

As they returned from Mass, with mouth-watering smells already seeping from the kitchens into the hall of the palace, the captain of Lord Aimery's galley appeared in an agitated state. "My lord," he announced in what John thought was a rude tone, "the wind has backed around to the north. If you leave now, we might just be able to ride that wind back to Kyrenia before the storm breaks.

If not, you may spend far longer here than you ever planned." He pointed dramatically toward dark clouds building up in the north.

"We can't just depart!" Lord Aimery protested, embarrassed by the man's tone as much as by his message. "Look at all that the Lord of Armenia has prepared!" He gestured toward the activity around them.

But a cold wind was lifting the tablecloths from the tables set up in the courtyard, making the servants run about to weight them down. Maria Zoë shivered and wished she had her cloak.

"That storm brings snow and ice!" the captain insisted. "It could close down sea travel for weeks in its wake. Do you truly want to be away from Cyprus so long?"

"What is the problem?" Leo of Armenia returned, having noticed that his guest had been waylaid.

"My fleet captain insists there is bad weather in the offing," Lord Aimery admitted with a frown, "but I'm sure he exaggerates. We wouldn't want to disrupt the plans you so graciously made for us."

"My lord," the captain turned to appeal directly to the Lord of Armenia. "Look to the north! That's a storm from beyond Taurus."

The Armenian prince followed the captain's pointed finger and he, too, felt the chill on the breeze. He nodded. "Your captain is right, Lord Aimery. There is a dangerous storm brewing, the type that brings snow and sleet and freezing rain on a wind like a razor's edge. We would not keep you here for the sake of merriment when you need to get your family to safety. Make haste."

By the time the fleet cast off, the overcast had blotted out the blue sky except for a last strip low to the horizon in the southeast. The sea was already choppy, with whitecaps scattered liberally on the lead-gray water. The oars were shipped and the covers battened down as the galley raced before the wind. Aimery stayed with Eschiva and his children in the main cabin, but the Ibelins, including Philip, kept to the deck, watching as the sky behind them grew increasingly dark and ominous.

By midday they were plunging through ten- to twelve-foot waves, and the captain had reefed all three sails. Maria Zoë clutched her cloak around her, the collar turned up so that it covered most of her cheeks right to the collarbone. Philip, on the other hand, was entertaining himself by trying to run up and down the poop, frequently staggering like a drunk because of the uneven lurching of the ship under his feet. John, annoyed by his antics, called for him to "stop being childish," but his father laid a hand on John's arm and shook his head.

"Let him be, John. Life will catch up with him soon enough. I wish you had had more years to be a playful colt. Of all the evil consequences of Hattin, one minor but nevertheless sad one was that it robbed you of your childhood."

Nonplused, John stared after his father, who had already turned away to follow the soaring of a seagull as it rode the wind overhead, cawing loudly. John had never thought about it like that, but with a twinge of guilty insight he realized that he was often sharp with Philip because he *envied* him his carelessness.

"I do hope we are ahead of that storm," Maria Zoë confessed her growing unease as the storm appeared to be inexorably catching up with them.

Her husband nodded soberly. "I admit, I'd feel happier in the *Storm Bird*. She could ride out anything!" He flashed a smile at John as he spoke, as if he knew these had been John's thoughts, too.

The captain was giving orders frantically, and shortly afterwards the helm was put up hard and the galley pitched down into the next trough, then lay hard on her side and seemed about to roll right over as they swung across the swells to head into the wind. "My God!" Maria Zoë gasped, clinging to the railing in terror. "What's happening?"

"I presume we're about to shorten sail again," Balian told her calmly, while Philip, frightened by this latest maneuver, sought proximity to his father. The four Ibelins stood together clinging to the rail and waited.

Sure enough, the crew made ready to hand the mainsail, casting the halyards off to the last turn, and ensuring the lines were free to run. For several nerve-racking moments, the booms of all three lateen sails shook and swung violently from side to side. The Ibelin party cowered at the very stern to be out of the way of the lashing and cracking canvas of the mizzen sail.

The galley was now pitching so violently that the bows came clear out of the water before plunging down violently as the swell swept aft. The long ram smashed into the sea to be smothered in foam, and once or twice water washed completely over the foredeck. As the rushing water collided with the forward deckhouse, it broke into cascades of spray that splattered on the main deck like drenching rain.

"You might want to go below," Balian advised his wife.

"What? Now? My dear, if we're about to go down, we stand a better chance of survival here on deck."

"I don't think we're in any risk of foundering," Balian reassured her, "but I think I just felt the first drops of rain." Maria Zoë glanced toward the low-hanging overcast, but could see no rain.

Meanwhile the crew had managed to drag the mainsail down, one handful of shivering canvas at a time. As soon as the upper boom was lowered, the crew lashed the sail into a rough stow. Meanwhile, the helmsmen fell off the wind and the bows swung around again. Once more, the passengers clutched the railing and felt their stomachs lurch as the galley turned broadside to the waves and rolled on her side, putting the leeward gunnel well under water. But the bows continued around, and she soon righted herself. In a moment they were again running before the wind—but now, with just the fore and mizzen set, the ship appeared lighter and fleeter. She seemed to ride the tops of the waves, racing the whitecaps.

"I'm beginning to like this ship," Balian grunted to his eldest son. "What's she called?"

"Something boring like the *Pilgrim Angel*."

Balian roared with approving laughter, and John grinned with pleasure. It was not easy to make his father laugh like that. Then again, he seemed to laugh more recently than he had in the years immediately after the Treaty of Ramla, much less in that hellish period between Hattin and the arrival of the crusaders.

With the ship settled into a comfortable stride again, Philip wandered away to the front of the poop, interested in watching the helmsman. John turned and asked his father, "What did you think of Leo of Armenia?"

"A very fine prince and a good man."

"He was so generous—he reminded me of Richard of England, somehow, for all that he was slight and dark rather than big and blond."

His father nodded. "Very observant of you, John. I think they do have much in common, and in some ways I admire Leo of Armenia more. His father was treacherously murdered, and his brother was taken captive and held for ransom, yet I have seen no indication that Leo has become bitter or overly suspicious of other men. He seems remarkably at ease in his own skin, candid and generous both."

"Did I understand correctly that he took the Prince of Antioch captive?" John asked cautiously.

"Yes, and he still has him, but he allowed me to meet with both Bohemond and his wife. They assured me they had been treated very courteously and provided with every luxury possible—except freedom. Leo's terms for their release were, if you like, mild, because he asked only that Bohemond accept Armenian sovereignty over Antioch—the exact reverse of the terms his brother had been forced to accept for his freedom. The problem is that while *Bohemond* was willing to agree to those terms, and sent his marshal to Antioch with Armenian troops to implement them, the citizens of Antioch were not. Since there were too few Armenian troops to resist the mob, they fled, leaving the citizens to proclaim Bohemond's son Raymond Prince of Antioch in his father's stead. This leaves poor Bohemond in an awkward position, to say the least. He is not sure what would become of him if he went home, but it also leaves Leo with a hostage of little value." Ibelin ended his narrative with a laugh. "Such is the absurdity of some diplomacy, John," he noted, glancing up at what he thought were more drops of rain.

At his inquiring glance, Maria Zoë again shook her head and declared, "I'm still happier here. Below deck, I promise you, half the inhabitants are violently seasick."

This was too true, so Balian turned again to John. "I like Leo, John, and he is a model of a good ruler, but there is a profound weakness in Armenia."

John looked over, surprised, and Balian continued, "It is in a sense a lawless land. Not that it *has* no laws, but strong men are too quick to ignore them. Central power is weak and only exercised when someone like Leo can win the loyalty of the scores of warlords who wield the real power. Such a system easily leads to despotism. Where power rests on strength rather than legitimacy, that power too often goes to the strongest rather than the best. Leo is a good prince, but his uncle was a very different man, who terrorized his people and plundered the wealth of the country. It is unimaginable that a youth like Baldwin IV could have ruled in Armenia; they would have torn him apart like wolves, or simply murdered him in his bed."

"But the disputes over who was the legitimate king of Jerusalem almost destroyed us," John protested. "Uncle Baldwin left, Tripoli made a separate peace, and then Montferrat and Lusignan undermined each other for years."

His father nodded as a rain shower pattered across the deck and then fled. "What do you think would have been better?"

It was very dark on deck because of the low clouds. Furthermore, with the wind howling, the deck creaking, the canvas moaning, and waves rushing under the keel, they had to raise their voices to be heard. Yet words were whisked away by the wind as soon as they left the speaker's mouth. It was almost as if they had never been said. So John risked it: "Didn't you ever think that you would have made a better king than either of them, Papa? Didn't you ever want to be King of Jerusalem?" As he spoke, John felt his mother's gaze firmly upon him, and he sensed her almost amused approval. That was good, but it was his father's answer he feared.

Balian gave his son the greatest compliment. He did not rebuke him or dismiss the question as impudent and inappropriate; instead he nodded thoughtfully and took his time answering. At last he looked John in the eye and admitted, "Yes, there were times when I thought I would make a better king than Conrad—much less Guy. But the price of grasping power would have been to make it dependent on force. Think of how Saladin lived in constant fear of someone doing unto him as he had done to others. Think of the Emperors of the Eastern Empire today—fearing the next assassin, the next palace coup. If I had seized power by force, I would have left an illegitimate legacy, one that secured *you* nothing. You would have had to fight for the Crown all over again—just as al-Afdal now fights for his father's legacy—indeed for his very survival." He paused to let this sink in, and his wife and son waited, sensing he was not finished.

"It seems to me, John, that the Constitution of Jerusalem is an excellent and wise foundation for government, because it gives precedence to the legitimate heirs of previous kings, while leaving to the High Court, much like the College of Cardinals or the monks of an abbey, the function of selecting between rival claimants the most suitable candidate. Certainly in the case of female heirs, the selection of the king consort lies firmly with the High Court, not the queen or her male relatives. If Sibylla and Guy had not bypassed the High Court at the time of her marriage, we would never have had the debacle of Hattin. It is the combination of hereditary and elected power that makes our Constitution strong. On the one hand it precludes the rise of adventurers and upstarts, but on the other hand it ensures that when a king *is* recognized by the High Court, then he has the support of his barons, bishops, and knights. That is something worth preserving, John. Henri de Champagne is not such a bad king, do you think?"

John's answer was drowned out by a shout from the bows. Land was in sight. They had almost made it home.

They scuttled into the harbor of Kyrenia as the last light of day was squeezed out by the rain that came thundering down on decks, sea, and quay. In fact, they were flung violently against the quay, as the following seas broke against the stonework. Within minutes everyone, including the Ibelins, were completely drenched and fled to the castle. By nightfall, the rain had indeed turned to sleet, and howled around the walls of the castle so furiously that the shutters rattled and the smoke was forced back down the chimneys. It was a dreadful night even for the highborn, much less the poor, but Lord Aimery had brought his wife and children safely home.

Chapter Twenty
A Crown for Cyprus

Nicosia, Cyprus,
May 1196

THE ARCHBISHOPS OF TRANI AND BRINDISI had been appropriately wined and dined, loaded with gifts, and bathed in praise. Now, at last, they had withdrawn to get a good night's sleep before continuing their journey via Limassol to Acre. There they were to prepare the way for the Holy Roman Emperor, who had announced his intention to lead an army to the Holy Land this year. Aimery had arranged for Barlais and Cheneché to escort his bishops as far as Limassol, and had no need to see them again before their departure. Eschiva, who had risen from her sickbed to gallantly play the role of consort with the grace and dignity innate to her, had retired exhausted. Aimery assured her he would come shortly, but first he needed to be alone, and so he dismissed his squires.

King Aimery—*Aimericus Rex.*

Aimery stared at the crown and scepter in awe. Having accepted his homage in proxy, Henry VI Hohenstaufen had entrusted the regalia of monarchy to the worthy Archbishops of Trani and Brindisi and tasked them with delivering crown and scepter to Aimery de Lusignan. The Emperor had also sent the message that he expected his "subject state of Cyprus" to welcome, provision, and support him with men, horses, arms, and supplies in his coming expedition to retake Jerusalem. It was to further this great cause that the Emperor had seen fit to accept the "submission" of Cyprus to his rule and had raised Aimery up from "lord" to "king."

The Emperor added the admonishment that Aimery must reconcile with the King of Jerusalem, the Archbishops had intoned. The kings of two Christian countries on the forefront of the struggle against the Antichrist, they lectured pompously, could not be enemies. As for the coronation itself, the Archbishops suggested that could best take place when the Emperor himself came to Outremer and could personally place the crown on Aimery's head.

Aimery had no objection. He could certainly wait a few months for the formal ceremony. The point was that both the Pope and the Holy Roman Emperor had *accepted* the principle that Cyprus should be a kingdom. The writs were signed and sealed. Jubail had done homage in Aimery's name. The crown and scepter lay before him. He would date his reign from this day: May 18, 1196.

Aimery took the crown and held it between his two hands. It was composed of a solid-gold base and large panels of gold, each encrusted with large stones: sapphires, rubies, emeralds, and opals. It was a "closed" crown after the Eastern fashion: two bands of gold, each nearly an inch wide, curved up from the sides to meet over the center of the head. Standing upright on the double-thick meeting point of these two bands was a cross with an amethyst the size of an almond set in it. It was very heavy: Aimery estimated four to five pounds. The inside of the crown was lined with velvet so it could be worn in comparative comfort.

Aimery looked around the room once more to be sure he was alone, and then he placed the crown on his head. It sat snugly on his forehead, not too tight nor too loose. But the cross unbalanced it somewhat, unlike a well-fitted helmet. He had to hold his head absolutely upright, or the weight of the cross tipped his head one way or another. He reached up and removed the crown from his head to look at it more closely.

The workmanship was magnificent. The Holy Roman Emperor had either spent a fortune—or he had captured it somewhere and held it in reserve for an appropriate occasion. Or, Aimery frowned, it might be Isaac Comnenus' crown. Richard of England had seized that as part of the loot he'd taken when capturing the island. Very probably it had ended up in Henry VI's hands as part of the English King's ransom to the Hohenstaufen.

The thought pleased Aimery as he turned the crown around in his hands, looking for indications of Greek workmanship that would support this theory. Aimery was not an expert, but he thought the settings of the stones were more Greek than Latin in style. Maybe Maria Zoë would know. At an appropriate time, he would ask her to look at it. He would also ask her about the crown she had sold to Isaac in the year after Hattin. It had been her coronation crown, sent with her from Constantinople. It ought to be a perfect fit for Eschiva, if they could only locate it in time. Aimery had not forgotten that he'd promised to make Eschiva a queen, and after all she had gone through this past winter, he was more determined than ever to see her crowned.

If this *was* Isaac Comnenus' crown—Aimery's attention returned to the crown in his hands—then it would establish an important bridge to the past. He hoped that his subjects (what a lovely word!) would be proud to be part of a kingdom. His Frankish supporters had definitely liked the idea! Barlais and Henri de Brie had been loudest in their glee—and immediately demanded the title of "baron." "We'll lay our hands in yours first thing tomorrow morning!" Barlais had declared. "Or, well, as soon as we return from seeing the Archbishops off."

Aimery had no objection to that idea, either. The sooner he bound these proud fighting men to him, the better. And not just them. Aimery had spent hours poring over maps of the island identifying, based on lists of Byzantine dignitaries and their landholdings, just how many fiefs the island could support. He estimated the island could support some three hundred knights and two hundred mounted sergeants. Nothing to what the Kings of Jerusalem had *once* commanded, but not so much less than the King of Jerusalem commanded *today*.

Aimery wanted those knights and sergeants to be his own men. He was fortunate, he reckoned, that so many of the Greek lords had already fled the island. They had been emigrating since the time of Isaac Comnenus, because of his onerous taxes and erratic behavior. The exodus had increased under Templar rule and during the tragic interlude under Guy. The Greek aristocracy, after all, usually had lands on the mainland or houses in Constantinople to which they could withdraw. The armed struggle had been left to the lower classes and led by the Church, not the nobility. Fortunately, Aimery suspected he would have had a much harder time putting down the unrest if he'd been facing fighting men rather than priests, pirates, and peasants.

Now, however, he saw an even greater advantage in their conspicuous absence: he had land to distribute. All he needed to do was lure the disinherited fighting men of Jerusalem to Cyprus—just as Cheneché, Brie, Jubail, Rivet, and the Ibelins had come already.

Obviously, if there were Greek lords still occupying their estates, he would not expel them, provided they did homage to him. So the first thing he had to do was send out clerks to the fiefs listed in the tax registers to find out which were de facto vacant and which were still occupied. He would then demand homage of those still present, and any man who refused would see his lands expropriated to the Crown. After that, he would know just how many Greek knights had accepted his rule and how many vacant fiefs were left over. Once he knew exactly what lands he had to bestow on worthy men, he could start recruiting.

As his eye fell again on the crown, however, he reminded himself that he did not want to end as Isaac Comnenus had—driven from the island by the indifference and betrayal of his own subjects. If the Greek Emperor decided to reclaim the island, the Holy Roman Emperor *might* send aid—or he might not. Or his assistance might arrive too late. He would not be able to hold the island against any hostile power, whether it was the Greek Emperor or the Sultan of Cairo, with just three hundred knights and two hundred sergeants— not if he had no infantry. And the infantry would have to be drawn from the Greek population.

Which was why this peace Ibelin had made with the Greek archbishop made so much sense. Let the Greeks have their own churches and their own laws, as long as they paid taxes to the Crown. And those taxes didn't have to be tithes for land. On an island as rich as this, he could tax (as the Greek Emperors had done) the timber and the mines, the tanneries, potteries, and glassworks, the wine presses and the oil presses, the taverns and bathhouses, the mills, and the markets. Not only that, there were harbor dues and anchorage, salvage, customs, and export duties. There were so many different ways of raising revenue that no single tax need be particularly high. The key would be to spread the burden across all layers of society and all professions. Manuel I had understood that very well, based on what the Cypriot tax officials had reported to him.

Again Aimery nodded to himself. Ibelin was wise. Restoring the laws of Manuel I not only quieted the fears of the native population and cloaked his laws in legitimacy, they also gave him more than adequate revenues—provided, of course, that the island returned to normal levels of economic activity. That might take a couple of years, even half a decade.

No matter. He had no need for coffers full of gold. He'd lived frugally all his life (in contrast to Guy), and Eschiva was anything but a spendthrift. She had always shown a prudent capability to hold their income together and prioritize expenditures, always meeting her own needs last. That was about to change. Even at current low levels of prosperity, the revenues of the Cypriot Crown vastly exceeded anything Aimery and Eschiva had ever had at their disposal in the past. They were, from what the clerks told him, at least double the revenues of his once rich father-in-law, the Baron of Ramla and Mirabel.

Then again, he would need a considerable fortune to outfit knights for a new crusade, if the Emperor really came to the Outremer. After a second, Aimery resolved to worry about that later. The Emperor might not come at all.

He was anything but pious, Aimery reflected cynically. In fact, he was a self-serving, cynical bastard—and Aimery, for one, would be happy for him to stay where he was. The crown was here.

Aimery took it again in his hands, full of wonder, admiration, and satisfaction—only to feel a stab of guilt. He was acting no better than the greediest sultan. Worse, perhaps. In sincere contrition, he dropped to his knees and closed his eyes. "Dear God, in the name of your Son, protect this crown and the men who will wear it. Protect them from excessive greed, excessive pride and hubris. Grant the men who wear this crown wisdom, compassion, and piety instead. Inspire them to rule over this island kingdom judiciously and prudently for the good of their subjects, both high and low, Greek and non-Greek, men and women. Most of all, dear God, make me worthy of this crown, that I may pass it to my sons with due humility and go to You when my time comes. Amen."

Paphos, Cyprus, September 1196

They had opened all the windows of the tower room to let the sea breeze inside in the vain hope of cooling it down. Although the breeze helped, the temperature at this time of year was still oppressively hot, and Ibelin had dispensed with stifling armor to dress in nothing but a yellow silk surcoat over a pale-blue cotton shirt and hose of the same color. His feet were shod in comfortable, low leather shoes, and his head was bare. Maria Zoë was likewise dressed for the heat of high summer in a loose silk shift, over which she wore a crinkled cotton surcoat with long, loose sleeves. The shift was cream-colored, the surcoat a transparent green, and both materials were so light that even the slightest breeze lifted and fluttered them.

John burst in on his parents excitedly. "Pomegranates!" he announced, carrying a small basket before him.

Maria Zoë looked over with a smile, exclaiming, "Isn't it too early?"

"They're from Troodos, the vendor told me. He said up in the mountains, the first frosts have come."

"Have you tried one?" Balian asked, coming over to inspect the fruit in John's basket. John watched his father's expression eagerly. Ibelin had been famous for its pomegranate orchards, and John knew that pomegranates were his father's favorite fruit. Now Balian could not resist taking one of the fruits, still half yellow, and with his eating knife he lopped the top off.

Maria Zoë came down from her perch in the window seat, and snatched a glass bowl from a mosaic table beside the cold fireplace to bring it to her husband. He was already intent on carefully cutting the outside skin of the pomegranate. When the fourth cut was finished, he set the knife aside and broke the pomegranate open over the glass bowl. Some kernels fell into the bowl, but more clung to the membrane of the pomegranate, and Balian started to pick them free with the tip of his knife.

John watched with satisfaction. This was a scene from his childhood: his father gently extracting the kernels of a pomegranate for his mother. It was a ritual. Maria Zoë loved the fruit nearly as much as Balian did, but hated getting her fingers stained by pomegranate juice or the squirts of juice (inevitable in the process of picking it clean) on her dress. The kernels of this pomegranate were a very light ruby color, rather than garnet, but when Maria Zoë reached for the first little handful her face lit up in delight. "Wonderful!"

"Are they?" Balian asked. As if he doubted her word, he helped himself to a generous handful. His expression gave him away before he nodded in satisfaction and looked over at the basket to remark, "I don't think these are going to last very long. Can you find the vendor again?"

John laughed. "I can do better! I was thinking, we should ask him to take us to the source. I could do with a long ride out of the city. What do you think?"

"If there's been frost in the mountains already, it should be much cooler there as well," Maria Zoë noted. "I'd like some respite from the heat."

"We could take a picnic," John enthused, "and make a day outing of it!"

Balian looked from his son to his wife. "Is this a conspiracy?"

"Hardly," Maria Zoë countered, "but you *have* been working very hard lately."

"There's so much to do," Balian countered with a sigh and a glance at the papers spread out across the table. He had been in Paphos almost a year, although he had not been officially granted the fief until Aimery had received the crown of Cyprus this past May. Ever since their arrival, however, Balian had sought to establish a functioning administration. He had attempted to engage the professional bureaucrats from Isaac Comnenus' reign or before—but some of these men had left, others were old or corrupt, and yet others were hostile to the Franks. Finding out who they could trust had been a painful process of trial and error.

At the same time, they had faced the acute need to re-establish law and order on the streets and offshore. Petty crime, theft, and even assaults were rampant in the city at night, and while Famagusta had been a pirates' nest, Paphos was a smugglers' den. The ships trading here were almost all merchantmen, roundships more than galleys, but their cargoes were mostly contraband. No one took kindly to someone trying to tax them. After a half-decade doing as they pleased and reaping 100 per cent of the profit, neither shipmasters nor merchants much cared if the duties Ibelin was trying to enforce dated back to the reign of Manuel I Comnenus or not.

No sooner had Ibelin reopened the customs house on the quay, manned entirely with customs officials who had previously served the Greek Emperor, than ships started trying to avoid the harbor and landing their cargoes at various nearby coves and bays. Ibelin had engaged Erik Andersen to patrol the coastline, offering him 100 per cent of the customs duties of any ships he seized and brought back to port for a full year—the contract to be renegotiated at that time. Andersen had raised credit from the Venetians, using the customs duties he anticipated as collateral, in order to build a small snecka. *Haakon's Ghost* soon struck terror in the hearts of the smugglers, and most preferred to pay customs duties rather than risk an encounter with the Norsemen. Still, resentment simmered among the ship owners and importers alike.

The hostility of the shopkeepers, millers, tavern owners, and bath keepers was if anything greater, because their profit margins were lower in the first place. There had been a minor riot in the market when Ibelin's men had come to collect the market dues. Another ugly incident occurred when the bakers went on strike to protest the higher cost of wheat, which they blamed on the fact that the new Latin landlords were now collecting rents again. . . .

Meanwhile, since the opening of the sailing season, more and more immigrants from the Holy Land were turning up in Cyprus generally and Paphos specifically. The news of the peace the previous fall had been rapidly overshadowed by the spectacular story of the Lady of Lusignan's kidnapping. Men hearing of that audacious raid concluded that Cyprus was still a wild and dangerous place. But when Cyprus was made a kingdom under a Latin King, men revised their opinion. It helped that King Aimery sent repeated invitations to "men with skills, trades, and courage" to join him in "rebuilding" the island.

Many of the newcomers were Syrian Christians, who despite speaking Arabic, shared most of the traditions and theology of the Greek Orthodox Church, but there were also Samaritans and Jews among the recent immigrants, as well as Latin Christians. What they all had in common was the loss of their homes, their possessions, and often their loved ones in the collapse of the Kingdom of Jerusalem following Hattin. Some had been in Saracen slavery; others had escaped only to find themselves homeless, penniless, and superfluous in the surviving Christian cities of Tyre, Acre, and Jaffa. On the whole they were willing and able to work, but they did not necessarily have favorable attitudes towards the Cypriots. There had been tavern brawls and even some more sinister acts of violence arising from the tensions between the native Cypriots and the immigrants.

All the problems eventually ended up on the Lord of Ibelin's plate, because he was now recognized—whether reluctantly or not—as Lord of Paphos.

"Come," Maria Zoë urged, reaching out to lay her hand on her husband's. "Let's take a day off and ride to the pomegranate trees—wherever they may be—tomorrow."

Balian took a deep breath and was about to say "yes," when a knock at the door interrupted him. He looked over, and John went to answer the door.

On the far side stood Ayyub ibn Adam, the apprentice mason. The young man was dressed like a Cypriot merchant or bureaucrat in a linen kaftan, belted at the waist. He was bearded and wore a wooden cross prominently on his chest. He bowed deeply to John and then, looking deeper into the room, to Ibelin.

"Ah, Ayyub!" Ibelin smiled and gestured for him to come forward—but then, noticing he was alone, he asked a little sharply, "Where is Master Moses?" Although bit by bit the drainage system had been repaired and whole sections of the city now had working sewers, the aqueduct was still not working. Balian had convinced himself that if he could get the fountains working again, the mood of the public might turn more favorable.

"Master Moses wasn't feeling very well this morning," Ayyub explained apologetically, bowing again in embarrassment.

Ibelin grimaced. The one-handed master builder was unquestionably a disappointment. Far from being grateful for this new opportunity, he had proved difficult. He complained about the tools, the workers, the prices, the food, and even the weather. He had excuses for every setback, never taking responsibility for his own mistakes or inaction. Recently he had also taken to drink. Ibelin frowned and snapped irritably, "What did he do? Drink too much last night?"

Ayyub looked down and squirmed in discomfort, but he answered loyally, "I think he ate some bad shellfish."

"It wouldn't have anything to do with the fact that he was going to report yet another delay, would it?" Ibelin snarled.

John and Maria Zoë exchanged a look. It was this irritability that they found both alienating and worrying. The pomegranates had for a magical moment brought back the Balian they knew and loved, but now he was frowning and angry again.

"My lord." Ayyub lifted his head and took a visible breath. "I think I've found a solution."

"Meaning what?" Ibelin asked warily.

"May I show you?"

Ibelin nodded. Ayyub stepped forward, pulling a scroll of parchment out of his sleeve. He rolled the drawings out on the table and began explaining them. "Here is the source," he indicated a spot in the upper right-hand corner. "The path of the Roman aqueduct ran here, through this limestone hill and out the other side. We have, as you know, cleared and repaired all the visible breaks in the aqueduct without water flowing. The only logical explanation is that something is blocking the water here—inside the tunnel."

Ibelin nodded.

"So, I climbed into the tunnel and followed it until I found where it had collapsed."

Ibelin cast the young man a look of approval that made Ayyub stand up straighter, even before Ibelin said, "Well done. And what did you find?"

"I went in from both directions, and a second time had men enter from the other entrance at the same time, measuring the distance. When we reached the blockages, we shouted and pounded on rock but could hear nothing of one another. If we measured the distance correctly, the two blocked passages are separated by a mile or more."

"That doesn't sound good," Ibelin observed dryly.

"No," Ayyub admitted, but he was still standing upright, and Ibelin saw excitement in his eyes. "I don't think we can clear the tunnel, my lord," he started in a slightly breathless voice. "It would be very dangerous work, and it would be very expensive. We'd have to prop up the roof of the tunnel at short intervals all along the way. What I thought, however," he hastened to get to the good news, "was that we could divert the water here." He pointed on the map. "I've surveyed the land, and with a detour of just four miles, we could keep the water flowing downhill to reconnect with the aqueduct down here."

"If it's possible, why didn't the Romans take that route?" Ibelin asked skeptically. Although what he'd seen of Ayyub had impressed him, he was still only an apprentice mason, and Ibelin had a hard time believing he could solve a problem like this. On the other hand, Ayyub didn't complain, and he worked very long hours while his master was lounging about in taverns or sleeping off the wine he consumed there. Ayyub had also picked up Greek at an amazing pace, and had started calling himself "Antonis" so he blended in better. He wore the cross, too, Ibelin supposed, to underscore that he *was* Christian, even if his native tongue was Arabic.

Ayyub shrugged uncomfortably. "I don't know, my lord. Maybe the Romans felt it was beneath their dignity to make a detour. The Romans liked straight lines."

To everyone's relief, Ibelin laughed. Then he looked more closely at Ayyub. "You really think you can do this?"

"Yes, my lord. And it's not just me. One of the Greek masons showed me the pass."

"Ah." That not only made sense, it sounded like cooperation. That was very good news. "So you've befriended one of them, have you?"

"Well, actually, I get along with *all* of them, my lord," Ayyub admitted immodestly. It was Moses who was constantly quarreling with them. His tendency to criticize, insult, shout, and blame had caused them to lose several of their best workers.

"I'm beginning to think I should have asked you to report to me alone before now," Ibelin concluded. Although it went against the grain to speak to a man's subordinate, there were times when it was necessary and valuable. "Ayyub—or should I say Antonis?"

"I prefer Antonis, my lord."

"Good. Antonis. This Greek mason, is he a master?"

"Yes, my lord."

Ibelin glanced at Maria Zoë, and she moved over to the far side of the table.

"Do you think this Greek master mason could take charge of the project?"

Antonis looked disappointed, but he nodded.

"Antonis, I want you to finish your training. It is the best thing for *you*. Equally important, nothing leads to resentment faster than raising an unqualified man above a qualified one simply because of his connections. If I put you in charge before you have completed your training—before you are a journeyman, much less a master—everyone would say it is because you are my protégé, because you came from the Kingdom of Jerusalem."

Antonis hung his head in defeat.

"If, however, you finish your training under this Greek master, you will gain credibility here—and, I promise, when you are finished, I will employ you. There is so much to do. I want a proper castle, for a start, and the Pope has promised to establish a Latin diocesan structure on Cyprus. I expect Paphos to be named an ecclesiastical see. A Latin bishop will want a proper Latin cathedral. Last but not least, I've already had letters from the Benedictines inquiring about a possible monastery here. If you get my aqueduct finished, you and this Greek master mason will be commissioned for the castle. Then—what?—five years from now?—you will be a master mason, and I can entrust you with the new projects. Does that sound fair enough?"

Antonis seemed to think for a minute, but then he nodded. "Yes, my lord. That is fair."

"Then I want you to bring me this Greek master mason. I need to meet him, but—"

The pounding on the door this time was not polite but urgent, and Ibelin spun about, frowning already.

The door opened without waiting for anyone to call "come in" and Sir Galvin burst in, shoving a man with his hands tied behind his back in front of him. "We got him, my lord!" he announced more grimly than triumphantly, as he pushed the man down on his knees.

Antonis instinctively backed out of the way as Ibelin crossed the room toward the prisoner. The man on his knees was middle-aged and fat, with a puffy face around small, watery eyes. For a criminal receiving this kind of treatment, he was exceptionally well dressed, in a long caftan over which he wore a cloak wrapped like a Roman toga. He had a gold collar and gold rings on his fingers to underline the point that he was not a poor man.

"Who is this, and what makes you so sure he's the man?" Ibelin asked. Sir Galvin had been sent to find out who was behind the brutal beating of a recent settler, a Jacobite from Maria Zoë's dower city of Nablus, who had set up a new bathhouse near the center of town. He charged the same prices as in Acre, which were substantially cheaper than the going rate in Paphos, and the Cypriot bath owners had come to Ibelin to protest. Balian had told them that they were overcharging and he had no intention of intervening. They had responded by spreading the rumor that Ibelin was taxing them more than the new immigrant, groaning that they were being ruined by his taxes. This had led to many natives boycotting the new establishment for a while, but the Latins and other settlers supported the newcomer. He had continued to prosper until two weeks ago, when he had been found in a gutter so badly beaten he was unconscious and slowly bleeding to death. He'd been carried to the castle, and Ibelin had sent for a doctor. Although the man was now on his way to recovery, Ibelin had vowed to find out who was behind this and publicly sentence them.

"His name is Niketas Blemidas. He owns the bathhouse near St. Solomoni, and one of his own customers betrayed him," Sir Galvin answered smugly. Ibelin just raised his eyebrows, and Sir Galvin continued readily, "Said's bathhouse has been closed ever since he was beaten within an inch of his life, and so people naturally went back to the other bathhouses. One of the customers overheard this pig bragging about how he'd 'put an end' to the 'Syrian's trade,' and with any luck his rival would either die or 'go back where he came from.'"

"Has he confessed?" Ibelin asked.

"You want a confession?" Sir Galvin asked, surprised. "Give me half an hour—if it takes that long."

"Wait," Maria Zoë interceded, not sure her husband, in his current mood, wouldn't give Sir Galvin permission to torture the prisoner. Coming across the room, she addressed the prisoner in Greek, "Do you know who I am?"

The man looked down and mumbled, "Maria Comnena."

"Yes. Correct. Do you know why you are here?"

"Your husband is determined to put me out of business. He hates me and all Cypriots."

"Did he just say what I think he said?" Ibelin angrily asked his wife. She made a calming gesture and continued with her interrogation. Starting (to her husband's outrage) with: "Yes, of course," before continuing, "That's why he's repaired the drainage, has stopped the smuggling, and is working on restoring water flow to the city. But given the fact that he hates all Cypriots, why do you suppose he's picking on you?"

"How should I know?" the man growled, sending Ibelin a look of loathing. "But if he tries to harm me, you'll see the whole city rise up in rebellion!"

Ibelin's Greek had been steadily improving, and he recognized the word "epanastatis"—rebellion. He had heard it all too often since his arrival here. He stiffened.

"Rebellion?" Maria Zoë asked back. "Why?"

"Because I'm a respected man from a good family. People look up to me!" the prisoner insisted. "Barbarians like your husband and his hounds have no right to lay a hand on me." He looked up at Sir Galvin with contempt.

Maria Zoë spoke to her husband in French. "I think Sir Galvin is right and that this is the man behind the beating. However, I don't think it would be wise to torture him just yet. He's a bully, and right now he believes he has many friends and supporters who will rally around him. If you put him alone in a dungeon and leave him there for a few days, he may start to see the world a little differently."

Ibelin nodded with resignation and gestured for Sir Galvin to take the prisoner away. He found the entire exchange very discouraging. "That man nearly murdered another man just because he works harder, and he calls *us* barbarians!" Ibelin shook his head.

Leaving, Sir Galvin nearly collided with the next party seeking an audience with Ibelin: Father Andronikos, accompanied by his wife and daughter. At the sight of Eirini, John's face lit up, and he hastened across the room to welcome her and her parents. Andronikos' wife, however, had caught sight of Maria Zoë and was intent on greeting her, her daughter in her wake. Father Andronikos was left smiling in the doorway. Because they were still separated by the language barrier, Ibelin called to his son, "John! I need a translator."

The last thing John wanted to do was leave Eirini's side, but he could not ignore a direct order from his father. Nor, in light of their fight the year before, did he want his father to think he had not grown up. With a bow to Eirini, he dutifully joined his father, who told him to greet Father Andronikos, assure him he was welcome, and ask his purpose.

Father Andronikos blessed Ibelin before answering John's question about his purpose. "Well, the girls insisted they needed to come shopping," he remarked with an indulgent glance toward his wife and daughter, "but I also have a request from Father Neophytos."

Balian indicated they should sit in the window seat, and the three men crossed to it. John sat next to Father Andronikos, so he had a clear view to Eirini, still dutifully standing beside her mother as the latter deluged his own mother with a flood of words.

"The good work you have been doing to clear out the pirates has reached Father Neophytos' ears," Father Andronikos announced and John translated.

Ibelin dismissed the remark with a deprecating gesture. "Andersen had been dealing with smugglers more than pirates," he noted.

Father Andronikos just smiled knowingly. "But it has not escaped Father Neophytos' ears that you have been just as harsh with the Pisans and Genoese as with the Greeks and Cypriots."

"Smuggling is smuggling," Ibelin answered firmly and John translated a little distractedly, because Ayyub/Antonis had joined the women and was engaging Eirini in conversation. The young man was bronzed by the sun, muscular and, John felt, far too good-looking. He certainly didn't like the way Eirini was smiling up at Antonis—practically the same way she smiled at him!

Father Andronikos was answering, and John had no choice but to focus on the conversation he was translating. "You may not know, but four years ago, when the Templars ruled the island, the Bishop of Paphos, a very wise and pious man by the name of Basil Kinnamos, felt he must personally bring word to the Patriarch in Constantinople of the terrible things that were happening here. He took ship at Paphos—but never arrived in Constantinople. There were no storms in the period he was traveling; it was summer. It is widely believed that he was seized by Pisan or Genoese pirates, who are known to have attacked a ship from Cyprus bound for Constantinople off Rhodes." John indicated that Father Andronikos should stop so he could translate this monologue.

As was to be expected, Ibelin was suitably outraged, but also quick to point out that he had no way of knowing what had happened four years ago. At the time, he reminded the Greek priest, he had been focused solely on the fight against Saladin.

"I understand, but Father Neophytos was hoping your Norseman might be able to persuade the Genoese and Pisans that fall into his hands to be more forthcoming about the fate of the good Bishop Basil."

"I can certainly ask him to question anyone—or indeed, *everyone*—who might be able to shed light on this incident," Ibelin promised. Meanwhile, Eirini's laughter floated across the room like the chiming of a bell, making John tense with jealousy.

"That is all we are asking," Father Andronikos assured him with a smile, adding, "Father Neophytos thinks it would mean a great deal to the people here if the fate of their beloved bishop could be discovered. If the men responsible could be brought to justice, it would *certainly* go a long way to reconcile the inhabitants of Paphos to the new regime," he added.

As John translated, the priest pushed himself back to his feet with his hands on his knees and declared, "And now I'd better go rescue your lady from my wife, who will otherwise talk her ear off. Good day, my lord. And to you, too, young—no, *Sir* Janis." He held out his hand to John, and smiled particularly warmly at the young man—before firmly taking his wife and daughter by their arms. With a bow to Maria Comnena, he escorted his daughter and wife out of the chamber.

John was left behind, frustrated and simmering with jealousy, as Ayyub/Antonis saw Eirini halfway to the door, bowing gallantly as she left.

Kyrenia, Cyprus, November 1196

It was one of those deceptively mild autumn days that Ibelin was already coming to expect on Cyprus. The sun warmed the air to summery temperatures. The breeze was light. The water was turquoise and aquamarine, and it sparkled like diamonds where the wind ruffled it. The ship gliding through the harbor entrance was flying all her bunting in a gaudy display reminiscent of a tournament field. Yet Ibelin's eyes were drawn to the banner flying from the mainmast, high above the other bright-colored banners: the simple white with gold of Jerusalem.

The sight of it as it stretched out on a puff of wind stabbed Ibelin's heart. No matter how much he *liked* being on Cyprus, the crosses of Jerusalem were an admonishment. He had not set eyes on the Holy City since the day he marched away after the surrender. And better so, men who had made the pilgrimage told him. The cross had been replaced by a crescent moon over the dome of the Temple of God, and the façade of the Church of the Holy Sepulcher was covered with Arabic graffiti.

Ibelin shook himself and concentrated on the present. On the deck of the ship gliding toward the quay was Henri de Champagne. He was dressed in rich robes of white silk trimmed with gold embroidery, and on his head he wore a flamboyant hat of cloth of gold bordered with white satin. He was not yet thirty years old, and looked young and fresh to Ibelin. Or was he himself just getting grizzled?

Trumpet fanfares sounded in welcome, and the population of Kyrenia had turned out in great numbers. They appeared flattered by (or at least curious about) a visit from the King of Jerusalem. Guards had to keep the crowds from flooding onto the quay, and people had clambered to the rooftops and crushed onto the balconies of the houses lining the harbor in such numbers that Ibelin wondered that the balconies didn't break.

With a gentle thunk Champagne's ship went alongside, and the gangway was hastily shoved out and onto the quay. Ibelin approached the foot of the gangway, and Champagne sprang lightly onto the other end. He crossed the gangway with easy strides, and when Ibelin went to bow to him, pulled him up into an embrace instead. "Father!" Champagne exclaimed loudly for the crowd, before turning to John and embracing him as well, calling him "Brother!"

"Welcome to Cyprus, my lord," Ibelin continued with the protocol. "If you are not too exhausted, horses await"—he gestured with his hand to the finely caparisoned horses waiting just beyond the quay—"so that I may escort you directly to my lord King of Cyprus at St. Hilarion. It is a ride of only five to six hours. We can make it before dark if we depart at once."

"Of course, of course," Champagne agreed at once, smiling graciously and waving to the cheering crowds around them.

He did it very well, Ibelin noted, with a boyish enthusiasm that was quite pleasing. Philip of France had always looked as if he detested cheering crowds, while Richard of England had acted as if cheers were his natural right. Champagne, in contrast, looked flattered by the applause—and that was endearing.

As they reached the horses, Georgios sprang down from his own mount to hold Champagne's off stirrup, while the king mounted the borrowed (but excellent) stallion. When everyone was ready, Ibelin led the way through the crowd with Champagne beside him. John and Champagne's entourage of six knights followed in their wake.

The noise of the crowd and their obligation to acknowledge it prevented conversation until they had passed out of the city. Here they picked up an easy trot for the first part of the winding road up the face of the mountain, and Ibelin addressed Champagne. "Did all go well in Armenia, my lord?"

"Splendidly! Bohemond has been released," Champagne exclaimed enthusiastically. "Bohemond's eldest son Raymond will marry Leo's niece, the daughter of Leo's elder brother."

Ibelin nodded; he had heard of this agreement from the men who came to inquire if King Aimery would receive Henri of Champagne on his return from Armenia to Acre. "It was Leo's plea that I reconcile with Aimery that was the last straw," Champagne added with a winning smile. "The High Court has been pressing me to make peace with him practically from the day he left the Kingdom, and the Bishops of Trani and Brindisi lectured me *ad nauseam* about the need for all Christian monarchs to join together—quite a piece of hypocrisy for two men representing the monarch who so vilely imprisoned my uncle!" Champagne could not resist noting with a disgusted snort.

"I think I could have ignored *them*," Champagne continued, "but not Leo of Armenia. He was so sincere. He appears to have loved your brother very well," Champagne ventured with a sideways glance.

Ibelin nodded. "My brother was a likable man—generous and jovial, and a good man to have beside you in a fight, too."

Champagne nodded, remarking dutifully, "I would have liked to have known him," before proceeding more hesitantly, "and yet I almost had the feeling Leo was more interested in this reconciliation between myself and Aimery for your *niece's* sake." There was an unspoken question in that statement.

"That could well be," Ibelin nodded again. "He hosted her after she had been seized by pirates, and he conceived a deep, almost paternal affection for her. He showed great understanding for her feelings and did not press her to show herself in public, but he was very solicitous of her welfare, bringing many doctors and priests to counsel her."

"Then she suffered maltreatment from the pirates?" Champagne asked in genuine shock.

"She was not violated, no, but she was at Paradisi to recover from an ailment that still plagues her—and the trauma of being seized, for a time bound in the hold of a ship, watching a failed rescue attempt, and then the weeks of uncertainty—they all took their toll."

Champagne nodded in sympathy. "Isabella was outraged, as you can imagine! She was desperate for me to *do* something, but what was I supposed to do?"

"That, I assure you, is the way we all felt. Aimery suffered a foretaste of hell until Erik Andersen could report who the pirates were and where they were headed." Ibelin hesitated, but since the conversation had turned to Eschiva anyway, he decided this was as good a time as any to warn Champagne. "You face more hostility from Eschiva than from Aimery, by the way."

Champagne looked genuinely startled. "Why is that? I swear I have always been as gracious and kindly to her as any man could possibly be—"

"Except for ordering her husband dragged from her bed and thrown into a dungeon for a deed he did not do," Ibelin pointed out.

Champagne looked at his father-in-law perplexed. "Is that the way she sees it?"

"Eschiva is less political than either my lady or yours," Ibelin explained simply. "She rarely thinks in terms of kingdoms and politics. She is loyal to her husband, and she believes he was wronged. In her eyes, you were unjust, and she has said she could *never* forgive you."

Champagne flinched—but then, frowning slightly, he sank into his thoughts. He focused on the climbing road that zigzagged back and forth up the steep slope ahead of them. Finally he turned to Ibelin and asked, "So is there any point in this visit?"

"Certainly! Aimery and I persuaded her that she should receive you and at least hear you out. You will have to exert all your charm to overcome her enmity," Ibelin warned solemnly before adding with a smile, "But I daresay you are up to the task."

"I will certainly do my best!" Champagne assured him.

By the time they dismounted in the forecourt of St. Hilarion, Champagne was as agog as they had all been the first time they saw the rocky mountain crest that housed the irregular and impregnable castle of St. Hilarion. "It might as well be an eagle's nest!" Champagne exclaimed, looking about in awe and nearly dizzy at the view down to the coast.

"Eagles do indeed nest all over the place," Ibelin answered, with a gesture toward the gnarled, wind-stunted trees around them in which many birds of prey made their homes.

"Those towers up there must give you a spectacular view!" Champagne admired.

"On a good day, they claim you can see all the way to Rhodes. It's not true, of course, but it *feels* like it. We certainly can see any ships approaching from the West long before they reach us. It's a wonder Isaac Comnenus was so surprised by your uncle's fleet. People must have seen it approaching for a day before it actually got here. But then, they may have kept the information to themselves, seeing how little they liked Isaac. Fortunately for your uncle and us, Isaac preferred the luxury of the palace in Nicosia to the semi-wilderness up here."

Champagne asked Ibelin to pause while he caught his breath. They had been climbing steadily ever since they left the outer ward, and it seemed like over two hundred steps. He let his eyes sweep along the northern coastline in wonder. "It is a beautiful place," he admitted.

Ibelin nodded, and they continued, their men behind them.

In the courtyard of the upper castle banners were hanging from the windows, and these flapped and curled in the stiff breeze. The arms of Lusignan fluttered proudly from all the surrounding rooftops, while the household knights and officials stood on the steps up to the great hall. Champagne paused to straighten his surcoat and his hat and then advanced through the narrow space that opened for him, with Ibelin a pace behind. He nodded acknowledgment to the men he knew: Henri de Brie, Barlais, the Chenechés, Jubail, and Bethsan.

They passed out of the fading natural light of dusk into the artificial light of hundreds of torches and lamps. Here the women were gathered in their finery, along with the clerics. On the dais at the far end of the room stood Aimery and Eschiva. Aimery had opted for armor and a silk surcoat with the arms of Lusignan—quartered with the arms of Jerusalem. That was an affectation Guy had started (legitimately), but which Aimery had now retained (provocatively, in the circumstances, Ibelin thought). Eschiva, in contrast, was in full Greek splendor: a dress stiff with cords of braided gold and studded with jewels that glistened in the unsteady light of the torches and lamps. Neither was crowned, of course, but then nor was Henri. Although both men carried the title of "king," neither had yet been anointed. It was something that helped make this meeting possible.

Aimery solemnly descended the steps of the dais to meet Henri halfway down the hall. The two kings embraced, kissing each other in a gesture of public reconciliation. "Jerusalem, welcome to Cyprus!"

"An honor, Cyprus, an honor."

Aimery turned and led Champagne up the dais steps and to Eschiva, standing immobile before the table.

Champagne bowed deeply before her and kissed her hand. "My lady! My lady wife, Queen Isabella, begged me to deliver a kiss from her." Although Eschiva caught her breath and drew her head back slightly, Henri ignored her obvious reluctance and took a step forward to deliver a kiss on both of her cheeks. As he did so he whispered, "Please forgive me, dearest Eschiva. I did wrong to arrest your husband, but for the sake of our children let us be reconciled."

Eschiva had not been expecting such a complete apology from Henri. She was genuinely flustered by it. She had prepared herself to be cold, inhospitable, disdainful, punishing. But how could she be, if he was so willing to admit he had been at fault?

Champagne drew back enough to smile directly into her eyes, his blue eyes pleading with her. "Please. At least let us focus on the present, the future. I long to meet your sons again. Ibelin tells me they are growing fast and are already showing signs of the Lusignan good looks." Again Champagne had aimed well: Eschiva was inordinately proud of her three sons, and any flattery of them won her favor.

"Come, my lord king, join us at the table," Aimery suggested, evidently unsure how Eschiva was reacting, and anxious not to prolong this moment in case her animosity toward Champagne still held the upper hand.

Champagne responded by bowing deeply to Eschiva and gesturing for her to precede him. She went around to the other side of the table and took her seat between the two kings. Maria Comnena sat beside her son-in-law, with her husband beside her, and Burgundia had been given the seat of honor on her father's far side. Champagne gallantly kissed her hand as he passed her on the way to his own seat. His "Enchanté" made the twelve-year-old blush with pleasure.

Champagne turned to Aimery. "I'm quite serious," he exclaimed, speaking across Eschiva but to her as well. "I'm most anxious to meet your sons—because, you see, they are the main reason I am here."

Aimery raised his eyebrows, and Eschiva frowned slightly.

"Marriages, as we all know, are the best means of burying bad blood. Leo and Bohemond are just the most recent example of a breach healed by bonds of marriage. The great Christian capitals of the East, Constantinople and Jerusalem, were united by my beloved mother-in-law's marriage to King Amalric." Champagne turned to smile at Maria Zoë. "So, you have three sons and I have three daughters; let us betroth them to one another."

"All of them?" Aimery asked, astonished.

"Exactly!" Champagne retorted with a smile, his eyes shifting from Aimery to Eschiva. He had taken her by surprise, he could sense that—she looked stunned—but it was hard to tell if she was also pleased or the reverse.

When Eschiva spoke it was to protest, "Your girls are still very little. The youngest, Philippa, is not yet a year old."

"And Guy is already a youth, I know," Champagne conceded, "but your middle son is not so very much older than my Alice, and your littlest, Hugh, is only months older than my Philippa. The reality is that children are fragile. We cannot know for sure if all our children will reach adulthood, and this alliance is too important to allow it to hang on the life of any single child. That is why

I think we should commit not to specific betrothals, but rather to the principle of marriage between the eldest surviving son of the House of Lusignan and the eldest surviving daughter of the House of Champagne-Jerusalem." As he finished, Champagne cast his eyes around the table to assess the reception to his proposal. He saw fundamental consent with the idea from both Ibelin and the Dowager Queen. Indeed, even Aimery was nodding. Eschiva was the only one who looked uncertain.

Aimery seemed to sense the same hesitation, because with a significant glance to his wife, he announced that they would think about the proposal and speak among themselves. Then he gestured to the food being brought in, signaled for the squires to pour the wine, and changed the subject.

The detailed negotiations lasted almost a fortnight, with Eschiva insisting tenaciously that the daughters of Champagne bring Jaffa as their dowry. Her argument was that Richard of England had bestowed Jaffa on Geoffrey de Lusignan, who had turned all his claims in the Holy Land over to Aimery. Champagne resisted the idea for a long time, until Ibelin pointed out that a Lusignan stake in the Kingdom of Jerusalem would make it more likely that the kings of Cyprus would expend Cypriot resources to defend Jerusalem. Champagne saw the logic of that argument, and it was agreed.

The night before Champagne was to depart, the festivities lasted late into the night. The mood was very good, and Eschiva let Champagne take her briefly onto the dance floor. She was too weak to dance for long, but as he brought her back to the high table she was exceptionally flushed, and Aimery bent over to brush a kiss on her forehead, remarking proudly, "You look like a young girl again." He was only partially lying: she did look younger than she had in years. "It's good that Champagne is leaving tomorrow, or I would have to fear he was seducing you," he teased.

Eschiva shook her head. "Never, my love. But will you forgive me if I go to bed now? Before the end of the festivities? I'm feeling dizzy."

"Of course! You've been holding up wonderfully these past weeks, but there's no need to overdo it." Aimery turned and looked around for someone to escort Eschiva. Philip d'Ibelin, who had been standing attentively behind the high table, came at once. "Bring the queen to her chamber; she needs to rest," Aimery ordered.

Eschiva pushed herself to her feet, and Champagne at once jumped up. With the perceptiveness of a well-mannered nobleman he asked, "Is something wrong, my lady?"

"Nothing except that you have exhausted me, my lord," Eschiva answered with a faint, yet contented smile. "That last dance. I think I overdid it a little—but I wouldn't have missed it for the world. I'm just a touch dizzy." Indeed, she was swaying slightly. Philip slipped his arm around her waist and half carried her off the dais into the solar.

Eschiva was hardly able to stand, and Philip called to another squire who happened to be there to come help him. They supported Eschiva on either side and together helped her up the stairs to her chamber. At the chamber door, Eschiva dismissed the strange squire and told Philip to help her to the bed.

"Should I send for Beatrice or one of your other ladies to help you undress?" Philip asked anxiously, feeling out of his depth in the bedroom alone.

"No, no. I don't need to undress just yet. I'll just rest a bit. Maybe I'll go back down to the hall later, when I feel better."

Although the words were reassuring, something about her demeanor made Philip hesitate. "Should I bring you something to drink?"

"No, no. I've had more than enough wine. Just lift my feet up onto the bed." Eschiva was sitting on the bed, and as she spoke she laid her head back on the pillows. Philip dutifully lifted her feet up onto the bed, slipping off her shoes at the same time.

Eschiva smiled at him down the length of her body. "Have I ever told you what a good squire you are, Philip?"

"Who? Me?" Philip asked, astonished. "John's the good—"

"Yes, John's a good young man. I'm sure he'll go far, but I've liked having you around me *more*. John was always so earnest, you know. You make me laugh. Whatever happens, don't lose your sense of humor, Philip."

"Aunt Eschiva?" (Technically they were cousins, of course, but because of the age difference Philip had always called her "aunt" in private.) "Are you sure you're all right?"

"Yes, Philip. Now hurry back so Aimery doesn't start worrying, but . . . "

"Yes?" Philip prompted, still uneasy.

"Your father. Tell your father no, never mind. He knows."

"Knows what?"

"What he has meant to me. All my life. Long before Aimery and the children . . . "

"Aunt Eschiva . . . you sound very strange. . . . " Philip admitted.

"Nonsense. I'm happy. Very happy. Things have turned out so well. So much better than I ever dreamed. I don't really care about being a queen, you know, but it means so much to Aimery to be king after all those thankless years groveling at Guy's arrogant feet. And I like the thought of our children . . . I'm so glad that Champagne came. So glad we could be reconciled. Go. I need to rest." She patted Philip's hand in a gesture of both reassurance and dismissal, and he slipped out of the room.

By the time Aimery came to bed, Eschiva was in such a deep, peaceful sleep, with a smile on her lips, that he did not want to disturb her. It was just hours before he needed to rise and escort the King of Jerusalem to Limassol so he could sail back to Acre. A formal escort of barons and knights would accompany him, so Eschiva had no need to join them. It would be better if she slept in late or whiled the whole day in bed to recover from the strain of the past weeks. He closed the door gently behind him, and slept in the anteroom.

The following morning the two kings set off side by side on the journey to Limassol. There they took leave of one another, with a great show of affection that was no longer staged. Both men had found much to admire in the other, now that Guy was dead and both felt more secure in their own realms.

It was not until Aimery, Ibelin, and the others returned to St. Hilarion five days later that they learned that Queen Eschiva was dead. She had passed away peacefully in her sleep the night before Champagne departed.

Chapter Twenty-One
One Wrong Step

Paphos, Cyprus,
September 1197

"YOU DON'T NEED TO COME IF you don't want to," Maria Zoë assured her
eldest son sympathetically. Today they were (at last) inaugurating the successful
completion of the aqueduct with a festival in the main square of Paphos. Tests
had been made and everything was functional, but the water had been temporarily blocked again to await this official opening. Today, in the presence of the
Greek Bishop of Paphos, Ibelin, and all the leading (and most of the common)
citizens of the city, the large central fountain (and others throughout the city)
would be flooded with water. The Bishop would bless the fountain, and there
would be street food, music, and dancing. At the banquet Balian and Maria
Zoë would honor the Greek master builder and his team, who had successfully
built a new channel that hooked up to intact remnants of the Roman aqueduct.
The master was to be given a large silver pitcher, and each of his masons would
receive a small silver cup.

The problem for John was that Ayyub/Antonis had completed his apprenticeship, and as a journeyman had obtained permission to marry. He had
requested the hand of Father Andronikos' daughter Eirini and had received a
positive answer.

When his mother addressed him, John was standing in the window niche,
gazing out to sea with a wistful expression on his face. Now he pulled himself
together and stepped down into the room. "I will come with you. This is one

of Papa's greatest achievements in Paphos to date. I would not want anyone to think I did not honor him for it."

Maria Zoë touched John's arm gently in approval. John was now a head taller than she, having caught up with his father. He was still very slender, and his face was almost gaunt, but it was a man's face. John had turned eighteen this past May, and he was his father's right hand in everything.

Maria Zoë nodded that she was ready to go, and John opened the door for her. They descended to the ward where Balian was marshaling their escort, with Meg already mounted on her flower-bedecked palfrey. At the sight of Maria Zoë and John, Balian called to the grooms to bring their horses, and in minutes they were all mounted and ready to depart. They crossed over the drawbridge and back into the town, which was bustling with subdued excitement. The harbor was more crowded than usual, and the crews of the ships were streaming from the port toward the center of town with the unique swagger of sailors freshly ashore. Carts, mules, and donkeys tethered to various buildings testified to the number of visitors, as people from the surrounding countryside flooded into the city to partake in the festivities.

A herald rode ahead of the Baron of Ibelin/Paphos and with short trumpet fanfares announced his approach. At the sound, people flocked to the side of the street and craned their necks to get a look at the Baron and his Comnena wife. There was no cheering, Ibelin noted, but he could sense no hostility, either. His eyes scanned the crowds looking for signs of trouble or resentment, but he found none. People appeared to be adjusting to Latin rule, and he supposed that (for at least today) they were mostly satisfied. Here and there people even waved to him. Bringing water back to the fountains was definitely a popular move, and well overdue. The public humiliation of the bath master who had assaulted his immigrant competitor had caused a small riot the previous year, and tensions between Greek and Latin, native and immigrant populations still simmered. But everyone could agree on the utility of functioning fountains. He hoped.

As they approached the large square on the site of the old Greek agora, the crowds thickened—and here, at last, men occasionally called out blessings or cheers. Ibelin could be fairly certain that most of the men wishing him well were newcomers, settlers from the Kingdom of Jerusalem, particularly from Nablus. Over the past year he had noted the unusual number of men from Nablus among the settlers; they appeared to have chosen Paphos, rather than Nicosia or Kyrenia, because they knew him and Maria Zoë.

Nevertheless, the fact that the Greek Bishop of Paphos had agreed to conduct the blessing was a good sign, too. The Bishop was flanked by scores of priests, all in their black vestments and long beards, which fluttered in the stiff westerly breeze coming off the Mediterranean. Ibelin had had word that the Pope had issued a papal bull this past winter naming a Latin Archbishop of Nicosia and suffragan bishops in Paphos, Limassol, and, surprisingly, Famagusta. While Ibelin welcomed the notion of Paphos becoming a bishop's seat, because it would bring additional wealth and prestige to the city, he was a little relieved that no Latin bishop had yet been named. This way he could bow to the Greek bishop in a gesture of respect that would, hopefully, help ease the latent tensions even more.

At the edge of the square, Ibelin and his party dismounted, left the horses with the squires, and advanced to greet the Bishop of Paphos with humility. Ibelin, his lady, and Meg all bowed their heads to receive a blessing before going together to the edge of the fountain. As they waited, apparently in prayer, a flag was run up on the tower of the customs house overlooking the square. This was answered by a flag on the tower of the outer wall. The latter could be seen by the men controlling the aqueduct cistern. Within minutes water rushed down the slope to bubble up into the fountain with a satisfying gurgle, followed by splashing. The latter ignited a cheer from the crowd around the square that became so enthusiastic it drowned out the Bishop's blessings. People started pressing in, dipping their hands in the cool water or filling jars and cups with it. Everyone was talking at once and jostling one another good-naturedly.

Ibelin, his wife and children removed themselves from the fountain with the bishop to stand on the steps up to the customs house. The bishop nodded benevolently at the crowds, as youths started splashing one another to the accompaniment of loud shouts. "This is a good thing," the bishop assured Ibelin above the noise. Balian's passive Greek had improved enough for him to understand remarks like this, but he was still reluctant to speak in Greek. So he answered in French, and Maria Zoë stepped in to translate.

While his parents exchanged pleasantries with the bishop, John's eyes found Ayyub/Antonis in the crowd. Sure enough, Eirini was at his side. She was dressed in a pretty gown with bright red embroidery, and she had hooked her hand through his elbow to walk beside him. She was very modest—indeed, she wore a scarf over her head and neck. She kept her head down, too, rather than shaking her curls and throwing smiles at all the handsome youths as some of the other girls did. But she didn't look glum or miserable, either. Rather, she was flushed and cast frequent admiring glances at Ayyub/Antonis. They were the same glances that she had once directed at John.

"Could you excuse me a moment, my lord?" John addressed his father formally.

Ibelin nodded absently, and Maria Zoë cast John a questioning, almost warning, look, but he ignored her. He wove his way through the crowds, skirting the press of people still surrounding the fountain to where Ayyub/Antonis was chatting to several of his fellow masons.

"Antonis!" John called out to attract attention.

Antonis turned around, surprised. When he caught sight of John, his face broke into a wide smile. He had no idea that John was in love with Eirini, and John knew that. Nor could John blame the Syrian immigrant for falling in love with the Cypriot maiden. Who wouldn't? What he couldn't understand was why Eirini had chosen Antonis over him.

As he joined the masons, John held out his hand to Antonis and congratulated him on successfully completing his apprenticeship.

"And my marriage! Eirini and I were married yesterday!" he announced, bursting with pride.

John was staggered to think it was already done—irrevocably and eternally. Not that he could have stopped it. He glanced sharply at Eirini, and she dropped her eyes, blushing bright red.

"Then I must congratulate the bride," John found himself saying smoothly, as he bent forward to touch his cheek to hers. It was self-inflicted torture, as he remembered the feel of her lips on his. How could she do this?

"I wanted to invite you and your lord father," Antonis was saying innocently, "but Father Andronikos convinced me we couldn't afford a feast worthy of a baron."

"My father, and indeed all of us, do not require extravagance," John countered, still feeling off balance and a little dizzy; "you should know that."

"Look! They're opening the casks of wine! Will you join us for a toast?" Antonis asked.

"Of course. I must drink to your good fortune and wish you many children," John agreed—although he didn't know where the words came from. Inwardly, out of pain, he wished them the opposite.

"Would you mind looking after Eirini while I fight my way through the crowd?" Antonis asked, with a smile so innocent it baffled John. Didn't he suspect anything?

John could only nod, however, and the next thing he knew Eirini was hanging on his elbow, while Antonis plunged into the crowd that had converged on the wagon with the wine casks. At first John couldn't bring himself to even look at her. He kept his eyes fixed on the crowd, watching Antonis' progress. Then it just burst out of him. "Why? Why did you marry him?"

"Because he asked me," Eirini answered bluntly.

"You mean you would have married *anyone*?" John demanded angrily, looking down at the first and only woman he had ever loved in his short life, anger smoldering in his breast.

"Not *any*one," Eirini answered firmly, "but Antonis is a good, honest man. He is hard-working and will go far. He is also very kind, and he loves me. Is that not reason enough?"

"What about me?" John protested. "Are you saying I am not good or honest? Or do you doubt my love?"

Eirini would not meet his eye as she answered, but she spoke firmly, almost bitterly. "You are Latin, and you are a knight. You would never have married me."

John felt he had been kicked in the gut. She was right, of course.

"I do not want to dishonor my father," Eirini rubbed the message in. "I was foolish to lead you on, but I'm not a child anymore. I want to be a respectable woman with a husband, home, and family. You could never give that to me. Antonis will."

John had nothing to say to that. He swallowed and looked for Antonis. He didn't want to be with Eirini a moment longer. He just wanted to run away. But he couldn't. He had to wait for Antonis to return. Eirini was now gazing at him. "Are you angry with me?" she asked, sounding for the first time a little unsure of herself.

John didn't dare to look at her. He kept his eyes on Antonis, who had successfully purchased three cups of wine and was returning cautiously through the crowds, intent on not spilling any of the precious liquid. "No," John told Eirini, unsure if he was lying or not. "As you say, we are not children anymore," he added. Inwardly he wondered: Could only children love without thought of the consequences? Did you have to be a child to just fall in love without calculating costs and benefits and risks? He felt very sad and very old, and had to force himself to smile as Antonis, grinning, offered him a cup of red Cypriot wine.

John raised his cup. "To the bride and groom! May you have many happy years together and a house full of healthy children!" He put the cup to his lips and gulped down half at once. Then, with another forced smile, he raised the cup again in salute.

"And to you and your father for making this all possible!" Antonis answered sincerely, lifting his own cup.

John raised his cup to clink it with Antonis', and as he did so he noticed a commotion at the other side of the square. He frowned and craned his neck. "Something's going on." He gestured toward a rider who was forcing his way through the crowd, making for the Lord and Lady of Ibelin/Paphos. The rider wore Lusignan livery and his horse was caked in sweat and dust.

"Something's going on. Excuse me." John handed his near-empty cup back to Antonis. "I must find out what has happened."

John forced his way back through the crowd as rapidly as possible, but it wasn't easy. People kept getting in his way. By the time he'd skirted the fountain, the rider had dismounted and gone down on one knee before his parents. They were both staring at him in obvious shock, while the Bishop of Paphos was crossing himself. Whatever news he'd brought, it was bad.

John pushed people aside to run the last few strides, pounding up the steps to his parents' side. Balian pulled him up the last step. "John! I need you to escort your mother to Acre at once. I'll come as soon as I can, but I need to regulate some things here first. Take her back to the castle to change and organize an escort of six knights. Take Sir Galvin and have him choose any other five knights he wants. Meanwhile, I'll find Andersen and have him get ready to put to sea immediately. *Haakon's Ghost* may not be as fast as the *Storm Bird*, but on this wind, she'll still get you to Acre faster than riding for Limassol and looking for another galley. Don't bother with horses. You'll have access to the royal stables."

"Yes, my lord," John replied without hesitation, but he couldn't help asking, "What's happened?"

"Henri de Champagne is dead. Some sort of bizarre accident. We don't know the details yet, but apparently he fell from a window to the courtyard and his death."

"Champagne?" John asked, incredulous, the images of him full of life, charm, and good spirits still vivid in his mind.

"I need to get to Bella as soon as possible," his mother told him.

"And I'm coming with you!" Meg declared resolutely.

Balian stepped back so John could take his mother's arm and escort her, and he didn't stop Meg from following. John elbowed his way through the crowds to their tethered horses. They did not speak. They did not need to. They all grasped what a horrible and unfair blow this was to Isabella. Just once did Maria Zoë exclaim: "God help me! She doesn't deserve this!"

Acre, Kingdom of Jerusalem, Mid-September 1197

Haakon's Ghost slipped into Acre as the wind died at dusk. The standards of Ibelin and Jerusalem were both flying from the masthead. The pilot met them off the outer sea wall. As the Norsemen manned the oars to enter the harbor cautiously, the pilot turned to sprint into the harbor. Imperiously, the pilot ordered one of the ships tied at the quay to clear a berth for the Dowager Queen's ship. By the time Maria Zoë, John, and Meg stepped ashore, horses were already waiting for them along with a small contingent of royal knights. Although Maria Zoë could not remember any names, she recognized several of the young knights from Champagne. They had come out with their lord on the last great crusade and had served Isabella since her marriage to Henri. They looked shocked and somber.

Standing with his mother and sister on the quay as they prepared to mount up, John was disturbed by distant shouting, screaming, and crashing. He frowned and lifted his head to listen more closely, and Barry lifted his head and ears as well. As a knight led a horse forward for him, John swung himself into the saddle and picked up the reins, but immediately asked the knight, "What's going on? It sounds like you're under assault!"

"In a way we are," the royal knight answered grimly. "Ever since their victory over al-Adil last week, the Germans have become insufferable! They've been demanding better lodging and complaining about market prices. Now they've run amok down in the Jewish quarter and are plundering and looting."

John stared at the knight in incomprehension. "And you haven't been able to restore order?"

"How can we? There's only a score of us, and we need to stay close to the palace to protect the Queen."

"You can't just let foreign troops run amok in the heart of Acre!" John protested.

"Well, you try to stop them, puppy!" the man answered with a sneer and a contemptuous look at Barry. Then he spurred his horse to the head of the column. John clamped his jaw together and followed behind the others, but his gaze was drawn again and again toward the sounds of rioting coming from the northwest. Where was the watch? Where was the Constable? John realized uncomfortably that he hadn't a clue who Champagne had appointed Constable after driving Aimery out of the Kingdom five years ago.

He cantered to catch up with his mother and sister near the head of the column, Barry loping behind him. As he drew up beside them, he pointed in the direction of the noise. "Do you hear that? Apparently the German crusaders are helping themselves to the property of the Jews. Someone's got to stop them! The Jews are citizens, too. Besides, if they can take what they want from the Jews with impunity, they'll attack the Syrians and then the other burghers next."

Maria Zoë looked over her shoulder in the direction John was pointing, and nodded. "You're right. You'd better see what you can do."

"Me?" John asked, astonished.

"No one else seems to be concerned. Take your father's knights and find out what's happening."

John drew a breath to protest, but then realized his mother was right. He was a knight, heir to Balian d'Ibelin, Lord of Paphos. His father's knights would obey him. "I'll see what I can do, my lady," he answered his mother formally.

He set his jaw and his expression turned to one of grim determination. As he inwardly assumed his father's role, he jumped down, put a lead on Barry, and turned the dog over to his sister. Then he remounted and rode back to his father's knights.

As he drew up beside Sir Galvin, he pointed toward the noise and again explained the situation. Sir Galvin didn't hesitate or question. He pulled his helmet off his pommel, set it on his head, and drew the strap tight. Then he drew his battle-ax from its leather case and weighed it in his right hand. Sir Sergios strung his bow and notched an arrow. The other four knights drew their swords.

They set out across town, following the sound of the disturbance. By now the sun had set and the streets were cast in shadow, but unlike most evenings in Acre there were no taverns spilling tables into the squares. There were no hawkers on the corners offering pre-prepared food, wine, or ale. The storefronts were closed and barred from the inside, and shutters were closed over windows.

The sounds of rioting grew steadily louder and nearer, and soon the smell of smoke reached them, too, making the horses skittish. Quite abruptly, as they followed a jog in the street, they came upon a large crowd of people cowering together in a cul-de-sac. They were keening and lamenting, some of the women tearing their hair and some of the men shaking their fists. Opposite them, a half-dozen soldiers were smashing open windows and doors or already dragging valuables into the street to stuff into their tunics. John felt a shudder run down his spine. Then he spurred his reluctant horse forward and clattered in among the looters, his sword drawn, to underline his shouted orders to desist.

The sight of an armed knight made the men drop what they were doing and fall back into the nearest alleyway. Delighted by this easy success, John and his men followed in pursuit. Unfortunately, the alley led to a larger square around the synagogue. The latter was already smoldering, although it had not truly caught fire. Here the number of men engaged in the looting numbered in the scores. John sat back and hauled his stallion to a halt. "I think they're too many for us!" he shouted at Sir Galvin. "We need reinforcements," John concluded.

Sir Galvin grunted in reply as he, too, pulled his stallion to a stop. He added, "I'll go rouse the f***ing garrison! The lazy bastards!"

"I'll try to bring the royal guard. One of you go back to *Haakon's Ghost* for help." John answered and asked his horse for a canter.

At the palace, the guard opened the gates for him without question, but John shouted down at them, "What the hell are you doing? There are hundreds of German soldiers looting and trying to burn down the synagogue!"

"Our orders are to protect the palace. You can't stop the Germans anyway. They're barbarians!"

"Where are the German nobles?" John answered, while his horse, responding to the restlessness of his rider, kept turning and scrambling on the cobbles.

"They're staying in the Archbishop's palace," the sergeant-in-command answered, gesturing to the large building diagonally across the street.

John swung his horse around and trotted across to the Archbishop's palace, snuggled up beside the Cathedral of the Holy Cross. Here the sergeants at the gate did not immediately recognize the Ibelin arms on his surcoat; it had grown too dark to distinguish color. They blocked his way belligerently.

John was getting increasingly desperate. He shouted at them, more forcefully than ever before in his life: "I'm John d'Ibelin, brother of the Queen, and I demand to see Conrad of Hildesheim immediately!"

John knew who to ask for, because the Imperial chancellor and commander of the German crusaders was the same man who had crowned Aimery King of Cyprus only two weeks earlier.

The guards caved in before John's imperious manner, and he found himself in the courtyard of the Archbishop's palace. He jumped down from his borrowed horse and took a moment to orient himself. He had been here only once or twice before, but fortunately for formal occasions, which meant he knew his way to the Archbishop's great hall. It helped that torches were lit along the inside of the arcade, and also up the stairs to the second floor. John took the stairs two at a time, conscious that the synagogue could be ablaze by now. Certainly the damage and destruction continued with each minute.

He burst into the Archbishop's great hall to find it already crowded with men milling about and, to his relief, the Archbishops of Acre and Hildesheim sat together on the dais. They were apparently in earnest discussion with a number of noblemen. John pushed his way through the seething crowds in the lower hall, unable to understand what was agitating the many occupants, because they were all speaking German. He sprang onto the dais, provoking a tardy response from a young knight in Hildesheim's service. The latter tried to put himself between John and the men at the table, but John shoved him aside so forcefully that two German noblemen sprang to their feet with their hands on their hilts.

"My lord of Hildesheim!" John called out to the Imperial Chancellor from

half a dozen feet away. "Your men are plundering and looting in the streets of
Acre as if they were in Damascus! And you have nothing better to do than sit
and drink?" The outrage in John's voice rang to the vaulted ceiling and reverberated there.

The German noblemen at once drew their swords and shouted back at
John, while behind him a general uproar erupted. The Archbishop of Acre,
however, leaned back in his chair with an odd smile on his face, and the Imperial
Chancellor gestured for silence, telling the noblemen to sheath their swords.

The level of noise dropped but did not fully die away. The Imperial Chancellor spoke into the lull, "It's young John d'Ibelin, is it not?" He spoke in Latin.

"Yes, my lord," John answered in the same tongue, because it was their only
common language.

"And you presume to give orders to me? The Imperial Chancellor of the
Holy Roman Empire?" he asked with raised eyebrows.

"My sister the Queen," John started deliberately. He was breathing heavily,
but he had a grip on himself. He answered slowly and clearly, speaking so every
man in the hall could hear him, "... is in grief and mourning. The *Dowager
Queen of Jerusalem*, therefore, tasked me with restoring order. And that I *will* do,
even if it means riding down and butchering your men," John bluffed. "I would
prefer, however, if you brought your men to order."

Behind him he heard men muttering "*Juden*" and "*Schweine,*" but he
ignored them and focused on the Imperial Chancellor. Hildesheim might be a
bishop, but he was a worldly bishop—and one who knew how to wield a mace.

"What makes you so certain you can stop thousands of fighting men from
obtaining what they believe is their just reward, young man?"

"My faith in God, my lord Bishop," John answered as forcefully as he could,
gulping air into his lungs to try to calm his racing pulse. "He knows that what
your men do is an offense against His people—the people he was born to—and
His Holy Gospel, for which He gave His sacred blood. Even now my men
are calling out the watch. If you do not take action, we will." John's heart was
pounding furiously in his breast. God help me! He pleaded silently. God help
me!

"Is this not what I have been saying for the last hour?" the Archbishop of
Acre spoke up, leaning forward and hissing to his fellow bishop: "You know it
is the right thing to do."

"My men won a great victory over the Saracens, and what have they got for
it? Nothing. No loot. No gold. Nothing."

"They have received the remission of sins past," the Archbishop of Acre
countered, "but *not*, I must stress, absolution for what they are doing *now*. The

sins they are committing here in the Holy Land against innocent people will take them all to hell, regardless of what they did to al-Adil's army!"

Hildesheim looked over at Acre with raised eyebrows for a moment, but then he pulled his feet under him and stood. He started distributing orders in German. The noblemen around him nodded, turned toward the hall, and started calling to their men. Abruptly all the men in the hall appeared to be scrambling to find their helmets and gauntlets. John felt himself quaking. If they were going to join their men in the looting, he—no, Acre—was utterly lost.

As if reading his mind, Hildesheim clapped him on the shoulder and remarked, "You win, boy. I've ordered my knights to rein in their men and move them out of Acre. We'll set up camp outside the walls—and then look for a Saracen city to sack."

John turned toward the Archbishop of Acre in amazement as Hildesheim swept past him, calling to someone to bring him his helmet and arms. He wasn't yet sure if he should believe Hildesheim or not.

The Archbishop of Acre had once upon a time been a priest at the Church of St. George in Lydda. He had known John's uncle and father. He smiled at John with nearly paternal pride as he remarked, "Well done, young man. You are truly an Ibelin."

Acre, Late September 1197

Ralph of Tiberius pounced on Balian before he had even dismounted. "Ibelin! Thank God you've made it." He grabbed Balian's bridle and held his horse for him as he dropped down onto the cobbles of the courtyard. Then in a low voice Ralph murmured, "Isabella must marry immediately! We need a king to take command of the Germans and confront al-Adil. We can't afford to take her grief into account. Too much is at stake."

Balian gave the young man a reproachful look and noted, "I've only just arrived, Tiberius. Let me at least speak to my wife and her daughter."

A groom emerged to take his horse, and Balian turned over the reins. He stepped back to tell his squires to see to his baggage, and then started immediately up the steps. Tiberius, however, clung to his side and continued speaking in a low, urgent voice. "My lord, don't mistake me as callous. I have the deepest sympathy for the Queen. No one would be gentler with her, yet more forceful with our enemies."

Balian stopped in mid-stride to turn and stare at the young nobleman. "Did you just suggest what I think you did? That you would be a suitable consort for Queen Isabella?"

"Why wouldn't I be? I'm a prince of Galilee," Ralph answered.

"A land we lost in 1187," Ibelin retorted briskly, before adding more wearily, "along with Ibelin and Ramla. I know. There's no shame in being landless, but the Queen needs a consort who is—"

The Lord of Caesarea, coming down the stairs, recognized Balian just as he came abreast of him, and at once stopped to grab him by the elbow. "Ibelin! Thank God! We need to call the High Court together."

"Of course," Balian answered with a glance at Tiberius. "But first I wish to see my lady and my stepdaughter the Queen."

Balian continued up the stairs, but Caesarea turned to flank him on his left, while Tiberius still clung to his right side. "Al-Adil has laid siege to Jaffa," Caesarea reported, pacing himself to Balian.

"And the Germans damn near burned down the synagogue," Ralph of Tiberius chimed in. "If your son John hadn't put a sword up the Bishop of Hildesheim's butt—"

"What?" Balian gasped, turning on Ralph in shock.

"Just a figure of speech, my lord," Ralph excused himself. "The German troops were running riot, helping themselves to whatever they wanted—and not just in the Jewish quarter—while the German knights and barons sat around ignoring it all. John stormed in and somehow convinced them not only to intervene, but to move their troops outside the city."

Balian was astonished—and very pleased.

"Jaffa's the bigger problem," Caesarea countered doggedly, with a frown at Tiberius. "Al-Adil still has some fifty thousand troops in the field, and the last we heard Barlais had sailed down to Jaffa with his wife and God knows what else, but certainly *not* troops. It was his pleas for help that forced Champagne to hire the Italian mercenaries. He was trying to address them from the balcony when it gave way under him."

Ibelin frowned. Aimery's selection of Barlais as the man to take control of Jaffa for the Lusignans had been dictated by the fact that Barlais had been Geoffrey's man and seemed to feel he was *entitled* to act as the Lusignans' lieutenant there. Aimery had also pointed out that Barlais had made more than enough enemies on Cyprus, and was better occupied elsewhere. Still, Balian wasn't surprised to find he was no match for al-Adil. Barlais was a sergeant—no matter what title you dressed him up in.

"Can't we send the Germans down to relieve Jaffa?" Ibelin asked Caesarea.

"*Who* are you suggesting should send them down?"

"The Queen."

This answer produced dead silence. Ibelin looked from one man to the other, and they both shook their heads mutely while not meeting his eye. Not a good sign.

Before they could say another word, however, the Archbishop of Nazareth emerged out of a door they were passing. He caught sight of Ibelin and exclaimed, "Thank God you're here, Ibelin! You need to summon the High Court at once! We have many urgent decisions to make! May I send out the summons?"

"Of course," Ibelin answered, surprised no summons had been issued already.

The Archbishop turned as if to take immediate action, but then stopped himself and turned back to lecture Ibelin (rather pompously, Balian thought): "The Kingdom has rarely been in a more precarious situation, my lord. You have no idea how close we came to losing the battle to al-Adil—right here outside our very gates." He gestured dramatically in the general direction of the Nazareth Gate. "The Germans would all have run away. It was the citizens of Acre, rallying to Champagne late in the day, who enabled us to hold their attacks and finally scatter them with a last charge."

"The Chancellor speaks the truth," Hugh of Tiberius spoke up hotly. He had come out of apparently nowhere to stand beside his brother. "The value of these German troops is far less than what we hoped."

"They're only good for terrorizing civilians!" his brother Ralph scoffed.

Ibelin looked from one to the other in dismay and then tried to continue, but now all three men kept pace with him, and he was next waylaid by the Lord of Arsur. "Ibelin! At last! We need to summon the High Court."

"Yes, I just told the Chancellor to issue the summons," Ibelin assured him, adding in a tone tinged with exasperation, "I expected the summons to go out before now."

"On whose orders?" Arsur asked, astonished. "You are the Queen's closest male relative. Or your son John, I suppose. . . ."

"No matter. It's done now. Although it looks as if most of the tenants-in-chief are already here," Ibelin noted with a nod to Pagan of Haifa, who had joined the crowd of men around him.

"Sidon hasn't shown up, and Jaffa is now held by Lusignan. We're also missing half the bishops," Haifa at once joined the conversation.

"What about the rear-tenants?"

"I haven't taken a count, but we could summon them to the Cathedral at noon tomorrow and see who shows up."

Ibelin nodded again, still somewhat astonished to find all these men awaiting his orders. While it was true he was arguably the most senior baron in the Kingdom, he had not imagined that the others would be so passive in his absence. No doubt the unexpectedness of Champagne's death had left them dazed and confused. No one had been prepared for a young king in the best of health to be suddenly taken from them.

He reached the entrance to the royal apartments. The heavy double doors were closed, and two sergeants stood in front of them, helmets partially hiding their faces behind wide nose guards. They stood with their legs apart and their hands on their hilts. They clearly had orders to admit no one and were determined to follow those orders.

Balian turned toward the door, and the men around him fell back respectfully.

"I'm Balian d'Ibelin," Balian told the guards simply. He did not even raise his voice.

The guards reacted smartly and promptly. One turned and opened the door, shoving it open and then stepping back and aside to allow Ibelin to pass. The other remained alertly in place, eyeing the men who had swarmed around Ibelin, ready to block them if they tried to follow. None of them did.

Balian stepped into the royal anteroom, and the door clunked shut behind him. The anteroom of the Queen's apartment was familiar. He had spent many hours there during the English King's sojourn in the Holy Land. The Plantagenet had housed his bride and sister in this palace, and Maria Zoë had spent a great deal of time with both ladies; he had often waited for her here. Then it had been bustling and cramped; now it was abandoned and empty. Carpets had been spread over the marble floors to dampen sounds, and tapestries had been hung on the walls for presumably the same reason. They were dark tapestries whose motifs he did not readily grasp, yet all were concerned with death, darkness, and grief.

He advanced through this room to the next, a private solar in which the Queen and her ladies usually read, spun, sewed, and conversed in privacy. It was a domain from which most men were prohibited. Again, it had been spread with carpets and hung with tapestries, making the room stuffy and hot. But here a sudden flutter of motion near the empty fireplace drew his attention.

"Papa!" Meg exclaimed as she jumped up, tossing her book aside to run to him. She was dressed all in black with black ribbons in her hair. "I'm so glad you've come!" she told him as she threw her arms around him. Then without taking a breath, she pulled him toward a marble bench they could sit on side by side. "It's been absolutely terrible!" Meg announced. "Isabella tried to kill herself before we arrived. Her ladies found her before she could bleed to death and bound up her wrists, but she'd barely recovered from that when she took a double dose of sleeping medicine—she says by accident, but Mother doesn't believe it—and she threw up all night long! Now she's refusing to eat, saying she can't face it, that she'll throw it all up. She's lost ten pounds at least, and she looks terrible!" Meg concluded.

"Looks are not all that matters, Dove," Balian reminded his younger daughter.

Meg rolled her eyes. "I *know* that!" she protested. Taking a deep breath, she met her father's eyes and declared forcefully, " . . . but they say something about us, too. Isabella is naturally beautiful; if she looks terrible, it's a reflection of the state of her soul."

"Hmm," Balian answered, impressed despite himself, but unprepared to admit that to his fifteen-year-old daughter. "So where are your mother and brother now?"

"I'm not sure where John is. He's been very busy. The very day we arrived, the Germans were rioting and looting down in the lower town. John tracked down the Bishop of Hildesheim and shamed him into taking action. I wish I'd been there! The Archbishop of Acre came to tell Mama all about it, praising John to the heavens, but John said he was quaking in his boots because he was bluffing about being able to ride the Germans down with his—meaning your—men. Meanwhile, Sir Galvin had roused the garrison watch, and Sir Sergios had fetched Andersen and his crew—who were spoiling for a fight, of course. Together with the Norsemen, they already had the Germans on the run even before Hildesheim and the German barons arrived."

"Good man!" Balian exclaimed. "I must find some way to reward him for that. And your mother? Where is she?"

Meg sighed. "She's in there with Isabella," she gestured with her head to the peaked door leading to the inner chamber.

"Is she all right?"

"You know Mama. She doesn't always let you see what she's feeling."

Balian smiled at that, then bent and kissed his daughter on her forehead. He stood to continue through the portal to the inner chamber.

"Papa?"

"Yes?"

"Isabella has to marry again, doesn't she?"

"That, or abdicate in favor of her daughter Maria."

"Oh!" Meg obviously hadn't thought of that. "But—But Maria's only five!"

"A regent would have to be appointed for her until she married. Traditionally, *constitutionally*," he improved his own phraseology, "the regent is a minor monarch's closest male relative. In Maria's case her closest male relative is her father's younger brother, Boniface of Montferrat. However, because she derives her right to the crown from her mother rather than her father, the High Court might rule that her mother's closest male relative takes precedence. In that case, the regent would be Isabella's half-brother, your brother John."

"John? But he's only eighteen."

"Only? That's more than old enough. The regency for a prince ends at age fifteen, remember, and from what you've just told me, John has already exerted authority and defended the interests of the Kingdom." Meg continued to look skeptical, but Balian told her, "Think about it, Dove. I must go to your mother and Isabella."

He advanced toward the door to the Queen's bedroom with the same determination and trepidation with which he led a charge against the Saracens. He knew he had no choice, and he felt nearly as helpless. He was in the hands of God.

Entering the bedchamber, he noticed that the air turned sour and smelly. It wasn't anything in particular, just a mixture of medicine, stale food, stale wine, maybe a whiff of vomit (perhaps that was just his imagination after Meg's comments), and sweat. Two women Balian only vaguely remembered jumped up in shock and alarm at the sight of a man entering the inner chamber, then recognized him. They dipped their knees and bowed their heads with a murmured "my lord" as they backed away.

Maria Zoë, dressed in black from her veils to her shoes, was sitting beside the bed, apparently reading aloud to Isabella. The latter was lying propped up on pillows inside the large box bed, which was hung with black curtains. Maria Zoë's voice faltered as she registered the intrusion; then her eyes met Balian's and her face relaxed. Something similar to a smile flitted across her face without reaching her lips. He advanced to her and took her hand as he turned to look down on Isabella.

Meg had not been exaggerating: Isabella did indeed look terrible. Her face was puffy and splotched with red as if she'd been crying all day and all night ever since the accident. The skin around her eyes was so swollen and red that it made her eyes seem small and pig-like. Her lips were chapped, but she had several pimples on her chin and beside her nose as well. Her hair was greasy and hung in limp strands around her face.

"My lady Queen," he greeted her formally.

"Don't call me that!" Isabella wailed, lifting herself up and reaching out her arms to him. "Hold me, Uncle Balian! Like you used to do when I was a little girl!"

Balian had no idea what he had been expecting, but certainly not this plea for comfort. It quite overwhelmed him, and he felt his throat tighten and tears sting his eyes as he knelt with one knee on the edge of the bed and pulled Isabella into his arms. They were both transported back to when Isabella had been a little girl of eight, dragged kicking and screaming from her home to live with her future in-laws at the order of the King. She had been imprisoned for three years in Kerak on the edge of Sinai, prohibited from even visiting her mother and stepfather. Balian and Maria Zoë had risked the wrath of the Lord of Kerak to go to her several times, and once Balian had gone alone. It had been during that visit that he had confessed his helplessness to rescue her from Kerak.

"I'm just as helpless as I was when you were at Kerak," Balian found himself confessing again as he held Isabella in his arms. She had been so little and skinny then. Now her figure was womanly and soft, but she clung to him in the same way. "I can't bring Henri back, any more than I could rescue you from Oultre-jourdain and his witchlike wife," he told her, his throat so tight with unshed tears that it was audibly strained.

"I just want to die!" Isabella wailed, tears flooding over her face. "I don't want to live without Henri. He was everything to me. He made life worth living. It's not the same as when Conrad died. We quarreled so much. He didn't really love me. Henri loved me, Uncle Balian. He really did!"

"I know he did, Bella," Balian assured her, squeezing her tighter for an instant. "He *still* loves you—from beyond the grave. It must break his heart to see you like this."

"What am I going to do?" Isabella asked, pulling back a little, so that Balian held her only loosely with his hands on her shoulders. "Mama says I have to go on living. That I am still Queen of Jerusalem. That I have no choice but to serve my kingdom."

Balian glanced at his wife, and then turned back to his stepdaughter. "You certainly have to go on living," he told her firmly. "If you take your own life, you damn your soul for all eternity, and so will be separated from Henri for eternity. He will certainly go to Heaven. You must know that?" he asked gently but reproachfully.

Isabella looked down and nodded.

Balian let go of her and backed off the bed, but remained standing beside it so he could hold her hand. "As for being Queen, if you truly want, you could abdicate and retire to a convent."

Isabella looked up at him hopefully. "Truly?"

"Of course," Balian assured her, despite the unhappy restlessness he could hear and sense behind him; Maria Zoë clearly did not approve of this advice.

"But, of course, you would not be allowed to keep your children with you. You would have to turn all four of your little girls over to the care of the High Court."

Isabella gasped, and then hiccupped eloquently. "That's not fair!" she protested.

"Bella," Balian reminded her gently, "a woman who renounces the world for God renounces all ties to her earthly family, and that includes her children. You know that."

"But if I remain Queen, I'll be forced to marry again!" Isabella protested. "How can I marry again, when I know I will never love another man? Sharing another man's bed would be abhorrent to me! Consummation would be rape!"

This much Balian had expected, and he nodded calmly as he stroked the back of Isabella's hand with his thumb. His calm acceptance of her outburst confused her, and she felt compelled to add, "I mean it, Uncle Balian. I could not bear to be intimate with another man after Henri. I would loathe him—and myself—for it!"

Balian nodded again and assured her, "I believe you, Bella, and I know how you feel. I know I could never share intimacies with another woman, if God should choose to take your mother from me before He calls me to Him."

"So what is left for me to do? I can't abdicate and retire to a convent without losing my children, and I can't remain Queen without losing my sanity by being forced to take another man to my bed."

Balian drew a deep breath. "The High Court will insist on a marriage, but they're hardly going to stand around in your bedchamber to enforce consummation."

"No, but what man would marry me for a crown and then risk losing that crown for lack of consummation?" Isabella shot back, making Balian smile inwardly. Isabella sometimes acted like she was all emotion, but underneath was a sharp brain.

To Isabella he simply weighed his head from side to side, trying to win time. He wasn't sure she was ready to really consider alternatives yet. He chose subterfuge. "Well, there are men like Humphrey who abhor sexual contact with women."

"Poor Humphrey!" Isabella exclaimed, and hiccupped again. Then she looked up sharply. "You don't mean . . . ? Surely the High Court—you told me they would *never* accept Humphrey."

Balian sidestepped the question about the High Court by reporting truthfully, "Humphrey has taken vows as a monk. He has joined a community of reclusive Greek Orthodox monks and vowed both chastity and poverty. But there are other men . . . like him," Balian noted cautiously.

Isabella did not seem taken by the idea. He risked going further, and shrugged slightly as he remarked in what he hoped was still a purely speculative tone, "Or, alternatively, a man who already *has* a crown would be less obsessed with securing a second."

"Kings don't exactly grow on trees," Isabella countered snidely. "And a man used to ruling will have little concern for *my* feelings. I'm not naive. I listened very closely to what Queens Joanna and Berengaria had to say about their marriages!"

"It's true. Kings are used to getting their own way, but if he felt as you did . . . "

Isabella frowned and sat up straighter, drawing her hand out of Balian's. "What do you mean, 'feels like I do?' How can anyone feel like I do?"

"You're right, Bella. No one could feel exactly as you do. You have suffered an exceptional blow. Henri was young and strong and healthy, and he had survived the battle with al-Adil only a week earlier. You must have seen God's grace in that and felt secure in His love for both of you. Nor is this like Conrad's assassination, because Conrad had made many enemies, and he had always lived on a knife's edge."

Isabella was frowning ever more intensely, and her body was taut. "You have someone in mind, don't you, Uncle Balian? You've already decided for me." She sounded resentful.

"No, Bella," he answered steadily. "I have not decided for you, nor can I. The choice will be the High Court's."

"Certainly!" Isabella spat out indignantly. "And whose voice will be loudest and strongest there? You know they'll do whatever you suggest."

"No, Bella, it's not that simple," Balian countered calmly. "Furthermore, I can assure you that none of us on the High Court would impose our wishes upon you. We may suggest candidates to you, but it will be your choice. The Church, if nothing else, insists on consent—as you well know. You cannot be forced into a marriage against your wishes."

"Who?" Isabella demanded.

Balian looked over his shoulder at Maria Zoë, because he had not had a chance to discuss this with her yet. He would have much preferred to consult her before sharing his idea with Isabella.

Maria Zoë got to her feet and joined him at the side of the bed. She said nothing, just looked up at him expectantly.

"I've spoken to no one about this—least of all the prospective bridegroom," Balian told his wife and stepdaughter. "And there's no need to discuss this immediately. I only—"

"*I want to know who you are thinking about!*" Isabella told her stepfather sternly and precisely, her lips clamped together.

"Balian didn't do such a bad job choosing last time, sweetheart," Maria Zoë reminded her daughter, leaning forward to stroke Isabella's arm as she spoke, while looking again at Balian with raised eyebrows.

"I was thinking of a man who is also in mourning. A man grieving for the woman he loved, the mother of his children, and yet a man who is already king and so would not marry you for a crown, but rather for sake of defending your kingdom *for you*. A man who has proven his worth on the battlefield many times, but is also wise in counsel—"

"Aimery?" Isabella gasped out. "Eschiva's Aimery?"

She sounded so shocked that Balian didn't dare speak. He nodded mutely.

"It would be like betraying Eschiva!"

"If it is just a formal marriage, as you want, without any intimacies, then how is that a betrayal of Eschiva?" Maria Zoë asked gently.

Isabella looked at her mother, then back at her stepfather. Her expression was unreadable, but Balian took it as a good sign that she was not shouting at him hysterically or telling him to get out of her sight.

"Sweetheart, nothing has to be decided right now," Maria Zoë suggested reasonably. "Why don't you let your ladies take you down to the baths, and then you could go visit your little girls, while I see about a proper meal. We can have a quiet family dinner with Meg and John to celebrate your stepfather's arrival. Then maybe you can get a good night's rest and we can talk again in the morning. What do you think?"

Isabella looked at her mother tensely, her mind clearly sorting through a variety of possible answers before she took a deep breath and agreed. "Yes, Mama. I think you're right. It's time I left this bed, washed, and dressed. Don't think I have agreed to this marriage!" she warned her parents sharply, but then continued in a calmer voice, "Still, I can't continue hiding from the future, can I? I have to face it, and it's easier to do that if I'm not a stinking wreck. Henri always wanted me to look and act like a queen. . . ."

"Because you are, Bella," Maria Zoë reminded her softly, her hand still on Isabella's arm.

Isabella looked at her mother as if she wanted to protest, but then she nodded. "Yes, I will concede that much: I would rather be queen than give up my little girls. I've neglected them, haven't I?"

"No," Maria Zoë answered with a tired but relieved smile. "You needed time to grieve, and it would have done your children no good to see you in this state. When you go to them, you need to be strong enough to comfort *them*."

Isabella drew a deep breath. It meant a great deal that her mother did not reproach her for her behavior—because deep inside, she felt guilty about it. She had been self-indulgent these past ten days, and she knew it.

Then she looked up at her stepfather. He was still looking concerned and uneasy. "You see, Uncle Balian? You've managed to drag me back from the precipice after all. How do you do it?"

"I didn't, Bella," Balian told her, reaching out to pull her into his arms again. "You did it all on your own."

Chapter Twenty-Two
The Last Kingdom

Acre, Kingdom of Jerusalem,
December 1197

THE ROYAL WEDDING WAS SET FOR the Saturday before the first Sunday in Advent, so that the feast would not be constrained by fasting. The fact that the German crusaders had marched north and taken control of first Sidon and now—if reports were to be believed—Beirut, meant that the subjects of the Queen of Jerusalem were (gratefully) among themselves. They had come to love their young Queen and wanted to give her a "proper" wedding, particularly since none of her three earlier weddings had been celebrated in great style. Her first wedding had taken place in a castle under siege when she was just eleven years old. The second had been hastily concluded in a tent during the bitter siege of Acre. Her third marriage, to Henri de Champagne, had been conducted in even more haste, barely a week after the assassination of her second husband. Not once had Isabella been celebrated by her subjects.

Now the commune of Acre buried their many rivalries and came together to plan festivities to mark the marriage of their Queen. To the wonder of the rest of the population, Pisans, Venetians, and Genoese worked hand in hand, while the guild masters and other communities—whether Syrian, Armenian, Latin, or Jew—likewise joined forces to plan a worthy celebration. Furthermore, all the various communities opened their coffers and engaged in a frenzy of preparations to make this event a testimony to their loyalty, their increasing prosperity, and their determination to survive as a kingdom. The King was dead; long live the King!

The streets had been scrubbed so clean that the stray dogs had moved out of town in search of food. The drunks and beggars had been rounded up and temporarily incarcerated in the city jail. The prostitutes were sternly ordered to wear "respectable" clothes or risk arrest. The churches had been decked in lavender and late-blooming roses, and from terce onwards their bells pealed in joy. Long banners of white stitched with crosses of gold hung from the windows of the houses, flapping and twisting in the breeze, while the arms of Jerusalem fluttered from all the rooftops.

Half an hour before midday, the large galley that had been lying offshore ran out her oars and started to maneuver towards the harbor entrance. Inside the harbor, the ships ran up their bunting and began to blow their foghorns in a cacophonous greeting.

At the same time, the gates of the royal palace opened and a long procession emerged. It was led by the exiled canons of the Holy Sepulcher, followed by the clerics of every church in the city—except the Cathedral of the Holy Cross, where the Archbishop and all his minions were preparing the wedding Mass. Behind the churchmen came knights in gleaming armor on brightly caparisoned stallions, both men and mounts bearing the arms of Jerusalem on surcoats and trappers. Next came the barons of the High Court, flanked by their ladies, ending with the Lord of Ibelin/Paphos and the Dowager Queen of Jerusalem. Immediately behind them, on a mare cleaned and curried to an almost perfect white and tacked with gold accoutrements, came Queen Isabella. For the first time in eighty days, she had set aside the black of mourning, and was dressed in purple and gold. Behind her came her half-brother John and half-sister Meg, followed by the rear-tenants, aldermen, and leaders of the commune of Acre.

Meanwhile, in the harbor, the blue galley trimmed with yellow had gone alongside the quay, the standard of Lusignan flapping from the masthead. The gangway was run out, and on deck the passengers waited, immobile and hushed. As the head of the procession emerged from beside the Court of Chain, a noticeable ripple of motion seized the men aboard the ship. As the clerics moved along the quay to make way for the rest of the procession, a man with a bushy mane of graying hair emerged from the aft accommodations of the galley. He was dressed in bright-blue robes trimmed with gold, and wore a closed crown on his head. He moved slowly to the end of the gangway and waited until the Queen of Jerusalem approached the edge of the quay. He then stepped up onto the gangway and waited again.

The Queen drew up and dismounted, causing all her escort to do the same. Her brother John stepped forward to hold her mare, and her sister Meg stepped behind her to carry her train. Slowly and deliberately the Queen advanced toward the gangway.

At last the King of Cyprus crossed the gap between sea and land, stepping down onto the quay to meet the Queen of Jerusalem. Neither bowed nor bent a knee. As equals they met, and as equals they kissed. The kisses were cool and formal, as if they were perfect strangers. Then the Queen turned to face her city and subjects, while the King took her elbow.

Together they walked along the prepared route between cheering crowds to the Cathedral of the Holy Cross. They walked slowly, nodding and waving to the crowds. Isabella managed to smile and wave, particularly for a youth sitting astride the railing of a balcony as he gestured frantically to get her attention and for a troop of excited little girls, who waved wildly at her and giggled in delight when she waved back. King Aimery nodded and lifted his hand now and again, but acted as if the cheers were all for the Queen.

They mounted the steps to the Cathedral and passed into a candlelit nave, the organ humming and the canons chanting. They proceeded directly up the central aisle with the barons, knights, and aldermen behind them. They were met at the screens by the Archbishop of Acre, and here the King and Queen halted. Behind them, the procession entered and spread out in the nave, along with many others who had tagged along, until the cathedral was filled to over-flowing.

It took a long time, but eventually a degree of imperfect quiet settled on the crowd. The canons finished their chant. The organ fell silent. The Arch-bishop raised his hands and blessed the King and Queen. He reached out and took Isabella's left hand and Aimery's right. He asked first Aimery and then Isabella if they were prepared to take the other in holy matrimony. They each answered in the affirmative, Aimery in a firm voice heard to the back of the nave, Isabella softly but without hesitation. The Archbishop placed Isabella's hand in Aimery's. The King of Cyprus drew a ring from his baby finger and prepared to slip it on Isabella's ring finger. When he noticed she was still wearing Champagne's wedding ring, he hesitated. He glanced up at her, but she kept her eyes down demurely. He pushed his ring over her knuckle and closed his hand firmly around hers for a moment. Then he turned to face the Archbishop again.

The Archbishop blessed them, then led them through the screens. Aimery took Isabella by her elbow and together they followed the Archbishop between the canons, who had started to sing again. In front of the high altar, satin-covered cushions waited for them. They knelt down to take communion, while the spectators remained behind in the nave.

Following the wedding Mass, Aimery and Isabella exited by the main portal into the street, to be met by a large crowd that broke into cheers of "Hip, hip, hooray!" and "Long live the King and Queen." Again Isabella waved graciously and Aimery waved with noticeable restraint. After a suitable time, some of Isabella's knights slipped past to clear a way for her to the royal palace and the waiting feast.

The wedding meal lasted over five hours, with numerous courses both savory and sweet. It was interspersed with entertainment from jesters, acrobats, troubadours, dancing monkeys in Saracen costumes, dwarfs dressed like Roman soldiers, and more. Each community in the city had selected their favorite entertainer for the occasion. During the feast, wedding gifts were also presented to the Queen. Each guild and commune strove to outdo their rivals by the beauty, craftsmanship, and expense of their offering.

Isabella seemed particularly moved when the Jewish community presented her with a carved ivory book cover that depicted scenes from the Old Testament. She asked the Talmudic scholar who had been selected to present the gift to come onto the dais. As he knelt before her, she thanked him earnestly, saying that she was touched by such generosity when the Jewish community had suffered so much damage at the hands of the German crusaders. The man, in his skullcap and long beard, bowed repeatedly as he assured her that the Jewish community was loyal to her and her house, and appreciated the protection her family had always provided to them. He glanced toward her brother John as he spoke. King Aimery at this point leaned forward and announced in a deep and clearly audible voice that the Jews could be assured of the protection of the House of Lusignan as well.

Later, after the last course of meringue roses and marzipan doves had been decimated, there was dancing. The Lord of Ibelin danced with the Dowager Queen, and many other barons likewise danced with their ladies. King Aimery was seen to address his wife, but she shook her head, and the royal couple remained on the dais as spectators. As the pace of the music increased, more and more of the older couples retreated, leaving the sweep of the great hall, cleared now of tables and benches, to the youth. John d'Ibelin led his sister Meg, but he was soon displaced by Hugh of Tiberius, Walter (the younger) of Caesarea, and a host of other young noblemen. Meg d'Ibelin was very pretty, lively, and (based on the peals of laughter that came from whatever part of the room she was in) witty and entertaining. She was also the sister of the ruling Queen, which made her a brilliant match.

After three hours of dancing, with the city long since embraced by the early winter night, King Aimery rose and offered his hand to Queen Isabella. She stood, and Aimery indicated the door off the back of the dais. Isabella turned and started toward it. At once the guests, now well inebriated, began clapping, chanting, and singing. Many, particularly the young men, surged toward the dais to follow the couple to their bedchamber and partake in the bedding ritual. They were stopped short by the knights of Ibelin, who came seemingly out of nowhere and lined the front of the dais, preventing anyone from mounting it.

There was some protesting, but as the Queen's household knights reinforced the Ibelin knights, the crowd recognized they had been checkmated. With some grumbling, they accepted that they would have to find their entertainment elsewhere. As neither wine nor food was being replenished anymore, the crowd started to disperse. The wedding feast was over.

Aimery knew his way around the royal palace of Acre, but he let Isabella lead. They had spoken very little, beyond the marriage vows and other necessities, and Aimery still could not see beyond Isabella's public façade to what she was really feeling. As they entered the Queen's anteroom, Philip and Fulk, Aimery's new squire (Dick had been knighted the year before), rose to meet them.

Isabella was surprised to see Philip; she smiled at him. "Philip! When did you arrive?"

"I came with my lord of Lusignan," the squire answered with a glance at his lord.

"You're still my brother," Isabella told him, and stepped forward to give him a hug and a kiss on the cheek.

As Isabella drew back from a visibly embarrassed Philip, Aimery told his wife, "I'll give you a few minutes to prepare yourself," and gestured with his head toward the door leading deeper into her apartments.

Isabella nodded and continued to the bedchamber, where her ladies awaited her.

When the door closed behind her, Aimery removed his crown and handed it to Philip, who reverently placed it on one of the small tables. Then Philip and Fulk helped Aimery out of his wedding robes and undergarments, right down to his silk shirt. This Aimery opted to keep on. "Is there water?" he asked.

"There's water, wine, bread, dried fruits, and oranges in the bedchamber, my lord," Philip answered.

Aimery nodded and looked about the room. Something was different about it from the days when Eschiva had served the English Queen, but he couldn't put his finger on it.

"It was hung with black tapestries, my lord," Philip explained, interpreting Aimery's look almost correctly. "We managed to get them all down, but didn't have time to find substitutes."

"The Queen is still in mourning—no matter what she wears or the color of her tapestries."

Philip nodded solemnly, and Aimery glanced toward the inside door, wondering whether it was too soon. He decided to wait a little longer, and gave Philip instructions to pack his crown in its leather case and stow it in a chest in his own suite of rooms at the other end of the corridor. "One of you should sleep here," he ordered, revising his instructions to: "Philip, as Isabella's brother, you'd better be the one to stay here. Fulk can sleep on the pallet in my chamber."

Both squires nodded, and Aimery glanced again toward the door nervously. He shook his head, and a strand of his long hair fell into his face. He ordered Philip to bring a comb.

Eventually one of Isabella's ladies appeared in the doorway and announced that the Queen was ready to receive her husband. Aimery nodded to his squires, dismissing Fulk to retire and ordering Philip to remain where he was. He then proceeded through the open door and across the day room to the bedchamber beyond. As he entered the latter, the other lady curtsied deeply to him before withdrawing, closing the door behind her.

Aimery found himself in a richly decorated chamber dominated by a large box bed with heavy velvet hangings. The room was lit only by one glass oil lamp hanging from the ceiling and a candle by the bed. Isabella was already in bed, her hair loose about her head, but the sheets drawn up over her body modestly. Only her neck and head were visible, propped up on the pillows.

Aimery walked to the side of the bed and sat down on the edge.

"Thank you for sending the revelers away," Isabella opened.

"Actually, it was your step-father's idea," Aimery admitted.

Isabella smiled faintly. "Dear Uncle Balian. I thought it might have been, since his men moved forward first, but you approved it. I appreciate that."

"Look, Isabella, I'm not here to humiliate or conquer you. I understand that you do not want any intimacies. For the High Court, your servants, and your subjects, I think it best that I spend the night inside this room, but I am prepared to sleep on the floor if you insist. Or, if you would be so kind, I will join you in bed but, on my word of honor, I will not force myself upon you."

"Thank you. I—I would not have agreed to this marriage if I had not believed you would respect my wishes. Yet, I—I want you to fully understand: I still love Henri." Although she spoke almost defiantly as she gazed at him, her lips were trembling and tears were shimmering in her eyes.

Aimery's heart went out to her. He would have liked to stroke the side of her cheek with the back of his hand. She had been brittle all day, and she'd been bound to break sooner or later. He was thankful that she had made it through the wedding and the feast without breaking down. He would have liked to take her in his arms as he would have one of his daughters, but he realized that any move to touch her would be misinterpreted. So he looked away from her and, staring at the candle, announced in a low and heavy voice, "And I still love Eschiva."

Isabella flinched, but Aimery didn't notice. His eyes were still focused on the candle rather than Isabella. "I think I've loved her longer than I even realized. Even in the early years, when I cheated on her with any woman who fired my loins, it never detracted from my love for her."

"That's a terribly male thing to say," Isabella told him bluntly. Aimery looked away from the candle to try to judge if she was bitter or reproachful, and Isabella smiled faintly at him. "I've been married three times before this, Aimery. I know a little about men."

"Fair enough," Aimery conceded—"but what I *wanted* to say is that my love for Eschiva grew with each year, each setback, each crisis." His eyes shifted back to the candle as he spoke in a voice heavy with memories. "Throughout that year in a Saracen dungeon following Hattin, it was the thought of Eschiva that kept me from going mad. Yet it was only after I went to Cyprus that I came to *rely* on her in a way I had not imagined possible." He paused and then admitted out loud for the first time, "She was the rock on which I built my kingdom— and she was gone before I could put a crown upon her head. I cannot tell you how much that hurts me to this day."

The pain in his voice reached Isabella through the darkness. She leaned forward and touched her fingers to his cheek so lightly that he could barely feel it. "I'm sorry, Aimery. For you and Eschiva both."

Aimery snapped his head around, and their eyes met. They were both on the brink of tears and they just gazed at one another. Then Isabella patted the bed beside her. "Come under the covers, Aimery, before you catch cold."

Aimery hesitated, but then he went around the bed, lifted the covers, and slipped in to sit beside, but still inches away from, Isabella. "Thank you."

"Why are you here, Aimery?" Isabella asked. "I don't mean in bed, I mean in Acre. Why did you accept this burden of a grieving widow, four frightened little girls, and a threatened kingdom, when you could have just stayed on Cyprus with your own family and a secure kingdom?"

"That's a fair question," Aimery admitted. "I didn't jump at the offer—in case Balian didn't tell you."

Isabella shook her head. "He didn't tell me any details, just that you had agreed to my conditions."

"I made him wait three days for my answer—and knowing how persuasive he can be, I wouldn't let him talk to me during that time. I spent a lot of time at Eschiva's grave, or just talking to her in my mind. I spoke to my confessor, and even asked my son Guy and Burgundia what they would think of such an extraordinary development. It was Burgundia who surprised me most. Her face lit up and she exclaimed, "Oh! Mama would have been so pleased!" He paused, because the memory was unmanning him. Tears were threatening to spill out of his eyes as he struggled to explain. "And that's the point," he continued, swallowing down his pain. "Eschiva never wanted anything for herself. She only wanted me to be successful and happy. She would have wanted me to be King of Jerusalem—not because she wanted Henri dead or you to be widowed. Don't think that—"

Isabella reached out to calm him. "I know that. Eschiva loved me like a sister and only wanted the best for me. I *know*."

"But she *hated* my brother Guy," Aimery confessed. "She always resented that he, unworthy as he was, had been made a king and dared to look down on me. She *hated* that." Suddenly he could hold his emotions in check no longer. He found himself sobbing helplessly at the memory of his former humiliations—and the irony that he was now King of Jerusalem but Eschiva was not with him to triumph.

Isabella opened her arms and pulled her husband to her breast. She held him and brushed her hands gently over his rough, graying hair as he shook with sobs. She did not speak, just held him until he had calmed himself.

That night they slept chastely in each other's arms, yet both found comfort and peace that neither had expected.

Acre, Kingdom of Jerusalem, December 1197

"Father!" Aimery greeted Balian with open arms.

"Spare me!" Balian answered. "My impudent daughter Meg is going to get her wish for a beardless bridegroom, simply because I can't *stand* the thought of yet another son-in-law who is older than I am."

Aimery laughed heartily and gestured toward a table in the open doors giving access to a balcony.

"You *do* know," Balian remarked, eyeing the open doors suspiciously, "that it was the railing of the balcony in the next room that gave way, sending Champagne to his death?"

"Yes, I know. Just one wrong step . . . But we're safe here. Come, sit down. I have a lot to discuss with the First Baron of my realm."

"You seem to be in remarkably good spirits," Balian noted with a penetrating sidelong glance. Aimery looked refreshed and energized as he had not since Eschiva's death.

"Indeed," Aimery agreed. "Surely you know that a young bride is the fountain of youth?"

"Hmm," Balian answered ambiguously. After all, he had been the one to convey Isabella's condition that the marriage be completely formal and unconsummated.

"You don't have to look at me like that. I have not broken my word, as your lady wife will be able to attest after she's seen Isabella. Nevertheless, Isabella and I are going to get along very well. We have already agreed on a number of things."

"That is very encouraging," Balian noted cautiously and a little warily.

"First of all," Aimery announced happily, "I don't know why Champagne was so reluctant for a coronation. It's past time Isabella was crowned and anointed. She's been Queen of Jerusalem since her sister died eight years ago—and had we crowned her then, my brother would not have found it so easy to bend England's ear. Conrad would certainly have insisted on a coronation, but Champagne's reluctance has denied Isabella her anointing these past five years, quite unnecessarily. I intend to set that straight, and will order that the Patriarch prepare a coronation for us both shortly after the turn of the year."

Balian nodded approval.

"Second—something you and I have talked about before—we need to pull together everyone's memories of the laws of Jerusalem and codify them, or at least record them before we forget."

Again, Balian nodded.

"Third, Isabella is very concerned about these German crusaders, who appear to take no account of her interests or those of her subjects. She does not trust them, and she fears they may do more harm than good. They failed to relieve Jaffa, and now it has fallen to al-Adil. What we're hearing is that they have plundered and slighted Beirut to the point where, reports say, it is no longer habitable. That's not in anyone's interest."

Balian sighed.

Aimery continued, "I need a Constable who can take command of Jerusalem's fighting forces and face down Hildesheim and his German barons."

"Did you have someone in mind?"

"Yes: you."

That took Balian by surprise. He started and then stared at Aimery with eyebrows raised in disbelief.

"But, of course, if you prefer to return to Cyprus as my lieutenant there, then I imagine I could find someone else. . . ."

Balian snapped for air, at a loss for words—but then he pulled himself together and replied forcefully, "I would indeed prefer to return to Cyprus, and I would be honored to serve as your lieutenant there."

"Good. That's settled, then." Aimery smiled, indicating he had expected this response, before continuing, "So that still leaves the issue of a Constable for Jerusalem."

"You know that Ralph of Tiberius was a rival for your position as husband to Isabella and King of Jerusalem?" Balian asked cautiously. He had bought the support of the Tiberius brothers for Aimery by agreeing to marry Meg to Hugh. To Aimery he stressed, "Ralph fought very well at Hattin, and both he and Hugh, I understand, distinguished themselves in this recent battle against al-Adil. You might think seriously about naming Ralph Constable as a means to cement his loyalty to you."

"You *do* remember why Champagne arrested me, don't you?"

"Of course."

"Well, it would be the same with me and Tiberius: I would never completely trust him. I want a Constable that I trust 150 per cent." He paused and waited for Balian's somewhat reluctant nod before adding, "I was thinking of your son John."

"John?" Balian could not believe his ears.

"He's stood up to Hildesheim once already," Aimery pointed out.

"John's mature beyond his years. He's got a good head on his shoulders. He's brave, but not foolhardy." Balian listed John's virtues readily, but then hesitated and added, "And he's only eighteen."

"Baldwin was fifteen at Montgisard," Aimery countered. "And I'm told Henry Plantagenet defeated his rival King Stephen at fourteen."

Balian nodded absently. Hadn't he told Meg only weeks ago that John was old enough to be regent? But that was different, because the title of regent was based strictly on blood ties. He reminded Aimery: "Kings automatically command loyalty; Constables need to earn it."

"Fair enough, but it's not as if I were a feeble old man or a minor child. I expect to command my own armies in any major conflict. I need a Constable for the working days, not for the crises. John is the Queen's closest male blood relative. Who else should hold my horse at the coronation?"

Balian nodded again, and then with a smile he conceded, "Then so be it. I am grateful to you for recognizing John despite his youth."

"*He* may not be so grateful," Aimery quipped. "Such prominence and responsibility will cut his youth short." Aimery was only half jesting.

"His youth was taken from him by Hattin," Balian countered, and then caught his breath.

"Yes?" Aimery prompted.

"If you take John from me," Balian opened, "then I want Philip back."

"I thought you might," Aimery admitted. "He's half Greek already anyway, and apparently Champagne had no less than four body squires, all of whom are idle and in need of employment. Sons of barons, of course."

Balian nodded. "Good. Was there anything else?"

"Just one thing."

Balian waited.

Aimery became deadly serious. "You could have advised Isabella to abdicate in favor of her daughter, confident that you would have been named regent of Jerusalem. Weren't you tempted?"

"Not really."

Aimery raised his eyebrows.

"We reap what we sow. I surrendered Jerusalem for forty thousand Christian lives, and Ibelin for fifteen thousand more. So I have no right to claim territory. Furthermore, I owe those people a livelihood. We can offer them that on Cyprus."

"In short, you chose Cyprus over Jerusalem."

Balian smiled faintly. "I chose Cyprus over *Acre*. If we *had* Jerusalem—and Ibelin, I might have made a different choice."

Aimery nodded in understanding. Part of him, too, preferred Nicosia to Acre, but the temptation to wear his brother's crown had been too great in the end. "So Cyprus will be your kingdom, then. The last kingdom."

"The last kingdom," Balian corrected, "is the Kingdom of Heaven."

Paphos, Kingdom of Cyprus, Epiphany 1198

They'd left Acre on a cold northerly and it had been a rough, wet crossing, but as they approached Paphos harbor the wind died away and milder air enveloped them. Within a half-hour the wind had backed around to the south, and although it was only a gentle breeze, it was enough to carry them through the harbor entrance. As they cleared the breakwater and the full harbor came into view, they were startled to find lanterns burning from the mastheads and on the decks of all the ships at anchor and along the quay. Not just that, but a snake of flickering light marked a procession making its way out of the city to the harbor. The chanting of the monks leading the procession reached them across the water as Ibelin, his wife, and his two youngest children stood on the foredeck of *Haakon's Ghost*.

"What is it?" Balian asked Maria Zoë.

"I don't know. It must be a local custom," she answered.

Balian turned around and signaled to Erik Andersen. "Don't take her to the quay just yet. Let's wait and see what's going on and what happens next."

Andersen ordered the helmsman to head the ship into the wind and then drop the sail, so that the snecka just drifted.

The procession was carrying an icon surrounded by candles on a litter. Acolytes swinging silver incense burners flanked the litter; the bishop and a dozen priests preceded it while the people of Paphos followed, dressed in their best. Eventually the procession reached the harbor, and the litter was set down on the edge of the quay. The crowd spread out around the litter and a respectful silence fell. The bishop held aloft a large wooden cross—and then, to Balian's astonishment, he flung it into the water with all his might.

Instantly, several young men launched themselves from the bows of the anchored ships and started swimming furiously toward the cross, in an evident competition to get to it first. From the shore and the ships, people cheered and encouraged their favorites. One woman's voice calling "Vasili! Vasili!" was particularly clear. As the swimmers converged on the floating cross, the excitement grew. There was some wild splashing, and then one young man held the cross above his head and the crowd cheered.

The victor swam with the cross to the quay, and the bishop reached down to take the cross from his outstretched hand. Others lay belly down on the quay to help the swimmer climb up the side and stand, dripping wet, beside the litter with the icon. A blanket was offered the swimmer, along with blessings from the bishop.

Singing broke out again, but now it was spontaneous and uncoordinated. Some of the men appeared to have brought wine with them and started to nip at it and pass it to their friends. The bishop turned and the litter with the icon started its journey back toward the cathedral, with many but not all the people falling in behind.

Ibelin nodded to Andersen that they could proceed, and the captain ordered the oars run out. They went alongside just as the last of the procession disappeared between the buildings lining the quay, but there were still a large number of people milling about peacefully on the quay.

The Ibelin family went ashore and began to walk the short distance to the fortress, but a woman, recognizing the baron and his family, blocked their way and gestured emphatically toward the city as she spoke in a flood of words too fast for Balian. "What's she saying?" he asked.

Both Maria Zoë and Philip answered. "She's telling us to hurry so we can catch up with the procession."

"Do you think we should?" Balian asked Maria Zoë.

"Yes, let's see what this is."

They changed direction and picked up their pace in order to catch up with the end of the procession. They soon found themselves winding their way through Paphos past open doors displaying house icons, all lit by candles. At the head of the procession, the bishop blessed each icon and the usually elderly woman tending each as he passed by. Nuts, dried fruit, and wine were offered to the people following in the bishop's wake. With each house they passed, the mood seemed to become less solemn and more joyous.

They must have tagged along for a quarter-hour or more before someone noticed and recognized Ibelin and his wife. Suddenly the names "Ibelin" and "Comnena" were being repeated up the length of the procession, like an echo that got ever fainter—until it started coming back the other way.

"*Ela! Ela!* Come! Come!" the voices said, and hands grabbed Balian's and Philip's arms, gesturing toward the front. Ahead of them people stood back to make way, and they were drawn forward through the length of the procession toward the front.

There was no question of refusing or resisting, but Balian was baffled by what appeared to be unmitigated goodwill. This wasn't the passive acceptance of last year, nor was it the support of the immigrants. The people here were almost all Greek, and they were smiling and nodding. He caught sight of Ayyub/Antonis with his wife and her family around him. Father Andronikos was nodding and smiling as if he could take credit for everything. Meanwhile, more and more women reached out to touch Maria Zoë's dress and murmur blessings for her as well.

As they reached the head of the column, the bishop broke into a wide smile and pulled Balian into his arms to kiss him on both cheeks. He exclaimed in Greek, in a loud voice that carried far: "My son! We thought you had abandoned us to return to your homeland, but you have returned to us! What a wonderful, additional reason to rejoice on this Holy Day!"

Maria Zoë caught her husband's hand and squeezed it. "I think we have come home," she whispered.

Balian d'Ibelin died in an unknown place on an unknown date of unknown causes. His grave no longer exists or has not been found. He was survived by his wife Maria Comnena, who died in 1217, and his four children. The House of Ibelin was to provide regents for both Jerusalem and Cyprus, seneschals and constables and queens, as well as scholars, jurists, and patrons of the arts. It was the most powerful family in Outremer for the next two centuries, yet never challenged the Crown.

Dear Reader,

If you enjoyed this book, please a take moment to write and post a review on amazon.com, Barnes and Noble, or Goodreads.

Thank you!

Helena P. Schrader

Historical Notes

First a word about the setting of this novel, as many readers may be surprised at how sophisticated, cosmopolitan and civilized the late twelfth century appears in this book:

- Although the bulk of the population in the Holy Land was still Christian at this time, the native Orthodox population spoke Arabic and used Arabic names; immigrants spoke their native languages and a smattering of Arabic. Second- and third-generation immigrants were bilingual, speaking both French, the language of the elite and administration, and Arabic, the language of the bazaars and the poor.

- The Holy Land under the Franks was an important crossroads of civilization. This resulted in considerable technological innovation and progress. Examples of this are: 1) wall fireplaces with chimneys. Although not known in the Arab world, the introduction of wall fireplaces and chimneys in Frankish homes predates their widespread use in Western Europe; 2) extensive use of glass in windows; 3) running fountains; 4) sewage systems that relied on water to flush out refuse.

Turning to specific historical events:

- Henri de Champagne ordered the arrest of Aimery de Lusignan, Constable of the Kingdom of Jerusalem, because he spoke up in defense of the Pisan community. Champagne suspected the Pisans of being in a plot with Aimery's brother Guy to depose him. According to the *Old French Continuation of William of Tyre*, Aimery was released because the grandmasters of the militant orders "and the barons of the Kingdom" went to Champagne and "upbraided him for having arrested the Constable. . . ." The text does not make clear that the issue here was a constitutional one, but the subsequent rebellion of the barons of Jerusalem against the Hohenstaufen kings hinges on precisely the issue that no member of the High Court could be arrested without an order by his peers (the High Court) —i.e., not by the King alone. I felt it was important to introduce this significant constitutional issue here.

- As I note in the introduction, there is no evidence that John d'Ibelin was squire to Aimery de Lusignan, but such a close relationship would help explain the otherwise surprising fact that King Aimery appointed John Constable of Jerusalem when still only eighteen or nineteen years old.

- In the Jerusalem Trilogy, Balian d'Ibelin was given a fictional younger brother Henri. He was invented when I wrote my first (unpublished) novel set in the Kingdom of Cyprus during the baronial revolt against Friedrich II. At the time, I was already trying to speculate on how the Ibelins became established on Cyprus, and hypothesized a younger son or younger brother who came to Cyprus with Guy, despite the hostility of Balian to Guy. Now that I've refined my interpretation of what happened, this fictional younger brother is no longer necessary.

- However, continued research turned up the fascinating fact that Balian had a nephew, the son of his maternal half-sister (whether Ermengard or Stephanie is not recorded) and her husband (first name unknown) de Brie. The Bries were powerful on Cyprus in the next generation. Hence the Henri d'Ibelin of the Jerusalem Trilogy has been reborn in this book as Henri de Brie, a nephew (rather than a brother) of Balian.

- In the Jerusalem Trilogy, I changed the name of Balian's brother Baldwin to Barisan to avoid confusion with Baldwin IV, the Leper King. However, as King Baldwin is not a character in this story, here I have used Balian's brother's real name, Baldwin.

- Due to confusion about when Aimery and Eschiva married and the dates of their children's births, and to avoid confusing name duplications, I used the name "Hugh" for their eldest child in my Jerusalem Trilogy, but have corrected that in this book to Guy. Hugh was not born until September 1195. On the other hand, to avoid the duplication of the name John, I have renamed Aimery and Eschiva's second son "Aimery."

- Despite the commonly quoted excerpt from the *Chronicle of Ernoul* that suggests Guy de Lusignan arrived in Cyprus in late 1192 to find a peaceful but depopulated island, there is substantial evidence that the revolt against the Templars continued throughout Guy's very short rule and into Aimery's reign as well. The Christian sources note that the Templars were driven from the island, and that the mightiest and wealthiest militant Order in Christendom *did not think they had the strength to hold it*—incredibly strong evidence that the revolt was very serious indeed. Even Ernoul's account implies that the male population was decimated—otherwise the new settlers would not have been urged to marry the widows. Most important, the Cypriot chronicler St. Neophytos talks of an extended period of violence, bloodshed, and disorder.

- Neither the exact date nor the cause of Guy de Lusignan's death are known. George Hill, in *A History of Cyprus, Volume 2: The Frankish Period*, claims Guy died "suddenly" in April 1194. The more reliable Peter Edbury says in *The Kingdom of Cyprus and the Crusades* that Guy died "at about the end of 1194" without venturing to suggest a cause. La Monte speaks only of "1194." I chose a date that suited the story line. As for the cause of death, since any violent death—whether assassination or accident—is more likely to have been recorded, we can assume that Guy died of an illness. For dramatic purposes, I have chosen to make it a slow, painful death. The symptoms described here are compatible with stomach cancer. Opium was widely available in the crusader states.

- Neophytos is a historical figure, later sanctified, who wrote an important chronicle of the period. His account alleges terrible oppression by Isaac Comnenus, and claims that the island was depopulated and impoverished before the Franks came. He also rails against the Franks, however, accusing them of further oppression. In fact, he systematically accuses all rulers, including Manuel I Comnenus, of poor governance, making it hard to know if one really was better or worse than the others. St.

Neophytos is known to have received visitors, and was revered in his own time. He also visited Palestine and Jerusalem before it fell to the Saracens.

- A conflict between the Latin Church and the Crown of Cyprus about tithes in the early thirteenth century makes it clear that the Greek Church was initially allowed to retain the tithes from their traditional lands—and that Ibelin's sons, notably Philip, supported the Greek—not the Latin—Church.

- Humphrey de Toron is said to have gone with Guy to Cyprus, and he was apparently dead before Aimery married the woman he still considered his wife, Isabella of Jerusalem. The date and circumstances of his death are not recorded. The notion of his joining a monastery is my own invention.

- Bizarre as it may seem, the incident of a Greek pirate named "Canaqui" (Kanakes in Greek) kidnapping Eschiva "and her children" is a recorded fact. The date of the incident is, however, unstated, and although at least one source says it was after Aimery was king, we know that Eschiva died before he was crowned. I have chosen, therefore, to place the incident in the winter of 1195-1196. It is also recorded that she was seized from "Paradhisi," on the coast. The *Latin Continuation of William of Tyre* explicitly states she had been "ill" and had gone to Paradhisi for a change of air—i.e., to recuperate. The nature of her illness is unrecorded.

- The rescue attempt by Magnussen is entirely fictional, but I thought it a fitting end for my Norse crusader.

- It is recorded in the Continuations of William of Tyre that Leo of Armenia secured the release of Eschiva and her children because of his "love" for her father, but it is not explained how he knew Baldwin d'Ibelin. We do know, however, that after abdicating his titles and turning his son and lands over to Balian in 1186, Baldwin d'Ibelin went to Antioch, a neighbor and, at that time, ally of Armenia. As a fighting man in search of new opportunities, the Armenian struggle against overwhelming odds might well have attracted Baldwin, and an early death in Armenia would explain why he was never heard from again in the Kingdom of Jerusalem.

- Aimery came to the Armenian port of Corycos to collect his wife and children, accompanied by "the best men in his kingdom" to bring his family home. It is reported that he was about to dine with Leo of Armenia when the captain of his fleet warned that if he did not sail at once, he would "stay longer than intended." He sailed just before a terrible storm and made it safely to Kyrenia.

- The Archbishops of Trani and Brindisi delivered the "royal regalia" to Aimery in "April or May 1196," according to Peter Edbury, who suggests that Aimery styled himself King from this time forward. Documentation from the period is very scarce.

- The visit of Champagne to Cyprus and the betrothal of his three daughters to Aimery's three sons is historical fact. It is sometimes mistakenly dated in 1194, but at that time Champagne did not yet have three daughters. Late 1196 or the first half of 1197 are the only possible dates for a triple betrothal. I've chosen November 1196 for the narrative of the story.

- Eschiva died of unknown causes before September 1197. As she was still a comparatively young woman (in her thirties), and there is no mention of an accident, death in childbed, or foul play, I believe she died of an illness—something supported by the Chronicles, which say that at the time of her kidnapping, she was in Paradhisi to recover from an illness. I have chosen to give her the symptoms of anemia, which can be fatal if not treated, and suggest that her captivity contributed to her weakness and so to her death.

- The "German crusade" led by the Imperial Chancellor, Conrad Bishop of Hildesheim, in cooperation with the forces of Jerusalem, defeated an invasion allegedly seventy thousand strong led by Saladin's brother al-Adil. The battle was nearly a defeat, and was saved by the commoners, who rallied to King Henri and held firm against a final Saracen assault.

- Henri de Champagne either stepped backwards out of a window or the balcony of a window collapsed under him on September 10, 1197. He died from the fall.

- Shortly after Champagne's death, Jaffa (which was held for Aimery de Lusignan by Barlais) fell to al-Adil.

- The German crusaders in 1197 reportedly behaved very badly while in Acre, throwing people out of their homes and plundering. Champagne called his nobles together and some recommended an assault on the Germans, but instead an unnamed "wise" German convinced the Germans to leave Acre and camp outside the town. This incident occurred *before* Champagne's death, but I chose to place it afterwards so that John could play a role in ending the incident.

- There are two literary justifications for giving John a role. First, Aimery named John Constable of Jerusalem just months later, while he was still only eighteen. I think it reasonable that he had done something that impressed the Lusignan with his capabilities. Second, roughly thirty years later, the commune of Acre proved tenaciously loyal to John, defying the Holy Roman Emperor to support him. An incident such as this, where John defended the rights of the citizens of Acre—especially against the Germans—makes a logical prelude to later events. Combined, these reasons made it convenient to portray John as a responsible and effective leader supporting the people of Acre, as a means of explaining his subsequent career. By giving John a role, I also had an excuse to include a real historical incident that would otherwise not have fit into the scheme of the novel. There is, however, no historical evidence that John d'Ibelin was in any way involved in this episode.

- Sometime in the fall of 1197 or early 1198, the German crusaders recaptured the coast between Acre and Tripoli, notably the city of Beirut, which was found—and left—in a ruinous state.

- Aimery de Lusignan was chosen as Isabella's fourth husband. He came to Acre in "the autumn of 1197," when Isabella and Aimery were married. They were crowned in January 1198.

- There is no record of who Aimery designated as his lieutenant on Cyprus after he went to Jerusalem. Thus, while there is no evidence it was Balian d'Ibelin, it remains possible that, were he still alive, he could have been appointed, particularly in light of Maria Comnena's value as a representative of the still popular and legitimate Imperial Byzantine royal family.

- The date, place, and cause of Balian's death are unknown. To my knowledge, neither his nor Maria's grave has been found.

Glossary

Abaya: a black garment, worn by Islamic women, that completely covers the head and body in a single, flowing, unfitted fashion so that no contours or limbs can be seen. It leaves only the face, but not the neck, visible and is often supplemented with a mask or "veil" that covers the face, leaving only a slit for the eyes between the top of the abaya (which covers the forehead) and the mask or veil across the lower half of the face.

Aketon: a padded and quilted garment, usually of linen, worn under or instead of chain mail.

Aventail: a flap of chain mail, attached to the coif, that could be secured by a leather thong to the brow band to cover the lower part of the face.

Bailli: a governor or appointed official of the Crown, but also the elected head of one of the independent commercial "communes" of the Pisans, Venetians, or Genoese.

Battlement: a low wall built on the roof of a tower or other building in a castle, fortified manor, or church, with alternating higher segments for sheltering behind and lower segments for shooting from.

Buss: a large combination oared and sailed vessel that derived from Norse cargo (not raiding) vessels. They had substantial cargo capacity but were also swift and maneuverable.

Cantle: the raised part of a saddle behind the seat; in this period it was high and strong, made of wood, to help keep a knight in the saddle even after taking a blow from a lance.

Cervelliere: an open-faced helmet that covered the skull like a close-fitting, brimless cap; usually worn over a chain-mail coif.

Chain mail (mail): flexible armor composed of interlinking riveted rings of metal. Each link passes through four others.

Chancellors: royal and baronial officials responsible for maintaining, filing, and archiving documents, particularly charters related to the transfer of property and the like. They were usually clerics, and served as advisers to their lords on legal matters.

Chausses: mail leggings to protect a knight's legs in combat.

Coif: a chain-mail hood, either separate from or attached to the hauberk.

Commune: the Italian city-states had assisted the land armies of the crusaders by blockading coastal cities and sometimes providing troops as well. In exchange, they had been granted territory in all the major coastal cities and the right to run their affairs more or less autonomously. The communes were governed by the laws of their founding city (Pisa, Venice, and so on), and had elected officials, headed by a "bailli" who represented them to the other sectors of society, particularly the feudal overlords of the territory in which they had settled.

Conroi: a medieval cavalry formation in which the riders rode stirrup to stirrup in rows that enabled a maximum number of lances to come to bear, but also massed the power of the charge.

Constable: the royal constable was the commanding general of the royal army in the absence of the king. The constable was responsible for mustering the army, ensuring it was adequately supplied, and carrying the king's standard or commanding in the absence of the king. The greater barons often had constables with similar functions, particularly mustering the vassals and securing the supplies of the baron's military entourage.

Court of the Bourgeoisie: the judicial body regulating and trying free, non-noble Frankish citizenry in the Kingdoms of Jerusalem and Cyprus.

Court of the Chain: the judicial body regulating maritime law and trying maritime cases.

Court of the Fonde: a court especially created to deal with commercial cases in market towns.

Crenel: an indentation or loophole in the top of a battlement or wall.

Crenelate: the act of adding defensive battlements to a building.

Faranj: (also sometimes Franj) the Arab term for crusaders and their descendants in Outremer.

Fief: land held on a hereditary basis from a lord in return for military service.

Fetlock: the lowest joint in a horse's leg.

Frank: the contemporary term used to describe Latin Christians (crusaders, pilgrims, and their descendants) in the Middle East, regardless of their country of origin. The Arab term "faranj" derived from this.

Destrier: a horse specially trained for mounted combat; a charger or warhorse.

Dragoman: an official of the crown or a baron responsible for representing his lord in the lord's rural domains. Although usually Franks of the sergeant class, they could be locals or knights. Their functions were very similar to English sheriffs. They were paid by their lord. The positions were not inherently hereditary, but custom favored the eldest son or a close relative of the previous dragoman.

Dromond: a large vessel with two to three lateen sails and two banks of oars. These vessels were built very strongly and were consequently slower, but offered more spacious accommodations.

Garderobe: a toilet, usually built on the exterior wall of a residence or fortification, that emptied into the surrounding ditch or moat.

Hajj: the Muslim pilgrimage to Mecca, one of the five duties of a good Muslim.

Hauberk: a chain-mail shirt, either long- or short-sleeved, that in this period reached to just above the knee.

High Court: similar to but more powerful than the English House of Lords, it was the council in which all the barons of the Kingdom (whether Jerusalem or Cyprus) sat to conduct the business of the state. The High Court was the legislature of the kingdoms, but also the chief executive body and the judiciary for the feudal elite. The High Court elected the kings, conducted foreign policy, and tried their peers.

Iqta: a Seljuk institution similar to a fief in feudal Europe, but not hereditary. It was a gift from an overlord to a subject of land or other sources of revenue, which could be retracted at any time at the whim of the overlord.

Jihad: a Muslim holy war, usually interpreted as a war against nonbelievers to spread the faith of Islam.

Kettle helm: an open-faced helmet with a broad rim, common among infantry.

Khan: a large building built around a courtyard, often with a well, that provided temporary warehousing for goods on the ground floor and housing/lodgings on the upper stories for traveling merchants.

Lance: a cavalry weapon approximately fourteen feet long, made of wood and tipped with a steel head.

Mamlukes (also Mamelukes and Mamluks): former slaves who had been purchased or captured and then subjected to rigorous military training to make them an elite corps of fanatically loyal soldiers. Although technically freed on reaching adulthood, most generally retained a slavish devotion to their former masters and could be trusted to serve with particular selflessness. A Mamluke could, however, also be rewarded with lands and titles (e.g., a iqta) or simply valuable gifts. In 1250, the Mamlukes would revolt against their Sultan, murder him, and seize power for themselves.

Marshal: a royal or baronial official responsible for the horses of his lord's feudal host, including valuing the horses of vassals and ensuring compensation for losses.

Melee: a form of tournament in which two teams of knights face off across a large natural landscape and fight in conditions very similar to real combat, across ditches, hedges, swamps, streams, and so on. These were very popular in the late twelfth century—and very dangerous, often resulting in injuries and even deaths to both men and horses. The modern meaning of any confused, hand-to-hand fight among a large number of people derives from the medieval meaning.

Merlon: the solid part of a battlement or parapet between two openings or "crenels."

Outremer: A French term meaning "overseas," used to describe the crusader kingdoms (Kingdom of Jerusalem, County of Tripoli, County of Edessa, and Principality of Antioch) established in the Holy Land after the First Crusade.

Pommel: 1) the raised portion in front of the seat of a saddle; 2) the round portion of a sword above the hand grip.

Palfrey: a riding horse.

Parapet: A wall with crenelation built on a rampart or outer defensive work.

Quintain: a pivoted gibbet-like structure with a shield suspended from one arm and a bag of sand from the other, used to train for mounted combat.

Rampart: an earthen embankment surmounted by a parapet, encircling a castle or city as a defense against attack.

Ra'is (also Rays and Rais): in the Kingdom of Jerusalem, a native (Syrian) "head man," "chief," or "elder" recognized by the native community as a man of authority. The position was usually hereditary, and the Ra'is usually occupied a larger house and held more property or more lucrative property (such as olive orchards, mills, or wine presses) than the average peasant in the village.

Rear-Tenants: men who held land fiefs from tenants-in-chief of the crown—i.e., the vassals of vassals. Most tenants-in-chief of the crown held large territories they could not themselves manage and owed scores of knights to the feudal levee. They met their obligations by dividing up their holdings into smaller segments consisting of a few villages, or in some cases feudal privileges such as mills and bakeries, and bestowing these holdings on individual knights in exchange for rents and feudal service.

Scabbard (also **sheath**): the protective outer case of an edged weapon, particularly a sword or dagger.

Scribes: in the context of Outremer, scribes were (obviously literate) officials responsible for collecting taxes and fees within a certain domain. They were usually natives (Syrian or Greek), but they were appointed by the lord of the domain and required his trust. They were often paid in land or payments in kind. There is no evidence that they were necessarily clerical.

Seneschal: the kings and great nobles employed this household official, who generally had responsibility for the finances of their lord—rather like the CFO of a major corporation today.

Snecka: a warship or galley that was very swift and maneuverable but had only a single bank of oars in addition to the sail, and so a low freeboard. These evolved from Viking raiding ships.

Surcoat: the loose, flowing cloth garment worn over armor; in this period it was slit up the front and back for riding and hung to mid-calf. It could be sleeveless or have short, wide elbow-length sleeves. It could be of cotton, linen, or silk and was often brightly dyed, woven, or embroidered with the wearer's coat of arms.

Tenant-in-chief: an individual holding land directly from the crown.

Turcopoles: troops drawn from the Orthodox Christian population of the crusader states. These were not, as is sometimes suggested, Muslim converts, nor were they necessarily the children of mixed marriages.

Vassal: an individual holding a fief (land) in exchange for military service.

Also by Nelena P. Schrader

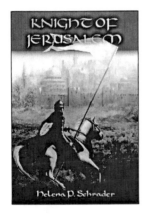

A leper king,
A landless knight,
And the struggle for Jerusalem.

Book I in the Jerusalem Trilogy. Balian, the younger son of a local baron, goes to Jerusalem to seek his fortune. Instead, he finds himself trapped into serving a young prince suffering from leprosy. The unexpected death of the King makes the leper boy King Baldwin IV of Jerusalem — and Balians prospects begin to improve…

wheatmark.com/catalog/knight-of-jerusalem-a-biographical-novel-of-balian-dibelin/

A divided kingdom,
A united enemy
And the struggle for Jerusalem

Book II of the Jerusalem Trilogy. The Christian kingdom of Jerusalem is under siege. The charismatic Kurdish leader Salah ad-Din has united Shiite Egypt and Sunnite Syria and has declared jihad against the Christian kingdom. While King Baldwin IV struggles to defend his kingdom from the external threat despite the increasing ravages of leprosy, the struggle for the succession threatens to tear the kingdom apart from the inside.

wheatmark.com/catalog/defender-jerusalem-biographical-balian-dibelin/

A lost kingdom,
         A lionhearted king,
                  And the struggle for Jerusalem
Book III of the Jerusalem Trilogy. Balian has survived
the devastating defeat at Hattin, and walked away a
free man after the surrender of Jerusalem, but he is
baron of nothing in a kingdom that no longer exists.
Haunted by the tens of thousands of Christians
enslaved by the Saracens, he is determined to regain
what has been lost. The arrival of a crusading army led by Richard the Lionheart
offers hope — but also conflict, as natives and crusaders clash and French and
English quarrel.

wheatmark.com/catalog/envoy-jerusalem-balian-dibelin-third-crusade/

CPSIA information can be obtained
at www.ICGtesting.com
Printed in the USA
LVOW11s1640291217
561233LV00002B/299/P

2